EX LIBRIS

VINTAGE CLASSICS

D1027219

# ALMS FOR OBLIVION: VOLUME II

Simon Raven was perhaps known as much for his controversial behaviour as for his writing. Born on 28 December 1927, he grew up reading and studying the classics, translating them from Greek and Latin into English and vice-versa. He was expelled from Charterhouse School in 1945 for homosexual activities, having first been seduced at the age of nine by the games master (an experience he described as giving 'immediate and unalloyed pleasure') and went on to join the army. Following his National Service, Raven attended King's College, Cambridge to read English. Raven later returned to the army but was asked to resign rather than face a court-martial for 'conduct unbecoming'. It was at this point that he turned his focus to writing. The publisher Anthony Blond paid Raven to write and to move away from London to Deal, Kent. His works span a multitude of genres including fiction, drama, essays, memoirs and screenplays. Simon Raven died in May 2001, having written his own epitaph: 'He shared his bottle – and, when still young and appetising, his bed.'

## OTHER WORKS BY SIMON RAVEN

### Novels

*The Feathers of Death*
*Brother Cain*
*Doctors Wear Scarlet*
*Close of Play*
*The Roses of Picardie*
*An Inch of Fortune*
*September Castle*
*The Troubadour*

*Alms for Oblivion* sequence

*The Rich Pay Late*
*Friends in Low Places*
*The Sabre Squadron*
*Fielding Gray*
*The Judas Boy*
*Places Where They Sing*
*Sound the Retreat*
*Come Like Shadows*
*Bring Forth the Body*
*The Survivors*

### Belles-Lettres

*The English Gentleman*
*Boys Will Be Boys*
*The Fortunes of Fingel*
*The Old School*

### Plays

*Royal Foundation and
Other Plays*

### Autobiography

*Shadows on the Grass*
*The Old Gang*
*Bird of Ill Omen*
*Is There Anybody There?
Said the Traveller*

*First Born of Egypt* sequence

*Morning Star*
*The Face of the Waters*
*Before the Cock Crow*
*New Seed For Old*
*Blood of my Bone*
*In the Image of God*

SIMON RAVEN

# Alms For Oblivion

## Volume II

The Judas Boy
Places Where They Sing
Sound the Retreat
Come Like Shadows

**VINTAGE BOOKS**
London

Published by Vintage 2012

2 4 6 8 10 9 7 5 3 1

*The Judas Boy*
First published in Great Britain by Anthony Blond Ltd in 1968
Copyright © Simon Raven 1968

*Places Where They Sing*
First published in Great Britain by Anthony Blond Ltd in 1970
Copyright © Simon Raven 1970

*Sound the Retreat*
First published in Great Britain by Anthony Blond Ltd in 1971
Copyright © Simon Raven 1971

*Come Like Shadows*
First published in Great Britain by Anthony Blond Ltd in 1972
Copyright © Simon Raven 1972

First published by Vintage in 1998

Vintage
Random House, 20 Vauxhall Bridge Road,
London SW1V 2SA

www.vintage-classics.info

Addresses for companies within The Random House Group Limited
can be found at: www.randomhouse.co.uk/offices.htm

The Random House Group Limited Reg. No. 954009

A CIP catalogue record for this book
is available from the British Library

ISBN 9780099561330

The Random House Group Limited supports The Forest Stewardship
Council (FSC®), the leading international forest certification organisation.
Our books carrying the FSC label are printed on FSC® certified paper.
FSC is the only forest certification scheme endorsed by the leading
environmental organisations, including Greenpeace.
Our paper procurement policy can be found at:
www.randomhouse.co.uk/environment

Printed and bound in Great Britain by Clays Ltd, St Ives Plc

# CONTENTS

# CONTENTS

# INTRODUCTION

'In a few days,' said an old friend, 'I am to be received into the Roman Catholic Church. I am very...exigent...about this, so I'm afraid I may turn into a bore, a religious bore. If so, I rely on you to stop me, even at the risk of offending me, because there is nothing more ghastly in the whole kingdom, in the whole universe, than a religious bore.'

My friend was not an Englishman: he was an intelligent and charming American Jew. But he was also anglophile to the highest degree, and he said what he said because he assumed, quite correctly, that this was the proper attitude to take among Englishmen in case of ardent religious conversion. The English, he thought, are a quiet, gentle-mannered people, who mind their own business and keep their troubles and obsessions to themselves. If an Englishman is about to do something that may vex his acquaintance, it is his social duty to warn them and to request them not to allow him to become a pest.

I fear he was out of date; for he was converted in the mid-1980s, by which time the English had long since ceased to worry about whether or not they were bores or pests. When I started to write *Alms for Oblivion* in 1962, it was still a concern among English people of whatever class that they should not irritate, nag, scold, embarrass or in any way incommode other English people of whatever class: that they should never interfere, pry or delate. True, ever since 1945 (in which year the narrative of *Alms for Oblivion* commences) there had been some deterioration in this respect, caused by the increasing publicity wished on to the rich, noble and famous, and the consequent priggery and spite. But in 1962 the old rules (keep your head down and hoe your own row) still held; and even a decade later, in the 1970s, during which

(1973) the narrative of *Alms* concludes and a little later in which (1975) I finished writing it, the English pride in a decent independence in all affairs remained pretty well unspoilt. I was therefore able to take for granted while writing, and my characters were able to demonstrate while being written, that an Englishman's home was still his fortress, inside which he could exist with privacy and according to preference, outside which he should bear himself modestly, i.e. without drawing attention to himself, and eschew enthusiasm or complaint.

By 1985, however, my Jewish-American-convert-Catholic chum's loyalty to what he conceived as the essential English ethos, the quiet English fashion of scepticism and moderation, was hopelessly outmoded. So far from being self-sufficient yet considerate in attitude and demeanour Englishmen had now become shrill, demanding and hysterical; self-pitying and unctuous; full of grievance at their own lot and envy of others' attainments. And things were to get worse between then and 1998. Who would have thought it possible, even in 1985 by which time the rot was visibly poisoning the fabric, that by 1998 disagreement about such items as 'race' and 'gender' should lead to sly censorship, seething accusation, and even to threats of imprisonment? That officials or 'social workers' should issue decrees about the poaching of eggs or the slicing of meat? That the police should conduct violent early morning raids on respectable households against which there were the merest rumours, witless and unfounded, of 'child abuse' or 'satanic' practice? Who would have imagined that a flighty, pea-brained princess with an addiction to publicity should become a cult almost in the degree of sanctity? Or that mental sloth should be condoned to the point of 'dumbing down' journals and broadcasts, of branding as 'élitist' the study of ancient civilisations or pure mathematics? And yet each morning's paper contains instances of such imbecility and indeed far worse – the tumults of popular rage which greet as 'unacceptable' verdicts of the courts however fairly and diligently reached, or the ugly, the obscene grief of adolescents whose favourite football team has been relegated. Cool England, indeed.

Here is another example of its coolness, this to help measure its general culture: in a recent re-print of the novels of Thomas Hardy, the editor of *The Return of the Native* finds it necessary to inform us in his notes that Nebuchadnezzar was a king of Babylon, that Tussaud's is a famous waxwork show, and that Adam was the 'first man in the world'.

What I should add to all this is that in the 22 years since the tenth and last novel in *Alms for Oblivion* was first published England had become a land which grudges reward or even tolerance of honest speaking (Enoch Powell) and indulges every whim of the idle and ignorant ('kiddies'). In case of accidental disaster a vengeful and sentimental public will not rest till thrown a scapegoat, however blameless: in case of wilful self-immolation 'lack of compassion' or 'deprivation' must be announced as the cause (never the 'victim's' inadequacy), while the *lacking* or the *depriving* will be attributed *instanter* to the Government, of whatever party, or even to the Queen.

The cry, 'If I can't, you mustn't', had some trace of justification, however sullen and unlovely the sound of it. Nowadays we hear instead an even less lovely cry, 'If I don't want to, you mustn't': i.e. 'It is just possible that I am, after all, missing out on something of value which you have been shrewd enough to detect and I haven't, and that wouldn't be fair and *equal*, now would it?' Once upon a time, however strong and righteous you considered your message, you scorned to become a pest: in 1998, however trivial your grievance, you find yourself encouraged and even 'morally obliged' to become not just a pest but a pestilence.

Enough. This little essay has been about certain types of mindless or sanctimonious behaviour which you will not find in *Alms for Oblivion*, except in small quantities deliberately introduced to be deplored, despised and mocked. These days you are not allowed to deplore, despise or mock them: they have become 'politically correct'.

Simon Raven
May 1998

# PRINCIPAL CHARACTERS IN
# *ALMS FOR OBLIVION*

The *Alms for Oblivion* sequence consists of ten novels. They are, in chronological order: *Fielding Gray* (FG), set in 1945; *Sound the Retreat* (SR), 1945–6; *The Sabre Squadron* (SS), 1952; *The Rich Pay Late* (RPL), 1955–6; *Friends in Low Places* (FLP), 1959; *The Judas Boy* (JB), 1962; *Places Where They Sing* (PWTS), 1967; *Come Like Shadows* (CLS), 1970; *Bring Forth the Body* (BFB), 1972; and *The Survivors* (TS), 1973.

What follows is an alphabetical list of the more important characters, showing in which of the novels they have each appeared and briefly suggesting their roles.

Albani, Euphemia: daughter of Fernando Albani *q.v.* (TS). Albani, Fernando: Venetial merchant of late 18th and early 19th centuries. Author of manuscripts researched by Fielding Gray *q.v.* in 1973 (TS).
Albani, Maria: wife to Femando (TS).
Albani, Piero: son of Fernando (TS). Not to be confused with the Piero *q.v.* of no known surname who lives with Lykiadopoulos in Venice in 1973 (TS).

Balliston, Hugh: an undergraduate of Lancaster College, Cambridge in 1967 (PWTS); retreats to a convent of Franciscan Friars near Venice, and is recognised in Venice by Daniel Mond in 1973 (TS).
Beatty, Miss: a secretary in the firm of Salinger & Holbrook (RPL). † 1956 (RPL).
Beck, Tony: a young Fellow of Lancaster College, well known as a literary critic (PWTS).
Beyfus, The Lord (life Peer): a social scientist, Fellow of Lancaster College (PWTS).
Blakeney, Balbo: a biochemist, Fellow of Lancaster College (PWTS); still a Fellow of Lancaster and present at Daniel Mond's funeral in 1973 (TS).

Blessington, Ivan: a school friend of Fielding Gray in 1945 (FG); later a regular officer in the 49th Earl Hamilton's Light Dragoons (Hamilton's Horse); ADC to his Divisional Commander in Germany in 1952 (SS); by 1955 an attaché at the British Embassy in Washington (RPL); by 1972 retired from the army and working at high level for a prominent merchant bank (BFB); pensioned off from the bank for indiscretion in 1973 (TS).

von Bremke, Herr Doktor Aeneas: a prominent mathematician at the University of Göttingen (SS).

Brockworthy, Lieutenant-Colonel: Commanding Officer of the 1st Battalion, the Wessex Fusiliers, at Berhampore in 1946 (SR).

Bunce, Basil: Squadron Sergeant-Major of the 10th Sabre Squadron of Earl Hamilton's Light Dragoons at Göttingen in 1952 (SS), and on Santa Kytherea in 1955 (FG); present at Daniel Mond's funeral in 1973 (TS).

Bungay, Piers: Subaltern officer of the 10th Sabre Squadron at Göttingen in 1952 (SS).

Buttock Mrs Tessie: owner of Buttock's Hotel in the Cromwell Road (RPL, FLP, JB, CLS), a convenient establishment much favoured by Tom Llewyllyn and Fielding Gray *q.v.*

Canteloupe, The Marchioness (Molly): wife of The Marquis Canteloupe (FLP, SR).

CANTELOUPE, The Most Honourable the Marquis: father of The Earl of Muscateer (SR); distant cousin of Captain Detterling *q.v.* and political associate of Somerset Lloyd-James *q.v.*; successful operator of his 'Stately Home' and in 1959 Parliamentary Secretary for the Development of British Recreational Resources (FLP); Minister of Public Relations and Popular Media in 1962 (JB); Shadow Minister of Commerce in 1967 (PWTS); Minister of Commerce in the Conservative Government of 1970 (CLS); still Minister in 1972, though under heavy pressure (BFB). † 1973 (TS).

Carnavon, Angus: leading, male star in Pandarus/Clytemnestra Film Production of *The Odyssey* on Corfu in 1970 (CLS).

Carnwath, Doctor: a Cambridge don and historian; an old friend of Provost Constable, and a member of the Lauderdale Committee; † early 1950s (BFB).

Chead, 'Corpy': Corporal-Major (i.e. Colour Sergeant) of the 10th Sabre Squadron at Göttingen (SS); present at Daniel Mond's funeral in 1973 (TS).

Clewes, The Reverend Oliver: Chaplain to Lancaster College (PWTS).

CONSTABLE, Robert Reculver (Major): demobilised with special priority in the summer of 1945 to take up appointment as Tutor of Lancaster College, Cambridge (FG); by 1955 Vice-Chancellor of the University of Salop, and *ex officio* member of the Board of *Strix* (RPL); elected Provost of Lancaster in 1959 (FLP); still Provost in 1962 (JB) and 1967 (PWTS) and 1972 (BFB); ennobled as Lord Constable of Reculver Castle in 1973 (TS).

Corrington, Mona: an anthropologist, Fellow of Girton College, Cambridge. Chum of Lord Beyfus *q.v.* (PWTS).

Cruxtable, Sergeant-Major: Company Sergeant-Major of Peter Morrison's Company at the O.T.S., Bangalore, in 1945–6 (SR); 'P.T. expert' at Canteloupe's physical fitness camp in the west country (FLP).


DETTERLING, Captain: distant cousin of Lord Canteloupe; regular officer of The 49th Earl Hamilton's Light Dragoons (Hamilton's Horse) from 1937; in charge of recruiting for the Cavalry in 1945 (FG); instructor at the O.T.S., Bangalore, from late 1945 to summer 1946 (SR); by 1952 has retired from Hamilton's Horse and become a Member of Parliament (SS); still M.P. in 1955 and a political supporter of Peter Morrison *q.v.* (RPL); still M.P. in 1959, when he joins Gregory Stern *q.v.* as a partner in Stern's publishing house (FLP); still M.P. and publisher in 1962 (JB) and 1970 (CLS), and 1972, at which time he gives important assistance to those enquiring into the death of Somerset Lloyd-James (BFB); inherits his distant cousin Canteloupe's marquisate by special remainder in 1973 (TS), and insists that the spelling of the title now be changed to 'marquess'.

Dexterside, Ashley: friend and employee of Donald Salinger (RPL).

Dharaparam, H.H. The Maharajah of: an Indian Prince; Patron of the Cricket Club of the O.T.S., Bangalore (SR).

Dilkes, Henry: Secretary to the Institute of Political and Economic Studies and a member of the Board of *Strix* (RPL, FLP).

Dixon, Alastair: Member of Parliament for safe Conservative seat in the west country; about to retire in 1959 (FLP), thus creating a vacancy coveted both by Peter Morrison and Somerset Lloyd-James *q.v.*

Dolly: maid of all work to Somerset Lloyd-James in his chambers in Albany (BFB).

Drew, Vanessa: *v.* Salinger, Donald.

Engineer, Margaret Rose: a Eurasian harlot who entertains Peter Morrison *q.v.* in Bangalore (SR).

Fitzavon, Humbert: otherwise called Lord Rollesden-in-Silvis. The man with whom the manuscripts of Fernando Albani *q.v.* are principally concerned (TS).

de FREVILLE, Max: gambler and connoisseur of human affairs; runs big chemin-de-fer games in the London of the fifties (RPL), maintaining a private spy-ring for protection from possible welshers and also for the sheer amusement of it (FLP); later goes abroad to Venice, Hydra, Cyprus and Corfu, where he engages in various enterprises (PLP, JB, CLS), often in partnership with Lykiadopoulos *q.v.* and usually attended by Angela Tuck *q.v.* His Corfiot interests include a share in the 1970 Pandarus/Clytemnestra production of *The Odyssey* (CLS); still active in Corfu in 1972 (BFB); still in partnership with Lykiadopoulos, whom he accompanies to Venice in the autumn of 1973 (TS).

Frith, Hetta: girl friend of Hugh Balliston *q.v.* (PWTS). † 1967 (PWTS).

Galahead, Foxe J. (Foxy): Producer for Pandarus and Clytemnestra Films of *The Odyssey* on Corfu in 1970 (CLS).

Gamp, Jonathan: a not so young man about town (RPL, FLP, BFB).

Gilzai Khan, Captain: an Indian officer (Moslem) holding the King's Commission; an instructor at the O.T.S., Bangalore, 1945–6; resigns to become a political agitator (SR). † 1946 (SR).

Glastonbury, Major Giles: an old friend of Detterling *q.v.* and regular officer of Hamilton's Horse; temporary Lieutenant-Colonel on Lord Wavell's staff in India 1945–6 (SR); officer commanding the 10th Sabre Squadron of Hamilton's Horse at Göttingen in 1952 (SS).

Grange, Lady Susan: marries Lord Philby (RPL).

Gray, John Aloysius (Jack): Fielding Gray's father (FG). † 1945.

Gray, Mrs: Fielding Gray's mother (FG). † c. 1948.

GRAY, Major Fielding: senior schoolboy in 1945 (FG) with Peter Morrison and Somerset Lloyd-James *q.v.*; scholar elect of Lancaster College, but tangles with the authorities, is deprived of his scholarship before he can take it up (FG), and becomes a regular officer of Earl Hamilton's Light Dragoons; 2 i/c and then O.C. the 10th Sabre Squadron in Göttingen in 1952 (SS) and still commanding the Squadron on Santa Kytherea in 1955 (FG); badly mutilated in Cyprus in 1958 and leaves the Army to become critic and novelist with the help of Somerset Lloyd-James (FLP); achieves minor distinction, and in 1962 is sent out to Greece and Cyprus by Tom Llewyllyn *q.v.* to investigate Cypriot affairs, past and present, for BBC Television (JB); in Greece meets Harriet Ongley *q.v.*; by 1967 has won the Joseph Conrad Prize for Fiction (PWTS); goes to Corfu in 1970 to rewrite script for Pandarus/Clytemnestra's *The Odyssey* (CLS); in 1972 is engaged on a study of Joseph Conrad, which is to be published, as part of a new series, by Gregory Stem (BFB); derives considerable financial benefit from the Conrad book, and settles temporarily in Venice in the autumn of 1973 (TS). His researches into a by-water of Venetian history cause trouble among his friends and provide himself with the material for a new novel.

Grimes, Sasha: a talented young actress playing in Pandarus Clymnestra's *The Odyssey* on Corfu (CLS).

The Headmaster of Fielding Gray's School (FG): a man of conscience.

Helmutt, Jacquiz: historian; research student at Lancaster College in 1952 (SS); later Fellow of Lancaster (PWTS); still a Fellow of Lancaster and present at Daniel Mond's funeral in 1973 (TS).

Holbrook, Jude: partner of Donald Salinger *q.v.* 1949–56 (RPL); 'freelance' in 1959 (FLP); reported by Burke Lawrence *q. v.* (CLS) as having gone to live in Hong Kong in the sixties; discovered to have retired, with his mother, to a villa in the Veneto 1973 (TS), having apparently enriched himself in Hong Kong.

Holbrook, Penelope: a model; wife of Jude Holbrook (RPL); by 1959, divorced from Jude and associated with Burke Lawrence (FLP); reported by Burke Lawrence (CLS) as still living in London and receiving alimony from Jude in Hong Kong.

Holeworthy, R.S.M.: Regimental Sergeant-Major of the Wessex Fusiliers at Göttingen in 1952 (SS).

Jacobson, Jules: old hand in the film world; Director of Pandarus/Clytemnestra's *The Odyssey* on Corfu in 1970 (CLS).

James, Cornet Julian: Cambridge friend of Daniel Mond *q. v.*; in 1952 a National Service officer of the 10th Sabre Squadron at Göttingen (SS).

Joe: groundsman at Detterling's old school (BFB).

Lamprey, Jack: a subaltern officer of the 10th Sabre Squadron(SS).

La Soeur, Doctor: a confidential practitioner, physician to Fielding Gray (FG, RPL, CLS).

Lawrence, Burke: 'film director' and advertising man (RPL); from *c.* 1956 to 1959 teams up with Penelope Holbrook *q.v.* in murky 'agency' (FLP); *c.* 1960 leaves England for Canada, and later becomes P.R.O. to Clytemnestra Films (CLS).

Lewson, Felicity: born Contessina Felicula Maria Monteverdi; educated largely in England; wife of Mark Lewson (though several years his senior) and his assistant in his profession (RPL). † 1959 (FLP).

Lewson, Mark: a con man (RPL, FLP). † 1959 (FLP).

Lichfield, Margaret: star actress playing Penelope in the Pandarus/ Clytemnestra production of *The Odyssey on* Corfu in 1970 (CLS).

LLEWYLLYN, Tom: a 'scholarship boy' of low Welsh origin but superior education; author, journalist and contributor to *Strix* (RPL); same but far more successful by 1959, when he marries Patricia Turbot *q.v.* (FLP); given important contract by BBC Television in 1962 to produce *Today is History,* and later that year appointed Napier Fellow of Lancaster College (JB); renewed as Napier Fellow in 1965 and still at Lancaster in 1967 (PWTS); later made a permanent Fellow of the College (CLS); employed by Pandarus and Clytemnestra Films as 'Literary and Historical Adviser' to their production of *The Odyssey* on Corfu in 1970 (CLS); still a don at Lancaster in 1972, when he is reported to be winning esteem for the first volume of his magnum opus (published by the Cambridge University Press) on the subject of Power (BFB); comes to Venice in the autumn of 1973 (TS), nominally to do research but in fact to care for Daniel Mond.

Llewyllyn, Tullia: always called and known as 'Baby'; Tom and Patricia's daughter, born in 1960 (JB, PWTS, CLS, BFB); on the removal from the scene of her mother, is sent away to school in the autumn of 1973 (TS). Becomes a close friend of Captain Detterling, now Marquess Canteloupe.

Lloyd-James, Mrs Peregrina: widowed mother of Somerset Lloyd-James (BFB).

LLOYD-JAMES, Somerset: a senior schoolboy and friend of Fielding Gray in 1945 (FG); by 1955, Editor of *Strix,* an independent economic journal (RPL); still editor of *Strix* in 1959 (FPL) and now seeking a seat in Parliament; still editor of *Strix* in 1962 (JB), but now also a Member of Parliament and unofficial adviser to Lord Canteloupe *q.v.*; still M.P. and close associate of Canteloupe in 1967 (PWTS), and by

1970 Canteloupe's official understrapper in the House of Commons (CLS), still so employed in 1972 (BFB), with title of Parliamentary Under-Secretary of State at the Ministry of Commerce; † 1972 (BFB).

Lykiadopoulos, Stratis: a Greek gentleman, or not far off it; professional gambler and a man of affairs (FLP) who has a brief liaison with Mark Lewson; friend and partner of Max de Freville *q.v.* (FLP), with whom he has business interests in Cyprus (JB) and later in Corfu (CLS); comes to Venice in the autumn of 1973 (TS) to run a Baccarat Bank and thus prop up his fortunes in Corfu, which are now rather shaky. Is accompanied by Max de Freville *q.v.* and a Sicilian boy called Piero *q.v.*

Maisie: a whore (RPL, FLP, JB) frequented with enthusiasm by Fielding Gray, Lord Canteloupe and Somerset Lloyd-James; apparently still going strong as late as 1967 (ref. PWTS) and even 1970 (ref. CLS), and 1972 (BFB).

Mayerston: a revolutionary (PWTS).

Mond, Daniel: a mathematician; research student of Lancaster College (SS) sent to Göttingen University in 1952 to follow up his line of research, which unexpectedly turns out to have a military potential; later Fellow of Lancaster and teacher of pure mathematics (PWTS). † in Venice in 1973 (TS).

Morrison, Helen: Peter Morrison's wife (RPL, FLP, BFB).

MORRISON, Peter: senior schoolboy with Fielding Gray and Somerset Lloyd-James *q.v.* in 1945 (FG); an officer cadet at the O.T.S., Bangalore, from late 1945 to summer 1946 (SR) and then commissioned as a Second Lieutenant in the Wessex Fusiliers, whom he joins at Berhampore; by 1952 has inherited substantial estates in East Anglia and by 1955 is a Member of Parliament (RPL) where he leads 'the Young England Group'; but in 1956 applies for Chiltern Hundreds (RPL); tries and fails to return to Parliament in 1959 (FLP); reported by Lord Canteloupe (CLS) as having finally got a seat again after a by-election in 1968 and as having retained it at the General Election in 1970; in 1972 appointed Parliamentary Under-Secretary of State at the Ministry of Commerce on the demise of Somerset Lloyd-James (BFB); appointed Minister of Commerce on death of Lord Canteloupe *q.v.* in 1973 (TS); soon after is in Venice to take a hand in industrial intrigues in Mestre.

Morrison, 'Squire': Peter's father (FG), owner of a fancied racehorse (Tiberius). † *c.* 1950.

Mortleman, Alister: an officer cadet at the O.T.S., Bangalore, 1945–6, later commissioned into the Wessex Fusiliers (SR).

Motley, Mick: Lieutenant of the R.A.M.C., attached to the Wessex Fusiliers at Göttingen in 1952 (SS).

Murphy, 'Wanker': an officer cadet at the O.T.S., Bangalore, 1945–6; later commissioned as Captain in the Education Corps, then promoted to be Major and Galloper to the Viceroy of India (SR). † 1946 (SR).

Muscateer, Earl of: son of Lord and Lady Canteloupe q.v.; an officer cadet at the O.T.S., Bangalore, 1945–6 (SR). † 1946 (SR).

Nicos: a Greek boy who picks up Fielding Gray (JB).

Ogden, The Reverend Andrew: Dean of the Chapel of Lancaster College (PWTS).

Ongley, Mrs Harriet: rich American widow; Fielding Gray's mistress and benefactress from 1962 onwards (JB, PWTS, CLS), but has left him by 1972 (BFB).

Pappenheim, Herr: German ex-officer of World War II; in 1952 about to rejoin new West German Army as a senior staff officer (SS).

Percival, Leonard: cloak-and-dagger man; in 1952 nominally a Lieutenant of the Wessex Fusiliers at Göttingen (SS), but by 1962 working strictly in plain clothes (JB); friend of Max de Freville, with whom he occasionally exchanges information to their mutual amusement (JB); transferred to a domestic department ('Jermyn Street') of the secret service and rated 'Home enquiries only', because of stomach ulcers in 1972, when he investigates, in association with Detterling, the death of Somerset Lloyd-James (BFB); joins Detterling (now Lord Canteloupe) in Venice in 1973 in order to investigate a 'threat' to Detterling (TS). Becomes Detterling's personal secretary and retires from 'Jermyn Street'.

Percival, Rupert: a small-town lawyer in the west country (FLP), prominent among local Conservatives and a friend of Alistair Dixon q.v.; Leonard Percival's uncle (JB).

Philby, The Lord: proprietor of Strix (RPL, FLP) which he has inherited along with his title from his father, 'old' Philby.

Piero: A Sicilian boy who accompanies Lykiadopoulos q.v. to Venice in 1973 (TS). Becomes friend of Daniel Mond. Not to be confused with Piero Albani q.v.

Pough (pronounced Pew), The Honourable Grantchester Fitz-Margrave: Senior Fellow of Lancaster College, Professor Emeritus of Oriental Geography, at one time celebrated as a mountaineer; a dietary fadist (PWTS).

Pulcher, Detective Sergeant: assistant to Detective Superintendent Stupples, *q.v.* (BFB).

Restarick, Earle: American cloak-and-dagger man; in 1952 apparently a student at Göttingen University (SS) but in fact taking an unwholesome interest in the mathematical researches of Daniel Mond *q.v.*; later active in Cyprus (JB) and in Greece (CLS); at Mestre in autumn of 1973 in order to assist with American schemes for the industrialisation of the area (TS); present at Daniel Mond's funeral.

Roland, Christopher: a special school friend of Fielding Gray (FG). † 1945 (FG).

Salinger, Donald: senior partner of Salinger & Holbrook, a printing firm (RPL); in 1956 marries Vanessa Drew (RPL); is deserted by Jude Holbrook *q.v.* in the summer of 1956 (RPL) but in 1959 is still printing (FLP), and still married to Vanessa; in 1972 is reported as having broken down mentally and retired to a private Nursing Home in consequence of Vanessa's death by drowning (BFB).

Schottgatt, Doctor Emile: of Montana University, Head of the 'Creative Authentication Committee' of the Oglander-Finckelstein Trust, which visits Corfu in 1970 (CLS) to assess the merits of the Pandarus/Clytemnestra production of *The Odyssey*.

Schroeder, Alfie: a reporter employed by the Billingsgate Press (RPL, FLP, SS); by 1967 promoted to columnist (PWTS); 'famous' as columnist by 1973, when he attends Daniel Mond's funeral (TS).

Sheath, Aloysius: a scholar on the staff of the American School of Greek Studies in Athens, but also assistant to Earle Restarick *q.v.* (JB, CLS).

Stern, Gregory: publisher (RPL), later in partnership with Captain Detterling *q.v.* (FLP); publishes Tom Llewellyn and Fielding Gray *q.v.* (RPL, FLP, JB, PWTS, CLS); married to Isobel Turbot (FLP). still publishing in 1973 (TS), by which time Isobel has persuaded him into vulgar and profitable projects.

Strange, Barry: an officer cadet at the O.T.S. Bangalore, 1945–6, later commissioned into the Wessex Fusiliers, with whom he has strong family connections (SR).

Stupples, Detective Superintendent: policeman initially responsible for enquiries into the death of Somerset Lloyd-James in 1972 (BFB).

Tuck: a tea-planter in India; marries Angela, the daughter of a disgraced officer, and brings her back to England in 1945 (FG); later disappears, but turns up as an official of the Control Commission in Germany in 1952 (SS). † 1956 (RPL).

TUCK, Mrs Angela: daughter of a Colonel in the Indian Army Pay Corps, with whom she lives in Southern India (JB, FLP) until early 1945, when her father is dismissed the Service for malversation; being then *in extremis* marries Tuck the tea-planter, and returns with him to England in the summer of 1945 (FG); briefly mistress to the adolescent Somerset Lloyd-James *q.v.*, and to 'Jack' Gray (Fielding's father); despite this a trusted friend of Fielding's mother (FG); by 1955 is long separated from Tuck and now mistress to Jude Holbrook (RPL); in 1956 inherits small fortune from the intestate Tuck, from whom she has never been actually divorced *pace* her bibulous and misleading soliloquies on the subject in the text (RPL); in 1959 living in Menton and occasional companion of Max de Freville *q.v.* (FLP); later Max's constant companion (JB, CLS). †1970 (CLS).

Turbot, The Right Honourable Sir Edwin, P.C., Kt: politician; in 1946 ex-Minister of wartime coalition accompanying all-party delegation of M.P.s to India (SR); by 1959 long since a Minister once more, and 'Grand Vizier' of the Conservative Party (FLP); father of Patricia, who marries Tom Llewyllyn (FLP), and of Isobel, who marries Gregory Stern (FLP); by 1962 reported as badly deteriorating and as having passed some of his fortune over to his daughters (JB). † by 1967 (PWTS), having left more money to his daughters.

Turbot, Isobel: *v.* Turbot, Sir Edwin, and Stern, Gregory.

Turbot, Patricia: *v.* Turbot, Sir Edwin, and Llewyllyn, Tom. Also *v.* Llewyllyn, Tullia. Has brief walk-out with Hugh Balliston *q.v.* (PWTS) and is disobliging to Tom about money (JB, PWTS, CLS). In 1972 is reported by Jonathan Gamp to be indulging curious if not criminal sexual preferences (BFB); as a result of these activities is finally overtaken by disaster and put away in an asylum in 1973 (TS), much to the benefit of her husband and daughter.

Weekes, James: bastard son of Somerset Lloyd-James, born in 1946 (BFB).

Weekes, Mrs Meriel: *quondam* and random associate of Somerset Lloyd-James, and mother of his bastard son (BFB).

Weir, Carton: Member of Parliament and political associate of Peter Morrison (RPL); later official aide to Lord Canteloupe (FLP, JB). P.P.S. to Canteloupe at Ministry of Commerce in 1972 (BFB); becomes P.P.S. to Peter Morrison *q.v.* when the latter takes over as Minister of Commerce on the death of Lord Canteloupe.

Winstanley, Ivor: a distinguished Latinist, Fellow of Lancaster College (PWTS).

'Young bastard': assistant groundsman at Detterling's old school (BFB).

Zaccharias: an officer cadet at the O.T.S., Bangalore, 1945–6; commissioned into a dowdy regiment of the line (SR).

# THE JUDAS BOY

# Contents

## AUTHOR'S NOTE

For the purposes of this novel, certain characters are supposedly employed by the British Broadcasting Corporation. Neither the characters themselves nor the "appointments" which they hold have any connection at all with actual persons or appointments within the Corporation as it is presently constituted or has been constituted at any time during its past. In real life, for example, I understand that the BBC comprehends a Head of Features Group, a Head of Science and Features, and a Head of Arts Features; but none of these has anything whatever to do with my "Director of Features", whose persona, title and function are totally fictitious. Similarly, "Miss Enid Jackson" of "Administration" is a complete invention.

S.R.

*PART ONE*

# THE ISLAND OF LOVE

*Trapped, he thought: there is no way out of this coach and there is certain death waiting inside it. Think. You have thirty seconds (with luck) to think.*

*But how could he offer resistance to an enemy that was invisible, impalpable? A piece on a chess board can offer no resistance because it is caught in a situation which has been devised by a mental power totally remote from itself. Except by that power the situation is unalterable; and so was the situation in which he himself was trapped now. It was of mathematical exactness, it could be represented by a classical syllogism: To stay is to die; but it is impossible not to stay; therefore it is impossible not to die.*

*Don't trifle, man: think. Unlike a piece on a chess board, you have a certain power of motion. You can at least move about within the square on which you are trapped. That square is this train, or rather, this coach. Move about it, dodge the enemy. But move where? Down the corridor. The enemy is waiting there too. Then move back again. Whatever you do, don't stay still. That's what the enemy, the remote intelligence, wants you to do — to stay still, to acquiesce, to accept the chess board convention. The convention ... the rules. The situation only exists within the convention, you're only trapped if you believe in the sanctity of the rules. Disobey the rules and you're free.*

*Because, you see, there's one thing the enemy forgot; and although he's everywhere, its something he can't possibly change, not now he can't. This isn't just any coach, its a wagon-lit. Get it?*

*It could never work.*

*It's your only chance, man. You've had your thirty seconds of thinking. Another thirty seconds and you're done for. Your last chance. MOVE.*

# 1
## ENVOI

"I HAVE only one eye," said Fielding Gray, "and a face like a broiled lobster. If I appeared on your television programme, old women and children would have fits all over the kingdom."

"No one is suggesting you should appear," said Tom Llewyllyn. "Have you the first idea what this programme is going to be about?"

"No. I don't follow television affairs. There is, thank God, no set at Buttock's Hotel."

"I'm surprised you're still living there. Now that things are beginning to go your way."

"Tessie Buttock's been very kind to me," said Fielding Gray, "and anyhow I detest change. There's never any change at Buttock's. Even the amount of dirt remains constant : never more, never less."

Tom Llewyllyn passed a hand through long wavy hair. It was, Fielding noticed, atrociously scurfy. Why didn't Tom's wife Patricia keep him up to scratch? His shoes were filthy, his shirt collar curled up like a piece of damp melba toast, his finger-nails were positively ghoulish. One could only conclude that Patricia liked dirt.

"But fond as you are of Buttock's," Tom was saying, "you wouldn't mind a nice little expedition? A temporary change of scene?"

One of the three telephones on his desk rang viciously.

21

"Llewyllyn," Tom said into it: "Today is History."

While Tom listened patiently to a yakking monologue from the other end, Fielding left his chair and walked to the window, from which he had a bird's eye view of the White City Stadium. How appropriate, he reflected, that the Dog Track should lie almost adjacent to the Television Centre. Both institutions recognisably belonged to the same world – a world, he now told himself, in which he had no business. He was a serious novelist, whereas Television – what was that revolting phrase? – was a popular medium. Being rather vague about his friend's position in the BBC (Tom had hardly been there a week), Fielding had imagined, when invited to call, that they were to discuss the possible dramatisation of one of his novels; but now it appeared that Tom's new appointment in this palace of nightmares was as Producer of something called "Today is History", and whatever that phrase might imply it could scarcely comprehend fiction. Well, if Tom wanted his help in broadcasting half-truths to the half-witted, he must look elsewhere.

"I've got him here now," Tom was saying into the telephone; "I'll tell him." He put down the receiver. "That," he said to Fielding, "was the Director of Features. He is an admirer of your work, and he hopes, like me, that you can do something for Today is History."

"Such as re-writing the nasty bits to reassure your imbecile listeners?"

"Viewers, we call them. Why are you so acid, Fielding?"

"This building, this office, these telephones. This isn't my style, Tom, and I shouldn't have thought it was yours."

"Then listen. They have given me *carte blanche* to prepare, without censorship or interference, six programmes, each of one hour, about any aspects of contemporary history which I care to choose. Don't say that isn't handsome."

"You're a writer, even a scholar. Not some kind of cultural whizz-kid."

"This is 1962, Fielding. This kind of thing is here to stay. It's a challenge which we must face."

"Don't talk clichés to me, Tom. Save them for your programme."

Tom's mouth drooped slightly and his eyelids blinked. Why is Fielding so foul to me? he thought. The arrogance of success? But he's not all that successful. Does his face hurt him, his poor ruined face? With an effort Tom said :

"There aren't going to be any clichés in my programme. I've got a large budget and I can afford the best writers. Such as you." Praise, he thought : writers – a few of them – may be able to resist money, but even the most honest will sell their souls for praise. "Your last novel," Tom went on, "put you in a new class. The first two were merely competent; but *Love's Jest Book* ... as a study in betrayal ... is really memorable."

"So it ought to be. It all happened, and I was the betrayer."

"Yes, yes, I know about that," said Tom soothingly; "but it doesn't alter the fact that the novel, as it stands, is a very fine piece of work."

"I don't see how it qualifies me to contribute to your programme."

"It proves finally and beyond doubt that you can write. Besides," said Tom, "I was thinking of another true story of which you have special knowledge."

"What can you mean?"

"Cyprus. You were there while you were still in the Army."

"Is that what you meant by a change of scene? I never want to see the filthy place again, Tom. The Cypriots, the Greek ones at any rate – they're the scum of the earth."

"Who's talking in clichés now?"

"They did this to me," Fielding hissed, and pointed at his

twisted mouth and bright pink grafted face. "They took one of my eyes and turned the other into a tiny red thing, like a pig's."

One of the three telephones rang. Tom picked up the wrong receiver, winced, grabbed another at random, turned out lucky.

"I entirely forgot, dear fellow," said the voice of the Director of Features (creamy, now, and disarming instead of its usual aggressive squawk), "to tell you what I really rang up for last time. A minor matter of policy. Just as well you should know about it while you're still at the planning stage."

"I thought I wasn't to be bothered with that," said Tom, while Fielding slunk away to the window again.

"No more you are, dear fellow. We value your intellectual honesty above everything. But we *should* be most frightfully grateful ... if you *could* just remember ... that *if* you do a programme about – er – people who aren't white ... emergent nations and all that sort of thing ... then it would be very nice if you needn't say anything nasty. If you see what I mean."

"I am very sympathetic," said Tom, "to emergent nations and that sort of thing."

"No doubt you are" – the creamy voice reverted to the squawk – "but sometimes the facts aren't."

"Then in such cases," said Tom firmly, "one's sympathy has to be qualified."

"Or" – hopefully – "the facts?"

"You can't qualify facts. You can only establish and state them."

"You can also assess them in the light of circumstance," the Director quacked: "intellectual honesty requires you to."

"If you mention intellectual honesty once more," said Tom, "I shall walk out of this building and never come back."

And be very glad to do so, he thought, as he put down the receiver and looked at the hunched and sulky shoulders by the window. As for Fielding, he thought, why bother with him? Have I not troubles enough? I have taken on this programme as a duty, because I feel that at last I should try to communicate to the people at large something which vitally concerns all of them – the way in which minute by minute history is being made under their noses. I want to tell them about the living process, and then give them true and powerful examples of the process at work; to demonstrate, above all, how very little, in the end, can come of human aspiration and planning, and how very much more results merely from time and chance, which happeneth to us all. This will be a difficult and unpopular message to put over, for it is opposed to all the preconceptions of a society which takes for granted that in this world, man is king. Although I myself am a socialist, dedicated to the progress and betterment of mankind (insofar as these are possible), I am to advance a philosophy of pessimism which will be ill-received at best and the only justification of which must be that it is true. To tell the truth is hard enough, even when one is promised *carte blanche*; and there are already signs that the promise is not wholly sincere ... for whenever people start talking about "intellectual honesty", one must reach for a lie-detector. With all this and much more to worry about, Tom thought, I should indeed be happy to quit this Tower of Babel and go straight back to writing my books. But if for the time, at least, I feel myself committed to stay here and try my best, one thing I can do to make life easier is not to employ tiresome and reactionary paranoiacs like Fielding Gray. There are plenty of other people, after all, who would be only too glad to be brought in.

So Tom Llewyllyn spoke within his heart, and then jutted his chin furiously at the obstinate back by the window. But even as he did so, he knew that he would persevere with Fielding, and this for two reasons. First, Fielding was one of the few able young writers in England who would understand and sympathise with the unfashionable thesis which Tom wished to put over; and secondly, Fielding was an old friend who could certainly use the money. He could not, Tom knew, be making much from the sale of his novels, despite their success of esteem, and although he also reviewed books, this would bring in peanuts. There was no risk of Fielding's being starved or cruelly pressed, but he had been in London for three years now, unable ever to quit it for more than a very few days, and for the sake of his health and his writing he needed a proper change.

And so now :

"The money will be very good," said Tom to the back at the window.

"Nothing can be very good after what happened to me in Cyprus," Fielding said without turning.

"It could even be," said Tom wearily, "that you might get a bit of your own back."

"How? By throwing bombs about like they did?"

"That's over now. There's peace. A truce, at any rate."

"So there was when they did this to me. An agreed truce of two hours while the bodies were being cleared up. And right in the middle of it . . . I tell you those people are scum."

"Then get your own back by proving it. That's why I want you to go there. The trouble's over now but there's more coming, because there are forces at work which have not been brought under proper control. The lull at the moment is only temporary because the Greek Cypriots are still up to something – something very unpleasant, by the smell of it. If you can prove to the world – and I mean *prove,* Fielding – that they're not the sturdy freedom-lovers of liberal legend but just a pack of cruel and treacherous bastards, then you'll have got a bit of your own back."

"More likely I'll just get the other eye blown out," said Fielding, still without turning.

There was a knock on the door, which was then opened, before invitation could be given, by a stringy young woman with a put-upon face and a sluttish cardigan.

"Miss Enid Jackson," she said; "from Administration."

"Yes, Miss Jackson?"

"You know why I'm here."

"I'm afraid not."

"Yes, you do. Your National Insurance Card. I've rung you several times. Now you're employed here we have to have your National Insurance Card."

"Yes, yes, I know," said Tom. "I'll stamp the thing myself. At home."

"You seem to have very rough and ready ideas about social administration, Mr Llewyllyn. It is your employers' responsibility to st—"

"—And I've just told you I'll do it for them."

"You can't," said Miss Jackson with prim satisfaction. "I must say, if everyone was as ignorant about welfare procedures as you appear to be—"

"—Look, sweetheart," said Tom, stalking round his desk at Enid Jackson, "I've been a bloody socialist all my life and I don't need you to lecture me on welfare. But I've always been working on my own till now, and if ever I had one of those footling cards I've certainly lost it. So be a good girl, will you, and rustle me up another."

"I'm afraid it's not as easy as that. Either you must produce a card fully stamped up to March the twenty-second, which is the day you joined this Corporation, or you must furnish me with a full explanation as to why it is not available."

"One or the other you shall have, sweetheart. I promise. But not just this minute . . . please."

"Very well. But I should add that until the position has been regularised your employment here is not on a satisfactory official basis. Good morning . . . Mr Llewyllyn."

Tom went back to his desk and put both hands through

his hair. Huge flakes of dandruff fell, like ashes from a bonfire.

"Help me, Fielding," said Tom in a small voice. "It's so strange here. I didn't want to come and I hate it. Help me. Don't refuse to be on my side now I've asked you."

At long last Fielding turned from the window and smiled his grotesque smile.

"If you put it like that, my dear," he said: "after Miss Enid Jackson, I can hardly refuse."

"So when will you be off, dear?" said Tessie Buttock that evening in Buttock's Hotel.

"Two or three days," said Fielding; "Tom's very urgent. But what I can't understand is what he expects me to discover. The trouble in Cyprus is over. They've got their independence, and that must surely be an end of it."

"But we've still got soldiers there?"

"Only in agreed bases on the south coast – for which we pay a whacking great rent. They can hardly start trouble about that."

"You trust naughty Tom, dear. He's got a nose for dirt." She scooped up Albert Edward, the hotel dog, who was glumly peeing on the sofa, and settled him in her lap. "Woozums, woozums," she cawed: "woozums remember naughty Tom? He was a bit vague about money," she said to Fielding, "but when he did anything he always had a very clear reason. He must have a reason for sending you off like this, and I don't doubt he told you."

"Yes," said Fielding, remembering what Tom had said after the departure of Enid Jackson; "but I'm not convinced."

"Tell us, dear, anyway. Albert Edward needs his mind taking off his poor old bladder."

"Well, he started by looking back a bit. He said that

Colonel Grivas devised a terrorist strategy – chucking bombs
at civilians and so on – because he couldn't hope to win on a
straightforward confrontation. He just hadn't the weapons
or the men. But even so, Tom said, Grivas was a brave man
with a fine war record, and it must have gone against his
nature to play it so dirty. By instinct and upbringing he was
a soldier and not an assassin."

"Nasty little runt he always looked in the papers."

"But nevertheless a fighter – as the Germans found out in
the forties. So Tom's theory is that he didn't want to adopt
terrorist methods – or at any rate not against unarmed
civilians – but in the end was persuaded into it."

"I'm not one to speak against Tom," Tessie said, "but if
you ask me, all you need do is look at that Grivas's face in
his photos and you've got all the explanation you need. We
wouldn't have him staying in our hotel, would we,
woozums?"

"I agree with you, Tessie. But *if* Tom is right – and he's
been right before about this kind of thing – then we're left
with an interesting question."

"You mean, who talked the little bugger into it?"

"Right. And where did he come from to do the talking?"

"Russia," said Tessie, for whom all evils had only one
source: "bloody reds, wanting us done out of our empire."

"The reds aren't the only people, Tessie, who want us
done out of our empire. But leave that on one side, whoever
*did* persuade Grivas (on Tom's theory) may still be around
getting ready to do some more persuading. There are a lot
of young Cypriots who tasted blood in the last affair, and
once young men have tasted blood they're bored by the idea
of going back to be peasants – or even pimps, which in
Cyprus is the only alternative. Which leaves them nothing to
do except sharpen their knives and listen to anyone who
wants to stir up trouble."

"Like the Russians," said Tessie, unshakeable.

"As to that," said Fielding, "we shall see. But I still think the whole thing's just been thought up out of nothing by Tom."

"So," said plump, kind Maisie in her Shepherd's Market flat, "this is the last time before you go off?"

"'Fraid so, Maisie," said Fielding: "let's make it nice and slow, to remember."

"It's you that's always so quick, duckie. Try the nineteen times table. They say it helps you to hold it back."

"Nineteen ... Thirty-eight ... Fifty-seven ... Sorry, Maisie, it's no good ..."

"Never mind, dearie. You can have that one on the house. Just get your breath back first, then have a look at these pictures, and we can do it again when you're ready."

"No one else coming?"

"Not for an hour or so. And the fact is, lovie, I want to tell you something. You've been coming here – how long is it now?—"

"—Three years—"

"—So we're old friends, really, and now that you're going away for a bit, I want to tell you something before you go."

Maisie waddled comfortably to the wardrobe and came back with a split of champagne and two glasses.

"This is on the house too," she said, "just this once. Now tell me, Fielding Gray: this Cyprus business – is it dangerous?"

Whenever Maisie called him "Fielding" or "Fielding Gray" instead of "dearie" or "lovie", he knew there was something unusual coming. So now he put aside the photographs and gave Maisie his best attention.

"Dangerous?" he said. "Why should you ask that? I thought you were going to tell me something."

Maisie scratched her naked bottom and plonked it down beside him on the bed.

"Dangerous or not," she said, "you're going to Cyprus to

try and dig up dirt. Which means that there's a certain kind of person you'll be dealing with. Always the same kind when there's dirt to be buried or dug up again, and I know that kind, because I had a lot of 'em in and out of this flat some years back, using it as a post office for that racket of Salvadori's. And what I found out, Fielding Gray, was this: they're poison all right, but they can't do you much harm provided you remember just one rule, which is what I'm going to tell you now."

She paused, took a gulp of champagne and fiddled briefly with his hair.

"One rule, Maisie? Only one?"

"Only one. Don't let them know anything at all about the *real* you."

"As if I would." What a miserable mouse, he thought, this mountain has brought forth.

"But you do, darling, you do all the time. We all do, unless we're on our guard. Even if you just go to a restaurant with someone, at the end of an hour they know what you like to eat and drink – something about the real you. Not very important, but something. I know something much more important: what you're like when you do . . . this." She tweaked him gently. "It's safe with me, but *their* kind 'ud use it all right if they knew. And there are more important things still – the things in *here*." She held two pudgy hands over her embosomed heart. "If you let them know what you've got in here, Fielding Gray, they'll have you cold."

"But why should I let them know?"

"Because it's always coming out without us noticing . . . in front of people we think we can trust. And the next thing you know it comes whirring back at you like a bloody boomerang and slices off your nut. So you make sure, Fielding Gray, that what you've got in there"—she traced a little circle round his left nipple with her finger-nail—"stays there good and tight. Promise?"

"I promise. Thank you, Maisie."

"That's my good boy. Now you drink up that fizz, and have a look at those nice pictures, and in no time at all you'll be feeling like the Albert Memorial."

Gregory Stern, who was Fielding's publisher and also Tom's, brought his wife Isobel, who was the younger sister of Tom's wife Patricia, to see Fielding off at Victoria Station.

"All I can say," Stern said, "is that this is a mistake. You've let yourself be soft-soaped into this nonsense of Tom's instead of staying responsibly at home and writing your next novel for me."

"Don't be such a boring old Jew," said Isobel: "you're only jealous because Tom's paying him so much more than you can."

"Gadding about in Cyprus," grumbled Stern, "thinking you're Paddy Leigh Fermor. You're old enough to know better."

"It's only for a short time," said Fielding, anxious to reassure Stern, who for three years now had been a generous publisher and a loyal friend.

"A short time, he says." Gregory Stern turned his eyes up to the roof and ran his fingers over his waistcoat buttons as though he were typing a letter of complaint on them. "A short time. So why are you going by the train, which is three days to Athens, instead of by the aeroplane, which is three hours?"

Since his marriage to Isobel the hitherto impeccably Etonian Stern had tended more and more to adopt a Yiddish idiom. This he did, in Fielding's view, in order to annoy his wife and make her unkind to him; for Gregory was something of a masochist (they said) and enjoyed being bullied.

"That's right," Isobel said now, inflating her huge breasts at Gregory and hopping from one thin leg to the other: "go and poke your snout into everyone else's business. Why shouldn't he go by train if he wants to?"

"It's just that I like trains," Fielding said to Gregory, "and if you'll excuse me, I think it's time I got on this one."

"No hurry, my dear. I've got something for you."

Unnoticed by Isobel, who was now busy leering at a sailor, Gregory drew Fielding on one side.

"For luck," Gregory said. He produced a cylindrical metal case about an inch long and one-quarter of an inch in diameter at the ends, from one of which he now prised out a tiny roll of parchment. "We call it a Mezuzah," he explained: "on one side is written a text, on the other the divine name, Shaddai. The case with the parchment inside it must be fastened to the outer door of a man's house. But if he travels, why should he not take one with him?"

He re-inserted the roll and handed the little tube to Fielding.

"Thank you very much, Gregory," said Fielding, touched. "But why should you think I need luck?"

"Don't we all, my dear?"

"Yes. But you've made this somehow special."

"You are special to me, Fielding Gray. I want you back in one piece to write more novels."

"That sailor's a pansy," Isobel said: "he isn't taking any notice of me."

"So he isn't taking any notice. So he doesn't like fat breasts and thin legs," said Gregory. And then to Fielding, "But why *are* you taking the train? They're very boring these days, you know. No one uses them, so there aren't any more madonnas of the sleeping-cars or anything jolly like that."

"Precisely. I shall have three days of entire privacy. No one, no one at all, can get at me or ring me up or dun me or make demands. I shall be sealed off in a travelling womb, without guilt or responsibility of any kind."

"I wish I could come with you," said Isobel, "and be a madonna of a sleeping-car."

A door was slammed by mistake farther down the platform, and a group of Americans flew into a screeching panic. In the midst of them one face suddenly stood out: a face like Mr Punch's, with a chin that curved up to meet the tip of a long, hooked nose, this being surmounted by spectacles which were glinting, from fifty yards away, straight into Fielding's eyes. I've seen that face before, he thought. It knows me and I know it. What's more, it's watching me. Who? Why? Where have I seen it before?

"Anything the matter, my dear?"

"No . . ."

"Then don't forget to go and see Detterling as you pass through Athens. I wired him and he'll be expecting you . . . Are you listening, Fielding? I was saying about Detterling—"

"—Yes, yes, I heard. Any messages?"

The spectacles had gone now. One moment they had been there, glinting straight at him. He had turned his head, only for a second, in response to Stern's insistence, and now that he had turned back they were gone. Where their owner had been, there were simply two wailing women, still under the impression that they were being treacherously left behind by the train, savagely jostling each other to get through a door.

". . . And tell Detterling," Gregory was saying, "not to worry about the Cavafy memoirs. I haven't yet found a translator, and anyhow I'm already doing too many bugger books this year."

More doors slammed, this time in earnest. Fielding backed towards the train. He didn't offer to kiss Isobel, though he had known her well for some time now, but she darted on to him and landed a great splosh on his little twisted mouth. Gregory looked on benignly, then himself came forward to kiss Fielding's cheek.

"God bless you, my dear. Keep the Mezuzah carefully."

"Of course, Gregory . . . I nearly forgot – where's Detterling staying?"

"The Grande Bretagne. I ask you. The firm is paying, so he stays at the Grande Bretagne."

"He would have done anyway," said Isobel; "and you're just a dreary, cheese-paring yid."

Gregory blushed so much with pleasure that his scarlet face shone as clear as a traffic lamp on the platform until the first bend chopped it from sight.

## 2
## EN ROUTE

THE MAN WITH THE SPECTACLES made himself known at Munich.

Fielding had seen nothing of him on the boat from Dover to Ostend, nor at dinner in the restaurant-car that evening, nor at breakfast the following morning. But just as the train was moving out of Munich, and as Fielding was walking along the Athens coach on his way to lunch, a figure advanced at him down the corridor, jutting its upturned chin and flashing its glasses like morse lamps.

"I was just coming," the figure said, "to suggest you joined me for a spot of food."

The figure put up a hand to smooth the very scant hair above its deep and pallid forehead, a precise yet nugatory gesture which at once prompted Fielding's memory.

"Percival," he said, "Leonard Percival. Göttingen, 1952. Wessex Fusiliers."

"I'm flattered," said Percival, "to be so accurately documented. Members of humble line regiments are easily forgotten."

"But you weren't, as it turned out, quite what you seemed at the time."

"Neither were you. Who would have thought that the pampered and pouting captain of Earl Hamilton's Light Dragoons would turn into a distinguished novelist?"

"Not distinguished yet," said Fielding, smug nevertheless.

"You might be if you stick to it. And if you don't waste time," Percival said, lightly but very clearly, "meddling with what doesn't concern you. Come on, we're blocking the corridor."

They walked through to the restaurant-car, where Percival ordered the cheapest menu at five Marks and Fielding the most expensive at fifteen, along with a bottle of Spätburgunder Walporzeim 1951.

"Always the best of everything," said Percival, "for Earl Hamilton's Light Dragoons. The gastronomic menu, the priciest wine on the list – and travelling by wagon-lit, but of course. A compartment to yourself, the attendant tells me."

"The BBC's paying." Fielding looked at Percival's exquisitely cut suit and manicured nails. "*You* don't look exactly ground down, come to that."

"I'm just mean," said Percival slyly. "I travel second class to save money ... and because I know my place as an ex-officer of one of the dowdier regiments."

"For God's sake stop harping on the Army. I've been out for over three years. And you were never really in it. You were a spy in Fusilier's clothing. Still spying ... Leonard?"

Percival said nothing while he was served with consommé and Fielding with crayfish in mayonnaise. Then:

"I still retain the knack," Percival said.

"The knack of hanging around sleeping-car attendants scrounging for information?"

"Paying for it. That's why I can only afford the cheapest lunch."

"It surely can't have cost much just to learn that I had a compartment to myself."

"Five Marks," said Percival severely; "or the equivalent of one good-size glass of that Spätburgunder Walporzeim."

"Then allow me to recompense you," said Fielding, pouring for them both from the bottle, "and also to enquire why you were so keen to find out. Are you hoping that I shall invite you to move into the upper bunk?"

The waiter thumped down a debased Hamburger in front of Percival and obsequiously presented Fielding with a veal steak smothered in cream on a lordly silver dish. When the subsequent ceremonies were concluded, Percival said :

"As it happens, you could do a lot worse. For the whole point is, Major Fielding Gray, that an empty bunk can be filled. Anywhere between here and Athens."

"Not if I've booked the entire compartment."

"The attendant, as we already know, is venal. If he supported the interloper, pleading, let us say, some obscure regulation about the priorities of travellers on official business, you'd be done for, wouldn't you ?"

"It would be disagreeable, certainly."

"Very disagreeable, I should say, if your companion suddenly pointed a long knife at you in the middle of the night and started asking rude questions about your interest in Cyprus."

Although this picture was melodramatic and absurd, there was a grating quality in Percival's voice which compelled Fielding to take him seriously.

"Why on earth should he behave like that?"

"Because," said Percival patiently, "his standard of manners would not be that of Earl Hamilton's Light Dragoons and he would be eager to have your answer."

"Which would be that I'm going to get material for a television programme on how the gallant Cypriots achieved independence and what they propose to do with it."

"As you very well know," said Percival, "neither topic will bear much examination. I think – don't you? – that your hypothetical bedfellow would want more convincing proof of your good will."

"Such as?"

"An immediate readiness to get off this comfortable train and take one going the other way. Quite unthinkable, of course : one doesn't take orders from foreigners."

Fielding crossly waved away a rich pudding, which Percival re-captured from the waiter.

"I'll have some more of that Spätburgunder, if you don't mind," Percival said, and poured a brimming glass.

"Is any of this in the least likely to happen?"

"That's just what I was spending all those Deutschmarks to find out. Were you to be alone, I enquired of the attendant, for the whole journey?"

"And was I?"

"Of course. The English gentleman had booked the whole compartment. The expected, the inevitable answer."

"Then why pay five Deutschmarks for it?"

"To observe the way in which it was made. Very much too glib. Not reassuring, I'm afraid."

Fielding hesitated before answering. He had last seen Leonard Percival ten years ago, when they were both serving, though in very different capacities, in the same barracks at Göttingen. What little he had then known of Percival he had not much liked, and it had subsequently appeared that Percival had been playing a discreditable role in a discreditable business. Nevertheless, that business had had official sanction at a high level, and there was no reason at all to doubt Percival's professional competence or (if one allowed for the obliquity which that profession involved) his present good faith. That Percival's motives were devious and, ultimately, quite unconcerned with Fielding's welfare was probable; but here and now, if Percival was warning him, he would do well to listen.

"All right," Fielding said: "then why not move in with me? That should settle any nonsense. I'm told that I snore rather badly, but even so a free bed for two nights should appeal to your sense of economy."

"A charming offer. But unfortunately I'm not much loved in Yugoslavia, so I must leave the train in Austria this afternoon. A pity: we could have talked about the dear old days in BAOR."

It was a measure of the ascendancy which Percival had obtained over Fielding during their conversation that Fielding, faced with this unexpected news, felt suddenly and totally vulnerable. Although the dining-car was grossly overheated, he found himself shivering as if he had been stripped to the skin.

"But . . . what shall I do?"

"Do, my dear fellow? Read your books. Look out of the window. Eat delicious meals . . . the restaurant-car which comes on at the Yugoslav frontier, by the way, is the best on this trip – or so I used to think when I was still allowed in it. The regime considers it a good advertisement, you see."

"Leonard. If, as you suggest, someone tries . . . to get at me . . . what shall I do?"

"Keep a stiff upper lip, old chap, and remember the honour of the regiment."

"*Leonard*—"

"—Don't tell me that an officer of Lord Hamilton's Horse is getting into a funk."

"I simply," said Fielding, pulling himself together, "want to know what course of action you recommend."

"Very simple. Tomorrow evening you will have a choice. Either you can eat an early dinner, at about six o'clock, in the Yugoslav dining-car before reaching the Greek frontier; or you can eat later on in the Greek car, which will be put on at the frontier station. Which will you choose?"

"The Greek one. I hate dining too early."

"You just don't listen, do you? I have already told you that the Yugoslav dining-car provides the best meals on this whole run. Take my tip, Major Gray: do your stomach . . . and yourself . . . a favour."

Percival rose to his feet.

"Ten per cent for service, isn't it?" he asked.

"You should know. You're so familiar with this line."

Percival counted five Marks and fifty Pfennigs, checked them carefully and put them on the table.

"The Greeks charge ten per cent too," he said, "and the Yugoslavs fifteen. But you're not the man to bother yourself about an extra five per cent, now are you?"

Smiling, Percival backed away down the aisle and raised a hand in farewell.

"Anyway," he said, "it's being paid by the BBC."

As Fielding re-entered his compartment after lunch, a face rose to meet him : his own. It was a clear second before he recognised himself in the looking glass over the hand-basin, and during that second a thick sweat of fear gathered in his groin. He had failed to know himself, as he realised when he was calmer, because Leonard Percival was still so much the same that he, Fielding, had been carried back in time and had forgotten, if only for a few moments, how he himself had changed. The face he had expected to see in the mirror was that of ten years ago : clear eyes widely set, Greek nose, voluptuous mouth and becomingly cleft chin. Now all that remained from that time was his hair, still thick and glowing auburn, better, he thought, than Percival can show or ever could. He stroked it fondly with both hands, watching them in the glass; my beautiful hair, he thought. And then, what shall I do? I'm already starting at my own shadow; what shall I do if ever the threat is real?

The trouble was, he thought, as he sat down by the window, that Percival's communication was on the one hand (if one thought about it properly for two seconds together) wildly improbable and yet on the other hand so authoritative. Its authority it derived from something in Percival's manner which had procured him Fielding's respect; and however laughable, however inconsistent what Percival actually said, Fielding felt somehow compelled to puzzle at it until it made sense. It was like being faced with a corrupt passage in a classical author: the words, as they stood, might be gibberish, but since they had been written by a great man there must be some way of emending and construing them so that their message would at last become clear.

What, then, had Percival been trying to say? And why couldn't he have come straight out with it? Even his manner, although it had won Fielding's reluctant attention, had been ambiguous. Perhaps he had been spying for so long that he was now incapable of doing anything directly: an occupational debility like tennis elbow or housemaid's knee. But this was no time for random speculation. Analyse: what had Percival said and what did he mean?

If one ignored the jokes about money and class, what it seemed to amount to was a series of warnings, each of a nature – and here was the confusion – to invalidate the one which preceded it. Percival had started by warning him off the whole project: stick to your work, he had said; don't meddle with what doesn't concern you. Having thus expressed his disapproval, however, Percival had then gone on to offer assistance or at any rate advice on the plain assumption that Fielding would see the journey through ("one doesn't take orders from foreigners"). He had told Fielding to be on his guard against a possible intruder, who might corner him in his compartment, with the connivance of the wagon-lit attendant, and start asking awkward questions. Leave aside the vagueness of all this (who would the intruder be? where and what his nation?), leave aside its sheer implausibility, one then came to the biggest *non sequitur* of all. For when asked what action should be taken to deal with the mysterious stranger, Percival had merely told him to dine, on the evening of the next day, not in the Greek restaurant-car but in the Yugoslav one. Percival evidently regarded this as a simple and obvious precaution,

but how it could help to thwart malicious intruders from
getting into one's sleeping compartment was more than
Fielding could compute.

Outside his window, April sparkled among the passing
pine-trees. A stretch of lake, a village with church and
tower, onion-topped, a green field with cows. Another
stretch of lake, another village with church, another field ...
As the countryside unrolled, strictly repetitive like the
background to an early Disney cartoon, Fielding's head
began to nod forward. Who had sent Leonard and why?
Would he turn up later, or did his assignment end when he
left the train in Austria? Where in Austria? If only Leonard
had been more plain ... but here he was in the compartment, now was Fielding's chance to get things straight. 'Tell
me, Leonard ...' But Leonard wasn't listening; he was
looking into the mirror, stroking his hair, which had grown
thick and curly and auburn, just like Fielding's. 'Do you like
my hair?' Leonard said. 'I've been using an expensive new
lotion – rather presumptuous in a member of the middle
class, but then I was envious of yours. Why should you
Dragoons always have the best?' He turned to face Fielding,
and he had Fielding's face as well as his hair, Fielding's face
as it had been ten years ago, in Göttingen, where the sun
sparkled among the pine-trees in the spring. 'I love you,'
said Leonard-Fielding, the ghost-Fielding from Göttingen,
'I love you so much, please give me a kiss.' But Fielding
knew that it was dangerous to be kissed by ghosts and he
shrank up against the window, while the ghost-Fielding held
out his arms and smiled wider and wider, obscenely inviting,
a living corpse cackling with laughter, its face splitting into
great sores of PUS PUS PUS, red and yellow like a Turner
sunset, POX POX POX.

Fielding woke to the heavy knocking on the door.

"No," he screamed, "no."

The door was flung open and a huge man thrust himself
through the narrow entrance.

"Gruss Gott, mein Herr," said the man reproachfully:
"Austrian customs, please."

Tom Llewyllyn and his wife Patricia lived in an angular flat
in Southwell Gardens. At about the time Fielding's train
passed over the German-Austrian frontier, Tom returned
home from the Television Centre, sat down in front of the
gas-fire, and said:

"Is the water hot? I need a bath."

But Patricia had forgotten to turn on the immersion
heater.

"It's hardly tea-time yet," she wailed.

"I couldn't bear that place a second longer. Anyhow, I
*have* asked you always to turn it on by three. Just to make
sure."

But Patricia had been out shopping, she explained, and
she had had to take Baby, their two-year-old daughter, to
the dentist, and she had been distracted later by a long
telephone call from her sister, Isobel Stern.

"What was Isobel on about?"

"She and Gregory went to see Fielding off at Victoria
yesterday."

Patricia hesitated, then picked Baby off the filthy carpet
and began to change her nappies.

"It can't," said Tom, "have taken Isobel very long to tell
you that."

"She'd had . . . one of her feelings."

Tom shrugged.

"Fine. Isobel's had one of her feelings and there's no hot
water. And another thing," he said: "when you change that
child you ought to wash and powder her."

Patricia, who before her marriage in 1959 had kept house
immaculately for her father, Sir Edwin Turbot, and had
been remarkable for strength of character, had changed in
the last three years. She had become sluttish and inefficient.

Tom thought that this was the result of her strong attachment to Sir Edwin, who from being a prominent statesman was now rapidly going ga-ga: Patricia, that was to say, was declining in her behaviour, out of an unconscious wish to share the old man's predicament. In which case, Tom could only hope that Sir Edwin would very soon die and so release Patricia from the need to emulate him; though of course it might work the other way – Patricia might develop an unconscious wish to share his coffin. Tom sighed heavily. It was all too complicated, would indeed have been insupportable had he not loved her very much.

Meanwhile Patricia had clumped reluctantly away to the bathroom with Baby and was now clumping back.

"No hot water, of course," she said, "so I couldn't wash her. But," with an air of pride, "I've turned on the immersion heater."

Baby began to dribble on Patricia's lap.

"That child smells," said Tom.

"That was what Isobel said," remarked Patricia impenitently, "about Fielding Gray."

"Rubbish. There isn't a more fastidious man in England."

"Not literally. It was all part of Isobel's feeling. There was, she said, a smell of death."

"She's just dramatising as usual."

All the same, Tom thought, I wish this hadn't come so soon after what I heard this morning. For that morning he had been visited by a man from the BBC department which handled sound-broadcasting in the Near East. He had heard, the man said, that Tom was sending a man to think up a programme about Cyprus. While it was no affair of his, and he did hope Tom wouldn't think he was interfering, he felt he ought to say that the time was ... ill chosen. Why, Tom had replied: there was no sign of present trouble, and if trouble should suddenly come, so much the more interesting for his writer on the spot. It wasn't as simple as that, the man observed: there wasn't going to be any trouble –

not for some time – but there were – *sensitivities*. In that case, could not the Cypriots have given the BBC a polite but firm warning to stay away for the time being? It wasn't so much the Cypriots who were being sensitive, the man said, as ... somebody else. Who and why? It was impolitic, the man opined, to ask such crude and direct questions about so very sensitive an area; after which cryptic pronouncement he had glided out of Tom's office.

Tom wondered now whether to tell Patricia about this and decided against it. She would only say that it confirmed Isobel's "feeling"; and since Tom, despite himself, was inclined to think the same, and was therefore furious with himself for being so weak and irrational, further discussion of the topic could only lead to loss of temper. Isobel, he told himself sternly, was a silly little ass, and the Near East man was a pretentious little ass, and best leave it at that.

"Isobel has too little to do," he said now : "why doesn't she have a baby?"

"They're trying very hard. Gregory wants one even more than she does."

"A baby," said Tom, looking with fond disgust at the drooling child on Patricia's lap, "should be enough to settle even her. Smell of death, indeed. The next thing we know she'll have bought a crystal ball."

"Once," said Patricia, "when we were children, she organised a seance."

"What happened?"

"Nothing really," Patricia said. "She pretended to go into a trance and shouted a lot of rude words. She claimed afterwards she'd never heard them before, but she was always hanging round the gardener's boy, so I expect she learnt them from him."

As the afternoon retreated from his window and the evening filtered slowly among the pine trees, Fielding alternately pondered and dozed. Most times that he fell asleep he was woken abruptly after a few minutes by acid heartburn which resulted from his gastronomic lunch. Once, however, he slept longer and was roused only by a tapping on the glass beside his head. This turned out to be Percival, who was standing on a platform and grinning. As soon as he saw Fielding was awake, Percival pushed his canines down over his lower lip in a rather good imitation of Count Dracula, waved, turned on his heel, and walked off with a swirl of his stylish overcoat towards the exit from the station, which, Fielding now saw, was called Linz. Apparently Percival had no luggage; nor, Fielding reflected, would one expect him to have any; like all vampires he doubtless travelled light.

Although Fielding's thoughts grew no clearer as the evening went on, by the end of dinner he had reached a decision. The meal, being Austrian, was poor and his appetite even poorer; but two whiskies and a bottle of brisk red wine helped him to formulate his plan with some confidence. Not that it needed much formulation, for it was extremely simple: he would just follow Percival's advice and see what came of it. He would stay awake, which should not be difficult after his comatose afternoon, until, in a few hours, the train crossed from Austria into Yugoslavia; he would then lock the door of his compartment and go to bed, fully dressed in case of night alarums; and for the rest, he would keep his one eye cocked the next day and in the evening would take great care, as Percival had urged, to dine early in the Yugoslav restaurant-car and eschew the Greek. Percival had assured him that this was the way to evade the danger that threatened; and though Percival's logic was obscure, the situation was Percival's production, so to speak, and Percival must be allowed to know best.

Having finally settled this over three large glasses of brandy, Fielding purchased a bottle of the same from the steward and went back to his compartment, where he amused himself (as he often did when slightly drunk) with reading his favourite passages from his own books.

When the train reached the Yugoslav frontier, there was less shouting and shunting than there had been at any frontier previous. Although Fielding had expected much activity from officials, these merely glanced at the pile of passports held by the wagon-lit attendant for his charges and passed on down the train.

Through his window, Fielding watched the Austrian dining-car as it was rolled away down a side-line (good riddance) and the Yugoslav one which was being moved up in its place. Now what, he thought to himself, can be so special about *that*, that Percival should have been at such pains to recommend it? No answer suggested itself, so he stretched himself flat on his bunk, half-anaesthetised with brandy, to sleep.

"Do you think," said Tom Llewyllyn at breakfast, "that we might have kippers occasionally instead of boiled eggs?"

"Baby can't eat kippers," Patricia said.

"Baby could have her boiled egg and *we* could have kippers."

"Then Baby would be jealous."

"Not if she can't eat kippers anyway."

"She doesn't *know* she can't eat them anyway."

Baby squirted half a boiled egg, carefully accumulated in her ample cheeks, on to Tom's dark suit.

"Oh dear," said Patricia. Her dressing gown fell apart to reveal the insides of two long, snaky breasts.

"Never mind," said Tom, breathing heavily, "I'll go to Shepherd's Bush in the check one."

"Oh, darling ... I'm afraid I forgot ... It's still at the

cleaners. But I expect a sports coat and flannels will be all right. I mean, for the *BBC* . . ."

"It just so happens that I'm having lunch with the Director of Features."

"Are you?" said Patricia, unimpressed. "Well, eat as much as you can, darling, because I've got to take Baby to the clinic and I'll be too tired to cook proper dinner."

Fielding had his breakfast in the Yugoslav restaurant-car. The head waiter, although he looked and moved like a retired wrestler, had a very graceful address.

"Eggs and bacon," he said, "for an English."

Fielding, whose liver felt like a badly blown up football on a muddy day, politely demurred; but when the head waiter's face started to crumple, he nodded assent after all and was served a few minutes later, with the best plate of eggs and bacon he had eaten in several months.

Gregory and Isobel Stern always had breakfast downstairs in the dining-room, fully dressed. It made, as Gregory put it, a crisp start to the day; and since they lived in Chelsea, where there was much laxity in the air, it was important to have as many crisp habits as possible.

Gregory ate some patent breakfast food compound of ground-nuts and sawdust, while Isobel knocked into a great plate of kedgeree, which she had cooked for herself.

"What are you doing today?" Gregory asked.

"Spring cleaning. What are *you* doing? Sitting in that office trying to cheat your authors, I suppose."

It was said with the malicious affection which of all her qualities Gregory loved most.

"I'm going to read some of the stuff which Detterling's been sending from Athens."

"That reminds me," Isobel said: "you know I told you I had that ... feeling ... about Fielding Gray?"

"Yes" – embarrassed and uneasy.

"Well, I had another last night in a dream. Fielding and I were looking at some old ruin somewhere. All I can remember is a large stone doorway, square and flat, with two animals carved above it, large dogs they looked like, sniffing up at a pillar. There was this same feeling of death I had at the station, only much stronger, as though the whole place was kind of ... seeped in it."

"Steeped in it," Gregory said.

"Well, there was a sort of *ooze*. That's seeping, isn't it?"

"But the verb is intransitive and so cannot be used in the passive voice."

"Passive yourself, you old cow. But the thing was," Isobel went on, "that there was another feeling too. With all that death about, Fielding was somehow enormously happy, quite radiant with it. 'It hasn't been like this for seventeen years,' he said."

"Seventeen?"

"Yes, wasn't it odd? If he'd said fifteen or twenty it would have seemed quite natural; but seventeen – so precise. That's why I remembered it."

Gregory champed his breakfast food.

"What was Fielding so happy about?" he enquired.

"The dream ended then. After Fielding spoke I saw a sort of blue flash a long way off ... and then the dream ended."

Gregory worked hard with his tongue to remove the coating of slush from his palate. The stuff might have been made of acorns. Why was it supposed to be so good for him?

"Could it have been the sea, this blue flash?" he asked.

"P'raps. Why?"

"Just a thought. You've never been to Greece, have you?"

"No. Why?"

"Just another thought. Tell me, Isobel my wife: what for must I eat this rubbish every morning?"

His eyes entreated.

"Because you're a weedy old Jew and it's good for you." Gregory chuckled.

"So I'm a weedy old Jew who must go now to work for my shekels. Will my wife be waiting this evening?"

"Waiting and ready," she said.

The Yugoslav countryside was green, rolling and interminable. During the morning Fielding read Richardson's *Clarissa*, which was even more interminable, and for lunch he had a glass of light beer and a piece of delicious but unnamed fish.

"Will the English not eat more?" the head waiter pleaded. "Our food is good, yes?"

"Your food is excellent. But I'm saving myself up for dinner."

Fielding pointed to a printed slip on the table, which begged to inform passengers in French, English, German and Italian (but not in Serbo-Croat) that dinner would be at 6.30 p.m. in order to enable them to conclude the meal in comfort before the train reached the Greek frontier.

"Ah, yes," said the head waiter, and ambled crab-wise away down the aisle.

"Fielding Gray, good," the Director of Features said: "Cyprus . . . not so good."

"Fielding knows about Cyprus," said Tom.

"And other places, I take it." The Director looked sternly at Tom's tweed jacket. "So why Cyprus?" he said.

"Why not? I told you I was sending him there some days ago. Why bring it up again now?"

The Director, being of privileged rank, was lunching Tom

in a private room in the Television Centre. A vegetarian, he had ordered the meal in advance: an undressed salad with some faddy kind of bread and for Tom, as a concession, a hard-boiled egg.

"What's your . . . line on Cyprus?" the Director of Features asked.

"That depends on Fielding. I've suggested he should start by checking back in the record for . . . inconsistencies."

The Director shuddered.

"Cyprus is an emergent nation now, you know that."

"No more so now than it was a week ago – when I first told you I was sending Gray. If you've got any new objections to his assignment, for God's sake be plain."

"When will he reach Athens?"

"In about twenty-four hours. Rather less."

"Send him a wire there," the Director quacked. "Tell him to hang on in Athens until further notice, as you may want him to research into something different after all."

"Is this what's known as *carte blanche*?"

"Simply a suggestion," said the Director, suddenly very mild, "which may be in everyone's best interest. Just ask him to wait. He'll probably be glad of a chance to have a good look round Athens."

"That's not the point, Director."

"I'm only trying to insure against . . . muddle. And that rings a bell. There've been complaints from Administration that you haven't turned in your National Insurance Card. See to it – there's a good chap."

During the afternoon, Fielding read more of *Clarissa*. It was, he decided, a work of obsession; its detailed and unhurried logic, its long and loving repetitions, demonstrated its author's total commitment and belief. The reader too believed, believed so completely that he became at first fascinated and then disgusted by a world clogged with so

much greed, complacency, prudishness and spite. Every time
Fielding reached a temporary saturation point, he looked
out of the window for ten minutes; but the Yugoslav
landscape still rolled about as boringly as ever, and the only
relief was an occasional crude farm building, some sullen
cattle, or a group of chunky children waving at a wayside
halt. Four o'clock, five o'clock, six. Nothing had happened
all day, and in half an hour he must go for his early dinner.


That evening at 5.30 plump Maisie had a visitor who was
called Somerset Lloyd-James, MP. This gentleman had been
a client of Maisie's for nearly eight years, with only a brief
interval some three years back when there had been,
through no real fault of either's, a minor misunderstanding.
Now, after he had finished pretending to be a newly
pubescent schoolboy whom Maisie, the under-matron, was
seducing in the sick-room, Somerset Lloyd-James said:

"Fielding Gray. He *did* come to see you before he left?"

"Yes, Nugent."

Nugent was the name which Somerset had chosen for the
schoolboy.

"That's enough of that for now. What I want to know is,
what did Fielding . . . seem to feel about this trip to
Cyprus?"

"Nothing in particular. Should he have done?"

"Lots of people would have been very pleased at an
assignment like that."

"He wasn't. He was sorry if anything."

"Ah," said Somerset: "why?"

"I don't think he likes the people much – after what they
did to his face."

"So that when he comes up with his stuff he'll do his
worst for them?"

"He certainly won't kill himself finding excuses for them."

"Thank you," said Somerset Lloyd-James, MP: "that's

what I wanted to know ... You can call me Nugent again now. Matron, I've got such a frightful pain – just here. Do you think I could have a day in the sicker?"

Maisie suppressed a sigh.

"I'm sorry to hear that, Nugent mi.," she said: "you'd better lie down there and let me have a look at you ..."

Tessie Buttock was sitting fatly on the fender in the front hall of her hotel.

"Woozums, woozums," she intoned to Albert Edward, who was lying in a rocking chair, "how we do miss that ugly Fielding, to be sure. All those interesting chats about his writing friends and all their filthy habits. Not to mention what he pays so regular for his room. We're not so full these days, woozums darling, that we can forget about that." She reached over and rocked Albert Edward's chair. "It might even be a mercy if they decided to pull the old place down. They'd have to pay quite a bit for the compensation. But then Fielding would have nowhere to come home to." A jagged smile cut into her mean, fleshy face. "You see, woozums, this is the only home he's got. All he's got in the world is those dirty writing friends, and some trollop up west, and the pair of us. I wonder – don't you wonder, woozums? – what he's doing now."

What Fielding was doing just then was walking down the corridor to the Yugoslav dining-car. Since this had been put on next to the wagon-lit coach for Athens, he had only a short way to go; and in fact it was even shorter than he expected, because the door at the end of the sleeping-car was locked.

Now he came to think of it, no one had come through to announce dinner; he had simply assumed that this would be at 6.30 as notified by the printed slip on his table at lunch, and he had therefore left his compartment promptly though unsummoned at 6.29. Perhaps there was some sort of delay (trouble with the cooking apparatus, trouble with the staff) and the door had been locked to fend off importunate diners till all was ready. Then surely the head waiter or one of his underlings would have been hovering with explanation or reassurance? But then again, he thought, this was an iron curtain country (more or less), and such places were notoriously careless of one's convenience. Perhaps the sleeping-car attendant would know what was going on.

The attendant had a cubby hole at the other end (the front end) of the sleeping-car. When Fielding reached it, its door was open and it was deserted. This in itself meant nothing. What was mildly worrying, however, was that the pile of passengers' passports, which were entrusted to the attendant and which Fielding had several times seen stacked on his table when going to and from the loo, had disappeared; and what was more discouraging still was that at this end of the car as at the other the connecting door was locked.

Calm, calm. Proceeding back along the carpeted corridor, Fielding knocked, one by one, on the doors of the compartments. One by one, as he received no answer, he opened them, only to find that in each case the compartment was empty; not only empty, but swept, garnished, pristine, unspotted by the least trace of occupancy past or present. When he opened his own door, which was half-way along, he stepped back, on sudden impulse, in case of ambush or trap; but it was exactly as he left it. Nor did this bring comfort, for a presence there, however alien, might have offered information, would certainly have offered human company, for which he suddenly yearned. The remaining doors, between his own and the end, he flung open, desperate and sweaty, without knocking. Nobody. Nothing. Once more he tried the door through to the dining-car: immovable as the gate of a tomb.

For some time now the train had been gradually slowing down. He looked out of the window. Dark now, nothing to see ... but surely ... lights, the lights on the rest of the train? But of course, unless the train was on a bend he wouldn't see them. One way to settle it. He forced down the window in the side door next to him and thrust his head into the night. Far away, in the direction from which the train had come, there was a single red light, receding: otherwise nothing, total blackness. And forward? Nothing at all, beyond the yellow-lit window at the front end of the sleeping-car, nothing at all except some kind of looming mass, darkness visible, as it were, which was near, how near? – nearer anyhow, suddenly all above him, *now* ...

The train (train?) must have been swallowed by a tunnel. Not four feet from him the light from the corridor window played on a furry black wall. The speed was still decreasing; but just as the wheels seemed about to stop entirely, they gathered way again, first slightly, then definitely, then vigorously. There must be a slope, he thought; there's nothing to pull it, nothing now except this lone car and me alone in it. Where? Why? How? Never mind that, only one thing to think about – escape.

Escape? From a runaway coach doing thirty miles an hour in a tunnel? Nothing for it. Wait. Perhaps it will slow down again, stop. Different noise from the wheels now, lighter, less confined, must be coming out. Slowly, surely. With God's grace it will stop. *God, make it stop*.

As the coach passed with a whoosh out of the tunnel, he put his head out of the window again. Far below he could see lights, as of a fair-sized town. The coach, so far from stopping, lurched violently round a bend. The thing was now quite clear. He was descending and rapidly accelerating round a series of loops, and at the next bend or the next but one the coach, unbraked, would simply ride off the rails into space.

Get out. Now. How? ... Jump *inwards*, towards the

hillside. But even so, rails, fences, wires, rocks, God knew what beside. Sleeping-car: *bedding*. He started back towards his compartment. The coach kicked and tilted, throwing him heavily against the side of the corridor; but after a grating of metal and creaking of wood the *status quo ante* was resumed. Last chance: out before the next corner. He flung into his compartment, seized the piled blankets from the upper bunk. The mattress, use it as a shield. Loaded with mattress and blankets, he staggered back along the corridor to the two side doors at its rear. He wrapped blankets round his loins and round his head; threw open the door which faced away from the gulf below; wrapped his arms and hands in two more blankets; clasped the mattress to his stomach, so that it shielded him from his face down to his lower shins; and then, as the wheels began to grind and squeal against the rails, he took off at a slant (head slightly forward) from the iron steps which descended from the open door. His last thought, as he fell into blackness, was of Gregory Stern's Mezuzah, which he was carrying, wrapped in a handkerchief, in the inner breast pocket next his heart: let the holy name of Shaddai save him if It would.

## 3
## INTIMATIONS
## AND INTIMACIES

"I BOUGHT this stuff for you off the peg," said Captain Detterling : "I hope it fits."

"It looks rather Greek," Fielding said.

"It came from the best men's shop in Athens. Now you get dressed, while I settle up with these hospital people, and we'll be on our way."

Detterling sauntered out of the room with a characteristic air of owning the entire building, and Fielding began to put on the clothes from the best men's shop in Athens. The shoes were hideous and the trousers disagreeably wide at the bottoms. Furthermore, while Detterling had bought him a grey homburg (of the type worn by old-fashioned Greek gentlemen when sitting outside cafés) which wasn't at all necessary, he had forgotten to get any underpants, which were. But who am I to complain? Fielding thought: I'm bloody lucky not to be wearing a shroud.

In fact, things could have hardly fallen out more fortunately. Less than an hour after the sleeping-car derailed itself a search-party from the town below had found Fielding, who was lying by the line suffering from multiple minor abrasions and immobilised by shock. Everyone had been extremely kind and helpful. He had been patched up by a competent doctor, made very comfortable in a private room in a local hospital, and treated with respect, the next morning, by an English-speaking policeman, who was distressed, however, that Fielding had no "piece of identification". At Fielding's suggestion, a telephone call had been made to Captain Detterling at the Grande Bretagne in Athens, and two days later here Detterling was, bearing the new clothes which the kind-hearted policeman had warned him Fielding would need after his violent misadventure, and having apparently fixed everything to everyone's satisfaction.

There was a knock on the door, and Detterling re-entered with a puzzled look.

"They don't want any money," he said crossly; "they say that in communist countries medical care is free."

"Are private rooms free too?"

"I mentioned that. They said that you were a guest who had suffered a grave misfortune in their country and was entitled to the best they could offer in recompense."

"The Greek thing about hospitality, I suppose. This far south the people are Macedonians rather than Slavs."

"I wouldn't know about that," said Captain Detterling, "but I find all this sweetness and charity very irritating. Personally, I like to pay the piper myself, so that I can call a disagreeable tune if I feel like it ... Do you approve of that homburg?"

"I'd sooner have had some pants."

"It's bad form," said Detterling, "to go bare-headed in foreign countries – particularly poor ones. It looks as if you're saying, 'Why should I bother to dress properly in a mucky little place like this?' The poorer the country, the more correct one should be in one's *tenu*."

"I don't doubt it. But I should still have liked some pants."

"We'll get you a pair on the way through Thessalonika."

"We're going by car?"

"Embassy car from Athens," Detterling said: "when one's dealing with these Bolshevik chappies it's as well to put on a bit of a show."

As the car thumped along the pitted roads towards the

border, Detterling explained how matters had been arranged. As a Member of Parliament, he had been well received at the Embassy in Athens, the First Secretary of which had luckily served during the war in his (and Fielding's) old regiment.

"Before your time, of course," Detterling said, "but when I vouched for you that clinched the matter. He made some telephone calls, including one to Belgrade, and turned over this jalopy complete with chauffeur, and by the time I got to the border on the way up there was a security big-noise waiting for me, waving your passport in the air and bursting to tell me the official story."

"Which was?"

"On their version, the police had had a tip-off, now thought to be bogus, that a pair of escaped prisoners had boarded the train at Skopje. So they stopped it for a check-up at some little station farther down the line, and of course the sleeping-car attendant had to get down and account for his bodies, of whom by that time you were the only one left."

"I remember stopping at several stations after Skopje, but I can't remember any kind of search."

"Well, according to my man the attendant was called out to show them your passport, did just that, and then went off back to his post in the sleeping-car. What they didn't know till later was that he never got there. He was found in the cleaning cupboard of the station loo some hours afterwards with a large lump on his nut and still hanging on to your passport."

"All right. But how did the coach . . . break loose?"

"They're not too clear about that. But the theory is that with the attendant out of the way some wicked person or persons were able to unlink all the carriages behind you, and unlink you from everything in front, and then shove you off on a branch line and send you whizzing down the mountain-oh."

"Pretty expert job."

"That's what I thought. Mind you, it's the sort of thing guerillas and that lot were always doing during the war, and Yugoslavia was swarming with 'em. I dare say they kept in practice ... Anyhow, it seems that about a hundred yards from where you were found the coach took off, plunged down the mountain, fell over a cliff and was smashed to pieces on some rocks at the bottom. There's not a particle of your kit to be found, my man said, and there wouldn't have been a particle of you if you'd still been with it. For all of which, I am to convey to you a hundred thousand apologies from the President and People of Yugoslavia."

"But do they know *why*?"

"Oh yes. The man told me with a poker face that it was probably an extremist group expressing their disapproval of the luxurious habits of capitalists and foreigners. A protest, you might say, against the International Company of Wagons-Lits."

"You didn't let him fob you off with that?"

"I was eating his luncheon, old man. It would have been rather pointed – don't you think? – to contradict."

"Darling," said Isobel Stern in London, "I *think* that at last this is it. Anyway, I'm late."

"We shall have a fine son," said Gregory.

"And I shall have a groaning," she said.

About twenty-four hours after they left the hospital in Yugoslavia, Fielding and Captain Detterling drove past Mount Olympus. All of it, except the lower slopes, was hidden in thick, fierce cloud.

"The gods must be sulking," said Detterling.

"I expect it's this."

Fielding felt in his breast pocket and took out Gregory

Stern's Mezuzah. He had found this, when he finally came
to his senses in the hospital, tightly clasped in his right hand.
Since it had been in the breast pocket of his coat when he
jumped, and since the coat, ripped half to pieces, had been
(he was told) some yards away from him when he was
discovered, this was not easy to explain. Fielding imagined
that he must have searched for and found the Mezuzah
while still delirious. Such a notion was curiously affecting
and much increased his regard, already considerable, for
Stern's gift.

"What is it?"

"A sort of Jewish charm. Just the thing to upset Zeus and
his crew. A present from Gregory. Which reminds me . . ."

Fielding went on to give Detterling the substance of
Gregory Stern's messages. When he finished, Detterling
said :

"He's wrong about the Cavafy memoirs. We must have
them if we can. If he won't pay for them, I will."

"He seemed very sure about it."

"I hope," said Detterling, "that this new Jewish act of his
is only on the surface. I've no objection to his giving you
amulets or whatever, but if he lets it affect his judgment . . .
if he suddenly wants to be forever doing Jewish books by
Jewish authors . . . then it'll be very awkward."

"There's no sign of that."

"I've been working with him for three years now. I'm
fond of him, and I know him really rather well, and I can
tell you for certain that any time up to six months ago this
Cavafy book would have been just the sort of thing to make
him dribble at the mouth. The memoirs of a modern Greek
poet who specialised in erotic themes with a strong historical
flavour . . . Quite irrestible. But now? Now he just dismisses
it as one more 'bugger book'. And why? Because Cavafy is
in the Hellenist tradition, whereas Gregory's getting obsessed
with the Judaic. I'm going to put a stop to that rubbish if I
have to beat it out of him."

In the seventeen years, on and off, that Fielding had known Detterling he had never seen him so heated. That this blasé and elegant aristocrat should suddenly fly into a passion on behalf of a minor Greek lyric poet was a real eye-opener.

"I never knew you were so involved," Fielding said.

"Neither did I," said Detterling, his voice crackling with irritation, "or not until a few weeks ago. I woke up one morning, after a late sitting of the House, with a terrible liver and one word hammering in my head: lies. I'd spent half the previous night, half the previous decade come to that, listening to politicians on both sides of the House mouthing out great big greasy *lies*. On the other hand, the one thing which had always impressed me, since I first joined in with Stern, was the extent to which those authors of his were concerned to tell the truth. They were a scabby lot, most of them, cranks and socialists and cheque-bouncers and niggers, but at least each of them, in his own dotty way, had a – how shall I put it? – a *hankering* for the truth. And suddenly that morning, while my liver festered and my head thumped, this seemed to be a remarkable and even a very moving thing. I became, as you put it, involved."

"And yet," said Fielding, "a good half of us are professional liars. Novelists, certainly. We record what never occurred."

"But unlike politicians you admit that before you start. Your truth has nothing to do with actual facts. Your truth consists in taking theoretical characters in theoretical situations and then tracing what you think would be the practical, moral and emotional consequences. If we, your readers, respond by saying 'Yes, yes, that is how it would be', then you have told the truth."

"Very often," said Fielding, "we just trick you into that response. Later on, when you close the book, you realise you've been conned ... that it's all been done with mirrors and not by real creative magic."

"An interesting point," said Detterling. "But I suppose in that case we can just be grateful to you for a brilliant illusion. At least you're only using your trickery to entertain, not to impose your own will on other people's lives ... Which brings us away from my involvement and on to yours. How are *you* involved?"

"In general—"

"—Not in general," said Detterling softly; "here and now. You are, it seems, at present involved in such a project and in such a way that someone has just tried to ... do ... you ... in."

"We can't be certain that what happened was deliberately aimed at me."

"No. But we can be certain – or at least I can – that the Yugoslavs couldn't wait to get you out of their country. No request, you notice, that you should stay and help with the enquiries. Just, 'So glad you've come, Mr Detterling, and please take him away as soon as he can move.' They know there's someone after you, you see, and they don't want your corpse on their hands. Or so I should surmise."

Fielding looked back at Mount Olympus. The clouds were less angry and were beginning to lift. Now that I'm receding, he thought, and taking the Mezuzah with me, the gods are starting to smile again. Perhaps the sacred name of Shaddai is not a blessing but, here at least, a curse.

"I was warned," he said to Detterling abruptly. "It's no good my pretending. I was warned, and so what happened must have been meant for me. What shall I do?"

"Take the first plane home from Athens."

"No. Not now I've come this far."

"Don't be obstinate, Fielding."

"It's not that. It's what you were talking about just now – a hankering for the truth." Fielding explained the genesis of his mission; how he had been reluctant at first, then half tempted by the chance to write revengefully of Cyprus, and finally won over by the personal nature of Tom's appeal.

"So you see," he said, "when I started I wasn't in the least concerned with the truth. Rather the reverse. But now ... now they've done this. . . . I must go on. To return now would mean that I'd allowed myself to be bullied – bullied out of my right to know."

"Idiotic pride," Detterling said.

"Partly. I don't like being denied. But there's also real curiosity. If someone has gone to such lengths, there must be something worth uncovering – don't you agree?"

"If someone has gone to such lengths, he'll go to greater."

"I shall ask for protection."

"If you ask for protection, you'll just be told to go home."

"There must be a way." His one eye pleaded. "*Res unius, res omnium,*" he said, quoting the motto of their old regiment.

"It's just conceivable," said Detterling at last, "that I know of someone who might help."

In London, Somerset Lloyd-James, MP, called on the Most Honourable the Marquis Canteloupe.

Lord Canteloupe was a conservative peer who had been given minor office under the Government, some years before, as Parliamentary Secretary for the Development of British Recreational Resources, an appointment considered apposite since he had been long and profitably engaged in exploiting his own west country estate as a popular pleasure ground. Although his efficacy on the national scale was somewhat impaired by a feudal manner and a low habit of mind, he had shown undeniable talents in the field of publicity and advertisement. He had therefore been put in charge of a newly formed Department of Public Relations and Popular Media, on the strict understanding that he should confine himself to devising propaganda and take no overt part in its dissemination.

The noble lord's job was to ensure, as far as possible, that the views which the nation formed of events domestic and foreign were the views which suited the Government. This was very far from easy; the newspaper editors, the radio and television producers, through whom, for the most part, he must operate, were not at all inclined to adopt Lord Canteloupe's line simply on Lord Canteloupe's suggestion. However, he had found that a *quid pro quo* in the shape of some juicy giblet of "inside information" would often win him a degree of co-operation, and he had become skilled in the confection of confidential items true enough to pass immediate scrutiny, false enough to give the impression he wanted to give, and apparently significant enough to earn editorial gratitude. In these semantic exercises he was assisted by a Member of Parliament called Carton Weir (who represented the Department in the Commons) and also, less officially but even more effectively, by Somerset Lloyd-James, who had long been editor of an influential journal called *Strix* and was happy to offer up his expertise in exchange for his lordship's patronage.

On this fine April morning their meeting had almost the appearance of an allegorical tableau: Somerset, with his scrawny limbs, bald head and pasty complexion, might have represented Winter in cringing withdrawal, while Canteloupe, with his vigorous and multi-hued presence, was for all his years the embodiment of sappy Spring. But any such interpretation of the scene would have been mistaken, for it was Somerset whose authority prevailed.

"Cyprus," Somerset said: "I don't like it."

"Not *more* wog-trouble?"

"Only if it's deliberately stirred up. We've been at great pains to put over a reassuring image. In Cyprus, we have conveyed, reasonable concessions have been made in response to reasonable and democratic pressures. So all, we have implied, is now peace and contentment; there has been no retreat, only a diplomatic adjustment."

" 'Please adjust your dress before leaving'," Canteloupe interjected. "Then you can pretend you never went in there."

"We therefore ring down the curtain," Somerset continued firmly, "amid restrained but real applause, and forget the whole affair. So the last thing we want, the last thing your Department wants, is for the drama to be started up again – and there is no immediate reason why it should be. But if someone goes out there deliberately looking for trouble, trouble there will certainly be."

"Well, it won't be our fault any more. Whatever happens there now, provided our troops stay in their bases and don't interfere, no one can blame us."

"As to that, you may be right and you may not. But suppose someone goes raking up the past? Suppose," said Somerset Lloyd-James, "that someone starts upsetting the mild and convenient historical version which we have at last persuaded the country to accept? Suppose someone gets up on television and demonstrates – *demonstrates,* Canteloupe – that from the start of the Cyprus business to the finish Great Britain was bullied and blackmailed and betrayed, and in the sum was cheated out of millions of money, hundreds of soldiers' lives, and a good slice of her rapidly dwindling prestige?"

"They can't cut *my* head off," Canteloupe said.

"You'd look very foolish. And your Department would have a lot of explaining to do."

"But why should anyone ... demonstrate all that?"

"Because it happens to be demonstrable – if someone should find the right clues. Now then. Tom Llewyllyn, who has an instinct for this sort of thing, has sent Fielding Gray, who is no fool and knows the background, out there to investigate. If Fielding picks up the clues, he'll follow them through to the bitter end, and Tom, who has been promised a free hand by the BBC, will broadcast the result on television. So what do we do?"

"We have a drink," said Canteloupe, and went to the cabinet by the wall.

"Not for me," said Somerset; "it's only ten-thirty."

"One needs to be flexible in this game."

Canteloupe poured himself a generous quintuple and followed it with a derisory squirt of soda.

"It is I," said Somerset, "who have been flexible so far. I got on to the Director of Features at the Television Centre and persuaded him to give an authoritative hint to Tom that a little delay would be appreciated."

"How did you persuade him to do that?"

"I promised him, in your name, that you'd let him do a documentary film of your place in Wiltshire. Private rooms and Rembrandts included. Free."

"Damn your beady eyes. I could have got thousands."

"It'll be excellent publicity."

"I don't need publicity. My place in Wiltshire," said Canteloupe proudly, "is at the top of the Stately Homes popularity poll."

"You don't need the money either. You're richer than half the Dukes."

"Half the Dukes are broke."

"Anyway," said Somerset patiently, "it was worth it. The Director had a word with Tom, and Tom, under protest, wired Fielding Gray in Athens and told him to hang on there for a possible change of instructions."

"And what did Fielding Gray do?"

"They haven't yet heard from him."

"Thousands of quid down the drain to get that telegram sent, and you don't even know he'll get it."

"He'll get it. Copies have gone to every major hotel and also to the airport. So at the very latest he'll get it when he goes there to catch his plane to Cyprus."

"All right," said Canteloupe, impressed; "but what then? All that anyone's agreed to is delay." He sucked down his whisky and poured himself another without noticing. "You say Tom Llewyllyn's been promised a free hand. When he thinks the delay's gone on long enough, he'll tell Gray to get going again, and what do we do then? *Give* the BBC my bloody house and ask for *more* delay? They'll probably want the park thrown in."

"You know and I know," said Somerset, "that there are other people even more concerned than we are to stop Fielding writing this programme. By engineering this delay, we have given them time and opportunity to ... er ... make their point."

"What a perfect swine you are," said Canteloupe happily. "But in that case, why not just leave it all to them? Why make the BBC send a million telegrams round the place, when all we need to do is *let* Gray go to Cyprus and get his come-uppance there?"

There was a knock on the door, through which floated a pudgy young man in a cloud of Chanel Eau de Cologne. Carton Weir.

"Get out," said Canteloupe.

Carton Weir floated out again.

"I'd give that fat little pansy the push tomorrow," said Canteloupe, "but the PM insists on my keeping him. I can't think why."

"He's particularly good at apologising to the people you insult. His *forte* is cleaning up messes. You may well need him – if there's a mess, for example, about Cyprus."

"I'd far sooner have you."

"I," said Somerset, "shall not be seen dead here if once there's a serious mess."

"I might have known. Well, while you are here," said Canteloupe, "answer my last question. If there are all these people so anxious to settle the problem of Gray, why not leave them to it? Why do we have to get in on the act?"

"Because," said Somerset, "if anything happens to him in Cyprus, it will be enquired why he was there and what he was doing, and this could lead to just the kind of revelations we deprecate. If, on the other hand, we delay him, thus giving other interested parties time to ... deflect him ... before he gets there, the connection with Cyprus will be far less pointed. And now I must get back to *Strix*. Please take my advice and be polite to Carton Weir."

When Fielding and Captain Detterling reached the Grande Bretagne Hotel in Athens, there was a telegram waiting for Fielding :

DESIRABLE YOU WAIT IN ATHENS UNTIL FURTHER NOTIFIED AMUSE TOI BIEN TOM.

"Somebody else getting the wind up," Detterling said. "Be a good boy and go home."

"He doesn't say that. He says I'm to wait here and amuse myself."

"The more fool him. Athens is about as amusing as Wolverhampton."

They went out into Constitution Square and took a taxi up to the Acropolis. For some reason this was closed, so they walked down-hill through the pine-trees and along a broad, noisy road to the entrance of the Agora. At the far end of this was a long portico of brash white stone. "The American School's reconstruction of the Stoa," said Detterling. "Personally, I prefer ruins to stay ruined."

"Let's try walking in it ... like philosophers of Athens."

The April sun was hot enough to make the shade very grateful, and the marble pavement, they found, favoured a steady yet effortless walk, as of two officers pacing the yard of Buckingham Palace between the Old Guard and the New.

"I'm going to wire Tom," said Fielding, "and tell him I want to move on straight away."

"Why not do as he says? He must have his reasons for asking."

They turned about, both of them unconsciously using the

standard parade-ground drill for the purpose, each in perfect time with the other, and marched slowly back along the portico.

"I suspect his reasons are too similar to yours in telling me to go home. I must move on quickly before they stop me altogether. If I get up enough momentum, they won't be able to. What was that?"

"What was what?"

"Something moved. Just behind us in that doorway."

They checked and turned, again with military precision. The door to which Fielding now pointed was locked; just to one side of it was a statue of a boy with a flute, ears pricked, eyes leering along the pipes, legs crossed daintily half way up the shin. Something about the full lips, as they curved over the flute, something about the firm but tenderly dented chin, made Fielding shiver all down his body.

"You're jumping at shadows," Detterling said as they resumed their march.

"It was that boy's face. I . . . recognised it as we passed."

"Of course you did. It's one of a thousand copies. Now then. If you're so set on going on with this business, I know a way you can get up momentum, as you put it, while obeying Llewyllyn's instructions at the same time. You remember I told you I knew someone who might help?"

"Yes."

"Well, just now he's on the island of Hydra. Two hours from the Piraeus by boat. You can go there for the day, to-morrow if you like, and be back for dinner. I may as well come too. Introduce you and all that."

"Who is it?"

"He's called Max de Freville."

"The gambler?"

"Right. He used to run a very big chemmy game in London."

"Then ran into trouble and came to live abroad with what he had left?"

"Which wasn't peanuts. Yes," said Detterling, "that's the chap. I think, though, he's now got some idea of starting a casino out here, if they'll let him. He's bored with doing nothing."

"How can he help me?"

"He had a kind of hobby. He used to pay informants all over Europe to let him know what was going on behind the scenes. His own private intelligence service ... very expensive. In the end, it became such an obsession that it nearly beggared him ... only he had the sense to pack it all in and move out while there was still time."

They turned about.

"Some three years ago," Detterling went on, "just before he left London for good, Max had a kind of boasting fit and told me a lot of what he'd learnt over the years. He was being pretty wild that evening, but some of it was true all right, and some of it was in much the same area as this enquiry of yours. That could be true too."

"Can you remember it?"

"Not in any detail. But I dare say Max can, and now he's had three years to calm down in, what he says should be worth listening to."

"I don't suppose he could ... protect me?"

"He can tell you who to stay away from. He might even know of possible allies. I gather he still does a bit of nosing about ... as far as he can afford it."

"And then," mused Fielding, "if he did give me a useful line, I could tell Tom I was really on to something and go right ahead – whether he liked it or not."

"But would the BBC go on paying?"

"The BBC is very generous. They paid handsome expenses cash down and also an advance of fifty per cent on my full fee."

"They might tell you to apply these resources in some other direction."

"They might but I shan't. They got me into this and the

least they can do is to let me see it through. Hydra to-morrow then?"

"Hydra to-morrow. I'll wire Max to expect us."

They marched away across the Agora. The boy with the flute piped silently on as the lock turned in the door beside him and a face almost as still as his own looked out after the two retreating Englishmen.

"Darling," said Isobel Stern to Gregory over their breakfast, "I was right."

"You're sure?"

"Either that, or I'm very, very late, which I never have been before."

"Then our son will be born at Christmas."

"Don't go getting ideas," Isobel said.

Above the little harbour of Hydra the plain but handsome white houses, built by the pirate captains of old, rise by steep tiers into the hills. In one such house, about a quarter of a mile above the northern wing of the harbour, Max de Freville put down his binoculars and said :

"They're just getting off the boat."

"Let me look," said Angela Tuck.

Angela was not Max's mistress but his comrade. For some years now they had spent much of their time together because they enjoyed taking care of each other. Although they often shared the same bed, they merely held hands in it, as innocent as the Babes in the Wood.

"I can recognise Detterling," Angela said now, "by the walk. As though he was wearing spurs. And there's a man with him dressed in the most ghastly suit and one of those homburgs. Are you sure that's Fielding Gray?"

"That's what the telegram said. I've never met him. How long since you did?"

"Seventeen years."

"Well then, of course he's changed. And he's been badly disfigured, or so they tell me."

"It's not that. He's got so fat, so coarse."

"So have you," said Max. "Let's go down and meet them."

They went through a little courtyard, out of a door and into an alleyway, along the alleyway and then down a flight of steps. At the bottom of the steps Detterling was consulting a surly islander, who was withholding information against the sight of money, while his companion in the homburg stood hunched against a wall. Max, pleased with this little piece of genre, screwed up the great furrows between his nostrils and the corners of his mouth in an expression which, intended for a smile, more nearly resembled the mask of tragedy.

"Welcome, old friend," he boomed.

The islander slunk off. Detterling and his companion turned, saw Angela, removed their hats.

"Your hair," cried Angela to Fielding; "at least you've kept your hair."

Fielding looked blankly at the large-limbed woman with the raddled, sexy face.

"It's been a long time," said Angela, resigned to not being recognised but nevertheless sad. "That summer in 1945. When me and Tuck had that house near yours in Broughton."

Fielding shook his head, not in denial but in rejection. He knew this woman now; he remembered the summer of 1945 quite as clearly as she did; and most clearly of all he remembered that she had done him harm.

"I know, I know," said Angela, reading his thought. She came down the steps and took his hand. "We'll talk about *that* later," she said. "First of all, drinkies."

Max and Detterling, who had been conferring together, started to loiter up the steps. Angela turned to follow them but Fielding took her arm and drew her back.

"It was all over long ago," he said: "no need to talk about it."

"As you wish." She put up her hand and quickly touched his hair. "I was just sorry that you were brooding about it after all this time. I don't want it to spoil your visit."

Fielding shrugged.

"We're taking the afternoon boat back to Athens," he said, and led off after the couple in front. Detterling now introduced him formally to Max, who looked him over sharply for a second or two, and then remarked:

"Angela was very excited when she heard you were coming. You mustn't disappoint her."

Before Fielding could think of a suitable reply, Max had turned back to Detterling.

"So I went to Rhodes first," he said, "but the authorities wouldn't hear of a casino there. Corfu, I knew, is just about to be fixed up anyway. So in the end I thought it might be worth taking a look round here."

They all went through the courtyard, Angela several paces behind the three men.

"Surely," Detterling was saying, "if they do grant a concession here, they'll want a Greek to run it."

"I know one who can front for me. An old chum called Lykiadopoulos. But somehow I don't think Hydra is right. Crowded in the summer, they say, but mostly with the arty set. All *they* bring to a casino is trouble."

They trooped through a large living-room and out on to a terrace which looked south over the harbour. The steamer which had brought Fielding and Detterling was now beating busily away to the south-west for Spetsai and the Argolid. As he looked across the wrinkled sea to the coast of the mainland, Fielding saw that clouds were beginning to rise, somewhere, it must be, in the direction of Nauplion. A line of Virgil came into his head: *moriens dulces reminiscitur Argos*; dying, he remembers his sweet Argos. Leonard Percival walked on to the terrace.

"Morning, all," he said. And to Fielding: "Nice to see you again."

Max introduced Percival to Detterling; Angela moved efficiently about with drinks and then went inside, muttering about the kitchen. Max and Detterling had already resumed their conversation about concessions, while Percival had seated himself in a canvas chair at the far end of the terrace and begun to polish his glasses. Fielding came and stood accusingly over him.

"What are you doing here?" he said.

"I'm an old friend," said Percival lightly. "De Freville and I enjoy exchanging gossip, you might say. So being in this part of the world, and knowing he was too ... I'm delighted you've decided to join us. You've come to the right place."

"What's that to you?"

"I am your sincere well-wisher," said Percival, "as you should have realised by now. I've already taken the liberty of telling Max about your assignment. You'll find him very helpful ... if you're polite."

"I've come here as Detterling's friend and on his suggestion. I didn't need you to interfere."

"My pleasure ... I was sorry to hear you had such an unpleasant time in Yugoslavia. All right now, I trust?"

"No thanks to you if I am."

"Come, come. I warned you, didn't I?"

"You should have warned me properly, told me to get off the train. You knew what was going to happen?"

"In broad terms. Rather an imaginative scheme, we thought when we found out about it, and very apt. You see, *they* wanted you out of the way for good, and the longer no one knew it was you, the better. So *their* idea was," said Percival with loving appreciation, "to dispose of you in a remote district of a barbarous country, in such a way that you would be quite unrecognisable, and to make sure that your passport was nowhere around to identify you."

"They don't seem to have been too clever about that. My passport was found soon enough."

"Enthusiastic amateurs, that's *their* trouble. No attention to detail."

"Who are 'they'? Cypriots, I suppose. And who are *you* for that matter?"

" 'They'," said Percival, "are people who resent you sticking your nose in where it isn't wanted. *We,* on the other hand, are anxious that it should not be cut off, as we are hoping you will sniff out delicious truffles."

"Then why did you bloody near let me get killed?"

"We wanted to make sure you were the right kind of man for our purpose. We had to know two things. One: were you a chap that would get cold feet at the first hint of danger? That was why I gave you a tip-off, told you to stay out of trouble and stick to your novels and so on – to see how you'd react. And true to your Dragoon upbringing, you didn't seize your luggage and run, you sat there on your arsehole and scowled. Good for you, chum. At the same time, you *were* cautious enough (quite rightly) to ask what could best be done, and this brings us to the second thing we had to find out. Granted you weren't the kind to scuttle away in a panic, were you competent to take care of yourself? Because if not, you were no use to us. So I was instructed to give you enough information to put you on the alert but not enough to let you know what was coming. All that palaver about restaurant-cars was to make sure you were awake and mobile about the time the trouble started. We owed you that, but the rest was up to you."

"And have I passed your test?"

"You're still here, aren't you?"

"And if I'd failed?"

"It would have been indisputably clear," said Percival, "for the most cogent of all possible reasons, that you were quite unable to help us."

"You bastard," said Fielding.

He reached down, whipped Percival's spectacles from his face, and drew his fist back to strike. Percival blinked up at him.

"Please return my glasses," he said : "I can't see anything without them."

The blinking, defenceless eyes were too much for Fielding.

"Here," he said, and handed the spectacles tenderly back.

"You should understand," said Percival equably, "that *we* are a perfectly respectable organisation, British and proud of it, with high-level sanctions for all we do. In assisting us you will have nothing to be ashamed of."

"What makes you think I'm going to assist you?"

"You already are. Because in any case at all your mission and your enquiry are exactly what we would wish them to be. Our only suggestion is, now that you've established your qualification in this line, that we should give you the benefit of our own expertise . . . in return, of course, for regular reports on your progress."

"And if I refuse?"

"Why should you? You'll be going ahead anyway, so why refuse the valuable support . . . the valuable clues . . . which we can offer. You see how highly we think of you."

Fielding looked south over the harbour. The steamer had disappeared, had probably rounded the cape into the Gulf of Nauplion, from which, he now noticed, the clouds were rising much higher and darker than before.

"Dirty weather on the way," said Percival, following his gaze. "Look, old man. We know, in outline, all there is to know about the Cyprus affair from way back. What we want is for someone to follow it all up and then construct a detailed and water-tight account. That someone is you. We can set you up with all the main headings, so to speak, and tell you exactly where to go to check everything up and fill in the gaps. We'll give you the whole thing on a plate."

"Then why not do it yourselves?"

"Because we, for obvious reasons, can't have anything to do with television. Not directly, at any rate. That's where you come in. Having got up your case, all the quicker and the surer for our discreet and unacknowledged assistance, you then present the incontrovertible facts to a shocked world. Believe me, you'll make quite a sensation."

"Which for some obscene reason will also suit you?"

"Yes, but why should you worry? You may even be glad when you know more about it."

Angela came round with more drinks.

"Lunch in five minutes," she said. And then, looking away to the south, "There's going to be a storm." She shivered slightly, pursed her lips at Fielding, and went over to Detterling and de Freville. Everyone had been very careful, Fielding now thought, to leave Percival and himself undisturbed.

"You do realise," he said, "that even if I agree to do what you want, my employers in the BBC are having second thoughts?"

"Yes," said Percival. "There are those in high places who want to let sleeping dogs lie."

"Why don't you then? You claim to be an official organisation . . . British and proud of it."

"Official interests can differ."

"Evidently. So what happens if those in high places prevail with the BBC and the whole thing's called off?"

"If you tell your friend Tom Llewyllyn what Max and I are going to tell you," said Percival, "nothing – but nothing – will make him agree to let it be called off."

At lunch it was agreed that in view of the nasty weather which was blowing up Fielding and Detterling would do better to delay their return to Athens until the following day.

"If it's rough," Max said, "the boat can't come into the harbour because of the narrow entrance. It anchors outside the bar and they row you out to it."

"Rather alarming? In a rough sea."

"They're very clever at it. But if it's really rough," said Angela, "the steamer doesn't stop at all."

Even as she was speaking a grey cloud moved over the face of the sky and the wind gathered strength through the alleyways.

"Goody," Angela shivered.

"That settles it," said Max. "I can lend you both pyjamas."

"And we shall have more leisure," said Percival, "to advise our friend Major Gray."

"Advise him about what?" Angela asked.

Angela did not take much interest in Max's intrigues, but she was rather interested, now that he had risen out of her past, in Fielding Gray. She had her own plans for his entertainment and was therefore anxious to know about other people's, in order to avoid unnecessary conflict.

"A little piece of journalism he's undertaken," said Percival. "Max and I may be able to help. This afternoon?" he suggested.

Angela glanced quickly at Max, signalling, as clearly as though she had spelt it out, what she had in mind. Max took the point and shrugged good-humouredly.

"Not this afternoon," he said to Percival, "tonight. As you say, we've plenty of time. After lunch, I for one am going to have a siesta."

Angela smiled at him gratefully.

"Snug," she said. "Nothing snugger than listening to the storm outside and having a siesta."

"Max mind?" said Angela. "Of course not."

She passed a hand along Fielding's flank and up towards

his chest, keeping the palm flat as it passed over his hips and his belly.

"Max knows what I'm like," she explained, "and he'd much sooner it was you than one of the local fishermen. Although he's a very civilised man, he's also rather a snob."

After lunch Max had disappeared. Angela had firmly offered Detterling and Percival a choice between back-gammon and siesta, of which they had elected the former. She had then led Fielding off, allegedly to show him the room which he would share for the night with Detterling, and taken him, instead, to her own.

"Max generally sleeps here at night," she said, "but he uses his own room in the afternoon."

After which, she had removed her skirt without ceremony and lain down on the bed in her stockings.

"Come on," she said: "show a bit of courtesy to your hostess."

So now Fielding was showing her all the courtesy he could muster, though not without misgiving. Every now and again he would think of his host and his social skill would flag. Then Angela would reassure him and set him going again.

"Turn over," she said.

As the rain rattled against the windows and Angela's fingers ran up and down his spine, Fielding thought of that far off summer during which Angela and her husband (now dead, it seemed) had occupied a house near his parents' on the coast at Broughton Staithe. He had desired her then, and she had first teased and later rejected him, and finally she had betrayed him. She had learnt his secrets and deliberately passed them to his enemies. So that now, now that it was himself, apparently, who was desired, he had the chance of revenge. The chance, he thought, but not the inclination; he was quite happy to lie there while this knowledgeable and still rather attractive woman kneaded his buttocks and his back. Yet why, he asked himself, *was* he desired? True, Angela could no longer afford to be so

choosy as she had been at Broughton, but she could at least
have found somebody whose face was still intact.

"Why now?" he muttered along the pillow. "Why not
*then,* when I was young . . . unspoilt?"

Angela, who was crouching over him with her stockinged
knees on either side of his own, lent forward to talk into his
ear.

"You're still young," she said, "and I like you spoilt. *Then*
you were perfect, I admit. But I could never fancy
perfection. I've always preferred something that was slightly
odd . . . even unwholesome."

She eased her thumbs up the insides of his shoulder
blades.

"That's why I seduced your friend Lloyd-James.
Remember?"

Fielding remembered very clearly. Somerset Lloyd-James,
his school friend and contemporary, had come to stay at
Broughton that summer, and Angela had invited them both
to her house while her husband was away in London. There
and then, she had as good as undressed Somerset under
Fielding's eyes and had only paused to order Fielding out of
the house before making Somerset free of her. To this hour
Fielding could still see them as they had been when he left
the house, Angela's great honey thighs and Somerset's
scraggy white ones.

"But of course," Angela was saying now, "if I'd known
that evening all that I found out later, it's you I'd have gone
for because it was really you that was unwholesome.
Somerset was just rather misshapen physically. But you" –
she ran both thumbs down to the top of the cleft between
his buttocks – "you were tainted all the way through. What
about that wretched boy at your school who killed himself –
what was he called?—"

"—Christopher," said Fielding, shivering with his distress
at the memory and with the pleasure that came from her
busy thumbs, "Christopher Roland."

"Christopher Roland ... What about *him*?" she said.

"I loved him, that was all."

"You loved him and he killed himself. What did you do to him, Fielding?"

"Must we talk about him?"

Somerset Lloyd-James had found out about Christopher and told Angela. Angela had betrayed Fielding to his mother. His mother—

"—Must we talk about Christopher?" he said. "It caused enough unhappiness at the time."

"Yes, we must," she said. "It excites me to talk about him. Turn over, Fielding ... It excites you too, doesn't it?"

As indeed it did. For all the misery, the guilt, the despair which Fielding had once felt about the boy, for all the sadness which he still felt and the almost unbearable recollections of his mother's part in the affair, talking about Christopher had excited him beyond anything which Angela's ministrations could have achieved, skilful as they were.

"Show me, Fielding. Show me what you did with Christopher."

"I ... Nothing. I wanted to be very gentle. So I put my arms round him, and I kissed him, and then he ... trembled ... and it was all over."

Angela chuckled and ran her finger-nails along his arm.

"Poor little Christopher. And the next time?"

"There wasn't a next time. Christopher wanted there to be, but at first I didn't, because he was ... changed somehow, and anyway I was afraid we might be found out. There'd been talk already ... Go on, Angela, don't stop."

"All right, if you go on about Christopher."

"Well ... later on, when I thought it was safe ... I wanted to do it again. But it was too late, because Christopher ... because ..."

"Because Christopher was dead."

"*Don't stop.*"

"Fielding. Show me what you would have done. What you would have done to Christopher if he hadn't been dead."

Later on, Angela said:

"What did he look like, the boy you wanted to do that to?"

"I don't really know how to put it. He was ... so finely made, so strong ... and yet so soft. I can't think of anyone like him. But yes," said Fielding, "yes, I can. Yesterday in Athens I saw a statue ... in that portico the Americans have built ... a statue of a boy playing the flute. The same legs, firm yet tender. The same lips, the same chin, the same face."

"Now," said Angela, "I'm going to be Christopher. I'm going to imagine what he'd have done to *you* ..."

At dinner they all reassembled, some having had a more interesting afternoon than others. Although the wind was still screaming down the alleyways, the rain had stopped, and Max proposed that Fielding should accompany Percival and himself to the tavern down by the harbour.

"Angie would only be bored by the discussion," Max said, "and you can tell Detterling about it later if you want to. He can stay here and keep Angie happy."

"Backgammon?" said Detterling to Angela.

"We'll see when they've gone," she said.

For the second time that day she looked gratefully at Max.

Max, Percival and Fielding sat at a table by the window of the Taverna Poseidon. Pressure lamps hissed and a group of sailors, in a far corner, muttered about the price of fish.

Outside, the wind swept the empty quay under the dim electric light, while the waters of the harbour slapped heavily at the rows of moored caiques.

"If it's only half as strong as this to-morrow," Max said, "they'll never get the steamer inside the bar of the harbour."

Spiros, the tavern-keeper, brought them a large can of wine, three tumblers and a plate of wizened apples.

"What do you say, Spiros? Will the wind keep up?"

Spiros turned down the corners of his mouth and moved away. The sailors, observing this, nodded to each other in approval: one did not give valuable information to strangers just for the asking.

"Disagreeable fellow, that," said Max: "they all are here. They don't mind tourists in the summer, if only because they can cheat 'em rotten, but they hate it if you stay for any length of time. They think you're prying into their secrets."

"Have they got any?"

"None. But their ancestors were pirates and they've inherited the pirate mentality. They regard this island as their lair and they don't care for people hanging about on it."

"Least of all rival pirates," said Percival; "one does see their point. But they ought to be grateful to you. If you start up a casino here, it'll bring 'em more tourists to cheat rotten."

"I've as good as decided against the place and they know it. I'll be moving on very soon."

"Where next?"

"It occurred to me that the Cypriots might be interested. I'm told they want to build up their tourist trade."

"What a lot of time we all spend," said Percival, "thinking about that wretched little island."

"Mind you," said Max. "I'd still need a Greek to front for me. I wouldn't trust the Cypriot Government to deal square with an Englishman. Not yet. Perhaps never . . . after what's happened. Which brings us," he said to Fielding, "to the information which Leonard here says you're after. Shall I tell you why I don't trust the new Government in Cyprus?"

"Because the Cypriots dislike us," Fielding said.

"But that's just the point. They don't dislike us. They never have. Which makes it all so much more sinister. If they'd just hated us, anyone could have understood their behaviour. But since, on the contrary, a lot of them even *loved* us, you'll agree that something very peculiar must have happened to set 'em off."

"Enosis," said Fielding; "all that hysteria about self-determination. Surely you don't need to look any further."

"You're taking the superficial view," Max said. "Of course they were ready to do a bit of shouting about Enosis and the rest of it, but they certainly didn't intend to have any real unpleasantness, any more than they did in the thirties. They just wanted a little excitement to liven up public holidays."

"At first, possibly. But once they knew they had official support in Athens – which they *hadn't had* in the thirties – they began to take it seriously."

"Superficial again," said Max. "British rule had its faults, but at least it was solvent and it was secure. It meant honest government, however short-sighted. Why reject this in favour of absorption by a corrupt and semi-bankrupt Balkan state, which would have taxed Cyprus into the sea and taken half its young men as conscripts?"

"The ethnic tie," said Fielding. "Besides, the Cypriots wanted to think they were choosing for themselves. They may have liked us but they hadn't chosen us. Here was their chance to assert themselves – with full encouragement in Athens from their own kith and kin."

"There was encouragement all right," said Max; "but the most important part of it did not come from their Athenian kith and kin."

"Oh come, come, come. I know the mainland Greeks don't care for their Cypriot cousins as much as they sometimes pretend to, but they were quite happy to lend a helping hand. If only to annoy the Turks."

"Happy to break a few windows and shout a few slogans, yes. Not to spend good money."

"Then where did the money come from?"

"Where does money always come from these days?" Leonard Percival said.

There was a long silence. Spiros came to their table, took away their wine-can although it was by no means empty, and returned with a full one. The sailors grinned at one another. Spiros had cheated the strangers of a good six drachmae.

"You're not going to tell me," said Fielding at last, "that the Americans—"

"—Look," said Max. "In the old days, as Detterling has told you, I used to spend the greater part of my money keeping myself informed. It started as a small service to check up on the people who came to my chemmy game – whether their credit was good; but one thing led to another and in the end I had correspondents all over Europe. Good ones too. Leonard here, for example, was one of them for years ... supplementing his meagre official income.

"Now, although I had to give up 'this amusing hobby some time ago, in the middle fifties my network was at its best, and one of the things I found out was this. The Americans, though they find us useful and don't really resent the little influence we still exercise, cannot and will not tolerate any survival of the imperial image. They cannot and will not suffer our retention of foreign *possessions*. This is not so much a matter of policy on their part as of sentiment: as long as any British colonies exist, they cannot forget that America was once a colony itself. Only by wiping out our entire colonial empire can they wipe out the indignity of their own colonial past. There are other considerations – it is much easier, for instance, to get American goods and industries into a place once you've got the British administration out of it – but paramount is the determination, as you might say, to trample on the red-coats."

"Neurotic envy," Fielding said.

"Very probably. What made them so furious about Suez, for example, was not what we were doing but the fact that we were the people doing it, in our old territories and in the good old way. With kettle drums and drawn sabres, which by this time, on the American reckoning, should have been safely rusting in museums. Anyway," Max continued, "the anti-colonial sentiment, whatever its psychological origin, is so strong that the United States, from time to time, have gone as far as actually to encourage and finance the subversion of our colonies. Secretly, of course, so secretly that on an official level no one even has to dream about it. But none the less Uncle Sam's helping hand has often been decisive … in Kenya for one place … and in Cyprus for one more."

"But *how*?"

"Flattery, advice and training for the local leadership; weapons and equipment; money. All provided on the q.t. by American secret agents. This was what they offered the Cypriots … partly direct and partly through Athens; and the Cypriots, for very shame, had to pick up the weapons and fight. Poor Cypriots. One day they were happily yelling about freedom in the market-place … and the next they found that someone had actually taken them at their word and given them brand-new rifles instead of empty ouzo bottles. It was now a matter of face: there could be no turning back."

"All this is rather nebulous," Fielding said. "Say what you like about the American secret service, on the face of it the Cypriot rebels were commanded by the patriot, Colonel Grivas, and armed with smuggled weapons."

"But who paid for the weapons? The Cypriots couldn't and the Greeks wouldn't. And as for the patriot Colonel Grivas," said Percival, "he was closely assisted at every step by a guerilla expert called Diomedes."

"And so?"

"And so Diomedes was the *nom de guerre* of an American secret serviceman called Earle Restarick."

"Restarick," repeated Fielding: "I seem to have heard the name."

"Perhaps. He was mixed up with me in that business in Germany ten years ago."

"That," said Fielding with distaste.

"That," said Percival. "A project, you may remember, which Britain and the US had in common, so at that time we were on the same side. I found him a very interesting man."

"And now you're claiming that this Restarick later became the brains behind Colonel Grivas?"

"The brains, and the bombs, and the cash."

"How can you be sure?"

Percival dipped a slice of apple in his wine and bit it in two with a snap.

"In this game," he said, "you get to know a man's style. I was working in Cyprus during the trouble, and more and more of the tricks pulled by the other side had what one might call Restarick's *idiom* ... which I remembered very well from the job we'd worked on together in Germany. And then, later on, I received information which proved that he was in Cyprus at the time. For that matter, he's still there now."

"Tell him about this idiom, this style," said Max.

"Restarick's favourite trick was a kind of four-dimensional feint. He would persuade his opponent to believe – to believe absolutely – in some situation, tactical, moral or intellectual, which simply didn't exist. In his response to the pressures of this mythical situation, Restarick's opponent would eventually take the action or strike the attitude which Restarick required of him, without Restarick's having to move a finger himself. In the end, this opponent would probably aim a desperate blow at some illusory figure of Restarick's creation – and the blow would go right through the shadow and land where Restarick wanted it to land. Several times in Cyprus he manoeuvred British patrols into firing on one another or on innocent crowds, he tricked British agents into denouncing one another, he even blackmailed an important officer into putting a time-bomb under the Governor's bed. Beautiful work," said Percival, "pure Restarick. He's quite indifferent, by the way, to the human or political results. He's only concerned with the immediate problem proposed to him and finding the neatest solution."

"Nevertheless," said Fielding, "although these exploits had Restarick's style, and although he was in Cyprus at the time, you can't *prove* that he was Diomedes."

"No," said Max; "not yet. But we can if we have just one more link."

"One more link," said Percival. "Pick up that link, achieve certain proof that Restarick was master-minding Grivas – and you can loose off the biggest anti-American scandal of a lifetime on twenty million television sets."

"And where is this ... link ... to be found?"

"Concealed on a dead body," said Max de Freville, "in a tomb eight centuries old. It sounds rather bizarre, I agree, but the explanation is really quite logical ..."

By the next day the wind had weakened, but not enough to allow the steamer from Athens to attempt the narrow entrance to the harbour. Two rowing boats were to convey passengers – at a cost of two drachmae per head for Hydriots, ten for other Greeks, and fifty for Fielding and Detterling – out to where the packet would anchor.

While Fielding and Detterling waited to embark, Max

gave Detterling messages for friends in London (whither Detterling must shortly return), Angela drank several large ouzos in the Taverna Poseidon out of sadness at her guests' departure, and Percival ran over the instructions which Fielding had been given the previous evening.

"Remember," said Percival, "that *they* don't know either that this object exists or where it is hidden. So they won't be guarding it."

"But they will be watching me."

"Certainly. But if you just pretend to poke about, as though you haven't any particular line to follow, and then give 'em the slip, they won't know where you've gone or what you're up to."

"Easier said than done. Besides, suppose they try some really radical expedient – as in Yugoslavia?"

"Unlikely. Restarick won't want to draw attention to Cyprus by murdering a well-known writer – who's there on behalf of the BBC – bang on the doorstep. Fielding Gray dead in Yugoslavia would have been well enough, but in Nicosia ... no. Odd as it may seem, the nearer you are to the centre of it all, the safer you'll be. From bodily harm at any rate."

"What other sort do you have in mind?"

"Restarick," said Percival, "is devious. He has his plans festering away for the future, so he doesn't want a lot of inquisitive flies arriving in Cyprus to buzz round your corpse – because while they were at it they might sniff out even nastier lumps of putrescence. This means he wants you alive – at any rate as long as you're in Cyprus – but he also, for obvious reasons, wants you silent. So what does he do?"

"You tell me. You're the expert on Restarick."

"He has recourse," said Percival, "to his favourite method. He brings pressure to bear on you by placing you in an exigent situation. Either a real one or, just as likely, an imaginary one which he's conjured up especially for you. In either case the pressure will be such – believe me, I've seen

him at it – that you will be mentally anaesthetised, quite
incapable of speaking a word in your own voice. That's the
kind of thing you've got to watch out for with Restarick."

The steamer came into sight round a headland and
sounded its hooter. Bare-footed boys ran round in circles
with luggage. Angela came red-eyed out of the Taverna
Poseidon.

"So," said Percival, "the best of luck. You're absolutely
sure where to find it?"

"Yes." Fielding shuddered. "You've made it very plain."

Angela swayed up to them.

"I do wish you weren't going so soon," she croaked.

"So do I," said Fielding, thinking of her gartered
stockings.

The oarsmen called from the rowing-boats. Percival
started to hum the Regimental March of Lord Hamilton's
Light Dragoons, and Detterling clanked along the quay in
time to it. Max took Angela's hand and gave his grisly smile
at her, while Fielding settled his deplorable homburg as
tightly on his head as he could.

"That's right, old man," said Percival: "hang on to your
hat."

Into a rowing-boat among a muddle of baskets, carpet
bags, caged chickens. Detterling breathing heavily beside
him: both facing to stern. Angela waving and slobbering,
Max saluting to the peak of his yachting cap, Leonard
Percival slowly parting his teeth in a grin like a portcullis.
Past a row of moored caiques, past a group of idle sailors
hawking and jabbering on a jetty, and so we say farewell to
dirty and dishonest little Hydra, and ... through the
harbour bar.

At once it seemed as if the boat were standing on its stern
and that chickens, carpet-bags, Fielding and all were being
sucked straight into the sea. But just as he felt himself finally
going the boat righted itself, dipped its bows, flung Detterling and himself back on to two squatting grandmothers in

black. No one else had turned a hair: it was routine. Fielding and Detterling apologised, picked themselves up, barked their shins on the cross-bench, received a mass of flying spray on their trousers, and were sworn at by the boatman, who looked like Charon but rather more malignant. Huddled together on the floor, they achieved some kind of stability for the next three minutes, at the end of which, hearing greetings from above, they looked up to see the cold, black side of the steamer. About seven feet above them was a square opening, ten feet by ten, from which two rope ladders were now let down to their rowing-boat.

First up, agile as spiders, were the two grandmothers. Then a deck-hand came halfway down the right-hand ladder and gestured to Charon. The latter passed up a suitcase, which the deck-hand caught with a swing of his arm and released again a split second later, so that it flew out of his hand and up through the opening in the ship's side. This procedure was repeated until all baggage was disposed of, whereupon Charon signed to Fielding to make the ascent up the left-hand ladder, the right-hand one still being occupied by the deck-hand, who was apparently telling Charon some kind of anecdote. Since the rowing-boat was lying in the lee of the steamer and was therefore rocking very little, Fielding anticipated no trouble in getting himself on to the rope ladder. This he gripped, then ran his hands up it while he manoeuvred both feet on to the rowing-boat's gunnel. It was at this stage that Charon pushed his craft clear of the steamer with a brisk lever movement of one oar, at the same time tossing up a large and rusty matchet to the deck-hand on the second ladder, who, using the same powerful swinging arm action as before but opening his fingers a split second earlier, launched the tool edge foremost straight at Fielding's head.

# 4

# THE CASTLE

TOM LLEWYLLYN went to see Gregory Stern in his London office. After congratulating Gregory on Isobel's pregnancy and hearing the gratifying details of an American paper-back deal in respect of his most recent book (*Queen Elizabeth II, The Bourgeois Monarch*), Tom said:

"I'm worried about Fielding Gray."

"I'm the one to worry," Gregory said. "First the BBC steal you, my best modern historian, to run their idiot programme, and then you steal my best novelist and send him off like bloody Byron."

"It wasn't *quite* like that, Gregory. And Fielding did need a change."

"So he's having his change and now you tell me you're worried." Gregory ran two fingers along his upper teeth and then prodded an incipient pimple on his jaw-bone. "So what's he done? Burnt down the Parthenon?"

"He rang me up yesterday," Tom said, "yesterday morning. I'd sent him a telegram asking him to hang on in Athens for a bit in case we wanted to revise his instructions. And now here he is ringing up to say that he was going straight on to Cyprus, that I needn't think I could stop him, and that anyway it wasn't safe for him to stay in Athens."

"Mad," said Stern, waving both hands in the air; "you've

paid him so much money that you've made him mad.
Cyprus ... He probably thinks he's Othello. Next time he
rings up he'll be Tamberlaine going to Persepolis or Jesus
Christ going up to his heavenly father. Why couldn't you
leave him as he was – quietly writing novels in Buttock's
Hotel?"

"Stop exaggerating, Gregory. Fielding certainly sounded
rather light-headed but he was perfectly lucid."

"Lucid, you call it? All that about 'not being safe for him
to stay in Athens'. What sort of talk is that?"

"There's still no need to exaggerate. I was hoping you
might be able to suggest some sort of explanation."

"How should I explain such *sotiserie*?"

"Well, I wondered," said Tom, embarrassed and reluctant, "whether Isobel had been having any more of those ...
hunches ... of hers?"

"Isobel has no time for such rubbish. She is too busy
bearing my son."

"Of course ... Gregory, you've known Fielding for as
long as I have. You know as well as I do that such
behaviour is quite untypical. Will you please try to say
something helpful."

"What can I say, my dear?" said Gregory more soberly
than he had spoken yet. "Except that I always thought he
wasn't so well balanced as he liked to appear."

"What would you *do* if you were me?"

"In a very few days now," said Gregory, "Detterling
will arrive back from Athens. Having spent hundreds
of pounds of my money in the Grande Bretagne Hotel,
he must at last condescend to come home and report.
He will have seen Fielding, and he will tell us all about
him. Detterling is an ex-officer and he will know what to
do."

"So are you an ex-officer. And so is Fielding, come to
that."

Gregory rose and went to the open window, through

which came April bird-song and the evening trill of typists released to their lovers.

"With Fielding and me," Gregory said, "it was only ever skin-deep. Although we may have looked the part, we always really relied on somebody else – usually the loyal and capable sergeant-major. But Detterling is the genuine article. He decides everything for himself and he relies on no one but himself to carry his decisions through."

"Then why did he end up as only a Captain?" Tom asked. "He had a regular commission and nearly six years of war to prove himself. Younger men than him were made Generals."

"I've often wondered about that," said Gregory. "One day . . . not yet awhile, but one day . . . I shall ask him."

Fielding Gray walked up the path towards the Castle of Buffavento. At the bottom of the path, a hundred yards below him, the road up the mountain had ended in a small area of sand and stone, on which his taxi was now parked with its somnolent driver inside it. Below this again the mountainside, rock and scrub and fir, fell away for hundreds of feet and then checked its descent to undulate gently into the plain of the Mesaoria, whose livid blues and lush purples and treacly yellows made a huge cloth of motley on which the distant minarets of Nicosia were set like a tiny silver cruet.

Above him, as he walked slowly but steadily up the winding path, Fielding could see the Castle: low and scaly, like a dragon crouching along the ridge, legs splayed to clasp it. The sun was burning down from the zenith; there was no wind; the cicadas hummed morosely. The knights castellan, Fielding thought, did they walk up this path, at noon-day, in full armour? And what kind of armour did they wear, those old crusaders? Chain mail, plate armour, leather jerkins? Plate armour was surely very rare when this castle was first built, and by no means every knight could afford a coat of chain; but leather? Leather, he knew, could keep out steel, for did he not owe his own life to the leather band inside his homburg, which had been proof against the flying matchet? Yet somehow leather seemed beneath the dignity of a crusading knight, even if he were so poor and unimportant that he was condemned to make up one of the band that garrisoned this castle, a younger son and a landless man, far from home and far from Jerusalem.

However that might be, even this suit (from the best men's shop in Athens) was uncomfortably hot. He stopped, set down the small grip which held his picnic lunch, lifted his homburg and wiped his forehead. Never mind; only another sixty or seventy yards to the top. Before starting again, he looked down at his taxi. How could the driver bear to stay inside that metal carapace (like plate armour) in this heat? And for that matter, the man ought to be up here with him if he was serious about his job. For the driver, Fielding knew, must be the man whom 'they' had told off to watch him. Whenever he asked the concierge at his hotel to send for a taxi, even for very short journeys inside Nicosia, the same man turned up in the same car. There could only be one explanation. Fielding did not resent his custodian and made no attempt to avoid him : better know by whom he was watched and how than tremble every time he passed a beggar. Besides, as he was demonstrating so clearly just now, the man was grossly inefficient – an amateur and not even enthusiastic. Lulled by several days' routine sight-seeing in Fielding's company – Bellapaix, Salamis, Paphos – he had doubtless decided that Fielding had nothing to go on and was simply killing time. At first he had lurked behind Fielding round temples and theatres and museums, but by now he seemed thoroughly bored. Too bored, thought Fielding, to climb the steps to the Castle of Buffavento; for what (he imagined the driver as thinking) could this

mouldering relic of the crusaders have to do with an up-to-
date intrigue in a world of time-bombs and taxis? Sleep on,
dull child of your age, soothed by the cicada.

Fielding replaced his hat, picked up his bag, and went on
up the path. After a little, this brought him to a flight of
straight and narrow steps, and these in turn to a small
natural platform. To his right, a path led away to the east,
along the very spine of the mountain ridge, between trees
which grew just below it on either side. To his left a rather
wider path ran some sixty yards to the castle gate, beyond
which an open court was visible. Ignoring the castle for
the moment, Fielding walked straight across the little
plateau. Far below him, the glittering sea stretched north
to the coast of Turkey, which seemed, in the distant haze,
like some long white flickering wave slowly rolling towards
him.

He shook his head to dispel this illusion and walked along
the path to the castle. Pausing in the courtyard, he could
have sworn that he heard the splash of water. Why not?
There must be a spring up here somewhere, or the castle
would have been indefensible. The pleasing noise reminded
him of coolness, and he walked on out of the courtyard,
through a wide stone doorway, and into a long and shady
gallery, in either wall of which, both to north and south, was
a series of magnificent windows that reached down from
arched summits just below the ceiling to sills at the height of
his waist, in all their depth framing nothing but blue sky. It
appeared that just here the ridge narrowed and sharpened;
for when he looked out to the north he seemed to be
hanging directly over the sea; and similarly, to the south, it
was as though a dropped stone would have plummeted
straight down into the Mesaoria.

More like a cloister than a castle, he thought. What could
this superb room have been? An ante-chamber, perhaps,
from which loiterers and petitioners might admire the view?
But no, he thought; surely – it had to be – this was where

the knights would have dined. Sitting on either side of a table which would have run almost the entire length of the gallery, they would have looked out of the windows into a sky which was somehow all the more immense for being framed, and then they would have risen, when the last of the Commanderia had been drained from the tankards, and looked down, either on to the spread chart of the terrain they were there to hold, or else on to the sea and then away beyond it to the land of the paynim, where Richard of England was riding under the Cross.

Fielding rested his bag on one of the broad window-sills and began to sort out his mid-day provisions. I too will dine here, he thought. I too will drink my wine where the castellans drank the sweet and heavy wine of Cyprus, and then dreamed of home.

Tom Llewyllyn and Gregory Stern were having lunch with Captain Detterling, who had arrived back in London the night before.

"So Fielding got a nasty shock," Detterling was saying, "the second inside a week, but he wasn't much hurt thanks to that homburg he was wearing. The Greeks were very apologetic. They explained that the matchet belonged to the sailor, who had lent it to our boatman, who was the sailor's uncle's wife's brother. The sailor was asking for it back, and the boatman wanted to keep it for another week, so they were having an argument ... at the end of which the boatman gave way and threw up the matchet. But just then the boat gave a lurch, the matchet was falling short, the sailor had to reach down too far and mistimed his swing ... etcetera, etcetera."

"And what do you think?" said Tom. "*Was* it an accident?"

"Impossible to say. But of course Fielding's mind was made up anyhow. The business in Yugoslavia – that cer-

tainly hadn't been an accident, and it was that which had
made him so determined to go ahead in the first place. And
now here was this fellow Percival telling him just how to set
about it – *and* saying that he'd probably be safer once he
was in Cyprus, a judgment apparently confirmed when a
sailor takes a shy at him with a rusty matchet. There was no
holding Fielding after that. The very next morning he rang
you up at the BBC and then took off for Cyprus. He didn't
even wait to buy himself some more kit, though he'd only
got the suit he stood up in. That was nearly a week ago, and
I haven't heard a word from him since."

"This man Percival," said Gregory: "is he to be relied
on?"

"He plays a pretty sharp game of backgammon,"
Detterling said, "and Max de Freville thinks well of
him."

"And what about Max de Freville?" asked Tom.

"He's good at giving the right marks to men like
Percival."

"And this story of theirs ... about the American who
called himself Diomedes?"

"If it's true," said Detterling, "it'll be worth every penny
you're paying to get it."

"I'd sooner have Fielding back home in one piece."

"Amen to that," Gregory said.

Both Tom and Gregory looked accusingly at Detterling.
He had failed to offer them a ready-made solution; the ex-
officer had let them down.

"Now you listen to me," Detterling said. He drank off his
port and put the glass down with a click. "I asked Fielding,
I urged him, to go back home. Since he refused to listen,
since he was dead set on carrying on, I procured him the
best advice I could about how to do so. Any complaints?"

This was too reasonable to be gainsaid. Gregory signed
the bill and they all three departed, Tom to the Television

Centre, Gregory and Detterling to the former's office, where they spent an acrid afternoon wrangling about Cavafy.

Fielding too had finished his food and wine. He put the remains of his meal back in his bag, then went to one of the windows in the south wall of the gallery. By craning his neck, he managed to get a view of his taxi, which was away below him to his left. The door was open and the driver's legs were sprawling out over the seat. Good. He had told the man he would eat and take his time up here, so that it would be a long while yet, even if the driver woke up, before his absence gave any cause for suspicion. There was no need to hurry. He picked up his bag, walked down the gallery and through another room, smaller and windowless, beyond it, and found, as he had expected, that there was a flight of steps leading down between two walls of stone to his right.

Somerset Lloyd-James and Lord Canteloupe were taking an afternoon walk in St James's Park.

"I've heard from the Director of Features at the BBC," Somerset said. "Some days ago, it seems, Fielding Gray rang up Tom Llewyllyn from Athens and said he was going straight on to Cyprus no matter what anyone said or did. He would hardly have acted with such precipitation unless he now has a definite lead."

"Which might," said Canteloupe, "be *any* kind of lead."

"Including the one kind which we don't want him to follow. If he *has* got on to that, then our Yankee friends are going to be very discommoded."

"Serve them right. They should never have interfered in Cyprus in the first place."

"But the point is," said Somerset, "that most of them haven't the faintest idea that they ever did interfere, and they'll be genuinely shocked when they find out. And what matters much more is that they're going to be made to look silly. Here, people will say, is the richest and most powerful government on earth, which is forever lecturing and hectoring the rest of us – and it doesn't even know what its own secret service is up to. This will be very irritating for the Americans, who will find some way of taking it out on us, although it isn't our fault. This in turn could be very damaging for the PM—"

"—Who will find some way of taking it out on me, although it isn't *my* fault."

"Precisely."

They paused on the iron bridge and looked down at the lake.

"Bloody ducks," said Canteloupe, "what do they care? It's all so unfair," he went on crossly. "This isn't a Fascist state. If the BBC sends a man to dig up the shit in Cyprus, what the hell can I do about it?"

"You are responsible to the Prime Minister," said Somerset, "for the suitable guidance of the popular media. If you fail, there are plenty of other people who will be glad of the place and the money."

"*Bloody* ducks," Canteloupe said.

"Of course," said Somerset, "I could have a word with Tom, but I hardly think he'd see the matter our way. He is very old-fashioned and still believes in publishing the truth, however manifestly inconvenient it may be. Whatever Fielding can prove, Tom will broadcast."

"There's always this Director chappie. He seems ready to help. What sort of man is he?"

"He's a vegetarian," said Somerset, "and therefore a crank. Like all cranks, he is self-important and obstinate. A little man, obsessed with his own rank ... which doesn't apply in this case, because Tom's been promised a free hand

and only comes under the Director for administrative purposes."

"He did what the Director asked about telling Gray to stay in Athens."

"He was bound to listen to suggestions ... at first. But now Fielding's settled all that by taking off on his own."

"Then it doesn't look as if either of them – either Llewyllyn or this Director – can be much use."

They walked on towards the palace. Bellies and buttocks squirmed on the grass all round them. Lechery, thought Somerset : oestrus. Aloud he said :

"The Director, because he is a little man, knows the rules very well. The rules, you will remember, were originally drawn up by Lord Reith, a puritanical Scotsman who deprecated scandal among his employees."

"Well?"

"Tom, although he is now respectably married, has a multi-coloured past. Now, it is just possible that his contract, as it extends over quite a long period, is governed by Reithian rules about correct moral behaviour, and that a public relapse into the habits of earlier days might disqualify him from his post. This much at least the Director will be able to tell us – the provisions of Tom's contract and the severity or otherwise with which these are currently enforced."

"I see," said Canteloupe. "If the rules are still a bit stodgy —"

"—And if they were picturesquely contravened by Tom ... who, after all, has endured three years of marriage and might be grateful, given opportunity, for some light relief—"

"—Then he would be liable to dismissal—"

"—And it wouldn't matter so much where Fielding went or what he discovered—"

"—Because when he got back Llewyllyn would have gone, and no Llewyllyn, no programme. Very neat," said

Canteloupe; "only what happens if he gets, say, the Billingsgate press to take his story instead of the BBC?"

"At least we've kept it off television. And Billingsgate talks the same language as we do."

"Billingsgate," said Canteloupe, "is a counter-jumper from the colonies."

"He still talks our language. And now," said Somerset, "I must go and have a word or two in that language with the Director of Features."

After going straight down for about twenty yards between walls on either side, the flight of steps which Fielding was descending emerged on to the open hillside, plunged steeply towards the sea for ten yards, and then swerved off to the left. Beyond this corner the steps continued some thirty yards further, now slanting gently across the slope between shallow banks covered with scrub; then they stopped, having deposited Fielding at the edge of a copse of fir-trees which grew out along a flat, wide spur. In the centre of the copse was a small open area, roughly circular and perhaps ten yards in diameter. Here Fielding put down his grip and carefully surveyed the scene in front of him.

'It is always said,' Max de Freville had told him, 'that the oldest Jewish cemetery surviving in Europe is in Worms. In fact it is at Castle Buffavento – if, that is, you can count Cyprus as being in Europe and a collection of three graves as a cemetery.'

And there they were: two square-topped head-stones, so deeply sunk that only three inches of either protruded above ground; and a long box-tomb, also sunk but still two feet in height and bearing, on the side which now faced him, an inscription in Hebrew characters.

'The Jew Elisha ben Habbakuk,' Max had said, 'made himself very useful to Richard I by lending him large sums of money while the king was on the island. Soon afterwards, when someone got up a nasty local programme in protest against current rates of interest, Elisha asked for help from Richard's followers and was given refuge, with his two daughters, up in Buffavento, which at that time was in English hands. All three were then murdered by the castle commander, who wanted the money Elisha brought with him, and buried just outside the precincts. The commander's knights, being offended by this treacherous behaviour, pushed the commander off the ramparts, announced that he had fallen when drunk, shared out Elisha's money between them, and raised a subscription to put up decent tomb-stones where the old Jew and his daughters were buried. Even then, it seems, hypocrisy was a British speciality.'

Fielding circled the box-tomb. He was not looking forward to what must come next.

'So much for the antiquarian background,' Leonard Percival had said. 'Now for some modern history. When the insurrection was at its worst, a Jewish-Greek schoolboy who was attending the Gymnasium at Nicosia accidentally learnt of a plan which some of his schoolfellows had made to blow up the local synagogue in protest against the neutralist attitude of the Jews in Cyprus. The boy informed the police of the plan and the incendiaries were caught in the act. Now, it was not at all unusual, as you will certainly remember, for school-children to chuck explosives about, but what was very unusual indeed was that someone should have dared to inform against them. Since that someone was obviously a Jew, and since there were very few Jews at the Gymnasium, they soon found out who had gone to the police, and Diomedes decided that a particularly striking example must be made, in order to deter other would-be delators. In fact he had the boy killed by the old-fashioned method of bending back two springy young trees, tying one of the boy's ankles to the top of each, and then letting the trees go . . . This on the edge of the main road from Kyrenia into Nicosia, with a large notice set up to inform passers-by that this was what DIOMEDES OF EOKA had in store for anyone who failed to mind his own business. It was improbable that the police would allow this exhibit to stay there for long, but it was thought that enough people would see it at daybreak for the world at large to get the message.

'But as it happened, the police were on the scene only just too late to rescue the boy and in time to cut down his remains before anyone at all had seen them. There was then a swift consultation, which ended in rather a surprising decision. The point was, you see, that although this very ugly murder could have been used to stir up indignation against EOKA, there was also no doubt that if it were made public it would have just the effect Diomedes wanted it to have – of deterring all informers whatever from then on. Since there were few enough of them as it was, this would have been most unhelpful for the authorities. It was therefore decided to hush up the whole business and hide the body – if that's what it could still be called – so securely that no one would ever see it or make any kind of report on its condition.'

'How do you know all this?' Fielding had asked.

'I was there when the boy was found . . . Even in these circumstances, however, good old British hypocrisy was in evidence: as much respect as possible must be had for the corpse. So since the boy was half Jewish, and since someone knew of this burial ground up at Buffavento, the body was whipped away up to the castle, where it would be right out of everyone's way but lying in ground that was more or less hallowed in its associations. The whole thing had to be done there and then and before it got light, without giving anyone a chance to know what was happening, so there was no time to make a coffin; and the most respectful thing to do – or so it seemed to the chap in charge – was to place the corpse in the hollow tomb which the knights had set up over old

Elisha. So that was what they did ... and drove back down the mountain some hours later, as though they were returning from a routine patrol, and nobody any the wiser.'

For some time, as he stood by the box-tomb, Fielding considered the Hebrew lettering. Although it was meaningless to him, its cabbalistic apparatus gave it a weird significance: such mysterious characters, he felt, must surely spell out a prayer or rune of the most powerful kind, perhaps a curse on any man who dared to disturb the grave.

He went back to his bag and took out a chisel and a small metal lever.

'You should not find it difficult,' Percival had said, 'to shift the slab on top. Though I'm told the police had quite a job of it ...'

Fielding inserted the chisel under the overlapping edge of the slab. He pressed the handle down and felt the slab lift very slightly; with his other hand he pushed the lever in beside the chisel.

'It was careless of me,' Percival had told him when instructing him what to look for: 'I should have taken it off the boy's remains as soon as we found him. But there were so many things to think about and just then it didn't seem important. All this happened, you understand, before I had really begun to equate Diomedes with my old colleague Restarick. It was only much later on, after I had left the island, that I finally became sure of this, and it was then I remembered what had been on that wretched boy's body. It went with him when they drove him away up the mountain. It *must* be there with him still.'

Fielding tested the lever. He would prise up the slab about six inches, he decided, get one hand underneath it and then the other (releasing the lever as he did so), and push the slab over until the far edge tilted to the ground. That should leave me plenty of room, he thought. Here goes.

Six seconds later he reeled back from the tomb and stumbled away to the trees, trembling helplessly and emitting great gouts of vomit. Gradually, however, he became calmer. At length he went to his bag, took out a bottle of water, dampened his handerchief and tied it over his mouth and nose, making a knot behind his head. Then he went back to the tomb and looked firmly and steadily down. Yes; that must be it – if Percival was right. He leant forward, put both hands down and round the neck, and began to fumble.

'Restarick/Diomedes,' Percival had said, 'isn't really a cruel man. He wouldn't have wanted to cause avoidable pain – not under his own nose. He would have been quite content with leaving the impression – such a very horrible impression – that pain had been caused. Furthermore, he would not have wanted noise or struggle. So what more natural than that he should have chloroformed the boy before he killed him? Or killed him *first* with chloroform? In the car on the way, perhaps. He would have soaked a handkerchief in chloroform to make a pad, held it to the boy's face until he ceased to struggle, and then, wanting to make quite sure but also to leave his own hands free to handle ropes and torches and the rest, he would have secured the pad to the boy's face with a second handkerchief, tied like a mask. Something like that. It must have been.'

'How can you possibly know?'

'Because there was a handkerchief tied round the boy's neck when we found him. I didn't take much notice, I thought it was the boy's own, which he had been sporting as some kind of neckwear. It was only years later, when I was finally sure that Restarick was Diomedes, that I remembered two things about that handkerchief. First, the knot was at the back of the neck – as though the handkerchief had been fastened round the face and then slipped down. And secondly, it had been immaculately clean and of very fine linen. Not at all the sort of handkerchief usually owned by sixth-formers from the Nicosia Gymnasium – though I was much too preoccupied and upset to think of that at the time. You see, the whole body, right up to the chest ... was bisected.'

Desperately, Fielding's fingers now clawed at the knot, which he had worked round to one side of the neck. Gangrene, he thought; people who muck about with dead bodies get their blood poisoned, it's always happening to students, the tiniest cut or flaw in the skin and the infection seeps through ...

'Now, one of the things about Restarick,' Percival had said, 'is that he's rather a dandy. He had beautiful suits. And he used to have all his personal linen specially made up by a firm in Dover Street – like all Americans, he greatly admired British clothes. And so if, as I'm sure, the handkerchief round that poor little Jew's neck was Restarick's—'

'—Then the firm in Dover Street will be able to identify it?'

'Very easily. On all his shirts and handkerchiefs and the rest he used to have his personal mark embroidered, like a kind of crest. A Maltese Cross.'

Fielding's sweaty fingers trembled and slipped. His hand touched the neck and his throat heaved. With a great effort he mastered himself and once more tackled the knot. Could any mere handkerchief be worth such torture?

'Surely,' he remembered saying to Percival, 'he'd never have left such a conspicuous object behind him on that boy's body?'

'I've no doubt he had every intention of removing it. But it didn't work out as he thought ... They arrive at the scene of execution and carry the body from the car. All in total darkness. They bend back the trees, which they have selected earlier by daylight. Two men secure them. Another man busies himself with the boy's ankles. Meanwhile

Restarick pulls the pad out from under the mask and starts to untie the mask itself. The knot is tight and it won't undo. Someone blunders or panics, the trees are released before Restarick is ready ... Then, when it's all over, he hears a car in the distance: the police. Hurriedly he tears at the knot in the handkerchief – standing on his toes, perhaps, because the parting trees have swung the body well clear. So he reaches up for the hanging head, and he can't risk a torch, and the car is getting closer. One final attempt to drag the handkerchief off the head, but it's tightly tied and he can't see and he's sweating with fear – so he runs for it with the rest of his men and hopes for the best.'

'Guesswork. All of it.'

'All except for one handkerchief of finest quality linen ...'

*This handkerchief,* Fielding thought now. The knot too tight to undo. '... One final attempt to drag the handkerchief off ...' Too tightly tied even for that ... then ... But now ... There is ... something different ... now. Slowly he peeled the linen up over the poor sunken face; clearly visible, amid the stains on the underside, was a Maltese Cross embroidered in green. The handkerchief stuck slightly and he gave a quick pull. The handkerchief came away and his knuckles rapped very sharply against the inside of the tomb. *Cuts; flaws in the skin.* Weeping with terror he threw down the cerement and ran for his bag. He scrabbled in it for the wine bottle, poured the lees over his knuckles, rubbed them well in. Would it be strong enough to disinfect? He must get back to Nicosia and find a doctor in case. But first there were things he must do. Still pouring with tears, he removed his own handkerchief from his face, dropped it on top of the filthy thing on the ground, gathered them up together and thrust them into his bag. Then he went back to the tomb to work the slab into its proper position. But no, he thought, there's something else I must do first, what is it, O God, what is it? Yes. *Yes.*

He felt in his breast pocket and took out the Mezuzah.

Gregory won't mind, he thought, as he placed it on the broken body.

"Forgive me," he cried out loud as the tears of terror and pity and disgust streamed off his cheeks, "please forgive me. Don't let there be a curse. Let the sacred name of Shaddai absolve me from your curse."

*PART TWO*

# ARCADIA

## 5
## APPRAISALS

"I'M SORRY," said Tom Llewyllyn to Fielding Gray in the Television Centre, "but it simply isn't enough."

"I quite agree."

"All you've produced," continued Tom, "is one handkerchief which you found round the neck of a corpse. True, you have been able to verify that it was sold to this man Restarick by a London firm of haberdashers; but what does that prove? Handkerchiefs are easily lost or stolen. Even if you can show that Restarick was in Cyprus at the time of the murder, that handkerchief does not necessarily prove that he was present at the killing, or that he was helping EOKA, or that he was Diomedes."

"But it does create a strong supposition that he was mixed up in it all somewhere?"

"In this sort of case we can't afford to deal in suppositions."

"I have already said that I agree."

"Then why," said Tom, "have you come back to London so soon? Not but what I'm very pleased to see you."

"I've come back," said Fielding, "to make quite certain where I stand. There have already been signs – that telegram to Athens – that the BBC isn't over-enthusiastic about this enquiry, and I don't imagine that the implications of what I *have* discovered will give very much pleasure. And so I want your assurance that if I follow this through, whatever

I later discover will be fully and fairly presented on television and not suppressed or laughed off."

"I'm in sole charge," said Tom, "of Today is History. You have my assurance – you always had it – that I will broadcast anything of value which you may discover in or about Cyprus. But are you sure you want to go back? Haven't you had enough trouble already?"

"Look," said Fielding. "I have persisted so far in order to find out the truth for myself. This I have now done to my own broad satisfaction, but, as we both agree, I have not yet come up with enough solid evidence to justify making the matter public. Since I think the matter should be made public, I am prepared to go back and hunt for more evidence, however disagreeable the circumstances, provided that I am assured of your support—"

"—Which you are—"

"—And also that you will now define exactly what sort of proof you will require from me before going ahead with an exposé."

Tom put his hands in his hair and his elbows on his desk. His eye was promptly caught by a large piece of paper which bore the memo *Call for Baby's Cod-Liver Oil and Malt,* an instruction which had been telephoned by Patricia just before Fielding arrived. He shuddered with irritation and re-addressed himself, not without effort, to the affair in hand.

"Difficult," he said. "What do you think you can offer?"

"My informant, Percival," Fielding said, "who was dead right about that handkerchief, has now come up with something else." Leonard Percival had in fact emerged from wherever he had been lurking to meet Fielding at London Airport the previous evening. In the taxi from the airport to Buttock's Hotel he had expressed satisfaction at what Fielding had achieved and issued crisp instructions for the next move. "Something else," Fielding said now, "of a rather different kind."

"Well?"

Fielding rose and went to the window which looked down on the White City Stadium. Tom, he thought, is not going to like this. Well, supposing he doesn't? I can just give the whole thing up, and that will be that. I've done what I wanted to; I've defied those who tried to bully me and found out the truth which they wished to hide; my honour is satisfied. I've won the game and I know it, and I'm surely a mature enough man not to care whether or not the result is made public.

And yet he knew very well that he did care. He cared, not on grounds of morality or politics or patriotism, but simply because he had an intense personal distaste for agitators – for all people like Restarick who (whatever their motives) went round stirring up trouble where there had been peace and quiet before. Such people made everything they came near ugly and uncomfortable. He, Fielding, resented them, he wanted them caught and humiliated and put out of the way. Until recently his hatred had been all for the Cypriots, who had taken one of his eyes and ruined his face for ever; but now, now that he knew what he did, it was Restarick he wanted to punish, not so much because Restarick was ultimately responsible for the events which had led to his disfigurement, as because Restarick was representative of those forces of disruption which were daily posing a more vicious threat to all the things he cherished.

For Restarick was the Enemy: he stood for Change. To be sure, he was the agent of an American organisation which existed to promote stability and good order throughout the world; but in this instance that organisation, inspired by jealousy of Empire, by sheer atavistic spite, was following a deliberate policy of rabble-rousing and revolution. Restarick had been sent to Cyprus to play the demagogue, to inflate trivial discontent to the point of obscene explosion. Restarick stood for disintegration, he stood for rant, for "protest", for subversion – and Restarick must be destroyed. Which meant that Restarick must be exposed; so that it was very important, as Fielding now recognised, that he should not give up at this stage, that he should persevere until he could bring a public case. For this he needed Tom's support; but Tom, he knew, would not be pleased when Fielding told him what must come next, and it would have to be put to him with care.

"Well?" Tom said.

"According to Percival," said Fielding, "there was a large notice left behind near that Jewish boy who was murdered. This specifically stated that it was Diomedes – not Dighenis, which was what Grivas called himself, but *Diomedes* – who had engineered this act of revenge. Never mind whether or not he was actually there, it was Diomedes who had given that order, and someone was evidently anxious that people should know this was the case. Now, who and why?"

"Perhaps Dighenis – i.e. Grivas – wanted to dissociate himself?"

"Precisely. Diomedes was making a stern and necessary example, as he thought, but Grivas reckoned that this particular piece of atrocity was going too far and would probably do harm to his reputation. This fits in very well with your 'Grivas was just a decent soldier' theory. He couldn't prevent Diomedes, if only because Diomedes was the agent of those who were providing the cash, but he wasn't going to be held personally responsible for *this* bit of beastliness. And so with or without Diomedes' knowledge, Grivas arranged for a notice to be left behind saying that it was all Diomedes' work."

"You're still no nearer proving who Diomedes was."

"Wait a little ... Now, in the event it didn't matter what the notice said because the mess was cleared away by the police before anyone knew about it. In fact, the whole thing was so carefully hushed up that only a handful of people know about it even to this day."

"All right. But where does all this get you?"

"It gets me to Athens. It gets me to the house of General Grivas, as he is now styled, telling him how much, as an ex-soldier myself, I admire his conduct of the campaign in Cyprus. True, I shall say, the terrorist element was unfortunate, but after all Grivas was outnumbered and had no choice. In the circumstances, he could be forgiven a few dead civilians, a few bombs in the markets and the taverns, because it was the only way to make his point. Indeed, I shall tell him, it is now generally agreed that the whole affair does him nothing but credit. So much so that BBC Television is very keen to do a piece about it – a piece which will demonstrate, in typical breast-tearing English fashion, that everything was all our fault and that our enemies were the most spotless and courageous of idealists."

"Go on," said Tom, frowning down at the memo about Baby's Malt.

"Well," said Fielding, "Grivas will sit there purring, and I shall then ask permission to put a few preliminary questions. Because, I shall say, there is one slight snag. Our investigations have revealed that there was one very nasty piece of work indeed, which up till now nobody knows about. The barbarous mutilation of a young Jewish boy, who was literally torn apart. No doubt about it : if necessary we can produce the body. Impersonal terrorism is one thing, I shall proceed, but this is quite another. Will the General kindly explain?

"Oh yes, yes, the General can explain : that particular murder was done against his wishes – he even had a notice put up to disown it. 'I'm afraid, sir, that I must ask you to be more precise.' Very well : it was arranged by his – er – assistant, Diomedes. 'And who was he?' Well, er . . . 'Come, come, General. Diomedes is just a code-name. It could mean anybody or nobody. Who was he? What was his role? Because if you don't tell me, the BBC will have to take a less tolerant view of your activities. I shall be compelled to report that I have inspected the remains of a victim – a mere child – whose manner of death was more revolting than anything since Dachau, and for whose murder General Grivas himself must be held responsible.' And what, Tom, does this gallant officer do then? Does he sit there and endure the stain on his honour? Or does he come up with the truth about Restarick?"

"He kicks you straight out of the house," said Tom, "if, indeed, he ever let you into it. I don't like it, Fielding. I don't like the way you propose to use threats in the name of the BBC—"

"—You can always say I exceeded my brief—"

"—And leaving that aside, I just don't care for your method. It's sheer blackmail – against all conscience."

"It's only *my* conscience that need be involved. Leave that to me."

"*I* shall be responsible for using the stuff."

"But not for getting it. You need know nothing about that."

"You've already told me what you intend."

"Pure speculation, dear boy. An imaginative version of the way things just might work out. Look, Tom," said Fielding, "what it boils down to is this: if I come back from Athens, bringing a signed statement from Grivas, or some other authoritative figure in this field, that Diomedes was the American, Earle Restarick, will you accept it as evidence?"

Tom breathed heavily and clenched both fists.

"Yes," he said at last: "if you can prove the signature."

"What about a tape recording?"

"Yes; if Grivas or whoever gives it his written attestation."

"And suppose I get the recording without his knowing?"

"Then I shall require one other witness, besides yourself, to swear that the tape is genuine."

"Fair enough," said Fielding. "So those are your conditions and you will stand by them?"

"I will," said Tom, wiping his palms on his lapels.

"Good," said Fielding. "I shall leave for Athens as soon as you send me an air ticket. First class, please."

"My budget isn't bottomless."

"It'll run to first-class air tickets for old friends. I shall be at Tessie Buttock's."

"Oh, all right," said Tom, and ground his teeth. "Give my love to Tessie."


"Tom sends his love," said Fielding to Tessie Buttock that evening.

"There's a dear boy, like he always was. How was he looking?"

"A bit harassed. I think this BBC job worries him."

"I hope," said Tessie, "that wife of his is feeding him proper."

"I doubt it. She was used to a big house in the country with plenty of servants. She hasn't taken to London."

"She could learn. I've no patience with these girls that put on airs."

"It's not altogether her fault," said Fielding. "For years now Tom has been making a lot of money, and he could easily afford a house or a large flat with a girl to live in and help with the work and the baby. Instead of which he insists on living in a poky little hole in Southwell Gardens and won't have a servant anywhere near the place. Something to do with his socialist conscience."

"But even socialists have servants," Tessie said. "Anyway, Tom was always in and out of restaurants, and he had people waiting on him when he lived here."

"Hotels and restaurants are different. You pay an agreed sum for an agreed service. But if you have servants in your own home, Tom told me once, it sets up a feudal relationship which is a denial of human dignity on both sides. His own words."

"What rubbish. Ask Albert Edward," Tessie said, and poked the snoring dog. "A fat lot he cares for his human dignity as long as he's warm and fed."

"I also think," said Fielding, "that consciously or not Tom's punishing Patricia for having had a rich and easy childhood. Whereas he himself – well, no one even knows where he came from."

"He once told me something," Tessie said, "which made me think his mother must have had a rough time. 'Four of us,' he said, 'and she could never be sure the money would come.' So perhaps he's punishing this Patricia because of his mother."

"Or perhaps he's sending his mother a lot of money to make up and can't afford anything better than Southwell Gardens after all. Anyway, the long and the short of it is that he's turning Patricia into a drudge and seems to regard it as the natural fate for a married woman." Fielding disengaged his thigh from the embrace of Albert Edward and rose from the fender-cushion. "So long, Tessie. I'm off out."

"Not staying in for supper, dear? I've got your favourite steak and kidney."

"Sorry, love. I've got a date."

"Made it with my own hands."

"Never mind," said Fielding, who knew as well as Tessie did that it had come out of a tin, "it'll make a nice treat for Albert Edward."


"I can't imagine," said Patricia Llewyllyn in Southwell Gardens, "what made you forget Baby's Cod-Liver Oil and Malt."

"I've had a difficult day," said Tom, "and I had more important things to remember. Anyway, why couldn't you get it?"

"Baby and I went to see Isobel, which is the wrong way for the chemist."

"How was Isobel?"

"Very energetic. She was cleaning out the attic."

"Why not follow her example?"

"We haven't got an attic."

"We've got a sitting-room," said Tom, looking despondently round it.

"Somehow," said Patricia, "I can't bring myself to care much about it. It's such a transitory kind of place. Now, Isobel and Gregory's house—"

"—Is all very well for Isobel and Gregory. I'm different. I've always lived in transitory places. I couldn't do anything else."

"What about me?" said Patricia.

"Come over here," said Tom.

When Patricia came to him, he took her on his knee and kissed her on the lips.

"Remember what I told you when we were married?" he said.

"Tom . . . Kiss me again."

"In a minute . . . Remember I said that I was a writer before I was a husband? And that in some ways my writing would always have to come first?"

"Yes."

"Well, this flat," said Tom, "is one of those ways. A writer is someone who lives in passage, and so this flat is just a place of passage. Soon we shall move to another. We shall never have a house like Isobel and Gregory, not even if I make a million pounds, until I am dead as a writer. Do you understand?"

"I think so. Tom, Baby's asleep. Come with me."

Later on, while they were eating Heinz Spaghetti on toast, Tom said:

"Have you seen my National Insurance Card? They keep asking for it at the BBC."

"I don't think you've ever had one."

"But I thought they came automatically."

"You have to stamp them," Patricia explained, "and send them in at the beginning of every March, and then they send you another one for the next year. If you've never had one, you'll never get one ... if you see what I mean."

"Have you got one?"

"Oh yes. That typist woman of Daddy's used to stamp them for all of us. I suppose she still does."

"But not for me?"

"Of course not, darling. Unless you gave her yours when we got married?"

"No. As you say, I don't think I've ever had one. No one's ever asked for it before."

"They don't, unless you take a job."

"But surely," said Tom, getting rather worked-up, "they ought to have sent me one when the whole business started. I mean, I'm a citizen, I'm *entitled* to a National Insurance Card."

"Darling, darling Tom," said Patricia, "you have such funny ideas about the Welfare State. *They* don't send you anything. *You* have to go and apply for it."

"Well, they must realise after all this time that I haven't got one."

"Not," said Patricia, "if you're a writer who lives in passage. You've never given them a chance to catch up with you."

"Come to think of it," said Tom, "when I was living at Tessie Buttock's, I did have an official letter one day, but I never even saw it. Tessie read it – she read all the letters – and then wrote 'Not known at this address' on the envelope and popped it back in the box. She told me about it later. You don't want to be bothered with muck like that, she said."

"Tom, darling," said Patricia cautiously, "you *do* pay income tax?"

"Of course," said Tom severely. "It's my plain social duty. Gregory employs an accountant for me and they deduct it from my royalties as they fall due."

"Well, that's a relief. I wouldn't want you to go to prison. But this other thing – what are you going to tell the BBC?"

Tom thought for a moment.

"I'll tell them," he said, "that I gave my card to you to get it stamped for me and that Baby went and tore it up. Then they can go ahead and apply for a new one. There's always a simple answer to this sort of nonsense."

Patricia giggled with sheer love.

"I can't help feeling," she said, "that someone will want to be told just a tiny bit more than that."

"Well, dearie," Maisie said to Fielding, "you *have* learnt a thing or two since you've been away. One of those dirty foreign girls, was it?"

"An old acquaintance, as it happens. Someone I met quite by accident."

"She ought to be ashamed of herself, showing you things like that. Old acquaintance, indeed. You were more than acquainted by the time you got through that little lot."

"It was rather revealing."

"Well, I hope *you* didn't do any revealing," Maisie said. "Remember what I told you before. Don't let on what's going on in there." She scratched the hairs on his chest. "Not when you're dealing with that kind of person. You never know who'll hear about it next."

"Not to worry," Fielding told her. "We only talked about things which happened a very long time ago."

"Old acquaintances met again by accident," Maisie said, "can be the most dangerous people of all. You start thinking you're young again, like you were when you first knew them, and there's no end to the silliness that goes on."

"Harmless silliness. And very delightful."

"That's as may be. Start behaving as though you're young all over again, and the next thing you know you've gone and ruptured a blood vessel ... So you're off back there in a day or two?"

"That's right."

"Well, you watch out for old acquaintances," said Maisie; "particularly if they start teaching you new tricks."


Angela Tuck, though she had too much sense to mourn long for departed lovers, would often wonder curiously what had become of this one or that. About Fielding Gray, after their brief encounter on Hydra, she pondered the more as there were several unusual items to add spice. These included their somewhat lurid connection in the distant past, the much talked of incident which had taken place while Fielding was boarding the steamer for Athens, and the strong impression she had otherwise received that he and Detterling were up to something on the sly. It also occurred to her, although she was not a book-loving woman, that it might be interesting to read the novels which Fielding had written.

When, therefore, she was passing through Athens a few days later (*en route* with Max for Cyprus) she called in at the large bookshop off Constitution Square and was impressed to find that all three of Fielding's novels were in stock. (She would have been less impressed had she known that they were the only copies in Greece, having been ordered by an English resident who had since been hurriedly repatriated.) After she and Max had established themselves in Cyprus at the Dome Hotel in Kyrenia, she was faced with two days' solitude (while Max moved hither and thither seeking preliminary reactions to his proposals for a casino on the island) and so had the ideal opportunity for a good, long read. She therefore sought out her glasses, sat down on the

English-style terrace overlooking the sea, ordered a bottle of sweet white wine, and then, having in some respects a very tidy nature, examined the three books to find out in what order they had been written and started in on page one of the first.

This she found of little interest. It was, she fancied, rather well written, but it also struck her as being frigid and superior in tone. Furthermore, it was concerned with the exclusively male world of the British Army on active service and came to a climax during an elaborate court martial, a form of proceeding which she regarded as pompous and absurd. As it happened, she had spent much of her own childhood and adolescence in military circles in India with a father who was later court-martialled for embezzlement, but this period of her life, which had ended abruptly with her father's dismissal, she considered as so irrelevant to her more recent destinies that she had scarcely given it a single thought in the last ten years. She was certainly not prepared to revive memories of it now in order to assist her appreciation of Fielding's novel – the scene of which, in any case, was set not in India but in East Africa.

The second book was rather more to her taste. It had to do with a native tribe, which was starving to death because the only food available was forbidden to it for religious reasons, and with the efforts of a young colonial officer, first to overcome the tribe's scruples, then to trick it into eating the prohibited meat. The problem was made real for her and the solution was ingenious; but once again the interest was largely professional, there wasn't a woman in sight, and the writing was so contemptuous of human folly and ignorance that she felt herself, along with all mankind, to have been viciously insulted. After this, she had almost decided not to bother with the third book at all – until a cursory inspection of the blurb made her open her eyes wider than she had opened them in some weeks and sent her back to work with a will.

Fielding Gray's third and most recent novel, published only a few months before, was called *Love's Jest Book*. As Angela had gathered from her glance at the blurb, the material was autobiographical and was drawn, what was more, from that period of Fielding's life when she herself had first known him : it embraced all the subjects and events which they had discussed on that memorable afternoon in Angela's bed on Hydra, and a great many more besides. Having opened with an account of how the hero (Fielding to the life) had fallen in love at his school with a fair and well-made boy called Alexis, the book went on to relate how Alexis was seduced and then deserted; how he sought consolation, was arrested by the police and was consigned to the care of a psychiatrist; and how finally, after a further and even more brutal exhibition of the Fielding-hero's treachery, he had blown his brains out with his father's revolver.

This was the central story. But there were also several passages about Angela herself, most notably those which described her liaison with the adolescent Somerset Lloyd-James (thinly disguised under the name of William Glyn-Davies) and the part later played by Somerset and herself in bringing about Fielding's exposure and disgrace. All of this Angela found fascinating. From noon until tea-time of the second day of Max's absence she sat on the hotel terrace absorbed in this violently romantic but (as she herself could vouch) substantially true tale of love and betrayal and death; and when she finally closed the book, she felt that Fielding's art had done justice to his matter.

"Clever," she mused to herself as she crossed the terrace to go indoors, "very clever. But it's more than that. He's obsessed. Even now, all these years later, he's obsessed."

"So," said Leonard Percival: "you know where to send to me if you've got any news?"

Percival was seeing Fielding off on the aeroplane from London to Athens.

"American Express, Rome," said Fielding. "And if I'm in trouble in Athens, I'm to go to 236a, Philhellene Street."

"Right. Though for the reasons I've explained to you, I think that from now on any pressures on you will be oblique. Not to be avoided, that is, merely by going to ground in Philhellene Street. Next point. You've got your story absolutely straight – the one you're going to use for getting an interview with Grivas?"

"Yes. Whatever he may have heard, I shall say, I've been misunderstood. Despite what happened to me personally during the Cyprus campaign, I'm not after making trouble. I admire his strategy and I want to make a sympathetic study of it ... not only for the BBC but for publication as a book. I shall write to him and say just that the moment I get to Athens."

"Good. Although he'll have been firmly warned against you, it might just work. Grivas dislikes being bossed about, by Restarick or anyone else, and the idea of meeting a man who fought against him in the field will appeal to the romantic side in him. Old enemies discussing past battles over a drink – like a scene from John Buchan. Grivas is quite innocent enough, quite old-fashioned enough to go for the idea."

"And if he doesn't?"

"Then you'll have to consider ways and means of breaking in on him, and either charming him or forcing him into giving you a hearing."

"If it comes to that, I'll need help."

"If it comes to that, you shall have it."

Fielding's flight was called on the loud-speaker.

"Time to take wing," said Percival: "don't fly too near the sun."

Earle Restarick, dressed in black silk pyjamas and a white silk scarf, was drinking coffee in the sitting-room of a villa above Bellapaix. The villa, which had once been a small monastery, could only be reached by a mule-track. From where Restarick sat, he looked straight along the track, which descended a gentle slope for about quarter of a mile and then dipped sharply out of sight down the hill-side. Restarick's eye, taking off from this point like a ski-jumper, hovered in the sky a moment and then dropped towards the Abbey of Bellapaix, hovered again, and then swept down through the foot-hills to the fort by Kyrenia harbour. He gave a long sigh of pleasure and turned unwillingly to the Greek Cypriot who was standing beside him.

"And then?" Restarick said.

"And then he told me to take him to Buffavento. At Buffavento he looked round and ate his lunch and told me to take him back again. Just another day's sight-seeing. The next morning I took him to Nicosia airport, where he caught the plane for Londino."

"Had he told you before that he was leaving?"

"He never told me anything. Only where to drive him. Otherwise he hardly spoke."

"But he was polite?" said Restarick.

"Yes."

"And generous with his tips?"

"Yes" – reluctantly.

"Then you have nothing to complain of."

"Except that he regarded me as just a part of the taxi. An important part, but otherwise no different from the rest of it."

"The English," said Restarick, "like to pay their own way and keep their own council. They do not understand that those whom they are paying expect to be treated as equals."

"But you Americans are different," said the Cypriot in a flurry of sycophancy; "you believe in human brotherhood."

"There is nevertheless a lot to be said," remarked

Restarick, "for the English point of view. Here is your money."

The Cypriot counted it carefully.

"But this morning," he said, "I have been away from my taxi. And now I must walk back down that accursed mule-track. All that time it takes, kyrios, all that time."

"If you snivel like that," said Restarick, "even we Americans will find it hard to regard you as a brother."

The man held out two hands towards him, but Restarick left his chair and walked out of the room without paying any further attention. He went down a passage and turned into a small study. At a desk by the window, which looked straight into the hill-side as it rose from the back of the villa, a stocky man with close-cut hair was fiddling with the insides of a short-range radio transmitter. Behind him, against one wall, was a much bigger one, and fastened to the wall beside it a large-scale map of the island.

"I've just checked by telephone with Athens," the stocky man said. "Gray arrived by plane from London last night."

"Thank you, Savidis. And I've been talking with that taxi-driver. He insists that Gray merely went sight-seeing here in Cyprus and then just left. If he drew a blank here, why should he be returning to Athens?"

Savidis shrugged.

"The BBC are paying him well. Perhaps he's persuaded them to let him have another try."

"But why did he go back to London at all? The BBC didn't send for him."

Savidis shrugged again.

"We must assume," said Restarick, "that he's on to something, something big enough to take him back to London for advice. Since he's been in touch with Leonard Percival, that's only too likely to be true. I've no idea how much Leonard knows, but he must know something, and the bastard's out to do us down. We've been squeezing the English service out of Europe and the Near East for years now, and even where they're still in the game nine times out of ten we've been first to find the honey-pot. But if they could get us publicly discredited over Cyprus, Washington might get nervous and call off some of our other Mediterranean activities, and then Percival and his buddies would have a fair chance to get back their old influence in their old stamping grounds."

"Can England still afford that sort of influence?"

"I wouldn't know. What I *do* know is that the British Government doesn't want any revelations about Cyprus because it doesn't want anyone to realise that we've made a fool of it, and it's therefore instructed Percival's branch, very firmly, to forget the whole affair. But that won't stop Percival's bosses – with their greedy eyes on our territory – if they can see a way round. And what better way round than using this man Gray to do the dirty work and dish it all up on television? That way, Leonard and his crowd would get everything they wanted – *and* they could tell their Government in London that they'd obeyed their instructions and kept out of it themselves. Go and complain to the BBC, they could say; it's this BBC man who's come out with it all, no good blaming us."

"All right," said Savidis. "It fits. So what do we do?"

"We hope," said Restarick, "that the British authorities will keep a sharp eye on the BBC and stop Gray broadcasting anything which either they or we wouldn't like."

"But we can't rely on this. We never could. Which is why it was decided to kill Gray at the very beginning – just in case, we said."

"Only both attempts were unfortunately bungled by your fellow-countrymen."

"I've been a naturalised American," said Savidis, "for twenty-five years. I agree in advance with anything you may care to say about the incompetence both of Greeks in general and of Cypriot Greeks in particular. Let us now revert to my point, which is simply this: if there was good enough reason to get rid of Gray 'just in case' before he even arrived here, there is far, far better reason now that he's apparently getting hot."

"Granted," said Restarick, removing his scarf as he spoke; "the only trouble is that it's now too late."

"Surely not."

"From the moment he arrived in Cyprus it was too late. Once he was here, the connection would have been too obvious. We all agreed about that."

"I know. But he's not in Cyprus now, he's in Athens."

"Meanwhile he's been back to London," Restarick said. He refolded his scarf and started to ease it back round his neck and under his pyjama collar. "He's reported to the BBC on his progress, which means, very probably, that he's had something to say about us. If we kill him now – whether in Athens or Timbuktu – his death will at once be imputed to us and his discoveries to date will get all the publicity Percival could ever have dreamed of."

"If Gray had proper proof," said Savidis, "he wouldn't have needed to come back. Since he hasn't got proper proof, he cannot have told the BBC anything *definite* about us, and therefore nothing definite can come out after his death. Provided it occurs *now*."

"Enough would come out to compel us to keep very quiet while the fuss was dying down. We're a long way from being finished here and we can't afford that kind of delay. No," said Restarick, making a final adjustment to his scarf; "Fielding Gray stays alive."

"And dangerous."

"Yes," mused Restarick. "Dangerous because intelligent. Dangerous because inquisitive. How does one stop a man being intelligent and inquisitive without actually killing him? Always an amusing problem."

He examined the map on the wall and sang a little song to himself, a song that had been popular just after the war.

*"Though it's only a cardboard moon,"* he sang,
  *"Sailing over a painted sea,*
*Though it's only make-believe . . .*
  *. . . Di-dee, di-dee, di-dee."*

"Forgotten the last line?" said Savidis.

"Yes. But the first three will suffice for our purpose. The Widow Tuck," he said, swinging round on his companion. "She's come here from Hydra with de Freville, we hear, and they're staying at the Dome Hotel down in Kyrenia?"

"Right. But what's she got to do with it?"

"The sailor folk on Hydra report that while Gray was there she spent a very long afternoon in bed with him."

"Ah, I see," said Savidis sarcastically. "We send the woman Tuck off to Athens, and tell her to go to bed with Major Gray and never let him get up? Until he dies of fornication, maybe?"

"For all your twenty-five years as an American citizen," Restarick said, "you still think like a Balkan peasant."

"And you think like a eunuch. Why not kill him and be done?"

"Eunuchs ruled Byzantium rather effectively for nearly a thousand years, Savidis. Do try to remember your own history."

"I live in the present."

"Like all peasants." Earle Restarick passed his fingers over the delicately embroidered Maltese Cross on his scarf. "Well," he said, "you have your uses, I suppose. You can demonstrate your efficacy in the present, my dear Savidis, by going into Kyrenia forthwith and discreetly making the following arrangements for the entertainment of Madame Tuck . . ."

## 6
## REVIVALS

"**M**AISIE," said Somerset Lloyd-James. "We'll get her."

"Who's Maisie?" said Lord Canteloupe.

"An old friend . . ."

"I still don't understand."

"Then have some more of this nice claret and listen carefully."

They were lunching at the Ritz, largely because this was about the only place left in London where the tables were still far enough apart for the occupants to converse unheard. Although Canteloupe was paying for the lunch, Somerset was ordering and organising it. Nor did Canteloupe object; for Somerset knew a lot about food and somehow hypnotised waiters into absolute compliance, like a snake.

"The Director of Features says," Somerset intoned, "that while there are no specific provisions in Tom's contract as to moral respectability, there is a clause which requires that he should be resident in the United Kingdom during the period of his appointment and that he should retain 'the necessary capacity to fulfil his obligations to the Corporation.' Obviously, if Tom went mad or broke his neck the BBC would be entitled to terminate the agreement."

"So where does this Maisie come in? Is she going to drive him potty or break his neck with a poker?"

"Maisie," said Somerset, "is a whore. A very accomplished whore."

"Lead me to her."

"I'll certainly give you an introduction, but that must come later. The point, here and now, is that Maisie of all people is qualified to make such a disastrous fool out of Tom that the BBC would have no alternative but to declare him thenceforth unfit 'to fulfil his obligations'."

"Tom Llewyllyn," said Canteloupe, "is not an easy man to make a fool of."

"Tom Llewyllyn," said Somerset, "used to be very, very partial to whores. In fact, Canteloupe, whores were all that he was partial to – though God knows he had enough opportunities elsewhere."

"You mean . . . he liked paying for it?"

"I mean he only liked it when he was paying for it."

"But since he's been married?"

Somerset shrugged.

"He'll have *missed* paying for it."

"However much he's missed it, that's no reason why he should let this baggage make a fool of him. Not to the extent that you seem to count on."

"You don't know Maisie," Somerset said. "She really is rather special. She's nothing much to look at, you understand, but she has a genius for her work."


While Somerset Lloyd-James was lunching with Lord Canteloupe, Tom Llewyllyn was lunching down in Cambridge, with Robert Reculver Constable, the Provost of Lancaster College.

"The programmes," Tom explained, "will be monthly. We are starting at the end of May with an analysis, conducted by Hugh Trevor-Roper, of resurgent Nazism in Western Germany."

"Very salutary," said Constable. "It's high time *that* cat was let properly out of the bag."

"I hope to let out a lot of cats – even fiercer ones," Tom

said. "I am particulary keen to emphasise the random nature of historical events. To show that we have very little control over anything that happens and that even when we think we know what we are doing we are usually doing something quite different."

"Hmm," grunted Constable, who was a good socialist and believed very firmly in planning. "Concrete instance, please."

"Cyprus," said Tom. "We thought we were dealing with a spontaneous demand for self-determination. In fact, however, the Cypriots were being unconsciously pressured into demanding something which they didn't want and then into using means they detested to get it. We weren't quarrelling with the Cypriots at all, really, we were fighting an American secret service conspiracy to humiliate and dispossess us. A perfect example of history making fools out of us all, since neither of the apparent protagonists – Britain and Cyprus – had the slightest control over anything that happened."

"But not exactly a random affair, even on your theory. At least the Americans knew what they were doing."

"Very few of them knew about it at all. And the only motive of those that did was atavistic jealousy of the British."

"Still not entirely random."

"Not far off it. There was no policy, only whim."

"Very well," Constable said; "and what evidence can you produce?"

Tom outlined what he hoped to be able to prove.

"If all goes well," he concluded, "I want to make this the subject of our programme at the end of June."

"And why are you telling me about it?"

"Gray himself," said Tom, "is too badly disfigured to appear on television. He will probably speak the narrative, which he himself will write, over the film sequences which we shall construct to illustrate it, but he cannot address the audience in person. In any case, I need someone more authoritative to do that: someone of prestige and known impartiality, who will summarise and endorse the proofs presented. In one word, Provost Constable, I need you."

"I'm an economist, not an historian."

"You are a figure," said Tom, "of the utmost academic repute. You are known as a man who will accept nothing without flawless evidence. That is what I need."

"That's as may be," said Constable, flattered despite himself: "but what makes you think that Gray's evidence will be flawless?"

"I can't guarantee that, of course. But if I give you immediate access to it when Gray returns, will you agree to assess it?"

"I don't see why not."

"And if you find it sound, will you appear on the programme and say so?"

"I don't much care for arc lamps and glamour."

"I wouldn't want you if you did. I want you to be bleak, even boring, and totally undramatic. I want you to sum up as precisely and as prosaically as the most scrupulous judge in the kingdom."

Constable rapped his coffee spoon on the table. First a few isolated beats, then a swift and continuous tattoo.

"I may write my own summary?" he asked.

"Of course."

"And I may examine the film sequences you propose to use to make sure that these do not distort fact or give rise to false emphasis?"

"Certainly. When they are ready."

"Very well," said Constable, "I'll do it. But if I were you, I shouldn't rely too much on this man Gray. Years ago, when I was tutor here, I had to refuse him admission to this college."

"So I've heard."

"But did you hear why? It was because he was found to

have deceived. To have deceived and betrayed people who loved him for the sake of his own squalid pleasure."

"I think you'll find that he's changed, Provost. Besides," Tom said, "if he tries to deceive us, no one will be quicker to find him out than you."

"He very nearly wasn't found out before," said Constable. "He might never have been if he hadn't lost his head. First he deceived, and then, at a critical moment, he gave himself away because he lost his head. Unreliable either way, you see."

"I think you're being rather hard, Provost. Years ago, when he was very young, Fielding Gray was pitiably exposed and then fully punished for all that he had done. Why not leave it at that?"

"I'll be glad to," said Constable; "but can *he* leave it at that?"

As soon as he arrived in Athens, Fielding had sat himself down in the Grande Bretagne Hotel and written to General Grivas in the terms already rehearsed with Leonard Percival. His experience of some years back, he wrote, while he was fighting against EOKA in Cyprus, had given him an immense respect for the General personally, and an abiding interest in the General's military techniques. However, since he had been engaged by the BBC to investigate Cypriot affairs, certain people (he was not entirely sure who they were) seemed to have misconceived his motives as hostile to the present interests of Cyprus and to the good name of those who had taken part in her liberation. If the General would grant him the privilege of an interview, he would undertake to remove these misapprehensions; and having done so, he would be greatly honoured if the General would condescend to answer certain questions about the strategies and conceptions involved in the Cyprus campaign. The information would be used to prepare a responsible television programme, and it was also hoped to produce a detailed study in the form of a book by the writer of the present letter ... who was, my dear General, yours sincerely Fielding Gray, sometime Major and Officer Commanding the 10th Sabre Squadron of the 49th Earl Hamilton's Light Dragoons (Cyprus 1956–8).

The next day, Fielding made an expedition by taxi to Delphi and did not return until late in the evening. Since he had been feeling more and more doubtful as the day went on about the reply (if any) which his letter to Grivas would elicit, he was surprised to find that an envelope had been delivered by messenger that afternoon and that it contained a very courteous note written (like Fielding's) in literary Greek. The General regretted that he must be absent from Athens for the next seven days, but would be delighted to entertain Major Gray to luncheon at one o'clock on the afternoon following his return. The General was conscious of the honour of receiving an officer from so distinguished a regiment as Earl Hamilton's Light Dragoons, whose bearing and dexterity he had much admired.

So that's it, Fielding thought. Nothing to do now but wait. He composed a brief despatch to Leonard Percival, c/o The American Express, Roma, and another to Tom at the BBC; then he settled down to prepare an elaborate schedule of sight-seeing and related reading to fill in the next week.

Angela Tuck, having finished Fielding's novels, had nothing much to do with herself, and was therefore not at all pleased when Max rang up the next morning to say that he must now spend a third day and a third night away in Famagusta, where he had found a building suitable to house a casino and also several allies who were well placed to help him obtain the good will of the Administration.

After receiving this telephone call, Angela fretted and fiddled the morning away, ate a large English-style lunch, slept through the afternoon, awoke cross and sour-mouthed at six o'clock, and contrived to spend the next two hours bathing and dressing. During these two hours she drank several large whiskies, and by the time she had put down a pint of red wine with what little she could swallow of her English-style dinner and then poured two neat brandies on top of the whole mixture, she was positively twitching for action. Max, she remembered, had spoken of a wine-shop called Clito's, where the drink was supposed to be good and the company various; so thither, having with some difficulty obtained directions from a disapproving hall porter, she took her crepuscular way.

Some years before, Clito's shop had been only a dank cave filled with barrels and his clientele largely masculine and indigenous. However, the praise which several bibulous men of letters had bestowed on his wines and his tolerance had made Clito famous and enabled him to move into more commodious premises, in which he was now (to the fury of the men of letters) operating as a considerable tourist attraction, with prices to match. The arrival of an unaccompanied female, which in the era of the dank cave would have caused grave displeasure, was nothing out of the way these days; and though survivors of the original clientele frowned into their glasses, a new and younger class of Cypriot customer perked up, looked knowing, and dragged on its trouser legs to reveal large sections of bare calf, which were then laid out on available chairs for Angela's inspection.

There was only one firm rule of the house – that no native might make a direct approach to a foreigner or overtly solicit a drink. Smiles and displays of calf were as far as the young jackals of Kyrenia might go, and to these Angela remained indifferent. Or so it seemed. In fact, she was quietly employing a calculus of her own from which, having first made rough appraisals of shoulders, biceps and hips, she was able to arrive at a computation of the probable priapic capacities of all present. Only when she had done this, and added in certain other factors, such as facial appeal, skin textures and colouring, would she arrive at her final selection; and being a woman of great experience, she took her time. Meanwhile, she tried a bottle of Cypriot rosé, changed to a coarse local brandy and soda, changed again to a more refined local brandy without soda, reflected that she was too old to risk inferior liquor, and grievously offended Clito, who retained a fierce pride in the vines of his island, by making him bring out the bottle of Remy Martin which he reluctantly kept in reserve for faddy drinkers.

After about three-quarters of an hour, Angela decided on a boy with thin, hairy legs and a smooth, pretty face. The contrast between the effeminacy above and the hirsute exhibition below titillated the perverse streak in her and also promised, when she consulted her mental records of this type, a graceful and not ungenerous sexual physique. So she called for another glass, raised the bottle of Remy Martin, waggled it like a pendulum, and beckoned to the goat-legged youth.

The youth rose, snorting and libidinous. Hardly had he reached her table, however, when a tall and bland-faced man, dressed in a beautiful suit of fawn gaberdine, took him by the shoulder, turned him smartly round, and pushed him back towards his friends. The boy turned at the man with a swift and saurian flick of the head, but as soon as he could see the interloper properly he nodded gravely and withdrew. The man sat down at Angela's table without speaking, waved at Clito, who was already bringing him a carafe of white wine, and then smiled at Angela, who had been about to issue a shrill protest, in a way that somehow seemed to offer untold riches in this world or even the next, to offer the Forbidden City, at the least, or the Golden Apples of the Sun.

"Mrs Tuck?" said the man.

What a come-down after that smile, she thought: a smile

such as a jinn out of the lamp might give to a princess of Araby – and then the two words as bare and flat as floorboards.

"Mrs Tuck," she said. "And you?"

Clito poured the stranger some white wine from the carafe and then, giving Angela a look in which distaste was now mingled with new respect, filled her glass with Remy Martin from the bottle on the table. Plainly, she thought, this man is someone; merely by sitting at my table he has raised my status.

"What do you want?" she said briskly. "And what do I call you?"

"Earle . . . with an *e*."

"Well, Mr Earle—"

"—Just Earle. I must apologise," he said in an American accent which was all but entirely anglicised, "for changing your plans for the evening. But I don't think you'll regret it."

Again the smile, promising undreamed of pleasures and enchanted islands in which to enjoy them. A pure con, thought Angela, and nerved herself to resist.

"You haven't changed anything yet," she said. "You've merely interfered and delayed."

"If you offered those boys a hundred pounds," he said, "not one of them would come near you now without my permission."

"Bloody conceit," Angela said.

She beckoned once more to the pretty face with the goat-legs. The boy stared straight back over her head and didn't move a muscle.

"You see?"

"Then I'll make do with my own company." She turned to Clito, who was hovering behind his counter. "My bill, please," she said.

Clito shrugged, shook his head, and spread his arms wide.

"He won't take your money."

"Then he can go without it."

Angela rose, walked steadily to the door and out into the empty street. As she went, the stranger said something in conversational tones and demotic Greek. There was a scurrying and a clattering behind her, and within five seconds she found that she was surrounded by the boys and youths from inside. They did not impede her; they merely formed a circle round her and walked along at the same pace as she did. Then the stranger, Earle, was beside her.

"We'll go to the harbour," he said, and took her arm.

The circular cortege turned down a side street, and then down another. From this it emerged on to a short quay, the far end of which sloped down, like a ramp, on to a beach of shingle.

"Where are you taking me?"

"A little al fresco celebration, Mrs Tuck. Believe me, you'll enjoy it."

They tramped across the shingle, away from the sea. Somewhere up on Ängela's left the fort was hanging in the darkness, while ahead was a mass of large rocks. One of the boys led the way to a gap between two of these; Earle followed him through the gap, gently pulling Angela along behind him; and the rest of the boys, some eight or nine of them, came in single file after Angela. The gap led into a rather wider passage, so that now she was able to come up with Earle and walk by his side.

"Intriguing, isn't it?" he said.

The boy in front led on for perhaps twenty yards, after which the passage narrowed once more and then immediately widened again to turn itself into an egg-shaped arena, closed off at the far end, of fifteen yards in length by some six or seven where the oval was widest.

"Nothing to be frightened of," said Earle in a soothing voice.

"I'm not frightened."

Nor was she. For one thing, she had had a great deal to

drink, and for another she was now pretty certain what was in train. Here was a rich American who was paying these boys to mount some sort of spectacle. For whatever reason, her own presence, or participation, was going to give him an additional thrill. So be it. If only he had come out with his proposition straight away in Clito's, instead of annoying her by putting on such a silly and pretentious act, Angela would have agreed to join in from the word go and would even have offered to share expenses. She liked a daisy chain from time to time, and the American himself, if too conventionally cut altogether to suit her tastes, was undeniably appetising. By and large, then, she was fully prepared to assist in anything which might be toward, and she looked with pleasure round the little grotto which had been selected. Her only regrets were that the floor was still of shingle, not sand, and that it would be too dark to appreciate the nuances of the entertainment.

Of this, it now appeared, she herself was to be the centre. All at once the boys from Clito's closed in on her. She just had time to notice that Earle himself had backed away against the rock, before she was lifted by a dozen hands and laid gently on the ground. The dozen hands now started to caress her in a dozen different ways, while out of the dark the pretty face she had fancied in the wine-shop loomed down from one side to kiss her on eyes, ears and lips. As the face hovered and dipped at her own, hovered and dipped again, always close enough to blot out what little she might actually have seen in the darkness, it began to seem to her as though it were this one boy alone who was making love to her but this one boy somehow endowed with so many limbs and so much skill that he could rouse pleasure simultaneously in every place of her body. Instead of being fumbled by a crowd, she was being gloriously embraced by an immortal god with a face like Cupid's and the magical ability to make one mouth do the work of ten, ten fingers do the work of a hundred. From head to foot, every nerve in her which was apt for stimulation was being stimulated; she was, literally, one mass of desire. As the tongues and fingers went on busily about their tasks, she felt her damp thighs being slowly prised apart. The god was poised, he was about to enter.

Then she was lying alone on the cold shingle, with only the disarray of her clothes to prove that she had not imagined the entire scene.

"Come back," she called; "come back."

"I told you you wouldn't regret it," said Earle, who was now standing above her. "An amusing idea, which originated with the Empress Theodora in her younger and jollier days."

"Bring them back."

"All right."

There was a quick flurry in the darkness and once again her god was loving her tenfold.

"What can you tell me about Fielding Gray?" said Earle.

"What's Fielding Gray to you?" she mumbled, while the pretty Cupid face brushed lightly over her cheeks.

"Tell me about him."

"Nothing to tell."

The god stopped loving.

"They're bored with your old body," said Earle. "You must excite them. Tell them what you did with Fielding Gray."

Angela started to tell. Slowly the god moved into action again, leaving her lips free to utter the phrases which roused his divine lust.

"I see," said Earle at length. "This boy the two of you talked about ... this boy that killed himself. Describe him."

Once again Angela's thighs were parted and the god was poised.

"I never saw him."

The god perceptibly withdrew.

"Christ, Christ," she screamed; "don't let him go away from me."

"Excite him then. Tell him about this boy. He likes hearing about boys."

Yes, thought Angela wildly, all gods are bisexual.

"I can show you a book," she babbled, "Fielding wrote a book. Fair-haired ... strong limbs but delicate too ... light silver hairs on his legs ..."

"Go on."

She felt the poised god move very slightly nearer.

"I don't know. Yes, I do. There's a statue like him. Fielding told me. In some porch or something the Americans made in Athens, a statue of a boy with a flute."

"How very convenient," said Earle.

He snapped his fingers, and the god sank his sacred flesh slowly into Angela's, working the while at her whole body with his tongues and his fingers and his other immortal members.

"No," said Maisie; "I won't do it."

"Didn't you hear properly?" said Somerset Lloyd-James. "Five hundred pounds, I said. To say nothing of an introduction to a new and noble client."

"New and noble clients are all right," said Maisie, "if they still want to come. But I won't do what you ask to this Tom Thingamabob at the BBC."

"All you've got to do is to meet him, get him started ... you know ... and then go there and kick up a thcene."

Somerset still tended to revert to his childhood lisp when he was excited or upset.

"I don't go out to work. I do it here. What you're asking," said Maisie, "isn't decent. It isn't fair and it isn't professional."

"Now, look here, Maithie—"

"—And you look here," she said. "I'm paid to make men

come. I don't mind which way I do it – as you very well
know by now – because that's what they're paying me for,
and as jobs go in this world it's as fair and as square as most
others I've heard of. But what you're asking's different.
You're asking me to make a fool of someone who's never
done me any harm and who's got his job to do the same as
I've got mine. If a man wants to knock on my door and
says, 'Maisie, here's a tenner, make me come', then I'll
do my best for him and welcome. But if a man wants
nothing to do with me, I want nothing to do with him,
and I'm not going out anywhere for the sake of stirring up
trouble."

"I dare say we could go a hundred higher."

"Court cases," said Maisie, "names in the papers. I'd
never have any peace and quiet again. So either get out of
here, Mister Somerset Lloyd-James, MP, or tell me what I
*can* do for you. Who do you want me to be this week? Your
governess? Or the chamber-maid at that hotel by the sea-
side? Or that jolly Aunt who played hot cockles with you in
the back of her Rolls on the way back from the circus? We
haven't had *her* for nearly a year now."

"None of those, I think," said Somerset, still lisping. "Can
we have the woman on the train? You know . . . when there
ithn't a corridor and she's thuddenly taken thort?"

Captain Detterling went to dinner in Chelsea with Gregory
and Isobel Stern. Although Gregory had finally agreed to do
the Cavafy memoirs, he was still proving obstinate in other
matters and relations at the office were rather strained.
However, it was understood that this dinner was a social
occasion, and since Detterling was far too well mannered to
talk business when he was not supposed to, all would have
been well had not Gregory himself raised the topic.

"Today," he said, "I signed a contract for a book which
propounds a new theory of the Crucifixion."

"What new theory?" Detterling asked.

"That the Romans were exclusively responsible."

"But we had all that," said Detterling, "ten years ago. Late in 1951, the Jewish historian Shalom Franklyn published an exceedingly long and detailed book about it. It's all been said, Gregory."

"Then it should be said again. Because people have already forgotten."

"They have not forgotten," said Detterling. "On the contrary, they remember very clearly that Franklyn was shown to be wrong. He succeeded in shifting a bit more of the guilt on to the Romans, and he blew up the notion that Pilate was a humane and civilised man; but he didn't prove, because he couldn't, that the Jews were spotless in the affair."

"This new book I have bought does that."

"Then its author is either unscholarly or deluded."

"Why are you so keen that the Jews should have killed Jesus Christ?"

"I'm not *blaming* them, Gregory. Christ asked for everything he got. I'm just saying that this particular controversy is dead."

"And if there were new documents?"

"Are there?"

"Professor Bamberger, the author, claims to have inspected—"

"—*Claims to have inspected*. What's the matter with you, Gregory?"

"So Bamberger is a liar?" said Gregory, thumping the table. "He is a Jew and therefore a liar? So that is it?"

"Boys, boys," said Isobel. "You don't want me to miscarry? Let's talk about something nice."

"So talking about Jews is not nice?"

"For Christ's sake shut up," Isobel said. "Has anyone heard anything more about Fielding in Greece?"

"You should know. It is you that is always dreaming of him."

"Not for a long time," said Isobel. "I used to think there was something psychic between Fielding and me, but since the baby's been coming it's all stopped."

"Nature," said Detterling: "I'm told she protects pregnant women against any form of worry by releasing a special secretion into the blood. Your body manufactures its own opiate."

"Yes," said Gregory. "Nature would not wish you to worry about Fielding at a time like this."

"I never worried. I just had hunches about what was happening to him. Or what was going to."

"I must say," said Detterling, "I should very much like to know."

"One morning," said Gregory, "he will wake up in Athens and say to himself, 'My God, how could I be such a fool?' Then he will come back to us and start writing novels again. *Love's Jest Book*," he said to Detterling, "is still selling slowly but steadily."

Isobel shuddered.

"I hated that book," she said.

"May one ask why?"

"There's a light, bright flicker of madness in it. Any sane man would have forgotten all that stuff years ago."

"No writer is strictly sane. Nor are people who have psychic hunches."

"Well, pregnancy seems to have stopped my kind of madness," said Isobel. "What can we do for Fielding's?"

"Make as much money out of it for him as we can," Detterling said. "Then when he finally goes raving at least he'll be able to afford a comfortable bin."


Earle Restarick flew from Nicosia to Athens. The minute he arrived, he took a taxi to the Agora and went straight to the reconstructed Stoa at the far end of it. He walked along this until he came to the boy with the flute, examined the statue with great care, and then knocked on the door beside it. When the door had been unlocked from within, he passed into a small and windowless room which contained several metal filing cabinets, a desk with one chair, and a lot of broken statuary.

"How's the ancient world?" he said to the man who had admitted him – a thin, short man, with a nose as long as a hockey stick and a sensitive mouth.

"Preferable to the modern one. How's the Great Game?"

"There is an interesting problem to hand. Does the American School of Greek Studies in Athens run to a knowledge of comparative ethnology?"

"Try us."

"That statue just outside in the portico?"

"A copy from a late Hellenistic original. Probably made about 100 AD. What's that got to do with ethnology?"

"Comparative ethnology. The Grecian type seems to have changed since the late Hellenistic period."

"There have been a lot of mixed marriages round here in the last 2,000 years."

"There must be some areas – remote areas – when you can still find the classic article."

"Only flukes, accidental throwbacks. For 2,000 years the whole of Greece has been swarming with Syrians, Romans, Franks, Lombards, Venetians, Egyptians and Turks. No area is remote enough to have escaped the attentions of that little lot. If you want the classical Greek type, there's only one hope for you."

"Oh?"

"Find a German got from the time of the occupation. There are a few about. Blond, blue-eyed, straight-limbed – a very passable imitation of the old Dorian strain. The only people in this country who still look like real Greeks," said the man with the hockey-stick nose, "were fathered in the forties by the Hun."

"And so," said Somerset Lloyd-James to Lord Canteloupe, "there's nothing doing with Maisie. Though she'll be glad to see you personally in her professional capacity."

He handed Canteloupe a slip of paper on which a telephone number was written.

"But," Somerset went on, "as regards Tom Llewyllyn there is another possibility."

Canteloupe sighed.

"Here we go again," he said.

"On the contrary, we don't go anywhere. This time we just sit absolutely still," said Somerset, "holding our breath and waiting for it."

"Waiting for what?"

"Nemesis," said Somerset with relish.

"Do you have to talk like a schoolmaster?"

"Nemesis," Somerset pursued, "which in this case will come, not as the scourge of pride, but as the scourge of innocence. It really is exquisitely funny."

He started to chortle, sounding like something behind the wainscot in a story by Edgar Allan Poe.

"If you don't stop that horrible row," said the Marquis Canteloupe, "and tell me what you're talking about, I shall hit you on your bald, yellow head."

Honking and wheezing with his macabre merriment, Somerset began to tell him.

# 7

# DIVERSIONS

THREE DAYS before he was due to see General Grivas, Fielding's sight-seeing schedule took him once more to Delphi, where he proposed to spend the night and make a more detailed exploration than he had had time for on his previous visit. He left Athens in a hired car (self-drive) at ten in the morning, stopped on the way at Thebes to look at the museum, and arrived at Delphi in time for a late lunch. Having then established himself in the Xenia, in a room which looked straight out over the gorge, he drove along the hillside to the ancient site and began his carefully planned tour of inspection.

After fussing about for some time among the "treasuries" in the temple enclosure, he sat down on a stone and read Pausanias' account (in the Loeb edition, which he had procured from the bookshop off Constitution Square) of the shrine and its environs. He then walked on up to the temple itself, peered down into the chasm from which the priestess had uttered the oracles, and started on a conscientious examination of the inner precinct. It was while he was doing this, and cursing himself, not for the first time, for his contemptible knowledge of archaeology, that he began to feel he was being watched.

At first the feeling was in no way uncomfortable; it was rather as though some tutelary spirit of the place, not the god himself but some otherwise unoccupied minor deputy, was courteously hovering nearby in case he should require direction or assistance. It was, he told himself, a compliment to the interest he was taking; he was being recognised as a worthwhile guest. As time went on, however, and the feeling that he was observed grew steadily more insistent, he began to wish that his companion (for as such he now regarded him) would find some means of declaring himself. Repeatedly he looked about him, hoping that the undeniable presence might take bodily form, but the only bodies visible were those of two crestfallen Americans and their voluble guide, who was issuing an interminable harangue, down by the treasuries, about the Amphictyonic Council.

Anxious to get out of range of the guide's clacking monologue, Fielding now left the temple and took the path up through the trees towards the theatre. The guardian presence went with him. Somewhere in the pine-trees, he could not be sure on which side of the path, an intelligence which wished to communicate with his own was lurking along beside him. An intelligence? Say rather a fancy, a dream, a vision: something, in any case, which wanted to draw nearer to him but which, as he now realised, could not declare itself further unless he himself were to perform some act of prayer or ritual, utter some word or think some thought, which would give the spirit shape and enable it to come to him.

What prayer? What word? What thought?

"Who are you?" he called. "What do you want?"

The presence lingered but came no nearer. Slowly he walked on up the path. He knew now that he needed more than mere words to speak; he needed to imagine something, or to remember something, or to feel something. A wish or an emotion? What? For if he could only make the mental effort required of him, he would be proved worthy and granted the vision. If not ... well, it would linger awhile as it was now, but before long it would go sadly away, betrayed by his own failure of spirit. He must prove himself before it departed. What did it want of him?

He emerged from among the trees and found himself standing at the top of the theatre, looking down the stone tiers on to the stage below, and then beyond it, to the gorge above which the eagles slowly circled, to the bare, black ridge on the other side, and then away to the west, where the sun was sinking above the Gulf of Corinth. As he watched the eagles gliding, and as he saw the sea come glittering and creeping up to the olive coast below, he realised, for the first time in his life and with a physical pang which stirred in his body like lust, what it meant to be in a sacred place. He sat down on the stone ledge at the top of the theatre and burst into tears.

For some time he kept his head lowered, while the tears dripped off his face and on to his feet. When he began to recover himself, he took a handkerchief from his pocket and put it up towards his eye. As he did so, he heard a voice which whispered into his ear the one word:

"Please."

He looked to his left and his right; he looked behind him; nobody.

"Please," the voice whispered, "please. Don't cry. Please."

My tears have let the presence speak to me, he thought. What more must I do to see it?

"Please. I am here. Please."

He raised his head again and this time looked down on to the stage. In the middle of it was a figure. A boy. Of course, he thought: in this theatre of all theatres the lightest sigh from the stage, the fall of a rose leaf, can be heard in every part.

"I am here. Please."

Fielding started to walk down the steps to the stage. As he drew nearer to the figure below, he saw that the boy's short fair hair curled above a square, creamy forehead; as he came nearer still, he saw that the eyes were mild and wide-set, that the nose was soft, that the lips were full and curved slightly downwards, and that there was a cleft in the chin. Dear God, he thought, he's been given back to me; that's what was promised in the pine-trees; for the price of my tears he's been given back to me.

"Christopher, oh Christopher," he called, "is it really you?"

The boy did not answer, but held out both arms and raised his mouth for a kiss.

Maisie rang up Tom Llewyllyn at the BBC.

"You don't know me," she said, "but I want to see you. I want to give you a warning."

"I'm afraid I don't quite understand."

"No, of course you don't, and I can't tell you more on the 'phone. Come round to my place at six this evening, and I'll tell you what I can."

"I don't think I can do that."

"Look," said Maisie. "You don't know me and I don't know you, but I know who you are and I know some of your friends. Fielding Gray for one – he's told me quite a lot about you. But it's not him I want to talk about, it's other so-called friends who are getting ready to land you in the dirt. So if you know what's good for you, you'll clean out your ears ready to listen and come round here this evening at six."

Then Maisie told him where to come and rang off.

In the room which looked out over the gorge, Fielding looked down on the firm, brown stomach and lowered his face to kiss it, while the boy moved his hands in his hair. Naked, the boy was just as Fielding had always remembered

him. But there were differences in other things. There was
no shyness, now that he had come back after all these years,
and no shame. Instead there was pride of flesh and
complicity in desire.

"Christopher," murmured Fielding into the brown skin,
"where have you been?"

"My name is Nicos."

"Now it is. But I shall still call you Christopher. Do you
mind?"

"It can make no difference." The boy went on playing
with Fielding's hair. "What happened to your face?"

"I was hurt in an explosion. Does it ... upset you?"

"It can make no difference," the boy said again, and ran
one finger down to the base of Fielding's spine.


"So you see," Maisie said to Tom, "Somerset Lloyd-James is
trying to do you down."

"But you've refused to help him, you say."

"He'll find someone else ... or some other way."

"Fore-warned is fore-armed."

"That's what I thought."

"Thank you," said Tom. "Why did you bother?"

"Because I didn't like the smell of it. And then, you're a
friend of Fielding's."

"Are you fond of Fielding?"

"I've known him a long time."

"I see ... I'll tell you something," Tom said. "Somerset
was right. If you'd set yourself out to do what he asked, it
could have worked. I'm married, and I love my wife, but it
could still have worked."

"Should I be flattered?" asked Maisie.

"No. It's not you, attractive as you are. It's the set-up. It's
... forgive me ... It's the brevity, the lewdness, the disgust.
That's what I always went for."

"I understand," said Maisie placidly.

Tom looked at her, panting slightly. His hand went towards his breast pocket, but then he closed his eyes, shook his head, turned firmly about and walked from Maisie's flat.

"I'm due in Athens in a day or two," said Fielding. He got off the bed, went to the window and looked out over the darkening gorge. "But once I've finished my business there, we can go anywhere we like."

"I'll go wherever you wish," the boy said, "but not to Athens."

"It won't be for long."

"Not to Athens."

"But why on earth not?"

"*Not to Athens.*"

The police, thought Fielding. Some trouble like that. Christopher was in trouble with the police, he thought, seventeen years ago.

"Then I must go alone. You can wait for me wherever you choose, and I'll join you as soon as I can."

"If you leave me," the boy said, "I shan't be able to wait for you. Anywhere."

"I don't understand."

"You've been very fortunate to find me – to find me once more, as you say. If you let me go . . . a second time . . . I shall have gone for ever."

"But why? *Why?*". . .

"Because I shall have been . . . recalled."

Like Eurydice, Fielding thought, sweating with fear.

"Come here," the boy said, "come to the bed."

As Fielding went towards the bed, the boy held out his arms as he had on the theatre stage that afternoon. He kissed the shiny pink skin, then took Fielding's head between his hands, cradled it in his warm belly, and stroked Fielding's hair.

"You must not leave me," the boy said; "you must not let me go again."


"Why are you home so late?" said Patricia to Tom in Southwell Gardens.

"Because I've been with a whore."

As Patricia slowly opened her mouth, a wail like that of a siren rose from somewhere down in her stomach and came spiralling out with steadily increasing volume. Baby, not to be left out of the act, emitted shrill screams of accusation at short intervals of deadly regularity.

"It wasn't what you think," said Tom.

He picked up the howling Baby, thrust her out into the little passage, then closed and locked the living-room door.

"It wasn't what you think," he repeated to Patricia, "but it might very easily have been. Because there's a hot, dirty, ratty side to me which I've never shown you yet but which has only been waiting to come out."

Patricia looked at him, silent now.

"I might have taken it out on that whore," Tom said, "and kept it from you that much longer. But I think it's time you knew about it, once and for all."

He forced her down on the sofa.

"For better or for worse."

He fumbled with her clothes and his own.

"Quick," he said, "hot, nasty and quick."

"Tom . . . *Tom*."

"Into the bushes," Tom hissed, "and do it before anyone comes. Standing up or like the dogs. Dirt. Sweat. Stink. Quick, Patricia, quick."

"Oh God," she whimpered, as Baby hammered on the door. "Oh dear God," she panted, "it's never been like this. Quick, Tom, quick. Like the dogs, Tom. QUICK."

I've got to go through with it, Fielding thought. I've got to see Grivas and get that evidence for Tom.

He looked at the sleeping boy beside him. The fair hair was plastered with sweat over the temples and the brow; the full lips pouted, as if ready to be wakened by a kiss.

No. Think. I've taken on a job, for which I'm being very well paid. Succeed in this, and it could mean more jobs, more money, later on. Fame. Anyway, Tom is relying on me, trusting me to do this for him.

But I could always say I'd been with Grivas and failed. (Those lips.) After all, I've been through a lot already, what right have they to force me into more?

But Tom didn't force me. He asked me if I wanted to go on with it, and I said yes.

Those lips, those cheeks.

But leave Tom aside, and to hell with the BBC, the job is one that ought to be, that must be done. I want to do it. I want to finish what I've started, now that I'm so near. I want to destroy Restarick, show up the whole rotten business, warn everybody what goes on.

But if I go to Athens, I shall lose him. For the second time.

Slowly, Fielding drew down the sheet. Chest. Belly. Loins. Thighs. Soft skin, silver down, catching the early morning light. The boy whimpered slightly in his sleep, and Fielding settled the sheet back over him, shuddering with joy at the sight he had just seen.

If I go to Athens, I shall lose it all.

I must go to Athens. For my career, for Tom's friendship, for truth.

But I am not due in Athens until one p.m. of the day after tomorrow. Two more days, two more nights.


"Take care," said Patricia to Tom at breakfast.

"Take care?"

"You know ... What you told me last night. What that woman—"

"—Maisie—"

"—What Maisie was warning you about."

Baby, who sensed peace and solidarity, gurgled happily.

"I'm grateful to Maisie," said Patricia, "for making it so much better for us."

"It was all right before."

"Not like that, though, never like that. And I'm grateful to her for warning you. You must take care, Tom. Why do they want to harm you?"

"I'm not sure. I think ... that they think ... that I may be going to broadcast something that will make trouble for them. There have been hints from other quarters."

"Must you go on with it?"

Tom shrugged.

"Yes," he said. "But if I keep my nose clean, there's nothing they can do."

Patricia kissed him gaily on the lips.

"Then keep your nose clean," she said.

Fielding and Nicos went for a walk along the shore of the Corinthian Gulf, between Itea and Galaxheidhi. For much of the way the olive trees came crowding down almost to the sea, leaving only a thin strand of beach. Since the afternoon was very hot, they walked mostly in the shade of the olive trees.

"Why do you not ask me," said Nicos, "who I am, where I come from? Such questions should be asked between friends."

"I'm not sure that I want to know the answers."

"Then I shall ask you. Who are you, Fielding Gray? Where do you come from?"

"I am a writer of books, and I come from England."

"And you have business in Athens. You will not go there now, I think."

"I must go."

Nicos pursed his lips and moved on ahead, kicking at the ground with every third or fourth step.

"But not yet," said Fielding as he caught up with him.

"When?"

"Need we talk of it?"

"Yes. I wish to know."

"In two days' time."

"You must not go. Please. You must not leave Nicos. You must not leave . . . Christopher."

He pronounced the name as if it had been Christopheros without the final syllable: Christopher.

"Why cannot you wait for me while I go?"

"I shall swim now," Nicos said.

"Take care."

"I am a good swimmer."

Nicos stripped down to his underpants, while Fielding settled himself on the ground, supporting his back against an olive trunk. From where he sat he had a clear view of the sea, and of Nicos as he bobbed and duck-dived some thirty yards out. Who is he? Fielding thought: where does he come from? But as he had told Nicos a few minutes before, he did not really want to know. It could make no difference. For on the one hand, Nicos was just a little pick-up, who had been waiting for a tourist, any tourist, and nobody wanted to know who pick-ups were and where they came from: while on the other hand, he was the gift promised by some god in a sacred precinct, and of such it was forbidden to enquire the origin. Enough, either way, that he was Christopher come back again, just as if Christopher had been reborn, when he died nearly seventeen years ago, and had grown up as Nicos, in a different land. Nicos' age was right for that, Fielding thought. He was slightly under seventeen, to all appearance, and could well have been born during that summer of 1945, when Christopher had been betrayed and died. Would Nicos die too if he were betrayed ... if Fielding went to Athens? But why should this be betrayal?

Fielding's head sunk forward on his chest. Eurydice, he thought. When she was taken for the second time (*ceu fumus in auras,* like smoke into the air, into thin air), Orpheus was forbidden ever to seek her out again. *Nec portitor Orci Amplius objectam passus transire paludem;* nor did the gatekeeper of hell suffer him any more to pass the barrier of the marsh. Eurydice, beyond the marsh in hell; Christopher, Nicos, beyond the marsh in hell. Or so he might be if Fielding left him to go to Athens. Like many that had been so beautiful. *Tot milia formosarum . . . formosorum . . .*

When he awoke there was no sign of Nicos in the sea.

"Christopher," he called at once; then "Nicos . . . Nicos."

*Ceu fumus in auras.*

"Nicos . . . *Nicos.*"

He rose to his feet and ran across the beach. But his legs had been infected with his panic and would not carry him; he sprawled full length and lay shaking and desperate, until a wave licked at his face. Then he raised himself on one elbow.

"NICOS," he screamed.

"Here I am."

There, at the edge of the olive grove. Quite naked now, legs crossed, leaning against a tree-trunk.

"I thought . . . I thought . . ."

"I was drying myself in the sun. You ran straight past me ... lying on the beach. I am sorry if you are upset."

"I'm all right, now. Oh, Nicos."

"Why do you look at me like that?"

"You know why."

Nicos grinned and flaunted himself.

"Come here," he said: "Then you can look as close as you please."


Tom Llewyllyn rang up Provost Constable at Lancaster College.

"I've just had a letter from Gray," Tom said; "he is to have an interview with Grivas in two days' time from now."

"As to that," said Constable, "we shall see what we shall see. But there's something else I want to talk to you about. Can you spare a few minutes?"

"Why not? The BBC's paying for the call."

"Ah," said Constable: "since what I have to say has nothing to do with your function there, it would be very wrong that the Corporation should be at charges. Kindly ring off at once, and then I will telephone you back."

Tom rang off at once and within a minute Constable rang him back.

"Now," said Constable, "the nature of power. The other day, when you came to luncheon here, you expressed certain opinions as to the random nature of historical events. Presumably these opinions are of some relevance to your thinking on the subject of power?"

"Certainly they are. Power too is a random affair. To begin with, it is almost impossible to see it as concentrated in any definite person or persons, if only because the world has long since become too complicated for even the most determined and intelligent individual to exert his will, except in very limited areas."

"Illustrate," snapped Constable.

"This isn't a *viva voce*, Provost."

"Illustrate . . . if you please."

"Very well," said Tom. "Power, in the simplest definition, is the ability to do or to act. You, as Provost of Lancaster, are supposedly the most powerful man in the College. Yet to what extent are you able to do or to act inside it? You can recommend, you can persuade, you can influence, you can intrigue. But when it comes to doing or acting, you cannot even dismiss one of the college servants without seeking ratification from the appropriate sub-committee."

"I should obtain their ratification if I sought in the right way."

"That makes you a diplomat, not a man of outright power. It makes your authority purely personal ... the kind of authority that extends only as far as you yourself are *seen*. Since you can make yourself seen over most of Lancaster, we may assume that you keep pretty effective control in that very limited area ... not because you are powerful but because, for the time being, people like to please you. So you'd better watch out, my dear Provost. If your Fellows were to start turning sour on you, you could end your days with your rule confined to a small bed-sitting room at the back of your own Lodge."

Constable laughed grimly down the line.

"Would you care to expand the thought?" he said. "To translate it into terms of the national or international scene?"

"Not on the telephone, no. The matter is too distressing. Telephones are only fit for making jokes."

"But if I were to invite you up here again—?"

"—For lunch one day? With pleasure."

"Or perhaps a slightly longer visit this time," Constable said: "power is a very large subject."


On the afternoon of the day before Fielding was due to return to Athens, Nicos said to him:

"Let us go to the museum, please."

They drove to the museum, which was by the entrance to the temple site.

"I have something to show you," Nicos said.

He led Fielding to the statue of the Charioteer. The face and figure were of bronze so worn and fragile that it must crumble, one would have thought, at a touch. The green skirts would disintegrate like sugar-icing, Fielding thought; and as for the sweet, calm face, one could surely push a finger through it as through a mask of papier-maché.

"I have seen this before," he said to Nicos, "but I'm glad you thought of coming here now."

I'm glad, he thought, because this is a timely reminder : a reminder that the Charioteer, according to Plato, stands for the principle of reason, which reins in the twin horses of the soul. I was in danger, he thought, of giving the wilder horse its head. I was in danger of yielding to desire, infatuation, call it what you will or whatever Plato called it, in danger of letting the reins go and leaving the chariot to run on until it crashed. Not now. Despite what I have seen stretched on my bed or cavorting among the olive trees by the sea, I know that I am a man of reason, and I am keeping a firm hold on the traces. This statue will remind me of that and give me strength – the noble Charioteer of the soul.

"Do you know the story of this man?" Nicos asked.

"I know . . . a kind of myth about him."

"I wonder whether it is the same as mine. In mine he is called Automedon, and he drove the chariot from which the warrior Achilles was fighting. One day, when they mounted the chariot, Automedon to drive it and Achilles just behind him, the horses spoke to Achilles and told him that the day of his death was drawing near. As for us, the horses said, we could run as swift as the West wind, which of all winds is the swiftest; yet even so we could not save you, for it is your fate to be slain in battle, by a god and by a mortal."

"I have heard that story," said Fielding, "but I cannot remember that Automedon had much to do with it, apart from just being there. The passage in Homer which describes it hardly mentions him at all."

"Automedon loved Achilles and wept for him."

"Homer says nothing about it."

"Automedon wept," insisted Nicos. "He wept so that he could hardly see to drive the chariot."

"Who told you this?"

"I know that it was so. When Automedon heard from the horses that his friend was to be taken from him, he started to cry. His face in this statue is calm, because he was a soldier and must not give way, but all the time he was crying inside himself – just as I am crying now – and he could not stop the tears from rolling down his cheeks."

Fielding turned from the statue to look at Nicos. Two huge tears were rolling down the boy's face, which otherwise, like that of the statue, was quite calm.

"Oh Nicos," Fielding said; "Oh Nicos, I must go to Athens."

He looked back at the statue.

"It's not Automedon," he said. "It's a man, any man, driving a chariot."

"A man, any man," said Nicos, "crying to himself inside because his friend must go away, leaving him alone."


"I must say," said Lord Canteloupe, "Maisie really is quite something. She's made me feel positively young again."

"So you've taken up my introduction," said Somerset Lloyd-James.

They were sitting in the pavilion at Lord's, watching the first match of the season.

"My dear fellow," said Canteloupe, "I'm hardly ever out of the place."

"Don't go overdoing it . . . and for God's sake be discreet. Your Department may not be much in the public eye, but you're not without name and importance, and if you're caught out it would mean a nasty scandal. Which is the last thing the Party can afford just now."

"Who's going to catch me out? And what if they do? Can't a man have a mistress?"

"A minister can't," said Somerset, "not even a junior one. These days all public men are supposed to be like the angels – devoid of private parts. And what do you mean, *mistress*? Maisie is a common bawd."

"I'm thinking of taking her away from Curzon Street and setting her up somewhere else. Just for me."

"You thelfish old bugger," yelped Somerset, shocked out of his usual calm : "I've been going to Maithie for yearth. What would I do without her?"

"I might let you share expenses in the new place. We could work out a rota."

"It 'ud cost me ten times what it does now."

"Well, if you're going to be stingy . . ." said Canteloupe. "My God, this cricket match is boring. If it doesn't improve soon, I'm going downstairs to telephone Maisie."

"She's booked for the whole afternoon. I rang her up this morning myself."

"There you are, you see. Much better have her nicely set up just between the two of us. Jesus Christ," cried Canteloupe, vibrating with enthusiasm, "she really is a bloody marvel. Nothing much to look at, as you said, but for sheer lust-making she's unique. I can quite believe she'd have settled Tom Llewyllyn's hash if she'd only been on for the job. How's all that going, by the way?"

"It's working out just as I hoped it would."

A man came marching towards them down the rows of empty white seats.

"Your cousin, Detterling," Somerset said.

"Good afternoon, you two," Captain Detterling remarked "Nice to have cricket starting again."

"You won't find this very amusing."

"Anything," said Detterling, "would be preferable to what I've just been through with Gregory Stern. Do you know what he's doing? He's decided to set up something

called the New Jewish Library, and he's got off to a
swingeing start by contracting for a three-volume commentary on the *Gemara*."

"What's that when it's at home?" said Canteloupe.

"The *Gemara*," explained Detterling, "is a commentary
on the *Mishnah*, which itself is a commentary on the
*Pentateuch*. A commentary on the *Gemara* is therefore a
commentary upon a commentary upon a commentary.
Apart from which, Gregory has also commissioned three
new books about Israel, all of them by Rabbis, and an eight-
hundred-page study of the Diaspora in Poland from 1840 to
1845."

"Not like him," said Somerset. "He's got the reputation of
being the shrewdest small publisher in the game."

"It's all started since Isobel's been pregnant."

"No connection, surely?"

"I don't know," said Detterling. "He's been hopelessly
over-excited about the whole thing. Because Isobel's
pregnant, he's suddenly seen himself as a kind of patriarch.
He's gone atavistic, you might say. He'll probably end up in
the Sinai desert with a tent and a camel before long, but
meanwhile he's expressing it all through his choice of these
ridiculous books."

"How long will it take him to go broke?" enquired
Somerset.

Detterling turned up his eyes.

"You'll see the vultures hovering when the time draws
near."

"He'll be up there hovering with them," Canteloupe said.


On the morning of the day on which Fielding was due to
lunch with General Grivas, he sent four telegrams from his
hotel at Delphi: one to Grivas himself, one to the Grande
Bretagne, one to Tom Llewyllyn in London, and one to the
firm in Athens from which he had hired his car. Then he

got into the car with Nicos and started driving west, heading for the ferry by which they proposed to cross the Gulf of Corinth and land on the Peloponnese, a few miles away from Patras. From Patras they would drive to Olympia, and from there over the mountains to Arcadia, that old country where the shepherds piped at noon.

# 8
## JOURNEY'S END

WHEN TOM LLEWYLLYN received Fielding's telegram, which informed him that there must now be an indefinite delay before Fielding could meet Grivas, he was both puzzled and annoyed. Why an indefinite delay? Either Grivas would meet Fielding or he wouldn't; there need be nothing indefinite about it. And why the lack of explanation? If it was safe to send telegrams on the subject at all, it was safe to offer a more circumstantial account. The whole matter was the more irritating as time for preparing the programme on Cyprus would soon be running short; and although a postponement would be in order, Tom did not relish the task of telling Constable that Fielding was behaving in a manner which made certitude as to dates impossible and did much to bear out Constable's uncharitable judgments, as to Fielding's obliquity, which Tom had been at pains to refute.

A telephone call to the Grande Bretagne Hotel in Athens revealed that Fielding had left the hotel some three days before. He had told Reception that he would be away at Delphi for one night only, but he had since wired – that very morning, in fact – to say that his date of return was now indefinite. That word again, Tom thought: something must have happened on Fielding's one-night excursion out of Athens to throw all his plans into total confusion. Had he been kidnapped and made to send the wires to prevent

171

anxiety in other quarters? Or was he funking his confrontation with Grivas? Or was he, perhaps, ill?

It was clear that if he had been kidnapped his captors would have made him insert in his telegram a convincing explanation of his inactivity. The absence of any such implied first that Fielding was quite free and secondly, this being so, that he had not explained himself simply because he did not wish to. Whatever had happened to cause the delay was therefore in some sense attributable to Fielding himself and almost certainly something of which he was ashamed. What could one do at Delphi of which one would be ashamed? Very little, Tom thought; it would be interesting to find out. He therefore sent for a guidebook, telephoned through (with some difficulty) to the principal hotel listed at Delphi, and was rewarded by discovering that the kyrios Gray had indeed stayed there for the last three nights. He had left that morning ... with his friend. His friend? Yes, the kyrios had – er – met a friend in Delphi, somewhat younger than himself, for whose accommodation in the hotel, as well as his own, the kyrios had paid before leaving. But where had he gone when he left? The kyrios had enquired the best way to the ferry at Antirrhion, so it was to be inferred that he had gone there.

By this time Tom did not need to be very acute to form a rough idea of what must have happened. Fielding had found something he fancied and driven it off. But why on earth had he driven it off in the wrong direction? Why couldn't he have taken it to Athens, since it was so important that he should go there? However much he fancied his new find, he could surely have borne a few hours' separation while he had lunch with Grivas as pledged. Clearly, something was badly out of order and something must be done. But what? It was a question of mounting an emergency operation to rescue Fielding (and with him his programme), and that meant finding a lot of money, which the BBC could be made to cough up, and a man of resource to send in pursuit, which was another thing again. Tom himself could not possibly go, having much urgent work on hand to get out the first programme in the series. The only person he could think of, there and then, was Captain Detterling (whom one automatically associated with expeditions of this nature), but Detterling was a Member of Parliament, and although he was much given to journeys he might not be able to take off just like that.

However, he was worth trying. A call to Detterling's chambers in Albany raised only a mealy-mouthed and unhelpful manservant, and a call to Gregory Stern Ltd raised only Gregory Stern, who insisted that Tom should listen for fifteen minutes while he read out a synopsis for a book on the Jewish problem in Mauritius. After this, Tom was just about to try the House of Commons, when there was a knock on his door, through which came the Director of Features and a man who looked like an upright crocodile in a bowler hat.

"Mr Llewyllyn," the Director of Features said, "something very grave indeed has just been brought to my notice. I can only hope that you will be able to explain."

I will have this, Fielding thought: I must have it. I am well over thirty years old and such a chance will never come again. I must go on having this for as long as I possibly can.

He was sitting on the steps of the Temple of Zeus at Olympia, watching Nicos, who was standing among broken columns somewhere away by the river. Behind and above the temple a small tree-covered hill rustled in the faint breeze of the afternoon. Tourists pottered singly about, for the most part keeping in the shade of pine or masonry. Only Nicos, standing among the broken columns by the river, remained out under the fierce white sun.

Yes, thought Fielding: I must go on having this for as

long as I can. But how long could that be? How long could he exist in this timeless state, measuring the hours and the days only by the recurring rhythms of desire, ecstasy, satiety and then, once more, desire? How long could he stay out of the world, thinking nothing of dates or money or obligations, living only in his coloured dream of love?

General Grivas, Tom Llewyllyn, Gregory Stern. Sooner or later he would have to return to their world and account to them for his absence. To Grivas he had wired that he was unwell and begged to be excused. To Tom he had wired that there must be delay. But sooner or later he would have to approach Grivas again, he would have to beg Tom's pardon for the hiatus (and all too probably for total failure, as Grivas might not prove so amenable to a second request), he would have to go home and propose some new scheme to Gregory and start earning his bread. He looked at Nicos, as he stood by the river Alpheius. How long could he go on having this? The answer was brutally simple: until the cash ran out.

So be it, then. If Nicos would stay with him, Fielding would keep him until the bottom of the purse was in sight. Then he would give him what he could and say good-bye, go back to Athens and start worrying about the bills. These would be heavy, and some of them, like the draft he had drawn on Tom's patience, might never be fully met. But that could not be helped. For the first time in seventeen years he had been in love, and this time he must not toss it away from him, as he had before, he must cherish it with all his strength and resources. The gods had offered him a second chance, which was perhaps the greatest privilege in their gift, and if he spurned it they would curse him for ever.

He left the temple step and walked through the scorching sun to where Nicos stood.

"You will stay with me?" he said. "Promise that you'll stay."

"If you will take care of me," said Nicos, "I will stay as long as it is permitted."

"Permitted?"

"We do not settle these things ourselves. You know that. There are powers much stronger than us who settle them for us. They let us meet; they will decide when we must part."

"The Fates, you mean? The stars? The gods?"

"There is one above all these. Necessity, that is what we have always called it in Greece. *Ἀνάγκη*," Nicos said: "Necessity."

"I was just thinking much the same thing."

Necessity. When the money ran out. Necessity was above everything, even above those gods who had given him his second chance.

"But meanwhile we can make the best of the time we have," Nicos said, and ran his tongue over his lips. "Nobody knows when Necessity will come, so there is no good thinking about it until it does. We will sleep the night here in the hotel and go on tomorrow. Sleep another night, at Tripolis maybe, and go on again. It is best like that."

"You think Necessity may take longer to catch up if we keep moving?"

"No. Necessity is everywhere at once. But it is nice to feel free, even if we can never be so."


"They both remained standing," said Tom to Patricia, "both the Director and the crocodile man, even when I offered them chairs. So then I knew something really bad must be coming."

"Oh, darling . . .'

"But at first it just seemed ridiculous. Apparently Miss Enid Jackson of the Administration Department had written to the National Insurance people to say that I had instructed her that my card had been inadvertently destroyed, and would they kindly issue a new one forthwith?"

"And would they?"

"No. They'd consulted their files and discovered I'd never had one at all. For a long time they'd been making attempts to get hold of me, the man in the bowler hat said – like that letter to Buttock's, I suppose – but they'd never succeeded. Now, at last, they'd caught up, and I must understand that I was to be prosecuted for fifty-two separate offences under the Act – i.e. one for every week that I'd failed to stamp my card over the last year, which is as far back as they're allowed to go. Since the maximum penalty for each offence is ten pounds, I could be fined over five hundred quid."

"We can surely find five hundred pounds, darling."

"They can also sue through the civil courts for contributions outstanding – in this case for at least as far back as three years, and possibly for the whole lot."

"We can still find the money. If you haven't got it all just now, I can sell some of the shares Daddy handed over last year."

"That was the line I took," Tom said. "I got my cheque-book out and asked the crocodile man how much he wanted. Let him name his sum, I said, and go away and leave me in peace. But he said it had gone beyond that now. The due processes of the law had been invoked, he said, and there was no stopping any of it. Then he went away and left me with the Director, who was practically flying round the ceiling."

"But why?" asked Patricia.

"Ah. This is where it all stopped just being boring and absurd and got absolutely loathsome. I was going to be publicly tried, the Director said. So what, I said: I'd plead guilty, pay up and get out. But for twelve years or more, the Director said, I'd deliberately evaded my obligations as a citizen. Rubbish, I said: it wasn't deliberate, I'd never even thought about it. But you *lied*, he said; you told Miss

Jackson your child had torn up your card when you never ever had one. A fraudulent lie – he was squealing with indignation by now – to try and evade paying out money for an invaluable social service. A squalid piece of deceit – *and* I'd had the effrontery to involve the BBC, to try to exploit the Corporation as the agent of my falsehood. I couldn't be trusted, I wasn't fit to work with decent people – let alone to give orders to them – I was evil, I was filth, I was slime . . . and I needn't bother to come back to-morrow."

"But Tom . . . He can't do that."

"He can't but those above him can – and have. There's a clause in my contract, something about my preserving the capacity to fulfil my obligations to the BBC. These, it seems, I have implicitly repudiated by my behaviour. Or so the Director has persuaded the gentlemen upstairs."

His head drooped and he looked very defeated.

"Tom. Darling Tom. After all your work."

"I don't think it would ever have been much good. For all their fine talk at the beginning, I think they were going to muzzle the series somehow – they've been making difficulties all along. But there's another thing."

He told her the story of Fielding, as he himself had construed it, and of his very worrying behaviour.

"God knows what sort of mess he's getting into. I was going to send someone after him – I could have got the BBC to pay. But now . . . well, I suppose I'll have to go myself. I can spare a few days, as things are."

Patricia drew a sharp breath.

"You won't be allowed out of the country. Not if you've charges to face."

"They'll accept security, I dare say."

"We haven't the money for you to go gallivanting all over Greece. Not with those fines, and all they're going to sue you for."

"I can manage . . . though I might have to ask you to cash some of those shares. Just as a loan, of course."

"That was for if *you* needed it. Not for anyone else."

"But Fielding's an old friend."

"Dirty pig." Her face was hard and pinched. "Running off with some filthy little boy from the gutter. If you go after him, I won't give you a penny."

"Patricia—"

"—Not a penny."

"Very well. I'll have to get hold of Detterling and ask him to go. He can probably afford the money. But when he asks me why, in all the circumstances, I'm not going myself, I shall have to grovel ... *grovel* ... and say my wife won't let me."

Patricia saw the danger signals working in Tom's face and realised that she had gone too far.

"Tom, darling ... I'm sorry I said that about Fielding. I didn't mean it."

"Yes, you did. I saw your face when you said it. It was obscene."

"I was upset, at the thought of you going away. Listen, Tom." She came very close to him. "Now that you've left the BBC, it's all over with the series. So what does it matter if Fielding doesn't see Grivas?"

She fingered him crudely and pressed up against him. He backed slightly away.

"It would be nice to know the truth, series or no. And then there's Fielding himself to think of."

Patricia fumbled with her skirt.

"Do you really think Grivas would have told him anything? And as for Fielding himself, don't you think he might be ... happy ... with this boy of his?"

"Perhaps," said Tom, looking down to where her hands were working.

"Then forget them all," she breathed at him. "You've no need to go to Greece, no need to grovel to Detterling either. Look at me, Tom, and say you'll forget them."

Tom stared fascinated at her violently circling fingers. "That's right," she said: "look at me, and forget them."

Fielding and Nicos motored over the mountains, through Tropaia (with its tiled roofs and blue balconies) and Dimitsana (terraced on its citadel of rock), and down into Arcadia, most of which consisted of bare hills, not at all Arcadian. But in the late afternoon, on the road between Tripolis and Sparta, they found a little valley in which were trees, wild flowers and a rocky stream. Here they stopped to discuss the night's harbour.

"Back to Tripolis or on to Sparta? From Sparta we could go to Gytheion or Monemvasia and take a boat to one of the islands."

"No," said Nicos quickly: "no islands."

"Whyever not?"

"The people are dirty and poor. Besides, there is a lot to be seen here in the Peloponnese."

"As you like," said Fielding rather shortly.

He stretched himself in the grass, and Nicos came and lay beside him.

"You are tired," Nicos said, "after driving over the mountains." He stroked Fielding's brow with the fingers of one hand. "It is a long way on to Sparta. Let us rest here a little and then go back to Tripolis, which is a pretty little town with market places and gardens. In the morning we can decide where to go next."

"All right."

The sun was warm and friendly in the evening, and the stream chattered quietly like well-mannered children playing at a distance, whose voices can still be heard though their words can no longer be distinguished. Fielding took the hand that was stroking his forehead and licked the palm.

"You have very soft hands, Nicos. Christopher had soft

hands. Warm and soft. You are like him everywhere ... here, and here, and here."

"You have soft hands too, and I like it when you touch me ... here, and here, and here."

So they trifled in the valley till the sun went down, then drove slowly back into Tripolis, where they found a hotel which overlooked a tangled garden in the middle of a small square.

In Athens, Earle Restarick went to the Stoa in the Agora and knocked on the door by the statue.

"News from London," he said. "The BBC has dispensed with Llewyllyn's services, and for the time being at least 'Today is History' is going into abeyance. The pressure is off."

"*E finita la commedia?*" said the man with a nose like a hockey stick.

"Yes. I must get back to Cyprus straight away. I want you to do something for me."

"Ring the curtain down?"

"And re-engage the principal boy. Talent like that must not be wasted. Here is some money for him, and an air ticket to get him to Nicosia."

Both of which Restarick now gave to his emissary, together with some brief and pointed instructions.

Fielding and Nicos walked up the path to Agamemnon's palace at Mycenae. The backs of their hands brushed as they walked. God, Fielding thought, looking sideways at Nicos, for seventeen years, for seventeen long years I've had nothing like this.

Ahead of them was the Lion Gate, square and flat, and above it two stone beasts craning their chins up on either side of a pillar. After they had passed through the gate and up on to the ramparts, they could see south beyond Argos and Tiryns to the bright bay of Nauplion; while just to the east of them rose the gaunt hill on which the beacon had flared blood-red, 3,000 years ago, as a sign to Clytemnaestra and her paramour that Agamemnon, Lord of Hosts, had taken ship from Troy.

And to the west, just over the road which led up from the village, was a car park, into which a Land-Rover now drove.

"There is a postern gate," said Fielding, "at the end of a long passage which leads right through the heart of the palace. Shall we go and find it?"

"Let us stay here," said Nicos, who was watching the Land-Rover.

A man emerged from this, walked out of the car park and over the road, and started up the sloping path towards the Lion Gate.

"I wonder," said Fielding, "what the Queen and her lover must have felt when the beacon flared at last. For ten years Agamemnon had been away ... 'far on the ringing plains of windy Troy' ... and then, one evening as they were settling to dinner, perhaps, the beacon blazed."

But Nicos was not listening. He was walking away from the ramparts and back to the Lion Gate. The man from the Land-Rover, a small man with a nose like a hockey stick, came through the gate, accosted Nicos as somebody known to him, and began to talk. Nicos nodded two or three times, then both of them passed back through the gate and started down the slope. Nicos did not look back to Fielding and made no sign.

"Stop," called Fielding, and ran down from the ramparts and through the gate in pursuit.

Nicos and the stranger with the nose turned to face him.

"Where are you going?"

"I am going away," said Nicos. "This gentleman has come from those who sent me, and says that he is to fetch me away."

It was uttered as a simple statement of fact, without emotion of any kind.

"Who . . . sent you?"

"I was sent to keep you away from Athens. Now it no longer matters, and this gentleman is fetching me away."

"Please, Nicos. Don't go. You don't have to go, Nicos. Please don't go."

"Why should I stay?"

Nicos and the man turned and walked on down the path.

"But do I mean nothing to you?"

Nicos and the man walked on.

"Don't you understand what you mean to me?"

Fielding circled round from behind the other two and started dancing absurdly backwards in front of them.

"Nicos," he babbled, "I have money. I will give you money to stay."

"This gentleman has brought me money. There will be more, he says. Much more than you could pay."

"Nicos, you're too kind, too young to talk like that."

"I am well over twenty. No, not seventeen, as you thought. I am not properly grown, you see. I wasn't fed when I was a child, and so now I go with those who will feed me and pay me best."

"But don't you realise what they'll do to you? The horrible ways they'll use you?"

"What should I care? For this week I have been pawed about and slobbered on and called by a dead boy's name. Next week there will be something else. That is all."

"Nicos. I love you."

The ridiculous ensemble (Fielding still skipping backwards) crossed the road to the car park. Nicos went to Fielding's car, pulled out the little bag with which he had been travelling, walked over to the Land-Rover and got in. The man with the nose climbed into the driving seat.

"Nicos," said Fielding, clutching the door of the Land-

Rover, "say something nice before you go. Say good-bye to me."

He looked into Nicos' eyes for some trace of pity or regret, however trivial, pleading with his own eye for some token of farewell. But the boy's face was without expression: without love or hate or friendliness or disgust, even without recognition.

"Nicos," Fielding said, "do you remember the Charioteer? Surely you meant what you said then? The way you said it—"

"—I was being paid to keep you with me. That is all."

The engine started. The land-rover backed suddenly, nearly throwing Fielding to the ground, and then roared out of the car park and away down the road.


In the Sterns' house in Chelsea, Isobel was toasting herself some Bath buns for tea. She had always had a healthy appetite, and these days she was positively voracious. As she stood over the grill, relishing the smell of the toasting buns and longing for them to be finished, she suddenly saw, as at a great distance, a flash of blue sea and felt a huge spasm of pain and misery pass through her entire body. It was as though she were being emptied of all capacity for joy or feeling, and emptied physically, eviscerated, at the same time. A sickly smell rose off the buns, then the acrid smoke of burning farina; but this went unnoticed by Isobel, who stood and moaned with her hands clasped to her belly while the cruel blood ran down her quivering legs.

# 9
## SWEET ARGOS

SOMERSET LLOYD-JAMES and Lord Canteloupe had dinner at the Connaught Hotel to celebrate. They had avocado pears stuffed with smoked and spiced cod's roe, a soufflé of turbot and lobster sauce, chicken cooked with *pâté de foie gras*, and a magnum of champagne to wash it all down; then they had stewed prunes, because these were good for their bowels, and shared a bottle of Taylor '27.

"So all's well that ends well," Canteloupe said. "No Llewyllyn, no programme; no programme, no trouble."

"Not for a while, no," Somerset said: "for a while the official version of the Cyprus business – rational concessions made in response to legitimate democratic pressures – will remain unchallenged. The Department of Public Relations and Popular Media has emerged unscathed, and you can now relax. Until the next time."

"The next time?"

"There's always a next time in this game. All celebrations must be provisional, even those at the Connaught Hotel. What's more, the next time may very well come tomorrow."

"Not Cyprus again?"

"No. I think you've heard the last of Cyprus for the next year or so. But there'll be plenty of other awkward affairs which will need explaining away. After all, Canteloupe, your job is to make the truth comfortable enough for the mass of the people to live with – to make the truth *acceptable*. It won't be long, with things as they are these days, before another unacceptable truth is dumped on your desk for treatment. And you won't be able to evade the issue as easily as we've managed to this time. It was sheer luck that Tom made a fool of himself like that, and even luckier that the Director was a jealous prig who was keen to make the most of it."

"I must say, I'm surprised he persuaded the high-ups to be quite so fierce with Llewyllyn."

"I don't know," said Somerset. "You see, Tom had committed the most serious error of all – he'd flouted a minor convention. He was too innocent to realise that that's the one thing people won't forgive. They'll forgive a murderer, but they'll never forgive a man who refuses to wear a black tie for dinner. Tom's silly little lie made a mockery of the system."

"Something in that," said Canteloupe. "Tell me, what'll happen to that chap Fielding Gray?"

"He's in luck. Since it's no fault of his that the programme's being dropped, he can just come home and claim the rest of his fee as promised. And talking of him reminds me: what arrangements are you making about Maisie?"

"Why does Gray remind you of Maisie?"

"Another old client."

"That's just the trouble," said Canteloupe crossly, "—all these old clients. Maisie say she's going to stay put in Curzon Street because she doesn't want to let her regulars down. Can you beat it? I've offered her comfortable quarters in Hampstead and a very handsome income, but she says that Hampstead wouldn't suit her because she can't stand the sight of all those pinkos in open-toed sandals."

"So you've offered her *otium cum dignitate*," said Somerset, "but Maisie prefers Curzon Street. A true professional. It does my heart good to hear about it."

"If you ask me, she just likes being on the game. Some of them do, you know."

"Then here's to Maisie," said Somerset Lloyd-James, MP, raising his Taylor '27, "to dear, plump Maisie, the girl with the crutch of gold."

"In bumpers," said the Marquis Canteloupe.

Both men drained their glasses and threw them over their shoulders, somewhat to the consternation of the Americans at nearby tables.

Fielding too was thinking about Maisie. As he lay on his bed in the hotel in which he had taken refuge in Argos, he thought about the warning which Maisie had given him and cursed himself for a fool. 'Don't let them know what's in here,' Maisie had said, running her finger round his chest. But he hadn't heeded Maisie, plump, fond Maisie, he'd ripped his heart right out for them all to get a good look. To get a good look and then spit on it. And then grind their heels in the spit.

And yet, he thought as he poured more brandy, would I have missed it if I could? For although it had all been false from start to finish, it had seemed true at the time. The illusion which Nicos had created had been very lovely while it lasted; and the fact that the illusion had been so cruelly destroyed could not spoil the happiness which it had brought him first. A man might catch a pox, he thought, but the ecstasy he had known while getting it could never be taken away. He, Fielding, had loved a mask, he had loved a dummy with human skin; nevertheless, he had loved.

And another thing, he thought in his misery; there had been appropriate revenge. Years ago he had betrayed Christopher; now Christopher had risen up from the dead and betrayed him. And again: he had used Christopher to make a tale, he had exploited him, in *Love's Jest Book,* to get money and a little fame; and now Christopher had come back as Nicos to exploit him in return – to exploit his love and turn it into money, to use his anguish to make a career. Fair's fair, he told himself : paid out in your own dud coin.

How long have I been lying here? he wondered. I came here yesterday and now it is evening again. I stink. I must get up and wash, go out and eat. Where does one eat in this scabby little town? This hotel? Class Gamma, the first I saw as I drove in yesterday evening, a den to hide in with brandy bottles, which aren't empty yet. Class Gamma : no food in this hotel, no hot water. Why bother? Lie here, blubbering and drinking and stinking, and let the night come down. I'm ugly; I stink; I'm getting old and rotten. Lie here, wallowing in stink and self-pity. Lie here and rot and let the night come down.

"So it looks," said Max de Freville in the Dome Hotel in Kyrenia, "as if something very handsome may come of it. Provided the island stays peaceful and the tourists come back."

"So what now?" Angela said.

"We stay here a few days longer, to approve the provisional plans for the Casino's equipment and decoration, and to tidy up the financial arrangements. Then we go to Athens to talk with Lykiadopoulos – he'll have to come in as the front name."

"Why? You seem to have got on very well so far by yourself."

"They're waiting for me to set it all up and pay for it," said Max. "Then, when it's a going concern, they'll grab it. The whole lot, down to the last spare roulette ball. But not if it's owned by a Greek. So we go to Athens and talk to old Lyki and bring him in as front name."

"Aren't you taking rather a cynical view?" said Mrs Ongley.

Harriet Ongley was of Franco-Russian stock, of English

birth, of American nationality (by marriage), and of substantial means (by widowhood). She was an old friend of Max's, having sometimes played, with her late husband, at his chemin-de-fer table in London, and she had run into him quite by chance in Nicosia three days before. She was now spending a few days with Max and Angela in Kyrenia before continuing her tour of the Near East. She had a sweet, round, placid face (young for her forty-two years), shapely and carefully shaven legs, a robust appetite for food, and an invincible belief in human goodness which she somehow contrived to reconcile with a keen intelligence.

"Why should they grab your Casino?" Harriet Ongley went on. "You're always saying how fond they still are of the British."

"But even fonder of money. So in a few days we go to Athens to see Lyki. And I think, Harriet, that you had better come too."

"But I'm scheduled to fly to Beirut, and I have no business with this Lyki."

"I have good works for you to do, Harriet. I have something right up your street. This morning I heard from an old correspondent of mine – Leonard Percival," he said aside to Angela, "—who tells me that somewhere near Athens Humpty Dumpty has fallen off his wall and shattered his delicate shell. All the king's horses and all the king's men are of little avail in such cases, but a good, patient woman, Harriet, with loving fingers, might just be able to fit the pieces together. At least she could sweep them up."

"No more broken egg-shells for me, Max. I've had my share of them." (Mr Ongley had died of martinis.) "Why should I bother with this one?"

"A work of corporal charity. You are a Roman Catholic, I think? I should be very grateful," said Max, "and very interested to hear how you get on. The case, you see, has a certain fascination."

And then, carefully playing on Harriet's known reverence for the creative arts and those who practised them, Max began to explain.

The morning after Captain Detterling heard about Isobel Stern's miscarriage he went to Gregory's office.

"I'm very sorry about Isobel," he said.

Gregory looked up coolly from his desk and fingered his waistcoat buttons.

"It was rather gratuitous," he replied. "I'm glad you're here. There are some things to discuss."

A secretary came in and put a bundle of files on his desk. Gregory started to flip briskly through them.

"During the last few weeks," he said, "I've signed some very foolish contracts."

"The New Jewish Library?"

"Yes. Fortunately it's early days yet, and we can get out of most of them in return for small down payments. This one, for example." He brandished a file. "The book on the crucifixion. You were quite right, of course. The thesis is unsound and in any case it has already been stated. And this – the commentary on the Talmud. The printing alone would have cost us a fortune."

"Why the sudden change of plan?"

"I've come to my senses, that's why. I've been in a state of infatuation which has now been dispelled. Next time Isobel conceives I hope I shall know better. After all, parenthood is a very commonplace affair."

"Well, don't go too far the other way," Detterling said. "Some of those books you commissioned are very promising. That Rabbi who's going to assess the strength of orthodox belief in Israel – that's a book we should certainly do."

"Granted. And one or two more. But for the most part – fwwhutt." He thumped his fist on the stacked files. "Now then. Tom, I hear, has left the BBC, and that also means an

end of Fielding's absurdities in Greece. I want a novel out of
Fielding in time for publication next spring, and a hefty
piece of polemics from Tom for the following autumn."

"Not much time, Gregory."

"I know. I want them both to be firmly reminded that
work is work – and is not to be confused with silly games in
Television Studios and Continental Expresses. So I'm going
to insist on an absolute deadline in both cases – but I'm also
going to offer them a twenty-five per cent increase on their
usual advances. Tom I am going to ring up this minute.
Where can I get hold of Fielding?"

Detterling shrugged.

"I suppose he'll come back from Greece in his own good
time."

"I want him back in my good time. That's the kind of
thing you're good at fixing. Please see that he gets a
message – wherever he is – telling him to be in this office one
week from today with a two-page synopsis, in type or fair
round hand, of an eighty-thousand-word novel."


Fielding's life in Argos had now settled into a routine. He
would get up at about eleven o'clock, hands shaking and
head buzzing, breakfast off Turkish coffee and some bread
and jam if he could face it, and then drive unsteadily to the
palace at Mycenae. There he would sit on the ramparts and
look towards the sea, thinking all the time of the days he had
spent with Nicos. Later on, when the hour came at which
Nicos had been taken, he would go over the scene minutely
and in every last detail, acting it out word by word and step
by step from the ramparts to the car park. As he did this he
would search desperately, in Nicos' remembered face, for
some sign that the parting was against the boy's will, for
some tiny sign that could mean sorrow or fondness; and
then, having failed to find such a sign, he would look south
again from the ramparts and sit there till evening.

When the dusk came, he would drive back to Argos, eat some kind of meal in a restaurant, buy a bottle of cheap Greek brandy, and go back to his room in the hotel, where he would lie on his bed and drink the brandy until he fell asleep, which he often did with his clothes on. Next morning he would wake quite early but would toss and groan on the bed until the heat in his little room grew unendurable. Then he would plunge his head in cold water, comb his greasy hair, and stumble downstairs to start his day once more.

'My dear Llewyllyn' (Constable had written to Tom) 'I'm sorry to hear that your series, and with it the Cyprus programme, must be abandoned. It would have been interesting to see what came of Fielding Gray's interview with Grivas.'

Well at least, Tom thought, I am spared having to tell him what went wrong with that.

'But the real point of this letter,' Constable went on, 'is to tell you, unofficially, that it has been decided to offer you a Namier Fellowship at this College. Invitation will be made to you in official form in a few days. I need not say how much I hope you will accept. I might also add that I think a period spent in academic surroundings will provide just the kind of discipline needed to complement the facile distinction of your talents and to enable you to treat worthily of power and correlated subjects, which clearly fascinate you as much as they do me.'

"What's a Namier Fellowship?" asked Patricia, when Tom had finished reading out the letter.

"A three-year appointment during which I should have to undertake some serious line in historical research. I should get a Fellow's stipend and all the rest of it, but I should not be expected to teach or administer. Only to get on with my own work."

"But what will Gregory say? He wants you to have something ready for him to publish next year."

"Gregory will have to wait. What I can now propose to him instead is a scholarly dissertation to which I shall have devoted three years' loving and detailed work in the peace and quiet of the fens. Up till now, I've been little more than a political journalist. A typical London opportunist. Now I've got a chance to do something of lasting importance . . . with the full recognition and backing of the most famous college in the world."

"You're going to accept this Fellowship, Tom?"

"Of course."

"But will Gregory want to publish a . . . scholarly dissertation?"

"I want to write one."

"But Tom . . . the money? With all those fines you've got to pay."

"We shall be much poorer, certainly. But it'll be cheaper, living in Cambridge. And at last I shall have proper work."

"But it'll mean . . . burying yourself . . . down there. You'll be forgotten in no time."

"You don't quite understand, Patricia. Robert Constable is giving me an opportunity – I'm pretty sure he's behind it all – to write about the anarchy which permeates historical processes and the deductions which follow as to the nature of power. Constable does not agree with, in fact he strongly disapproves of, the line which I am going to take. Nevertheless he's giving me a chance to state my case because he thinks that it should be stated. It's a magnanimous offer and a magnificent challenge. I wouldn't refuse it for anything."

"Tom," said Patricia stubbornly, "I think I'm pregnant."

"Are you indeed? Well, you can be pregnant just as well down in Cambridge as you can up here."

"Tom . . ."

She came towards him, smiling her invitation.

"Oh yes," said Tom, not unkindly, "we can do as much

of that as you want. But we're still going to Cambridge, and there's an end of it."

Harriet Ongley paused in Athens for just long enough to enquire at the Grande Bretagne Hotel whether there had been any further sign of Fielding Gray. She was told that there had not, but that someone had telephoned for him from London and left a message. This message, which was the one Detterling had been trying to pass on as requested by Gregory Stern, Mrs Ongley read and put into her handbag. She then set out, as instructed by Max, for the Isthmus and the Argolid.

She drove a hired car and sang to herself as she drove, arias from Verdi and passages of counterpoint from Bach. She was very happy because she was going to meet a new and "creative" person, someone, above all, who wanted her help; for while it was true, as she had told Max, that her husband's deathbed had temporarily drained her of charitable impulse, she was a woman who needed to be needed and she had secretly dreaded the prospect of touring the Near East with no one to mind but herself.

Seeing no necessity to go hungry, she stopped for a substantial lunch at the Xenia in Old Corinth. Then she drove on down the road towards Argos, trying to remember a line which she had read in a paperback translation of Virgil. Yes ... that was it: "and dying he remembers his sweet Argos." What a lovely line, she thought, blinking her eyes as she drove.

After a time, she turned left to Mycenae, drove through the village and on up the hill to the palace; and as she got out of her car in the car park, she saw the most extraordinary sight.

A young man was capering backwards down the path from the Lion Gate. He was waving his arms and seemed to be pleading with somebody, though there was nobody with

whom to plead. He came skipping on down (still backwards), past the little booth where tickets were sold, over the
road and into the car park. Then, at last, he turned, and
looked in despair at the only car in the park other than her
own. It was as if he were watching someone go to the car,
do something and leave it again; and then as though that
someone were coming towards herself, for the young man's
gaze followed an invisible person across the car park and
gradually rose until it met her own. She saw that he had
only one proper eye, from which tears were streaming down
over a filthy and distorted face.

But now the young man was moving. He staggered across
the car park until he came to her own car, through the front
window of which he started to look so intently that for a
moment Harriet too thought that there must be somebody
within.

"Nicos," the young man said, "do you remember the
Charioteer? Surely you meant what you said then?"

Whatever answer the young man received, it was
evidently final and unbearable; for he leapt back from
Harriet's car as if he had been shot, and then sank on to the
ground, where his whole body heaved and throbbed in a
grotesque orgasm of grief. Harriet took a deep breath, then
went to stand over him.

"I have a message from your publisher," she said as
firmly as she could, "which I found in the Grande Bretagne
Hotel. You are to present yourself in London with a synopsis
for a new novel in four days from now."

"Christopher, oh Christopher," whimpered the young man
on the ground.

"You're hysterical," said Harriet. "You need a bath and
some fresh clothes and a meal. We will go in my car to
Nauplion, where we will stay in a dear little hotel on that
island in the harbour. There you will write a synopsis for
your novel, and we will then fly back to London and show it
to Mr Stern."

"Who are you?"

"My name is Harriet Ongley, and I have come to take care of you." She stooped down and put her face near his. "Please let me take care of you. Don't send me away."

She started to stroke the greasy, matted hair and took out a handkerchief to dry the wet, pink cheeks.

"There, there. Time to stop crying. Time to come home and start all over again."

She moved her face even closer, ignoring the foul breath which came from him, and kissed him on his twisted lips.

# PLACES WHERE
# THEY SING

# Contents

*PART ONE*

# SCHOLARS' MEADOW

"THAT'S IT," thought Ivor Winstanley: "the *coup de grâce*."

Away on his right a spiteful little bell tinkled in confirmation.

"Winning gallery," squealed the professional's boy from the net-post: "game, set and match to Doctor Helmut."

Ivor waddled into the corridor which ran along the tennis court while Jacquiz Helmut stalked patronisingly behind him.

"Your game's holding up very well, Ivor," he said, "but you must remember to keep the ball away from your opponent's forehand when you're on the hazard side."

Opponent's foreskin, thought Ivor crossly; how maddening these Jews could be, even the well-bred ones. Suppressing the temptation to remark that he had been playing tennis when Jacquiz was still in his kosher knickers (what a sight he must have looked, legs like the stalks of hock glasses), and remembering the universal tolerance which the modern age and his own calling required of him, he merely said, rather sadly:

"This will be our last game, I suppose, until the autumn."

"I've never understood why they close the court for the summer term."

"They don't close it," Ivor said; "it's just not done to play royal tennis during the summer."

Jacquiz wound a scarf of many colours round his neck, then draped himself in a still more improbable blazer.

"Why not?" said Jacquiz, almost whining. "The pro stays here, and so does that boy of his, both of them drawing good money."

"Nevertheless," said Ivor, slipping on his battered sports

203

jacket, "the custom is quite clear: no tennis from the first day of the full summer term till the last of the long vacation."

"Why have a custom so wasteful and restrictive?"

"You're a historian," Ivor said, "and you understand this kind of thing as well as anybody. Now, the essential point is that the custom does not apply to the university strings who are to represent us against Oxford at Lord's during July. So plainly the original idea was to keep our only court clear so that the top strings could practice whenever they wanted to; but rather than have a rule, which people would have disliked, they started a custom, which everyone, this place being what it is, was delighted to accept."

By now they had left the University Library behind them and were passing through the new court of Clare—two white-flannelled figures, one a foot taller than the other, grotesquely in step; for Ivor Winstanley had an accommodating nature, was, moreover, very sensitive about seemliness, and he would have found something scandalous in walking out of step with his companion.

"When?" snapped Jacquiz. "When did they start this custom?"

"I don't know," sighed Ivor. "It was certainly observed when I came up in the late 'twenties."

"And you did nothing to stop it?"

"I never was the interfering kind."

"Well, it's high time somebody did," said Jacquiz. "I myself am not exactly radical, as you know, but I resent being deprived of my tennis."

"All right, then: do something."

"All right. I shall."

Ivor and Jacquiz had had this same conversation, almost word for word, every April since they started playing real tennis together, which was now a long time ago. The truth was, however, that tennis was only one of Jacquiz' minor pleasures, and he had no intention of doing anything at all. Although they both knew this perfectly well, they would not have dreamt of omitting this discussion, which had become for them as significant a feature of the natural calender as the return of the cuckoo. Summer was icumen in, and this was their rite of welcome.

"I remember," said Ivor happily, "the first time you said that. It was in April 1953 – a few days after you'd been elected to your fellowship and a few weeks before the coronation. You had some lunatic idea that the best way of beginning a new reign was to scrap a lot of old customs. But it is now 1967, and tomorrow is the first day of full summer term, and the tennis court will then be closed, as it always has been, to all but the university strings, and you would sooner fly off the roof of the chapel than do anything whatever about it."

They both nodded with profound satisfaction, and turned to look at the gate of Clare New Court, which they had just left.

SUI MEMORES, the inscription read, ALIOS FECERE MERENDO.

"'Made other men remember them,'" translated Ivor, "'by their deserving.' Worrying, you know. As a classical man, I am very unhappy about the use of *alios* in this context."

"Why?"

"The plural of *alios* is normally used in pairs . . . some did this, others did that. *Alios* by itself is very dubious usage. However, the only alternative reading is *aliquos,* and if we adopt it the passage would mean, 'Made *some* men – i.e. some *only* – remember them by their deserving.'"

"I can't see much wrong with that."

"Cynical."

"Since when," said Jacquiz as they crossed the Queen's Road and turned right under the trees, "has cynicism bothered you?"

"It has no place on a memorial gate like that one."

"But that's the whole point. The memorial gate says *'alios'*, which isn't cynical."

"But *is* doubtful Latin. Doubtful Latin has even less place on memorial gates than cynicism."

"So what do you conclude?"

"That they should have chosen another quotation."

"*'Dulce et decorum est pro patria mori'?*"

"No. Untruthful. Perhaps, '*Aspicit et moriens dulces reminiscitur Argos.*' 'He looks up to heaven and dying he remembers his sweet Argos.' "

"Applicable?"

"Perhaps some of them remembered their college as they died. I think . . . I think perhaps I might have done. But if you want my choice of a suitable quotation, it comes in plain English : 'Dead is dead' . . . A turn in the Fellows' Garden before tea?"

"With pleasure."

They recrossed the road and went up to a tracery gate; Ivor felt in his pocket and produced a key; Jacquiz smiled and opened the gate without one.

"Since when," Ivor asked, "has that gate been kept unlocked?"

"Since the College Council met in March. You were away in Greece. The Council, after strong urging by Provost Constable and others, decided to grant the undergraduates' request that they be allowed free access to the Fellows' Garden at all times."

"Oh," said Ivor, as if suddenly winded. "I hadn't heard." He waddled slowly over the lawn, past the Judas Tree and towards the summer house. "What others?" he asked at length : "what others beside the Provost?"

"Tony Beck – very vociferous *he* was. If, he said, we clung to out-dated privileges, then something called 'the new awareness' would ensure they were forcibly taken from us. Daniel Mond and Tom Llewyllyn said much the same."

"Oh . . . oh," puffed Ivor painfully. "So now . . . the Fellows' Garden of *Lancaster* College . . . is open to anyone who wants to walk in?"

Jacquiz shrugged.

"Does it matter?" he said. "They ruined the garden anyway when they built the new hostel right on top of it."

Both men turned their faces to a prominent red-brick building which stood where there had once been a grove of lady-birch and now glowered over the rest of the garden as if threatening to advance and occupy it all in the name of utility and progress.

"The garden was a lost cause already," Jacquiz said as he glowered back at the hostel; "but it is important we should not lose any more. So I hope you will make a point of being at the Council tomorrow? I'm whipping all our people in."

"What's up tomorrow?"

"The College is up . . . by a very large sum of money from the sale of those farms in Lincolnshire. The question is: how is it to be spent? There are people who would like to see more of *those*" – he gestured, almost obscenely, at the new hostel.

"Where? Here?"

"Worse. In Scholars' Meadow."

"But they can't do that," wailed Ivor. "Scholars' Meadow is set aside by the statutes . . . *qua currant et ludant pupillares* . . . for the exercise and sports of the students."

"They haven't exercised or sported there for over a century. Not since the new playing fields were purchased."

"Even so, the statute still protects it. Anyhow," Ivor went on sullenly, "it looks very nice as it is, and to build on it would wreck the view of Sitwell's from the backs."

"Reformers," said Jacquiz, "disdain aesthetic considerations. And radical reformers, which is what we're dealing with, hold even statutes in contempt."

"That's not to say they can break them."

"There are ways of getting round them, Ivor. Bequests, trusts, statutes – you can subvert the lot these days. All you need do is claim that it's in the best educational interest of the college to do so, and no one will dare breathe a word."

"And why should it be in the best educational interest of the college to build over Scholars' Meadow?"

"Because it would mean we could take more students."

"And who in his right mind wants to do that?"

"For God's sake, Ivor. You must know *something* of what's been going on in the last ten years."

"Yes. I heard we were to have sensible changes. Sensible changes, gradually introduced here and there, to make things better and fairer. Fewer tied scholarships, that kind of thing – and quite all right by me. What I did not hear was that we were going to ruin one of the finest views in Europe simply to increase our numbers."

"But that's just what it's all about, Ivor. Increased numbers equals democracy in action equals absolute good. Fine views equals privilege equals absolute bad. We have a large area called Scholars' Meadow, which looks nice but serves no purpose. Its beauty provokes as much resentment as its uselessness, and certain people will not rest until it is covered from the Queen's Road to the river with square, grey blocks of cheap and nasty bed-sitting-rooms—"

"—Full of cheap and nasty students, all reading sociology. Don't tell me. Well, it's got to be stopped." Ivor Winstanley breathed heavily through his nose, while little flecks of foam appeared at the corners of his mouth. "A hostel in the Fellows' Garden is one thing; a tactful concession to the times, you might say. But to build on Scholars' Meadow – an act of vandalism on that scale means the end of everything."

"So you'll be there tomorrow?" said Jacquiz.

"With sword and buckler. We've got a majority. Even now, we've got a majority on the Council, and if all good men and true turn out, we have nothing to fear."

"Except," said Jacquiz, "that it's no longer up to the Council. Or not entirely."

"You mean the Government may make trouble?"

"Perhaps. But we can deal with them, because they talk the same language as we do and acknowledge much the same rules. I'm afraid, though, that there are far more sinister opponents than Governments – even Socialist ones."

"I find you very puzzling, Jacquiz."

Ivor wiped his mouth with the sleeve of his coat and led the way, rather quickly for him, back towards the gate. Indignation had made him hungry for his tea.

"There is," said Jacquiz, "a new element in these affairs.

An element undreamed of in your philosophy or in mine. Until now."

Ivor produced his key, as of long habit, to unlock and relock the gate.

"No," said Jacquiz, twitching his cardinal's nose, "no key. The undergraduates wouldn't like it – remember?"

"Most of them aren't up yet," said Ivor, huffy and illogical.

"But tomorrow is the first day of full term," said Jacquiz: "they'll all be up tomorrow."

Among those who were up already was an undergraduate called Hugh Balliston, who inhabited a room in the hostel by the Fellows' Garden. Hugh's room looked over the Garden, so that he would certainly have seen Ivor Winstanley and Jacquiz Helmut, had he been anywhere near his window. But as it happened he was lying face downward on his bed with Hetta Frith underneath him.

"Castro," cried Hetta, "you can't half do it. Castro, Lenin, Engels. Mao . . . *Christ.*"

"Christ?"

"Sorry – *Marx* . . ."

"Soon?"

"*Soon.*"

She snorted like a Derby winner and took in a great suck of breath.

"Mao," she whimpered; "Mar*cuse*," she moaned with a mighty shudder; "Fidel, oh Fidel," she yelped, and at last subsided quivering with, "Che . . . Che . . . Cheeee . . ."

Hugh, who had come to climax at the same time but had characteristically kept quiet about it, eased himself off Hetta and off the bed and marched to the wash basin. Hetta watched him with pleasure: the thin, sinewy legs; the pale, narrow back, with the three large pimples on the left shoulder blade; the upper arms of alabaster, the fore-arms sprinkled with short, black hairs, disappearing round his body to do their hygienic work. Castro, but Hugh could do it! And now perhaps he would come back to the bed, talk to her for a while of what he had done during the vacation and what he proposed for the coming term, and then, with a little luck (Marx, Castro, *Che*) start doing it all over again.

But Hugh had other plans.

"Get dressed, duckie," he said. "You've got to go."

"Oh Hugh . . . What about tea?"

"What about it?"

"Wouldn't you like some?"

Hugh turned to face her. He had a thin line of hair which ran down the very centre of his chest, the last place, Hetta reflected, where most people had any. Below his navel the stomach was flat and silky, inviting Hetta's kisses. She leapt off the bed, fell on her knees, threw her arms round his hams, and nuzzled her cheek against the soft skin. Firmly but kindly Hugh disengaged her, then took a hand towel and started to dry himself with minute and particular care.

"I've got some work to do," he said.

"But just a quick cup. After all, it is tea-time."

"No, it isn't," he said: "tea-time's at half past six. You mustn't keep reverting, Hetta. I know it's hard for you with Daddy a parson in Godalming and all the rest of it, but once you come over there's no going back to the rectory style – not even for the odd cup of tea."

His voice was low, unaggressive and confident, easy yet precise; a gentleman's voice, one might have said, had it not been for a very slight grating of the 'a's. This one did not exactly hear; one just realised, some moments later, that it was present. Hugh's voice was like certain kinds of white burgundy, which are agreeable to swallow but leave an undertaste of phlegm on the palate. Or, as Hetta had sometimes told herself, it was like the de-odorant spray which Mother used for the kitchen: from being fresh and light, it turned, within seconds, to a smell of warm metal. Sniffing this smell now (so to speak) and being disappointed of her tea, Hetta was provoked to mild counter-revolution.

"The sort of people who have tea at half past six," she said, "would not approve of sex in the afternoon."

"I know. We're going to change all that. We're going to educate them to understand that there's nothing wrong with sex in the afternoon."

"Then they'll realise there's nothing wrong with tea at four o'clock either."

Hugh laughed and nodded, conceding her point. Overwhelmed by this generosity, Hetta at once felt ashamed of having been "mardy" and skipped into her knickers.

"I don't want to be in the way," she said, really meaning it.

"There's a good girl. I wouldn't do this to you, but I've got to get ready for a tutorial this evening."

"A tutorial? But it isn't proper term yet."

"Tony Beck wants to go over something with me. Something special."

"That's because you're his special pupil. What with your First last summer, and that University Prize in the autumn . . . The Members' English Essay Prize," she proclaimed proudly. "Awarded to the undergraduate with the largest member," she giggled, and tweaked it fondly.

"We've had that joke before," Hugh said stuffily, considering his academic success to be somehow tainted by such ribaldry. "Now for God's sake take your hands off before I get another horn on."

He put on a striped flannel shirt (collarless) and a pair of denim trousers, and went to his desk by the window.

"What is it you're doing for Mr Beck?"

"Just a short essay. I've got to make a fair copy before I see him."

"All right. I'm going. What about tonight?"

"No good," he said without turning. "I've got a meeting. The old men are up to something."

"Oh?"

"They've got their hands on some money, and we aim to see they spend it properly. Although Lancaster's a filthy rich college, it's too much to hope they'll send it somewhere else where it's needed. And we can't make 'em – not yet. But at least we can try to see they do something decent for the college itself."

"Like what?"

"Like we're going to discuss tonight."

"How interesting. Can't I come to the meeting?"

"Sorry, love. Private. Get going, will you?"

"I'm at the door. Wave to me, Hugh."

Briefly, Hugh turned his bright simian face, already crinkled with concentration, towards the door. He put his hand through his black hair (thick, curly hair, but tidily trimmed at the nape) and then waggled four long fingers at Hetta. Hetta waggled four rather stubby fingers back, hitched her jeans over her lovely round bottom and on to her ample hips, and flicked a long blonde wisp away from her mouth in order to smile at Hugh. It was half a smile of innocence, bold and sweet and trusting; and half a prostitute's leer (want a dirty time in a taxi?). Hugh quivered with tenderness, gurgled slightly and then turned back with a shrug to the papers on his desk.

"Go along, bottykins," he said softly. "Come tomorrow at twelve."

Although Hugh had told Hetta she could always go through the Fellows' Garden if she wanted to, Hetta felt this to be wrong unless she was accompanied by a member of the college. On leaving the hostel, therefore, she walked a hundred yards down the tarmac drive to a side-road, turned left up this and walked a hundred yards to the Queen's Road, then turned left up that and walked yet another hundred yards to the back gate of Lancaster College, which was exactly opposite the gate of the Fellows' Garden. Thus Hetta's residual bourgeois scruples had already made her walk three times further than she need have done; and even now they continued to operate. For although anybody in the world was at liberty to walk through Lancaster College, Hetta felt that one who had a lover in the college should not do so unless escorted by that lover, in case she should seem to be assuming proprietary rights; and she was now seriously considering going all the way round through Trinity, which would have taken her another mile out of her way. In the end, however, common sense prevailed, and she started up Lancaster Walk, under the elm trees and towards the Willow Bridge.

On Hetta's left, as she went, was Scholars' Meadow. What sort of playground it had provided for the scholars, and what games they played there, were now questions beyond any conjecture; for Scholars' Meadow was no longer, to speak properly, a meadow at all. Its most prominent feature was two magnificent copper beeches which grew on the summit of a small, steep mound. The mound itself was at the centre of a rectangle, perhaps two hundred and fifty yards long by a hundred and fifty across, which was covered by thickets of shrub and small, wispy trees, these being diversified by patches of moss, daffodil and pheasant-eye, and interlaced by little paths which wound hither and thither, stopped here, started again there, dashed across one another and whipped back to cut across themselves, with no pretensions either to purpose or convenience. The wonder was that they survived at all, as no one ever walked along them and no one, indeed, was ever seen to enter the "meadow", which (the story went) was tended by an unknown gardener who arrived at dusk and was gone again by dawn.

It had often been suggested to the undergraduates of Lancaster that, since the Meadow was dedicated by statute to their pleasure, they should frequent it more often . . . a suggestion which had been renewed when they started to agitate, the previous winter, for unrestricted use of the Fellows' Garden. But the student committee which was conducting the affair had replied that they were not to be fobbed off with what they didn't want; and when asked why they didn't want it, they had answered that as no one had walked in the Meadow within living memory (since 1856, in fact, when the "new" playing fields had been procured), the place had acquired an air of remoteness and even of hostility which they found uninviting.

This, of course, was a rationalisation : all the committee really wanted was to embarrass and annoy the Fellows by challenging their exclusive right to their own property. Nevertheless, there was something in the claim that Scholars' Meadow was unwelcoming; for, despite its gay flowers and pretty paths, it had an intimation of mortality about it, as though it had been the last retreat (if allowance were made for botanical differences) of a decaying Emperor who was waiting hopelessly until the barbarians should come to sack Byzantium.

Why it should have given this impression was difficult to say. Though it was sometimes described as a "wilderness", the word was used only as a conventional term of landscape gardening, and the area was in no way gone to seed or overgrown; quite the contrary, whatever the truth about the mysterious gardener, it was as trim, in its informal way, as the Fellows' Garden itself. Perhaps this was the explanation : for there is, after all, something rather sinister about a well kept plot of ground which has no visible gardener. However this might be, the general feeling persisted that Scholars' Meadow was mildly numinous in an undefined but disagreeable way, and people just did not care to set foot in it.

And yet, perversely enough, they loved it. They gazed at it in deep silence, from all angles, at every hour of every day. As did Hetta now. How pretty, she said to herself as she looked down a little path which ran through a mass of daffodils, jumped a stream on a tiny bridge, curved round a young green beech, and disappeared between two bramble bushes. How . . . how satisfying, she thought, pausing a moment opposite the central mound; and then, passing along the upper half of the Meadow, "why is it so sad?" One thing that made it sad was the lonely and nameless old horse, who was always grazing in the only piece of real meadow that remained, a narrow strip which lay between the upper end of the "wilderness" and the river bank. And what made it even sadder, she reflected, was the long line of willows (half of them weeping) along the bank itself. These ran all the way from the far top corner of the Meadow to just short of Willow Bridge, where the line ended in a group of four trees which leaned out over and into the water, whether in grief or supplication Hetta could not tell. Melancholy, she told herself, but knew the word was wrong. Hugh could tell me the right one, she thought, he's so clever at English. Doleful? No. Mournful? Not really. Dismal? Definitely not. The word for which Hetta was looking and could not find was perhaps "elegiac"; but it is doubtful whether Hugh Balliston would have told it to her, as it was not a word of which he approved.

The bridge was crowded with people who were staring down at the Meadow, and with others who were jostling for good places against the balustrade. Most of the men turned to look at Hetta, but she kept straight on with what she thought to be a disdainful carriage, not knowing that this sort of carriage only emphasised the twin oscillations of her delicious buttocks. To her left there was now a huge and beautifully mown square of grass; and at the far end of this, facing its entire width, was an elegant eighteenth century building (Sitwell's), in which, she knew, most of the dons and a few rich undergraduates (a very sore point with Hugh) had large and lavish rooms. Straight ahead of her, the gravel path she was on passed through a gap between the south end of Sitwell's and the College Hall (an engaging piece of Gothick pastiche), then led on into the Great Court of Lancaster; while to her immediate right were the steps which mounted to the main entrance of the Provost's Lodge, a late nineteenth century erection with a commonplace yet somehow imposing frontage. Hetta gave this a glance of angry contempt, as it contained the principal and therefore the most villainous of all "the old men", and then walked on quickly, through the gap between Sitwell's and the Hall, and into the Great Court.

It was now her paramount duty to get through the Great Court without taking any notice of the chapel. This was less than a furlong away to her left, forming the north side of the court, and was one of the finest pieces of perpendicular in the kingdom; but she had been warned against it by Hugh during one of the most solemn passages of her "re-education". "We can learn lessons from the past," Hugh had said, "but we must not be distracted or corrupted by it. The great thing you've got to realise about that chapel is that it stands for a system of thought which is false, outmoded and repressive. You must not succumb to its charm." Mindful of this, Hetta marched straight ahead, arms swinging and bosoms bobbing, eyes and nose pointing resolutely to her front. But Hugh or no Hugh, the chapel could not be long ignored, for the good reason that Hetta had to turn left at the top end of the path round the court in order to come at the gate. This meant that she could not avoid seeing the south-east tower and at least two of the southern buttresses . . . unless she looked down at the ground instead, which Mother had taught her was a furtive and slovenly habit. So Hetta turned left and lifted up her reluctant eyes to the chapel, and now as always the sight was too much for her.

"Castro, how fucking marvellous," she said.

Re-education forgotten, she turned towards the statue of the Founder, King Henry VI, who stood over a fountain in the centre of the grass.

"Beate Henrice," she whispered, "ora pro nobis."

Then, having enjoyed this self-indulgence but full of guilt at her betrayal of Hugh, she hacked on to the Market Place, where she caught a bus out to the Institute of Pediatric Training in the outskirts of Cherry Hinton.


Robert Reculver Constable, Provost of Lancaster College, had seen the passing Hetta snarl at his front door. He had been sitting at the desk in his study, had looked up from his work and through the window to refresh his spirit with the sight of the back lawn, and had observed Hetta very clearly, on the gravel path below his casement, as she flicked the fair hair from her mouth and formed her lips into a priggish pout which (Robert Constable surmised) was intended for a scowl of moral disdain. It happened, however, that just as Hetta's disdainful walk was even more sexy than her ordinary one, so her disdainful look was even more fetching than her face in repose. So much so that the Provost was tempted to fling open the window and ask her in for tea. This (he reflected) would be more or less permissible as he had actually met her, in the company of one of his own young men, Hugh Balliston, who had been walking her round the Fellows' Garden a day or two before. Since the Provost knew and liked Hugh, he had stopped him to speak a friendly word and had been, rather grudgingly, introduced to Hetta. Even so, he now reminded himself, asking stray girls in to tea was something which Provosts of Lancaster did not normally do, and something which he, Robert Constable, most certainly did not do. Besides, Hetta's scowl, however fetching, was a scowl nevertheless, and so it was reasonable to assume that she would have refused the invitation.

But *why* had the girl scowled? He supposed that she must have been listening to Balliston, who had said something to make her hostile. But again, why should Balliston do that? Constable had always made a point of being pleasant to the boy, whom he recognised as a very able scholar and a potential credit to the college. True, Balliston was a left-winger and anti-authoritarian of the most insistent kind, as he had made plain by his work on student committees and by several talented articles in undergraduate journals; but then the Provost himself was a Socialist of long and impeccable standing and had bent over backwards, during his reign at Lancaster, to promote reform and relax discipline to the furthest degree consistent with passably good order and the peaceful pursuit of knowledge. Surely that must be enough, even for Hugh Balliston?

But somehow Robert Constable was not quite reassured. There had been signs lately that some people (exactly who he could not have said) wanted yet more change and wanted it very much quicker. And not just change, the need for which Constable understood, but a new kind of change, the precise nature of which no one had explained to him, beyond hinting that the demands about to be made were no longer matters for debate and negotiation in carefully defined terms but were somehow both unrefusable and limitless. Beyfus had said something of the sort a few weeks ago : "It isn't a question of adapting the existing structure any more," Beyfus had said; "one must acknowledge the principle of total fluidity." Whatever that might mean. (Trust Beyfus to be both contentious and obscure.) But if it meant what he thought it meant, Constable did not in the least like it, and he could only hope Hugh Balliston had not been taken in. After all, the great things that had been fought for and achieved since the war could not be allowed to go up in smoke (total fluidity?) just because of some new and extremist fad. Balliston, Balliston of all people, must be of calibre to understand that.

Whichever way you looked at it, however, Hetta's scowl meant trouble from Balliston and those like him. So once again, why? It was only a few weeks since the Council had yielded over the Fellows' Garden : surely there couldn't be another point of dispute already? "Total fluidity," rasped Beyfus' voice in his ear. All right, but even so, and however limitless and unrefusable the demands to be expected, such demands must come in concrete form; one at a time or a hundred at a time, they must be *distinguishable*. So what was it that Balliston and his cronies wanted now? What was it that had caused pretty Hetta to pout so appealingly but with such evidently savage intent? Constable shook his marmoreal head (that of a late Emperor, one might have said, risen from the ranks in Bithynia or some such place, but not without breeding – a small local chieftain's son perhaps?) and passed a large, hard hand through closely cut grey hair. There was, he thought, one concrete and distinguishable issue which, above all others conceivable, would appeal to the disaffected just now : the disposal of one quarter of a million in sterling money.

For the college had sold land to the North-West of the Wash, and sold it for just twice its value as this appeared on the books (which still carried land valuations as last made in 1947). Of the monies realised by the sale, the statutes decreed that one half, i.e. the capital sum which the land had theoretically represented, must be re-invested immediately; but the other half, all £250,000 of it (not subject to Capital Gains Tax), was surplus – it was money to be spent. The cash was presently to hand, and with it trouble for the Provost. For naturally enough, the intended sale had been widely known about. The actual processes had taken so long (well over three years) and had been so hideously boring, that popular interest had lapsed; but there remained certain acute and concerned observers, within the college itself, who had followed the business right through and were well aware that it had at last been finally settled. It was men such as these who were now mustering : determined men, all with plans of their own, plans fully forged and highly polished, which they would thrust at the Provost like so many bristling swords the first moment that the news was officially broken.

Which would be at the College Council the next morning, on the first day of the full summer term in this year of our Lord 1967.

Once more the Provost lifted his wary eyes to seek refreshment from the lawn and from Scholars' Meadow; once again he brought them back to the gravel path below and this time saw no Hetta to enhance the scene. He sniffed fiercely and bent his head to the blank sheet in front of him. Tomorrow he was going to be set about by clever men who would have diverse and cherished schemes for the spending of two hundred and fifty thousand pounds. He was going to be made to listen to appeal, threat, common sense, moral blackmail, political rancour, sweet persuasion and idle dreams. He must be ready for all of them; how, then, did the dispositions lie?

First, he thought, myself. I would merely wish that the money should be invested in equities (which should appreciate considerably between now and the end of 1968) and left to increase until everyone who wishes has had time to present detailed suggestions which can then be calmly considered on their practical as well as other merits. What I do *not* want is that some theoretically plausible plan should be hastily adopted on moral or political principle and that we should thenceforth

be committed to this and this alone. But that is just what the
activists, in their different ways, will try to force us to. Very
well then: who will emerge as the leaders and under what
banners will they lead their men?

"Right wing," he now wrote: "Balbo Blakeney and Jacquiz
Helmut.

"Helmut is opposed to change for snobbish, aesthetic and,
to do him justice, for intellectual reasons. Ideally, he would
like nothing at all to be done with the money for as long as
conceivably possible. He might therefore support me in advo-
cating delay. On the other hand, since he knows the money
must be spent sometime, he may well want it used straight
away (i.e. before the sum can grow by investment and become
an even greater menace) and used, of course, on something
neutral and familiar.

"In any case, it is far more likely that any positive suggestions on the right will originate with *Balbo Blakeney*. He has
the upper-class gift of leadership (in which his foul tongue
helps rather than hinders him) and an undeniable streak of
imagination despite his narrow scientific training. What does
Blakeney want? (Apart from ever increasing quantities of food
and drink.) He can hardly expect us to finance his researches
into the chemistry of the blood, which are already generously
underwritten by his Faculty. Or again, while Blakeney loves
buildings, and not only traditional ones, like Helmut he loathes
the notion of admitting larger numbers of undergraduates. He
could, I suppose, urge the erection of a College Laboratory
for the convenience of our science students – were it not that
his contempt for all students whatever is so pronounced he'd
as soon see them to the devil. He could propose more bath-
rooms and lavatories – were it not that those in his own set
are quite adequate and he wouldn't dream of worrying about
anyone else's. All in all, I'm afraid I must admit that I cannot
begin to foretell what Balbo may put up: I must resign myself
to its being a surprise, almost certainly a disagreeable one."

And what following, thought Constable, laying down his
pen and looking across the lawn to the rose-brick wall at its

far side, would Blakeney command? He would certainly command Helmut; but the important question was whether he could also take with him those who represented more moderate right-wing opinion. The chief of these were three in number : Ivor Winstanley, the Latinst and celebrated Horatian; the Hon. Grantchester FitzMargrave Pough, Senior Fellow, Professor Emeritus of Oriental Geography, and a noted mountaineer in his day; and the Rev. Andrew Ogden, Dean of Chapel. Such was the prestige and amiability of this trio that where they went all men who were right of centre, by however small a margin, would follow. Indeed, if Winstanley, Pough and Ogden were in accord, it was even possible that some of the moderate left might join them. That they would be in accord was like enough, as they frequently were; but would they be behind Blakeney? This must obviously depend on the line Blakeney took, and about this, as the Provost had already told himself, there could be no knowing. The only reasonable surmise was that Blakeney, realising that he depended on the support of Winstanley and the other two to make up his numbers, would temper his propositions to their tastes.

These reflections he now committed to paper with the rest, fully and accurately and without grudging a second of the labour : for it was Provost Constable's one vanity that he wished to leave behind him a record and a justification of his entire career; and he was therefore assembling notes, day by day and blow by blow, for a autobiography of such huge dimensions and such minutely interlocking detail that it would surpass anything that had ever been produced in its kind, even by the most tortuous of Alexandrians or the most prolix of Victorians.

So much for the right, he now thought as he penned his last sentence on the subject : tactics unpredictable and strength as yet undetermined. What about the left.

"The leadership of the left," he wrote after some thought, "will certainly go to Lord Beyfus. A life peer of recent creation, veteran of countless Commissions and Committees, he enjoys such enormous prestige both as a public figure and a social theorist that the left has no other choice. The point to mark, however, is that Beyfus himself will be led, in this as in all else, by Mona Corrington; and the kind of thing Mona will put him up to can be readily guessed at.

"At a recent meeting of the Girton Anthropological Society, to which I was bidden as guest speaker, she deliberately turned the discussion from the formation of élites in primitive societies (the proper business of the evening) to the survival of privileged élites in our own. This unwarranted transition she effected (as usual) by sheer effrontery; she simply remarked that dissolution, being the opposite of formation, was a subject relevant to our brief, and then asked me what was my 'personal thinking, as controller of a residual élitist institution, on available methods of eliminating discrimination and eradicating bourgeois/hierarchical systemisations in order to finalise the comprehensivisation of educational resources and exclude all elements of social or intellectual selectivity.' Uncertain whether it was her impertinence or her abuse of the language that more merited rebuke, I simply replied that entrance to my college was at present determined, as far as might be, by mental competence alone, and that once here men either did their work properly or were promptly dismissed.

"Mona immediately went into more jargon about 'the fascist connotations of subjective standard-maintenance', and then switched, when I was least expecting it, to being brutally concrete. Lancaster College, she said, was rich and getting richer : what were we doing with all that cash? Before I could draw breath, she told me what we should be doing, which was to make the fullest use of our space and resources in order to house 'a much enlarged student-body, drawn from all sections of the community and indeed the entire human race, with complete disregard of outmoded notions of academic attainment'. Mercifully, she was interrupted by the arrival of cocoa and stale biscuits; but she had said enough to show me what kind of nightmare she will try to inflict on us through the agency of her double-ganger Beyfus.

"Although we shan't know the details of Mona's scheme until Beyfus parrots them out at the Council tomorrow, I am pretty certain that young Tony Beck will go along with him. Beck is a shrewd critic of English literature with a keen and muscular style of setting down his opinions; he, if any man living, must realise the importance of academic standards; and yet, although nothing on earth would make him drop his own, he seems to think that the 'new culture' requires their general replacement by something which he calls 'co-operative evaluations'. These, as far as I understand it all, are arrived at in committee or even, ideally, in public assembly. They represent the highest common factors, as it were, in mass appreciation – i.e. the highest level to which all members of the populace, given their own sincere effort and every educational facility, can be expected to attain. Necessarily, this level is very low; but to insist on a higher one is apparently an offence against new social theory, which holds that to transcend the prescribed level of understanding is an aggressive exercise of mental privilege. Apparently it causes 'undesirable tensions', both in those who cannot follow and therefore feel themselves 'deprived', and in those who can and therefore feel themselves 'apart' – which for some reason is considered a hideous fate these days. How Beck reconciles his own undeniable 'apartness' with his advocacy of these modern methods (under which, presumably, everyone would be awarded an identical degree) God alone knows.

"To leave all that aside, however, it is clear to me that any plan of Beyfus's which would sacrifice standards to numbers, and destroy both distinctions and distinction, would have Beck's support, if only because Beck delights, above all, in the discomfiture of established men. But how many others would back Beyfus here? Once again, we come to the all-important moderates. There are, I think, two respected left-wing moderates whose attitudes will substantially influence all other left-wingers. There is also a joker in the pink pack who cannot be dismissed out of hand for reasons I will come to in a moment.

"But first, the two moderates. These, of course, are Daniel Mond and Tom Llewyllyn. Although Daniel is a quiet, introspective character and Tom very much the opposite, they have been great friends since Tom came here in '63 and have one thing very much in common : both of them have seen enough of the world in action to make them sceptical of untried theories for the improvement of any part of it.

"Their respective experiences have been very different in kind. Daniel's were all concentrated into a brief period of time and a small geographical area – i.e. into a summer spent in Göttingen where he went to do research in 1952. God knows exactly what happened to him (though I believe Jacquiz Helmut knows more than most of us), but whatever it was cost him both the power of speech and the power of will to do any further creative work. He remains a very sound man in his own fields of pure mathematics (Finite Series and the Tensor Calculus) but only as a teacher of conventional methods, no longer as the brilliant originator which he promised to be before he left for Göttingen. He went away, I remember, an eager, innocent boy; when he returned he was a little old man, unable to speak above a whisper, his physical health and his intellectual enterprise alike entirely shattered. And yet he is never bitter or morbid; although he has lost half and more of what life meant to him, he is tender in his manners and humorous in his whispered comments, a loyal servant of his college and his faculty, content to pass the rest of his life in the routine work of an obscure academic station. But the important point for my present purpose is that he was once subjected, and that most rigorously, to 'a crash course' in the ways of the world.

"If Daniel has been pitched about by the world, Tom has bustled in it. Prestige journalist, popular historian, BBC producer, he has spent many years amid the smoke (and the vices) of Rome, learning to move at ease with the near-great and to survive among the violent and corrupt. Although he was very glad to come here, and will stay, I think, as long as we let him, he will always keep one foot, or at any rate a big toe, in his old arena. Part of Tom will always be a Grub Street man, however seriously the rest of him is working on the treatise which he is here to write; he has been and still is a frequentor of coffee houses, market places, drawing-rooms and great assemblies, one ear to the arras and one eye to the keyhole; and this is his great value to us here and now. Thank heaven we waived the rule which bars Namier Fellows from college administration and elected him to the Council. For Tom, a socialist by his birth, which was both low and Welsh, has none of that moral smugness and intellectual arrogance which attach to your middle-class socialists by conviction. Any smugness he might have had has long since rubbed off in taverns and posedas, while his training as a working journalist has taught him to despise anyone who claims a monopoly on intellectual truth. What Tom will bring to the Council to-morrow is the much needed reminder that all crops depend on dung and dung comes from the anus.

"So much for Tom and Daniel. There remains the question of the left-wing joker . . . the Rev. Oliver Clewes, the College Chaplain. He is one of these new progressive clerics who hardly seem to believe in God at all and apparently picture Christ as some kind of revolutionary guerilla from South America. As a nominal Christian, Clewes is mistrusted by most of the left, while as a declared socialist he is mistrusted by all of the right. The few people remaining merely despise him as an equivocating opportunist. The one important thing to be said of him, therefore, is that he will discredit whatever cause he may adopt in the eyes of everybody at all, so that one can only hope he will not support a good one."

Not without satisfaction, Robert Constable read through what he had written, gathered the sheets together, then held them up vertically and tapped them gently against his desk until they were absolutely flush. His thoughts were now in order against whatever the morrow might send, and he could ring with good conscience for tea . . . when, that was, he had done just one thing more. With great care, he fastened the sheets together with a stapler (exactly half an inch from the top edge and half an inch from the left-hand edge), then carried them over to some long shelves of files and secured them with an elaborately sprung device in a file marked, 'Lancaster College: Academic Year October '66 to June '67.'

Having replaced this file with a happy sigh, Constable pushed the bell by the door: one long and three shorts, these latter meaning that today he would have three chocolate biscuits instead of his usual two (surely he had deserved them). He then cleared a small table and placed it near his desk to hold the tray; for he would not extend his indulgence to taking his tea in idleness, and he proposed, during this brief collation, to revise the whole of his new paper for the Keynes Society, thus alloying his pleasure but increasing his self-esteem.

Thirty seconds since he rang the bell: where was that damned woman?

And indeed, just as he sat down at the desk, there was a knock on the door.

"On the table just here," Constable said without turning.

"Yes, dear," said Mrs Constable.

"You're sure it's strong enough?"

Constable liked a sergeant-major's brew which would have killed most sergeant-majors.

"Six spoonfuls, dear, and two for the pot."

"Thank you. That's all."

While Elvira Constable fled gratefully through the door, her husband reached for his paper (Moral Justice and the Taxation Structure). But before he read the first paragraph (which would give the tea nice time to settle), he allowed himself one more look over the back lawn. Strolling across this very slowly, on a diagonal from Willow Bridge to the north end of Sitwell's, were Tom Llewyllyn and Daniel Mond. Tom's head was turned to Daniel's ear and his hand rested lightly in the crook of Daniel's right arm. While Tom mouthed fluently, Daniel nodded gently, and then, as Tom paused for breath, brought his free arm across his body and touched Tom's hand where it lay inside his own elbow. Robert Constable felt rather than saw the smile with which Tom responded; and for a moment his head drooped over his desk, as he thought to himself how sweet a thing it must be to walk across a lawn in April arm in arm with a friend.

Tom Llewyllyn and Daniel Mond were talking about an old acquaintance they had in common, a novelist called Fielding Gray. The reason why Daniel had touched Tom's hand was that Tom had become vehement about Gray's irresponsible behaviour some four years before (when Tom, as a BBC producer, had commissioned him to write a programme for television) and Daniel, who deprecated vehemence, wished to calm his friend down. So he brought his hand over to Tom's, and Tom, as Provost Constable had sensed from his window, smiled in response.

"Not that it made any difference," Tom now said. "For a variety of other reasons that programme would never have got on the air in any case. But the fact remains that Fielding simply rode off into the blue with some bloody Greek boy while he was being paid a lot of money to prepare a script for me, and not a word did I hear until weeks later, after he'd been picked up near the palace at Mycenae, crying drunk and stinking like a corpse."

Since there was a threat of further vehemence here, Daniel patted Tom's hand once more and whispered :

"Fielding always had good taste in his choice of settings. Where was the boy?"

"He'd pissed off by then. That's why Fielding was in such a state. Anyway, along came some interfering Yankee widow woman and scraped him off the ground – quite literally, from what I hear – and took him off to Nauplion to be dried out and deloused. After a bit she brought him back to London and got him writing again, and I'm bound to admit that he produced a bloody good novel. *Operation Apocalypse*. It won the Joseph Conrad Prize for 1964."

Daniel screwed up his eyes in his pinched, sallow face.

"I didn't care for it," he muttered.

"Why on earth not? It's the best thing he's done – except possibly for *Love's Jest Book*."

"It's based on . . . some events . . . which happened to us both at the time I knew him. In Germany it was, in 1952. I was there researching, you see, and he was with his regiment. Somehow he's made it all false."

Daniel broke off into a series of quick, painful little croaks. Although their pace was sedate, both halted, and Tom was silent until Daniel had had time to recover what was left of his voice. Then,

"How was he false?" Tom said.

"When it all happened," said Daniel moving slowly forward again, "I was in great fear. I had good reason to be afraid, and Fielding knew this – indeed he was very kind to me for as long as he could be. But in this novel he makes out that I was just being hysterical – that I was a pathetic paranoiac suffering from persecution fantasies. This hurt me very much."

"Perhaps it isn't really you. Perhaps he used what he remembered of your situation but gave it a different slant."

"I was in the most terrible distress. He should not have used such distress for his work unless he was prepared to treat it honourably . . . with compassion."

"Novelists," said Tom, "are cannibals. Worse: they eat you *alive* for their nourishment. It's not surprising if odd things happen while they digest you."

"You take a lenient view, Tom."

"I once wrote a novel myself, Danny. Have you never tackled Fielding with this?"

"I've never seen him since that summer in Germany."

"Then he's changed a lot since you knew him."

They rounded the north end of Sitwell's.

"A quick cup?" said Tom.

"That would be nice."

They went up the staircase nearest the chapel and turned into the front chamber of a set on the first floor. Although the furnishings were mean – three sleazy armchairs, a scruffy desk, an oval table smeared with ink and dry sweat – it was a tall and lordly room.

"Mind you," said Tom, kneeling to light the gas-ring, "I didn't meet Fielding till after he left the Army in 1958. What was he like back in '52?"

"Beautiful. Rather drunk. Thoughtful. Bitter. Accustomed to being obeyed – that was the Army, of course."

"He isn't beautiful any more," Tom said, "and the only person who obeys him is Tessie Buttock."

"Tessie Buttock?"

"She owns a hotel in the Cromwell Road, where he stays when he's in London. But he spends a lot of his time in the country these days, and not very far from here. Broughton Staithe, on the Norfolk coast. He does all his work there – two novels in the last three years, not up to 'Apocalypse' but not bad at that."

"Is that woman – the Yankee widow woman – still with him?"

"Yes," said Tom: "though he's finding her rather stifling. Or so I gather from chums. I haven't heard from him or seen him since the Greek fiasco, which is absurd when we live so close."

"Write and ask him over here. One of you must break the silence. I'd like to see him . . . despite what he did to me in that novel . . . now that he's no longer beautiful. Perhaps," added Daniel wistfully, "that explains it all."

"I'm not sure he'd come. This college was always one of the things he was most bitter about."

"I know. He was kept out of here because of some trouble at his school. That was one of the first things he ever told me. It upset him, he said, because he'd always wanted to be a don."

"I see his point. It's an attractive life."

"You've only had a few years of it," whispered Daniel, "and you've got special work to keep you happy."

For a moment he looked very withered.

"Even when that's finished," Tom said, "I want to stay. If the college will have me."

"They might. Your Namier Research Fellowship was renewed after its three-year term, which is very unusual. They elected you to the Council – which for a Namier Fellow is quite unheard of. They must think highly of you. But why do you want to stay, Tom?"

Tom Llewyllyn looked into the palms of his grubby hands, then rubbed them up over smooth cheeks and on into his abundant and gritty hair.

"It's peaceful," he said; "and as far as it goes, it's genuine. On the whole, the men in this college try to discover the truth in their own line and then to act on it."

"But suppose," croaked Daniel, "their own line is irrelevant to anyone or anything else? It sometimes happens, you know."

"It is still valid in itself. Satisfying, therefore, to the scholar."

"Such truth can be horrible, believe me. The more horrible because you are alone with it."

"But always genuine."

"And totally destructive of this peace you talk of. But as for that," said Daniel, "it's threatened anyway. Even those who are still lucky enough to enjoy this peace of yours will soon find it can't last."

"Why not? Guilt?"

"Nothing as subtle as that. The threat, the danger, is on an everyday level and of the crudest possible kind."

He was interrupted by a series of sharp gasps in his throat.

"There's a lot of trouble coming to us, you know," he said at length.

His manner was casual, as of one who predicts a spell of disagreeable weather during the month of February.

"What makes you think so?" said Tom, uneasy but trying to maintain the same tone.

"The undergraduates. They're getting difficult."

"Undergraduates have always been difficult."

"Not in the same way. They used to be wild or lazy or lecherous or cranky, but they always accepted the framework. Drinking men, hunting men, whoring men – to use the nineteenth century idiom – dissenting men or reforming men, they all knew that if they went too far they would be disciplined or even dismissed, and they accepted this, much as they accepted that the world was round, as a natural condition of existence."

"They still believe the world to be round, I imagine."

"They also believe that its shape can be altered to suit their convenience." Daniel put his cup down on the oval table and fingered the grimy surface with distaste. "There's a theory about it, far too loose and speculative to be strictly applied, but it will give you some idea of what I mean. According to this theory, the present generation of students was the first to be treated, when babies, after the precepts of Doctor Spock. Whenever they so much as whimpered, they were lifted out of their cots and petted and pampered until they stopped. The result is, the theory says, that over the years they have come to believe, to believe absolutely, that they can have anything they want simply by whimpering for it."

Daniel paused to wheeze for twenty seconds.

"Now, so far," he went on hoarsely, "they haven't whimpered for anything very important, just for small concessions here and there, so that we have found it politic to yield. But very soon now they are going to start whining, if not for the moon, then certainly for something far too valuable to be given them. And when they are denied, for the first time since birth, mark you, they are going to scream their little heads off."

"Well," said Tom, who was becoming angry at this prospect and was only controlling himself with an effort, "we mustn't be reactionary. We must find out . . . now . . . what they want and discuss it with them like civilised human beings."

"Do children ever know what they want when you ask them? Even if they do, they want something else two seconds later."

"You really can't go on equating our undergraduates with children and babies."

"*Spock babies*," I said. "It's a metaphorical way of describing an attitude: I WANT THAT TOY *NOW*. And there's an obvious corollary: if a Spock baby is not to be refused, neither is it to be restrained. If a Spock baby wants to defecate," Daniel said, "it defecates there and then. And Spock babies, of course, are often turned loose without nappies."

"So what it comes to in your view," said Tom crossly, "is that either we give the students some belated potty training or else we get ready to pick up the shit."

"Have it thrown at us, more likely." Daniel backed towards the door. "See you in Hall?"

"I'm afraid not. Patricia's expecting me home."

"Tomorrow at the Council then. There's going to be big money talk, I hear."

The white silk scarf, which Daniel always wore round his throat like a bandage, had worked loose during his exegesis and now slipped down slightly to reveal a long, flaring lesion. It was not the first time this had happened; now as ever Tom opened his mouth to ask the question he longed to ask, and now as ever, seeing the hunted look on Daniel's face as he lifted and tightened the silk, he thought better of it.

"Money talk, Danny?" he said lamely.

"Yes," rasped Daniel. "'If there were dreams to sell, what would you buy?' There's plenty of money come in, they tell me, and so there'll be plenty of dreams floating round the Council. To say nothing of all the Spock babies' dreams when the students get to hear of it."

"What are your dreams, Daniel?"

"Approximately those of William Morris," said Daniel, opening the door; "so as far as I am concerned, it is unlikely that the college can command the appropriate currency."


Provost Constable, in accordance with his schedule, finished revising his paper for the Keynes Society at the same moment as he took his last sip of lava-like tea. Having wiped a thick crust of sugar from his lips, he placed his cup on the tray, then crossed the room and placed the tray on the carpet near the door, thus ensuring that Mrs Constable, when summoned, would either (a) hit the tray with the door, or (b) just miss the tray with the door but put one foot right in the middle of it, and (c) and in any case at all, have to bend down to pick it up. Having made this disposition with some care, the Provost rang the bell and returned to his desk, picking up *en route* the latest popular work by Professor Parkinson, which he had been invited to review in the columns of *The New Statesmen*. Normally, he only reviewed academic treatises, but he was presently distressed, being an honest man, by the fact that Parkinson's plausible common-sense contentions had for the most part been simply ignored by the left-wing press instead of being properly refuted. This he considered a shabby evasion, and so, busy as he was, he had accepted the *New Statesman*'s invitation.

The main thesis of Professor Parkinson's book was that a high rate of taxation discouraged personal effort and was incentive only of quick spending on consumable goods, which could not, once consumed, be made subject to a later wealth tax. Since Constable's mind, after revising, "Moral Justice and the Taxation Structure", was very much tuned to such questions, he went to work with a will.

"The late Sir Stafford Cripps," he wrote, "is known to have believed that the British people would tolerate taxation to any amount. Despite the objections of the cynical or merely frivolous . . ."

And so on, about our seemly puritan heritage, for the best part of 300 words. However, just as he was framing the sentence which was to clinch his first paragraph, Mrs Constable, who had heard the bell but had been delayed while adjusting her surgical stocking, knocked on the door.

"Come in," called Constable, looking up from his review while he rehearsed, at lightning speed, the rebuke he would deliver when the door hit the tray.

The door opened cautiously. There was a sound of very heavy breathing but no more. The door closed.

With a sulky pout, Constable resumed his composition. It now occurred to him that two key phrases on the sheet before him had been unconsciously copied straight out of "Moral

Justice and the Taxation Structure". Although the phrases
were apt and the piracy, in the circumstances, venial, Constable scorned to fob off the literary editor of the NS with
second-hand goods. He struck the two phrases from his text,
with difficulty found two more that would serve, realised that
a slight shift of emphasis which resulted would disrupt the
rhythm of all he had written so far, and then, gritting his
teeth, tore the page to honourable shreds and began all over
again.

When Hugh Balliston had finished writing a fair copy of his
work for Tony Beck, he made himself a cup of Bovril (having
time in hand but feeling bound, after his remarks to Hetta, to
eschew tea) and relaxed for ten minutes, during which time he
amused his mind with the imagined sexual antics of Provost
Constable. He even constructed a scene in which the Provost
tried to seduce Hetta; but when the shadowy Hetta refused to
be contained by her allotted role as proud daughter of the
proletariat, and instead flopped on to Constable's lap with
jolly whoops of lust, Hugh desisted from this entertainment
and set out for Tony Beck's rooms in Sitwell's.

As he crossed Willow Bridge, he saw Daniel Mond, who
was returning after his tea with Tom Llewyllyn to his own
rooms in Willow Close. This was a three-sided court, which
occupied the space between the Provost's Lodge and the river,
being open to the latter and facing across it to the west. The
southern wing of the court came right down to the river and
separated Lancaster from its neighbour in that direction; the
northern wing stopped about a cricket pitch short of Willow
Bridge and some few yards to its right (as Hugh was facing),
allowing one to fork right as one stepped off the bridge and
cut across on to the little lawn which was central to the Close.
Set into the river-edge of this lawn was a stone quay for the
mooring of punts, and overlooking the quay was a large weeping willow, which Daniel had now paused to inspect.

Since Hugh had a minute or two to spare and was fond of

Daniel, whom he met often at meetings of the Cabbala (the college essay club), he waved and went across to him.

"Another term tomorrow," whispered Daniel; "the last of another year."

"Oh, Daniel. You make it sound like the last there'll ever be."

"It could be, from my point of view."

"You're surely not leaving?"

"Not that I know of, Hugh."

"Then why so gloomy?"

"Because this way I am prepared for anything at all to go wrong and shall be delighted out of all proportion if even one tiny thing goes right. It's a form of insurance. Like taking a mackintosh with you on a sunny day. A precaution which you seem to have neglected this afternoon."

"So have you."

"My gloom serves instead of one. But *you* have neither gloom nor a mackintosh. That is presumptuous. I shouldn't be at all surprised if you were struck by a thunderbolt."

The words were uttered from so straight a face that Hugh could almost have thought they were meant seriously.

"I'm only going to Sitwell's," he said, "to see Tony Beck. I might just make it that far."

"Let's hope so. And if you *do* arrive safely, give Tony my love and remind him that he has had my copy of the late Professor Hardy's little book for the last eighteen months."

*"A Mathematician's Apology?"*

"Yes. I shall now go indoors to compose my own. It will never be published, but perhaps God will give it his attention."

Daniel raised his hand to his forehead in a quasi-military salute. He moved off towards the south wing of Willow Close and disappeared through the entrance to staircase Omega, in which he had rooms that overlooked the river.

"I met Daniel Mond on the way," said Hugh to Tony Beck in Sitwell's a few minutes later: "he says you've had his copy of G. H. Hardy's 'Apology' for the last eighteen months. He was behaving rather oddly, I thought."

"Hardy was one old woman," said Beck, "and Daniel's another."

Tony Beck was a short, stout man with a very thick neck and an agreeably lop-sided face. Whenever he was displeased, however, he inclined his head to the left side, on which it was smaller, thus causing the right cheek bone, which was normally no more than noticeable, to jut out laterally in a massively aggressive fashion. This was a pity, thought Hugh, observing the phenomenon now, because it destroyed Beck's usual appearance of coarse good humour and substituted one of truculent conceit.

"Well, do you want to read my essay?" said Hugh. "Or shall I read it to you?"

"No. I want to give you my ideas on the subject. On several subjects."

"It took me a lot of work," said Hugh.

Beck leaned over, whipped Hugh's essay away from him, screwed it into a ball, and tossed it through an open door into his bedroom.

"Now," said Tony Beck. He ceased to jut his cheek bone and smiled at Hugh with crude charm. "You are an undergraduate just turned twenty and in your second year of residence. At the end of your first year you took a starred first in Part One of the English Literature Tripos. You are going to take two years reading for Part Two; you therefore have no examination this summer and plenty of time at your disposal. But what do you do with it? Exactly the same as you would have done if you had been taking Part Two in a single year. You read hard, wide and deep; you write your very clever and percipient essays. And that's all."

"What's wrong with it?"

"Limited. Limited and limiting."

"I went in for that prize last autumn. And got it."

"And what did you do to get it? You simply wrote yet another clever and percipient essay."

"I've done a lot of stuff for the Cabbala."

"More essays."

"And for undergraduate magazines."

"*More* essays," snarled Beck. "My point is, you haven't involved yourself in anything active."

There had been a time, and that not so many years before, when this would have meant that Hugh should play more games or take part in dramatic productions. At this time, however, and to these two, it could only mean one thing: politics.

"Oh yes, I have," said Hugh. "I've sat on student committees, drafted memoranda and resolutions, I've even drawn up declarations of right. Who do you suppose was behind the student demand to be allowed to use the Fellows' Garden?"

"That's just it. You were *behind* it. You *drafted* the resolution and you doubtless *composed* the letter of demand. All of it cerebral, Hugh. You've done the whole lot at a desk. It's time you took a turn at the barricades."

"This is England," said Hugh: "we don't have barricades."

For the moment Tony Beck let this pass.

"This essay I asked you to do" – he gestured through the door to the bedroom – " 'The Politics of the Novelist'. Kindly tell me your broad conclusion."

"If you'd had the patience to read it, you'd have found a complete analysis."

"I'm sure I should. I've read a lot of those in my time, Hugh." From Beck's tone, one might have thought he was rising sixty instead of barely thirty. "Here and now I'm interested in your conclusion. Which was . . . ?"

"That a novelist's political beliefs should be implicit in his novels."

"Why not explicit?"

"Because explicit statements in the novelist's own voice," said Hugh firmly, "irritate the reader and, more important, undermine the structure of the novel. Take the early George Eliot—"

"—I'd prefer to leave her just now. You're saying," said Beck in a hectoring voice, "that novelists must eschew open declarations of political allegiance because these vitiate their art?"

"As you know very well for yourself. And as you also know very well, this does not prevent them making whatever political declarations they please in the form of separate tracts or essays."

"Which they produce, just like their novels, sitting on cushioned chairs in cosy studies. But when, Hugh, do they get off their bottoms and *act*?"

"In times of crisis or oppression. Otherwise they should do what they are best at, which is, presumably, writing. Provided society is stable and tolerably fair, a novelist must get on with his work just like anybody else."

"But society is the whole world, Hugh. The world is not stable or tolerably fair. The world is riddled with crisis and oppression. We must *all* get off our bottoms and act."

"Look, Tony," said Hugh. "For the last seven years you've been sitting in this college teaching English literature and doing distinguished work as a critic. Although you have made no secret of your politics, you have not allowed them to affect your judgments as to literary merit; and although you have engaged in polemics up to a point, you have certainly not got off your bottom, as you put it, to act. So why are you preaching at me now?"

"Timing, Hugh. Until just recently, whatever was the case with the world at large, there remained in privileged England enough *national* stability to make any kind of radical action unpopular and futile and therefore thoroughly impractical. So I just got on with my criticism and did it as well as I could in its own terms, in terms, that is, of objective literary judgment. One should always play a game according to its own rules, Hugh, otherwise there is no enjoyment to be had from it; and that's why I kept politics out of my criticism. But it *was* only a game, and the time for it is nearly over. The national, the purely local stability which made it possible for me to play it in peace has been rotted right through to the piles and will soon collapse completely."

During this exordium, Beck had been strutting up and down the room, which was amusingly furnished with Victoriana. He now sat down in a grandfather chair, as on a throne, and threw off the rest of his speech like an edict.

"Even though I've been observing closely," he pronounced, "I'm not at all sure why or how this has happened. I suspect that British energies have been sapped by a mixture of guilt for an imperial past and resentment at imperial decline. But the important point is that it has happened, and nothing can halt the process now, certainly not a flabby Labour Government with half-baked right-wing policies and sentimental left-wing sympathies. From here on, the order of the day, in England as everywhere else, will be crisis and flux : disobedience and mutiny on the part of the so called lower classes; despair and desertion on the part of the upper. In short, Hugh, things are just going to fall apart.

"This being so, there is no longer place and leisure in this country for well-fed men in warm studies to write novels upon which other well-fed men in warm studies will comment. The only relevant occupation must be to go out and burn away the stumps of diseased wood which remain from the old edifice and still clutter the site, and then to build anew in concrete, glass and steel. Destruction and reconstruction. So what part, my good Hugh, do you propose to bear in all this? Reading pretty essays to the Cabbala Club will hardly be enough."

"What part do *you* propose to bear, Tony? The scene is of your setting."

Tony Beck gave Hugh his asymmetrical look of displeasure.

"I'm going to show solidarity," he said, "with the forces of the future."

"Since this apparently necessitates the use of clichés," said Hugh, "let's have another one : you're going to climb on the band-wagon."

"If you like." Beck grinned like a small boy caught playing "doctors" with his sister. "At least I'll be allowed an instrument to blow a tune."

"Not of your own choosing. And suppose you turn out to be wrong? You'll look awfully silly climbing off again."

"Timing, Hugh. Although it's time to warn friends like you

what will happen, it's still not quite time to commit oneself."

"Then why expect me to? All that stuff about manning the
barricades."

"That was overstating it, I grant you. Just have a look round
them, that's all I meant. Get the feel of them. Then pick up
a few cobblestones and take some practice shots through
middle-class windows. You might call it 'protest'."

"Only hooligans break windows . . . for practice or protest."

"I'll tell you what it is with you," sneered Tony Beck;
"you're yellow. You'll use up gallons of ink writing mani-
festoes, you'll gas away all night about progress and social
justice, but when it comes to the crunch, you're yellow."

Hugh flushed.

"I don't care for violence," he said. "Of course I know that
in certain countries it's been necessary as a last resort, and I
honour those that have used it for that reason. But here . . . no.
Here we can still settle things like civilised men."

"That's all done for, Hugh. The rot's gone too far. What
people want is speed and certainty. They want violence; for
violence is the instant detergent which will scour away filth
and wash the world bright again. That is what the masses feel,
Hugh – the masses of deprived people all over the globe. To
pretend otherwise is sheer cowardice; it's hiding your head in
the—"

"—*Must* we go on having these clichés?"

"People like clichés," scowled Beck. "They have a warm,
familiar ring. So if you take my advice, you'll start learning
some yourself. Whose side are you on anyway? Don't tell me
the old men have won you over with a starred First and the
Members' English Essay Prize."

"Why are you baiting me, Tony?"

"I'm just trying to wake you up."

"Then tell me something particular which needs doing. Stop
mouthing about decay and violence and show me some one
thing which needs setting right. And then, if I really have to,
I'll throw cobblestones with you. But not just for practice."

"Very well," said Beck, leaning his head to the left. "As you know, the College Council has sold some land and made a sack of money."

Hugh nodded.

"You told me yesterday," he said, "that there was to be a meeting about that this evening. A preliminary meeting to decide what the students of this college want the money spent on. The only thing which bothers me is that most of the students aren't up yet."

"Precisely," said Beck. "They'll be consulted later. Tonight's meeting is not exactly what you might have expected. The fact is, I want to introduce you to a friend of mine called Mayerston. He's only a year or two older than you, so I thought I'd bring you both together and then leave you to work out what action those of your age-group might take to see that this money is properly used."

"We must first decide on a proper use for it."

"That, as you have suggested, is for the students at large. But there's no reason why you and Mayerston shouldn't . . . discuss general tactics."

"Look," said Hugh: "who the hell is this Mayerston?"

"He's . . . not of this college," said Beck evasively.

"Then what's it got to do with him?"

"This business is of more than parochial interest, Hugh. There's a lot of people who feel very strongly about this money."

"If Mayerston's not from this college," persisted Hugh, "which one is he from?"

"He's from outside the University."

"Then what's he doing here?"

"I suppose a human being has a right to be in Cambridge . . . even if he doesn't belong to the University."

"Of course. I'm sorry, Tony. But what's his line?"

"He'll explain that better than I can. You'll find he has a very unusual and compelling point of view."

"At least you can give me some idea of it."

"For our present purpose, it amounts to this. Whatever the

Council decide to do with this money . . . even if they vote to spend it in the most enlightened way possible . . . their decision must be protested."

"Why, for Christ's sake?"

"Simply because it *is* the Council's decision. As Mayerston sees it, the students must decide."

"Then let the students ask for consultations with the Council before it takes its final vote."

"No. This isn't an exercise in co-operation. The whole point is that the students should impose their own absolute will. They must make the Council back down from any position whatever which it adopts."

"Suppose the students have nothing better to offer?"

"Then they will simply say 'no' to the Council and go on saying it."

"Not very constructive."

"It's not intended to be. The important thing is to beat down the Council."

"Of which you are a member. I think it stinks," said Hugh.

"You may think differently after Mayerston has explained the philosophy behind it."

"I doubt it. I suspect he's going to talk a whole lot more of your old bollocks – a diseased society and violence the only way to cleanse it. It's not even original, Tony: it's been used by a great many people – most notably by Adolf Hitler."

"You'll find Mayerston more subtle than that."

"I shan't, because I'm not even going to meet him. Good evening, Tony. Let me know when you expect another essay."

Hugh navigated a velour-hooded chaise longue and a bronze-clad family lectern, and walked towards the door.

"Hugh . . ."

"Yes, Tony?"

"You must listen to Mayerston, you know. If only in order to refute him."

For five seconds Hugh stood dithering on the carpet

(pistachio-green and eglantine). There was a knock on the door.

"Come in," called Tony Beck. ". . . Good evening, Mayerston."

"In conclusion," wrote Robert Constable, "it is important to face up to Professor Parkinson's charge that a high rate of tax on earned income draws off creative and inventive energy, too much of which, he claims, is now unproductively employed in devising new methods of tax avoidance. There is some evidence to support this assertion; but the assertion itself demonstrates and strengthens precisely those attitudes of mind which modern social philosophy is concerned to discredit and destroy. For personal ability or talent must no longer be regarded as a means to personal enrichment but as a commodity, held in trust by some fortunate individual, whereby he may serve and enrich mankind. Indifferent to monetary returns, such an individual should find his satisfaction in the exercise of his skill (grateful that it releases him from the drudgery by which most men must earn their livelihood) and in the knowledge that he is providing pleasure or amenity for his fellow human beings. Such grace, I fear, is still far to seek; and it will certainly not be found in any quantity as long as influential writers like Professor Parkinson continue to regard society, not as an area of tillage to be held and harvested in common, but as a barren and bloody arena in which men mangle one another in pursuit of acclaim and gold."

That, thought Constable as he lifted his head, is putting it a bit strong. Although there are real gladiators, the iron men of industry and commerce, for the most part the circus is occupied by perfectly decent fellows who are hoping, in return for a conscientious display of talent, to achieve a quiet independence and retire to a Sabine farm. But then again, thought Constable, if society is to be truly co-operative there is no place even for such temperate self-interest as this. It's not the economics of the thing that matter so much as the moral attitude . . . the idea that one will make a part of human society for only so long as it takes to raise enough money to opt out of that society and buy a pretty house on the hill way up above the noise and the suffering and the stink. If society were justly ordered, thought Constable for the millionth time, if wealth were fairly spread, then no ability would win enough money to escape the suffering and the stink, and all ability would therefore be used to mitigate them. This, then, must be the argument for heavy taxes on earned money – that independence, even when earned, is a crime against humanity.

Yet of all men, thought Constable, I am by nature the most independent and by situation the most aloof. True, I serve society in that I educate its young, but I do so in circumstances of such calm and privilege that for many years now I have been unreached by its cries of pain. Perhaps, he thought, that is why the young are now so restless : they hear the cries from the world outside and cannot bear them, and are determined that those like me should hear them too. But where is the good in that? If one listens to those cries, one becomes unmanned, unfit for the task of curing the ills that cause them. In order to help the world, one must get knowledge first, and while getting it one must stop one's ears and live behind thick walls. The walls of Lancaster, thought Constable, are strong and shall remain so, for I am their guardian : I, like the knights who were my ancestors, am Castellan.

About an hour and a half after Daniel Mond had left him, Tom Llewyllyn finished the chapter on which he was working (An Analysis of the Random Element in the Reform Act of 1867) and walked across the Great Court to the Lauderdale Gate. He left his rooms, as he always did, with regret; for it was here that his work was done, here that his life was now centred, and he returned each night to his house in Grantchester with a bleak certainty that the day could now hold little more either of value or of pleasure. He loved his wife and he loved his daughter; but they represented a domestic duty which was at odds with the independence proper to a scholar, and, what was worse, they called him away from the company of Daniel and the rest at the evening hour, just when that company would have been sweetest. To dine with like-minded friends was the crown of any man's day; but even when he found excuse to dine in college, the occasion was spoilt by the nagging sense that Patricia was waiting and that he must leave directly after the dessert.

"Good night, Wilfred," he said to the porter on duty in the Lodge.

"Good night, sir," said Wilfred, looking up and smiling with tactful sympathy, as though (Tom thought) he had divined the reluctance with which Tom now stepped through the gate.

For a moment, as he saw his old Lagonda on the College Stones outside, Tom's spirits lifted. It was a lovely evening for a spin. But a spin, he thought, of barely three miles; and after that . . .

. . . "So you're home," said Patricia, as he had known she would; "not staying *there* for dinner?"

. "You know I always warn you," said Tom, sitting down very heavily, "if I'm staying in college for dinner. What have you done today?"

"I took Baby into Cambridge . . . by bus . . . to have her plate adjusted."

"Let's have a look, love."

Tom put his arm round his seven-year-old daughter's waist and drew her in between his legs. Baby squirmed away from him.

"I hate my plate," she yelped.

"That dentist's no good with children," whimpered Patricia: "now, if we were in London—"

"—I've told you. You can have it all done there if you want to."

"Privately?" Patricia mocked. "And you a socialist?"

"Don't be bloody-minded, heart. Do you want it, that's the thing?"

"It's such a strain going up and down."

"Then go up for a whole week. Stay in a hotel. Go up, and get her teeth fixed as you want them, and enjoy yourself."

"And you?"

"I'd be all right. I could sleep in my rooms in college."

"You'd like that, wouldn't you?" she breathed.

"And so would you," he said levelly: "you could get yourself some clothes while you were about it."

Patricia looked down at her worn tweed skirt and then at two holes by the left knee of her thick brown tights.

"Hotels, private dentists, new clothes . . . We can't afford all that any more."

"Rubbish. I know I don't get much from the college, but there's all those back royalties coming in, and there's that money your father left—"

"—*That's* to be kept for Baby, thank you very much—"

"—To say nothing of all we save by living down here in the country. There's plenty of money if you care to make the effort."

"Just so's you could be free to live in that hateful college for a few days. That's all you want, isn't it? Sometimes I think you'd be glad if Baby and I were dead."

Baby started snivelling to stress the point.

"Don't be silly, heart. You're tired and so's Baby. Put her to bed while I get the supper."

"Wirr, wirr, wirr," Baby went.

"Tired I may be," Patricia said, "but strong enough to say this. When we came here, *you* said it was for three years. I hated the idea, as you very well knew, but you were so keen, and you promised it would only be three years, so I said I'd come. But now what? We've been here nearly five, and God knows how long to go. Why couldn't you keep your promise?"

"I wasn't to know they'd renew my fellowship."

"You could have refused."

"Wirr . . . wirr . . . wirr."

"I hadn't finished my book."

"Your *book*. As if anyone will want to publish that. By the time we get back to London – if we ever do – they'll have forgotten you ever existed. How can you expect Gregory Stern to risk his money on a million-page sermon, about a subject which interests nobody, and written by a provincial has-been."

"I should have thought," said Tom, nettled, "that Power was a subject to interest a lot of people."

"Not the way you're writing about it. All split hairs and preach, preach, preach. Remember what happened to those specimen chapters you sent Gregory? They came back without comment."

"I don't think this is quite Gregory's thing. I rather thought the University Press might be more suitable."

"There are some things," said Patricia with spiteful glee, "which even the University Press can't swallow. Have you tried them yet?"

"I've sent them the odd hundred pages . . . as you know."

"Six months ago – and not a word from them."

"The University Press works very slowly."

"Everything about the University works very slowly. They can't even bury their dead. So they just leave them lying there rotting – like that ghastly Daniel Mond – and pretend they're still alive. That's what'll happen to you, Tom. You'll start to rot, but they'll tell you you're still alive, and you're so besotted you'll believe them."

"Wirr," howled Baby, "wirr, *wirr, WIRR*."

"You need two things," said Tom quietly. "An intelligent interest and a vigorous lover. You've let your mind go to pieces and the the rest of you's following." He looked at the holes by her knee. "Fast," he said.

"*CHRIST*," screamed Patricia, and struck him over the chops. "It's you I want. Why won't you do it to me like you used to?"

"I can't."

"Of course," she snarled, "I know I'm not what I was before I had that miscarriage . . . brought on by the move down *here*."

"It isn't that," said Tom. "I just can't. I love you very

much, but I can't do that for you any more. Not for you or for anyone, any more."

"Wirrrrr."

"You don't know what you're saying, Tom."

"Oh yes, I do. It's stopped, Patricia. Nothing stirs it at all. I look at young girls in the street, and I think, surely, a juicy little thing like that, plump buttocks, smooth thighs spreading, the little dark triangle and the red lips moist and open . . . but it's no good. My cock doesn't even twitch. It's all over for me. Dead . . . Now take that grizzling child to bed while I get the supper."

I wonder, thought the Honourable Grantchester FitzMargrave Pough (pronounced Pew) whether I should ask Dinkie and Dudu to Sunday luncheon again. Dinkie and Dudu were the two choristers at the east end of the front row south. At this moment they were banging through the Magnificat in great style though without assistance from the organ, as this was a day for unaccompanied evensong.

The uncharitable, thought Grantchester Pough, may remember that it was these two I invited last time I gave a Sunday luncheon. If, therefore, I invite them to the next, the uncharitable might draw scandalous inference. On the other hand, my last Sunday luncheon was over a month ago, just before the Choir School broke up for the holidays. There has been a goodish interval. The choristers started their new term yesterday, the college starts a new full term tomorrow, and that means a clean sheet. You start again from scratch, last term's lists having long since been torn up, and there is therefore no reason why Dinkie and Dudu should not be at the head of *this* term's list of guests for my Sunday luncheons.

But then again, will they want to come? Pough, as always when perplexed, seized a large handful of his beard and scrabbled in it, as though hoping to find truffles. He glared down at Dinkie and Dudu from the Senior Fellow's stall, defying them to refuse his invitation. Even if they did not care for the wholesome vegetarian fare which he offered, they should find compensation, as had generations of choristers, in his tales of the Eiger and the Matterhorn. And of the narrow failure on Everest (that need not have been a failure if only his colleagues had trained, like himself, on raw cabbage instead of steak). What more could any proper boy want? And yet, he thought sadly, there were signs these days that his stories were not as popular as they had been. For the last three years or so, the choristers had listened with a certain lack of respect; not indeed with disbelief (for even they knew that it was all in the record) but with mild contempt, as though wondering why any sane man should be at agonies to climb a mountain the summit of which could be comfortably viewed from the cockpit of a light aircraft. Modern boyhood seemed to have got its values botched up; he must have a word with the Headmaster of the Choir School about it – though he knew in advance exactly what the wretch would say. He would say what he said to every complaint, whether about the deterioration of the Choir School's cricket or the lack of gloss on the choristers' top hats: "What you forget is that my boys are the first children of the space age."

And now Dinkie and Dudu, those twin children of the space age, as alike as two little robots, were going gaily through the Gloria, what time the Chaplain, the Reverend Oliver Clewes, was cringing up the nave to the lectern.

Oliver Clewes, though humble in demeanour, was inwardly full of gleeful pride at the shock he had in store for the congregation. A small congregation, as on any week day, but with igneous elements in it. Pough, the Senior Fellow, would be just plain furious. Andrew Ogden, the Dean of Chapel, who was conducting the service, would be bitterly insulted. And even Balbo Blakeney might be roused from his contemplation of the Screen to mutter some indignant obscenity. With the spiteful relish of a man about to plunge in a detonator and blow a sleeping garrison to shreds, Clewes ascended the steps up to the lectern. Amen, carolled the space children, and flirtily arranged themselves to listen.

"The second lesson," said Clewes, "will be taken from the thirteenth chapter of St. Luke's Gospel." He paused, hands on the plunger. "It will be read in the new translation."

Oh, what a dreary fellow, thought the Reverend Andrew Ogden, wiping his palms down his rusty surplus. I knew he was up to something – he's been walking round all day like Titus Oates. And now this is the best he can do. He really thinks he'll get my bate by reading the Parable of the Prodigal Son in the new translation. On the contrary: I've always thought it was a silly story, and I'm delighted that this flat, boring English will make it sound even sillier.

How very convenient, thought Grantchester Pough. I've been meaning to look at the new translation for months. I should be able to judge from this specimen whether it will be worth the trouble . . . No, he thought after three sentences, it certainly will not.

God, what a cur, thought Balbo Blakeney, as he sat in the Inductor's stall high up behind Dinkie's and Dudu's blond heads. (The Inductor was the College Officer who lead new Scholars forward to take the oath from the Provost; he received a special emolument of two and a half guineas a year, payable every Lady's Day.) What a dribbling, mangy cur. To disgrace this building with *that* rubbish. Not that anything said in here makes the slightest sense; but at least the old words made the right kind of noise. And that reminds me, he thought. The singing's getting patchy. Quality still good, on the whole, but those little eunuchs down there need to concentrate harder. They need more discipline, and if they're not getting it it's the fault of that poxy Headmaster. Morale in the Choir School has been low for some time, and it's his business to set it up again. I'll not have this building discredited by so much as half a botched verse in the whole bone-aching psaltery.

His eyes moved up the carved stalls opposite, then up the coloured windows (dull but still rich in the fading light), and then to the ringed roses sculptured on the ceiling. Gazing at these, he remained seated for the whole of the rest of the service (including the Creed), and had to be roused by the verger forty minutes later when it was time to close the Chapel for the night.

Short gowns flying, Eton collars gleaming in the dusk, toppers rakish on the leaders and straight as chimneys on the infants in the rear, the Choir rattled off in file, all along Sitwell's and then sharp right for Willow Bridge.

"I saw Gloozer Pough looking at us," said Dinkie to Dudu.

"Everybody looks at us."

"Not as hard as Gloozer Pough. Perhaps he'll ask us to lunch again."

"It's not our turn."

"He was looking at us so hard I don't think that matters."

"If only he'd give you a proper lunch."

"His stories aren't bad."

"The first time you hear them."

"Shall we go if we're asked?"

"Oh, I think so," said Dudu. "It would be very unkind not to, if he looked at us like you said... Look, there's Lord Beyfus."

"He's not a proper Lord. It was only Mr Wilson made him one."

"He doesn't look like it either. He's so small . . . and sort of black."

"That's because he's a Jew and never comes to Chapel."

"That lady with him . . . she looks nice."

"Why is she wearing trousers?"

"I expect she's got horrid legs. But her *face* is nice."

"I don't know. There's something . . . unfair . . . about it. As if she was hoping to find someone enjoying themselves just so's she could spoil it."

"Lord Beyfus doesn't look as if he ever enjoys himself."

"Not with her around, that's certain."

But in fact Lord Beyfus was really quite happy; for Mona Corrington was back after being away nearly a week, and

during that time some interesting things had come up which
they were now about to discuss. As the choristers went twitter-
ing off into the twilight, he took Mona's arm to guide her down
the narrow and bicycle-cluttered passage (between the Hall
and the end of the Provost's Lodge) that led into Dawley's
Court, a small gravel close bounded by the College Library
and four staircases of comfortable but unfashionable rooms.
Having released her as soon as they were out of the passage
(for Mona severely rationed their physical contacts, however
innocent), he hovered fussily about her as they approached his
staircase (Theta), and then followed her up to the second floor.
Not until they were inside his rooms with the door closed did
she open her mouth (a life spent in a women's college had
given her a horror of being overheard), and when she did it
was to say :

"Sherry."

Beyfus poured two glasses of Dry Fly and gave one to Mona.
She tossed hers down with a single gulp and put the glass
firmly away from her on the mantel-shelf. One drink before
dinner was Mona's rule. Straddling in front of the gas-fire, she
started to boom at Beyfus.

"I am a bearer of good tidings. The atmosphere is becoming
more propitious every day. London, Paris, Rome, Berlin –
everywhere it's the same story. I've seen more than twenty
distinguished Anthropologists in the last six days, and most of
them were implicitly agreed that from now on we must ditch
the past and concentrate on the future."

"But surely," said Beyfus, carefully and deferentially, "the
whole object of Anthropology is to establish the human
patterns of the past. Only when you've done that can you turn
to the future."

"They were *implicitly* agreed, I said. The feeling is that the
past shouldn't be researched any more but *codified*. The helpful aspects, that is, will be marshalled to form a definite body
of knowledge. Instead of seeking to qualify this, we shall take
it as established, once and for all, and use it as an instrument

to analyse the conditions of the present – and so to predict the future."

"A dangerous game, Mona. The present is fluctuating too fast for precise analysis. And prophets look very silly when they make mistakes."

"By predict we mean ordain. In the light of past experience, we shall say, if present behaviour patterns are so and so, then future behaviour patterns can only be such and such. Provided we say this often enough and authoritatively enough, governments will deliberately enforce the patterns we foretell. They will regard them as historical necessities."

"In other words, you're going to adopt my function. You're turning yourselves into sociologists."

"With this difference," said Mona : "we shall have introduced our historical instrument. Where *you* say the present is fluctuating too fast for analysis, we shall say that our anthropological knowledge can distinguish certain human constants which are being arranged and re-arranged by the operation of random variables – i.e. by day to day events. Where *you* say these variables are changing too fast for you to cope, we shall say that our ability to recognise salient human constants enables us to plot a basic pattern (whatever the variables at work), and that any one present pattern can only be succeeded by a limited number of others, all of them known to us and all similar in type. In other words, we shall claim to have a formula."

"A formula based on selected anthropological data which, you say, will no longer be subject to addition or investigation but simply accepted as holy writ. What sort of scholarship is this, Mona ?"

"Don't start up about the purity of learning, Beyfus. Academic learning is of no value except in so far as it can be used to determine social method."

She gave him a brief but very intense look, and started to put on her cloak.

"You've booked our usual table at the Arts Restaurant ?" she said.

"Yes."

"Then dinner."

"Yes . . . But look, Mona. Your body of anthropological data. To put it bluntly, you're just going to select what suits your political purposes."

"Yours too."

"Arbitrarily selected data could make an unreliable instrument."

"It'll make a good enough stick to beat them with," she said: "dinner."


"I've heard a good deal about you," said Mayerston; "all of it interesting."

Mayerston was clean-shaven and neatly dressed in a suit of dark checks. He had appealing hair (straight, blond hair of moderate length) and a seductive smile. He also had plenty of money; for when Hugh had suggested that they went to eat at Haq's, an eating house of low cost and demotic cuisine, Mayerston had simply announced that they would go to the Arts Theatre Restaurant and that dinner was on him. What was more, the Head Waiter had treated him with respect on their arrival and though obviously hard up for space had found the two of them a corner table which could easily have accommodated four.

"Yes," Mayerston was saying now: "I've heard more than you might think."

"From Tony Beck, I suppose," said Hugh. "You know, he made you sound so foul that I didn't want to meet you. If you'd reached his rooms two minutes later, I'd have been gone."

"Tony Beck is a good critic," said Mayerston, "but he'd make a bad novelist. He has no eye for people. No ear for them either." He sipped the two guinea claret which he'd ordered. "What did he lead you to expect?"

"A wild-eyed ranter in a boiler suit."

Mayerston laughed. He had a deep, easy laugh and a deep,

easy voice, both of which made a slightly disconcerting contrast with his boyish appearance.

"That's for children," he said, "for frightened children who want a uniform in order to be safely one of the gang. Though surely there can't be anything very strange to you about all that? You must have plenty of friends in the boiler suit set?"

"Yes. But they belong here and you didn't, which was the first thing against you. And then Tony made you sound very extreme."

"And are none of your friends extreme?"

"They are all constructive, whatever else."

"And Beck told you I wasn't?"

"He said your plan was to go on saying 'no'. Not to suggest anything, not to . . . participate . . . just to say 'no'."

"As far as that goes, Beck is perfectly correct."

Hugh felt a disappointment which amounted almost to misery. From the first moment that Mayerston had walked into Tony's rooms, Hugh had felt that here was a man who had something to contribute. Of course, there was no rational ground for supposing this; it was just something about the way in which Mayerston had carried himself, had shaken hands, had looked Hugh up and down with a thoroughness which might have been insolent but in fact seemed only appreciative. Here was a man of candour and intelligence, Hugh had thought; an ally. He had been further impressed when Mayerston cut short a pompous speech which Tony had started about the international freemasonry of students, and then, ignoring Tony's protests, suggested to Hugh that they should leave together at once. He had been childishly flattered by Mayerston's invitation to dine at the Arts; he had been charmed by the courtesy which Mayerston had shewn as his host; he had been amused by Mayerston's comments, spare and well placed, on their fellow diners. But above all Hugh had been expectant; he had been waiting for a message, even perhaps for a vision; and now . . . now it seemed that all he would hear was the same barren tale as he had already heard from Beck.

"Perfectly correct, Beck is," said Mayerston, "as far as he goes."

"Mere negation . . . obstruction. Is that all you can offer?"

"It's all I'm going to offer to Beck. One doesn't tell men like Beck more than one can help, Hugh. No more than one needs to get one's way with them. Because men like Beck are greedy. They steal."

Hope stirred again in Hugh's stomach.

"Why have anything to do with them?" he said.

"They have influence. They know people. They know you, for example, and introduce you to me. They have many uses. But one doesn't share one's ideas with them, because they steal."

Mayerston waved a casual hand. The wine-waiter rushed from the far end of the room, where he was in the middle of taking another order, and bowed with pleasure at Mayerston's request for cognac.

"Then who," said Hugh, trembling with excitement, "does one share one's ideas with?"

"Grammar, Hugh. With whom does one share one's ideas? With those who are worthy."

Hugh opened his mouth but Mayerston lifted a hand to silence him.

"Before you ask any further," Mayerston said, "understand this: not all men have the same needs. You, for instance, have certain mental needs, because you are a man of intellect. Others have other needs at other levels. They are not inferior to you, but their needs are different and must be catered for in a different manner."

The wine-waiter brought them two brandy glasses and a bottle of vintage cognac, which he left on the table.

"He knows I like to pour for myself," said Mayerston, doing so liberally and passing the bottle to Hugh; "he knows I must be catered for in my own way."

Out of sheer nervousness, Hugh poured himself about twice as much as Mayerston had taken.

"I'm sorry. I—"

"—It'll do you good. Drink it slowly."

Mayerston produced a leather cigar-case and carefully chose a medium-sized cigar.

"Now then," Mayerston said: "people's needs. Although these are different, there is one basic need which almost everyone has in common: to feel that he has some say in his own destiny. The difference lies in the various ways in which this basic need is expressed; from the crude ways, like demanding more money, to the relatively subtle ways, like seeking justice or fulfilment or personal recognition – or, as in your case, trying to determine intellectual truth. But in the end, satisfaction, for every man, lies in being able to assert himself – or to think he is asserting himself – on his chosen level. You agree?"

"Yes," said Hugh, and took a gulp of cognac.

"Slowly, I said . . . Now, the trouble with contemporary society is *not* that it prevents people from asserting themselves on their different levels but that its responses are both feeble and dishonest. It gives in almost at once and provides whatever is demanded – but provides it in a form that it knows to be worthless. The higher wages, for example, lose their extra value almost as soon as they are awarded; improved status means the same old dreary job under a higher-sounding name; and so on. Hence the general discontent; and hence our problem, which is to reward those who assert themselves with something genuine in response to their demands, on whatever level these may be made. Otherwise the whole affair is a mockery."

"And so it is bound to be," said Hugh, "as long as their demands are self-centred. More money for *me*; higher rank for *me*. What people are demanding are *distinctions* . . . which can mean nothing at all unless they are confined to small minorities."

"And that, of course," said Mayerston with just a hint of irony, "we cannot possibly allow. So the answer must be to persuade people to demand the kind of thing which is in both genuine and plentiful supply. In this way, they will be asserting themselves to some purpose. They will have a good chance of actually achieving what they're aiming at."

"And what is that to be?"

"Never mind what it is just yet," Mayerston said. "The thing you have to get straight first of all is that people have to be persuaded . . . or even compelled . . . to want it. They must be forced to give up their old aspirations and to desire what we wish them to desire, because we know that it is only this which is worth having. In short, Hugh, we are not going to give people what they want; we are going to make them want what we have to give."

"I see. You are going to dictate."

"To educate. To persuade."

"You said 'compel', 'make' . . . 'force'."

"Careless of me . . . though our arguments will certainly be forceful and compelling."

"*Our* arguments, Mayerston? How can I join you before I know what these . . . forceful and compelling arguments . . . will advocate?"

"Are you worthy to know, Hugh?"

Mona Corrington and Lord Beyfus came in. They sat down at a table in the corner opposite Hugh and Mayerston. Lord Beyfus, who knew Hugh slightly, smiled across at him. Hugh smiled back, and Mona, unexpectedly, simpered.

"You know Beyfus?" said Mayerston.

"A little."

"A dedicated man but unoriginal. He is not worthy to know. I think . . . I hope . . . you are."

"Tell me then."

Here, surely, must be the message. The rest had been cautious and preliminary. Now . . . surely . . . the good news.

"We are to persuade people to want," said Mayerston, "something genuine which we know is there to give."

"So you have been saying."

"Fellowship," said Mayerston. He spoke quietly and deeply, clutching his brandy glass very tightly, one hand over the other. "Fellowship. Brotherhood. Love. Here in Cambridge, a University which shall know nothing of privilege and ambition, of menial services rendered and paid for, nor anything of that learning which is bought and weighed and sold again. A University in which men will gather round other and equal men to listen and to receive the wisdom and knowledge, which these, their brothers, have to offer, freely and as a right. A University which will refuse none and smile on all. An Alma Mater, Hugh; a kindly mother of her sons."

There was a long pause. At last:

"And where does the Arts Restaurant come into all this?" was all Hugh could think of to say.

"No one, in that University, will want the Arts Restaurant."

"Not even you? You seem very fond of it."

"I shall be gone by then. Doing the work of persuasion elsewhere."

"Where they still have restaurants – until, of course, you've done your work and gone on to the next place."

And yet Hugh was moved by what Mayerston had said. The message was there; the news was good . . . or seemed so after all this cognac. He felt rather ashamed of himself for making pert remarks about Mayerston's taste in restaurants; but surely the point was valid?

"When in Rome," said Mayerston pleasantly, "one may as well enjoy her amenities. Until such time as they are swept away. And then . . ."

Mayerston shrugged in resignation, but not quite, Hugh thought, in abrogation. Wherever Mayerston was, one felt, there would somehow continue to be exclusive restaurants. Yet did this inconsistency matter very much? Perhaps a man of Mayerston's . . . authority . . . could be trusted to make his own rules.

"What you propose," said Hugh, "co-operation and fellowship, have always been realisable. The difficulty is to persuade people to want them. You are obviously very sensitive to this difficulty. How shall you meet it?"

"Before one can build up Love the Beloved Republic," Mayerston said, "one must first pull down the Scarlet City to make room. There will be plenty of volunteers for *that* part of the work."

"Yes. People enjoy smashing things. Even metaphorically."

"How strait-laced you are, Hugh. Have some more cognac."

Mayerston poured; Hugh did not demur.

"So demolition," said Mayerston, "is no problem. The problem is how to persuade people to start re-building once the Old City is down."

"They'll be too busy looting and raping, you mean."

"If you like. *That* is when persuasion will really be needed. But I think I have the answer. To use your own terms, we let them gorge themselves on loot and rape, and then, when disgust sets in, we seize on their repentance and tell them to purge themselves of their guilt by building temples."

"And the impenitent?"

"To them we shall suggest that they contribute their loot and their energies to erecting comfortable brothels – for by this time they will be tired of fornicating in the rubble. We shall provide the ground plans – and when the buildings are up the impenitent will discover that they too have been making temples unawares. Temples of love."

"That's trickery, not persuasion."

"Justified – for Love the Beloved Republic."

"The men who thought they were building brothels may not think so."

"Ah, but they will," said Mayerston, very earnestly. "When they see the Beloved Republic, they needs must love it. No man can help himself. They will forget their brothels and fall down on their knees to give thanks . . . and a very elevating scene it will be," he said, his earnestness suddenly gone; "but here and now it is time to discuss a few practical details."


"Who," said Mona to Beyfus, "is that young man over there? The one you smiled at."

"An undergraduate from Lancaster."

"His face has character. And his friend?"

"Him I don't know."

"At their age, they shouldn't be drinking so much brandy. They shouldn't even be here."

"A special treat, perhaps."

"This is no time," said Mona, "for special treats. Work – that's what's wanted. And from now on you and I are going to have a lot extra."

"I can't possibly take on anything more just now."

"You can take *this* on. We're forming an International Committee of Anthropologists. Me and some of these people I've met this last week. We want you as Vice-Chairman, to make the thing reputable."

"I'm not an anthropologist, Mona, and I'm quite sure it will be reputable without me."

"We need a solid name. Some of the others are rather flashy."

Beyfus shuddered.

"Sometimes," said Mona, "I think you're just a fussy old bourgeois at heart."

"So you have this committtee," said Beyfus, refusing to be baited. "So you have me as Vice-Chairman. So what do you do then?"

"We issue a pamphlet. The International Committee of Anthropologists issues a pamphlet called Educational Patterns in Megalopolitan Cultures."

"Megalopolitan Cultures," said Beyfus, "aren't your business. Your business is savages."

"Our business is the study of man. In this pamphlet we shall prove that all city-centred cultures throughout history have been compelled to adopt a quantitative approach to education."

"Meaning?"

"That more people – many more people – have to be educated, despite the obstructionism of a tradition-orientated élite."

"Meaning?"

"Higher numbers and fuck standards."

Beyfus tittered.

"You are a funny girl," he said.

"No, I'm not. I'm a serious middle-aged woman, who's trying to publicise the most vital truth of our century – that in an urban/industrial society we must use the last ounce of our educational plant to one hundred per cent capacity. *And* build more all the time."

"But everyone knows this already."

"So they may, but they don't act on it. This whole town is full of lawns and parks and gardens and tennis courts and God knows what. Good building land, Beyfus; land on which they could erect *sky-scrapers* if they turned their minds to it. Like that new one by Tottenham Court Road Tube Station. Just think, Beyfus, how many students we could pack into *that*."

At High Table in the Hall of Lancaster, conversation turned on how the Chaplain (who was absent, skulking in his room) had read the Second Lesson from the new translation.

"It sounded," said Balbo Blakeney, "just like the scabby jargon in one of Beyfus's sociological tracts."

"Flabby, not scabby," said Andrew Ogden, the Dean of Chapel. "And not jargon. Just clear but utterly sapless English."

"Perhaps," said Provost Constable, "it really will lead to a better popular understanding."

"Which will be disastrous for the Church," said Tony Beck, gleefully. "The Church is as good as rumbled already, and if people really understand what it's saying, they'll die laughing."

"I understand you were there, Senior Fellow," said Constable to Pough : "what do you think?"

"I think," said Pough, "that these carrots are out of a tin. Since I pay extra money for the services of an under-chef to prepare my vegetarian diet, I do think I might be given proper carrots."

"The nutritive values," said Balbo Blakeney, "are identical."

"I was thinking of the taste."

"At your age," said Balbo, taking a huge portion of steak and oyster pudding from the serving-man's dish, "you should be thinking only of your arteries. Childer," he called to the wine-butler, "red burgundy."

"You've already had a bottle of white," said Ivor Winstanley in admiring tones.

"And now I'm going to have a bottle of red."

"What," enquired Jacquiz Helmut, "will happen to your arteries?"

"They'll seize up, in laymen's terms, by the time I'm sixty. And don't think I shan't be glad. Do you suppose I want to go on living in a world run by pinkoes and pansies?"

"The trouble is," croaked Daniel Mond, "that they may not seize up quite finally. You may just have a very nasty stroke, and stay alive but paralysed and imbecile. That is the sort of joke which God enjoys."

"Come, come, Daniel," said Andrew Ogden mildly.

"As a Jew," said Daniel, "or rather a half-Jew, I know a lot about God and His jokes. We invented Him, remember."

"And killed Him," said Pough.

"So the joke was on God," said Winstanley. "Childer, I'll have half a bottle of what Mr Blakeney's having."

Constable wished that the conversation was more edifying, but failed to remember a time when it ever had been.

"I hear," he said, "that Mona Corrington is back. My wife saw her with Beyfus earlier this evening."

"Where has poor old Mona been?" asked Jacquiz languidly.

"On the continent," said Tony Beck, "getting up trouble."

"She's a grand girl, Mona," Balbo Blakeney said: "she stirs up the shit wherever she goes. Her politics are sheer cow's piss, of course, but I do love a spunky girl like Mona who goes round stirring up the shit."

". . . All of which reminds me," Mona was saying to Beyfus in the Arts: "this new surplus Lancaster's got. Half a million."

"Quarter of a million."

"Quite enough to build with."

"Yes. I'm going to propose a new building on Scholars' Meadow."

That at least should please her, he thought. But it didn't.

"Cost?" she snapped.

"A hundred thousand plus."

"Then why only one new building?"

"There are other things to be done, Mona dear."

"No, there aren't. Not these days. Now, Beyfus, you listen to me . . ."

First with depression and then with mounting horror Beyfus listened.

"And that," she said at last, "is what you will propose."

As Beyfus opened his mouth, Mona gave him a long, hard look which could only mean one thing: do this, or there'll be no more of *that*. So Beyfus took a big drink of Vichy Water, which he supposed to be good for his nervous stomach, and then nodded humbly.

"Just as you say," he said.


". . . So you see," Mayerston was telling Hugh, "these are not the methods of reform but the methods of revolution."

"Peaceful revolution," insisted Hugh. For of course, he kept telling himself, all this talk of demolition and so on *was* only metaphorical.

"Radical in any event. *Radix*," said Mayerston, "meaning root. The roots come up."

"But painlessly," said Hugh, "because first we shall have been careful to dig the soil away."

"All right. And who more suitable for the task than our chums in boiler suits?"

"They don't like hard work," said Hugh disloyally.

"Then occasionally we give them a little treat. We let them move some of the soil by a quicker and more amusing method."

Demolition again, Hugh thought. He did not like it, even as

a metaphor. On the other hand, he believed in Mayerston and wanted to go with him. Why, he thought, do I believe in this man, whom I have only known for a few hours? It's not the cognac and it's not the straight fair hair; it's not the beautiful deep voice; it's not even the vision of the Beloved Republic. It's just . . . that I want to follow this man. It would be the same if he were starting a club or making a film or proposing a two-man crossing of the Pacific. Whatever he's up to, I want to be there, I want to bear a part. I want to laugh when he does, to cry when he does – and to mean it. Above all, I want him to turn to me and say, "Well done."

"Where do I come in?" Hugh said.

"So you will come in?"

"Yes."

"Despite your obvious reservations?"

"Yes."

"And you will do all I ask of you?"

"If you ask. Not if anyone else does."

Mayerston smiled, revealing very white but rather unevenly placed teeth. The left-hand upper canine noticeably overlapped its two neighbours and protruded over the lower lip with gauche and innocent charm.

"Good," said Mayerston, and Hugh was pleased.

"But what must I do?" he said.

"You have a name for academic brilliance. You are . . . somebody of repute. I want you to set an example to all those who have no repute . . . to all those sullen, dirty young men in beards and boiler suits. And more than set an example: inspire them."

"You could do that better than me."

"I can't be everywhere at once. I have a lot to attend to. You will do for them," said Mayerston eyeing him closely, "what I am doing for you."

Hugh paused to consider this. He knows his power, Hugh thought: well, and why not? Then, shaking his head modestly,

"But what must I do in terms of action?" he asked.

"You must initiate and encourage certain movements,"

Mayerston said, "which will in time shake down the whole structure of this University as it now stands. Or, to use our other image, you must conjure the wind to blow away the soil that nourishes the roots."

"A rather . . . nebulous programme?"

"You," said Mayerston, "will make gestures. The denim-clad mass will stir and charge. And down comes all."

"Another metaphor, Mayerston. What do I *do*?"

"You direct your attention," said Mayerston, "to the large sum of money which your college has just received from the sale of land. You find out what are the early proposals for using this money – Beck will tell you that, one of his many uses. And what you then do, in the first instance, is this . . ."

For something over an hour, with great precision and much practical detail, Mayerston proceeded to tell him.


After the Fellows of Lancaster had drunk port, claret, madeira and Château Yquem in the Senior Common Room, they dispersed for the night. Daniel Mond, making tracks for Willow Close, found Jacquiz Helmut at his elbow.

"A word or two in your ear," Jacquiz breathed.

When they reached Daniel's rooms over the river, Jacquiz spread himself out full length on the window seat and called for Orangeade.

". . . With ice," he said; and then, when Daniel had stopped fussing about, "Where do we stand *in re* tomorrow's Council?"

"We?"

"We Jews."

"What's that got to do with it?"

"There are three of us. Beyfus will do what La Corrington tells him. I shall support the *status quo*. What shall you do, Daniel?"

"I shall listen to all the suggestions and support the most sensible."

"Suppose none of them is sensible? Or suppose that no sensible suggestion has any chance of getting through? For anything to be passed, remember, there must be 75 per cent of the Council in its favour."

"If there is a sensible suggestion," wheezed Daniel, "I shall support it, whether or not it has any chance of getting through. If there are no sensible suggestions, then I shall support none at all. But I still don't see what being a Jew has to do with it."

"People are going to get very angry, Daniel. When they get angry, they look for faces to punch. Jewish faces, because they tend to be sensitive and clever, are the most satisfying kind."

"Perhaps, too, because they tend to be sanctimonious."

"Good point," Jacquiz said. "And the moral is, not to look sensitive or clever or sanctimonious when fists are flying. Now Beyfus, of course, is going to look all three; but Beyfus is the darling of the left, so there'll be no fist in the face for him."

"There are still," said Daniel, "a few right-wing fists about."

"I'm delighted to hear it, but I doubt whether they will be much help to *us*. Both of us, Daniel, if we allow for our political differences, will be standing for good sense and moderation. Neither quality is popular in times like these, and neither is ever popular in Jews. They make us look superior."

"Then let us cultivate modesty and get on with our work. You with your life of Garibaldi, me with my Tensor Calculus."

"We must still attend the Council and vote. This will expose us to attention. In all our Jewishness."

"The Council is not noted for anti-semitism."

"And the students outside it?"

"The students are committed absolutely to racial tolerance. It's the best thing about them. Why all this fuss, Jacquiz?"

"I felt it my duty to talk to you about the dangers. To ascertain your attitudes."

"Thank you, Jacquiz. Dangers there certainly are, but not, I think, of the kind you mention."

"I'm glad that is your view, so long as it gives you peace of mind. You see, Daniel, I was afraid that you might have been thinking along the same lines as myself and that you might have been getting ready to . . . er . . . to—"

"—Play the poltroon?"

"Let us say, to come to some accommodation with the extremists. I'm glad to be reassured."

"Look," said Daniel, "you had that reassurance almost as soon as you got into this room. But you still had to carry on at length about these . . . dangers . . . you envisage. Why, Jacquiz? Were you trying to frighten me?"

"Only to test you, my dear. To make absolutely certain. I mean, after all you've been through . . ."

"After all I've been through, Jacquiz, I don't believe in bogymen. I've seen the real thing. Fairy tales don't bother me."

"And yet . . . you *have* got fears, you say?"

"Not as a Jew, Jacquiz: as a scholar."

"No one can discredit your scholarship."

"They can say that it is irrelevant."

"Why should they say that?"

"Because from their point of view it is true. I am not a scientist. I am not even a creative mathematician any more. I am just a guardian of a body of abstract truth which is expressed in certain symbols. This truth, beautiful as it is, has nothing to contribute to the new society as they see it. Nor, come to that, has the study of Garibaldi."

"But Garibaldi himself was a revolutionary."

"Was. They are not interested in the past, Jacquiz. They are not interested in truth for its own sake, whether it has to do with your Garibaldi or my mathematical series."

"Then in what are they interested, for Christ's sake? Why are they here at all?"

"They are here to better themselves. To get more of what is going . . . by which I do not mean knowledge, but social status and worldly goods. They have decided that they are not getting more enough quick enough, and so they are now turning nasty with us and all we stand for. You must know that."

"I knew they resented our privileges," Jacquiz said. "But our scholarship . . . why, we are offering to share it with them."

"And they don't want it, because very few of them can understand it, let alone enjoy it."

"Then why not just leave it to us?"

"Because if they don't want it, no one else is going to have it either. Anyone that did might get pleasure from it, you see – a pleasure which they can't share, *ergo* a privilege. For scholarship *is* a privilege, Jacquiz, and it's going to be destroyed with the rest."

After the goodies in the Senior Common Room were finished, Balbo Blakeney had invited Ivor Winstanley and Tony Beck to drink brandy in his rooms in Sitwell's. Since these were on the staircase nearest to the college hall and therefore to the Senior Common Room which adjoined it, the journey was short and the three men managed it without disaster – though in Ivor's case only just.

"So," said Balbo Blakeney, gathering up the Prunier Grande Champagne 1928 from his eighteenth century sideboard, "the boys are back tomorrow. What trouble," he said to Beck as he handed him a generous half-tumbler of cognac, "are they hatching up this time?"

"The usual stuff, I expect. Protest against privilege and divisiveness. Justifiable resentment at the frivolous uses of superfluous affluence. And so on."

"And where do you stand?" mumbled Ivor Winstanley into his brandy.

"Where I always did," said Tony Beck. "Waiting to join them when I'm certain they've won. And they will win, you know."

"Then why not join them now?"

"Because I want to enjoy the old things in the old way for the very short time that's left."

"If you leave it too long," said Ivor, "they might not let you join at all."

"Don't you worry," giggled Balbo, his gnome's face pursed in affectionate malice, "our little Tony is taking care of all that. He may not have joined them yet, but he's dishing out hints on the sly. He's telling them that for the time being he can be more help to them where he is, listening to our counsels among the flesh-pots and then passing the word along."

"I am showing," agreed Beck good-naturedly, "discreet sympathy with the student cause."

"Which means," said Balbo, "that he can go on guzzling with the rest of us right up to the night of the long knives. When that comes, he slips away from high table, changes into his dungarees, and hey presto, there he is waving his sweaty nightcap in the middle of the mob. You are a bloody bastard," he said, waving the bottle at Beck; "have some more of this stuff."

"The point is," said Beck, having some, "that I shan't be in the middle of the mob, I shall be at the head of it. Grateful for my past advice and good offices, appreciative of my experience and maturity, the students will ask me to be their leader. Which is lucky for reactionary jackals like both of you, as I may be able to protect you."

"Send us to labour camps," muttered Ivor, "instead of hanging us from lamp-posts."

"You wouldn't protect your own mother," said Balbo happily. "You'll sentence us all to be drawn and quartered, in order to show revolutionary fervour, and then you'll set about finding yourself a pretty uniform and a big white horse."

He went to the side-board for another bottle.

"Don't let's get over-excited," said Tony Beck. "All that is in question . . . at least for the time being . . . is a new kind of university. The young are discontented with what they've got and want something different."

"Like what?" said Ivor, and slumped.

"Something which will make them feel more important," sneered Balbo.

"That's about it," said Beck. "They have a legitimate aspiration, as they would say, to become a force in the present government and future planning of this university. Now as ever – now more than ever – youth will be served. But no one is talking about labour camps or lamp-posts or big white horses. Simply about radical change, which has now become a necessity."

"Ah," said Balbo, "necessity. I have an old acquaintance, a certain Captain Detterling, who is very fond of the expression. He uses it in the Greek sense, ἀνανκη, which as Ivor here will agree – wake up, you fat bag of guts – means essentially that which is unchangeable. Necessity, my dear Tony, is a conservative word: there is no such thing as necessary change."

"Inevitable change then."

"Change of some kind there will inevitably be, as things do not, unfortunately, stand still. But no particular kind is inevitable, Tony. Have some more booze to sharpen up your wits."

"My wits," said Ivor, staggering to his feet, "are clean undone."

He went quickly through the door and was heard being sick in the sink on the landing.

"Poor old thing can't hold his juice any more," said Beck. "Now then, Balbo. I agree with you that we can't determine exactly what change there will be; but the general direction is clear enough. There is an idealistic movement towards equality. The young will have it so."

"Not all of them or even most of them. Most of them just don't care. In the good English tradition, they are moderate men."

"Apathetic would be a better word. Apathetic but slightly uneasy, because they somehow feel that idealism is the new thing and that they would be safer as idealists. So when the movement gathers way, they will go with it."

Outside the door, Ivor started down the stairs, keening loudly.

"It takes more momentum than you think," said Balbo, "to move a mass of the apathetic."

"There will be very considerable momentum. You haven't met my new friend, Mayerston. A prophet, Balbo, to bring the people out of Egypt."

"The people always end by throwing prophets out, Tony. They nag too much."

"Precisely. And that is when worldly men like myself step in. Mayerston the prophet does the donkey work and brings the people through the desert. When they're heartily sick of Mayerston and the short rations he imposes in Moab, I take over just in time to lead them into the land of milk and honey."

"And the land of cognac, Tony? Of red burgundy and white?"

Balbo proffered the bottle.

"Yes," said Tony Beck. "We allow all those things again once Mayerston is dead and we're out of the desert. Or at least, since they're probably in short supply, we allow them to our leaders and those we value."

"Privilege, Tony?"

"Of course, Balbo. Revolutionaries are only human, after all. I would wish to see you among the privileged in Canaan."

"I don't want to go to Canaan. I like it here in Egypt and shall stay behind."

"There is no staying behind. You know that. When God's children depart, Egypt is smitten and accursed. You come with us or you die of plague."

"I am a scientist. My skills will keep me alive."

"Because of those skills we shall insist on taking you with us. We shan't want poor puffy old Ivor, but we shall insist on taking you."

Both drank deep.

"So whether you like it or not," said Beck, "you will come to Canaan. If you come quietly and work well, you will share my palace and my cognac, my burgundies red and white."

"And if not?"

"You will be thrown into Golgotha."

"I thought," said Balbo, "that we were only discussing changes in this university."

"The allegory holds at all levels."

"All right. So Mayerston/Moses is dead and you've come to the promised land, where you start relaxing a bit. Or so you hope. Because you seem to have forgotten that the Ark of the Covenant is still right up with you, and who should be there carrying the bloody thing but Lord Beyfus and Mona Corrington? Who will speak in the voice of their egalitarian Jehovah to rain curses on your palace and your cognac."

"Unless, Balbo, they have started relaxing too. Even Mona and Beyfus must relax sooner or later. They might even be relaxing now. Do you suppose he fucks her?"

"I've often wondered," Balbo said. "I saw his cock once, in the Fellows' loo. It was like a cooked snail."

Both drank deep and then deeper.

"Of course," said Beck, "you can't really tell unless you've seen it erect. It wasn't erect in the Fellows' loo, I take it?"

"No."

"Not a snail but a limpet?"

Both of them honked with laughter and drank deeper still.

"But none of this proves," said Beck after long thought, "that he doesn't fuck Mona."

"Can you imagine Mona opening her legs? There'd be a sort of rending noise—"

"—Like the veil in the Ark of the Covenant when Jehovah rent it—"

"—Or like Ivor being sick—"

"—And Beyfus would come bouncing up like a balloon—"

"—And Mona would give one squeeze of those huge thighs—"

"—And Beyfus would burst with a plop—"

"—But Mona would mend him and blow him up again—"

"—So that whenever he spoke it would just be Mona's hot air coming out—"

"—Which is what happens anyway," said Balbo; "therefore Beyfus fucks Mona, q.e.d."

Balbo poured more cognac and goodness, how they both laughed.


But in fact Beyfus wasn't fucking Mona at all. He was sitting bolt upright beside her on the leather-covered sofa in his room, while Mona explained, at some length, how they were going to serve the cause of humanity during the whole of the next quinquennium. Having told him just how she proposed to manipulate the new International Committee of Anthropologists, and having firmly outlined his own tasks in the reconstruction and "detraditionalisation" of Lancaster College, Mona passed from the realms of speculation (for even she admitted that her plans depended on highly volatile contingencies) into those of fantasy.

"By about 1970," Mona said, "we should be ready for the coup in reverse."

Oddly enough, Mona was a keen and courageous gambler, being especially fond of Chemin-de-Fer, and from time to time she flavoured her speech with expressions picked up in the gaming house.

"The coup in reverse?" said Beyfus, who was not familiar with the idiom.

"You run your bank as long as you dare," Mona explained, "and then, when you reckon it must be beaten on the next coup, you reverse the situation. You let the bank pass; somebody else takes it on – and you go 'banco' against your own bank, and win."

"It sounds very pleasing."

"It is."

"But I don't quite see—"

"—A simple analogy. The present government, which, for the want of anything more radical, you and I support, can stay in office, run its bank, until March '71. But if it stays that long it will almost certainly be beaten in the elections, so the better plan is to pass the bank voluntarily, i.e. resign, in 1970 – and then instantly challenge the new bank with a call of 'banco'. Which means, Beyfus, that one's going for the whole damn kitty. In this case . . . the Monarchy."

"*Mona*," said Beyfus, deeply shocked.

"The moment parliament reconvenes, the new Labour opposition will demand a plebiscite on whether or not the country wants to keep the Queen and the Royal Family. The plebiscite will be refused, whereupon the idea will gain great appeal in all quarters. The sheer novelty will guarantee that. From then on, the new Conservative government will appear as an oppressive tyranny which has refused the people's right to free expression. The Cabinet will lose its morale and any impetus it ever had, the people will go on hankering for the plebiscite – and in five years' time they will certainly return Labour on the strength of our promise to give it to them. In this way we achieve re-election in 1975. But if we hang on till 1971 before dissolving, and then adopt only the conventional processes of opposition, we may stay out until 1981 or even longer."

"Which way would the plebiscite go?"

"That doesn't matter. The plebiscite is only a ruse."

"But it does matter," said Beyfus petulantly; "because if the Monarchy goes, my peerage goes with it."

"Why should you care? You only took it on as a duty, because Harold said he needed men like you to make themselves heard at Westminster."

"I've got very fond of my peerage." Beyfus hesitated guiltily. Then, "You know," he blurted out, "I get an almost sexual thrill of excitement every time someone calls me 'my lord'."

"I don't want to hear any more infantile nonsense of *that* kind . . . Time I was going."

"But first," said Beyfus, his little dark eyes pleading, "can you? Will you? Please, Mona."

"Apart from this prattle of peerages," said Mona, deliberating, "you've really been quite a good Beyfus. Not very good, of course, but certainly not bad. So the answer is . . . yes. Go and get ready."

Full of happiness, Beyfus hurried into his bedroom and changed into his pyjamas.

"Ready," he called out.

"Have you washed your teeth?"

"Sorry. Forgot."

He cleaned his teeth carefully at the hand basin.

"Ready *now*," he called.

Mona came in and sat down on the bed. Beyfus clambered up beside her and nuzzled against her shoulder. Mona stroked his hair.

"Beyfus baby," she said fondly.

Still nuzzling, Beyfus placed his hands together.

"Our Father," he said, "who art in heaven, hallowed be Thy name. Thy kingdom come . . ."

Mona stroked his hair and heard him out. Then she helped him into bed and tucked him up.

"Why a Church of England prayer?" she asked. "Jewish prayers are much stronger."

"And was not Christ a Jew? This was Christ's prayer, Mona. It belongs to no church."

Mona went to the bedroom door and put her hand up to the light switch.

"Lights out now," she said. "Good night."

"Good night, Mona. Thank you for my nice evening. See you in the morning."

"See you in the morning . . ."

Mona turned off the light and closed the door very gently. She paced across the sitting-room, gathering up her cloak as she went, turned off the lights by the outer door, and walked down the stairs. Outside the stars were shining, Bootes and the Bear, which men also call the Wain, which ever circles in its own place and watches Orion. But Mona, who did not much care for Homer, looked neither for the Bear nor Orion. She stuck her head forward, fixed her eyes on the ground five yards in front of her, placed her hands behind her back, and then strode away through the sleeping college, thinking of good battles past and the better ones to come.

# PART TWO

# THE KING'S MATTER

"BENEDIC, DOMINE, NOBIS," intoned Robert Reculver Constable, Provost of Lancaster College, "*et his consiliis nostris.* Amen."

"Amen," repeated the nineteen other Members of the Council, each standing behind his chair at The Great Table of the King's Matter, which was a massive rectangle of oak, twenty-five yards in length, and used only for such assemblages.

"Why do you summon us this day?" boomed Grantchester Pough, as Senior Fellow, from his place at the bottom of the table.

"To lend ear and give counsel."

"And shall we speak with truth and without fear?"

"With truth and without fear and in good fellowship, for our Sovereign Lady the Queen will have it so."

"Then God save our Lady the Queen," bawled Grantchester Pough, meaning every word of it, "and God be merciful to the soul of our good Lord and Founder, the Blessed Henry of Lancaster. Amen."

And from all, "Amen."

"Is it your will that I proceed?" the Provost resumed.

"It is our will."

All sat except the Provost himself.

"What matter, Master Provost?" called Pough up the table.

"Listen and mark."

Since this exchange made an end of the preliminary formalities, Balbo Blakeney and several others lit cigarettes. The Provost rootled among some papers, cleared his throat, then rootled again. From behind him the portrait of Provost Lauderdale, who had been butchered on the College Stones

279

when denying entry to the Parliament men, scowled over his head and all along the table. Jacquiz Helmut arranged his scarlet gown to his liking, while the Senior Fellow produced, from somewhere about him, a Rabelaisian throat spray and with a noise like a cataract squirted his yawning tonsils.

Then there was silence in the Long Chamber while they all waited for what they knew the Provost must say.

"Principal Bursar," the Provost said.

The Provost sat. The Principal Bursar rose, it now being a quarter past ten of the clock, and occupied them, until lunch time, with a reading of the accounts as cast on All Fools' Day. None might leave while this went on, and none might join the Council for the first time after it was done. The rule was quite clear : either members attended from the very first word of the meeting, or they stayed away. A very good rule it was too : for since the condition of being allowed to speak or vote on any measure was that a man must first sit through at least three hours of the Principal Bursar's arithmetical recitation, the frivolous or impatient, should ever such be elected in error to the Council, were speedily discouraged from bearing any part at the Great Table of the King's Matter.

At half past one, the accounts being by now threequarters read, the Council adjourned for the traditional collation of spiced herring and small beer.


"Shall I like this Mayerston?" said Hetta to Hugh, over a sandwich lunch in a riverside pub.

Hugh had an uneasy feeling that she wouldn't.

"You'll find out when you meet him tonight," he said.

"Why not until tonight?" asked Hetta. "I mean, if it's all so urgent and exciting."

"I expect he's busy until then," said Hugh, who suddenly had another uneasy feeling that perhaps Mayerston, like Dracula, never emerged from his lair until sundown.

"And you say there's an important part for me?" persisted Hetta.

"Very."

"Then why not tell me?"

"Mayerston will explain it far better."

"No one explains things better than you."

"It's not just a matter of explaining," Hugh said. "We want you to *believe* in what you're going to do."

"So long as you want it," said Hetta, "I'll believe in it."

Hetta was still feeling guilty about her little display of weakness in the Great Court of Lancaster the previous afternoon.

"Nevertheless," said Hugh, passing her a sandwich, "you'd best hear about it from Mayerston. So eat up your nice salami, and then we can go."

"Back to your room?" said Hetta eagerly.

"Not this afternoon. It's so nice I thought we'd take a punt down to Grantchester."

"That's not your sort of thing at all. Punts down to Grantchester . . . Like a lord in an Edwardian novel."

"It's one of the things," said Hugh, "that I want us to do while we still can."

"What can you mean? You really are being most frightfully peculiar today. It's something to do with this Mayerston. I can feel it."

"Look," said Hugh: "either eat up that fucking sandwich and come with me on the river, or go home. But for Christ's sake stop ticking like a bloody clock."

Hugh, though sometimes brisk with Hetta, had always been tender at bottom. But the speech which he had just made now was not tender, at bottom or anywhere else. There was a new and ugly tone in his voice which made Hetta both resentful and fearful. Nevertheless, she bit back her tears and her salami sandwich and then, not asking for time to go to the loo though she wanted to rather badly, accompanied Hugh to the boat house which adjoined the pub.


At a quarter past four in the Long Chamber, Lord Beyfus was well under way. The Principal Bursar had finished his reading at half past three; the accounts had been put to the vote and passed; and the Provost had ordered that they would now discuss possible uses for the quarter-million pound surplus to which full reference had been made in the statement they had just approved. Lord Beyfus had then risen (underneath the portrait of Provost Dawley, who, having lost his faith in Christianity one bright morning in 1873, had hanged himself from the top of the south-east tower of the chapel soon after breakfast the same day) and asked the Provost's leave *"orationem severiorem exigere"*—to push out a stiffish oration, i.e. one longer than the fifteen minutes which custom prescribed as the normal limit. Constable had bowed and consented; Jacquiz had reminded everyone within earshot that in any case Beyfus, as a peer of the realm, did not need special permission; and now, at a quarter past four, Beyfus was coming round on his last lap. Or so everybody hoped.

". . . All of which considerations," quacked Beyfus, "moral, social, educational, spatial and financial, can be satisfied by a scheme which I will summarise as follows :

"One. The erection, on Scholars' Meadow, at the approximate cost of £100,000, of a students' hostel to hold one hundred extra students.

"Two. The erection, on the rear lawn of the college, again at the rough cost of £100,000, of a second hostel to hold a hundred more extra students."

"On the rear lawn of the college?" said Ivor Winstanley, in tones which combined horror at this proposal with something like reverence for its sheer enormity.

"I have the ear of the Council," snapped Beyfus.

"But the rear lawn—"

"—Lord Beyfus has our ear, Mr Winstanley," said Constable sternly. "Lord Beyfus . . ."

"Three," said Beyfus. "The £50,000 which will then remain from the surplus should be spent on providing the two hundred extra students in their new hostels with a variety of attached amenities of an experimental nature. It will be neither possible nor desirable to cater for these students on the basis of the present facilities and social routines of this college : not possible, because there is simply not the space – in Hall, for example, or in the Junior Common Room, or in the College Library; not desirable because such facilities and routines are in any case retrograde. We must therefore experiment with new oecological patterns of a kind appropriate to the new society for which we are striving.

"The two principles behind these experimental patterns must be (a) rationalised co-operation in environmental function, and (b) social integration within the norm. The first requires that all domestic management should be undertaken by the students themselves : meals must be provided, cleaning and repairs performed, *by* students *for* students on a system of rota which will ensure that all bear an equal part. I do not propose to go into detail here and now; but a good example of what I envisage is the Student Co-operative Cafeteria, which will replace, for those in the new hostels and ultimately for every member of the college, the outdated institution known as Hall. Servants will of course be unknown. All service will be self-service. All food will be purchased, prepared and cooked by teams of students. No resident in the hostels will be exempt from taking turns of duty : even graduates and Fellows will assist in the meanest chores – which, however, will be much mitigated by the use of the most modern machinery and techniques."

Beyfus looked to left and to right, surveying the looks of incredulity or disgust which had now appeared on nearly every face except that of Constable, which was frozen in regal indifference, and that of Tony Beck, which wore a sly grin as if to say, "Catch me doing the washing up." In one quarter and one only was there evidence of friendship unalloyed : Oliver Clewes, the Chaplain, was staring at Beyfus with a fatuous look of devotion such as would have discredited a half-witted Spaniel. Beyfus hurriedly removed his eyes from Clewes and raised them to the portrait on the opposite wall; this was of Dean Peregrine Runcible-Walpole, who, in 1897, had published a volume of lyrical verse containing the famous stanza :

The boys on Belmont beaches
Do as nature teaches,
    If no one's there to frown :
When from high the kind sun reaches,
They toss away their breeches—
Show behinds like ripened peaches
    With the same soft down.

Finding Runcible-Walpole's gooey gaze almost as intolerable as Clewes's, Beyfus flicked his eyes one portrait to the right (the 14th Lord Seymour of Saxmundham, a rather moderate major-general of Division in World War I) and launched himself down the home straight.

"The second principle behind the experimental patterns to be embodied in the new hostels," he said, "I have designated as social integration within the norm. By this I mean the encouragement of behaviour that emphasises communal awareness rather than personal preference. Communal awareness will already, of course, have been fostered by the common performance of domestic tasks; but the concept must be taken a stage further, to include hours and methods of study and even leisure pastimes.

"For it is no longer acceptable that certain individuals, who have a liking for intellectual pursuits, should be allowed to enjoy these in privacy for as long as they choose and at the expense of their fellow students. I say, 'At the expense of their fellow students', because by shutting themselves off from their contemporaries they are not only making a claim to be different from them but also making a bid to achieve better degrees, and so higher esteem and reward, than the average student can expect.

"Thus the average student, going about his normative pleasure-cycle while the few remain immersed in their books, is made to feel excluded, guilty, insecure and inferior. To prevent this, students will be accommodated by threes : three students to a good-sized bed-sitting-room, which latter cannot possibly be regarded by any single student as a place of privacy or retreat. If a student wishes to work, he must go to the hostel work-room, which will be equipped with specially programmed audio-visual devices (thus reducing individualistic elements in study-processess), and which will be open from 9 a.m. to 1 p.m. and from 4.30 p.m. to 6. This will ensure that outside the approved working hours no student will be able either to advantage himself by extra effort or to withdraw himself from the community into a closed and selfish world of scholarship. All will be compelled to participate in the normative leisure patterns appropriate to their age-group.

"Such patterns, in the past, have had a regrettable tendency to be distorted by aggressive and individual pleasure-pursuits. So in order to ensure that patterns of a strictly modern typology are developed and conformed to, we shall spend a large part of the £50,000 balance on recreation rooms of a socio-creative play-potential.

"In this way," Beyfus concluded, "the numbers of the college will be doubled, a large amount of unproductive land will be utilised, and new ideals of social obligation and community-orientated function will be introduced among us. I should add that to make the experiment really worth while, the residents of the hostels should be of both sexes. There is nothing in the statutes to prevent this Council from declaring that the college shall henceforth be co-educational – a reform much to be desiderated according to current theories of moral hygiene and sexual equality."

Phew, thought Beyfus as he sat down; what I go through for Mona. I only hope she'll be pleased by what I've said, because nobody else will be.

But in fact he was to be proved wrong in this before many hours were out; even there and then, he was not wholly without allies. True, when the Provost called for a preliminary vote to determine how many members of the Council favoured the general sense of Beyfus's proposals, the only people who signified support were Tony Beck and Oliver Clewes; but Tom Llewyllyn and (surprisingly) the Senior Fellow both announced that they wished to make further propositions on not wholly dissimilar lines. When, therefore, the council adjourned for tea at half past four, the Baron Beyfus felt his cause was not entirely dead.


During the tea interval, Tom Llewyllyn remembered the conversation which he had had with Daniel Mond, the previous afternoon, about Fielding Gray. Bored and fretful after the slow hours of words and figures, he felt a sudden compulsion to make contact with someone – with anyone – outside Lancaster College, whose tedious business was holding him a prisoner in the Long Chamber through this bright day of gaudy spring. So he sat down at the writing desk in the Fellows' Parlour and wrote a brief note in which he suggested that Fielding propose himself for an overnight stay any time after May the first.

"As you probably know," he wrote, "Daniel Mond is here. He thinks you owe him an explanation, and I agree with him. But however that may be, we shall both be very pleased to see you here. It's been far too long . . ."

He did not know Fielding's exact address in Broughton Staithe, so after some hesitation he addressed the envelope to Major Fielding Gray (he'll like the old title, Tom thought) c/o Gregory Stern the publisher – Fielding's as well as his own. He then dropped the letter in the box for franking and despatch, and felt very slightly better. A door which had long been closed was about to be re-opened.


"Tea on the lawn?" said Hetta at Grantchester when Hugh suggested this. "You'll be reading Rupert Brooke next."

"What's wrong with tea on the lawn?"

"You said yesterday that no one must have tea till half past six. To be like the workers, you said."

"When in Rome," said Hugh, "one may as well enjoy her amenities. Until they are swept away."

"That doesn't sound like you," said Hetta suspiciously.

"Do you or do you not want some tea, for Christ's sake?"

So nasty was his tone that Hetta wanted to say, No, she

didn't; but her need to piddle was now scarcely containable, and she supposed that the tea place would run to a ladies' lavvy.

After tea, the Senior Fellow addressed the Council in the Long Chamber. Like Lord Beyfus, he said gleefully, he too was going to suggest an experiment. Mindful that their Royal and pious Founder had ordained that his college should be a place of "godliness and good learning", he would like to depose that neither of these virtues was encouraged by the daily and swinish consumption of butcher's meat, which fuddled the intellects and overheated the blood. It was time this abuse was checked. He, Pough, therefore put forward the following scheme : let them build a new hostel, on Scholars' Meadow if nowhere else could be found for it, for the accommodation of up to one hundred students; let all these students be fed from a vegetarian kitchen which would be attached to the hostel, and let them give their solemn undertaking that they would not indulge at any time either in the flesh of fish, foul or quadruped, or in alcoholic beverages. At the end of two years after the erection of this hostel, let them compare the moral and academic records of the hundred vegetarians with those of the other undergraduates in the college. When they were satisfied that the former were incomparably superior, let them set about making plans for re-organising the kitchens of the entire college on a vegetarian basis, and for the total prohibition of alcohol within its walls.

It was typical of the old gentleman that he should have satirised his own fads in order to ridicule someone else's. When he finished, there was a low murmur of appreciation from all except Beyfus, Clewes and Beck. Sanity had now been firmly re-established, everyone felt, and high time too.

"Better now?" said Hugh when Hetta came back from having her pee.

"Yes. I mean no. There was never anything wrong with me."

"I'm sorry if I've been stroppy, Het. The thing is . . . I've been upset. By Mayerston."

"I thought you admired him . . . Goodie, what lovely scones."

"I do admire him. But the more I think about him . . . and I think about him all the time . . . the more I feel there's something wrong."

"Don't you trust him?"

"I trust him all right."

"Then don't you *like* him? Try this yummy cream."

"I *do* like him. I find him very attractive."

"*Hugh*, you don't mean . . . ?

"No, Het. It's not a physical attraction. I only wish it were, because then it could be easily explained. As it is . . . I almost feel as if there'd been some sort of transference . . . as if in some way he were beginning to possess me."

"Like a witch?"

"You mean a warlock. No. Warlocks use demons to do their work. Whatever . . . is affecting me, is coming from Mayerston himself."

"If you ask me," said Hetta, "it was all that brandy you drank. Half a bottle each, you said. No wonder you still feel peculiar."

"I dare say you're right. Dear, sweet, uncomplicated Hetta." He raised her hand from the table and kissed it.

"Oh my goodness me," said Hetta, flustered with pleasure: "can I have some more scones?"

"We ought to get back."

"There's plenty of time."

"No, there isn't. You've got to go out to Cherry Hinton and change."

"*Change*, Hugh?"

"Me too. Before we meet Mayerston."

After Pough's little triumph, Tom Llewyllyn told the table a few home truths.

"It is not acceptable," said Tom, "either by the Government, or by the informed public, or by the student population throughout the country, that a college should occupy as much space as this one does and yet should have such a comparatively small role of undergraduates. Leave politics aside, you must still face up to the general view that Lancaster is an educational luxury . . . that it is *uneconomic*. I say this with regret, because in my opinion it stands for something which is not reckonable in terms of utility; but that is how the world reckons, and these days we must reckon with the world. When it is generally known that on top of everything else we have just acquired a surplus of £250,000, the cry will be for a visible and practical investment in the future of the nation's youth.

"Rather than have importunate suggestions thrust on us from outside, we must be ready with a scheme of our own. It should be a scheme prominent enough to satisfy the Government, utilitarian enough to satisfy the philistine public at large, and radical enough to satisfy student aspirations. It should also be . . . malleable enough . . . to fit within the existing framework. In short, gentlemen, it must be a scheme which combines a maximum of ostensible bustle with a minimum of real change."

Elegant, thought Constable, but flippant. Still the journalist.

"You may find such a dictum surprising in the mouth of a socialist," Tom continued, "but the truth is that the only valid motive for changing anything is to improve what is bad while preserving what is good. Schemes of the kind which the Government, the public, the students at present favour would do neither. Such schemes simply represent change for the sake of change – as futile a thing as speed for the sake of speed.

"But this is not to say there is no room for improvement here. The college *is* rather too ample for the student body it contains; and while over-crowding will always bring banality and deterioration, under-crowding can make for sterility and smugness. I think, then, that institutional health and social justice alike require that we effect an increase . . . a very carefully calculated increase . . . in our numbers."

My word, thought Beyfus, Mona will have a fit when she hears about this. Particularly if he gets his way. And what's more she'll blame me. She won't tuck me up for a month. She's so unfair, Mona is, even when a fellow does his best.

"On my view," Tom was saying, "we could contain 25 per cent more students, i.e. about sixty, without seriously compromising our standards. On my view also, that represents the minimum scope of the change we must make in order to remain unmolested. A 25 per cent increase will combine duty with prudence. But since it is, after all, a bare minimum, it will be necessary to publicise it in somewhat inflated terms. That is what I meant by bustle.

"So there must be a fanfare of trumpets, gentlemen, followed by the immediate announcement that there is to be a new building on the Western half of Scholars' Meadow. The noisiness of the announcement will satisfy the Government. The mean-spirited intention to build over a pretty wilderness will satisfy the parsimonious public. The breach of statute and tradition will satisfy the disgruntled students, who will conceive that a stone laid on hitherto protected property is a stone worthy of the New Jerusalem. As for ourselves, we shall not be without comfort if we examine the scheme closely. We shall still have half our Meadow, for it is, let me repeat, only on the Western half that we shall build; and since we need only build for sixty people, and have a great deal of money with which to do it, we can make ourselves a building both small and beautiful which will enhance rather than hamper the view of Sitwell's and the Chapel."

A preliminary vote of eleven members (i.e. more than 50 per cent) in favour of Tom's general sense guaranteed that his project would now be debated in detail. Should it receive, after debate, as many as twelve votes (60 per cent), it would then go on a short list of selected proposals, one of which would ultimately be adopted. For ultimate adoption, a proposal would need not only more votes than any other on the short list but also a minimum of fifteen (75 per cent), so that even after it was established which proposal on the short list had majority support, a bloody-minded caucus of six could keep it out indefinitely. However, all that was still a long way off; Tom's job here and now was to win the extra vote needed to get his scheme short-listed; and this meant that he must throw some enticing inducement to one of the members who had voted against it. Tom would not get the chance to do this himself until he exercised the proposer's privilege of winding up the debate; in the meantime, therefore, while Jacquiz Helmut was making a pithy speech of objection, Tom studied the list of his opponents, pondering whether he had in his pocket a carrot red enough for this or that donkey.

The opponents of Tom's scheme were: Jacquiz Helmut, who was clearly quite beyond redemption; Lord Beyfus, who doubtless considered that Mona would not approve anything so moderate; Oliver Clewes, who was infatuated with Beyfus; Tony Beck, who presumably (like Mona/Beyfus) wanted something more extreme; Ivor Winstanley, an old ally of Helmut's; Andrew Ogden, the Dean of Chapel, a respected and temperate conservative; the Senior Fellow, Grantchester Pough, another temperate right-winger, who had previously supported the idea of a new building but had obviously done so only in order to introduce his own little joke; the Lay Dean, a man of no account except in this, that he had never been known to change his mind; and Balbo Blakeney, who had done nothing all day except smoke cigarettes and look bilious.

Of these nine, then, it was clear to Tom that only two might conceivably be converted to his cause in time to swing the impending vote. One was Balbo Blakeney, for the good reason that Balbo was fascinated by architecture and might well respond to Tom's appeal for a really beautiful and expensive building which would set off and not disgrace Balbo's beloved Chapel. Against this was the fact that Balbo had as yet shown no sign of responding, having scarcely even deigned to listen; he had simply sat there scowling in a cloud of smoke and had cast his adverse vote without hesitation. This confirmed what Tom and others had already surmised – that Balbo was incubating some scheme of his own and was hoarding his entire will and energy for its later prosecution. And what, Tom wondered, would it turn out to be? As to that, time would show; meanwhile he must concentrate on his only other potential convert.

This was Andrew Ogden. True, Andrew usually voted with Winstanley and Pough, and he had done so firmly enough just now; but he differed from the other two in this, that he was very much more sensitive to the body of Christian precept and in particular to those parts of it which advocated, to use the rough lay equivalents, the qualities of "fairness" and "decency". These, to Andrew, were more than mere gentlemanly attributes, they were a religious passion. It followed that one might probaby get through to him, not by advancing politic reasons for letting sixty new students in, but by urging that it would be "unfair" and "indecent" to keep them out. This meant, thought Tom, that his method would have to change from the rational to the emotional – no bad thing, perhaps, in a speaker who was winding up. Having settled his tactical approach, he assumed a mild and ingenuous expression, and beamed charitably across the table at Jacquiz Helmut, who was now concluding his address.

". . . Only necessary to say," perorated Jacquiz, "though without any malice, that Mr Llewyllyn's suggestion has the audacity of total inexperience. For he is, after all, only a temporary Fellow, only recently co-opted as a colleague on our Council, and we need seek no further than this to explain the crudeness of his proposal and the simple-minded facility with which he has preferred it."

Tom went on beaming at Jacquiz until he was seated, then turned his eyes up languishingly at Tony Beck, who had risen in the place next his own.

"The truly disgraceful thing," said Beck, who wished to place himself on record, in case of future investigation, as having expressed the orthodox new-left attitude, "is that Mr Llewyllyn should be so impervious to real human need. He has suggested that all of this huge sum be expended on a building which will hold only sixty students, and he is clearly far more anxious that it should be aesthetically pleasing than that

it should fulfil any social function. In the face of such heart-
less irresponsibility, one can only respond with amazement and
indignation. Let Mr Llewyllyn look out from his ivory tower
at the mass of young faces which are turned towards us –
bright, eager faces, hungry for truth and knowledge – and then
let him tell them, if he dare, that he has room for only sixty of
them because a larger building would block his cherished
view."

This speech cheered Balbo Blakeney up enormously. He
positively rocked with pleasure all through it, and clapped his
hands loudly when it was over.

"You beautiful, rotten bastard," Balbo said; "you keep it
up like this, and you'll be king of the revolution."

But after this little outburst he slumped back into his cloud
of cigarette smoke and there remained while speaker succeeded
speaker and Tom himself at last concluded the debate.

". . . There is a lot," said Tom, turning his eyes on Andrew
Ogden and beginning to blink a little, "in what Mr Beck has
said about the heartlessness of denying entrance to those who
are seeking for knowledge and truth." A decided shift in
emphasis from my first speech, he thought, but by this time of
the day memories are short. "With Mr Beck, I say to you that
it would be . . . shameful and indecent . . . to turn such away
from our gate." Andrew Ogden was twitching : but was it in
sympathy with his words or in contempt at his ploy? "At the
same time, since we cannot admit the whole world, let us
ensure that those we do admit – and surely sixty is a substantial
number – are received into surroundings and accommodation
worthy of their noble and aspiring youth."

Loathing himself for being capable of such a speech, Tom
sat down to wait and see whether it had done the trick. When
the Provost took the vote, it was revealed that Tom had lost
one supporter, in Daniel Mond, but that he had gained two –
Andrew Ogden, as he had hoped, and also Oliver Clewes. On
the final count, then, Tom now had twelve votes for his proposal, which would therefore be entered on the Provost's
Tabula Rerum Graviorum, or short list.

"All right," said Mayerston to Tony Beck: "what happened in there today?"

Beck told him. Then:

"When are you seeing Hugh Balliston again?" he asked.

"Very soon now. And his girl friend with him."

"A word of warning," said Beck. "The girl is honest."

"So is Hugh."

"Hugh is also clever and proud of it. He prides himself on being able to follow people, to appreciate their deeper meanings. Since he wants his appreciation to be appreciated, he is liable to go further than he would really wish in making it evident. To prove that he has understood, he acts out his understanding."

"In short," said Mayerston, "he is obliging because vain."

"Whereas Hetta, you will find, is neither."

"She obliges him, presumably."

"She loves him."

"Then she will do what he tells her."

"Unless," said Tony Beck, "she should think it unworthy."

"Unworthy of her?"

"Unworthy of him. At bottom she is rather old-fashioned, you see, despite her parade of contemporary opinions. If Hetta has a friend or a lover, she is eager for his honour."

"Why, Danny," asked Tom, "did you vote against me?"

"What does it matter? You got your way."

"And not a bad way. You were in favour of it at first. So why did you change?"

"Because I didn't care for your last speech."

"I had to do something . . . to get extra votes."

"But you did yourself a disservice," said Daniel, "by making yourself cheap."

"Andrew Ogden didn't think so. I won him over."

"You also," said Daniel, "won over Oliver Clewes. Not a recommendation."

"Yes, that did surprise me."

"It shouldn't have done. Clewes has an instinctive affinity with the spurious. That is why he supported Beyfus earlier on."

"But my proposal was not spurious."

"Your speech was."

"Don't quarrel, Danny."

"I shouldn't dream of it," Daniel croaked. "You've got your way for the time being, and not at all a bad way either, as you remark. For most people . . . even for Constable . . . that is enough. But I value you, Tom, more than I value your proposal, and I was sad that you could be so false."

"Shall you go on voting against me?"

"No. Provided you argue honestly from now on, as you did in your first speech, I shall support you . . . unless a better proposal is made by someone else."

"Fair enough, I suppose . . . I've written to Fielding Gray, Danny. Asked him to come over for a night."

"Good."

"But they say this Yankee woman of his doesn't like to let him out of her sight. I hope she doesn't tag along."

"Fielding has a sense of the appropriate," said Daniel. "He knows that women can't stay in this college."

"But does she? Anyway, Yankee women love pushing their way in where they're not wanted."

"All women do."

"And once they're in, it takes a steam-crane to get them out."

"I shouldn't worry, Tom. Fielding has a knack of gliding away when it suits him. Or had when I knew him. He just used to . . . disappear . . . often when one wanted him most."

"Like he disappeared with that Greek boy, damn him."

"So if he decides to give his American lady the slip for a night," said Daniel, "no power on earth will stop him."


When Hugh and Hetta met Mayerston in the Eagle Tavern as arranged, Mayerston was dressed in a roll-neck sweater and whip-cord trousers. Since Hugh was in his best (and only) suit and Hetta was got up to the nines (on Hugh's instructions) in a shimmering cocktail outfit, this was rather disconcerting.

"How nice you both look," said Mayerston, "but you shouldn't have bothered. I thought," he said to Hugh, "that we might try that place you mentioned last night. 'Haq's', didn't you say?"

"Dinner's on me," said Hugh stiffly.

"As you like. But let's make it Haq's, eh?"

Hetta began to hate Mayerston already, and they went to Haq's, where they sat at a square plastic table with legs of differing length. Hugh had a jet black mixed grill, Hetta dropped a noodle in her lap because the waiter jogged her elbow, and Mayerston ate a huge plate of fried meat balls in curry sauce with evident enjoyment. On Mayerston's suggestion they all drank something called Seven Up, though Hetta made it quite clear that she would have preferred Coca Cola. What made things even worse was that Mayerston said absolutely nothing during the entire meal, except to ask the waiter for three more bottles of Seven Up, which Hetta thought, he should have left to Hugh. Only when three cups of gritty and light brown coffee (Turkish) accompanied by some cubes of scurfy gelatine (Delight) were set before them did Mayerston at last open his mouth with any purpose other than to shove curried meat ball into it.

"That was very nice," Mayerston said. "How clever of Hugh to know about this place." He sipped his coffee. "Delicious," he said to Hetta : "don't you agree?"

Hetta was too miserable to do anything but shrug.

"Cheer up," said Mayerston : "there's a treat in store for you."

"What?" said Hetta.

"Tomorrow night," said Mayerston, "you're going to sleep with Hugh in Lancaster."

"*What?*" said Hetta.

"All night long," Mayerston said.

"It's a protest," said Hugh, and looked exceedingly silly.

This was too much. Suddenly and fiercely, Hetta started to

blubber. She couldn't find her hanky, and her nose was blocked by snot which bubbled like a cauldron every time she tried to draw her breath.

"Never mind," said Mayerston, passing her a large silk affair which smelt of Verbena, "use this. And then, I think, we'll have a change of scene."

The change of scene turned out to be a tiny pub near Little St. Mary's. Mayerston led them into a back room, where there was a sideboard on which stood a pot of coffee and several kinds of liqueur. Comforted by a cup of the coffee, which was very sweet and very strong, and then further consoled by two large glasses of something white which tasted deliciously of greengages, Hetta began to feel happier than she had all day. Although she still didn't care much for Mayerston, she was quite ready to tolerate him, and when, a few minutes later, he started talking, she listened politely and calmly, while sipping a third glass of the greengage drink which someone had thoughtfully poured for her.

"Let me explain," said Mayerston, "what this is all about. At the meeting of Lancaster College Council today, Lord Beyfus made a remarkable and far-seeing proposal of what might be historic importance." He gave a brief précis of Tony Beck's account of this. "And what is more," he went on, "he also suggested that all this be implemented on a co-educational basis."

"Don't be soft," giggled Hetta; "they'll never let women in there."

"Why not?" said Hugh fiercely.

"They'd spoil it," said Hetta. "Women spoil anything like that, if you let them interfere. It's our nature. Like reading private letters which people leave about, or making people talk when they just want to sit quiet and read."

"Nevertheless," said Mayerston, "and although you may disagree with certain details, Beyfus has put forward a scheme of revolutionary significance. You do see that?"

"By Castro, yes," said Hetta, banging down her glass.

"And what has happened?" said Mayerston.

"Well, what?" said Hetta.

"The College Council declined even to discuss it. Instead, they discussed at length, and then placed on their short list for later consideration, a miserable apology of a plan, which was supposedly liberal in conception but was in fact just a clever piece of reactionary obstruction. The Fellows of Lancaster are trying to fob society off by building a kind of glorified summer-house."

"Now hold on," said Hugh: "a new building to house sixty undergraduates, I heard."

"In relation to modern educational problems," insisted Mayerston, "they might as well build a potting shed. Here is this golden opportunity, and no one except Beyfus has the imagination, or even the inclination, to rise to it. Beyfus has been turned down like a piece of bad fish. So what do we do?"

"We pro-*test*," said Hetta, throwing her glass over her shoulder.

"Right," said Mayerston. "And this is how we do it. We shall give out, all over Cambridge and all over England, that in protest against Beyfus's rejection you and Hugh are going to sleep a whole night together in Hugh's room in the Fellows' Garden Hostel of Lancaster College."

"What's that got to do with Beyfus's rejection?"

"It's a magnificent gesture. You'll be breaking the oldest and strictest rule of them all. You'll be asserting your human right to freedom and to love."

"Love," said Hetta, "is just as much fun in the afternoon."

"But you have a *right* to love at night."

"Beds that size are a bloody bore for a whole night," said Hetta, "and a girl needs her sleep. I'm quite happy with things as they are, thank you. A good fuck in the afternoon or soon after supper, and then home sweet home to cold cream and beddy-byes."

"Your personal preference is not at issue," said Hugh. "The point is, we have a right to nights."

"Do stop that ridiculous jingle," Hetta said. "A rightful Night full of Petting and Sweating," she improvised. "I just don't want it."

"Well, you're bloody well going to have it."

"Just think of the slogans we can get up," said Mayerston. "'They may muzzle Beyfus, but they can't Lock Out Love.' You see the association? Love equals freedom equals Beyfus's proposals for co-educational hostels."

"I can't imagine anything drearier."

"You'd be the heroine of the campus."

"They don't have a campus here," said Hetta, "and I don't want to be a heroine. I like being private."

"If I can risk my career," said Hugh, "you can risk your privacy."

"And that's another thing – it's all a wicked waste. They'd just chuck you straight out of Cambridge the very next morning."

"Just let them try," said Mayerston with relish. "We'd get up a mass demonstration. We'd threaten so much trouble they wouldn't dare."

"Demonstrations," said Hetta, "threats. It's all people like you can think of. Why must there always be people like you," she snarled at Mayerston, "to come along and spoil things."

Mayerston looked at Hugh, who came very close to Hetta.

"Hetta," Hugh said, "you do believe in all the things I've been teaching you? All the things we discussed last winter – you do believe in them, don't you, Het?"

"Yes. But what's that got to do with it?"

"A time comes, Het, when you have to show that you believe."

"I'll tell anyone who wants to listen."

"You have to *act*."

"Is that what he says?"

She glared across at Mayerston.

"Not only him. And anyway, heart, it's true."

He put his mouth to her ear and whispered. Hetta slumped.

"All right," she said dully, "I'll do it."

"That's not enough. You must *want* to do it."

Hetta made a great effort. She drew in her breath and shook her hair back and smiled up at Hugh.

"I believe you, Hugh, and I believe in you. I want to do it for your sake."

"For its own sake."

"For its own sake *and* yours."

"All right, heart."

Hugh looked up and nodded at Mayerston. Mayerston smiled back at him, and Hugh felt a rippling surge of satisfaction like that which comes to a man when he rises and stretches his muscles after a long day in a narrow seat.

"Tomorrow night, then," Mayerston said.

"As soon as that?"

"Tomorrow night."

"I've decided," said Patricia to Tom out at Grantchester, "that I'll do what you suggested last night. I'll take Baby to London to have her teeth done there."

"Good. Take your time about the arrangements. I want you to have a really nice little holiday. You look tired."

"So do you, Tom."

"This Council meeting. I had to make two speeches."

But Patricia wasn't interested in the Council.

"Tom," she said, "this afternoon, at that place down by the river, there was a boy and a girl having tea together on the lawn. I saw them when I was walking past with Baby. I'd seen the boy before – when I came to your college once." She described the boy at some length. "Can you tell me who it was?"

"Second year man called Balliston," Hugh said. "He reads rather good essays to the Cabbala."

"The Cabbala?"

"College essay club. Why do you want to know about him?"

"He had a look of you. When we first met."

"I hadn't noticed."

"You wouldn't. It's not a resemblance, Tom, it's something in the eyes. He wanted something, just like you did then."

"I wanted success."

"You already had it."

"And I wanted you."

"Why?"

"Because I loved you."

"There was something more . . . something different."

"Very well. I also wanted somebody . . . before whom I could bow down. Bow down and abase myself."

"That's it," Patricia said : "that's what that boy wanted. But the girl who was with him was no good for that. *She* wanted to bow down to him."

"He'll find someone suitable," said Tom : "there are plenty of father figures around the place for him."

"*Father* figures?"

"The sex doesn't matter. It's just a question of finding someone convenient with a large pair of feet to grovel at. In Cambridge there are more male feet than female ones, so the odds are he'll end up venerating some don."

"How unhealthy."

"Why? Do you want him to venerate you?"

"Don't be so *silly*," Patricia said, and went to heat up the tinned stew for supper.


"So they turned you down?" Mona said to Beyfus.

"Absolutely flat."

"Then they must be *made* to understand."

"So what do you want, Mona? That I should put a bomb under the table?"

"We must talk to people in London. There must be pressure."

"But my dear, if this proposal of young Llewyllyn's goes through, people in London are going to be perfectly satisfied. A new building, they will tell each other, and sixty more undergraduates – what more can we ask for, they will say, than that?"

"It's not enough, Beyfus."

"Everyone else thinks it is, Mona, except you."

"And you, I should hope."

"And me. And Tony Beck."

"What will Tony Beck do about it?"

"I think he will try to make trouble through the students."

"In that case, Beyfus, we must join in."

"For God's sake, Mona. Do you want I should be carrying banners and throwing bricks? At my age?"

"If I can do it, so can you. And there's no need to throw bricks. We just lend our support by showing ourselves."

"Exhibiting ourselves is what you mean. Like two creatures in the Zoo."

"If you're going to talk like that, Beyfus, I shall leave."

"No, Mona. Please stay."

"Only if you promise to do what I say. After all, the students will be supporting you; why shouldn't you support them?"

"All right, Mona. I promise." Beyfus heaved an enormous sigh. "Provided you will always be there to."

Mona grasped his hand for a moment.

"Silly old Beyfus," Mona said.


"You were very quiet today," said Tony Beck to Balbo Blakeney.

"I had nothing to say."

"I should have thought that scheme of Llewyllyn's might have interested you. I can't support it, of course, but it sounded rather good."

"I know a better," Balbo said.

"Oh?"

"You're going to hate it."

"Try me."

"You wait till tomorrow." Balbo giggled and postured like a garden dwarf. "If I tell you tonight, you might have me murdered in my bed."


"That Council again tomorrow?" said Mrs Constable in the Provost's Lodge.

"Tomorrow and tomorrow and tomorrow," her husband replied.

"Oh dear . . . Shall I turn the television on?"

"Why?"

"There might be some news."

"Do you remember," said Constable, "how in the old days the announcer on Radio sometimes simply said, 'There is no news tonight'?"

"That can't happen these days. People feel entitled to news, so news there has to be."

And news there was. When the television set had warmed up, a voice said:

"Late night news flash from Cambridge University."

The grey screen flickered and heaved, then gave birth to a grinning and greasy young man with daintily permed hair.

"The students of Lancaster College, Cambridge," said the young man in a superior brand of common voice, "are preparing a protest against the rejection of a scheme proposed by Lord Beyfus, the well known expert on social problems, for the erection of new student hostels."

The screen flicked, and a still picture of Lord Beyfus appeared.

"We understand that Mr Hugh Balliston, the well known Lancaster student, has invited his girl friend, Miss Hetta Frith, to spend tomorrow night with him on the college precincts, to claim the right of all students to self-determination and freedom of choice. No woman has spent the night in any part of Lancaster College, except the Provost's Lodge, since the college was founded over five hundred years ago."

Lord Beyfus was replaced by a still of the Chapel.

"Our correspondent informs us that Mr Balliston's gesture is intended to draw the attention of the college authorities to the demands of youth and the future and to demonstrate student solidarity with Lord Beyfus and his radical proposals."

Constable switched off the set and went back to his book (Spengler's *Decline of the West*).

"What are you going to do about *that*?" said Mrs Constable.

"I'll decide in the morning."

"You could become a laughing stock."

"If you don't mind, I'm trying to read."

"You haven't much time, you know. Tomorrow night, the television said."

"So I heard, and thank you. But as far as I am concerned, 'There is no news tonight.'"

When the Council was seated the next morning, Balbo Blakeney asked and obtained leave to make an "orationem severiorem".

Let him draw the Council's attention, Balbo said, to the chief glory of the college: its Chapel. It was for this, and for the music that was made inside it, that Lancaster was known all over the world. Now, at the moment the Chapel, as far as was known, was in excellent structural condition; but it would be no news to members of the Council that other and older buildings throughout the country were deteriorating so fast that they could hardly be held together even by the most expert and diligent repairs, which were, incidentally, costing astronomical sums of money. The reason for all this was very simple : the surveys conducted at the critical period, i.e. when the buildings had attained an age of about five hundred years, had been inexpert and negligent, with the result that small but important flaws, having been patched over or simply ignored, had spread and multiplied until they constituted a massive and often radical threat to the entire fabric. Had proper attention been paid when such flaws first appeared, had their basic causes been sought out and fully investigated when found, then an early and comparatively inexpensive programme of restoration would have secured the future safety of such buildings as, say, York and Canterbury for many centuries to come. As it was, York Minster was propped about by brackets and crutches like a paraplegic, and Canterbury Cathedral was permanently encased in scaffolding like an old whore in a corset.

"My point is," said Balbo, "that our own Chapel has now just reached the critical age when the first serious flaws and lesions must be expected to originate. I have already, I think, detected a crack in that section of the roof which is over the choir stalls. It is quite plain what we must do if we are to avoid the disasters which carelessness has occasioned elsewhere: we must start, now, on an exhaustive survey of the Chapel from the foundations to the pinnacles, find out what faults are developing, and have them aborted, so to speak, in the womb. I will not trouble you with technical details; but I must stress that this is *not* to be merely a perfunctory routine inspection : every angle must be measured and re-measured, every inch of fabric must be examined, and the setting of every last pane of glass must be checked and tested.

"Furthermore, it will be necessary to determine what effect the continual passage of motor traffic just outside the college is producing on the Chapel's structure. If motor cars are found to constitute the slightest threat," said Balbo with relish, "then they must be stopped. As a Royal Foundation, we have powers within the University and the Borough (or City, as I believe it now calls itself) which can easily encompass the compulsory diversion of traffic. It will also be necessary to compute whether or not a serious threat is posed to structure or fabric by other forms of modern beastliness, present or foreseeable, such as supersonic aircraft. In such cases, remedies may not be so easily found as with the cits and their motors, but we are not incapable of exerting pressure in the highest places.

"All in all, then, this survey and the work which will be done as a result of it will be both long and costly; but neither as long nor as costly as it would be in fifty or a hundred years' time, when labourers and artisans will doubtless be even more pampered and overpaid than they are now. Indeed, if we neglect this opportunity we might never be able to afford another. We are entrusted, gentlemen, with one of the finest buildings in Christendom. By taking a relatively easy course of action now, we can ensure its survival, in its present and excellent condition, for perhaps another thousand years. Postpone this course of action, and the small patch of rot which we might find and root out today will become the loathsome and pervasive disease which is past cure tomorrow . . . just as the spirochaete multiplies from the single primary sore until the whole body is a mass of festering ulcers – and down comes all."

So far, Balbo's proposal had been sensible enough; after all, no one could seriously maintain that the preservation of one of the most famous buildings in the world was a frivolous or unworthy object. But all those who knew Balbo were aware that he would never rest content until he had contrived to hurt or annoy someone. Even his most sane and sound suggestions had to be used as weapons; in his hands, even the most peaceable instrument must somehow be converted into a bodkin that could puncture somebody's hide and be twisted in somebody's entrails. In the present case, it seemed almost impossible that so beneficent a scheme could be sharpened, as it were, to draw blood; yet everyone at the table knew that this would soon be contrived, the only question being how.

"In concrete terms," said Balbo, "I propose that £200,000 of the money which has come into our hands should be set aside to pay for an immediate Grand Survey of the Chapel and for the immediate action which that survey shows to be necessary. Any monies then remaining in this fund can be kept for the subsequent works which, however thorough we are now, time and chance are bound to impose on us. However, you will notice that of the quarter-million surplus there is still £50,000 for disposal; and I propose that it be used as follows:

"For the Choir School, gentlemen. The provision of sacred music of the proper standard is becoming annually more difficult and expensive. More difficult, because parents in this deplorable age think their children are better employed playing with technological gadgets than singing in choirs – even when they receive large bursaries to do so. More expensive, because private schools of the size of our own Choir School are now uneconomical to run. The Choir School contains twenty-four choristers and sixty others – a total of eighty-four. The economic figure for such a school is now estimated at a minimum of one hundred and fifty. The Choir School therefore runs at a substantial loss, reserves are being depleted, the headmaster is a worried man, petty saving, particularly on food and entertainments, is the order of the day, and morale is low.

"The result of all this is easy to see. The obtuseness of parents means that good choristers are harder, and in some years impossible, to come by; the standard of singing falls; and even that standard which is still maintained is compromised by the discontent and uneasiness which is induced in the choristers by the shoddiness and penury of their school. Children respond instinctively to such conditions – with cynicism, slackness and contempt.

"However, the standard of music is still tolerable. Our Chapel is not yet disgraced. All will be well if we spend money, first on increasing the choristers' bursaries and so winning over mean-minded parents, and secondly on subsidising the School itself, to the extent that it can become a place of which pupils – and, once more, parents – may be proud, instead of a third-rate lodging house. More money, much more money, for the Choir and the Choir School, gentlemen : a fund of fifty thousand pounds."

So there was Balbo's twist. He was proposing that £50,000 of the college's money should be spent on a preparatory school, thus provoking to bitterness and rage all those who were hostile to the private system of education, but at the same time ensuring the support of all the conservatives, who could never resist baiting the left on this particular issue. It was therefore a brilliant exercise both in malice and tactics : there could be, for Balbo, no more certain way of mustering a dependable body of friends and of causing real pain to his enemies

The attitudes expressed in the subsequent debate were predictable. Beyfus and Beck utterly condemned the notion that a great college should condone and enhance private privilege;

Tom Llewyllyn regretted that a proposal in many ways so enlightened should be vitiated by such insolent disrespect of contemporary opinion in the field of education; and Clewes, the Chaplain, proclaimed that Christianity was concerned, not with monuments to its dead past, but with "the sweet and humane spirit of its living future." The conservatives, on the other hand, spoke blandly and smugly of their duty to preserve "all that was precious in Architecture, Music and Religion" for the benefit of aspiring humanity and "of the newly literate masses who now, for the first time, are educated to the higher enjoyments." The more ill-tempered the left, the more smoothly public-spirited became the right; and at the end of it all Balbo's proposal was adopted for the short list by a vote of 13 to 7, the seven against it including Provost Constable. The Provost's vote, however, carried no more weight than any other man's; while the credit which the opposition might have had from his name and *auctoritas* was more than cancelled out by the shaming adherence of Clewes.

By the time the vote on Balbo's proposal had been taken, it was a quarter to one. So far, no reference had been made by any member of the Council to Hugh Balliston's threatened act of protest, although several of them, like Constable, had heard of it on television the night before and most of the rest had read short but prominent paragraphs about it in the morning newspapers. The reason for their reticence was one of protocol: Hugh's behaviour was an immediate matter for college discipline and might only be discussed, therefore, at the instance of one of the college officers, such as the Tutor or the Lay Dean, who were responsible in this field. Since the senior officer present who was directly concerned with discipline was the Provost himself, no one might raise the topic until he did; and since Constable's plan was to play the whole affair down, he had deliberately kept quiet about it when the Council assembled, in the hope that his omission would indicate to all that he did not regard Hugh or his protest as being of importance. Plainly, however, he must say something sooner or later, so he said it, briefly, now.

"This business of young Balliston and his woman," he remarked; "we shall simply ignore it. The college servants have been instructed to do likewise."

"And the Press?" asked the Senior Fellow. "The photographers?"

"If we ignore the whole thing and do nothing, there will be nothing for them to photograph. All that will happen is that at some time this evening Miss Frith and Mr Balliston will arrive at the Fellows' Garden Hostel and at some time tomorrow morning they will leave it again. A very dull picture that will make."

"The other students may demonstrate in their defence," said Andrew Ogden.

"If we do nothing, there will be nothing for the other students to defend them from."

"They might stage a celebration."

"What celebration?" said the Provost. "If they wish to sing bawdy songs outside Mr Balliston's door, then as far as I'm concerned they are welcome."

"They might form a sort of guard of honour . . . with banners and things . . . when the pair of them arrives at the hostel. That," said Ivor Winstanley, "would make quite a good photograph."

"The public," said Constable, "is sick and tired of photographs of foolish young men with banners."

"This one will have special interest . . . in the circumstances . . ."

"Just think of it," said Balbo: "banners saying FUCK FOR FREEDOM and things like that."

"I have thought of it," said Constable; "and let me assure you all that provided you take no notice of this puerile protest, nothing more will be heard of it."

He's got something up his sleeve, thought Tony Beck.

I hope Mona won't make me be in the guard of honour, thought Lord Beyfus.

I wonder whether I could bless the union as they go into the hostel, thought Oliver Clewes.

"So I rely on you, gentlemen," said Constable with finality : "if we behave as though nothing were happening, then in effect nothing will happen."

We'll see about that, thought Tony Beck.

Although Patricia Llewyllyn hated Cambridge (with much the same sort of jealousy as other wives hate their husbands' regiments or clubs), she loved the walk there from Grantchester along the river. Normally she had to go by bus, because the walk was too much for Baby, and this of course made her hate Cambridge all the more; but this morning, since she had managed to park Baby with a neighbour, she was free to go on foot, and her enjoyment of the journey mollified her feelings towards her place of destination.

In any case, it would have been unreasonable in her to resent Cambridge just now, as she was going there entirely of her own free will. Usually she went only if there was some necessary chore to attend to, like special shopping or a visit to Baby's dentist, but today she was going because she felt like it. She had no particular plan; there was nothing which she especially wanted to see; nobody was expecting her. She just felt like it. The walk will do me good, she thought : I need to get right away from Baby for a few hours. In which case, she thought, why am I not walking in the other direction, which would serve as well if not better for exercise? Why am I walking towards this town which fills me with loathing, as a rule, whenever I even think of it?

For the time being, it was easy enough to look down into the river reeds and evade the question. She imagined that she was in a punt, and that the punt was moored in among the reeds, secret from all the world, and that she was lying on her back looking up at the chasing clouds. The clouds were moving fast across the blue sky, but there was no wind where she lay in the punt; there was only the sun, warming her along all the length of her body, wooing her patiently and gently, yet gradually growing fiercer and more greedy as it rose from morning to noon. There was no one else there in the punt, only her, so she could take off her clothes if she wanted to and expose herself to the quickening rays . . .

She looked down at herself as she walked, imagining her large white limbs stripped and prone in the punt – and noticed, to her surprise, that she was wearing her best costume and a new pair of stockings. She had made no conscious decision, when dressing that morning, to put on any but her ordinary day clothes; yet here she was, dressed almost as if she were to meet someone for luncheon at Fortnum & Mason, her sister Isobel perhaps, except that she had no hat and was wearing sensible shoes. For a moment she panicked : had she indeed promised to meet Isobel in London that day, remembered when she got up but forgotten later? No, she told herself firmly. Lunch with Isobel at Fortnum's was in three days' time; she had arranged it on the telephone last night, so that they could discuss plans for when she brought Baby up to see the dentist. (She had hoped Isobel might ask them to stay in her house in Chelsea, but Isobel, though she seemed pleased they were coming, had made no mention of this on the telephone.) Confused and annoyed with herself, for she could not afford to wear out her best costume walking through meadows by the river, she found herself asking a second and more difficult question about the purpose of her walk. It was no longer, Why am I walking to this town I detest? It was, Why am I walking there all got up as I haven't been for years, except on special occasions?

Patricia shook her head and walked slowly on. Once more she looked down into the reeds by the margin of the river, and once more she willed herself into her secret punt, where she lay without moving, embraced by the kindly sun.


Hugh Balliston spent the morning reading Matthew Arnold's essays on Heine, Keats, Wordsworth and Shelley, and T. S.

Eliot's essays on Arnold, Shelley, Wordsworth and Keats, in order to strike a balance. He analysed the limitations of Arnold as a critic and those of T. S. Eliot as a poet writing criticism. He considered the defects of Heine as deposed by Arnold and of Shelley as deposed by Eliot, and then calculated to what extent these really were defects, as opposed to being virtues from a proper understanding of which Arnold and Eliot were precluded by their limitations as earlier determined by himself. Having spent a very happy four hours doing all this, Hugh left the Fellows' Garden Hostel, walked through the Fellows' Garden, across the Queen's Road and up the avenue past Scholars' Meadow, skirted the rear lawn and headed through the Great Court (without looking at the Chapel) toward the Lauderdale Gate, outside which he was to meet Hetta for lunch.

But before he was out of the Great Court, he was stopped by Tony Beck.

"I'm very glad to see you," Hugh said. "In your view, is Arnold sound on Heine?"

"Arnold's sound on most things, given his limitations. I've got a message for you to pass—"

"—Agreed. But what exactly were his limitations?"

"The same as yours," said Tony Beck. "At heart, he was an academic who wanted nothing to do with human life or emotions if he could possibly avoid it. When do you see Mayerston? To make final plans for tonight?"

"Early this evening," said Hugh, his face falling at the thought.

"Well, pass this on. The old men have a plan to deal with this protest of yours. They're simply going to ignore it."

"Good," said Hugh.

"What's that?"

"I'm glad there's not going to be any trouble."

"There'll be trouble," said Beck, "because trouble is what Mayerston wants. But it may be a bit harder to raise it if the old men deliberately don't react, so you'd best warn Mayerston what they're planning."

"Anything else?"

"Yes. I think the Provost has some other plan in reserve in case the Press shows too much interest."

"What plan?"

"He didn't tell the Council. Damned ill-mannered, I thought."

"Could it be," said Hugh, "that he doesn't entirely trust some of the members?"

Hugh smirked and passed out through the gate. No Hetta – though he himself was five minutes late. But what there was was some kind of tourist woman, sitting on the low wall which marked off the College Stones, and eyeing him as if she wanted to eat him. I wonder, thought Hugh, very theoretically, if she'd pay me. And then : but isn't there something faintly familiar about her? That really rather fine and statuesque appearance, and that face, worn but commanding, like the Lady Volumnia's? However, there was no time for further reflection along these lines, as panting Hetta now arrived at the double.

"Bus late," she spluttered.

"Never mind, heart. Lunch."

He doesn't recognise me, though Patricia Llewyllyn as Hugh and Hetta walked away. Well, why should he? We've never met properly. And after all, I ought to be content : I've *seen* him, which I suppose is why I came. But what shall I do now? I can't follow them. I can't go on sitting here. Would Tom give me lunch, if I went in and asked? But no, she thought, he'll be having a special lunch with that Council of his, all tucked away in private where no woman can get at them. I'd better just go home, she thought. Home to Baby. And not come here again. No one here wants me, not even Tom, and certainly not . . . *him*.


But if Patricia Llewyllyn didn't know where the Council was lunching, Mona Corrington did. She wasn't allowed in there, but she jolly soon had Lord Beyfus brought out.

"This protest," she said; "tonight in the Fellows' Garden Hostel."

"What do you know about it?"

"More than you, I dare say. One of those young men telephoned from *The Observer*. He'd heard, he said, that there was to be a special demonstration when the young couple arrived at the hostel. Did I know who'd be there?"

"And did you?"

"I knew of two people, and so I told him : you, Beyfus, and me."

"Hetta," said Hugh : "if you don't want to go through with this, you needn't."

"Do you want to go through with it, Hugh?"

"I'm asking you, Hetta."

Hetta gave him a stout look.

"Now you ask," she said, "I don't much care for the idea. But we've promised your friend, Mayerston, so there's no going back."

After lunch, the Provost invited members of the Council to put up further proposals for spending their quarter of a million pounds. There were several such. Jacquiz Helmut suggested that the money should simply be invested and the considerable income used to award a series of lavish grants for travel and research; but the general view was that since a large investment had already been made with funds realised from the sale, the quarter million of profit should be spent *in toto* on some proportionable undertaking which would otherwise have been beyond their means. Grantchester Pough was in favour of a new boat-house which should include a modern gymnasium, an indoor swimming pool and all the facilities of a Kurhaus or health-centre – an idea which attracted so few others that it was not even debated. Finally, the Senior Tutor advocated the rebuilding of the College Library, which, as he pointed out, was badly overcrowded with books and was now almost impossible to work in. Enough members approved of this scheme for it to be put to debate; but despite a husky speech in its support by Daniel Mond, who reminded them that the library was the main point of the whole college, no more than 10 people voted for it at the finish.

So the upshot was that no further proposals were placed on the short list. This meant that there must now be a straight two-sided contest between, on the one hand, Tom Llewyllyn's motion for a single new building on Scholars' Meadow and, on the other hand, Balbo Blakeney's plan for surveying and restoring the Chapel and for subsidising the Choristers and their school. The comparative merits of both plans would be further debated the next day; and whichever of the two received the more votes, provided it also received a minimum of fifteen, would be finally adopted. After this, a committee would be formed to work out the details; but the general sense of the scheme adopted must be made public as soon as the Council rose, which should be, with any luck, by noon on the morrow. Although Constable would be very relieved, as he reflected, to prorogue this time-consuming assembly, he was not looking forward to the promulgation of its decision. For whichever way the vote went now, the plan he must announce would be a moderate one; and while he himself approved of this, he also knew that in an immoderate age nothing would be more suspect, more resented, more persecuted, than moderation.

"So you see," said Mayerston to Hugh and Hetta in the Bath Hotel, "however the old men may choose to react, we already have the publicity to make a very big splash. I tipped off the television people in time to get us a nice little puff last night. And the Press this morning was gratifying."

"A bit too gratifying," Hetta said. "The Warden at Cherry Hinton was on to me like a battleship."

"How did you cope with that?"

"Cherry Hinton isn't a real college, only a kind of lodging house. The Warden's supposed to be a sort of sympathetic aunt – she's got no real power over what you do, provided you don't hold orgies in the place itself. But she did ring up my parents."

"And how did you cope with *that*?"

"I rang them up myself a little later and told them not to worry, it was only a student rag. I'm fond of them, you see," Hetta said, "and I don't want them to be hurt."

"A bourgeois attitude."

"My attitude."

"Well, you'll have a lot more to explain away to them to-morrow," said Mayerston, "if things go properly tonight. Because I've arranged a full-scale reception for you when you get to the Fellows' Garden Hostel, and the Press will be there in force."

"You've *arranged* a reception?" Hugh said.

"The word's gone out all over Cambridge about what's happening, so a lot of people will turn up out of sheer curiosity. Among them will be certain special friends of mine who will . . . liven things up."

This made Hugh and Hetta very silent. Mayerston went over to the bar and bought them stiff whiskies.

"Drink this," he said, "and start smiling. Your carriage will be here in ten minutes."

"Our *carriage*?"

"That's right. Horse-drawn. The Press likes a bit of a spectacle."

"Spectacle is right," Hugh said.

"The ground's damp," said Beyfus; "I knew I should have put on my galoshes."

Beyfus and Mona were on their way to the demonstration.

"Never mind," said Mona: "I'll find you a nice dry place to stand when we get there."

"It's getting there that's the damp part."

"For Christ's sake, Beyfus. Think of yourself as a soldier."

"A soldier, she says. Next thing, she'll have bought me a cannon."

Grantchester Pough, Jacquiz Helmut and Ivor Winstanley were approaching the hostel through the Fellows' Garden. It was very dark, and Ivor, who was slightly drunk, kept making spook noises to amuse himself.

"Wheee – aiiieee – eeecchh," Ivor went. "What time does the balloon go up?"

"We have plenty of time," said Pough.

They went through a back door, which led into the hostel from the garden, and down a long white corridor. At the end of this was a college porter in a bowler hat, which he raised as they approached him.

"Everything in order, Powell?"

"Yes, sir. There's a lot of them out in the drive, but there hasn't been no trouble yet."

"Good. Then we'll all just wait quietly in your office."

Robert Constable was bringing his autobiographical matter up to date.

"A demonstration," he wrote, "is promised for this evening, but I am fairly confident that we have the situation in hand. What worries me, however, is that once this sort of thing starts, there is never an end of it. People get addicted to protest, just as actors get addicted to public performance or young guerillas to drawing blood. And then again, it gives the idle and restless a specious excuse to neglect their work, on the ground that they 'are fighting for their beliefs' or 'serving their ideals'. Anything rather than mind their books.

"The problem of maintaining authority in such circumstances is almost insuperable. For if one quashes a protest, there is a further and probably more numerous demonstration to protest against the method of quashing; if one gives way and yields what is demanded, another demand follows the very next morning; and if one simply ignores the whole thing, the protestors are liable to walk right in and smash the furniture, for not to be noticed is more than they can endure. Nevertheless, I believe that the last policy is the best, always providing that one arranges certain safeguards, as I have done in this present case . . ."

When Beyfus and Mona turned into the asphalt drive which led up to the main entrance of the Fellows' Garden Hostel, what they saw was this.

On either side of the drive, which was lit by lamps similar in design to those in the yard of St. James's Palace, were long lines of young people waiting amicably for something to happen. To the left of the hostel entrance was a small brass band in a travesty of Hussar uniform; in front of it was a group of mature young men, all of them unknown to Beyfus except for the fair-headed boy he had seen dining with Hugh Balliston in the Arts, and all of them dressed very much alike in elegant yet somehow proletarian garments of leather; and loitering about on the left were Tony Beck and Oliver Clewes, the former trying to pretend that the latter did not exist. Also scattered around the region of the entrance were some six photographers, two of whom were inspecting a pile of placards which lay directly in front of the leather-jackets.

As Mona and Beyfus started uncertainly up the drive, Tony Beck walked up to the fair-haired boy and drew his attention to them; whereupon the fair-haired boy gave a flick of his hand, the band played several bars of a fanfare, and a number of leather-jackets took placards from the pile and raised them aloft. These were of ingenious fabrication, their messages being spelt out in small electric light bulbs which the bearers could switch on and off. Most of the slogans seemed to be about Sexual or Academic Freedom, but at least three, Beyfus noticed, were about Beyfus, and they were extremely flattering in their purport. One proclaimed him the prophet of the new liberty, the second demanded that he be given a fresh hearing by the Council of Lancaster, and the third appeared to assert his virility – BEYFUS, it announced, FOR SEX. Confused but rather pleased, heartened by the polite applause of the boys and girls who were flanking the drive, Beyfus went trotting on towards the hostel, Mona striding at his side, and was about thirty yards short of it, when there suddenly came from behind him a loud PIM-POM PIM-POM PIM-POM, and he found that he had been snatched off the drive, by two solicitous young men, only just in time not to be run down by a large ambulance which careered on up to the entrance. (Mona, who had resisted a similar rescue party, very nearly bought her lot.)

What happened now was stately and impressive. The figure of the porter, Mr Powell, came out through the swing doors with the measured dignity of a Major-Domo and gestured coolly to a second porter, who emerged behind him. Mr Powell held back one swing door, his colleague the other; and in the frame thus provided there appeared the Honourable Grant-chester FitzMargrave Pough, limping very badly and supported on either side, indeed virtually carried, by Jacquiz Helmut and Ivor Winstanley. An ambulance man ran to their assistance; the driver of the vehicle started to turn it round (not an easy matter in the small space available); and Mr Powell approached the photographers. Removing his bowler hat with regal courtesy, he started to address them. Beyfus, who by this time had worked his way nearer the entrance, caught the phrase, "Gentlemen of the Press", followed by others such as "celebrated attempt on Everest", "bad fall on his evening walk in the garden", "feared gravely injured". Meanwhile, the leather-jackets had been compelled to make way for the crippled man and his attendants, the band had been dispersed by the sorties of the turning ambulance, and many of the placards had been trampled on by people anxious to get a closer look at what was doing.

Just as the Senior Fellow was being lifted into the ambulance, there was a hubbub at the far end of the drive. Some sort of horse-drawn conveyance, it seemed to Beyfus, had tried to gain admittance; but since the kindly and intelligent spectators had realised that the drive was too narrow to accommodate both this carriage and the ambulance *en passant,* the former was now being waved firmly on down the road.

Immediately after this a different hubbub started up at the hostel end of the drive, this caused by the gentlemen of the Press, who, having avidly photographed the disabled Pough, were now clamouring to be allowed to accompany this still famous man in the ambulance and get his statement of what had occurred; for although Mr Powell had been very plain that Pough was hurt by a fall, the reporters, who belonged to a simple-minded class of person, insisted on somehow connecting the injury with the demonstration they had come to witness. Since they would not be put off, Pough graciously yielded; whereupon the ambulance hurtled off into the night, taking every reporter and every camera with it.

By this time, the crowd had already begun to disperse, feeling, as assembled Englishmen always do in the case of death or accident, that decent respect for suffering required no less of them.

"They're all going home," said Hetta to Hugh.

They were sitting in an open landau some way down the road from the entrance to the hostel drive. Out of this the crowd was now streaming, turning away, for the most part, in the direction of the Queen's Road. The few people who came down towards the landau walked sedately past, ignoring it completely.

"That ambulance which came out," said Hugh : "someone must have been hurt." And then to their coachman, "What are your instructions?"

"I were to put you down at the Fellows' Garden Hostel of Lancaster College," the man said in a heavy fenland accent, "and that were all."

"Well, I think you'd better go home. Thank you very much."

Hugh climbed out and helped Hetta down. The landau drove off along the road, away from the diminishing crowd.

"I wonder," said Hetta, "where on earth Mayerston found that thing."

Mayerston came out of the drive, paused, spotted them, waved, and walked down towards them.

"Well?" said Hugh.

"Home," said Mayerston. "Never reinforce failure."

"What happened?"

"I'm not quite sure, and I don't much care. The important thing is to do better next time."

Hugh's heart sank within him. If only Mayerston had not been so cool and unconcerned, if only he had shown depression or ill temper, then Hugh would have warmed to him, would have soothed him with kind words and listened to excuse. But as it was, Mayerston's confidence about "next time" and his bland assumption that everyone else shared it made Hugh so miserable and so hostile that suddenly, for want of any other relief, he stamped his foot hard on the pavement.

"How much more have I got to put up with?" he snapped.

"Come, come," said Mayerston; "beaten already?"

"It was such an anti-climax."

"So that's it," said Mayerston. "The star of the evening was cheated of his role."

"It isn't that at all. It's the waste of time."

"I don't know," said Hetta, wanting pleasantness. "It was a lovely ride. Where did you get that landau?"

"I saw it in a farmyard near Waterbeach, when I was out there walking. I like long walks," Mayerston said: "you must both come with me one day."

And all at once the idea of lazing through the countryside with Mayerston, in quest of landaus and God knew what other curiosities, seemed so attractive that Hugh forgot to be angry and petulant and was eager to start walking that very moment.

"When?" he said. "When shall we go?"

"We'll arrange it when we all meet tomorrow," said Mayerston, "which will be at 6 p.m. in the lounge of the University Arms. Bye-bye till then."

He saluted Hetta and strode off towards the Queen's Road.

"No point in hanging round out here," said Hugh. "Want to come in to the hostel?"

"You heard what Mayerston said. It's all off."

"There's no reason why you shouldn't come in for half an hour. It's still quite early."

"For once," said Hetta, "just for once, I simply don't feel like it. Anti-climax, I suppose, like you said. I think I'll walk up through Lancaster and get a bus."

"Want me to come?"

"I know the way," said Hetta, "so it would be rather a waste of your time, now wouldn't it?"

In the summer the back gate of Lancaster was left open until ten o'clock. As it was now only just after nine-thirty, Hetta's notion of walking up to her bus through the college was entirely feasible. But things did not go quite as she had planned.

In the end, Hugh saw her over the Queen's Road and waved her off through the back gate. Since she was irritated with Hugh, who, she felt, had been both querulous and grovelling towards Mayerston, she hardly returned his wave but stuck her nose in the air and lit off at a smart light infantry pace. Half way up the Avenue, however, she began to feel that she had been petty and unkind. After all, Hugh had offered to take her to her bus, which was pretty good as manners in Cambridge went nowadays, and there was certainly no reason why she should not have said a proper goodnight. Never part in anger, her mother always said. Thinking of all this, Hetta slowed to a dawdle and then to a complete halt, wondered whether she shouldn't go back, imagined how nice it would be in Hugh's bed with Hugh on top of her (Marx, Castro, Che, whatever could have made her say she didn't feel like it?), turned round, thought how cross Hugh would be to see her if he had started on some work, turned back again bus-wards – and found herself looking straight into a gnomish face.

"Balbo Blakeney," said the face.

"I know," said Hetta. As part of her course in Pediatrics

she had once had to attend a special lecture by Balbo on abnormal blood-conditions in infant children.

"And I know a bit about you, Miss Hetta. I've got something to tell you. Come and have a drink."

"I was just going to get my bus."

"You didn't seem too sure about that. Anyway, Missy, you ought to hear what I've got to say. It's about your young man."

"Hugh?"

"Young Balliston."

So Hetta, who was of a trusting disposition, suffered herself to be led away to Balbo's room and given a huge glass of the vintage cognac.

"Now then," said Balbo, "I'm not the interfering type, but I've got you up here to warn you. To warn you to warn young Balliston. Because if he doesn't take care he's going to spoil a very good thing."

"Why not tell him yourself?"

"He wouldn't listen to me. He thinks I'm a fascist hyena."

"So do I."

"But you're a woman, so you'll listen to what a man tells you. And what it all comes down to is this. Tony Beck – that's what it comes down to. Tony's got young Balliston into all this, but he won't lift a finger to get him out of trouble – not unless it suits his book, and that book's so complicated that there's no knowing what'll suit it for two minutes together."

"How do you know?"

"I know Beck. And a very amusing fellow I find him. But he's no good for young Balliston. Young Balliston's got a great deal going for him, but he'll lose the lot if he listens to Tony Beck."

"Why are you taking all this trouble? You're not on Hugh's side. If you had your way, Hugh and everyone like him would be kicked right out of this college. You'd never have let him come here in the first place."

"Wrong, Missy. He's a scholar, and here we've always liked

scholars. Anyhow, I thought that by telling you this I'd be doing *you* a good turn. I like the look of you, Miss Hetta; I like it a lot."

And Hetta found herself liking the look of Balbo Blakeney. Well, not exactly his look, she told herself, but his fatherly approach. Being given advice by Balbo was a curiously warming experience. So in order to lengthen her stay she told Balbo about Mayerston.

"I've heard a bit about him," said Balbo. "Tell me, where does he come from?"

"No one seems to know. But what bothers me is this hold he's got over Hugh. It bothers Hugh too."

"Then tell him to cut loose."

"He can't. He starts to sometimes, but Mayerston always knows exactly what to say to him, and Hugh falls flat on his face worshipping."

"Not good, Miss Hetta. You want to pump some sense into him."

"But it's so difficult. Because in a way Hugh's quite right to admire Mayerston. Mayerston's trying to do something that really matters."

"That's what makes him dangerous. Beck's bad enough, Missy, but people see through Beck, and that's an end of it. They don't see through Mayerston because he believes in what he's doing."

"And so does Hugh. And so do I."

"I can't say anything about that. But look at it this way. What is young Balliston best at in all the world?"

"His English," said Hetta without hesitation.

"Then tell him to stick to that. People should do what they're best at – if they're lucky enough to have the chance."

"I suppose you're right," said Hetta, who was liking Balbo more and more. "But how can I convince Hugh?"

"Lysistrata."

"Lysistrata?"

"A Greek play, Missy. All the girls in Athens told the men,

'No more nice games of hot cockles until you stop this ridiculous war.'"

"Oh," said Hetta doubtfully; "did it work?"

"Yes."

"But that was a play."

"Can you think of a better plan?"

"No."

"Then try this one," said Balbo; "and if you want a shoulder to cry on, you know your way here."

When the College Council assembled the next morning, the Provost made a brief statement:

"As most of you will have heard," he said, "nothing came of the student demonstration planned for last night. A crowd did indeed gather by the Fellows' Garden Hostel, among whom there was evidently a small body of organisers, these being equipped with placards and so forth. In so far as they had time and opportunity to display this apparatus, it would seem that they were protesting against our recent rejection of the proposal by our colleague, Lord Beyfus, that large experimental hostels should be built on Scholars' Meadow and the rear lawn."

Lord Beyfus shifted his papers about and looked silly.

"However," Constable went on, "before the demonstration could reach any kind of climax, a regrettable accident, totally unconnected with the demonstration itself, occurred to the Senior Fellow in the garden nearby. The arrival of an ambulance effected what could not have been achieved by a whole brigade of policemen – i.e. the immediate and peaceful dispersal of the crowd. There is a moral here, on which those who advocate strong measures on such occasions might care to reflect.

"All reporters present transferred their attention to Mr Pough. The student Balliston entered the hostel unaccompanied and without incident at about 9.45 p.m. There is no report of the demonstration in the morning papers. Finally, you will be glad to know that the Senior Fellow, though unable to be with us here today, has returned to his rooms in college, where he is entirely comfortable in the care of the college nurse."

Tony Beck pulled a sceptical face.

"This is all very well, Provost," said Andrew Ogden; "but we cannot suppose that this will be the last of these demonstrations, and the next time one occurs we cannot rely on the opportune arrival of an ambulance."

"We can continue to rely," said the Provost, "on a show of dignified indifference . . . and on the uses of our own good sense. And now, gentlemen, to the business of the day. I have before me on my short list two proposals, as to the relative merits of which I now invite you to discourse and arbitrate..."

"Castro," squawked Hetta, "it's never been so marvellous. Castroooo. Equaliteeeeee. Che . . . Che . . . Cheeee."

A little later Hugh got off the bed and washed himself while Hetta looked lovingly on. But when he came back to her, she pulled herself together and prepared to tell Hugh what she was now convinced that she must say to him before it was too late.

"What time," she began, "are we due at the University Arms? To meet Mayerston?"

"Six o'clock, he said last night."

"Well, don't let's go."

"Hetta?"

"Don't let's go."

Hugh stretched himself beside her on the narrow bed and began to fidget nervously with one of her thighs.

"Listen, Hugh," said Hetta, taking this as a promising sign, "you've done your bit. Ooowwwh," she said, as he pinched a piece of thigh.

"Sorry, Het. Didn't mean to hurt."

"You've done all that he can expect. You agreed to make this protest last night, and you did everything he asked—"

"—You too, Het—"

"And it's not our fault it went wrong. Now it's all over and we want nothing more to do with him."

"We can't just walk out on him now. What he's doing is work that should be done. Anyway, I'm committed."

"No, you're not," said Hetta evenly.

It was clear to her that Hugh was ready to listen, because otherwise she would already have been silenced and sent home. The problem was, how to go on from here. She wondered whether to tell Hugh what Balbo Blakeney had said, but decided that any overt reference to Balbo would certainly weaken her case.

"You promised to help Mayerston with his work," she now said carefully, "but that work isn't what you thought it was. Can't you understand, Hugh? He's just trying to smash everything to pieces."

"Only as a beginning. So that he can rebuild it all from scratch."

"No, Hugh." She pushed Hugh's hand away from her crutch, at which his fidgeting fingers had now arrived, and replaced it with her own. "Smashing things is all that interests Mayerston, and he won't care the teeniest bit if he smashes you as well. And if that happens, don't think Tony Beck will help you either."

"How can you know all this?"

Hugh's voice was cross but also uncertain. He was still ready to listen.

" . . . I just feel it. I love you, Hugh, and I feel . . . I *know* . . . that you're in danger. You've got so much, Hugh, so much that's worth doing. Why risk it all for Mayerston and Tony Beck?"

"To hell with Tony Beck. But Mayerston's another thing. I think, I *believe*, that his ideals are worth fighting for."

Oh God, thought Hetta miserably, if only I could talk like he does, make things plain in the way he can. How shall I convince him? How?

"I've told you," she said: "all Mayerston wants is to pull

everything down. Pull it down, and leave a pile of ruins, and move on."

"So you say. And I say he wants to build something far finer instead. Why should I be wrong, Hetta?"

The question was not rhetorical. His voice was pleading with her to find a reason.

"Listen, lovely Hugh," she said. "Of all things in this world I love being here with you like this. But now I've got my hand over my cunt, and there it stays until you agree that you'll have nothing more to do with Mayerston. And if you don't agree, I shall get up off this bed, and put my clothes on, and go home, and I shan't make love with you ever again – until you break with Mayerston. It will half kill me to do it, but do it I shall, because I believe, believe, believe, darling Hugh, that you must free yourself, while you still can, from this man Mayerston."

There, she thought. I've said all this because of you, Balbo Blakeney; because you wanted to help me and I trusted what you said. But what help can you be, kind as you are, Balbo Blakeney, if Hugh denies me? For if Hugh denies me, then I must keep my hand on my cunt and deny him (though at this very moment I long to open my legs to him as wide as the golden gates of heaven), and what help can you be then? You offered me your shoulder to cry on, but what use is a shoulder to a girl like me?

"And my promise to Mayerston?" Hugh said quietly.

"He got it under false pretences."

Hugh put his hand on Hetta's and tried to move it, but it clung as tight as an oyster shell. Refusal roused him further; he seized Hetta's free hand and placed it on his groin; but the hand just fell limply away from him.

"You mean it, Het."

"Yes."

"You're crying, Het."

"Yes."

"Why, Het?"

"Because it breaks my heart, but I'm going to do it."

With a burst of blubbering and a flurry of her splendid limbs Hetta heaved herself over Hugh and off the bed.

"Wait."

She waited.

"If I . . . do what you want, I must tell him. I must go to the University Arms, where he'll be expecting us at six o'clock, and tell him straight out that I'm finished. I can't just leave him there. You do see that?"

Hetta stood pondering by the bed, then nodded.

"Well then?" he said.

He held out his hand to her. She shook her head.

"Not until you've gone and come back."

"But if I promise you, Het?"

"Not until you've told him."

"I swear that I will tell him as soon as I see him this evening. You can come yourself and hear me."

"You swear, Hugh?"

"Yes, heart. Come to bed."

"Go on, then : swear."

"I've already sworn."

"Swear again."

So Hugh swore a second time; and then Hetta – trusting, randy Hetta – leapt blithely on to the bed and opened her legs as wide as the golden gates of heaven, that her lover might come in.

"So they're still talking," said Mayerston to Tony Beck in the lounge of the University Arms.

"Yes . . . though I think we'd all hoped to get the Council finished with today. But it seems a lot of people have a lot on their minds. Some reckon that Llewyllyn's idea is a sensible compromise which will keep the college out of trouble or controversy for a long time to come, and this appeals very much. They'd all like to feel safe."

"Then why don't they settle for that?"

"Because Balbo Blakeney has struck a strong chord. They're

proud of their chapel, and they see the sense in his suggestions for preserving it."

"And his suggestion about the Choir School?"

"As most of 'em see it, that's pretty sound as well. If you're going to have a Choir and a Choir School, you may as well pay a bit extra and do the thing properly."

"When will the debate be finished?"

"Some time tomorrow, I'd say. There's nothing more to be said, but there are still a few who'll want to repeat what's been said already."

"Which way will it go?"

Beck shrugged.

"Does it matter?" he asked. "You'll be against them whatever they decide."

"It could make a difference to our tactics. For example," said Mayerston, "if they should decide to spend the money on the Chapel, well, the Chapel is actually standing there as a . . . possible centre of our activity."

Beck raised an eyebrow and said nothing.

"But until we know the Council's decision," Mayerston said, "we can only be sure of our overall strategy. This must be to go on mounting protests and demonstrations until finally the authorities are compelled to take some action."

"Such as?"

"Sooner or later they will have to discipline somebody. They'll probably panic and do it clumsily, but even if they behave calmly and sensibly, their act can be misrepresented so as to stir up the indignation of a great mass of moderate students, who will hitherto have had nothing to do with us."

"You're sure they'll join you?"

"Yes. Suppose things had gone better last night, and suppose Hugh Balliston had been sent down—"

"—But that's just the point," said Tony Beck. "The Provost was quite determined that no one should be sent down. As he said, if we ignore what is happening, then in effect nothing will have happened."

"He can't go on like that. Sooner or later, if we keep making a nuisance of ourselves, your Provost or somebody else in the University will have to put his foot down. If he loses his temper first, so much the better, but in any case at all down will come his foot—"

"—Preferably on Hugh Balliston—"

"—Or some equally respected individual, and then we shall have a martyr. Once we have a martyr, the big battalions will rally round him at our call. as has been their habit throughout history. From being a mere nuisance, we shall have become a serious threat."

"And then?"

"As you know," said Mayerston, "I have a number of skilled assistants. These will immediately assume leadership of the battalions, in the way they have been trained to do, and then we shall be ready to strike."

"Strike at what?"

"As I've already indicated to you," said Mayerston blandly, "that question is best deferred until we know which way the Council has decided. Some time tomorrow, you think?"

"Yes," said Beck sullenly, and put his head on one side.

"And meanwhile," said Mayerston, "we must revert to the phase which we are actually in. Our job at this moment is to provoke authority into making a martyr for us."

"Well, here's your boy," said Tony Beck, as Hugh Balliston entered the lounge.

"I wonder where the girl is."

"Do you need her again?"

"No. But she was invited to come here. If properly handled, she has a useful influence on Balliston."

Although Mayerston could not know it, the reason why Hetta, the "useful influence", had stayed away was to show Hugh that she trusted him to keep his oath without her supervision. Hugh himself was very touched by this delicacy of spirit; and now, as he looked round the lounge and signalled recognition to Mayerston, he was determined to be worthy of it. He advanced on Beck and Mayerston with poker face and measured tread.

"Drink?" said Mayerston.

"No thanks. I've only come to tell you that from now on you must do without me."

"Now you look here—" began Tony Beck.

Mayerston gave him a quick look which killed the rising words.

"You look tired, Tony," Mayerston said. "You need a rest and a bath before your dinner. See you tomorrow."

Beck opened his mouth, stopped another of Mayerston's looks, then heaved himself up and shambled out.

"Not a good man when things go wrong," said Mayerston, raising one arm. "Now sit down, Hugh, and have a drink."

Hugh remained standing. A waiter appeared beside him. Mayerston looked from Hugh to the waiter and back again.

"What'll it be?" Mayerston said.

"I . . . er . . . a pint of bitter, please."

"No pints in the lounge, sir."

"A half of bitter."

"No draught beer in the lounge, sir."

"A lager."

The waiter withdrew and Hugh sat down on the chair which had just been vacated by Tony Beck.

"We must arrange that walk," said Mayerston. "Some time next week, perhaps? I shall want to know how you're getting on."

"You needn't worry about that," said Hugh. "I have a great deal of interesting work to do, and I shall get along very nicely."

"I don't doubt it. But I shall want to know your opinion of what's happening. You see," said Mayerston, "there'll be quite a lot happening in the next few days, and naturally I'll be glad to hear what impression it's made on a . . . spectator whose intelligence I respect."

The waiter brought Hugh's lager.

"Who said anything about being a spectator?" Hugh said. "We shall have plenty to say in Lancaster about all this, and we're quite capable of standing up to the Council. In our own way, Mayerston, which isn't yours."

"You disapprove of my way?"

"It's too extreme."

"We went into all this the other night, Hugh. You seemed quite satisfied then."

Hugh took an unhappy gulp of lager.

"I liked you," he said, "very much. And I still do. But I've come to understand—"

"—*Liked me?*" said Mayerston. "You said you *believed*."

"I believe in your ideals but not your methods. They're so wasteful."

There was an echo here ("It's all a wicked waste," Hetta had said) and Mayerston was quick to catch it.

"Ah," he said. "So little Miss Hetta, the girl from the home counties, has been having second thoughts. Hetta, the playtime revolutionary, has discovered that the toys are sharp and dangerous after all, so she's taken her little Hughie by the hand to bring him indoors to bed."

Hugh went scarlet.

"Hetta believes as I do," he said. "She wants equality and justice. Not blood."

"Who said anything about blood? I'm disappointed in you, Hugh. An intelligent and independent man, as I thought, but what do I find? You've been got at by a woman."

"That's not true."

"Oh, but it is. You're like a suburban husband who's being nagged at by his wife because he wants to change his job. 'What'll become of me and the kiddies?' " he trilled, in a very fair imitation of Hetta. " 'What'll become of our dear little semi-detached?' So of course the poor sad sod knuckles under in two minutes flat. But at least he's got the excuse that he has his children to care for, whereas you, Balliston, all you're thinking of is yourself and your books and someone to tickle your knob. You're throwing me over because you want to go on writing your precious essays and being told how clever you are by a silly slut from Surrey who doesn't know Kafka from

Cavafis but thinks you've got a cute prick. I'll tell you what it is with you, Balliston: you're just a mimsy little scholarship boy who's been swallowed whole by a cunt."

Hugh was not certain which in all this he disliked the more – the venom or the obscenity. Never before had Mayerston shown a trace of either. But there was also something else which Hugh found more sickening than both together: the substantial truth of the accusation. For he had (he could not deny it) been won over by Hetta's tears, by her appeal to him not to throw himself away, and last but not least by her threat to refuse him his pleasure. He had, in truth, been got at by a woman.

"You're not to talk about Hetta like that," he said feebly.

"I'm sorry," said Mayerston, smiling penitence, "but I hate to see a good man breaking up. People like Tony Beck, it doesn't matter what happens with them. But you, Hugh . . ."

"You shouldn't have said those things. It wasn't like you."

"No. But I was upset. Wounded. Betrayed."

First contempt, thought Hugh, now sorrow; and the sorrow because I gave cause for contempt.

"Perhaps I was too sudden," he said.

"No. Better be sudden than equivocate. You were quite right, Hugh. You've got your life to live, when all's said." Mayerston lifted his glass of Pimm's and took a long drink. "Now then; about that walk. I thought we'd drive out to Cottenham and take the footpath over the fields to—"

"—I don't want to hear about anything else until we've cleared this up first. I must know what to believe, Mayerston. You said you wanted to destroy in order to build. Hetta says you want to destroy in order to destroy. Which is true?"

"Although Hetta is an honest girl, Hugh, she is not a clever one. She hasn't understood."

"Hasn't she, Mayerston? Can you prove she's wrong?"

Mayerston leaned forward, took both Hugh's hands in his, and looked straight into his eyes. Mayerston's irises were blue flecked with brown, by no means an unusual arrangement, except that the brown flecks seemed somehow to recede, as though some were more distant than others, as though they were minute clouds in a tiny sky, some riding higher than the rest and others higher still, so that as Hugh looked from one to the next he was drawn on and upwards into a blue empyrean that had no end, until he was hanging there in space, way up above the highest of the little brown clouds, supported only by the warm, dry, infinitely reassuring clasp of Mayerston's soft hands.

The hands released his; there was a terrible moment of panic as he started to fall, very fast, from what must surely be an immense height; then the hands clasped his again, and he was sitting in the lounge of the University Arms.

"You must believe me," Mayerston said, gently kneading Hugh's wrists. "Hetta means well, of course; but between you and me, Hugh, there is a different and much more powerful link. You felt what happened just now? When I let you go for a moment."

Falling and falling, faster and faster, from a great height . . . Hugh nodded bleakly.

"You understand then?" said Mayerston. "Next time I let you go, Hugh, it will be for good."


Despite her resolution not to come near Lancaster again, Patricia had once more parked Baby and walked into Cambridge, where she had spent most of the afternoon hanging round the College Stones, hoping to see Hugh. Since Hugh had been in bed with Hetta, Patricia had been out of luck; and after Wilfred the porter, who recognised her, had come out of the lodge for the third time and asked her whether he should fetch Mr Llewyllyn, she had given up and gone back to Grantchester.

By a quarter to six that evening (at which hour, had she still been on the Stones, she would have seen Hugh leave Lancaster *en route* for the University Arms) she had made up her mind what to do. First, she rang up her sister Isobel; then she started to pack for herself and Baby; and then, as soon as Tom arrived home, she said:

"I've decided to take Baby up tomorrow. Isobel's fixing rooms in a hotel."

"Rather sudden?"

"I want to go at once."

"As you like," said Tom, who was too tired, after his day at the Council, to wonder why. "Have you arranged with the dentist?"

"No. I'll do that when we get up there. Isobel knows a good man that Gregory goes to."

"It may be some time before he can give Baby an appointment."

"Gregory will arrange about that."

"Gregory or no Gregory, it may take some time."

"Then I'll have to stay longer," snapped Patricia. "Do you really care?"

"I want you to enjoy yourself. Not just to hang around up there waiting on the convenience of a dentist."

"And what do I do down here – except wait on the convenience of Tom Llewyllyn?"

"One of the porters tells me," said Tom in a puzzled voice, "that you were waiting on the College Stones for two hours this afternoon. Was it me you were wanting?"

"No," said Patricia, "it was not."

"Then what's all this about waiting on my convenience?"

"It's your fault," she said, "that I was waiting there. And it's your fault that I'm going to London a full week early and with nothing properly arranged. But I shouldn't let that bother you, because now you can do what you've wanted to for years – you can go and live in that precious college of yours until I get back."

"And when will that be?"

As there was real anxiety in his voice, Patricia relented slightly.

"I'll let you know as soon as I can," she said.

"Yes, please do," Tom said seriously. "The college is having

great trouble getting servants these days, and the Domestic
Bursar will want to know how long I'll need a bedmaker."


Hetta was waiting for Hugh when he returned from the University Arms to the Fellows' Garden Hostel. Since Hugh had
had a large dinner with Mayerston and Hetta had only had
scrambled eggs, which she had cooked over the gas-ring in the
gyp-room, Hugh was at a strong advantage.

"You're wrong about Mayerston," Hugh said.

Hetta shrivelled slightly and said nothing.

"He's convinced me that he means what he says," Hugh
went on belligerently; "so I must stick to him, Hetta. Can you
understand that?"

Hetta still said nothing.

"Can you understand that?"

"You swore to me," said Hetta. And then, in a very small,
tired voice, "How did he convince you?"

"He . . . he just did," blustered Hugh. "You wouldn't
understand. You haven't understood anything."

"I suppose not," said Hetta. "Do you know, it just did not
occur to me that you could break your oath?"

"I only swore because you said that Mayerston was a fraud.
He only wanted to destroy, you said. Since I now know that's
not true, I am absolved from my oath."

"You swore," said Hetta, "because I wouldn't let you have
me until you did."

"That's not true. I meant to keep my word, and I did . . .
at first. I went straight up to him and told him it was all
over."

"And then?" said Hetta. "I suppose he talked you round."

"Yes. But in a very special way." Hugh shook his head
angrily. "You couldn't understand."

"I'm tired of being told that. I think I shall go."

"Het . . . I'm doing what I know to be right. You won't
desert me now?"

"No, Hugh. I shall come to you and listen to you whenever

you wish. But I meant what I said: I shan't make love with you again until you've broken with Mayerston."

"But I've just told you. I can't."

Hetta shrugged miserably and moved towards the door.

"Tell me one thing," she said: "what does he want you to do now?"

"It's a secret. It has to be. You'll find out when it happens – which will be soon enough."

"Hugh . . . sweet Hugh . . . don't do anything to make them send you away from here."

"How like a woman. All you can think of – degrees, careers, respectability."

"I'm not thinking of that. I'm thinking of the work you love so much."

This went home. At first Hugh's face just crumpled; then it reassembled itself, only to fall to pieces again in sheer fury.

"God damn you to hell, you blackmailing bitch," he screamed. "Stop interfering, will you? Just stop interfering and get out."

Hetta got out, smiling and waggling her fingers to him, out of old habit, as she went.


"That's bad, Miss Hetta," said Balbo. "That's very bad."

After leaving Hugh, Hetta had come to cry on Balbo's shoulder.

"Oh, Mr Blakeney," she sobbed, "what shall I do?"

"Put your head in my lap," Balbo said. "Sit there, on the floor, and put your head in my lap."

This was taking fatherly behaviour a little too far. Hetta's face went rigid and she shook her head.

"Don't be scared, Missy. I know what's good for you."

He put an arm round her waist, a surprisingly strong arm, and forced her slowly off the sofa and on to the floor. Then, holding her down with both his hands on both her shoulders, he shifted his own position in order that he might clasp her between his knees.

"Don't be scared," he said.

Hetta wasn't scared, but she regarded all this as uncalled for. When she tried to get up, she found that Balbo's knees had her tight. When she tried to wriggle out frontways, all she managed to do was to turn slightly, so that now, when Balbo leaned forward, his stomach pressed against her cheek.

"What are you going to do?" she said.

"What your mother did when you were small."

Balbo produced a comb from his breast pocket and started to comb her hair. Sometimes he scratched, very delicately, at the roots; sometimes he passed the comb firmly but strongly through the long outer tresses; sometimes he stretched a lock taut from the scalp and played the comb over it as a violinist might play his bow over the strings. Whatever he did was soothing and delicious; before very long Hetta relaxed completely, sticking her legs out over the floor and nestling her face against Balbo's friendly little pot.

"What shall I do, Mr Blakeney?" she murmured. "What shall I do about Hugh?"

"From what you say," said Balbo, steadily and sensitively combing, "he's infatuated. Only one thing you can do, Missy. Let him go his ways and get ready to pick up the pieces."

"Will you help me, Mr Blakeney?"

"I'll help, you Miss Hetta. And will you help me?"

"How can I do that?"

"By coming here, every so often, and letting me comb your beautiful hair."

"But of course you may. You do it so gently, so marvellously."

She turned her face up to smile at Balbo, and saw that two big tears were running down his face, one on either cheek.

"Oh, poor Mr Blakeney. Why are you so sad?"

"Brandy, Miss Hetta. It makes one remember things."

"I thought it made you forget them."

"So it does – the little things that don't matter. But the big things, Miss Hetta, it brings them up as clear as yesterday."

Hetta had the sense to pursue this no further. If he wants

to say anything more, she thought, he will. But Balbo simply
went on combing her hair, now sweeping grandly through
great skeins of it, now nibbling exquisitely at her scalp with
the points of the teeth, while Hetta closed her eyes and wished
that he need never stop.


The College Council concluded its discussion just before lunch
time the next day. There had been a great many speeches,
most of them repetitious, but what it all boiled down to was
this : the extreme left, Beyfus, Beck and Clewes, were against
either of the short-listed proposals, considering them to be
merely impertinent, yet would support Tom Llewyllyn's for
want of a better; the moderate left, headed by the Provost,
also supported Llewyllyn; and the right, of all shades, was
now solid for Balbo.

There were, however, certain subtleties in the situation. The
continued absence of Pough reduced the Council to nineteen
but did not reduce the number, fifteen, which would constitute
the 75 per cent majority necessary to pass a motion for final
adoption. Without Pough, moreover, Balbo's supporters were
now reduced to nine; for though he had obtained a vote of
thirteen to get his plan short-listed, three of those thirteen had
been moderate left-wingers, who sincerely felt that the problem
of preserving the Chapel should be fully aired before the
Council but were nevertheless far more inclined, now it had
come to the crunch, to support Tom's new building and the
25 per cent increase in student numbers. When the Provost
took the vote, therefore, there was a count of ten for Tom's
proposal and nine for Balbo's, which simply meant deadlock.

The procedure in such a case was clearly laid down. The
Provost must now dismiss the Council with the warning that
it would be reconvened to give another vote in seven days'
time. By then, the theory was, private suasion and intrigue
might have issue in a decisive majority one way or the other.
But in practice, of course, such weekly reconvents could
succeed each other for months without any perceptible re-

alignment of the Council; and there were very few of its members, apart from the extreme left-wingers, who would not be entirely satisfied if something of the kind occurred. Tom was certainly in no hurry. Balbo knew that the Chapel and even the Choristers could wait another year and be little the worse for it. And Constable, as Provost, considered that a certain amount of mystery and delay (though more than six months might be dangerous) would invest the final decision with higher dignity. In any event, since nothing had been decided, nothing need yet be promulgated, which meant grateful respite from the world's comment. With a feeling of some relief, Constable rose to give his colleagues the formal word of dismissal:

"Nil est peractum, socii. Go hence and meditate, and return when seven nights have passed."

Gregory Stern, the publisher, and Isobel Stern, his wife and Patricia's sister, lived in a jolly house in Chelsea which Isobel kept very bright and clean. Hither came Patricia and Baby, neither of whom looked bright and clean, as soon as they reached London; and Isobel served them a delicious soufflé of turbot, which she had cooked herself, for lunch.

The soufflé was wasted on everyone except Isobel. Patricia, whose culinary method was limited to the incompetent manipulation of "convenience foods", was jealous of the achievement and in any case regarded it as somewhat immoral. Baby, sensing her mother's displeasure and playing up to it, splashed her share round her plate and whined for fish fingers. The prospect for the long afternoon ahead would have been very grim indeed, had not Isobel, who wanted a tête-à-tête with her sister, taken one very sensible precaution. Shortly after the beginning of the meal she had given Baby a glass of orangeade in which she had dissolved a liberal quantity of aspirin; this Baby had swilled down, with bestial sucking noises and much discharge of nasal mucous, in twenty seconds flat; so that five minutes later, just as she was opening her mouth to grizzle about the soufflé or demand more orangeade (she had not yet made up her mind which), sleep fell on Baby like a hammer and stretched her prone in her chair. Isobel bore her off and deposited her, none too gently, on a couch in Gregory's dressing-room, then returned to catechise Patricia.

"You and that child," she said, "are in a bigger mess than ever. What's the matter with you, Patty? You used to think so much of yourself."

"I still do," said Patricia, miserably surveying her best costume. There was no doubt about it : the skirt was considerably the worse for her recent expeditions by the river. "I may not look very elegant," she said querulously, "but let me tell you, it's not very easy for me, living down there in the country with hardly any money and—"

"—Knackers," said Isobel. "You lived in the country for years before you got married. You know how to manage in the country as well as any woman that breathes. And as for money, you're rolling in it. We both got exactly the same when Daddy died, and I know what it was to the last penny. You could carry on like the Queen."

"That must all be saved for Baby," said Patricia primly. "It's Tom's business to provide for me, and now he's at that revolting college he earns practically nothing."

"Balls."

"I tell you, Tom earns practic—"

"—Balls to not spending Daddy's money. By the time Baby's grown up, the way things are going, it won't be worth the piddle in her plastic potty."

Isobel splayed her long, thin legs on either side of her chair and leant over the table, her huge breasts bouncing on the edge of the soufflé dish.

"I know what's wrong with you," Isobel said. "You look to me as if you haven't been fucked in months."

"I . . . I don't care much about all that."

"Yes, you do. We're a very sexy family. What's the matter with Tom? Can't he get his pecker up?"

"He . . . hasn't been very attentive."

"Then you must find a little something on the side."

"*Isobel.* Do you?"

"No, because Gregory *is* attentive. But I jolly soon would if he wasn't. Haven't you got someone you fancy?"

Patricia shook her head firmly. Then, because it had been her habit over many years to be honest with her sister, she started nodding it instead.

"Who?"

"An undergraduate. I don't know him. I haven't even spoken to him. But oh," said Patricia greedily, "how I could love that undergraduate."

"Then love him."

"He's got a girl friend."

"They're hot at that age. He'll have plenty of energy for you too."

"But look at me."

"Spend some of Daddy's money and do yourself up. You've got lovely strong legs and a beautiful bloody great bottom. Your undergraduate will love that – if the rest of you's half way passable. I'll tell you what," Isobel said. "While you're here in London, we'll set you to rights. We'll buy you clothes and get your hair fixed and have your face put together again. We'll send you back to Cambridge looking like a lioness, and you can *eat* your undergraduate."

"But it's wrong, Isobel. Wrong, wrong. That's why I came up to London early – to get away before I did anything silly."

"Let's get this straight. Are you afraid of sinning or just of being silly?"

Patricia thought a long time.

"I don't think Tom would mind," she said. "He's as good as told me. I should probably be much nicer to him . . . if I had something to look forward to every so often. But I don't want to look a fool, Isobel. How . . . how do I make the first approaches?"

"Will he respond to the mother act?"

"The what?"

"Will he accept your authority? You have quite a presence, you know."

What was that, thought Patricia, which Tom had said the other night? Something about feet which were convenient to grovel at?

"Now you mention it," she said, "I think he might prove quite obedient."

"Then drop something," said Isobel. "Tell him to pick it up for you and call a taxi, and to see you home in it because you're upset. Then, when you get home, tell him that *this* is how you're both going to spend the afternoon, because Mother knows best. He'll have to join in, if only out of politeness."

"But suppose it's a failure?"

"I was coming to that. It's your job to see that it isn't. You're Mum and you've got to do the work. You've got to busy yourself round your little baby boy. You've got to feed him and clean him and change his nappies and kiss his little bottom and show him how to point his little prick. Do you understand?"

"Not quite."

Isobel sighed.

"That girl of his," she said; "with her it'll have been very straightforward. Boom, boom, boom. With you it's got to be different. You're the older woman; the guide to secret places, the priestess of mysteries, the dispenser of curious pleasures."

"Oh. I don't know much about those."

"Hasn't Tom . . . ever . . . ?"

"No. As you would say, he is – was – very straightforward."

"You'd better come upstairs then," Isobel said. "Gregory has a very interesting collection of books."


"It is a commonplace of all administration," said the Leading Editorial in *The Times* the following morning, "that important decisions must only be taken after much thought and discussion. On the face of it, therefore, it is by no means unsatisfactory to learn that the Council of Lancaster College, Cambridge, has not yet committed itself to a definite course of action as regards the disbursement of the £250,000 surplus which has recently become available to that venerable institution. One may conceive that the Provost and Fellows are conducting exhaustive and responsible deliberations about the best possible use of this substantial sum for the betterment of the services which the college has long tendered to the public weal."

So far, thought Provost Constable, sipping his thin coffee and averting his eyes from Mrs Constable's flannel dressing gown, so good.

"However," the leader continued, "information has reached this journal which gives rise to disquieting reflections. According to a reliable source" (Master Beck, I suppose) "the choice before the Council is now limited to two alternatives: a small new building for the accommodation of approximately sixty extra students; or the extensive survey and restoration of the College Chapel, together with increased subsidies for the upkeep of the Choir. Of the former proposal, it may be said that many will deem it inadequate, in view of the extensive funds in hand, to the needs of a rapidly expanding student population; of the latter, that, while the sacred architecture and music of Lancaster College must at all costs be preserved for posterity, there is nevertheless something of perverseness, at this difficult juncture of our social history, in applying to the premature refurbishing of a stone erection (however famous) what will rightfully be looked upon as the due of aspiring and at present underprivileged young people . . ."

Great God, thought Constable, what unctuous drivel. Has the editor turned to jelly?

"There's a funny bit here," said Mrs Constable, rattling an organ of the Billingsgate Press, "by a man called Alfie Schroeder. Shall I read it out to you?"

"No."

" 'Dons delight to bark and bite,' it says, 'and those in Lancaster College, Cambridge, have certainly chosen some mouldy old bones to scrap over. Presented with a surplus of quarter a million pounds, the learned Fellows are squabbling like a load of Gorgons – about what? About whether to provide accommodation for a handful of extra students, or to pay more money to the Choir Boys, who've been letting their top notes get a bit grotty of late. But just in case anyone agrees with me that £500,000 is a little too much to lay out on improving the plainsong (dowdy old chants left over from the middle ages), perhaps they'd like to join me in reminding the dons of Lancaster that we live in an age in which science and technology'—"

Constable had been just about to tell his wife to hold her tongue (in so many words), when she was interrupted by a knock on the breakfast-room door. Bidden to enter, the Head Porter presented himself, wearing tails (since it was a saint's day) and carrying a silk hat.

"Mr Provost . . . Madam," the Head Porter said bowing. "Someone has been a-writing rude things on the rear lawn. You, sir, I must ask to come and read them. You, madam, I must warn to avert your ladylike gaze."

So Constable and the Head Porter went up to Constable's study, whence they could look out on the rear lawn. Constable saw two things. He saw a small, bent man, whom he knew to be one of the college gardeners, standing under the study window and crying; and he saw, burnt into the grass in letters ten feet high:

> LOSE LLEWYLLYN;
> BUGGER BLAKENEY;
> FUCK THE CON;
> BUILD WITH BEYFUS.

"Who," said Constable after some thought, "is the Con?"

"First three letters of your own name, Mr Provost. Making a Frenchie word, or so I understand."

"I never knew they called me that," said Constable. "I must be getting out of touch."

## PART THREE

# MADRIGAL FOR A MAY MORNING

"ALL IN ALL," wrote Robert Constable, who was making up his record of the seven days which had passed since the writing had appeared on the lawn, "this has been an uneasy and indecisive week. When I first saw what had been done to the back lawn, I was exceedingly angry, though I think I managed to conceal this from the Head Porter, who was with me at the time. What made it so much worse was the sight and sound of the third gardener, who was sobbing his heart out because his life's work had been destroyed. No one had thought of that, of course: it just had not occurred to the young men responsible that their fine and easy gesture had destroyed, in a few minutes, the achievement which had taken a fellow human being thirty years. Nor had they reflected that the human being in question was one of the 'workers' they are always ranting about.

"However, I managed, as I say, to control myself, and having dismissed the Head Porter, I settled down to consider what should be done.

"Although I had been thinking of the culprits as 'them', I now reflected that a single man could easily have done it on his own, and that whether or not this had been so, one agent in the affair must certainly have been Hugh Balliston. Why did I pick on him? Because Balliston, who is a great purist and a stickler for correct English usage, was the only man in the world who would have bothered to *punctuate* such a message and in such a medium. The careful semi-colons at the end of each line and the full stop at the end of the whole were as good as a signature. True, the crudely alliterative

349

slogans lacked Balliston's usual elegance, but they were terse and quotable, which was everything for their purpose. I was in no doubt about it : Balliston was my man.

"So what was I to do? My tactic so far had been simply to ignore all protests and demonstrations; but whereas one can ignore the flouting of unimportant regulations and can even ignore personal insult (for in the end those that insult me merely insult themselves), one cannot ignore wanton destruction.

"In the end, I decided to back my hunch. I sent for Balliston (who came most promptly), told him that I knew he was guilty and whence I had inferred his guilt, and asked him to explain to me how he, of all people, could do such a horrible thing. Balliston, being a strictly truthful boy, admitted the crime; and then, being if anything even keener on self-justification than I myself, started to expound to me why I should not take his act to reflect adversely either on his intelligence, his morals or his aesthetic sense.

"The basic theory behind his actions, he told me, is that the University as it is must be destroyed so that a better one can be substituted. He had, on his own admission, destroyed beauty; but it would be urged by those who were behind him, first that such beauty was an irrelevance or even, much worse, an insult to the underprivileged, and secondly that in recording his 'justifiable resentment' he had been performing 'an act of conscience'. Any punishment would thus be interpreted as 'victimisation', and would lead to mass indignation, which he and his friends would be able to exploit for their initial purpose of destruction.

"Very well, I said : but did he really believe in the basic tenet behind his actions – that the University as it stood must be destroyed to make place for a better? Did he conceive that such an object was practicable? At this he became very shifty; he muttered something about the necessity for faith and his having encountered someone who had inspired him with faith, and then fell silent. Although he did not abandon his claim, although he even put a proud face on it, it obviously embarrassed him nevertheless, because with some part of himself he still knew that he had been cheated or charmed into betraying his critical intellect, that he was suffering from a temporary alienation from reason – to say nothing of plain common sense. So then I understood what was happening to Master Balliston. He was being piped by the Pied Piper (like many better men before him), and the question was, how to rescue him before he was piped away under the hill.

"With this problem in mind, I asked him whether he ought to have told me so much about his friends' strategy. Surely, I said, he had given away secrets? Oh no, he replied, he was perfectly certain that I had always understood what was doing, he just wanted me to know that he understood too, so that I shouldn't think him a fool. But I did think him a fool, I told him, for ever accepting the revolutionary programme in the first place – for accepting, that was, that an existing good should be destroyed for the sake of an improvement which was wholly putative. But my opinion shouldn't bother him, I went on, since potential martyrs must be prepared to put up with a reputation for folly and fanaticism as part of the burden of martyrdom. This, as I knew it would, made him both angry and unhappy. Master Balliston may be ready to assume a crown of thorns, but he wouldn't be seen dead in a dunce-cap.

"Even so, the piper's tune was still in his ears. Clearly, he was going to see the thing through. 'I burnt those slogans into the lawn,' he said, 'and I can show you a jar still half full of the chemical they gave me to do it with. Although I'm sorry about the lawn, I'm not sorry about the implications of my act. Now go ahead and punish me.' The punishment, I remarked, must fit, not only the crime, but the degree of responsibility for the crime. It was clear to me that he was not vicious, merely misled. I therefore proposed to hold him at the very considerable expense of having the lawn returfed where necessary . . . which would be a suitable and durable reminder to him that he had allowed himself to be duped. The debit would be recorded in a suspended account against his name, and he could pay it off over the years ahead. And let his friends make what propaganda they could out of *that*.

"Since then, a week has passed and all, so far, has been quiet. But there is a very nasty smell in the air, and some of it, I think, is traceable to the sour frustration I have caused among the extremists by behaving so non-committally about Balliston. His friends wanted a martyrdom and have got instead a text-book example of liberal dealing; so they are (one may fear) turning nastier than ever. Yet what can they do without their martyr?

"The Council met again this morning, the Senior Fellow being back in his place again. He is voting, predictably, for Balbo Blakeney's proposal, which received ten votes, as did Tom Llewyllyn's. Deadlock. I don't imagine the vote will change for months to come; and I can't make up my mind whether this will help or hinder the promoters of future protests. Neither, I should say. The extremists' ostensible complaint is that Beyfus has been decisively rejected, and nothing can now alter that. Can they, one wonders, use Beyfus alone, without a martyr in his cause, to stage their holocaust? No. A martyr they must have, and it pleases me mightily to have withheld him."

What the Provost did not understand, since he had been brought up to respect the truth, was the facility with which Mayerston and his associates were capable of tailoring the facts to fit their purpose. A formula had been readily devised to transform Constable's moderate treatment of Hugh Balliston into a deed of grinding tyranny, and the popular version which was now being put about went something like this:

"Hugh Balliston of Lancaster has committed an act of moral and social conscience in protesting against Lancaster's rejection of Lord Beyfus's progressive proposals. In order to make his protest significant, Hugh was compelled to deface college property. Since Provost Constable holds property more sacred than conscience, he is making Hugh pay for the damage."

So far, the formula kept within hailing distance of the truth, but at this point there was an abrupt switch of the tiller.

"Hugh is a student of working class background" (the formula continued) "who can not afford to pay the sum demanded even if his political creed permitted him to do so. But if he doesn't pay up by the end of the term, he is to be rusticated until he does. Since he will never be able to, he is in reality being sent down from the University and deprived of his degree – all because he has spoken up for equality and justice in defiance of age and privilege."

"So you see," said Mona Corrington, who was elaborating on this theme to Lord Beyfus, "there has been a gross abuse of authority by your Provost. A week has passed since he penalised Mr Balliston in this intolerable fashion, and yet none of you in Lancaster has done anything about it. Why not?"

"Because," said Beyfus wearily, "what you have been saying is mistaken. Mr Balliston is not to be rusticated, nor is any other pressure to be put on him. As I understand it, he has his whole life-time in which to pay."

"That's not as most people understand it."

"Then most people have not understood it."

"They've got the main idea," Mona said; "they know that Balliston is being punished for disrespect of college property, and they won't stand for it."

"See here, Mona. Outside, on the College Stones, is parked a smart, green Jaguar. Yours. If you went out now and found someone scratching slogans on it with a chisel, you would do your best to detain him and make him pay for the damage. Right?"

"It would depend," said Mona, "on the slogans. Any right-wing rottenness, and I'd call the police at once. But if I approved the message, and if I felt it had come from some warm and youthful heart—"

"—Then you'd pat the culprit on his curly head," said Beyfus, "and you'd drive to your garage, where you'd shout and scream at the foreman until he promised to respray your car with absolute priority over all other cars whatever. And when the bill came in, you'd send it on to this college, claiming that your car was on college ground when it was damaged and that the porters should have been guarding it more carefully. I know you, Mona. You have everything both ways . . . you have everything a hundred ways."

"If you're going to take such a stupid tone, Beyfus, I shan't be at all nice to you for a long time" – she paused for this to sink in – "and I shan't tell you the most important thing which I came here to say."

"What's that?"

"Apologise first for being so offensive."

"Mona, my darling," said Beyfus contritely, "I wouldn't hurt you for the world. It was only my little joke."

"I've told you before, Beyfus: the times we live in are too serious for jokes. Now then. The big news is this. Although all of you in this college have been too flabby to do anything about Hugh Balliston, others are getting ready to march to his defence. The story has been put round, Beyfus, and anger is growing."

"Everything seems quiet enough to me."

"That's as it should be. Though indignation is already blazing, discipline is being used to contain it until the right moment. The authorities are being lulled, Beyfus. And meanwhile the troops are massing in the dark, ready to attack with the dawn, when the sleep of the authorities is always deepest."

"And who told you all this, my dear?"

"I am in touch with the organisers."

"That boy, Mayerston?"

"Those who help him."

"Hmmm," said Beyfus. "He does know, I take it, that if he spends too long lulling the authorities he will also lull his own troops?"

"He knows that, Beyfus. He knows just how long he can keep the flame of anger burning, and he will strike when he has kindled it to its fiercest."

"He certainly seems to have made an impression on you. All these fancy metaphors."

"Don't be flippant, Beyfus. When the soldiers of liberation go over the top for the dawn attack, you and I must be with them."

"Mona, sweet Mona. Let us have *either* the kindling flame of righteous anger *or* the massed troops of liberation. Let us please not have both. Let us for preference have neither. Exactly what is to happen, Mona dear, and when?"

Dropping her fancy metaphors and using the most precise and concrete of terms, Mona proceeded to tell him.

"Tell me, Miss Hetta," said Balbo Blakeney, as he drew the comb slowly through her hair, "have you seen young Balliston?"

"Yes," said Hetta miserably.

"What does he say about this fine? Does he reckon it's fair?"

"He doesn't say anything much. He's got some secret, but he's not telling it to me. All I know is that he's sticking to Mayerston."

"And you're still trying to prise him loose?"

"I've begged him," Hetta said. "I've told him how lightly he's been let off over this lawn thing, that next time they're bound to send him away, that he's ruining all he's worked for. But he won't listen to anything I say."

"So you're still staying out of his bed?" said Balbo carefully.

"Yes, and I can't bear it. He looks at me and says, 'I need you, Hetta.' And I say, 'All right. Just give up all this rubbish with Mayerston.' 'I can't do that,' he says, 'not now; but Hetta,' he says, 'if you'll only trust me and love me, I'll tell you what we're planning. I'll show it's not rubbish. I'll tell you everything, Hetta, if only you'll come into my arms.'"

"But you won't?"

"No."

"So all of this is getting you both nowhere." Balbo grazed her scalp very gently with the sharp points of the comb. "He gets no love and you've not the slightest idea what he's up to."

"Not the slightest."

"But he's up to something, Miss Hetta. Although it's been so quiet, they're all up to something – that I know. If we knew what, we might be able to help him before it's too late."

"Then shall I make love to him after all, Mr Blakeney? Then he'll tell me what's going to happen, and I can tell you, and it can all be stopped."

"You couldn't do it, Missy. If he told you, he'd be trusting you. You'd choke to death if you tried to breathe a word of it, to me or anyone else."

"What can we do, Mr Blakeney?"

"There's one thing. I can try to find out what's going on from Tony Beck. I doubt they've told him, but he may know something."

"Will he tell you if he does?"

"He might drop a hint without meaning to. I know him very well, Missy, and I'm good at picking up hints."

"And then?"

"We'll see what we can make of it all and do whatever we can."

"Kind Mr Blakeney. Oh, I do want to help him, to comfort him . . . to have him comfort me. I need him so."

"And I need you, Miss Hetta."

For a long time, while Balbo went on combing, Hetta was silent. Then :

"Like . . . like Hugh does, Mr Blakeney?" she said.

"Not quite like that. It'll be very easy for you, I promise."

"Show me then."

He took her hand and showed her.

"No," she said after a while. "Not like that. You're kind and good and patient. You deserve better than that."

She shifted herself between his knees until she was kneeling up before him.

"Go on combing my hair," she said, and lowered her head towards his lap so that he might do so.

"How much will it cost?" croaked Daniel Mond to Tom Llewyllyn.

They were standing together on the rear lawn, watching the last of the re-turfing. The damaged circle of grass which had represented Hugh's grammatical full stop had been cut clean out and a fresh and verdant disc, exactly measured, was now being eased into place.

"More than Balliston can pay."

"He doesn't have to pay," said Daniel: "not until he's older. If then."

"Even so," said Tom, "if anyone wants to twist it all to make trouble, it won't be difficult. A poor scholar is being put at charges to maintain a luxurious feature of the college decor. That's all the provocation they need."

"You think they'll rise to it?"

"Of course. Not that it makes any difference. They'd have found or fabricated some 'legitimate grievance' in any case. Once we turned down Beyfus, they were bound to."

"Then why didn't you support Beyfus?"

"Why didn't you?"

"Because," said Daniel, "one cannot give in so easily. One cannot stand by and say nothing while everything is pulled to pieces."

"Exactly. That's why I framed my scheme. It was workable, it conceded a measure of necessary change, and I hoped – I just hoped – that it would satisfy all parties for the time being and give us breathing space. But this plan of Balbo's for the Chapel – the mere fact that it's being entertained at all – will infuriate absolutely everyone. And with this affair of Balliston's thrown in . . ."

"Everything seems quiet."

"It aways does – until the next time. By the way, Fielding Gray's written. He's coming to spend next Saturday night."

"Oh good," said Daniel. "We'll all be able to listen to the Madrigals. He'll enjoy that."

In London, Isobel Stern cooked a gala dinner in Patricia's honour, as Patricia was returning to Grantchester the next day. Although Isobel knew that her sister would not appreciate the attention, she was glad of the excuse, being very fond of food, for an extra special blow-out.

Luckily the chambermaid at Patricia's hotel had taken to Baby (God alone knew why) and had volunteered to baby-sit. So Patricia was able to come to Isobel's unencumbered, which was an unusual blessing, and arrived looking absolutely stunning. For Isobel had been as good as her word; during the last week she had had Patricia refurbished cap-à-pé. The result was somewhat in the Empire mode: a hair style of tight curls to frame the bold, seignorial face, and a loose and simple gown which disguised the slackness of Patricia's bosom while emphasising the strength and amplitude of her buttocks and her thighs.

"My word," said Gregory Stern, "Tom's in for a nice surprise."

Neither Isobel nor Patricia bothered to explain that Tom was beside the point.

"You might tell him," Gregory went on, as he tucked into his langouste flan, "that I'm anxious to discuss this book he's writing."

"Did you like the chapters he sent you?"

"Yes," said Gregory, putting down his fork and rapidly fingering every button about his person one after the other, "and no. You see, it's a very important subject, the nature of power, and Tom's aperçus are undeniably very subtle, but it's all – what shall I say? – it's all rather donnish. Tom's public is used to something less demanding . . . more friendly in tone."

"So what are you going to do about it?" said Patricia. "Whenever it's finished, that is."

"I hoped Tom might make certain cuts and concessions. To please his loyal public and his loyal publisher."

"Isn't it about time," said Isobel, "that you published a donnish book? Instead of grubbing after money all day long."

"I dare say," said Gregory, "that Tom will be thinking about money too."

"He certainly ought to be," said Patricia. "I'm sure I've got none to spare. Not after paying for Baby's dental treatment."

"Mean bitch," Isobel said. "I hope young thingamabob comes off all over your new dress."

"*What* did you say?" said Gregory.

"Nothing. Just an old nursery joke."

Partly out of politeness and partly out of naivety, Gregory allowed this to pass without further comment. So, from different motives, did Patricia. For the truth was that Isobel's remark had conjured up so vivid a picture of Hugh Balliston in priapic flood that Patricia was half faint with lust and anxious to change the subject back again while a vestige of self-control was still left to her.

"What you must know about Tom," she said firmly, "is that these days he is not in a mood to make cuts or concessions to please anyone. That college has destroyed his sense of obligation."

"Hark at her," said Isobel, and set down a dish of truffled chicken's breasts cooked in cream and framboise.

"It's true," Patricia insisted. "All he wants for his book is the applause of the Provost and Fellows of Lancaster College. Nothing else matters to him."

"Good for Tom," said Isobel, "and one in the schnozzle for poor old Fagin here."

Gregory smirked. He always enjoyed it when Isobel insulted his Jewishness.

"That's all very well," said Patricia, "but he can't stay in that mutual admiration society for ever. At least, I hope not. It's time he started facing up to the world again."

"When he sees you tomorrow," said Gregory, "back home and looking like an Empress, he will do whatever you say." He raised his glass. "To reunion," he said.

Having no ready excuse for refusing, Patricia joined in the toast.

"Have some more hock, Miss Hetta."

"Thank you, Mr Blakeney. It's delicious."

Balbo was giving Hetta lunch in his rooms.

"Now then, Missy," he said, having poured the wine, "I did what I said I would. I've been to see Tony Beck, and I have to tell you that I got exactly nowhere."

"He couldn't tell you anything?"

"Couldn't or wouldn't. Whatever they're up to this time, and whatever part they've fixed for young Balliston, they're keeping very close about it."

"Oh."

"So I'm afraid I've been no help to you at all. Which being so, if you don't want to see me any more, I'll quite understand."

"But you have been a help, Mr Blakeney." Hetta drunk a healthy draught of hock and lowered her glass. "Don't you *know* how I enjoy coming here to see you?"

"Coming to see a wizened old thing like me?"

Hetta walked round the table and leant over Balbo from behind. She clasped her hands across his chest and kissed his neck.

"You're sweet and gentle and clever," she said, "and you've done all you can about Hugh. I still worry about him dreadfully, but he's a big boy now, and if he wants to behave so sillily, we'll just have to let him."

Then she went back to her place and whacked into her lobster mayonnaise. After a little while, Balbo said:

"I've hired a car for the afternoon. A car with a chauffeur."

"Goodness, how grand."

"No, it's not. I've never learnt to drive, you see. I thought we'd go to Long Melford. It's a beautiful place, you'll find."

"Isn't there a famous church?"

"Yes, Miss Hetta, there is. I particularly want to show it to you."

"Do you know," said Hetta, gaily cracking a claw, "I think that's the best thing that anyone's ever said to me."

A luncheon party of a very different kind was going on in Tony Beck's rooms : beer and cheese sandwiches, to give the occasion what Beck considered a suitably proletarian air, while at the same time saving him money. Present were Hugh Balliston, Mayerston, and Mayerston's principal lieutenant, a squat and snake-eyed youth who sported a fringe of beard and a light blue anorak.

"So you all understand," said Mayerston, "exactly how it's going to work?"

They all nodded, Hugh rather glumly.

"It's particularly important," Mayerston said to him gently, "that you should have the right sort of look on your face while it's all going on. You're the centre-piece of the whole show. Try not to look as if you were just about to be hung."

"I'm the martyr. Isn't that how martyrs look?"

"No," said Mayerston. "They look long-suffering but radiant."

"Not easy."

"Agreed. We may have to give you a shot of something before we put you on. You can arrange that, Job?"

"Yup," said the light blue lieutenant.

"One thing you haven't told us," said Tony Beck edgily : "when is it to happen?"

"From what the lads tell me," said Job in a voice like tyres scrunching over broken glass, "the student boys and girls have bought this martyr bit about Balliston here. Indignation is running higher all the time – in Cambridge and in other places too. But unless something new happens, they'll start to cool early next week, and once they do that we'll have to blow very hard to get the fire up again."

"Thank you, Job. I think that makes our best time pretty clear, gentlemen. This week-end. Sunday, Sunday at . . . half past twelve o'clock."

"But the Madrigals won't be over," said Hugh stupidly.

"The Madrigals?"

"This Sunday," explained Beck, "is Madrigal Sunday. They are sung between noon and 1 p.m."

"What are madrigals?" scrunched Job.

"Madrigals," said Mayerston, "are songs of love set for un-accompanied voices. They are beautiful but somewhat repetitious, and I'm quite sure that by half past twelve on Sunday everyone will have heard enough."

While he was working in his room that afternoon, Tom Llewyllyn received two telephone calls.

The first was from the Cambridge University Press. It appeared that the Syndics had considered, with great interest, the specimen chapters which Tom had submitted to them, and that they now wished to express their provisional readiness to publish his book on its completion.

The second call, which came only a few minutes later, was from Patricia.

"Patricia, oh Patricia, the University Press wants to publish my book."

"Well, if that's what you want . . . I'm very happy for you, Tom."

"Thank you, darling. How's everything in London?"

"I'm not in London, Tom. Baby and I came down this morning."

"Oh. Why didn't you warn me?"

"I didn't know. The dentist was much quicker than I thought." She started to gabble. "He saw Baby at once, and he gave us appointments every day – you know how clever

Gregory is at arranging all that – and before I knew where I was it was finished. But Tom . . ."

"Yes, Patricia?"

"There's no need for you to come back to Grantchester just yet if you don't want to."

"But of course I must come back now you and Baby are home."

"Listen, Tom. How long did you arrange to stay in the college?"

"Till the middle of next week. But now that you and—"

"—Tom. You said that the college would have a lot of trouble arranging bedmakers and things. If you told them next week, you must stay till next week. It's not fair to mess them about."

Which was true enough, Tom thought. And not only that: since Fielding Gray was coming to spend Saturday night, the week-end arrangements would be very much easier and more enjoyable if he himself were still living in college. But it was most unlike Patricia to take such a liberal line; really most unlike her.

"Are you quite sure," he now said, "that you and Baby will be all right?"

"Quite sure, darling. I've had a simply marvellous time, and I feel absolutely wonderful, and the last thing I want to do is upset your plans. Now today is Thursday, so I'll expect you back today week."

Well, thought Tom as he rang off, I was certainly right to make her go to London; it's done her a power of good. Thoroughly contented, he turned back to the quarto page before him. Now that he knew the University Press was backing him, the labour already seemed lighter. But it would never do to become over-confident. Careful with your words now, he told himself, you can't be too careful with words.

"True authority," he began to write, "must depend on reciprocal good will. There must be competence and justice on the one side, respect and trust on the other. But even where such conditions obtain, there is room for endless misunderstanding and mischance. Let just one clever dissident plausibly misrepresent the motives of one faltering minister, and the trust that has been won by a century of stable government can be shattered overnight . . ."

The following morning Patricia parked Baby with her obliging neighbour, got herself up to kill, and went slamming into Cambridge as fast as her rather large feet would carry her. There were just two things she wanted: one of them was to meet Hugh Balliston and the other was not to meet Tom. The former at least must be mainly a matter of luck, but Friday, she reminded herself, had always been her lucky day.

Not at first, however. She drew a blank in the Fellows' Garden and spent an unrewarding hour hovering round the back gate of the college. The easiest way, of course, would have been to march straight into the Fellows' Garden Hostel and ask for Mr Balliston's room; but she had an idea that such a direct proceeding would be not only indiscreet but also presumptuous, for if God meant her to meet Hugh, He would arrange it at His Own pleasure. She was bound, she thought, to wait; and she now decided on King's Parade as the next place to wait in. The quickest route thither lay straight through Lancaster and, as she reflected, right under the windows of Tom's rooms; so she mopped her brow and heaved a heavy sigh and walked all the way round by the Mill Bridge.

In King's Parade she had a cup of nasty coffee, spent half an hour reading the University Notice Board in front of the Senate, another half hour looking at college scarves in the window of Ryder and Amies, and then, heart sinking and hope fading, turned up past Great St Mary's to patrol the Market Square. Three times round and no joy. Into Heffers'. Out of Heffers'. Up Petty Cury and down again, across to Bowes & Bowes, back to Heffers', thence to the Ladies in the square to patch herself up (and did she need it). Up the steps, through the parked cars, along to the entrance of the Arts Theatre, look at the playbill (some modern rubbish about a Bolivian bandit), off down Bene't Street – are you mad, woman, cavorting round like this? – past the front gate of Lancaster (quickly, before that officious porter sees you) and straight on to the University Notice Board – for after all, someone might have put up a new notice since you were last there.

And so someone had. It announced that the Rylands Prize for Shakespearian Studies was awarded to HUGH EDWARD BALLISTON for his Essay on Shakespeare's Theories of Kingship. And here – merciful Jesus – was Hugh Balliston himself, pale, worried and nervous but unmistakably Hugh Balliston, coming down King's Parade in order to read about his triumph . . .

. . . There's that ferocious tourist woman again, thought Hugh as he walked down King's Parade. Reading the University Notice Board. What the devil has it got to do with her? . . .

. . . Very much to Patricia's surprise, Hugh did not turn aside to look at the Notice Board but kept straight on. He's seen it already, she thought. He's seen it, or he knows about it, and he's walking straight on and out of my life. And then she thought, perhaps he doesn't know, perhaps it just hasn't occurred to him, anyway I must try it, now or never—

"—Young man," she positively bellowed, "come here and read this . . ."

. . . Patently mad. Keep going. No. Don't just leave the poor thing there, you can't. Humour her. Wild, gleaming face, dress rumpled between quaking thighs, hair one crazy mess of decomposing curls – I should have kept going but it's too late now . . .

"Read this," Patricia said.

Hugh read it, then read it again.

"Hugh Edward Balliston," she said. "That's you."

He nodded.

"Aren't you pleased?"

"It's all so unreal," he said. "I wrote that essay and sent it in – why, months ago now. I'd almost forgotten. I thought they'd decided not to award the prize," he burbled; "they often don't, you know, if none of the entries is good enough. So when I didn't hear, I thought—"

"—Never mind what you thought. Darling, darling Hugh, you've won the bloody prize."

This peculiar statement brought him to his senses again.

"How did you know my name?" he said.

"Never mind that. Is it a big prize?"

"Not in money. But it's a good one to win, because anyone can go in for it. Graduates, dons, anyone."

"You beat them all," she said, her voice ringing with pride: "you beat the bloody lot."

"Do you always say 'bloody' so often?" Hugh asked. "Who are you, anyway?"

Now or never.

"I'm Tom Llewyllyn's wife, Patricia" – he'd have to know sooner or later – "and I want to talk to you. We've never met but we were once at the same party. The Provost's party last Michaelmas. So we do know each other in a way."

Her voice urged this with such a note of pleading that he could only nod assent.

"We will get a taxi in the Market Square," said Patricia, remembering just in time that it was her role as laid down by Isobel to command and not to beg, "and drive to my house for lunch."

What am I doing in this taxi with this huge, ramping woman, who is shamelessly rubbing her knee against me and smelling of sweat? What ogress is this who has swept down from her lair to carry me off? Tom Llewyllyn's wife, she says. I thought someone told me that he'd married rather grandly – a Tory ministers' daughter. *That's it:* the eldest daughter of Sir Edwin Turbot, grand vizier of the Conservative Party, now some years dead. Well, he'll be turning in his marble tomb if he knows about this lot – his daughter capering round Cambridge like a public whore . . .

. . . What shall I do with him now that I've got him? He's not responding to my knee. Never mind, there's the whole afternoon. Do as Isobel told me : just announce what's going to happen and take it from there. I'm Mummy, and Mummy knows best . . .

. . . A nice face really, under that upper-class arrogance. Vulnerable. Deprived. All very sad – and very clear. Tom Llewyllyn's died on her in bed, so she wants to be consoled. Badly, by the look of it. Well, she's not getting anything from me. Hugh's for Hetta . . . Or is he? Hetta's not for Hugh. She hasn't been for over a week. Over a week, and not a peck on the forehead to show for it. And then again, this woman, this Patricia, it's not just sex she's after, it's me : she knew who I was, she was happy that I'd won that prize, she wasn't waiting just for anybody, she was waiting there for me. "I want to talk to you," she said. And all this clumsy business with her knee – it's quite plain she's never done this kind of thing before, she just doesn't know how to begin. Humour her. Why not? Hetta's dried up on me, and Sunday may well be the end of everything, and it's a long walk home from wherever we're going. So play up to her, Hugh Edward Balliston : cast your bread upon the waters, and see what the gods send back on the tide . . .

. . . He's pressing back against my knee. Bless his heart. But why does he look so white and ill? He ought to be so happy about that prize. Perhaps he hasn't been getting enough to eat, they're very poor, some of these boys, I must feed him up . . . so what have I got in the house? *Christ.* Beans. Tinned sausages (skinless). Heinz Spaghetti – but no bread to make toast. Why didn't I think? I could have gone to Fortnum's yesterday before leaving London. Stop at a shop? Of course. But I haven't any money, I only brought two shillings and that went on the coffee in King's Parade, how to pay the taxi, there's no money at home either. Oh Jesus, Jesus Christ . . .

"Please let me."

Seeing her distress, Hugh had at once taken out his purse and paid for the taxi.

"But I like Heinz Spaghetti and tinned sausages."

. . . Well, he'd eaten it all, and there'd even been a cup of Camp Coffee – no milk, of course, but he said he didn't mind about that. And now she really must assert herself, get the upper hand, dominate like Isobel said. Mummy knows best.

"You look tired, Hugh," she said. "Come upstairs and lie down."

. . . And really it wasn't too bad. She seemed to have got hold of some pretty way-out ideas from somewhere, and this one at least was a bit ambitious for a woman of her build, but it wasn't going badly at all . . . even if she was a bit fierce with those huge teeth.

"Patricia, nice Patricia," he said.

"Hugh, nice Hugh. Aren't bodies fun?"

"Yyyoowww. Try the other way again. Between your breasts."

"All right, but don't look. My breasts are horrid. Like snakes."

"Lovely long snakes, sliding and sliding. Go on . . . go on . . ."

"Mrs Llewyllyn," called a female voice from downstairs, "oh, Mrs Llew-yyyllll-yn. I saw you come home in your taxi, so I've brought Baby back a bit early." And then lower but clearly audible through the open door, "Go on, Baby darling. Run upstairs to Mummy."

"Mummy, Mummy, Mummy . . ."

"Into the wardrobe, Hugh."

"Mummy, Mummy, Mummy . . ."

"That's it. Mind your . . . Hugh, I've *got* to shut the door. *Get it out of the way.*"

"Mummy, Mummy . . ."

"Down between your legs – like *that*."

Slam. And a rush of little feet on the landing.

"Oh Mummy, you do look funny. Why haven't you got any clothes on?"

"Because I took them off and put them in the wardrobe."

"Why?"

"Because I've been resting."

"But you *haven't* put them in the wardrobe. They're down here all over the floor. So what are you doing by the wardrobe?"

"I was just going to get some other ones out."

"Can I help you choose them?"

"No. I've decided to put those ones on again after all."

Patricia crossed the room, scooped her clothes off the floor and started to dress herself under the close and malicious inspection of Baby. She was very afraid lest Baby might notice Hugh's clothes, which were piled neatly on the chair by the dressing table, but she needn't have worried, as Baby was too fascinated by her mother's anatomy to have eyes for anything else.

"And now," Patricia said, as she tugged her dress down over her sweaty rump, "Mummy and Baby will go for a nice walk."

"Where?"

"By the river, I suppose." And then rather louder, so that Hugh could hear in the wardrobe, "We'll go for a nice walk by the river and not get back till tea."

"Shouldn't we make the bed first?"

"No. We can do that later. So we'll forget it, Baby. We'll forget it," she called bleakly towards the wardrobe, "just forget it. We just won't think about it any more."

Mummy knows best.


As soon as all was quiet, Hugh extracted himself from the wardrobe (having not sustained any very serious personal injury), put on his clothes, and set out for Cambridge. Since Patricia and Baby were to be in the region of the river, and since it was clear that Patricia did not wish to set eyes on him again, he walked along the by-road to Trumpington, where he caught a bus.

As he was carried along the Trumpington Road and past the Botanical Gardens, he attempted to cast an account of the day's events. First, the Rylands Prize: excellent. Second, this incident with Patricia Llewyllyn: that too would have been good in its way, if it hadn't had so ludicrous an ending. What a pity, he thought; we were both enjoying it so much; but as things turned out, it may have done positive harm. Not indeed to me, he thought, though it has left me jumpy and dissatisfied, but to poor Patricia, who may well think in terms of divine intervention (or something of the sort) and never attempt to rebel against her lot again. Certainly, her last few words before she left the bedroom with Baby had shown a grim determination to call the whole thing off for good.

But perhaps, he thought, that was only her first reaction to the shock of interruption. Perhaps she will think again. If so, do I want to go on with it? On the whole, he was disposed to think not. It had all been unusual, rather moving and very educative, and there was no doubt that Patricia's physical attributes were both ample and curious. But as against all this, it would be neither comfortable nor prudent to have an affair with the wife of a don. It was obvious that the obliging neighbour who had delivered Baby must already have smelt a sizeable rat, and though Tom Llewyllyn would doubtless take a fairly enlightened view of such quadrupeds, there was no denying that they carried dangerous fleas and were best left undisturbed behind the arras. And so, while Hugh was deeply regretful that the antics on Mrs Tom Llewyllyn's bed had not reached their proper culmination, he was, by and large, disinclined to make or even take any opportunity for their renewal.

In any case, he thought, as he walked from the bus stop to the main gate of Lancaster, God knows where I shall be after this business on Sunday. If the worst comes to the worst, I may not even have time to collect the Rylands Prize, let alone go a-wooing to Grantchester. I wish it were over, he thought: it is the right thing to do and nothing will stop me doing it, but I wish to God that Sunday was over and myself safely back with my books. And with Hetta, if she'll have me. The trouble is, he told himself as he walked into the Great Court, that this sort of thing never *is* over. Revolution is self-perpetuating. Once you start, you have to go on to the end – to the ever-receding end – or there's no point in starting. Mayerston will never set me free, unless he's defeated and got rid of; and if that happens, I may have to go too. I'm trapped, he told himself: I have no way out, ever . . . except by deserting Mayerston . . .

He was nearing Willow Bridge now, and among those who were standing on it and staring over Scholars' Meadow was Hetta. Or someone very like her. He quickened his step. Yes, surely it was. If he asked her, she would come to his room, listen to him, hear his troubles. She might even take pity on him, when she knew how unhappy he was, and give herself again despite her vow.

"Hetta," he called, as he hurried towards the bridge, "oh, Hetta."

Hetta turned and waved.

"Oh, Hetta . . ."

"Never mind her," said a voice by his side; "I want a word with you. Now."

Tom Llewyllyn.

"Here he is," said Tom to Daniel Mond.

Tom had led Hugh fiercely across Willow Close and up into Daniel's rooms on staircase Omega. Daniel was lying full length on his sofa, looking pale and persecuted, fiddling uneasily with the silk scarf which he always wore round his throat. Tom shoved Hugh forward, like a police constable propelling a vagrant toward the station sergeant's desk, and then fell back to hover alertly by the door, as though he anticipated that Hugh was going to run for it at any moment.

"Oh," said Daniel, and then, "Ah . . . I've just heard about the Rylands Prize, Hugh. Well done. It must have been a wonderful essay."

This was not what Hugh expected in the circumstances, and plainly not what Tom expected either. He now advanced and stood, almost threateningly, over Daniel's head.

"We are here to discuss a different piece of writing," Tom said. "Show him, Daniel."

"Oh . . . er . . . yes," said Daniel, and passed Hugh a sheet of folded quarto.

This was an anonymous letter, which said that Daniel was a reactionary Judas who had betrayed the prophet Beyfus. Daniel, it seemed, was also a high priest and a Pharisee, the false Jew who had spurned the oppressed and the humble among his people, whose voice was the voice of Beyfus. Daniel was a filthy Jewish Fascist and Daniel was Fascist Jewish filth.

"Your gang wrote that," said Tom when Hugh had finished reading.

"No. Why should they? What good can it do them?"

"*Some one* wrote it."

"Not me. Why show it to me?"

"Jacquiz Helmut warned me," said Daniel in a placating voice, "that this sort of thing was likely to happen. He warned me weeks ago."

"It's the work of a psychotic," said Hugh, "or some one with a personal spite against Daniel."

"Jacquiz said," persisted Daniel, who was obviously finding it an effort to speak at all, "that people would get angry. When they get angry, he said, they look for faces to punch, and they prefer Jewish ones."

"Why?" asked Hugh, genuinely concerned to know.

"Because Jewish faces are clever and self-righteous."

"Well, he was certainly right about that."

"Thank you, Hugh . . . Your candour is appreciated."

"Never mind all that," said Tom. "The real point is that people can easily get out of control. You know that, Balliston. You know, as well as anyone, that once you start stirring people up they may do anything. This," he said, snatching the letter from Hugh, "and far, far worse. So why," he screamed into Hugh's face, "have you helped your rotten, scummy friends to do this to Daniel?"

"How unfortunate," said Daniel inconsequently (deprecating Tom's noise and fury but uncertain how to quench them), "that this had to happen on the day Hugh has won the Rylands prize. Well done again, Hugh. I am pleased."

"I wish I was. It's all been spoilt."

"You've only got yourself to blame for that," said Tom, who had sensed Daniel's distaste for his honking and was now speaking in a low voice that was parched and crackling with hate. "I dare say you didn't write this thing, but you're to blame, because you've licked up the slime of envy from the gutters and gone round breathing it out in rant."

Hugh ignored this.

"You don't look at all well," he said to Daniel. "Is there anything I can do?"

"Yes," said Daniel. "Stop making this horrible trouble for us all. Write your essays and give us pleasure. Don't let your good name get mixed up in all that," he pointed a limp finger at the letter which Tom was still clutching. "Stay away from that."

"But can't you understand?" said Hugh wearily. "That letter has nothing to do with the people I'm working for or the cause I serve. It's something different, separate, totally irrelevant."

Tom grunted with anger.

"And *can't* you understand," he said, "that if only you and your kind had kept quiet in the first place, this letter would never have been written? You set the climate, for it, Balliston; you whipped up the hatred from which it sprang. What does Daniel care who actually wrote it? All he wants, all any of us wants, is to be left in peace."

"But that's just it," said Hugh. "You're all so complacent that we have a duty to rouse you. You've let your consciences become so lethargic that if we don't make a row we'll never wake you up."

"Look here, Hugh," said Daniel, "would you mind going away? I realise that your motives are pure and high-minded, and I'm quite sure that the young have a lot to teach us all, but will you kindly go away and leave us in peace and quiet?"

"*I* didn't ask myself up here," said Hugh huffily, and flounced out of the room.

When Hetta saw Tom confront Hugh and lead him off to Daniel's staircase, she knew at once from Tom's face that something unpleasant had happened. At first she was minded to stay on Willow Bridge until Hugh came out again and then ask him what was up. But as the minutes went by, she realised that she was now late for her tea-time appointment with Balbo, and since it wasn't fair to keep the poor old darling waiting (and since she was in any case very hungry), she moved herself smartly off towards Sitwell's.

And so it came about that when Hugh left Tom and Daniel he did not, as he had hoped and expected, find Hetta waiting for him. Forgetting the friendly wave which she had given before he went off with Tom, he now assumed that she was deliberately avoiding him, and this, after his frustration at Grantchester and the disagreeable scene in Daniel's room, put him in a very bitter mood indeed. It was quite intolerable that the world should so misuse the winner of the Rylands Prize: who did they all think they were? Well, by the time he and Mayerston had finished with them, they were certainly going to find out: parasites, reactionaries, decadents, that's what they were, Tom, Hetta, Patricia, Daniel, the lot, and it was going to be made very plain to them that there was no longer any place for their sort in a well ordered modern society. Come 12.30 on Sunday, now only some forty-four hours away, he, Hugh Edward Balliston, was going to give them a very nasty shock.

"There's something very odd about that young man," said Tom to Daniel as soon as Hugh had gone.

"He's sound at heart," said Daniel: "tiresome but genuine. Not at all odd as boys go nowadays."

"I didn't mean that. I meant something particular – something I only noticed just as he was leaving. Daniel . . . Balliston had a deep bite on the lobe of his right ear."

"And so?"

"Biting ear-lobes is a trick of Patricia's."

"For Christ's sake, Tom. Biting ear-lobes is a trick of any woman's."

"It's a trick of Patricia's when she gets excited. She does it almost without knowing – and very painful it can be. Right across the top of the lobe, drawing blood. Balliston had blood there, Daniel."

"Patricia doesn't even know him. She never comes in from Grantchester."

"Yes, but that's just where she saw him. Weeks ago, Daniel, she saw him there and asked me about him . . . in some detail. And she *does* come into Cambridge. The other day, so Wilfred the porter told me, she was waiting about outside the college for a good two hours. Wilfred went out and spoke to her: she was rather peculiar, he said."

"Tom, Tom, Tom. What's that to do with Hugh Balliston?"

"And since she's been back from London, she's been acting totally out of character. She's encouraging me to stay here in college. She doesn't want me back in my own home."

"*Tom* . . ."

"It fits, Daniel. Anyway, there's something up with her, and I mean to find out what."

Tom crossed the room to the telephone on Daniel's desk.

"Tom . . . you're not jealous?"

"No," said Tom between his teeth; "just curious."

He lifted the receiver.

"Tom dear," said Daniel, "put it down."

"Why?"

"You're being unreasonable and unkind. You're getting worked up because of a coincidence which probably means absolutely nothing."

"There's something going on, and I know it."

"Whatever it is, let her tell you when she wants to herself."

"Suppose she doesn't?"

"Then you'll have lost her confidence, in which case you'll have only yourself to thank."

"That's the one thing I couldn't bear. I don't mind what she does, Daniel, as long as she tells me. Now, if I ring up and ask, she will tell me, because she's a very truthful woman, and then I can tell myself I'm still in her confidence. But if I don't ring . . . and she says nothing . . . what am I to tell myself then?"

"The truth. That you've failed her and she no longer trusts you," Daniel paused and started breathing very heavily. "Tom," he said in a voice so small and thin that he sounded like a man calling for help from the depth of an immense chasm, "please do as I ask. Please, Tom. Don't do anything unkind. I couldn't bear it now if you did something unkind. You're all— Oh dear, oh dear, whatever am I saying?"

"Danny . . . what on earth's the matter?"

Tom put down the telephone receiver and came to stand over Daniel.

"I'm sorry, Tom. I'm not well. My throat. It gets infected again sometimes, it opens inside, you see, and it hurts me so much, Tom, and all this to make it worse."

"*Opens inside?* What in God's name have you got?"

"I tried to kill myself once – oh, a long time ago, and I can't ever tell you why – and . . . *this* is what I did."

He clawed his silk scarf away to show the flushed, puffy lesion, six inches long.

"But it's worse inside, Tom, and it flares up at me. I've got anti-biotics, but I have to use the tablets more and more often, and every time they take longer to help. *Stay with me, Tom.*"

Tom looked down at Daniel and at last, briefly but gravely, he nodded his head.

"I'll stay, Daniel. But in a little while, I'm going to have you taken over to my rooms, because they're bigger and so we can both sleep there. And there I will be with you and take care of you, until you are quite better. And then you will come back to your own rooms here, and I will go back to Patricia. You understand what I am saying, Daniel?"

"Yes, Tom. You are saying that you are not a man who disappears when he is most wanted. The way Fielding Gray used to disappear."

"Remember, Danny, I come from the people. Disappearing when you're wanted is very much an upper-class habit."


Ivor Winstanley, calling on Jacquiz Helmut, was surprised to find two large packed suitcases standing at the ready by the door.

"Going away, Jacquiz?" Ivor said. "In the middle of full term?"

"I have to consult a specialist about my health. Yours might benefit if you did the same."

Ivor pondered this for some time. At length:

"There's nothing the matter with my health," he said with some contempt.

"No? I should have thought your drinking was wearing you down a bit."

"Nevertheless, Jacquiz, I'll stick it out here. I may be a decaying old sot, but I know whose salt I've been eating all these years."

"Don't make heroic gestures, Ivor. Ageing and overfed scholars," said Jacquiz Helmut, "can seldom carry them off."


"I am bound to admit," wrote Robert Constable in his record, "that matters are not turning out as I had hoped. Despite my lenient treatment of Hugh Balliston, the extremists have managed to twist the affair in such a way as to cause mounting indignation throughout the whole University and beyond it. If Balliston isn't exactly a martyr, he's not far off it, and something has occurred to increase his face value (so to speak).

"For he has just won the Rylands Prize with an essay so distinguished that the judges have recommended its publication at the expense of the Chest. As far as that goes I'm delighted, but there's no doubt that this achievement will turn Balliston into a more prominent figure than ever and make of him an even more powerful tool in the hands of his exploiters.

"These must surely be planning to make use of him as soon as possible; but *how*? If only I had the smallest clue, I might devise some workable tactic. As it is, however, they have learned their lesson from the failure of the Garden Hostel protest; they now realise that to advertise their intentions is to vitiate them, and they have kept very close indeed about their next move. Even that ass Tony Beck has given nothing away. One can only stand to, as it were, and be ready for anything from any direction, a nerve-racking predicament which I have not experienced since the war; and come to that, I could almost wish I still had my old company of Gurkhas at my back to see me through . . .

"One minor nuisance. Jacquiz Helmut has left for London this morning, on the plea that he must have a series of important consultations with his heart specialist. He says he must be away at least a week, and this will make trouble over the history supervisions at the worst possible time, just before the exams. A headache for the Tutor, who is not the most resourceful of men.

"And one routine bore. Tomorrow is Madrigal Sunday, and I must give the customary luncheon party in the Lodge after the madrigals. This kind of occasion brings Elvira out at her silliest. Although we have the five most competent college servants in to cook and serve, she somehow contrives to put even these off their stroke and turn the thing into a fiasco. Last year would have been catastrophe, if it hadn't been for some memorable jokes from Tom Llewyllyn, who just managed to save the situation. But this year we shan't have Tom to depend on, for he tells me that he is seeing after poor Daniel (who is ill and also badly upset by an anonymous letter he has received) and doesn't care to leave him. All in all, though, perhaps this is just as well, because it seems that Tom has invited that contemptible fellow Fielding Gray for the weekend, and if Tom were coming to the lunch I suppose Gray would have to come too, which would really be most disagreeable to me after all that has happened over the years . . ."

Tom, Daniel and Tom's guest, Fielding Gray, were having dinner in Tom's rooms in Sitwell's. Because of Daniel's throat, Tom had ordered only the wettest dishes offered by the kitchen; but even so Daniel was making heavy going, this being due less to the state of his health than to the distaste which he felt at the appearance of Fielding Gray. When Daniel had last seen him fifteen years before, Gray had been a handsome if somewhat dissipated man of twenty-five; this evening he was not only middle-aged and obese but hideously disfigured in the face by the injuries which he had received while on active service in Cyprus in 1958. As Daniel had been warned of this, it should not have come as a shock, and indeed at first he was quite unworried by it; but as the evening went on, Gray's one red eye and pink plastic cheeks seemed to Daniel such an obscene travesty of the human countenance as to be proof positive of an evil which lay deep seated, not in Gray himself, but in God. This being so, Daniel tried to blame God and suffer Fielding Gray, which, given Gray's proximity and God's absence, was not an easy task.

"So you're never going back to London?" Tom was saying to his guest.

"Except for odd days, no. Tessie Buttock's been on at me

about it – tired of London means tired of life, she says, it's the
only quotation she knows – but I can do without London from
now on. Anyhow it doesn't suit Harriet."

"Harriet?"

"Harriet Ongley. My rehabilitator and companion. She
thinks London is bad for my character."

"And is it?" said Daniel.

"I wouldn't know, Daniel. You see, I haven't got a character
any more. I've never really had one since I was rejected by
this college."

"So you told me," said Daniel, "the first time we met. It
was false and self-pitying then, and it's much worse now. You
were a perfectly adequate soldier – as far as I could understand it – and you're now a successful novelist. Which reminds
me : I must tell you, Fielding, that I strongly resent the way
you twisted the real facts in *Operation Apocalypse.*"

*"Apocalypse* was a novel, Danny. It was not intended to
render events which actually happened but to tell a story which
would entertain readers. Although it was *suggested* by what
went on in Göttingen that summer, there is no further connection."

"That's what I told him," said Tom.

"Then why use my character?" said Daniel.

"To save myself the effort of inventing one."

"But if you use my character, you should respect it."

"The character in that novel," said Fielding Gray, "is
simply a collection of words. It does not exist as a real entity,
and there is therefore no question of respecting it as one respects a real human being. One merely disposes of it – i.e. of
the words of which it consists – in such a manner as to hold the
attention of the reader, thus encouraging him to pay out ready
money for one's next book."

"So that is your opinion of your art?"

"I never said I was an artist. I am an entertainer, Danny.
I arrange words in pleasing patterns in order to make money.
I try to give good value – to see that my patterns are well
wrought – but I do not delude myself by inflating the nature of

my function. I try to be neat, intelligent and lucid : let others be 'creative' or 'inspired'."


In Grantchester the conversation was less thoughtful but equally acrimonious.

"Bed time now, Baby."

"No."

"Nice bath first with Quacky Whacky, then into lovely warm bed."

"No, *no,* NO."

Christ, thought Patricia wearily, sometimes I wish she were dead. But better her for company than no one at all; at least there'll be some other human creature in the house during the long night to come.

"All right," she said : "one more game of Snakes and Ladders, and *then* bed."

Snakes and Ladders; "lovely long snakes, sliding and sliding"; Christ.


"You must understand," Fielding Gray was saying over the brandy, "that I do not want money out of greed. I want it only as a means to being independent."

"Independent of Harriet Ongley?"

Gray tightened his grip on his brandy glass and pursed what passed for his lips. Clearly this topic, though he himself had introduced it earlier, was not a welcome one.

"That's another matter altogether," he said thinly. "What I'm talking about is making oneself independent of the system . . . being in a position to tell all the bloody bureaucrats and politicians to go to the devil. I want to be beyond any man's interference."

"Independence as a denial of power," said Tom slowly; "a very respectable ambition. But doomed, Fielding. The bureaucrats and the politicians, the men who relish power, are determined to tie down every last one of us. At the moment, as you say, money can still procure a modest freedom; but this is an affront to the power boys and they're stopping it as fast as they can. First they tax your money; then they forbid you to use it except as and where they see fit; and finally they'll just sequester it – or render it worthless. Money as a means to independence is all but finished."

"So you think there's no hope?"

"I think," said Tom, "that very soon the only way of achieving independence of movement or action will be through winning power for oneself first. You're trying to evade the power boys, Fielding; but under modern conditions the only way to do that is to beat them at their own game. You can't be independent of them any more, but you can rise above them."

"Of course," said Daniel, "there is an easier way. If one is prepared to settle just for *intellectual* independence, there's not much they can do to stop you."

"They can stop you publishing."

"But they can't stop you thinking your own thoughts."

"Can't they?" said Gray. "A person who is thinking his own thoughts has a calm and satisfied look on his face which is very easy to recognise. As soon as *they* see that look, they can come and wipe it off."

"Then one must live alone."

"They can soon stop that. Rational use of available accommodation, they'll say: at least five people to every house – and one of them a government informer in case anyone presumes to think his own thoughts."

"Do we have to depress ourselves like this?" said Tom. "It's such a beautiful evening."

They all stood by the window and looked down on the Great Court. Someone was playing the organ in the Chapel ("Where my sheep may safely graze") and Henry VI pondered piously over his fountain.

"'Sitis boni pueri,'" said Fielding, "'mites et dociles, servientes Domino.'"

"What's that?"

"I should have thought you'd have known. It's what Henry VI said to a group of scholars when he met them one day near Eton. 'Be good boys,'" he translated, "'gentle and biddable, serving the Lord.' There is worse advice than that."

"It hardly conduces to independence," said Tom.

"But it could make for peace of mind . . . Who's that," said Fielding, "that young man walking down by the Chapel? *He* doesn't look very gentle or biddable."

"That's Hugh Balliston. He's a good boy really," said Daniel, "but just lately he's had rather a confusing time."

Early though it was, Hugh was going home to bed. He was unhappy and bored and lonely and also very afraid, so that temporary oblivion was really the only answer. And anyhow, tomorrow would be a long day.

I wish Hetta was with me, he thought. It's so lonely without her. Besides, that's just what I need to help me to get to sleep.

"Miss Hetta?"

"Mr Blakeney?"

"Were you asleep?"

"Yes . . . but I'm glad you woke me up."

She tweaked him and giggled softly.

"Next week," said Balbo, "I thought we'd look at more churches. If you'd like to."

"I'd love to. You explain them so beautifully."

"We might start with Ely Cathedral. 'Merrily sang the monks in Ely,'" quoted Balbo,

> " 'When Cnut, King, rowed thereby;
> Row, my knights, near the land,
> And hear we these monks' song . . .' "

"Oooh," shivered Hetta, "couldn't we go tomorrow?"

"No, Miss Hetta. We need a whole day for Ely, and tomorrow's the Madrigals. You wouldn't want to miss them, after all I've told you about them?"

"The Madrigals tomorrow," said Daniel, as they turned away from the window.

"I thought that was in May Week," said Fielding, "at the end of term."

"It is. The Cambridge Madrigal Society sings them from punts on the river. But tomorrow it's the Lancaster Madrigals – sung by our choir in front of the West Door of the Chapel. Immediately after Matins."

"Very handy," said Tom, "Right under my back window."

"But surely," said Fielding, "Matins and Madrigals don't mix."

"This college," said Tom, "has always taken the Chaucerian view . . . that God should be heartily thanked for *all* his gifts. Although I am not a believer myself, I find a lot to be said for it."

Although the spirit of Madrigal Sunday might be, as Tom Llewyllyn had observed, Chaucerian, the scene which was set for the singing of the Madrigals was more Edwardian than medieval. The Great West Door of the Chapel was open, giving a view of the interior as far as the screen, which thus formed a distant back-drop. Immediately outside the open door, on the two top steps, were ranked the adult members of the Choir, dressed in morning tails and grey top hats, the Reverend Andrew Ogden being on one wing and the Senior Choral Scholar on the other; while on the next step below them, in single line, were the Choristers, who were got up in Eton suits and straw boaters, the latter bound with ribands of the royal purple which divided, at the rear, into two strands and flowed down to the Choristers' bottoms. On the gravel path beneath the steps, arrayed in velvet cap and quartered tabard (red rose, lion rampant, lion couchant and white lily),

stood the Master of the Musick. In his right hand he held a
baton which resembled a Prussian Field Marshal's, and with
this he would presently elicit song. At the moment, however,
he was turned away from the Choir and watching the audience
assemble on the north eastern corner of the rear lawn.

The grander or more far-sighted of this audience were provided with comfortable chairs, of which there were three
crescent-shaped rows cutting off the tip of the lawn. Behind the
chairs, people strolled or sat about on the grass, some of them
dressed, like those who were seated, in grey frock coats, and
almost all of them conforming to the custom of the day, which
was to wear, on the right hand lapel, a large spray of red and
white flowers, white for the purity of the Blessed Henry's
soul and red for Lancaster. A few of those seated, as well as a
very few of those on the lawn behind them, wore pansies of
the royal purple, a privilege reserved to such Lancaster men as
could trace a true line of descent from knights or noblemen
who had served King Henry VI in court or field or castle.

In the front row of the seats (all but two of which were
now filled) was the Honourable Grantchester Pough, totally
recovered, one would have said, from his recent mishap and
concentrating his gaze on the choristers Dinkie and Dudu,
whom he was to entertain to luncheon when the Madrigals
were done.

"Gloozer's giving us that look," said Dinkie.

"Shut up, will you. We're just meant to stand here and look
pretty."

"I shall start giggling if he goes on gloozing at me like
that."

"Well, look at someone else. Look at Lord Beyfus. He's with
that lady you said you liked so much."

For Lord Beyfus and Mona Corrington were also there in
the front row.

"Ready?" said Mona.

"I'll do what you made me promise. But I do wish they
wouldn't interrupt the Madrigals."

"Madrigals," snorted Mona : "hey nonny nothing."

This was not the view which Balbo Blakeney was expressing to Hetta Frith, with whom he was sitting in the second row.

"I wish," said Balbo, "that I could write a madrigal for you, Miss Hetta."

"What would you say, Mr Blakeney?"

"I should say that your hair is golden and your lips are ruby. And that the smell of your flesh is like new-mown hay."

"I don't think," tittered Hetta, "that it would be a very original sort of madrigal."

"But I should mean every word of it. You in that pretty white dress . . . the spirit of summer."

"I'm glad you like my dress. I bought it specially. You did say white was the colour? White, with red and white flowers?"

"Yes, I did."

"Then why are you wearing a purple pansy?"

Very modestly, Balbo started to explain, and was overheard by the Most Honourable the Marquis Canteloupe, the shadow minister of Commerce, who had been taking part in a debate in the Union the previous evening and was now sitting in the third row with Somerset Lloyd-James (MP), his friend and jackal.

"I never heard such snobbishness," said Canteloupe. "Fellow in front boasting that his family goes back to Agincourt."

Somerset took a squint in the direction indicated by Canteloupe.

"I think that's Balbo Blakeney the biochemist," Somerset said. "If so, he's a second cousin to Blakeney of the Marsh – you know, the Norfolk lot. They were made knights after Agincourt and barons at Henry VI's succession."

"Nothing to boast about. Every Tom, Dick and Harry who could still stand up was knighted after Agincourt."

"Not a bad occasion for it, all the same. There weren't many Canteloupes at Agincourt."

"Nonsense. My ancestor, Gilbert Tyrrel, was in charge of

the other-rank brothel for the whole campaign. He came back
to England with 40,000 marks, a thundering great dose and
a grant of arms as an esquire. So much," said Canteloupe,
"for the sort of rubbish which went on at Agincourt."

This conversation had been heard but not heeded by Mrs
Harriet Ongley, who was looking for Fielding Gray. Early
that morning, as soon as she woke up, she had a sudden
intuition that Fielding was either drinking too much or otherwise getting up to mischief, and so she had decided to come to
Cambridge and fetch him home to Broughton. She had looked
for him all over the lawn and was now carefully scanning the
seats. What she didn't know was that Fielding was with Tom
and Daniel in Tom's set at the north end of Sitwell's, from the
rear bedrooms of which they would have good sight and sound
of the Madrigals. They also had sight of Mrs Ongley, whom
Fielding now pointed out to his friends.

"Bloody bitch has come sniffing after me," Fielding said.
"I suppose I should be flattered."

"Does she often do this."

"Only when I go somewhere associated with my past. She's
afraid I may get sucked back into it."

"What do you want to do?" said Tom. "Shall I ask her
up?"

"No. She hasn't seen me, thank God."

"She'll enquire at the Porters' Lodge," said Daniel, "and
they'll send her here."

"Then I'll go quietly," said Fielding; "but until then we'll
forget her. I see bloody old Somerset Lloyd-James has got himself here."

"There's worse news than Somerset," remarked Tom.

"What can you mean?"

"You see that tubby little man with the huge hat? About
forty-five degrees and ten yards from your Mrs Ongley."

"Yes."

"Well, that," said Tom, "is Alfie Schroeder of the Billingsgate Press. He used to be a reporter but he's been a columnist
for some years now."

"I met him once," said Daniel. "A very decent little man."

"Decent or not," replied Tom, "Alfie means trouble. He's devoted to his wife and family, and nothing would bring him all the way here from Willesden on a Sunday morning except for a very hot tip."

"Perhaps he wants the cultural experience? To embellish his column."

"In that case he'd bring his wife. If Alfie's here alone, wearing that hat, Alfie's smelt trouble."

Which was exactly what Alfie had smelt. Although he enjoyed this kind of occasion (since he knew a good thing when he saw it), he would never have sacrificed a domestic Sunday to the Madrigals had he not expected a sensation in Three-D and Technicolor. Meanwhile, however, he was looking forward to hearing such of the Madrigals as would be sung before the sensation, and noted with pleasure that the Master of the Musick was now looking at his watch and tensing himself as for action. Which followed speedily. The ranks of Choral Scholars and Choristers parted at the centre; down the steps, from within the Chapel, came Provost and Mrs Constable; the Master of the Musick saluted them by raising his baton to his forehead; and the Provost, having bowed first to the Master, then to the Choir and then to the audience, handed his wife to one of the vacant chairs in the front row. He's wearing one of those purple pansies, thought Alfie (who did not know why they were worn, or that the Constables had held Reculver Castle for Henry VI and for many kings before him): he's wearing a purple pansy, Alfie thought, and he looks as proud as the very devil, and I wonder how he'll come out of this lot, when it starts.

And now the Master of the Musick held his baton high and all were silent. Even Mona Corrington was awed, and Harriet Ongley was frozen where she stood. Hetta clasped Balbo's hand; the Marquis Canteloupe, who badly wanted a drink, did not dare bring out his hipflask for very shame; and Somerset Lloyd-James forbore to sneer. Tom blinked back tears and Daniel closed his eyes to hide them; Fielding Gray forgot his wounded face; while Dinkie and Dudu, taut with anticipation, slightly parted their lovely lips and—

"—Spring, the sweet spring, is the year's pleasant king;
Then blooms each thing, then maids dance in a ring,
Cold doth not sting, the pretty birds do sing :
Cuckoo, jug-jug, pu-we, to-witta-woo."


". . . My sweetest Lesbia, let us live and love
And though the sager sort our deeds reprove,
Let us not weigh them : Heav'n's great lamps do dive
Into their west and straight again revive
But soon as once set is our little light,
Then must we sleep an everlasting night . . ."

"What's that they're singing?" said Daniel to Tom, whose attention, after half an hour of madrigals, was beginning to wander.

"Campion," volunteered Fielding Gray: "a translation of Catullus. I once translated that poem myself. Very difficult because it's so simple. Luminous in Latin but trite in English, probably because—"

But this particular essay in comparative semantics, though holding its own in competition with Campion, was now to be silenced for ever by a new sound : that of a massive brass band, which struck into "Jerusalem" like a battery of heavy howitzers. The noise, which totally swamped the singing of the Choir, came from the region of the Willow Bridge; all eyes, which had hitherto been aimed at the West Door, now turned through an arc of 180°; and what they saw was this.

Marching off the bridge and on to the south west corner of the rear lawn was the band which had just begun "Jerusalem", scarlet, gorgeous, trimly moving, and led by two white-booted drum majorettes whose thighs were exposed right up to their lacy knickers. Clearly, thought Alfie Schroeder, this ensemble had mustered in the avenue on the other side of the bridge,

under cover of the trees; but even so, it was a tribute to the
singers that no one, apparently, had noticed what was going
on. For to judge from what now came into view there must
have been a great deal going on. Swaying off the bridge behind the band was a large platform, borne aloft by some
twenty men, on which a lone youthful figure was posed in an
attitude of aspiration and defiance; and behind this again came
a forest of placards (like the insignia carried behind the Roman
Emperor in some extravaganza of the screen) bearing bold and
lapidary legends which denounced Lancaster, its Chapel and
its dons, while praising Beyfus, Balliston and various aspects
of progress. Behind the placards marched a small but deadly-
looking platoon of leather-jacketed boys; following them was
a second platform and a second tableau, this one consisting of
a huge and evidently vinous papier mâché cleric who was
trampling sadistically on the belly of a real, live and absolutely
naked girl; and after this there came a column, a very long
column indeed (so Alfie could now discern as he peered into
the distant trees) of young men and women.

First reactions were various. Harriet Ongley, who had lived
for a long time in America, assumed that all this was a planned
part of the festivities and was utterly entranced, forgetting for
the moment her anxiety about Fielding Gray and her irritation
at failing to find him. A surprisingly large number of the inferior spectators seemed to share her view of the matter and
made way for the band with respectful admiration. Among
those seated, however, there was no doubt that something was
amiss: even the Marquis Canteloupe, who was not well up
in the forms of Cambridge life, detected something untoward
and remarked to Somerset Lloyd-James that "this show"
might well "fuck up" the Provost's luncheon, to which they
had both been bidden, so hadn't they better think of finding
some bloody pub to eat in? Others were bound to take a less
detached attitude, not least among them the Provost himself,
who signalled to the Master of the Musick to get the gaping
Choir into song again, and then walked round to the rear of
the seats to confront the now rapidly approaching procession.

In the Provost's wake went Ivor Winstanley, who had no clear idea of what he meant to do but imagined (wrongly) that Constable would be glad of his assistance.

"And I will stand at thy right hand," shouted Ivor (who was not strictly sober, having celebrated Madrigal Sunday with elevenses of a sweet and thick Marsala), "and guard the bridge with thee."

Constable answered with a glacial nod, then held up his right hand to halt the scarlet bandsmen. Just for a moment, such was the authority in his manner, the bandsmen seemed to waver in their march; but when Ivor Winstanley unintentionally parodied the Provost's gesture with a pompous imitation, all hope was gone. The band came on apace, while the two drum majorettes, having planted their long batons in the lawn, tackled Ivor and the Provost respectively, tossing both well clear of the axis of advance with two simultaneously executed movements of elementary jiu-jitsu.

Meanwhile, the squad of leather jackets had come doubling up on the left flank of the column and were starting to clear a passage through the rows of seats. This they did quickly and competently, only pausing to brush aside anyone who attempted to prevent them and to punch him in the teeth if he persisted. One such was Grantchester Pough, who punched back – very hard and very low, since the circumstances, as he saw them, rendered the Queensbury Rules irrelevant. What deeds he might have done that day, or what black fate might have overcome him at the last, it is interesting to conjecture; but in actual fact, realising that he had responsibilities which precluded his brawling like a common sailor, he suddenly broke off from the mêlée, gathered up the Choristers (who were still gallantly celebrating the sexual obsessions of Catullus) with one sweep of his long arm, formed them into file with a crisp order, and led them away across the Great Court to the safety of his rooms.

It was at this stage in the proceedings that even Harriet Ongley realised that more than a mere carnival was afoot. She longed for her true knight to ride up and save her (where *the dickens* was he?), but her true knight, who opined that Harriet deserved everything she got, continued to enjoy the scene from Tom Llewyllyn's window.

"That chap they're carrying," he said. "He's the one we saw skulking about last night."

"Hugh Balliston," said Tom crossly. "And a perfect damn fool he looks."

And felt. Despite the banner which was carried in front of him and announced that he was both the victim of a dead age and the embodiment of a new, Hugh felt like a twit. Although he had fiercely declined to take the pills he was offered before the march began, he now wished he'd accepted them. The grinding and self-conscious effort to look like a cross between Rodin's "Thinker" and Joan of Arc was making him sweat through his shirt and grind his teeth in mental rage. Too late now. He hadn't taken the pills and must find some other analgesic. Watch the antics, then; no better distraction from one's own ills than the observation of human antics.

These were manifold, but the two most entertaining at the moment were, first, those of Somerset Lloyd-James, who was running away towards the side gate beyond the Chapel as fast as his spindly legs would carry him, pursued by howls of laughter from Lord Canteloupe; and second, those of Lord Beyfus, who had placed himself at the head of the procession, in front of the majorettes, and was leading the way up the Chapel steps towards the West Door. On and up he went, his bottom sagging and wagging like that of a worn out catamite, his head held high, his arms outstretched in front of him, on and up he went, like a fat little Moses ascending Sinai, towards the cowering ranks of Choral Scholars – only to plant his right foot in a boater abandoned by the fleeing Dudu and fall flat on his face, his left ankle at the same time becoming gaily cross-gartered by the long purple ribands which Dudu had sported from his hat.

Some were later to allege that Beyfus bounced when he fell. What is quite beyond dispute is that the charitable Andrew Ogden came down from the top step to Beyfus's aid, reaching him at the same time as frantic Mona Corrington, who had rushed up from the gravel. Together they got Beyfus on his feet; but since his right foot was stuck through the straw hat and his left was much impeded by the riband which joined the hat to his left ankle, he promptly fell down again, this time on his back. Both Mona and Andrew blamed the other for this; the difference being that Mona was now resentfully determined to manage Beyfus all by herself, whereas Andrew Ogden, forgiving her with all his Christian heart, was still eager to co-operate. What ensued was a tug-of-war, each of them heaving away at one arm of the supine Beyfus, to no effect whatever except repeatedly to jerk up the poor old Hebrew's napper and bring it cracking down again on the edge of the stone step beneath it.

And now most assuredly would this farcical scene have dissolved everyone present into unquenchable laughter and thus broken up the entire demonstration (ah, would that it had indeed been so), had not Mayerston emerged from nowhere in particular and given a quick, quiet order to a mature-looking leather boy. The latter gathered five more; the six of them moved up the Chapel steps like panthers; and within ten seconds they had made a kind of bundle of Mona, Beyfus, Ogden, boater, riband and all, and carted the whole lot off like one large parcel.

Whereupon Mayerston mounted the steps and things became serious again.

Mayerston's first action was to gesture politely but dismissively at the two rows of Choral Scholars, who, doubtless feeling that they had stood their ground for as long as could be expected, obediently dribbled off the steps. Mayerston then turned towards the band (which for some minutes now had been marking time while continuing to play), pointed his right forefinger at one drum majorette and his left at the other, turned about to face the West Door, and marched lightly and smartly through it. The majorettes pranced up behind him and the bandsmen followed, neatly forming their four ranks into file as they went in order to negotiate the door which, though wide, could not accommodate four men in line with bulky instruments.

After the band rode Hugh, rigidly triumphant on his platform, and after Hugh the papier mâché clergyman, who, being nearly as tall as the door itself, had to be eased inch by inch under the lintel, while the naked girl beneath his foot diverted public attention from the awkwardness of this manœuvre by screaming and squirming in realistic agony. Meantime, the leather boys had been sorting out the column of student marchers in the rear. This now stretched diagonally across the lawn, over the Willow Bridge and along the avenue (so Alfie made out) right down to the Queen's Road. Clearly there was not room for this entire mob in the Chapel, and equally clearly the organisers were determined, from whatever motive, to avoid overcrowding; for the leather boys were now both marshalling and thinning out the column, despatching at least two persons in three to join a rapidly growing group round the statue of Henry VI in the Great Court and only admitting to the Chapel a carefully selected minority. Quite what the principle behind the selection was, Alfie could not determine: it had nothing to do with physique or gender, though it was possible, he thought, that those allowed into the Chapel were chosen as the dirtiest and most ill dressed. The reason for this preference was obscure to Alfie, but the basic strategy behind it all was as plain as the nose on his face. Those left outside the Chapel in the Great Court, quite apart from perpetrating casual outrages, would be amply able to deal with any resistance which the authorities might now attempt to rally and with any external threat to those gathered inside the Chapel, who could set about their business (whatever *that* might be) without fear of interruption. Inside or outside, Alfie asked himself; and decided that the big news lay within.

But how to get in? The column was now being very smoothly processed. The chosen were being waved swiftly up the steps and through the West Door, the others efficiently diverted into the Great Court. If the leather boys wanted you out, you stayed out. "Press," shouted Alfie, wagging a card and waddling up the steps – and was ushered in with deep bows of gratitude and respect.

"But they won't let me in so easily," said Balbo Blakeney, who had observed this little incident.

"Why do you want to get in?" asked Hetta.

"To keep an eye on the old place."

"There's nothing you can do. It's a blessing you can't get in."

"But I think I can, Miss Hetta. There's a little door into one of the side-chapels. Unlocked, as a rule."

"Don't go, Mr Blakeney."

"Must, Miss Hetta. Got to keep an eye on the old place."

"Then I'll come too."

"No place for you, Missy. You cut off home."

"I'll come too."

"And so will I," boomed the Marquis Canteloupe, who had been listening to this exchange and now found himself (despite his earlier aversion) liking both Balbo and Hetta very much indeed.

"Right," said Balbo, "but don't make so much din about it. Noise gets on my nerves."

And he led the way round the north west tower of the Chapel and then eastwards along the north wall. This was an area seldom visited by anyone, as it consisted of a strip of rank grass (lying between the north wall of the Chapel and the southernmost building of the neighbour college) which had once been the Lancaster coal dump and was now used for dustbins. Although the smell was abominable, the arrangement always pleased Balbo who was amused by the medieval juxtaposition of grandeur and squalor. Canteloupe and Hetta were not so amused and started to retch, but Balbo led on stoutly, and when they were about forty yards from the east end of the Chapel, he suddenly darted behind a buttress, pushed through a cluster of waist-high nettles, and seized a rusty ring which hung from a low studded door.

Alfie Schroeder, meanwhile, had been wafted down the Chapel on a wave of precedence and prominently ensconced in the Provost's stall against the east side of the screen, with a full view of the chancel. This was somewhat disconcerting, even to a man of Alfie's agnostic temperament, as the altar had been cleared to make room for Hugh Balliston, who was now enthroned on top of it and was gazing in the rough direction of Alfie with a fierce look of misery that might just have been taken for revolutionary zeal. Alfie wasn't fooled for a moment: that boy, he told himself, is rueing the day. Of even more scandalous interest, however, was the deployment of the papier mâché cleric, who had been set up so that his buttocks were supported by the lectern (which was some thirty yards to the west of the altar and slap in the middle of the aisle) and his two feet were straddling his female victim, the latter being prone on the floor with her bottom aimed in a suggestive manner as for a long range shot at the West Window. The band, which had at last dispensed with "Jerusalem" and gone on to a samba instead, was drawn up in two long lines, which stretched down, one on each side of the aisle, from either wing of the sanctuary to the eastern end of the choir; and for the rest, all seats whatever, from the Doctors' and Masters' stalls down to the meanest Chorister's bench, were crammed with the scruffiest, hairiest and most hang-dog assemblage which it had ever been Alfie's luck to contemplate. I was right, he thought: it *was* the dirtiest they were letting in here – the dirtiest because the most resentful. So what does that point to?

But this question was not to be answered for a while. Even the practised leather boys must have time to arrange the rest of the congregation in the west end of the Chapel, and to judge from the racket that arose from the far side of the screen this would take some minutes yet. Alfie did not know whether to be glad or sorry about the delay. The more delay, the more chance of intervention and anti-climax (notwithstanding the massed guard in the Great Court) and the less chance of a scoop for Alfie's column; but the less chance, also, of some really sinister outcome, such as Alfie (knowing a good thing when he saw it) would deprecate in surroundings like these. In any event, there was nothing to do but wait.

This, at first, had been what Tom and Daniel felt as they watched the events below, from various of Tom's windows.

"Best stay put and keep quiet," Daniel had said.

But as more and more filthy boys and girls piled into the Chapel, and as the crowd grew larger and larger round Henry VI's statue in the Great Court, Tom became restless.

"I can't bear it," he said.

"What can we do?"

"We can go up into Jerusalem," said Tom allusively, "and perish with him."

"With whom?"

"Can't you see what they're going to do? They're going to pull down that statue."

And indeed a small group of leather boys was already surveying King Henry's statue and the fountain at its base, while another such group was coming through the crowd with pickaxes and coils of rope.

"Stay here, Tom," Daniel said.

"No," said Fielding Gray. "Tom's right."

"It's nothing to do with you. You were never even in the college."

"I was elected a Scholar. They turned me away before I got here, but I was elected a Scholar." Fielding turned to Tom. "I'll come with you," he said.

So Fielding and Tom (having persuaded Daniel, though he pressed to come too, that in his state of health he could only be an embarrassment) went up into Jerusalem, which in this instance lay down in the Great Court. Fielding, however, never quite reached his destination. The moment he emerged with Tom from Sitwell's, he was boarded, so to speak, by Harriet Ongley, who came running up on her strong, shapely legs, while her globular face (usually placid and benign) exploded into reproach like a flying sea-mine.

"Just where do you think you've been?" she screeched, seizing Fielding's left arm with both hands. "I'm taking you home right now."

If Tom expected any resistance from Fielding, he was disappointed. Hanging his head in shame and resignation, Fielding suffered himself to be towed away, lurching and stumbling, round the edge of the crowd and off to the front gate.

So here I am, thought Tom, and what do I do now? He eased his way through the crowd in order to see what was doing near the statue. Round Henry's neck were tied two ropes, two teams to pull on which were now being recruited by the leather boys. Tom supposed that if this failed to shift the statue they would then start work with the pick-axes, which for the present lay discarded in the ground, just by the rim of the basin into which the fountain was playing from under King Henry's piously pointed feet. Tom eyed the pick-axes and pondered within his heart: it could work; they might call his bluff, and God knew what would happen then, but it could just work. Anyway, he thought, there was no time for delay. The two teams to pull on the ropes were already made up; the two ropes, forming an angle of 40°, were already stretched taut from the poor king's neck. At any moment the order would come to heave. Now or never.

Tom bent down and seized a pickaxe. He struck a nearby leather boy hard on the head with the flat centre of the pick, gave him, as he reeled, a shove in the mid-riff with the helve, and sent him tumbling into the shallow water in the basin. He then climbed in after him, stood astride the unconscious body, and raised the pickaxe on high. All this he did in about five seconds, so that scarcely anyone even began to take in what was happening until he gave a demoniac squeal for silence.

"Listen to me," he called, in the high-pitched, fanatical chant which he remembered from the Welsh chapels of his childhood. "If any man pulls those ropes; or if any man seeks to harm that statue; or if any man comes near me: then I shall strike down with this pickaxe into this man's throat beneath me."

From the outer crowd rose a hum of curiosity, but in the region of the statue everyone was quite silent. Tom, lifting his weapon even higher, wildly contorted his face, in the hope that he would look mad enough to mean what he said; and for the time at least the mob seemed to believe him. In any event, no one moved. But for how long? And for how long, Tom thought, can I go on dilating my eyes like a dervish and holding up this pick, which is already weighing a ton? No, he thought, if I'm to stay here I must devise distraction, not so much for the crowd as for myself from my own discomfort; a distraction which will leave me still alert, will indeed help me to remain so, but will also help me to forget the dull ache in my face and my arms.

So he opened his mouth and started to harangue. In the crazy manner of the Welsh preachers he had heard so often before he escaped from his own people, he lilted and babbled and chanted of sin and damnation and death. Yet his burden was secular : the hell of which he spoke was of this world, the hell of envy and sloth, and the salvation which he offered was also of this world, by grace of intelligence, truth and hard work.

A sermon of a not wholly dissimilar kind was going forward in the Chapel. This was delivered by Mayerston, and took the form of a series of violent denunciations of the church, the clergy and the entire academic establishment, which was still associated with them. Each denunciation was framed like the verse of a psalm; and after every verse Mayerston would pause while Tony Beck and two assistant leather boys inflicted brief and vicious assault on the papier mâché cleric by the lectern, who was thus being slowly and symbolically dismembered.

"Let them consume away like a snail," howled Mayerston, "and be like the untimely fruit of a woman : and let them not see the sun."

Bash, wallop, and away went a papier mâché arm.

"They grin like a dog, and run through the city : and the foam of their jaws doth stink like the bowels of dead men."

RRRiiippp, and off came half the surplice.

"Behold, they were conceived in beds of dung; and their sons and their daughters coupled together in the filth of sewers . . ."

How very jolly it would be, thought Lord Canteloupe, if one could use language like that in the Upper House. And I must say, he thought (wrinkling his battered but still fruity face into a sumptuous leer), I rather like the cut of that girl. Like Maisie doing that trick with her bum when I'm slow getting off the mark. I wish I could get a better look . . .

For although the little chantry in which Canteloupe and his companions were secreted was almost opposite the lectern, the view which it afforded was poor, since there was a great deal of elaborate stone tracery screening side-chapel from upper chancel, to say nothing of a high box tomb, which blocked the line of sight where the tracery divided, and the row of bandsmen who flanked the aisle. Canteloupe now decided that he would try to peer round the tomb, and was edging cautiously past the Maltese Cross which was carved on one end of it, when Balbo plucked him back.

"Mustn't be seen," Balbo whispered.

"Quite right. Sorry. What are you going to do?"

"Nothing as long as they just go on like this. They're not doing the place any harm."

But in fact the proceedings were now changing dramatically in nature, though whether or not they threatened what Balbo would consider harm was still uncertain. The papier mâché cleric, having suffered a final indignity in the groin, had now tottered to the floor, and the girl had arisen from among the remnants, freed at last, as one was intended to assume, from ancient oppression. This release she celebrated by giving a few rather clumsy hops and skips mimetic of her new autonomy, in which, however, she was not long allowed to indulge herself.

"You are free of your old tyrant," boomed Mayerston from his place; "now go to your new comrade."

Whereupon Tony Beck took her by the wrist and led her briskly up to the altar, on to which (not without vigorous upward pressure applied by Beck to her posteriors) she at length managed to clamber. Hugh Balliston bent down from his throne in welcome; the girl looked up and spread her arms in adoration; and after fifteen seconds of preparatory endearment, it became only too plain what was now about to happen.

"By God," said Canteloupe: "they're going to do it on the altar."

"Desecration," said Hetta.

"But no damage," said Balbo; "that's the important thing."

But someone else thought otherwise. Out of a small door (which led into a vestry at the east of the choir and the south side of the Chapel) there now hurtled a furious and gibbering priest: Oliver Clewes, who disapproved of the Madrigals and had been sulking in the vestry ever since Matins. Surprised and cut off in his lair by the advent of the demonstrators, Clewes had doubtless deemed it prudent to lie low; but no clergyman, however revolutionary his opinions, could tolerate fornification on his own altar. Straight for this he now went; he grabbed up off the floor a pair of heavy candlesticks (which had been removed from the altar when Hugh was installed on it), and had time to administer two or three punishing strokes on Miss Liberty's succulent fesses before a tide of blue jeans and greasy hair surged up the chancel, burst on the steps of the sanctuary, and swept the wretched girl away from him.

Clewes now disappeared from sight, and Canteloupe, who had taken advantage of the interruption to move himself to a better peep-hole in the tracery, began to hope that the programme would be resumed. But there must be considerable doubt whether Miss Liberty was still in the mood, and in any case that of the mob had now altered drastically. It had been defied and it was out for vengeance, or so at least it was now told by Mayerston, who yelled from his stall the one word:

"SMASH."

"For Christ's sake, man," protested Alfie beside him.

"SMASH," yelled Mayerston again.

"Smash, smash, smash," the cry was taken up.

But no one seemed too sure what to smash (the miserable

Clewes having been pulped already), except for Tony Beck, who now saw his chance to put his name for ever on the record.

"Smash," he cried, and seized a candlestick.

"Smash," he screamed, and climbed on to the altar.

"Smash," he howled, and scrambled on to the foot-wide ledge at the top of the reredos.

"Smash," he roared, taking back the candlestick and poising himself to strike through the most beautiful East Window in England.

But Balbo was there beneath him, standing on the altar and tugging at his ankles, and Hetta was there beneath Balbo.

"—Oh, wicked, wicked, wicked," Hetta shouted.

—And Canteloupe was there doing his best to protect Hetta from the mob that hated her for loving Balbo for loving the window, and Hugh Balliston was there, trying to redeem himself in his own eyes by fighting side by side with Canteloupe.

"How could you all be so wicked?" Hetta cried, just as her mother would have done, "how could you all be so wicked in this lovely place," while Beck fell from the reredos and Balbo was dragged from the altar (but the Window, the East Window was safe), and Canteloupe and Hugh thrashed out all about them with their fists and feet, and someone (no one would ever quite know who) seized the candlestick which had been dropped by Beck and smashed it down on poor brave Hetta's skull.

When the police arrived (summoned by Somerset Lloyd-James, who was not a poltroon and had run away only for this purpose), they found Tom on the verge of collapse but still just retaining his authority beneath the statue. They then penetrated the Chapel, to find Balbo, Hugh, Canteloupe, Miss Liberty and several students in various but not serious states of injury and shock. Clewes they found to be severely though not lethally broken up. Hetta they found dead before the altar in her white dress. Tony Beck and Mayerston they did not find at all.

"I'm so glad you came," said Hugh to Patricia Llewyllyn.

Patricia had come to Hugh's room in the Fellows' Garden Hostel. Mummy to the rescue.

"I had to, after I heard. That poor girl . . . And what's going to happen to you?"

"I've been forgiven. They've put it round that I was the victim of moral blackmail while suffering from mental strain due to overwork. And after all," said Hugh with just a trace of bitterness, "I was wounded fighting for the right side."

"Wounded?"

"A cracked rib."

"I hope that'll give you a good lesson . . . not to go in for things which you don't understand."

Mummy knows her boy.

"I understand quite a lot about them . . . now. I rather wish I didn't."

"Forget it," said Patricia : "it's all over and done."

Briskly, she unzipped her skirt.

"Now then," she said : "where did we leave off?"

"Snakes," said Hugh : "lovely long snakes, sliding and sliding . . ."

"So remember, next time," said Mona Corrington, "to look where you're going."

"Will there be a next time?" said Beyfus, who was propped up against the pillows wearing a bandage like a turban round his head. "I should have thought most people have had enough."

"I haven't, for one."

"No," said Beyfus, "I don't suppose you have. So what's your next step?"

"The International Committee of Anthropologists. It's time

that made a bold bid for the bank. In fact I'm starting on a round trip tomorrow to try and get things buzzing."

"You're going away, Mona? When I'm ill."

"Only for three days."

"Mona . . . This last time before you go?"

So Mona sat down on the bed beside him, put his head on her bosom, and heard him at his prayers.

"What I can't understand," said Jacquiz Helmut, who was now back from his medical consultations, "is why the police took so long to come. You say this chap Lloyd-James telephoned them almost at once."

"Yes, from the Porters' Lodge in Caius. But the police couldn't get into the college," explained Ivor Winstanley, "until they had the Provost's permission; and the Provost, like me, was out stone cold on the grass. So naturally it took some time before they were put in touch."

"A fine piece of clowning . . . And what's been done about Tony Beck?"

"He's vanished. With Mayerston, they think."

"There's certainly no future for him here."

"Nor much with Mayerston. They say," said Ivor, "although nobody can prove it, that it was probably Mayerston who hit the girl."

"What was *she* doing there, I'd like to know? She wasn't even a member of the University."

"Nor were half the others, it seems. A lot of them – particularly those in the Chapel – had come by coach for the day from places like Essex and Sussex. I thought they looked too awful to be ours, even in the distance. You don't realise how lucky we still are."

"Perhaps," said Jacquiz; "but this kind of thing has come to stay."

"Well, next time it happens I hope you'll stop here and lend a hand, instead of going off to your specialist. How did he find you, by the way?"

"Ticking over," said Jacquiz. "He recommends plenty of royal tennis this winter but no disagreeable exertion. He certainly wouldn't want me to get mixed up in revolutions. I pay him far too well."

"The extraordinary thing was," said Tom to Daniel, "that Fielding didn't say a single word of protest. He just hung his head and went with her."

"Leaving you in the lurch. I told you he was never there when wanted."

"But this time it was different. He was removed by someone else, you see. Obviously she must have a very strong hold over him."

"Perhaps that's what he wants people to think," said Daniel, "so that he's always got an excuse for disappearing when it suits him. Tom . . . ?"

"Yes, Danny?"

"When are you going to disappear?"

"How can I? These are my rooms."

"But very soon now I shall be well enough to go back to my own. And you'll have to go back to Grantchester. Oh, it's quite all right, you warned me clearly enough, but I'd just like to know when."

"Not for a long time, Danny. Even when you go back to your rooms in Willow Close, I shall go on living here in college. So it'll be almost the same as now."

"But how can you? Patricia . . ."

"Patricia," said Tom, "is a very honest woman, and I'm happy to tell you that I have kept her confidence. This morning she told me something which leads me to suppose that she will have no need of me for some while yet. Sooner or later, Danny, I shall have to go back to her. But this summer at least we can both enjoy together."

"A very instructive business all round," wrote Constable for his record. "It has left me with two intentions, One is to learn jiu-jitsu, and the other is to dismiss the Master of the Musick. He actually allowed the choir to stop. Not for long, but it was only because I ordered him to that he got them singing again, and as everyone knows, no Master of Musick is worth his salt unless he can keep things going right through the last trump.

"In many respects, quite a lot of good has come of it all. Balliston has at last learned his lesson, and by pardoning him we have been able to give a public exhibition of liberal tolerance which will stand us in good stead in many quarters. Beck has gone – good riddance, on the whole – and so has Mayerston. Clewes has shown that he has got some spunk in him. And Tom Llewyllyn's courageous performance should guarantee him a permanent Fellowship when the matter comes to the vote.

"Even the death of poor Hetta Frith has its brighter side. There's nothing like a death to sober people up, and Hetta's should be worth a good two years' peace to Cambridge . . . particularly after the very gruelling account in that journalist Schroeder's column.

"Meanwhile, the tedious question of what to do with our quarter million surplus is still dragging on. The Council voted on it for the fourth time this morning. Result : still ten each way . . ."

After the Memorial Service for Hetta Frith in Lancaster College Chapel, Balbo Blakeney stood awhile under the tablet which had been set up.

HETTA FRITH
1948–1967
One Great-heart.

"Ah, Miss Hetta," Balbo whispered, "there were so many churches I wanted to show you."

"She'd like that," said the Marquis Canteloupe, who had come up behind Balbo and was pointing at the tablet; "Bunyan, isn't it?"

"How did *you* know?" said Balbo before he could stop himself.

"My old nanny used to read it to me," said Canteloupe, quite unperturbed. "I've never forgotten. 'My sword, I give to him that shall succeed me in my pilgrimage.' Splendid stuff."

"That's from a different passage."

"But saying the same sort of thing . . . My word, old fellow, you do look low."

"I miss her so much, Canteloupe."

"I know what. I'll introduce you to a friend of mine. Name of Maisie. Maisie will take your mind off it."

"Who's Maisie?"

"Maisie's a tart. Not all that to look at, but believe me, she'll take your mind off poor little Hetta."

Balbo considered this.

"So soon?" he said at last.

"The sooner the better," said Canteloupe. "Hetta won't mind. Even if she knows, she won't mind. She'll want you to enjoy yourself."

"You talk as if you knew her. Yet you only ever saw her that one time. You didn't even know her name until she was dead."

"That one time was enough. A girl who could stand up to all those yobs like that would never grudge you a romp with Maisie."

"I don't see that that quite follows," said Balbo, "but you're certainly right about Miss Hetta. She never grudged anybody anything."

"Then that's settled. Here's a card of Maisie's with her telephone number" . . . Canteloupe scribbled on the back . . . "and my recommendation. If I was you, I'd run up to London this very afternoon. But give her a ring first. She gets very booked up."

Balbo looked from the card to Hetta's tablet and back again to the card.

"She bought a white dress for Madrigal Sunday," Balbo said. "She hadn't a penny in the world, but she bought a white dress, because I'd told her white was the colour."

"Good for Hetta."

"But why do you think she bought it?"

"To please you, I expect, and because girls like to be seen in the right thing."

"No," said Balbo. "Miss Hetta didn't give a curse what she was seen in, and she knew she'd please me well enough if she turned up in rags. She bought that dress," said Balbo, "because I'd told her that white was in memory of King Henry's innocence. She was doing honour, Canteloupe, HONOUR, to a dead king because she thought of him in some sort as her host."

"Don't upset yourself, old fellow."

"I'm just trying to explain what Miss Hetta was really like. A jolly, sexy girl with bags of guts, yes; but so much more besides. She was . . . so delicate, Canteloupe. So delicate."

Balbo put Maisie's card in his pocket.

"Delicate but dead," he said, "so thanks for the tip. Come on, and I'll give you a drink."

# SOUND THE
# RETREAT

# CONTENTS

CONTENTS

## PART ONE

# THE ASPIRANTS

LATE IN NOVEMBER 1945, as His Majesty's Troop-Ship *Georgic* was approaching Port Said, the O.C. Troops said to the Captain:

"No shore leave for the Cadets, I think. They'd only go and get clap."

"Or worse," the Captain said.

"Precisely. But I think we ought to arrange some kind of treat for them. To make up."

"I know," said the Captain; "we'll have a conjurer on board."

"But we *always* have a conjurer on board at Port Said."

"The Cadets aren't to know that. They'll think that it is, as you say, a treat."

And so at Port Said the usual Egyptian mountebank was engaged to come on board and entertain the 300 Officer Cadets. This he did in the First Class Lounge, which would not be needed that day since all the Officers, and for that matter almost everybody else except the Cadets, had gone ashore, despite the risk of getting clap. All this, as the O.C. Troops had foretold, had made the Cadets feel left out and resentful, so that at first they were in no mood to pay attention to a smelly old Gyppo and his nursery magic. There were sullen and sceptical faces everywhere; much blowing of noses and shuffling of feet.

The Egyptian, being used to sullen audiences on Troop-Ships which were heading East, was not at all put out when his first offering – streams of coloured handkerchieves hauled out of his capacious sleeves – was received with something like a jeer. He simply went to the second item in his programme (an old routine of smashing eggs into a fez and pulling out live chickens in lieu), fully conscious that this too would be received with contempt, which at this stage was just what he wanted. And so with his third trick, his fourth and his fifth – the last being greeted with unrestrained booing, which fell sweetly on the magician's ears; for from this he knew that at last he had the spectators in exactly the frame of mind (mutinous and sceptical) which had always been most propitious to the illusion which he now proposed to work on them : an illusion which, by contrast with what had gone before, would so surprise and delight the Cadets that they would crowd round him with admiring smiles and liberal handfuls of coinage before waving him with honour on his way.

The trick which he was about to perform, though it was the pride of his repertoire, was in essence very simple. He would put one of his audience under an hypnotic spell and would order him to get into a coffin, which would then, with much ceremony, be closed, hammered down, weighted and thrown overboard by the magician and three apprentices. After the off-loading and sinking of the coffin and much keening by the Egyptians, the ship would be searched, and at length the victim would be found to have been 'resurrected' from the deep, usually in some faintly ridiculous posture, e.g. sitting on a lavatory seat. (As for the coffin, this was subsequently recovered by diving boys at nugatory expense.) Over the years, the conjuror had found that this combination of the macabre and the facetious had a particular appeal to British audiences, and since the mechanics had never once failed him, it was with absolute confidence that he now went into his preliminary stratagems.

"Gully, gully, gully," he articulated : "please will one gallant officer come forward as volunteer."

The Cadets were not put into better humour by his affecting to believe that they were officers. Nobody moved.

"Gully, gully," wailed the old charlatan, rather pathetically; "one gentleman . . . please . . . please."

It was at this stage that Peter Morrison arose, a large and slightly shambling Cadet with a huge round shining face. In fact Morrison was more bored than most by this performance, considering it to be not only inept in itself but of a kind suited only to the frivolous; yet at the same time, knowing that it was what his superiors had ordained for him, he felt it to be his duty to show an interest and try to keep the show going. He was also rather sorry for the conjurer, who seemed to be having a thin time. All of which being so, Morrison got up and approached the magician, who welcomed him with open arms and a low salaam, and at once began to hypnotise him.

Since Peter Morrison was a young man of intelligence and iron will-power, this might have been very difficult. But because he was keen to help, and also rather curious to find out what would happen, Morrison allowed himself to sink into an apparently trance-like state (while in truth keeping all his faculties) and was the better able to sustain his pretence as he had once seen a hypnotist at work on his victim in a music hall in Norwich during the war. When ordered into the coffin, he obeyed with sombre dignity; and even while the lid was being closed over him (an experience to perturb the most sanguine) he continued to simulate the repose which befitted his role.

There was now a hammering of nails and a wailing of neophytes for two full minutes, during which time the bottom of the coffin swung downwards and deposited Morrison in the cushioned interior of a hollow catafalque with a small thud which went unheard in the prevailing racket. The coffin bottom then swung upwards and clicked back into position, as did the false and velvet-covered top of the catafalque, which was similarly hinged and sprung. By this time Morrison had a pretty fair notion of what was to happen and was resigned, as he always had been, to letting the whole affair take its foolish but innocuous course.

And so, doubtless, it would have done, but for just one divergent factor. All went smoothly – the funeral procession down to 'C' deck, the sinking of the weighted coffin and the smuggling of Peter Morrison from the empty lounge – until the assistants so charged came to arrange Morrison for his 'resurrection'. Since their master had ordained that on this occasion the victim should be discovered supine on a dining room table and stripped down to his underpants, and since they had good reason to suppose that Morrison was still under trance, they started to undress him cap-à-pié. Nor would Morrison have resisted this, for it was respectfully done and he was a good-humoured boy who could take a joke at his own expense, had it not been that through some inadvertence of the ship's laundry he was without underpants on that particular day. When, therefore, the Egyptians began to remove his uniform trousers, he remonstrated firmly both with voice and gesture; whereupon the apprentices, startled by such sudden autonomy in one whom they had thought to be no more than a breathing corpse, fled screaming and cackling on to 'C' deck to find the sorcerer in chief.

He, meanwhile, was enjoying some esteem. As always happened, the contrast between the shabbiness of his earlier tricks and the impressive scope of this one had considerably enlivened his audience. A clever piece of ventriloquism had raised a scream from the coffin as it sank, and there were even those who hoped that Peter Morrison, whether through the malice or incompetence of the conjurer, had indeed been sent to the bottom. It would make something to write home about. All, therefore, were eagerly awaiting the next stage in events – when the assistants came gibbering along the deck and fell at the feet of their master.

The latter, when he understood what had happened, was perturbed. That Morrison should come out of the trance (as the magician saw it) before being woken by the person who had put him into it was unprecedented and might be dangerous. The worry and displeasure on the mountebank's face, being clearly genuine, at once communicated themselves to the Cadets . . . who correctly deduced that something had gone wrong, incorrectly concluded that this could only mean harm of some kind to Morrison, and then, in tones which variously conveyed dismay, indignation, fear, affection, racial hatred and pessimistic relish, demanded an explanation. Since none, in the circumstances, would have been audible, the magician was somewhat relieved when Peter himself now appeared to provide one with his presence. But as it turned out the explanation thus rendered was inopportune; for Peter, regretting his disruption of the assistants and wishing to provide an appropriate climax to the trick, had soaked himself in a sea-water shower, in order to give the impression that he had indeed returned *de profundis*. All of which would have been well enough, had it not been for the current mood of the audience. For the Cadets, having watched the magician become more nervous every moment and being convinced by now that something was badly amiss, remembering, also, the terrible scream from the coffin, instantly assumed that the dripping Peter had in truth been submerged in it and had only been saved by his own resource and exertion. This ridiculous notion would never, of course, have persisted for more than a few seconds; but before those seconds were up, a mass of Cadets, led by Peter's friend Alister Mortleman, had cruelly man-handled the luckless wizard to the gangway and thrown him headfirst into a lurking bumboat, which folded together, on the impact, like a closing penknife, and sank in ten seconds flat.

"Now then," said the O.C. Troops: "I am commanded to make an. enquiry into yesterday's little affair. Stand easy, gentlemen, please."

The O.C. Troops looked up reproachfully at the ten Cadets who were crowded into his day cabin, then screwed in his monocle and started to read the paper in front of him:

" 'It has been deposed before the British Consul in Port Said by Mustapha Duqaq, professional magician, that on the 25th day of November, 1945, being by official invitation on board His Majesty's Troop-Ship *Georgic* in the harbour of Port Said, he, Mustapha Duqaq, was flung by a party of Officer Cadets from the deck of the aforesaid vessel into a small boat, his own property, which was waiting to carry him off: that he himself sustained bodily injuries to the value of 73 pounds sterling and 14 shillings—' "

"—Sir," said Alister Mortleman, coming to attention like the clap of doom, "how could he possibly have worked that out so quickly?"

"Don't interrupt," said the O.C. Troops, blinking behind

his monocle. " '. . . That his boat, value 270 pounds sterling, was stove and sunk, that items of equipment pertaining to his profession and valued at 185 pounds sterling were lost or damaged beyond recovery—' "

"—But all his equipment was in the First Class Lounge, sir—"

"—Pray don't interrupt, sir. '. . . And that two of his servants, who were manning the boat, were drowned; estimated value one pound and ten shillings sterling *per caput*. It is desired that these allegations be investigated forthwith and that those responsible for the assault be placed under close arrest. An immediate report will then be rendered to both the Civil and the Military Authorities in Port Said, the latter of which will instruct you as to arrangements for handing over the culprits to the appropriate Egyptian authority. I am, Sir, di-da, di-da, J. Kershaw, Brigadier, B.M.C., Port Said.' You see," said the O.C. Troops petulantly, "what your little prank has ended up in?"

"But, sir, we didn't mean—"

"—For Christ's sake, man, shut up. Every time you open your mouth, you make things harder all round. . . . That's better," said the O.C. Troops, as apprehensive silence ensued. "Now, gentlemen: we are going to hear the principal witness of what occurred, Sergeant W. T. Pulcher of the Military Police. Listen to him carefully and do *not* interrupt."

"Can we cross-examine him later, sir?"

"If you want to"—this with an unexpected giggle: "S'arnt-Major, bring in Sergeant Pulcher."

". . . Leeft, right, leeft, right, halt."

". . . State your evidence, S'arnt Pulcher."

"SIR. On the 25th of November I was keeping the gangplank with the Ship's Officer of the Day. At approximately 1515 hours there was a yelling and a screaming like a load of banshees, and a crowd of Officer Cadets runs up with what looks like a bundle of manky washing, and chucks it past my lughole into the harbour. SIR."

"But in fact the bundle of washing was an Egyptian?"

"Sir."

"Didn't you recognise him?"

"No, sir. Just some thieving Gyppo – that's what I thought."

"But, Sergeant. The conjurer comes on board every time we drop anchor in Port Said, and you've been on this ship for over a year. You must know him by now."

"Sorry, sir. All them wogs are all the same to me."

"What about the Ship's Officer? Did he recognise him?"

"Ship's Officer, sir, had gone to drain his snake."

"Well then . . . could you recognise any of the Cadets responsible? Are there any here, for example?"

Sergeant Pulcher surveyed the Cadets with the courteous disdain of a reigning prince in a brothel. "Sorry, sir," he said at length, "but all them Cadets are all the same to me."

"So you can't help me any further?"

"No, sir."

"And do any of you gentlemen wish to cross-examine? No? Dismiss, please, S'arnt Pulcher. . . ."

"So," said the O.C. Troops a few minutes later, "no one saw properly what happened, and no one recognised the victim or any of his assailants. And yet those assailants, with perhaps one or two exceptions, are all in this cabin before me now. So someone, you deduce, must have recognised them after all. Ponder this mystery, gentlemen. An informer from your own ranks? Perish the thought. Myself? I was ashore. One of my staff? So were all of them – except, of course, for Sergeant Pulcher. Who has a wife and five children in Wolverhampton, gentlemen, and might appreciate a testimonial of how much you have enjoyed your voyage – when, that is, we arrive at Bombay in two weeks' time."

The O.C. Troops paused for this to sink in.

"Yet although evidence is so scanty, gentlemen, I can assure you that this would not be the end of the affair, were it not" – he glanced through a porthole – "that we are now safely out in the Red Sea. You may perhaps wonder why the ship was not detained at Port Said or Suez. The answer can only be that someone . . . someone or other . . . must have been dilatory. With the result that instead of a full scale police investigation, with the conjurer in person to assist, all we have to deal with is this radio message." He flourished the paper from which he had been reading earlier. "In short, the whole matter is now left to me."

The O.C. Troops lit a cheroot and glinted through his monocle.

"And since I can discover nothing, nothing can be done. No one can be sent back to Egypt, even if there were the means to send him. Although serious damage has been done, although two Egyptians have been drowned – and all because of a childish panic which in aspirant officers was a scandal and a degradation – yet nothing at all will be done. You know why not, gentlemen?"

"Because," Alister Mortleman began, "there aren't any witnesses to—"

"—For God's sake don't be a bigger fool than he made you."

The O.C. Troops inhaled a lungful of smoke and sent it back at the Cadets in a thin, hissing stream.

"There are just two reasons, gentlemen, why nothing will happen to any of you. First, because we – the British – are still in control. We may not be for long, we certainly shan't be for ever, but for the time being we are still able to arrange things to our liking at ports like Said and Suez and in countries like Egypt.

"And the second reason why you are being protected is that while on this ship you are my men. That you are also Officer Cadets makes no difference – I would do just the same for private soldiers. You are my men, I am charged to bring you safe to Bombay, and I *will not* leave any of you behind in Egypt or anywhere else. It is, you might say, a matter of honour; for the first and the last obligation which an Officer owes to those under him is *never*, in any circumstance whatsoever, to desert them. I give you good afternoon, gentlemen. Mr Morrison, you will be so good as to stay a moment. . . ."

When the rest had gone, Peter was invited to sit down.

"Now then," said the O.C. Troops; "none of this was really your fault, but I should like to give you a warning."

"Yes, sir?" said Peter, part smug and part resentful.

"Yes, sir. You see, once having embarked on a certain course – in this case, that of helping the conjurer by pretending to be hypnotised – you should have seen it through. Unless a grave emergency had arisen."

"It did arise, sir. I told you. Those Egyptians were going to uncover my private parts."

"Their intention was innocent."

"But everyone would have seen."

"Don't be such a baby," said the O.C. Troops. "Only the lower classes bother about that. And there's another thing. After you'd scared those Egyptians off, you decided to douse yourself in a shower. Why?"

"I *told* you, sir. Although I didn't care for being mucked about like that, I wanted to make the trick end well."

"Very commendable. But what you were doing, Morrison, was this. You were obtruding an additional factor into a situation of which you were totally ignorant. A very dangerous thing to do."

"I knew pretty well what was meant to happen."

"But you didn't know what was actually happening. You didn't know that out on deck that conjurer was in trouble. Or why. And so you did the one thing which was bound to make the trouble worse : you made a dramatic appearance that confirmed those boys in their wildest suspicions and turned them into a mob."

"I hadn't the slightest intention—"

"—My dear fellow, of course you hadn't. No one ever has. But all this fuss would have been avoided if only you'd obeyed the old rule : – never interfere. That was your crime, Morrison; you *interfered*; you did the wrong thing – the most calamitously wrong thing – for what you thought was the right reason. So be warned. It happens every day," said the O.C. Troops, "and every day it brings another promising military career to abrupt termination."

"That O.C. Troops," said Alister Mortleman: "a smooth performer."

"What they call a man of the world," said Barry Strange.

"Devious," said Peter Morrison.

The three of them were leaning over the rail and watching the flying fishes. These they found pretty sad entertainment after the first thirty seconds or so, and disillusionment had led to moroseness.

"He has simply taken advantage of his position," Peter went on, "to fix the whole thing."

"Just as well for me, I s'pose," said Mortleman, who was tall and very chunky in his jungle green shorts.

"And for me," said Barry, who looked like a radiant fourth former on Sports Day, his golden hair well matched by golden thighs.

"His example is a disgrace," said Peter, whose shorts hung down dismally below the knee. "How can one expect Cadets to treat Indians properly if they see a senior Officer behaving like that to Egyptians?"

"Behaving like what?"

"Ignoring their appeal for justice."

"I expect he thought it didn't really matter," said Barry very sincerely, "because Egyptians are so immoral and disgusting. But Indians are so much decenter – you know, loyal and clean – that we shall *want* to be nice to them."

"Shall we?" said Alister. " 'All them wogs are all the same to me,' " he quoted.

"You shouldn't use that word," said Peter primly. "It means that you consider them inferior, like Sergeant Pulcher or the O.C. Troops."

"I *do* consider them inferior. And for Christ's sake stop nagging on about the O.C. Troops. If it hadn't been for him, me and Barry and the rest might be rotting in a dungeon in Port Said."

"I suppose," said Barry, "that we really have heard the last of it? I mean, there won't be people waiting to arrest us at Bombay?"

"You heard what the gentleman said. They wouldn't know who to arrest."

"You're sure, Alister?"

"I'm sure, Barrikins."

"What do you think, Peter?"

"I think," said Peter, "that you've both been very lucky—"

"—We did it for you, for Christ's sake—"

"—And that it's up to you to redeem yourselves now that you've been given a second chance."

"Oh dear," said Alister. "I do see why you were head of your house at school. Heavy."

"Dependable," said Barry, and looked shyly at Peter.

"Bossing. It was the same at my place. If you went round all the boys and chose the ten longest faces with those spiteful sort of sticking out teeth, they'd be the ten heads of houses."

"Peter's teeth don't stick out. And his face is round."

"It gets a bit ovoid from time to time. He's bound to be made a J.U.O. when we reach Bangalore."

"J.U.O.?"

"Junior Under Officer. Responsible to the Platoon Commander for the conduct and turn-out of the Platoon."

"In which case," Peter said. "I'll have to do something about my own shorts."

He started to turn them up on the inside.

"Do you think I could do this and then sew them?"

"Don't you bother," said Alister. "We shall be refitted with new kit at the Transit Camp near Bombay, and then with still another lot when we get to Bangalore."

"How do you know?"

"Sergeant Pulcher told me. No one ever comes to the Far East, he said, without getting at least three different issues of tropical kit. Dhobi-man's shit, he called it."

"Dhobi-man?"

"Indian for washerman."

"But surely," said Barry, who had a careful mind, "it won't be worth issuing us with new stuff at the Transit Camp if they're going to change it again at Bangalore."

"We may be at the Transit Camp for months," Alister said.

"Nonsense," said Peter: "we are due at Bombay on December nine and at Bangalore not later than December sixteen."

"The official version, Peterkin. But people get lost in transit camps. They get forgotten. Every day," Alister said, "they go to the office for a movement order, and the Sergeant-Major says it hasn't come through yet, and then a new Sergeant-Major comes who doesn't know them, and *he* says he can't find them on *any* of the lists, not even on the ration strength, so they can't get any food or any pay, and they just totter round the camp like ghosts until they forget their own names and either die or go native."

"Oh no," said Barry, shocked.

"They can't lose 300 Officer Cadets," said Peter, reassuring.

"Why not? The war's over and nobody really wants us. I shall be very surprised," said Alister, "if we ever get commissioned at all."

"You've been too long on this ship," Peter said: "you need proper exercise."

"You can say that again. I haven't had a crap for a week. God, these flying fish are a bloody bore," Alister said: "whatever was Kipling on about?"


"Brahmin," announced a skinny and pallid Major in the uniform of the Madrasi Rifles, "are priests and teachers. Caste colour, red. Kshatriya are rulers, noblemen and warriors. Caste colour, white."

The 300 Cadets were assembled in the Main Lecture Hall of the Transit Camp at Khalyan, some forty miles from Bombay. They had already been there for ten days and had twice been issued with new sets of tropical kit, both of which had now been withdrawn, so that they were compelled to wear the thick shirts and battle-dress trousers in which they had left England six weeks before. However, they were told that they could expect yet another tropical issue any day now – as soon, in fact, as a train had been arranged to take them South to Bangalore. But here was the trouble. The Rail Transport Officer was not empowered to order a train until the Senior Quartermaster at Khalyan had fitted the Cadets with the correct Drill, Khaki, O/Cadets in Transit for the Wearing of;

and the Senior Quartermaster, for his part, was not empowered to fit out the Cadets until a definite date had been fixed for the train. A little good will between the two Officers concerned would soon have overcome this difficulty, but good will was in short supply at Khalyan, and the affair had now reached a draw by perpetual check. Meanwhile, the Cadets idled sweatily through the days and were occasionally summoned to hear improvised lectures about the Empire which they had come to inherit.

"Vaishya," said the skinny Major (who was in open arrest while awaiting Court Martial and so, being relieved of all other duties, was free for this one): "the common people, tillers and traders. Caste colour, yellow. Sudra: servants, slaves, what have you. Caste colour, black.

"Outside this structure of Hindu society, we also have other people, who cannot come near the Hindu without polluting him – the Untouchables, Pariahs or Outcastes. Some of them are so degraded as to be Unseeable as well as Untouchable, and may only emerge after nightfall."

There was a long pause, during which the Major, who considered that he had now exhausted his subject, tried to think of some felicitous formula of conclusion. Before he could accomplish this, however, his escort, a tubby red Captain of Indian Ordnance, pointed reproachfully at the lecture hall clock and murmured something about another thirty minutes still to run. The Major sighed deeply, scraped into his harassed mind for something more to say, and then went grinding on:

"Between the castes or *Varna*, there were, and are, very strict rules governing their relations. A Brahmin can kill a Sudra for the cost of a cat. Or so they told me when I was a Cadet, but that may have gone out now. On the other hand, if a Sudra kills a Brahmin, he is ferociously punished right there on the spot – quite how I'm not sure – and is also considered to have damned himself for eternity. This kind of thing certainly makes a chap know his place."

The Major let out a despairing snort. He looked at the Captain, who shook his head gently but firmly.

"Hack on, old fellow," the Captain said.

"The point is, though," the Major whined, "that these wallahs here in India accept all this. They really believe in it. For these people, what we would call salvation is merely a matter of keeping in one's place. You don't have to *do* anything, you just have to stay in the right place and go through the motions.

"Suppose you're a Merchant. What you do is set up a notice saying, 'C. Hasri, Merchant', and then just sit underneath it. Going through the motions, you see. No one cares whether you actually buy or sell anything; just sit quiet under your notice, and you'll rake in tons of salvation marks, and the next time you're reborn you'll have gone up in the scale. You'll be a Kshatriya, say, a warrior. Now to be fair, the warriors are the one lot that do *do* what they're meant to. They're very good at fighting, as you'll find out."

For a moment the Major seemed to have been quite restored by this thought, but then he became glummer than ever.

"The only trouble is, they don't much care who they're fighting against, because they get their salvation marks just for fighting, you see, and it's all one to them whether they're bayoneting the Japs or scalping your mem-sahib. Provided, that is, they've been told to by their officer, because obeying your officer means you're staying in your right place, and it isn't your biswacks to bother whose windpipe you're splitting if once he's given you the say-so. So that's why we have to be so frightfully careful about what Indians we allow to be officers. There have always been Viceroy's Officers, of course, and now we're beginning to have King's Indian Officers, but it can be terribly tricky, because with these chappies you never know which way they're going to jump unless you're holding the whip yourself. So it's inconceivable that any of 'em should ever be given more than a very subordinate command. . . ."

"Was it true – what that Major was saying?" asked Barry Strange that evening.

"He made sense," said Alister Mortleman; "except that

some of the time he almost seemed to think that the war was still going on."

"I thought he was rather unhinged," said Peter Morrison. "He's going to be court-martialled, you know. Embezzling Mess funds."

They were walking in the cantonment fair ground. The Dive Bomber, unpatronised, hung athwart the sky. A few private soldiers, mostly young members of the Transit Camp's permanent staff, scuffed their way along the stalls.

"Of course," Peter said, "he was only talking about Hindus. Mohammedans are very different, I'm told."

Since none of them had ever met either, this remark passed without comment.

"Wall of Death," said Alister, pointing; "let's go in."

But the half-caste at the door said no, they couldn't. The motor-bicycle had gone wrong, he explained : could they come back next week? Whatever was wrong with the motor-bicycle, no one seemed very urgent to repair it; for it was standing a few yards away, its rear wheel propped in a bracket and its nose turned to the wall. Sitting on its saddle, the wrong way round, was a florid and seedy Englishman of about forty, smoking a thin, black cheroot.

"Sorry, chaps," he said.

"Is that the motor-bicycle?"

"Yes. We're waiting for the fair ground manager to stump up for a new back tyre."

"And are you the rider?"

"Yes. When there's any riding to be done."

"But surely," said Barry kindly, "when you get your new back tyre there'll be lots of people coming to watch."

The death rider took his cheroot from his mouth with thumb and finger.

"Don't you believe it," he said, pinching off the live end of the cheroot with his nails. "The old soldiers – the ones going home – they've seen too much to bother with me. And as for the boys who are coming through on the way out – this fair ground makes 'em home-sick and they stay away."

"Who does come here then?"

"The odd pen-pusher from the Camp. Hoping to pick up a girl." He put his half-cheroot in his breast pocket and lowered his voice. "There's a few blackie-white jobs about. Ten chips a throw and not too bad at the price. I can introduce you fellows if you like."

"No thanks."

They turned and walked away.

"Good luck with the bike," Barry called back.

"Sordid type," said Peter.

"It can't be much fun, being stuck in this dump with a burst tyre. . . . . What did he mean – 'ten chips'?"

"Slang for rupees."

"Well," said Alister, "if we're here much longer I shall have ten chips' worth myself."

"Ten chips' worth of disease," said Peter. "We'll be off in a day or two, don't you worry."

"But if we're not," said Barry, "we must come back next week and see the Wall of Death. I'm sorry for that poor man."

"Barrikins wants an introduction to a blackie-white job," Alister teased.

"I think that's disgusting of him," Barry said, looking at Peter, "but I'm sorry for him all the same."

"We'll be off long before that tyre's mended," Peter insisted.

But despite this assurance, depression hung over the party as stark and ugly as the Dive Bomber.

"Come on," said Peter, feeling a duty to raise morale : "I'll stand us all a ticket for the Tattooed Rhinoceros."

The Tattooed Rhinoceros was stuffed.


Four days later they were still at Khalyan, so it looked as if Barry would be able to see the Wall of Death after all; and indeed Alister had promised to go with him the next day, which would be Christmas Eve. Meanwhile, there was some considerable excitement because an Officer had flown from Delhi especially to address them. He was called Lieutenant-Colonel Glastonbury, he looked like a taller and flabbier brother of Douglas Fairbanks Junior, and he was something very important (Peter told them all) on Lord Wavell's staff. The Officer Cadets thought he had come to explain the delay in moving them to Bangalore; but so far from doing that, he didn't even seem to know that there was a delay. He had come to talk to them, he said, about their military careers.

"A good hundred of you," he drawled, "have come out here as Indian Army Cadets of Infantry. But I must inform you that it is most unlikely that more than a handful of you will ever be officers in the Indian Army."

("What did I tell you?" whispered Alister fiercely to Peter. "They don't want any of us. I can see by the look on his face.")

"The probability is," Colonel Glastonbury droned on, "that at least ninety-seven per cent of all of you will be commissioned into British Infantry Regiments of the Line, and will join units of those Regiments still in the Far East as soon as you leave Bangalore."

He repeated this in a great many different ways for the next twenty minutes, and then asked if there were any questions.

"Can you tell us, sir," asked Peter, "*why* so few of us will be accepted for the Indian Army?"

"Because the new policy will be to commission native Indians."

"Then why were we accepted as Indian Army Cadets?"

"Because no one had anticipated the new policy."

"Are we *still* Indian Army Cadets?" Peter persisted.

"As far as that goes, yes. It's no good getting all het-up with me, my dear fellow. I'm just a messenger boy from Delhi. Anyhow, I'm a cavalry man myself" – this with tired complacency – "and I don't really understand what the Infantry wallahs are up to. With you or anyone else. But there's one thing I do understand, and you'd better understand it too."

He looked down on the assembled Cadets like a benevolent Jeremiah.

"It's all coming to an end, you know, out here. There's no future in the Indian Army, even if you do get into it. Because the show's over, chums. It may take a year or two to wind it up, but the Durbar's done. So if you stay here long enough, you can help put up the shutters and pull down the flag. And that's what's in it for you."

Before Lieutenant-Colonel Glastonbury left Khalyan, he went, on behalf of the Cadets, to the Commandant of the Transit Camp and asked how soon they could expect to be sent on to Bangalore. The short answer was that the Commandant didn't know and didn't care, and so he told Glastonbury, bidding him mind his own business for good measure.

"Pure nerves," as Glastonbury explained good-humouredly to the deputation of Cadets which accompanied him to the local air field. "He's not a bad little man really, he's just worried stiff about what's going to happen to him when the poor old Raj packs up."

"Even so, sir, he might have been more civil," Peter said.

"He didn't like the cut of my rig." Glastonbury's regiment, a British one, was the 49th Earl Hamilton's Light Dragoons, and his uniform, even in a tropical version, was distinctive. "And he don't care for visitors from Delhi. They seldom bring much comfort with 'em. . . . Thank you for seeing me off, gentlemen. When I've got any more news in your line, I'll look in on you all at Bangalore."

All of which was well enough but left the Cadets still mouldering in Khalyan, where, they must now presume, they would be spending the twelve days of Christmas. So the next day – Christmas Eve – Alister Mortleman and Barry Strange set off, late in the afternoon, to visit the Wall of Death and enquire whether it was now functioning. Peter, who was suffering acutely from the local variant of diarrhoea ('Khalyan squirt'), stayed behind in order to be near the lavatory.

"You know what," said Alister to Barry : "I think I'm going to have one of those blackie-white girls that chappie was telling us about."

"Do you know how?"

"Of course. You just – well – you know."

Barry, who didn't, nodded.

"What about you?"

"I wouldn't mind," said Barry, who liked to please and therefore adapted his moral tone to his company of the moment; "but I haven't got enough money."

"Ten chips? I've got enough for both of us."

They entered the fair ground. The Dive Bomber was still at precisely the same angle as when they had last seen it.

"Suggestive," Alister said.

"I don't want to catch anything."

"You won't – not if you use one of these."

Alister passed his friend a small envelope. They approached the Wall of Death, outside which the rider was sitting on the motor-bicycle; like the Dive Bomber, he did not appear to have moved since they last left him.

"I think," said Barry, "that we ought to be getting back. There's a carol service in the Garrison Church at six."

"Rubbish," said Alister. And then to the rider, "Hullo there."

"Hello again," the death rider said.

"We . . . we want you to introduce us to two of those girls you were talking about."

"Gladly. But you haven't got time."

"Plenty of time. Not even a muster parade till the day after Boxing Day."

"Your lot's packing up to go," the rider said.

"Nonsense. We only left them a few minutes ago."

"Have it your own way."

"But I mean to say . . . *on Christmas Eve*."

"It's all one to me," the rider said. "If you want two girls, you can have 'em. Ten chips each and five for me."

To Barry, as he looked across the twilight fair ground, down the rows of silent stalls and on to the hill which spiralled up behind them like a thin, malformed cone, there came some lines of verse from his childhood :

> True Thomas lay on Huntlie bank;
>     A farlie he spied with his e'e;
> And there he saw a ladye bright
>     Come riding down by the Eildon Tree.

True Thomas had taken the road to 'fair Elfland', and Barry, he now saw, had done the same. True Thomas had been doomed to wander for seven years – indeed, if Barry remembered aright, 'he never gat back to his ain countrie'. Barry must get back to his while there was still time. Already, perhaps, it might be too late, and he would find that he was cut off on an island in empty space, condemned to the fair ground for ever. Barry shivered, whirled about and bolted.

"Sensible young fellow," said the rider to Alister: "why don't you do the same?"

But Alister stood his ground. "Here's fifteen rupees," he said. The rider took the money but didn't move.

"Through the entrance," he said to Alister, "first door on the left and up to the gallery."

"And then?"

"Take your pick. There's everything you need up there."

"Not very private."

"What did you expect for ten chips?"

Alister drew a deep breath and marched through the entrance.

When Barry got himself back to the Cadets' quarters in the Transit Camp, everything was in turmoil. An Emergency Movement Order had just come through (nobody quite knew whence, though the word 'Delhi' was in many mouths) and the 300 Cadets were to be entrained at midnight. Since most Cadets had scant belongings, packing presented few problems; but the formalities to be gone through were massive. Resentful Colour Sergeants clumped hither and thither with huge lists in triplicate; while groups of muttering officers, whom no one had ever seen before, stood around beating their calves urgently with canes.

". . . Morrison, P."

"Here, Colour Sergeant."

"Mortleman, A."

"He's just gone for a walk. He'll be back soon."

"He'd better be, laddie."

"He couldn't know that this was going to happen."

"*Couldn't know*, laddie? No more could I, and I'm here shouting the odds, ain't I? On parade when I'm wanted, Christmas Eve or Doomsday, it's all one to me. Murphy, J. . . . Muscateer, Earl of . . . Zaccharias, W. Outside the lot of you, and get fell in."

"Please, Colour Sergeant. My diarrhoea."

"Follow the column to the stores at your own pace, and keep your cheeks together. What you lot need is a nanny."

"Please, Colour Sergeant?"

"Yes, my lord? Lost your coronet, my lord? No? . . . Only your Part One pay book? Is that all you've lost? Well, you'd better find it, Mr Lord Muscateer, sir, you had indeed, because if somebody asks you for it and you don't 'ave it, you'll be a man without a name – won't you, my lord? – and that means you'll be doubled away to a dungeon and never 'eard of again. OUTSIDE."

". . . Morrison, P."

"Colour."

"Bush jackets three, O/Cadets in Transit for the Wearing of, slacks three, shorts three. Sign there. Still keeping your cheeks together, I 'ope?"

"Only just, Colour."

"Mortleman, A. He's the one that's gone walkies. One of you young gentlemen had better find him, I promise you that, because if he's not on that train tonight they'll have him for desertion – absent when under warning to move. What's his size? . . . Big bastard, eh? Well, you take that lot for him, Mr Morrison, P., and hurry off out of here before you drop your tripes in my nice clean stores. Murphy, J. – bush-jackets, slacks, shorts – and here's 'is lordship again, I've got a special lot for you, my lord, in silk. . . ."

God, thought Peter, as he sat on the can with all Alister's tropical kit and his own piled about his ankles, it's like scalding water going through. Shall I go sick? *Go sick and miss the train?* It might be weeks before I got sent on; they might back-squad me to a later intake, they might say I'd lost my chance altogether – just send me home. Khalyan squirt – *ouuucchh* –

but there'll be a lavatory on the train, one must stay with one's friends in strange countries, one mustn't fall out for a small thing like Khalyan squirt – Phheeeuuwww, but that should do the trick for the next twenty minutes.

Someone came into a nearby cubicle and was violently sick. As there were no doors, Peter looked in as he passed. Alister, reeling and retching over the seat.

"Alister."

"Peterkin. I'm so *drunk*. Better now, but so tired. So tired. Help me to bed, Peterkin."

"No bed, Alister. You've got to get into this tropical dress, and fit up your equipment web, and get on parade at 2300 hours to get on to the truck to get on to the train at midnight."

"God, I feel awful. You look rotten too. Bed."

"No bed. Back to fit up our kit. But I think . . . I'll have to have another shit first. . . ."

So Peter had another shit and Alister was sick again for fellowship; and then they staggered to their basha (hut) and despite Peter's injunctions lay down on their charboys (beds), while Barry fussed about them fitting together their equipment web and asking prurient questions of Alister.

"She gave me this stuff," Alister said. "Not alcohol, I think, after all. Something to make me do it better, she said, very expensive, thirty chips extra, and it certainly worked and—"

"—And now it's made you ill," said Barry primly. "Lift your behind, please, Alister, or I shan't be able to get your slacks up. That's right. I'll just see how Peter's getting on, and then I'll come back to help you with your big pack and pouches. . . ."

". . . Morrison, P."

"Colour."

"Mortleman, A. . . . Glad to see you at last, Mr Mortleman. I hope you had a pleasant walk, sir, even if it has turned you bright green. Murphy, J. . . . Your lordship . . . Zaccharias, W. And now, all of you, up into that truck. Allow me, Mr Mortleman. (Jesus Christ, sonny, what have you been drinking? You stink like a Parsees' tower. Didn't they warn you never to take a drink from those girls?) And so up with the tail – thank you,

Mr Strange – my compliments, gentlemen, and a pleasant journey to Bangalore. You'll find it a nice place enough, but one last tip : never eat the orange meringue pie in Ley Wong's Chinese Restaurant."

When the Christmas sun rose on them, they were passing through Poona; their Christmas dinner they ate in a siding at Sholapur.

What with Peter's Khalyan squirt and Alister's repeated vomiting, the night had been a fitful one. Since there was only one W.C. for each coach, and since each coach contained two Platoons of Cadets, and since over-excitement had produced a strong propensity to evacuate even in those who didn't have Khalyan squirt, there were considerable problems of hygiene and logistics. However, Barry did what he could to mitigate his friends' discomfiture, and was stoutly assisted by the Earl of Muscateer, who devised an ingenious contraption, with an oil funnel and some mess tins, for the desperate Peter when the loo was occupied, and used most of his best eau de Cologne in cleaning up Alister. By the time they had passed through Poona, order of a kind had been achieved; and when 'dinner' was served at Sholapur (a thick stew, ladled into their mess tins from containers on the platform) both Alister and Peter were strong enough to dismount and queue up with the rest.

To make matters better, the late afternoon was mild and grateful where they were, and amusement was provided for them in the form of an Indian shanty village just below the embanked siding. Standing on the platform, they could observe the colourful and picturesque antics of a thousand-odd natives, whose total living space, it appeared, was just a little larger than a fair sized croquet lawn.

"Quarters for the Untouchables, do you think?"

"Like a nest of cockroaches," Alister said. "Thank God we live in a country which can never get as crowded as that."

"Can't it?" said Lord Muscateer.

"Can you imagine people in England ever living like that? Look at that squalid little girl – shitting on her own doorstep."

"After last night," said Peter, "one can hardly find fault with that. Where," he said to Muscateer, "did you get that oil funnel? Not the sort of thing one carries around."

"My governor told me to bring one. 'Whenever a man goes East of Calais,' he said to me, 'he should always take a large oil funnel. You've no idea how handy it can be.' It seems my governor was right."

"I'm very grateful to him – and you. It must be awkward to pack."

"At least it's not easy to lose. Not like a Part One Pay Book. I still can't find mine," said Muscateer miserably: "do you think they can make a row about it?"

"A bit of a row, yes. It's rather the same as an Identity Card. I should own up."

"What did that Colour Sergeant mean, by the way?"

"About doubling you away to a dungeon? That's rubbish, of course."

"No, not that. About not eating orange meringue pie in Ley Wong's Chinese Restaurant. Why on earth should he tell us that?"

"I didn't hear that bit," said Peter. "How many Indians do you suppose actually sleep in one of those huts?"

"I've just counted ten going into one," said Barry, "and no one's come out."

But oecological conjecture was now interrupted by a summons back to their wooden seats. The train pulled out of the siding and rattled away with them across the dusty Deccan towards Gulbarga. For a while they looked across the yellow, stony plain, until the sun sank behind the Western Ghats and all the ways were dark. Then they wrapped blankets round their thighs and stomachs, dozed and shivered, nodded off and nodded on, snored and dribbled and whimpered, while the distressful night crept by and slunk away at last before the kind old sun.


Not so kind, however, by twelve o'clock noon, when the train stopped at Kadur for lunch, which was thick slices of fibrous beef in a slimy gravy, garnished with undercooked potatoes. Now the sun was an enemy, an enemy who became more brutal with every minute of the slow afternoon, as they crawled across the flats towards the hills. These they reached at early evening and blessed the cool; until, as the sun sank and the train climbed, the cool turned to chill and the chill to bitter cold, which sent them to cringe in misery under their mean little blankets, like workhouse children waiting to be whipped.

At dawn, the coastal plain. By mid-morning, Madras. At Madras a breakfast of stewed tea and tiny pale yellow fried eggs (one each), and then a change of train.

"Last lap," said Peter to Muscateer.

For now they would ride due East to Mysore State and Bangalore; back over the coastal plain and then a slow ascent to the plateau, just high enough to temper the sun but not to reach the cold; and so into a promised land of blue days and whispering palm trees, an imperial land furnished with riches and tranquillity, a fabled land of chukkhas and barra pegs and tiger hunts, a comfortable land where Cadets were waited on by squads of bowing servants and Commissions were handed out like bright bouquets at a ball. With a lurch and a skip the train was out of Madras: Bangalore this evening, the cry went down the coaches; Bangalore for dinner – PASS THE WORD.

They arrived at Bangalore at 2.30 in the morning.

Once there, however, they found that they were very much expected. A motherly Sergeant-Major, overseen but not interfered with by a pug-faced Captain of Gurkhas, sorted them into Platoons and marshalled them into a fleet of open trucks, which carried them through a narrow bazaar and then through outskirts of shadowy, spacious houses, and stopped on a flat arena of sand, apparently in the middle of nowhere but in fact in the middle of the O.T.S. For out of the night on either side of the arena loomed long grey buildings with low verandahs, each of which, they were informed, was a Mess; and in one or other of these they were all swiftly and copiously fed.

Indian bearers had meanwhile assembled in strength and were now dished out, by the motherly Sergeant-Major and two placid assistants, at the rate of one bearer to four Cadets. Each bearer promptly gathered up the kit-bags of his four young sahibs and then, having first excused himself courteously for being unable to carry their valises as well, led them off at a short-arsed trot (no quicker than the Englishmen's walk) to their quarters in the Cadets' Lines, which consisted of parallel and single-storeyed bashas, each basha containing fifteen separate rooms and thus housing a Platoon of thirty Cadets in companionable pairs. The beds were made up with clean sheets and mosquito nets; there was hot water in the adjacent showers; there was a tumbler and a carafe by each pillow : but also by each pillow, and less for their comfort, was a polite note welcoming Mr —— (as the case might be) to the O.T.S. and requesting him to be on parade in the arena between the two Messes at 6.15 the following morning. It was already 4.45.

So at 6.15 they mustered (having been woken by their bearers with tea and green bananas at 5.45) and now everything was made very plain. They were to be formed into three Companies, two of three Platoons and one of four; A and B Coys would use one of the two Messes ('Clive'), while C Coy with its four Platoons would use the second and slightly smaller Mess ('Wellesley'). Each Platoon would be commanded and in large part instructed by a Captain of the Indian Army with the disciplinary assistance of a Cadet Junior Under Officer; each Company would be commanded by a Major of the Indian Army, who would be assisted by a Sergeant-Major (British) and a Cadet Senior Under Officer. There were six other Companies of Cadets at present in the O.T.S., all at various stages of the normal training, and also an Indian Company (Experimental), whose status was uncertain and whose members, should they chance to meet any, they must treat with polite indifference. The whole shooting match (as the motherly Sergeant-Major explained) was commanded by the Commandant, Brigadier Percy de Glanville Manwood, O.B.E., formerly of the Chota Nagpur Lancers – "and don't ask me why an Officer of Horse is training Officers of Foot, because I'm a simple man, gentlemen, who minds his business. Which is now to invite you to proceed in order of Platoons to the Contractor's Store, where you will be issued with the correct kit and lovely black tin trunks to put it in."

Whereupon 1 Pl. of A Coy was marched off by the Cadet considered the most likely candidate for the office of J.U.O. (a quondam Corporal of Military Police) and the rest settled down on the verandahs to wait.

"They needn't have got us up this early just to hang around here," said Alister crossly.

"Everyone," said Peter, "has to get up early in the East. It isn't healthy to stay in bed."

"And at least," said Barry, "we can hang around together."

For so it had luckily turned out. Cadets had been allotted to Platoons on a basis which was partly alphabetical and partly snobbish, those from the public schools and the better regiments being firmly segregated from their less fortunate comrades, since it was felt by Brigadier P. de G. Manwood (official policy to the contrary notwithstanding) that people were happier with others from their own social background. However, it was also felt that lip service must be paid to official doctrine in the matter; and so a judicious compromise had been reached whereby each Platoon was socially cohesive but each Company, taken as a whole, presented a social mixture – there being in A Coy, for example, one Platoon of upper-class boys, one of minor public school boys and one of what Alister called oiks. (This was the one which had just marched off under the ex-policeman.) Now, Peter Morrison, Alister Mortleman, the Lord Muscateer and Barry Strange all belonged to an upper/upper-middle alphabetical block which was to constitute No. 2 Pl. of C Coy; and so, while they indeed had the pleasure of hanging around, as Barry said, together, they also had to hang around for a very long time, since 2 Pl. C Coy was low in its numerical if not in its social order. They were still hanging around, in fact, some two hours after lunch (or, more properly, tiffin).

"I thought," said Barry, "that in India everyone had siestas."

"They gave that up in 1941," Peter told him: "it wasted too much time which might have been devoted to valuable training."

"But surely, that's why we get up so early – to do the valuable training before it gets too hot."

"Up here it never gets too hot. This is a Grade I Weather Station."

"So they think they can have it both ways," grumbled Alister: "drag us out at vulture-fart *and* keep grinding us the whole afternoon."

"Officers," Peter reminded him, "must be prepared to work long hours. This is no place for the shop steward mentality."

"Anyhow," said Muscateer, who liked hanging about, "you can't say they're exactly grinding us just now."

"It's surprising they haven't found something useful for us to do," said Peter. "I haven't seen an Officer since that one at the station last night."

(But what Peter didn't know was that all Officers of the O.T.S. were attending a special conference, convened by Brigadier Manwood on receipt of urgent orders from Delhi, in order to discuss the modernisation of the curriculum – e.g. whether or not the Cadets should still be instructed in stick drill.)

"I wonder," said Barry, "what sort of Officer we'll have for our Platoon."

"Indian Army in any case," said Alister.

"Does that make a difference?"

"I had a great-grandfather in the Coldstream," said Muscateer, "who had to transfer to the Indian Army after a row about some other fellow's wife. Usually, after that sort of row, they just sent you to a line regiment to get you out of London. But my great-grandpapa was so awful that they sent him all the way out here. Do you suppose *that's* any guide to the form?"

"What happened to him then?"

"He got mixed up in a duel with a Rajah. On elephants. But the next day they heard that he'd inherited, so they hushed it all up. He always said afterwards that Indian Army Officers were the most frightful tuft-hunters. —But some of you chaps are for the Indian Army, aren't you? Sorry and all that."

"I've got an Indian Army Cadetship," Peter said, "but that man who came to Khalyan didn't fancy my chances."

"I'm hoping for the Rifle Brigade," said Alister, pointing to his cap badge with some insistence.

"And I'm for the Wessex Fusiliers," said Barry proudly; "my brothers were with them, you see."

"Yes," said Muscateer : "I do see."

"What regiment are you going into, Muscateer?" – this from Alister.

"I've been with my county mob so far – the Wiltshires."

"I'd have thought you'd have gone into the Guards."

"They haven't been too keen on us since great-grandpapa's little affair. Anyway, my old governor says a man ought to join his local lot. He says that's what the best chaps always did, and that your smart London regiments are just a load of shit-stabbing grocers."

"Rather strong?"

"My old governor always puts things strong," said Muscateer with a lazy smile of love. "Here's that nice Sergeant-Major. I think it's our turn at last."


At the Contractor's Store, each of them was issued with and required to sign for : five new suits of khaki drill, these being of rather poorer material than any of the several previous issues : a fly whisk; a bicycle; three pairs of lumpy flannel pyjamas (whether they wanted them or not); ten pairs of brief white drawers, of a kind difficult to manipulate when one was peeing and guaranteed to cause and exacerbate tinia cruris; a jungle hat; a tent; a camp bed; a camp wash-stand;

a leather hip-flask; a bible and a prayer-book (for conducting burial services when no Minister of the Church was available); and a split swagger cane. They were also given, as the motherly Sergeant-Major had foretold, one black tin trunk apiece, in which to put everything except the bicycle. For some reason that was not very clear they must pay for all this themselves, the Contractor told them, in instalments which would be deducted from their emolument (henceforth equivalent to that of a junior Sergeant) over the next six months. When everything had been checked and stowed, their bearers came trotting up from the Lines to collect the loaded trunks, while they themselves rode off to tea on their new bicycles, all of them, that is, except Lord Muscateer, who had never learned to ride a bicycle and had to wheel his instead.

The next day they started their training in earnest. From 6.15 a.m. to 7.45 they had stick drill with their new split swagger canes. After breakfast they had Urdu, which was taught to them in groups of four by grave and white-robed Munshis, who addressed them as 'Sahib' and expected the courtesy to be returned. Peter Morrison was glad they were learning Urdu, because he thought this meant that he had a better chance of getting into the Indian Army: after all, as he said to Barry, why should the authorities make them learn Urdu unless some of them at least were going to need it? Barry, who liked people to be happy, agreed with Peter about this; but Alister, who was fast developing a nose for Indian proceedings, said that Urdu lessons were simply an old habit which the authorities were either too lethargic or sentimental to abandon.

Later on in the morning, they were introduced to the Officers of their Company. G Coy was to be commanded by a man called Major Baxter, a cheerful and loud-mouthed little chap from an Indian regiment so unsmart that it was quite famous for it. Major Baxter had a head the size of an elk's and wore shorts which came down to about a foot below his knees; which was just as well, perhaps, because his legs resembled those of a spider with stockings and shoes on. As for the Platoon Commanders, there was one called Captain Better-edge (handsome and morose) for No. 1 Pl., and another called Captain Lafone, who had a voice even commoner than Major Baxter's, for No. 3 Pl., and yet another for No. 4 Pl.; but for some reason No. 2 Pl. hadn't yet got a Commander, which made them feel rather left out. However, Major Baxter said that an Officer would be coming to them very shortly and that meanwhile Peter Morrison, who had already been appointed J.U.O. on account of his large and reliable face, would be responsible for their welfare and deportment.

The C.S.M. of C Coy was a disappointment. They had all been hoping that they would get the motherly Sergeant-Major, who had so far been controlling everybody and everything single-handed; but it now turned out that he was to be C.S.M. of A Coy, while C Coy was to have a man called Sergeant-Major Cruxtable. This Warrant Officer, who came from the Wiltshire Regiment, was prematurely obese and had a sideways look like that of a pi-dog who was afraid lest someone might kick it out of the way before it had finished crapping. Although Muscateer, loyal as ever to his own 'mob' and his own county, pretended to find Cruxtable satisfactory ('the sort of man who's been about a bit'), everyone else disliked and mistrusted him on sight. In truth, however, and as they later found out, they might have happened on much worse; for Cruxtable was simply a slut and like most sluts was happy to leave all men in peace providing only that they served him similar.

Having been introduced to their superiors, the Cadets were then lectured by Major Baxter on the conduct and esprit which would be expected of them. In the main, exhortation was negative: the Cadets were *not* to get drunk, borrow money from native money-lenders or frequent native women (in which category, for all practical purposes, Eurasians were included); they were not to interest themselves in Indian politics or walk about with bare feet (in case they picked up hook-worm); and in no circumstances whatever were they to complain about anything that had to do with the O.T.S. Let them only observe these simple and sensible conditions, Major Baxter said, and they would all have a pleasurable six months' course with Commissions thrown in at the end of it. Failure was unheard of at Bangalore (since it cost the Government so much to send people out there) except in case of insanity, death or thrice repeated venereal infection, which was why they were requested not to sleep with natives. If they had any personal problems, they might always come to him, but frankly, gentlemen, potential officers were expected to keep their troubles to themselves and not go whining round for pity like a shower of illiterate conscripts. And so good morning to them all, and a very pleasant week-end . . . oh, and just one thing more. Although there was no formal Church Parade at the O.T.S., it was held to be desirable that some thirty per cent of the Cadets should attend Matins at the Garrison Church each Sunday. Sergeant-Major Cruxtable would therefore select one man in three by lot, regardless of individual creeds, as future Officers must learn to subordinate private belief to public duty. The only Cadets who would be exempt when the lot was drawn were those who had been selected to take part in the O.T.S. Cricket Trials, which would start on Sunday at 11 a.m. and were to be honoured by the presence of H.H. the Maharajah of Dharaparam. Should His Highness approach any Cadet in a familiar manner, such Cadet was warned to be cautious but very polite.

Several Cadets from the new intake had been chosen, on account of their school records, to take part in the O.T.S. Cricket Trials that Sunday. Two of these were Peter and Alister. Peter, who had just failed to get into his School XI in a good year, bowled slow off-breaks all so exactly similar in flight and pace that they soon bored even the most wary opponent into some contemptuous and fatal error; while Alister was a flashy batsman who used too much right hand but had played for Winchester.

The proceedings were undistinguished but pleasant; for the O.T.S. Cricket Ground was agreeably sited and had one of the few grass wickets in all India. 'Napier' (Peter's and Alister's team) was first in the field and dismissed 'Curzon' (three of whom had been bored out by Peter's off-breaks) for 194 runs. Batting after tea, 'Napier' swiftly put on 97 for 2 (with the help of an aggressive 34 by Alister at first wicket) and then settled down to plod slowly and without risk towards a very probable victory. When the score was 150 for 3, Peter, who was to bat No. 10 and did not expect to be called upon, suggested to Alister that they should take a turn round the ground, if only to avoid the succulent giggles with which H.H. the Maharajah of Dharaparam was favouring Alister from his box in the pavilion.

Taking a turn round the ground in the opposite direction were two men in light civilian suits and panama hats. Although one of them was large and loose and the other was stringy and sparse, they kept perfect step as they walked together and made a model of easeful and elegant progression.

"That's Colonel Glastonbury," said Alister: "the chap who came to Khalyan."

"And the smaller one's called Captain Detterling," said Peter. "I've met him once or twice in England – down at my school. He's the only man who ever made a double century in a school match. Before my time, of course."

As Glastonbury and Detterling approached the two Cadets, they lifted their hats in effortless unison. Detterling sported the Butterfly riband, Peter noticed, and Glastonbury the Eton Ramblers'. After the introduction of Alister to Captain Detterling and the shaking of hands in all other required permutations, the two Officers replaced their hats and turned about as if to accompany their juniors.

"But we," said Peter politely, "will walk your way."

"No," said Detterling. "You two are players; we're only spectators."

"So we walk your way," Glastonbury said.

Before Peter had time to consider the full implications of this courtesy, Glastonbury launched into an explanation of their presence. He himself had come from Delhi to impress upon the Commandant of the O.T.S. that certain rather radical changes were now necessary in the Syllabus of Instruction.

"We asked them to fix it up themselves," Glastonbury said. "and let us know what they'd done. In fact they've done precisely nothing, so I've been sent to chivvy them along. They're still teaching you Urdu, I hear?"

"Yes," said Alister; "*and* stick drill. That's about all they have taught us so far."

"Well, Urdu will certainly go," said Glastonbury, "but stick drill will probably stay."

"Why, sir?" said Alister petulantly.

Glastonbury simply opened his eyes slightly wider at Alister, as if the answer should have been obvious to any sane person, and changed the subject.

"Captain Detterling has come here as an instructor," Glastonbury said, nodding across at his companion.

"For our Platoon? We haven't got one yet?"

For no evident reason, Detterling and Glastonbury exchanged guilty glances.

"I'm afraid not," said Detterling. "I'm to teach Military Law and Infantry/Tank Co-operation to the whole O.T.S. I'm cavalry, you see. The same regiment as Giles here."

It occurred to Peter that if these two were friends and near-contemporaries, as seemed to be the case, then there was a marked contrast in their comparative rank; no doubt Glastonbury's Colonelcy was only temporary, but there was no reason why Detterling, after nearly six years of war, should not have achieved some similar brevet. It also occurred to Peter that the last time he had seen Detterling, which was at their old school in England only three months before, Detterling had been newly appointed to the job of sifting recruits at the various Primary Training Corps in order to find suitable candidates for the Cavalry. Since posts like this required long experience, they also carried long tenure; which being the case, Detterling's arrival at Bangalore required elucidation.

"I dare say," said Detterling, anticipating the question which Peter would have been too well mannered to ask, "that you wonder what happened to that job of mine in England. Cavalry (Armoured Corps) Selection Officer. The thing was, my dear fellow, that I wasn't getting any recruits for them. On the contrary, I simply put everyone off."

"Why was that?"

"I could never get up any enthusiasm about tanks. I kept on telling them how nice it would have been if we'd still had horses but how horrible it was having tanks."

"Are you going to tell us that? When you teach us Infantry/Tank Co-operation?"

"I don't suppose we shall do much of that when it comes to the point – eh, Giles?"

"It will be in the new syllabus," said Glastonbury in tones of mild rebuke.

"But since there are so few tanks in India," said Detterling happily, "we shan't have any to practise with."

"You can always do the theory."

"The theory's all right," said Detterling; "it's the tanks themselves I can't stand. Nasty lumps of metal, making such a bloody awful smell. . . . I think I'm going to like India," he said, looking across the Cricket Ground to where two old ladies, attended by turbaned syces, sat in an open landau. "There's rather the sort of atmosphere there used to be in Malta, when I first joined the Regiment in '37. You know, a guard of lancers for the G.O.C. and all those randy wives in long white dresses."

"It may not last," Giles Glastonbury said.

"That's part of its charm. Incidentally," said Detterling, "there's a sort of cousin of mine here somewhere. Muscateer, he's called. Does anyone know him?"

"Yes, sir," said Alister quickly.

"Well, rustle him up, there's a good chap, and we'll all go out to dinner . . . if you're free, that is."

Peter and Alister said they were free and Wellesley Mess was appointed as the initial rendezvous for the evening. A few minutes later 'Napier' made the winning hit, which they all four applauded, though Detterling grumbled bitterly about the quality of the stroke. Then there was much flurry of puggrees and cummerbunds; the two old ladies in the landau sailed serenely off the grass; His Highness, still giggling, was driven away in his 1924 Lagonda, which was painted in the Old Harrovian colours; and Peter and Alister rode in rickshaws through the sweet, gritty Indian dusk, to find Muscateer (who had spent all day learning to mount his bicycle) and change for Detterling's dinner.

Since Glastonbury and Detterling were too fastidious about their food to risk dining in the Bangalore Officers' Club ('Brown Windsor Soup and boarding house curry, I expect'), it was decided that they should go to Ley Wong's Chinese Restaurant, where the cuisine was versatile, Giles Glastonbury told them, and credit was as long as anywhere in the East. Not that Detterling would need credit for this dinner; but it might prove useful to the three Cadets to have Glastonbury's personal introduction to Ley Wong, who would then let them cash cheques whenever they wanted to and would also avail them of his superior services as a procurer at special rates.

"He always lets me off twenty-five per cent," Glastonbury said in the horse-drawn gharri that took them there, "and he makes the girls do the same."

"How do you know him so well?" asked Detterling. "You were never stationed here that I'd heard of."

"I did him a good turn some years back. It was when I first came out here – you remember" – this to Detterling only – "just after that spot of bother I had in Tunisia."

Detterling remembered and nodded. Alister opened his mouth to ask what 'the spot of bother' had been, but was silenced by a look from Peter.

"Well, when I first appeared in Bombay," Glastonbury said, "no one really knew what to do with me – my arrival being rather sudden, you see – so they put me in charge of what they called the Hygiene and Amenity Board (South India). I had to go round with a Medical Officer and a Padre inspecting all the cinemas and restaurants and bars, and then report back about whether or not they were suitable for clean-limbed British soldiers. You get the idea?"

They got the idea, and Muscateer remarked that his old governor had done much the same sort of thing in France in 1944.

"And a proper pantomime he made of it," said Detterling; "your old governor dished out Army Licences to every cat-house between Calvados and the Ardennes, just to annoy

Montgomery. They had to send someone round after him to close them all down again."

"Well, in course of time," Glastonbury continued after this parenthesis, "the Hygiene and Amenity Board passed through Bangalore, and the first place we had to inspect was Ley Wong's Chinese Restaurant. Before we even started, an Indian informer came to see us, and said that Ley Wong had been cashing cheques drawn on a Japanese Bank, i.e. trafficking with the enemies of the King Emperor. Needless to say, this informer was the owner of a rival restaurant, but the charge still had to be investigated. In fact it was my plain duty to go straight to the police.

"But there was something so outlandish about the idea of a chap cashing Japanese cheques that I thought I'd have a word with him myself. And a very nice little man he turned out to be. His story was that he had a good client, a British Officer, who'd left some money in a Japanese Bank before the war and didn't see why he shouldn't get the benefit now. Nor did Ley Wong – especially as his client was prepared to have his cheques discounted at fifty per cent. And anyway, Ley Wong told me, it was an interesting challenge."

"And he managed to get the cheques cleared?"

"Yes, bless his oriental heart. He simply passed them through neutral territory. Not that this was as easy as it sounds of course. But Ley Wong got up some sort of pipeline, and fed the cheques through to Japan, and had the ready money fed back again. He had to pay the agents a small fortune, and he lost heavily over exchange rates en route, but the end of it was he made twenty per cent on the deal and everyone concerned was quite happy. And so, now I came to think of it, was I. After all, if the Japanese were fools enough to pay out on cheques drawn by an Englishman, who was any the worse off?"

"Unless," said Muscateer apologetically, "there were coded messages or something on the cheques?"

"There was no question of that game," said Glastonbury, "because the Officer who issued them was in the Grenadiers. So of course it must have been all right, Ley Wong told me, and naturally I agreed."

Detterling sighed very gently.

"So what did you decide to do?" he asked.

"Well, the Grenadier had moved on by that time, and no harm had been done, as I saw it, and it seemed to be a very pleasant sort of restaurant, so I told Ley Wong I'd forget it. The informer wouldn't make any more trouble, Ley Wong said, because he was in such bad odour with the police about something or other himself that he wouldn't dare go near them. Which was why he'd come to me instead."

"But he'd also told the Doctor and the Padre on your Board," said Detterling: "how did you keep them quiet?"

"Took 'em for a slap up dinner at Ley Wong's and told 'em the whole story was rubbish. It seemed simpler than going into detail."

"And they were happy with that?"

"I suppose so. As it happens, I never saw them again. They both had killing hangovers the next morning and had to stay in bed; and meanwhile some cousin of mine had found out I'd got to India and where I was, and wired me to come to Delhi juldi juldi to take up a post on his staff. So to Delhi juldi juldi I went. But whenever I've been here at the odd time since, Ley Wong has always shown himself most grateful."

"Those girls at cut rates?"

"Not only that. He once gave me an ivory casket with a collection of gold coins inside it minted by the Mogul Jehangir."

"Rather . . . valuable?"

"I dare say," said Glastonbury with superb indifference; "a very touching present, I thought. Apparently Ley Wong had somehow got into his head that my hobby was collecting coins. Of course I've never cared anything about that, but I didn't want to hurt the poor fellow's feelings."

"So what did you do with the coins?" said Detterling casually.

"They're knocking around somewhere in my bungalow up in Delhi. . . . And there's Ley Wong now. Grinning all over his face."

But to Peter it seemed, as Ley Wong bowed them through

the entrance and on into a private room, that the little China-
man's grin was not wholly amiable. There was a lack of elasti-
city about it. Perhaps, thought Peter, Ley Wong was getting
tired of accommodating the Glastonbury Sahib with cut-price
girls and Mongol gold. But if so, there was no further sign of
his resentment. Long chains of waiters, under the personal
supervision of Ley Wong, came and went with course after
course of classical Chinese delicacies and bottle after bottle of
rare White Burgundy. The waiters came ever faster, and Ley
Wong bowed ever deeper with the presentation of each new
dish; while Alister grew ever more loud-mouthed, Muscateer
more agreeable, Detterling more laconic, and Glastonbury
more confidential. It seemed to Peter that all the inner mysteries of Delhi were being revealed to him and that these made
a truly Byzantine spectacle of levity, betrayal and decay.

"You know what's happened?" Giles Glastonbury said.
"They've lost their confidence. Everyone from His Excellency
downward. They've been told so long and so often that they've
no right to be here that they've begun to believe it. Which
means they've stopped believing in themselves and their function. When that happens, everything starts running down –
no, not just running down, but *falling apart*."

"You don't appear to be falling apart, sir."

"It's different with me. You see, I never really believed in it
much; I just took it as it came from day to day, because I only
ever came here by accident. I'm just someone who's passing
through, Morrison. But the old hands out here . . . the men
who are the core of it all . . . they *loved* what they were doing,
they even loved the Indians in their way, and they did their
damnedest to get it right. They got a lot wrong, of course, they
were nagging and self-satisfied and they couldn't understand
that to most Indians custom matters much more than cleanli-
ness – all that kind of thing; but at the same time they really
did try to bring in justice and sound administration, to stop
people starving or selling their eight-year-old bodies, to increase
wealth and knowledge. Up to a point they succeeded, and up
to a point they were thanked, and so they thought they could
stay for ever. They made this their country, and even stayed on

when they had to retire, some of them, because their *lives* were here.

"But now what's happened? They're being told they're not wanted and never really were. The Government in England is embarrassed by them, the Americans mock at them, the educated Indians are screaming for their jobs, and the very cows in the street seem to hate their guts. So not unnaturally, they're rather hurt. Hurt . . . and dispossessed. Soldiers and civil service – it's the same with them all."

"And so they've turned vicious, you say?"

"Not exactly that. When things fall apart," said Glastonbury, "you get a feeling that nothing matters any more . . . that you can just let yourself go. All those things you've wanted to do for so long and haven't dared to because of your career – well, you can ahead with the lot now, and what the devil? Girls, boys, booze, hashish, telling the boss upstairs to piss in his own navel – you can do it all when the barbarians are banging at the gate and the world's about to go up in flames. What's to stop you?"

"Decency?"

"Well, yes. And that's what's keeping the show going. If we've got to hand over, some of them are saying, let's do the pukka thing and see that everything's in good order first. That's the best chaps, of course. But the middling sort – they've just ceased to care and started shouting for the belly dancers. They've not turned vicious . . . but irresponsible."

"Not here," said Peter; "not yet."

"You wait and see. You're the last lot of British Cadets which will come to Bangalore. From now on it's going to be Indians only. With Indian instructors for the most part. So as far as the white Officers are concerned – whether they're Indian Army or British Army – this is the last term at the old school. And when that comes round," said Glastonbury, "when people are doing the old things for the last time, they're too depressed to trouble very much how well or how badly they do them. Irresponsibility again, you see; a more honourable kind than the other, but it comes to much the same in the end."

The waiters set a final dish before each of the diners: a

creamy confection topped by a light crust of sugar and flavoured (so Peter thought as he tasted it) with grapefruit or sweet citron.

"Anyhow," said Glastonbury, "there's one way in which all this is certainly going to affect you here. Would you like to tell them" – this to Detterling – "or shall I?"

"You seem in a teaching vein, Giles," said Detterling languidly: "you do it."

Glastonbury nodded. He pushed his untasted sweet away from him and beckoned to a servant to remove it. But since Ley Wong was out of the room the servant was dilatory, and before he could collect the bowl from in front of Glastonbury it had been seized by Muscateer.

"Sorry and all that," said Muscateer, "but waste not, want not. Fascinating taste this stuff has."

Detterling, as host, signalled to the servant to return to his place against the wall.

"Your grandmother always had a sweet tooth," said Detterling in extenuation of Muscateer's conduct. "All right, Giles, you tell 'em the form."

"It's like this. As I've been saying to Morrison here, from next month onwards the O.T.S. is going to take in Indian Cadets only, with Indian instructors. But there aren't many Indian Officers who've had experience at that, so they're going to let 'em have a practice go on your lot. Or rather, they're thinking of it – and Delhi's in favour as it'll be a sop to Indian nationalists to see Indian Officers training white Cadets. But before the final decision's taken, they're going to run a test to see how it works. And they're going to run this test on your Platoon. 'No. 2 Pl., C Coy,' the bumf says." Glastonbury turned to Peter. "'J.U.O.: O/Cdt. Morrison, P.'"

"So that's why we haven't had an Officer yet."

"You'll have one at 6.15 tomorrow morning. Captain Gilzai Khan of the 43rd Khaipur Light Infantry."

"A Moslem?"

"Yes. There was a bit of feeling about that. The Hindus only came round when we reminded them that if the test flopped the Moslems would get all the blame and if it succeeded they'd both share the benefit. I should tell you that Gilzai Khan has been chosen as an Officer of forceful character who is fully expected to succeed."

"I don't understand," said Muscateer: "my old governor said that native Officers were called Jemadars and Rissaldars – things like that."

"Jemadars and Rissaldars only hold the *Viceroy's* Commission. Gilzai Khan has his from the King."

"Your governor was always a bit behind the times," Captain Detterling remarked.

"A wog," said Alister bitterly: "a wog Officer for *us*."

"There are wogs *and* wogs," said Detterling blandly. "I'd drop the word if I were you. Gilzai Khan might not care for it much."

"You're on their side, sir?"

"We're on nobody's side," said Glastonbury. "We're just warning you what's going to happen. Morrison here may have a tricky time as J.U.O. As his friends you'll want to help him."

"Why didn't Major Baxter warn us?" said Alister shrilly. "He's the Company Commander. It was his job, not yours."

"You have a point, Mr Mortleman," Colonel Glastonbury said, "though I cannot applaud your manner of making it." He drummed a little tattoo with his fingers on the table, glanced at Muscateer, who was sweating rather a lot, sucked his lips in and resumed. "Major Baxter," he said, "is a war-time Officer of good record, but he is not by nature a diplomat. He himself is well aware of this defect; and when I told him that I knew some of you, he asked me to take on this task for him."

"We're most grateful, sir," said Peter. "But in a day or two you'll be going back to Delhi. If there should be trouble, we shall need a diplomat to represent us. Since Major Baxter, on your showing and his, is hardly the man to apply to . . ."

". . . You may apply," said Detterling, "to me. I can manage Major Baxter for you."

There was a heaving and a choking and then another heaving, and Muscateer was very, very sick.

"Why is it," said Glastonbury crossly, "that whenever I dine here with people they get ill?"

"Too much of that pudding . . ."

"What was it?"

"Orange meringue pie," said Glastonbury; "Ley Wong's famous for it."

"Funny. I thought it tasted of grapefruit."

Muscateer went on being sick.

"If you ask me," said Alister, "it's the idea of being ordered about by a bloody wog."

Detterling looked at Alister coolly but said nothing. Many waiters appeared with buckets and mops. Soon afterwards, when Detterling had paid the bill, they all took Muscateer home to his basha. He retched desperately all the way but managed to say one thing, this to Detterling: "You won't tell my governor, will you, sir? He'd feel so dreadfully let down."

# PART TWO

# THE KHAN

AT 6.15 on the morning after the Cricket Trials and Captain Detterling's dinner, the Cadets of C Coy paraded for P.T.

Muscateer, who was looking very wan and feeble, had mustered with the rest of them. Although he survived the initial routine of 'deep breathing' and 'knees bend', when invited to vault the horse he collapsed along the top of it like a rag doll. The British Sergeant Instructor who was taking No. 2 Pl. scraped him off, shook him out and set him on his feet.

"Try again, laddie," the Sergeant said : "take your time."

So Muscateer walked ten paces away from the horse and tottered back at it once more. When he was only a yard or two short, his knees sagged under him and he fell flat on his face, smacking his nose against one leg of the horse as he went. This time, when the Sergeant picked him up, he was streaming with blood and staring into nowhere with a fixed smile which reminded Peter Morrison, oddly enough, he thought, of Ley Wong's grin when he had welcomed them to his restaurant the evening before.

"Go and sit in the shade, laddie," the Sergeant said.

Muscateer didn't move. The Sergeant beckoned to Peter and Barry, who helped Muscateer into the shade of a large banyan tree on the edge of the Physical Training Area. While they were making him comfortable and trying to arrange his long legs in a more or less dignified position, a short, thin man, who had a large, bald head like that of a chess pawn, walked round from the other side of the tree. He was wearing Khaki Drill with shorts, boots and puttees wound up to the knee; his two thumbs were tucked into the twin shoulder straps of a black Sam Browne belt, from the left side of which hung an empty sword-frog.

"I," he said, "am Captain Gilzai Khan. Who are you?"

"Cadet Morrison, sir. J.U.O."

"Cadet Strange, sir . . . and this is Cadet—"

"—Let him answer for himself."

"Muscateer," mumbled Muscateer from the roots of the banyan tree.

"You are Officer Cadet the Earl of Muscateer," Gilzai Khan stated flatly. He squatted down on his hunkers. "Listen to me, bahadur. You are my man now, and my men do not fall out of the ranks unless they are dead or unconscious."

"But he's ill, sir," Barry said.

"Hold your tongue, little boy, until I ask you to use it."

"Sir."

"Not 'sir'."

"Sahib?"

Gilzai Khan spat like a cobra.

" 'Sahib'," he said, "is for a box-wallah or a munshi. My men call me . . . Gilzai Khan."

He looked carefully at the limp and ashen Muscateer. "Muscateer bahadur," he said, "you will get up and follow me and vault over that horse."

Still squatting, he put a hand in Muscateer's left armpit, then slowly flexed himself upright, dragging Muscateer up with him.

"Come," said Gilzai Khan.

Keeping his hand in Muscateer's armpit, he stepped out on to the Physical Training Area. He released Muscateer (who staggered but remained standing), ran towards the horse, clapped his hands twice before his face, and vaulted neatly over on both hands, while his black sword-frog lifted from his rump and fell back just as he landed. He turned to Muscateer and beckoned.

"Bahadur," he called.

Muscateer took two painful steps and stopped. His throat was working and the sweat was rolling down his face in drops the size of cherries.

"Bahadur," called Gilzai Khan.

Muscateer lurched forward. His head went down and he

ran straight at the horse. His absurd legs looked like flapping rope's ends and his arms were stiff along his body. When he was about four feet from the horse, he skipped crazily and then hurled himself into the air, arched over the horse like a length of hose-pipe, and was caught by Gilzai Khan, who held him, bottom upwards, in an inverted 'U'.

"Good, bahadur. Very good. But now you are unconscious," remarked Gilzai Khan, "and now, therefore, you may fall out."

He hung Muscateer over the horse, saluted the gawping Cadets, and strode fiercely away.

"Tactics, gentlemen," said Gilzai Khan: "Lesson Number One, The Frontal Attack. But first . . . where is the Bahadur Muscateer?"

"They took him to hospital, Gilzai Khan. After P.T., while we were having breakfast. The M.O. thinks he's got jaundice."

"Thank you, Morrison huzoor. This evening we shall visit him. All of us, gentlemen; together. And now, the Frontal Attack. When . . . Cadet Mortleman . . . do you think that we use the Frontal Attack?"

"When the enemy is in front of us," Alister said off-handedly.

"That, Cadet Mortleman, is usually the case. But we do not usually employ the Frontal Attack. In what special circumstances do we do so?"

"When we're late for lunch or in a hurry to get home."

"I have a name, Cadet Mortleman, and a title. Kindly use them when you address me."

"A title?"

"Khan."

"I thought that was part of your name."

"No, Cadet Mortleman. It means that I am descended of a princely house of the tribe of the Gilzai."

"And who are they, when they're at home?"

"Frontier men. Warriors. As you would say, real bastards," said Gilzai Khan, laughing lightly, "who do not take insolence from schoolboys. You will write out five hundred times, Cadet Mortleman, 'Officer Cadets must learn the manners of gentlemen', and you will deliver your work to me at first parade tomorrow."

"Like all these wogs," muttered Alister to his neighbour; "can't take a joke."

"What was that, Cadet Mortleman? I did not quite hear you."

"You weren't meant to . . . Genghis Khan."

Whatever the Cadets might have expected by way of retribution for this silly remark, they were disappointed. For Gilzai Khan merely threw his head back and laughed.

"Haw, haw, haw," he chortled, "how I love your British humour. Genghis Khan – that is good, very good, Cadet Mortleman – such powers of thought, such clever play with words. Haw, haw, haw – we have a jester in our midst, brothers, we must show our appreciation. All together now: haw, haw, haw."

"Haw, haw, haw," went the Cadets, swept along by Gilzai Khan's irresistible example: "haw, haw, haw," they went, while Alister sat glowering and champing in humiliation: "haw, haw, haw, haw, HAW."

"Enough, gentlemen; enough, my children. The days will go faster for us now we have one among us to make jokes . . . one – how do you say it? – buffoon. But we must not neglect our work. Life is not all jokes. The Frontal Attack, my Cadets, is no joke at all. Now when . . . Mr Zaccharias . . . do we use the Frontal Attack?"

"I suppose," said Zaccharias, who was a tubby boy with a bland face and a mean mouth, "that we use it when there is no safer way . . . Gilzai Khan," he added hurriedly, as the huge pawn's head made a sudden thrust towards him.

"You are right, Mr Zaccharias." Gilzai Khan pronounced 'Zaccharias' with the stress on the second syllable. "You are right, and yet you are wrong. We use the Frontal Attack when there is no cover, because when there is no cover we must go the shortest way."

"That's what I meant, Gilzai Khan."

"That I know, and so far you are right. But you are also wrong. Why is he wrong ... Mr Murphy?"

"He hasn't mentioned fire-power," said Murphy, a glum, spotty youth, who was even fatter than Zaccharias and was reputed to masturbate four times a day. "If you have superior fire-power, Gilzai Khan, you can blast the enemy to bits and then walk straight on to his position."

"No, you cannot, Mr Murphy. That is what the Yankees thought. They thought they could destroy the enemy with bombs and shells from a distance, while they sat on their bottoms drinking Coca-Cola and reading comic papers. Afterwards, they thought, they could just drive through the enemy lines in their jeeps without fear of opposition. Time after time they made the same mistake – and time after time they and their jeeps were wiped out when they reached their objective. And then they thought they had been heroic, whereas in truth they were simply lazy. They refused to realise that if the enemy is properly entrenched he will survive almost any bombardment; and that in order to take ground, you must engage those who hold it hand to hand and kill them man by man."

"What about the Atom Bomb, Gilzai Khan? No enemy could survive that."

"We are discussing Tactics, Cadet Mortleman, not Grand Strategy. They do not issue Platoon Commanders with Atom Bombs. Platoons must attack their enemy over the ground. If there is no cover, they must attack the shortest way – from the front. So much was correctly implied by Mr Zaccharias. But he said something that was wrong, and I am still waiting for somebody to tell me what. Morrison huzoor, cannot you tell me?"

"Zaccharias lacked confidence, Gilzai Khan. He seemed to think that a Frontal Attack is a last resort."

"So it is. It is much better to advance close to your enemy under cover and then pounce from the flank than to run into the muzzle of his rifles over open ground. Believe one who knows, huzoor: charging over open ground is not enjoyable. No. Mr Zaccharias was wrong in something else. What was it?"

Gilzai Khan moved his black eyes from Cadet to Cadet and then let them rest on Barry Strange.

"Officer Cadet Strange," he said. "They say you had brothers who were soldiers. So tell me, little Officer Cadet: what would *they* have said in this matter?"

"Zaccharias used the word 'safe'," said Barry. " 'When there is no safer way,' he said. My brothers, Gilzai Khan, would have told him that when a man starts thinking of what is safe, he starts thinking of the quickest way home."

Barry, who had surprised himself and everyone else, sat back and blushed.

"Good," said the Khan.

He walked round behind Barry, rested his hands on his shoulders and started to massage the top of his spine with his thumbs.

"Listen, my Cadets," he said. "Officer Cadet Strange has spoken what I wished to hear. In battle there is a right way and a wrong way, a near way and a long way, a fast way and a slow way; but a *safe way* there can never be except for the way home, and that way, my children, we do not take."

That evening the whole of No. 2 Platoon went to the Garrison Hospital to see Muscateer. They marched there in column of threes, commanded by Gilzai Khan, who marched at their head; not behind them, or off to one side of them, or slopping along at his own pace as many Officers would have done, but right there bang in front. This pleased the Cadets very much, though they would have found it hard to say quite why.

But it did not please Alister.

"Why couldn't he let us walk over in our own time?" he said to Peter, as they all crowded into the hospital.

"I think . . . that he sees it as a ceremony."

"Since when was visiting a chap in hospital a ceremony?"

"Gilzai Khan," said Barry, "is not just visiting a chap in hospital but doing honour to a comrade."

"Fiddle di rum-tum-bum," said Alister. "And talking of

bums, you'd better watch yours, little Officer Cadet. All those Moslems are buggers, and this one fancies you."

Barry flushed like a pillar box. "Don't be foul," he said. Then they all followed Gilzai Khan, who himself followed the Matron, who, having seen the Platoon arrive, had recognised the quality of the occasion and turned out in person to conduct them all to Muscateer's bed.

Captain Detterling, who was there before them, sitting by Muscateer and looking worried, rose to bow to the Matron and greet Gilzai Khan.

"He seems rather low," Detterling muttered, and then took the Matron on one side. Peter, who watched them walk slowly down the ward together, caught the words, 'Father in Wiltshire . . . cousin . . . what shall I write to him?', as they went.

Meanwhile the Khan was rallying his man.

"We have come to see you, bahadur," he said rather unnecessarily : "we wish to know when you will return."

"I feel rather low just now," said Muscateer, echoing Detterling.

The Cadets gathered round the bed in a half circle. Gilzai Khan pushed aside Detterling's vacant chair and crouched over Muscateer like a lion over a carcass.

"You must not feel low," he said. "You did well. Muscateer bahadur, *you will come back to us soon*?"

"All this fuss," muttered Alister to no one in particular, "about someone he hardly knows. But he knows he's an Earl all right, and that's why he's making the fuss."

"If you fellows don't mind," said Muscateer to the Cadets, "I would like a little more air. It's awfully kind of you all to come and see me like this – please don't think I don't appreciate it – but I do feel a tiny bit shut in."

The Cadets moved back a little. Muscateer smiled his thanks and closed his eyes. Even the Khan, crouching silently over the bed, seemed at a loss what to do next. Muscateer opened his eyes again.

"Near our house," he said, "there is a river which flows through a wood. When the spring came and the summer, my governor and I used to row down the river in a little boat, through a long tunnel of green trees – until suddenly we'd come out into the open, into a meadow which there was. Although I loved the trees, it was a wonderful feeling when we came out into the open, into the blue sky and the sun. I was reminded of it just now, when you fellows moved back. Just for a moment, it was like coming out of the trees into the sun."

His voice, hitherto precise, now wandered slightly.

"Into the sun . . . into the meadow. A meadow by the river it was, the sort you see in those old pictures, with coloured flowers, each one by itself . . . all alone . . . as though it had been specially painted into its place. And there were always grasshoppers singing. Do they sing, do you think? Anyway, making that chirruping noise of theirs. And I used to imagine a knight riding through that meadow, in a long robe, carrying one of those guitar things, with his 'squire riding behind him and two dogs with those kind of greyhound faces, leaping about round the flowers. Not far away was the spire of Salisbury Cathedral – *really* was, I mean, not like the knight, who was imaginary . . . except that he wasn't *only* imaginary because I knew he had been there once, hundreds of years before, because my governor used to tell me about him. He was a sort of ancestor of ours, you see, and one day he'd ridden out to visit his lady-love – just as I've told you, the robe and the lute – but he was murdered on the way by six black knights in armour, who'd been sent by the lady's husband. 'Bloody shame,' my old governor used to say, 'what a rotten mean lot of spoilsports.' So they struck him down in this meadow, six to one, soon after he came out of the wood. You'd think they'd have killed him in the wood, wouldn't you, where no one could see them, but there was only a narrow path by the river and the trees were very thick, so perhaps there wasn't room for all their horses. That was how the 'squire escaped : he rode back into the wood, leaving the poor knight dead in the meadow and the silly dogs whimpering in the flowers."

Muscateer closed his eyes and fell asleep. Gilzai Khan, who was still crouching close over the bed, straightened up and shook his head briskly.

"We shall come again soon," he said, half to Muscateer and half to the Cadets. "You may return to your quarters in your own time, gentlemen. Officer Cadet Strange, you will come with me."

"Was he delirious, do you think?" said Alister.

"Jaundice doesn't make you delirious."

"Perhaps they'd given him some drug that made him peculiar."

"He was certainly rather odd," Peter said. "We'd better step out a bit, Alister. You've got those lines to do tonight."

"Lines?"

"Five hundred lines for the Platoon Commander. By first parade tomorrow, he said."

"You don't suppose I'm going to take any notice of that."

Peter heaved a deep sigh.

"I don't yet know much about Gilzai Khan," he said, "but I do know that if you set yourself up against him you're going to come off worst."

"Supporting him, are you?"

"I'm his J.U.O."

"And you're my friend."

"As your friend," said Peter, "I am advising you to write those lines."

"You make it sound like an order."

"You already have your order. From the Platoon Commander."

"A conceited, pushy wog. And what's he doing with Barry, I'd like to know?"

But even as Alister spoke Barry came running up behind them.

"Gilzai Khan," he said breathlessly to Alister, "says you needn't do those lines."

"Mighty big of him. And why not?"

"He says that you must have been upset this morning because of Muscateer and didn't mean what you said."

"Damn his eyes. I meant every word of it. Who does he think he is to start reading my mind?"

"He's let you off," said Peter. "Just leave it at that."

"Then why couldn't he tell me himself? Why use *me* as an excuse for hob-nobbing with Barry?"

"*You* were only an afterthought," said Barry, rather cuttingly for him. "He wanted to talk to me because he thought I'd be able to explain that story of Muscateer's. About the knight in the meadow."

"Simple enough, I should have thought. Horny chap goes riding out to shaft another chap's wife, so the second chap has him ambushed and done in on the way."

"Gil' Khan didn't find it simple."

Barry paused. All round them in the dark was a whirring and a chirruping (grasshoppers? or did they have some special Indian name?) and in the distance was the slow, dull clank of cow-bells. Under their feet the dust of the path on which they were walking squeaked very lightly with every step they took.

"Gilzai Khan," Barry said, "was worried about the 'squire. I had to explain just what a 'squire was in those days, and then he asked me if the knight and the 'squire would have been . . . you know . . . keen on each other."

"How very embarrassing."

"Funnily enough, it wasn't. The idea seemed so ordinary to him that I found it seeming ordinary to me too. But I told him I didn't think they could have been, because the knight was so obviously keen on ladies. So then Gilzai Khan said that that needn't make any difference: the knight could have been keen on ladies *and* on his 'squire too. Is that right?" said Barry to Peter.

"Yes," said Peter unhappily; "I think it is."

"But what really worried him was this. Whether or not they were keen on each other, he said, the 'squire should never have run away. He should have stayed and died with his master. I suggested that perhaps the knight had *told* the 'squire to run away (especially if they *were* keen on each other) but Gil' Khan said that even then the 'squire should have stayed and died. 'From 'squire to knight,' he said, 'or from boy to lover, the duty is clear. If it were you and I, huzoor, you would not leave me.' "

"What did you say to *that*?"

"Nothing. What could I say? But then he pressed me. '*Would* you leave me, huzoor?' he said. 'Would you?' 'I should obey your orders, Gil' Khan,' I said, 'because you are my Platoon Commander.' 'I am your *Captain*,' he said: 'say it.' 'You are my Captain, Gil' Khan,' I said. 'That is true, huzoor. Now good-night and go well. You know how to answer? Stay well, you must say.' 'Good-night, Gil' Khan,' I said: 'stay well.' "

Barry came out of this narration with a flushed look on his face; flushed and excited.

"What's that you called him?" Alister said.

"But just as I was going," Barry went on, ignoring Alister's question, "he called me back to tell me that you needn't do those lines because you had been upset. Then, 'Good-night, huzoor,' he said again: 'go well.' 'Stay well, Gil' Khan,' I said, 'stay well.' "

Something about this ancient formula had evidently caught Barry's imagination. For as he repeated it now his eyes shone and his lips quivered with pleasure.

"What's this new name you've got for him?" Alister insisted.

"New name?" said Barry, puzzled.

"His name is Gilzai Khan."

"That's what I called him."

"No, you didn't. Gil' Khan, you've been calling him. Several times."

"Oh," said Barry; "I hadn't noticed."


"Now, my Cadets," said the Khan: "this is the Assault Course. While you are going over it, live ammunition will be fired over your heads. The regulations state that the Bren Guns from which it is fired must be firmly secured on tripods, having first been so aimed as to fire twelve feet above your heads. And so they will be – except for the gun from which I myself will fire.

Morrison huzoor, assemble the Platoon by sections on the start line. . . ."

As they jumped the first obstacle (a pit with barbed wire at the bottom) Gilzai Khan fired quick bursts which seemed almost to scrape the soles of their leaping feet. As they climbed the hundred-foot net, the bullets cut the strands a bare six inches above their scrabbling fingers. When they emerged from the long crawl through the underground tunnel, it was to find puffs of sand spurting right up their noses. By the time they reached the finishing post, limp, tottering and drenched in sweat, they had a very lively idea of what it was like to be under fire, as distinct from what it was like merely to go over an artificial Assault Course while careful instructors fired on a fixed line many feet above them.

"Now," said the Khan : "I see that some of you have soiled your trousers. Do not be ashamed, gentlemen. The first time I was so close to real bullets I stank of fear for the next week."

"Please, Gil' Khan, can we fall out and change?"

"Indeed you cannot. Where on a battle field could you fall out to change your breeches? You are stuck with it, my brothers, until the end of the morning."


"Now, gentlemen," said Captain Detterling : "Military Law. What you have to understand is this. Whereas there is a lot of ill-informed chatter about the harshness and injustice of the Military Code, in fact this is simply a faithful reproduction of the Civil Code as adapted to military circumstances. The same rules of evidence are insisted upon, the same safeguards are applied, the same rights, in all essentials, are guaranteed. Indeed I have heard it said that the Military Code is often more fair to an accused person than the Civil, in that far greater freedom is in practice allowed to the defence in the style and method of presenting its case . . .

". . . And so, gentlemen," Captain Detterling concluded at the end of the period, "we are confronted with the paradox inherent in all systems of discipline : the most powerful sanctions are those which are never applied. For every time a sanction is applied there is a risk that it may fail of its object and so appear less formidable. Or to put it another way, any overt exercise of authority is apt to cheapen authority, because it reveals that authority must first have been questioned. *The ideal authority is one that is never questioned and is therefore never invoked.* So a final rule of thumb, gentlemen : to prefer charges is a sign of failure; but if you must prefer them, make absolutely sure that they stick."

Captain Detterling gave the class a Machiavellian look.

"Did anyone go to see Muscateer yesterday?" he asked. "I was tied up."

"I did, sir," said Alister. "He seemed in much better shape. He says he's much happier now he's got a room to himself."

"Hmmm," said Detterling. "Nasty business, jaundice. It drags on for ever, and even when it's over I'm told you can't drink for months. I'll pop up and take a look at him tonight."

"On the word of command 'one'," said C.S.M. Cruxtable, not very briskly, "Cadets will place their canes under the left arm-pit in a horizontal position. Cadets will then remain motionless during the intervening chant of 'two, three', and at the next word of command 'one' they will release their canes with the right hand and bring the right arm smartly down to the side. Now then :—

"ONE – two, three – *One*. Horrible," said C.S.M. Cruxtable good-naturedly, "perfectly horrible. Like a lot of old women waving to their fancy boys in the park. So we'll try it again, gentlemen. Kindly remove your canes from under the left armpit and hold them in a vertical position, flush with the right forearm and down the right side. . . ."

"Map Reading," said the Khan : "Lesson Six. Last week, my friends, we were discussing contours. Today I will show you how to use those contours to draw a cross-section of the terrain as between one point and another. Pencil, paper and instruments, gentlemen, please. And where, Cadet Mortleman, is your ruler?"

"I forgot it, Gilzai Khan."

"I have told you : when we have map reading, bring pencil, paper, compasses, divider, protractor, set square, and *ruler*."

"And I've told you : I forgot it."

"Then go and get it."

"Oh, I say," said Alister. "It's a good half mile back to the basha."

"I know, Cadet Mortleman. And you will not take your bicycle. You will run all the way there and all the way back. And if you are not back in seven minutes, you will do it again."

And then, as Alister did not stir, "Juldi, juldi," he rasped, seizing the chair from under Alister's bottom and brandishing it with one arm above his head; "juldi, juldi, *pi-Cadet*."

Alister turned pale and then puce. He clenched his fists and he ground his teeth. Then he slouched from the classroom and was back with his ruler in seven minutes flat.

"I am glad that you have come, huzoor. There is one thing I must know."

"Yes, Gil' Khan?"

"Your friend, Cadet Mortleman. Why does he hate me so much?"

"That is something you should ask Peter Morrison," said Barry. "He's the J.U.O., Gil' Khan, and he understands it all much better than me."

"Come, huzoor; truth between friends."

"All right. It's because you're an Indian. What he would call a native. He doesn't like having to obey you."

"Why is that? I know my trade. The others all obey me. You too, huzoor : you obey me, do you not?"

"Yes, Gil' Khan. . . . You are my Captain."

"Come here, then, and sit. Is it my colour that Cadet Mortleman dislikes?"

"It could be."

"So. . . . And you, little Officer Cadet? Do you dislike my colour?"

"No, Gil' Khan. I like your colour."

"Do you, huzoor? But I have scars, big, white scars. Do you think that you would like those too?"

"I . . . I don't know."

"Then I shall show you and you will see. Do not be shy, huzoor. I am your Captain, and it is a great honour to be shown your Captain's scars."

"Where's Barry?" said Alister.

"The Khan sent for him," said Peter.

"To go to his quarters?"

"I think so."

"Why?"

"Does it matter?"

"It matters very much. If that beastly wog thinks he can start playing games with Barry . . ."

"There is no reason to suppose anything of the kind. Gil' Khan likes Barry and he wants to talk to him. And Barry's not the first to go there; I've been several times."

"You're the J.U.O. And he doesn't fancy your ring."

"Gilzai Khan is an Officer of the King. Barry is one of his Cadets – and old enough to take care of himself."

"Is he? *Is* he, Peter?"

"Look, Alister," said Peter uneasily, "why not drop all this about the Khan? I like him, we all like him except you. And as for Barry – it'll be time enough to start complaining about that if Barry starts complaining himself. He's got a tongue in his head and he's got good friends to come to if he needs them."

"He might be afraid."

"Afraid? He half worships the Khan."

"That's just it. The Khan might take advantage."

"Listen," said Peter. "If I see Barry looking unhappy, I'll take it up with him, I promise you that. But meanwhile, Alister, just stop making trouble. I've had some experience with this sort of thing, and *believe me*, it's fatal to interfere unless and until there is very clear reason. For the rest, you'd make life a lot easier for me and for everybody else including yourself if you'd stop flaunting your ridiculous pride and trying to hate up Gilzai Khan."


"Now this," said Captain Detterling, "is what they call good tank country. Nice and flat, you see, for the beastly things to roll over."

They were standing on a low ridge and looking out over a dreary plain of sand which was unbroken except by occasional dried-up nullahs. Formerly fertile country, all this had been appropriated by the O.T.S. as a training area at the beginning of the war; but beyond the desert which the military had made over the years, and still within the Cadets' field of vision, were kinder sights – small patches of green, scattered wooden shanties, and, just discernible, a yoked bullock plodding interminably about a well.

"You may be hoping," said Detterling, "that those nullahs would put a stop to any nonsense with tanks, but not a bit of it. They're not deep enough. The tanks would just crash in, nose first, and then heave themselves out the other side. It's astonishing what purchase they can get with modern tracks. No, gentlemen; there's nothing to stop tanks for as far as we can see from here, unless some of those fields in the distance turn out to be paddy fields. But as it happens, they're not paddy fields. Can any of you," said Detterling with a self-satisfied air as of one who had been in India thirty years instead of barely thirty days, "explain how I know that?"

Since he was obviously itching to tell them himself, the Cadets maintained a tactful silence.

"Paddy fields," said Detterling, "are always below the level of the surrounding countryside because they have to be flooded. And since they're flooded, they sometimes bog down tanks. However, none of these fields appears to be lower than the rest of the land, *ergo* they're not flooded, *ergo* they wouldn't bog down tanks, *ergo* we've got the whole damned area to play with.

"Now, gentlemen. Let us imagine that we have at our disposal one Sabre Squadron, with which to support one Rifle Battalion of Infantry."

"*Sabre* Squadron, sir?" said Cadet Zaccharias.

"It's what we call a fighting squadron of Cavalry," Detterling said, "even though we now have bloody tanks. In battle, my Sabre Squadron would consist of a Headquarters Group and three Sabre Troops of four tanks each. Each Troop would support a Company of Riflemen and each tank would support a Platoon. You infantry chappies would use the tanks as carriers and cover and sources of supporting fire. To illustrate how it all works, and at the risk of boring us all to death, I have devised a theoretical manœuvre which we shall now carry out on this charming plain."

They spent the rest of the morning wandering over the plain, some of them pretending to be tanks and the rest of them being the infantry. In fact Captain Detterling's manœuvre was quite interesting, because it had been clearly thought out, it progressed by definite stages and it proposed a number of dramatic problems. It was rather difficult, however, to connect such very sedate proceedings with actual warfare, especially when they remembered what it had felt like, on the Assault Course, to have real live bullets spitting dust up their nostrils. Indeed Detterling himself felt bound to point out how artificial it all was.

"I've not seen much action myself," he told them, "because I kept out of it whenever possible; but I've seen a bit, and of course it's not at all like this. On this exercise we have a plan and we're following it. In action the plan has to be changed every five minutes, and anyhow everyone's too frightened to remember what it is, even supposing they ever knew in the first place. So you just muddle on and hope for the best."

After hearing this, they executed several more precisely ordained movements, until Captain Detterling announced that the enemy was defeated and that it was time for lunch. By now they had arrived at the far end of the sandy plain, where they were gratified to see a large marquee which had just been erected by the mess servants. They could not, of course, eat their lunch in the open because the kite-hawks would have spoilt it by swooping at their food.

"It's this sort of thing," said Detterling as he sat down next to Peter, "which did for the Italians in the desert. The Officers insisted on a proper lunch, so every day at noon everything else had to stop while a marquee was put up by the men and their Officers were served with the whole damn rigmarole from antipasta to zabaglione."

"You were in the desert long, sir?" Peter asked.

"No longer than I could help. It was perfectly foul," said Detterling crossly, "what with the heat and the cold and nothing to drink and that bloody man Montgomery sucking up to the troops, it made one despair of the human race. The only sensible people there were the Italians, who did nothing but surrender, so *they* didn't last long, and when they'd gone the British and the Germans got so enthusiastic that it positively turned your stomach. Even Giles Glastonbury got enthusiastic and took it all seriously, so much so that he shot a sentry because he found him asleep on guard duty. Of course that was going too far, and so they told him, but it was the *kind* of thing everyone was doing, otherwise Giles wouldn't have got away with it so easily."

"Was that why he was sent on to India?"

"Yes. Mind you, there's good precedent for shooting a sentry who goes to sleep – I think it counts as desertion in the face of the enemy – but it's not what one expects of one's friends. Giles ought to have been more tolerant. And while we're on the subject of Giles, he ought to have known better than to talk like he did the other night. All that stuff about getting his whores from Ley Wong on the cheap. He's very rich, and he's a sort of cousin of the King's, and a man in that position jolly well ought to pay full price. How can one respect one's sovereign if his cousin's being stingy in knocking shops?"

This question being quite unanswerable, Peter turned the conversation to Gilzai Khan.

"I hear he's rather a success," Detterling said. "He wanted to come on this affair today – said he was jealous of other people taking his Platoon without him – but I persuaded him to go and spend the morning cheering up Muscateer."

"He'll like that. They both will."

"Yes. . . . He says there's only one thing which really bothers him, and that's your chum Mortleman. I was afraid there might be trouble there."

"Alister's been very silly, but I think I've made him see sense."

"Good. You see, they're an odd lot where Gilzai Khan comes from and they've got a funny streak. If Mortleman goes on taking the piss, the Khan might turn up nasty – and I mean nasty – and that," said Captain Detterling, "would be rather a pity for all concerned."

"I have to tell you, sahibs," said the Munshi, "that today has been our last lesson. Your study of Urdu is to be discontinued. For myself, I am sorry, as I shall no longer be employed; for my country, I am glad, as it means that the British will soon be departing."

"Why are you so keen to get rid of us, Munshi sahib?"

"Because, Morrison sahib, we wish to order our own affairs. We shall not order them as efficaciously as you do, my God, no, but then efficacy is not important to us, you understand."

"No, Munshi sahib; I don't understand."

"We do not set the same values on the same things. And that is all."

"But you aspire to be a modern nation?"

"Politicians' talk, Murphy sahib. We merely aspire to be left in peace."

"And if you starve?"

"We have always starved. Many of us are starving at this minute."

"Not nearly as many as will starve when once we're gone."

"You are right, Mortleman sahib, but there is no need to sound so pleased about it."

"It's your fault. You will insist on the British leaving."

"Partly because we do not like being spoken to in that tone of voice. But let us not quarrel on our last morning together.

It is important that we should part in amity. And so : salaam, Morrison sahib, it has been a pleasure knowing you and you have done well. Salaam, Murphy sahib, you have been idle but in no way offensive. Salaam, Mortleman sahib, and may God lend you gentleness. And the last of our little group, my Lord Muscateer, he is still in hospital, poor boy?"

"Yes, Munshi sahib."

"You will take him my salaams, then, and say that I am sorry to have seen him so little. Wish him health and wisdom and a safe return to his father, for a great inheritance is no light matter. And now, sahibs, go in peace."

Murphy smiled politely but vaguely, while Alister muttered something.

"Stay in peace, Munshi sahib," Peter said.


"True Mohammedans," said the Khan, "do not eat pig and do not drink wine. They also have their foreskins cut."

He surveyed No. 2 Platoon with a fierce grin.

"For myself," he said, "I eat pork and I drink alcohol and I do not give a good God-damn who has a foreskin and who has not. Indeed, I have reason to believe that a foreskin keeps the flesh tender and – how do you say? – sensitive, and so makes for an increase of pleasure."

He grinned again, rather as if he had a stock of foreskins at his disposal which he would be happy to distribute on request to those deprived.

"And so," said the Khan, "I am not a religious man. I am unclean. I am defiled." He put his left hand down to his flank and started to fiddle with the empty sword-frog which hung there. "I acknowledge Allah and I respect his prophet, but there is an end of it. If I went into a Mosque, I should take my shoes off, but I should not go inside to pray, I should go inside looking for Subadar Doraini Mahmet, a religious man if ever there was one, who lost fifty rupees to me at dice ten years ago, when I too was a Subadar, and has not yet paid. So every time I see a Mosque, I say to myself, 'Perhaps that hound Doraini Mahmet is in there praying, I will go in and demand my due.' I have not yet found him, my Cadets, but one day I shall, and it will be a black day for Doraini Mahmet, that I promise him.

"But why do I tell you all this? Simply to show that I, Gilzai Khan, am not a man for prayer or fast or thrusting my God upon my fellow men.

"In brief, my brothers, I know and mind my business, and I expect others, whether Mohammedan or Hindu, to mind theirs. But this is what they will not do. Hindu and Moham- medan, they are for ever calling down curses upon each other and draining each other's blood and slicing off each other's parts because the foreskin has been cut or not cut, as the case may be.

"And so what is a man to do? Ignore this folly you say; but this folly is everywhere in India and may not be ignored. A sea of folly over the earth, my brothers – which will turn to a sea of blood the first minute the King Emperor withdraws his might and his men. Ignore it? We shall be swimming in it – those of us who are still here. As for you, you will be gone. But as for me . . . this is my country, so here I must stay. And when the knives come out, mine too must come out, to protect my own people. I cannot stand by and watch while Hindus slaughter Moslems, however much I may condemn the folly of both. A man must fight for his own kind, and if that kind and another kind take arms against each other in the one country that both believe to be their own, then a man were better un- born than live to see it."

And then one evening a few days later they heard that Mus- cateer was dead.

"Dead, sir? Dead of *jaundice*?"

"They say he had a dodgy liver," Captain Detterling said. "Funny, that. His old governor's is made of brass."

"Bad news, Molly. Muscateer's done for. I've just had a wire from his Commandant."

"Oh. Oh dear. Oh dear. Oh dear. Oh dear."

The Marquis Canteloupe handed his wife the Commandant's telegram and went to the window. Outside, February lay long and blank over the Wiltshire fields.

"I thought," said Lady Canteloupe eventually, "that cousin Detterling's letter said he was all right."

"Some time ago, that was. Poisoned in a wog cook-shop, Detterling said, but not to worry. Seems he was wrong. Jaundice, that telegram says. Something to do with the liver, ain't it?"

"My father had it. Twice."

"I s'pose Muscateer gets it from him. Not your fault, old girl. Pity it's too late for another, though." He turned back to look through the window. "When there's all this."

"He was such a kind boy," Molly Canteloupe said.

"It'll all be wasted on my bloody brother Stephen. Or Alfred. Should either of 'em live to collect it."

"Why should this happen to such a kind boy?"

"Ask me another," Lord Canteloupe said.

And with that he left the room and then the house, and walked sharply across his demesne to a small boat house which, until now, no one had ever entered during the winter. Someone had locked it until the summer should come, but Canteloupe, knowing what he wanted and being a man unaccustomed to hindrance, kicked the door in with one blow of his foot, and then dragged a rowing boat down into the creek which lapped into the open end of the shed. Once seated in the boat, he fitted the oars in the rowlocks and coaxed his way down the narrow creek, shoving at the banks with his oar-blades to gain passage and correct his course.

Very soon he reached the river. Without hesitation he turned upstream and rowed towards a distant wood; but Canteloupe, facing to stern as he rowed, could not see the wood : his view was of marshy flats lined with willow that stretched silently away, growing dim and white in the lurking mist; and ever between him and this view, sitting in the stern and holding the steering ropes, was a lightly flickering shade, now of a little boy in baggy shorts, grinning gaily at the start of a new day—

'Daddy, daddy, Mr Synge at school says there's going to be a war soon. *Is* there? And when will it be my turn to row?'

—now of a furry and pustular ephebe in worn corduroys—

'Father, I'm worried about mother. She gets so lonely while you're away fighting.'

—and now of a fine young man, stretched lazily across the seat with his long legs thrust out in front of him and crossed at the ankle, with eyes that smiled even when his face was grave, with large, brown capable hands—

'So you've come home, Papa, just when I'm going off to join up. Lucky for me the war in the East is over, though I don't care for the sound of this new bomb.'

So Canteloupe came, as they had always come, to the trees which spread their branches over the river; only now the trees were leafless and he could see the low, grey sky above; and when he came out on the other side of them, into a meadow which there was, it was not like coming out of a dark tunnel (as it always used to be) but more like emerging from a narrow street into an empty square. But if this was different, the voices were the same: 'Daddy, Daddy . . . Father . . . Papa. Tell me the story about the knight, the knight who was murdered in this meadow.'

And when he heard these voices, the unhappy man at last bowed his head and wept. Hitherto he had kept his face straight and stern, like a face on a tomb, as became a nobleman of ancient line who was visited with great misfortune; but now that the voices had asked for the story which he had told so many times, he shipped his oars and bowed his head and wept, babbling out the story as the tears ran down his face, interrupting it, now and then, to pray for the souls of the murdered knight and his own lovely son . . . until the kindly river, seeing that he would row no more that day, took his boat in its slow stream and carried him back again through the trees, the way that he had come.

"Your trousers are muddy, dear."

"I've been down to the river."

"I see. I've been thinking. We can have him brought home, you know. Even if they've already . . . We could still have him brought home. Then he could be here, which is only right."

"He'll sleep sound enough where he is," said the Marquis Canteloupe. "Look 'ee here, Molly. We'll speak no more of Muscateer in this house. He was our boy, and now he's dead, and there's an end of that."

And so Geoffrey Humbert Charles fitzAvon Julius d'Azincourt Sarum, called by courtesy of England the Earl of Muscateer, went to his long home in Bangalore, riding on a gun-carriage drawn by his comrades, as a soldier should. Gilzai Khan and Major Baxter marched in front of him and Sergeant-Major Cruxtable waddled behind, while the drums and bugles of a nearby British Battalion played him bravely on his way. In the graveyard of the Garrison Church, amidst the hideous but durable monuments of three generations of sahibs, he was received by a Chaplain with the rank of full colonel, who introduced him to his new quarters with unctuous aplomb; after which a firing party let off several rounds of blank over him without serious misadventure. Captain Detterling, as the nearest relative present, then cast the first dust upon the coffin; the Commandant of the O.T.S. succeeded him; and it was just as the Commandant was returning the trowel to the Chaplain that something quite appalling occurred.

Gilzai Khan began to keen.

At first no one knew what it was or who. There was a sound that might have been the wind on a winter shore, followed closely by another which might have been made by a rutting cat, and then a series of long wails reminiscent of faulty plumbing in a Bloomsbury hotel. Everyone looked about in some alarm, while Major Baxter took the trowel from the Chaplain and did his bit with it, but no one was any nearer to an explanation either of the noise or its meaning until C.S.M. Cruxtable, who knew a thing or two in his quiet way, moved quickly round the grave in order to accost Gilzai Khan, who was standing behind Detterling and the Chaplain and was therefore concealed from the other mourners. What Cruxtable intended to do when he reached the Khan nobody would ever know; for before the confrontation could take place, the Khan moved forward to take his turn with the trowel, and while he was doing this he really let rip.

By this time it was clear to all present what was happening and why, and reactions were various. C.S.M. Cruxtable shrugged his shoulders and rolled back to his former place. The Chaplain stood with his mouth open, rather as if he expected someone to put a jelly baby into it. The Commandant gritted his teeth and flared his lips, like a neighing horse. Major Baxter scratched his arsehole vigorously. Alister Mortleman was working his face in fury. And the other Cadets looked sad and foolish because a man whom they trusted was letting them down. Only Captain Detterling seemed unaffected by what was happening, and he it was that saved the situation. As Gilzai Khan stepped back from the grave, flourishing the trowel over his head and screeching like a banshee, Detterling stepped forward to embrace him, and in a loud, clear voice that all might hear thanked him, in the name of the Marquis Canteloupe, for the tribute which the Khan had paid to his son.

"The noble Lord his father shall hear of this," said Captain Detterling, "and send his greeting over the ocean to Gilzai Khan."

This remark settled everyone, including Gilzai Khan. The senior men present were comfortably confirmed in their view that only white men could deal with natives, while the Cadets, except for the furious Alister, felt that Gil' Khan, after all, had done something rather splendid after his own fashion.

So it was in an atmosphere of relief and good will that they all adjourned to Ley Wong's Chinese Restaurant for the wake.

Why Ley Wong's should have been chosen for this purpose rather than Wellesley Mess, no one was quite sure. Possibly Detterling (who was in charge of this part of the arrangements) had thought that Ley Wong would do the thing better;

possibly the Commandant had persuaded him that to have a funeral feast going full blast in the middle of the O.T.S. at noon would be bad for discipline. However this might be, Ley Wong's was where they went, and a very nice change it made.

Present were all members of Muscateer's Platoon with their Commander, Captain Gilzai Khan, and also the Commandant, Major Baxter as O.C. C Company, Captain Detterling, Sergeant-Major Cruxtable and the Bugle-Major who had led the Drums and Bugles during the morning's ceremony. So although they had been allotted the largest private room, there was rather a crush; and since Ley Wong had laid on a Chinese banquet of thirty-five courses, each one more elaborately spiced than the last, their faces were soon dripping with sweat, which was mopped up by two attendants who made an unceasing circuit of the banqueters carrying towels soaked in buckets of jasmine water. After the fifteenth course, Cruxtable and the Bugle-Major retired, being the only two present who did not either hold or aspire to commissioned rank; after the twentieth course the Commandant withdrew to keep an appointment with the Resident; and after the twenty-fifth Major Baxter excused himself on the ground of work waiting for him in the Company Office. This left only the principal mourners, if you could call them that, who by this time, with the exceptions of Captain Detterling and Peter Morrison, were exceedingly drunk. As Gilzai Khan had told the Cadets, his nominal adherence to Islam did not inhibit him in the article of alcohol, of which he consumed twice as much as anybody else with perhaps two-thirds of the effect; and even Barry Strange, who was normally cautious when the wine-cups glistened, had caught the spirit of the occasion and was busy downing bumpers with Wanker Murphy.

As drunk as anyone else, but by no means as happy, was Alister Mortleman, who gave the impression of biding his time. This he judged to have come when he saw Gilzai Khan leaning across the table to associate himself in a bumper with Murphy and Barry. As the Khan's glass came across to touch those of the other two, and as Barry smiled a welcome first to the Khan's glass and then to the Khan himself, Alister pushed back his chair, lurched round the table, and rapped the Khan sharply on the shoulder three times.

"Yes, Cadet Mortleman?" said the Khan, not looking at Alister but smiling back at Barry instead.

"British Officers," said Alister, "don't do that sort of thing. They don't make a beastly caterwauling at a funeral."

"I am not a British Officer," said the Khan, still smiling at Barry.

"You hold the King's Commission. *The King's Commission*," Alister screamed.

Whereupon everyone else was silent and the Khan, though still looking at Barry, no longer smiled.

"That does not prevent me," said the Khan, "from sorrowing for a dead friend."

"But he *wasn't* a friend," said Alister in a high, wild voice : "you hardly even knew him."

At last Gilzai Khan turned to face Alister.

"He was my man, and I knew his quality."

"You stinking black snob."

Gilzai Khan got to his feet, slapped Alister smartly but not very hard across the cheek, sat down again, raised his glass to Barry, and drained it.

"I could report you for that," Alister squealed; "you'd be sacked."

"But you won't, Cadet Mortleman. Because you are an Englishman, and whatever your faults you do not bear tales. Besides, it was, as you know, a challenge."

"Now look here, you two," began Peter Morrison from across the table. He turned to Detterling for assistance, but Detterling pursed his lips and poured himself more wine.

"Necessity," Detterling said. "Those two were bound to have a row in the end."

"But a challenge, sir? A duel?"

"It's often happened in the best circles."

"They're both drunk."

"So much the better. Neither of them will get hurt."

And Detterling looked across with interest to see how the affair would progress. As for the Cadets of No. 2 Pl., what with the heat and the succulent dishes of food which were still being served, what with the pools of spilled wine and the broken glass and the ubiquitous scent of jasmine, most of them clearly regarded the whole business as totally unreal, as a kind of cabaret got up to round off a memorable entertainment; and even those who were more alive to what was going forward took their cue from Detterling and looked on without apprehension or partiality. Apart from Peter Morrison, only Barry Strange seemed to fear any serious threat; but when he started to get up, presumably to intercede between his two friends, the Khan shook his head and frowned so heavily that Barry at once huddled back into his seat.

"Now," said the Khan to Alister. "I am the challenger, so the choice of weapons is with you. But since I shall destroy you, with any weapon known to either of us, within thirty seconds, you will allow me to make a suggestion. A contest, Cadet Mortleman, which will injure neither of us and will therefore make no scandal; a contest in which, indeed, I shall have the advantage of experience but you will have the advantage of youth; a contest for which we are both somewhat unmanned by drink, but you no more than I."

And with that Gilzai Khan clapped his hands and beckoned to Ley Wong, into whose ear he whispered at some length.

"Now, gentlemen all," he said, as Ley Wong bowed himself from the room, "what you are about to see is to be a secret between us as comrades of the same Platoon. By the memory of the friend whom we have buried, you will all swear yourselves to silence. All raise your right hand and repeat after me. . . .

"By the memory of the Muscateer bahadur do I swear to keep silence when I leave this room."

Three minutes later, a string of six girls was ushered through the door by Ley Wong. Two were Indian, slim and delicate; two Malayan, plump and dimpled; and two were Indo-Burmese half-breeds, childish in face yet full in figure: and all were naked above the waist.

"You choose first, Cadet Mortleman," said the Khan: "one, two or three. The contest is this: which of us shall prove his manhood the more times in twenty minutes. So choose up to three girls and then go about it as you please; they will obey your slightest order. But remember one thing: when I say 'prove your manhood', you must be seen to have done so. You understand?"

Alister nodded.

"And the judge of that," said the Khan, turning to Peter, "shall be you, Morrison huzoor. You, so to speak, shall award the hits."

"Oh, I say," Peter began, but the Khan ignored his incipient protest and turned away to strip. As did Alister. Two couches were now deposited by servants in the narrow but adequate space between that side of the table, which was opposite Peter, and the wall; while those sitting in that area withdrew their chairs to either side in order to give Peter a clear view. It was a measure either of the Khan's authority, or of the amount that had been drunk, or of both, that no one except Peter seemed to think any of this in the least extraordinary. Indeed many Cadets were making fairly obvious preparations to enjoy themselves fully on their own account.

When Alister and Gilzai Khan were both fully stripped, Alister chose two girls, a Malayan and an Indo-Burmese, and motioned them both to sit on his couch. Of the remaining four, the Khan chose three, two of whom, rather surprisingly, were the Indians and the other the second Malayan. While the un-selected girl slipped quietly from the room, the Khan instructed one Indian to go to his couch and his other two girls to stand off on one side. He then looked at Peter.

"Give the signal, huzoor," he said. "Remember: twenty minutes."

Peter gaped. Detterling produced a gold hunter and placed it in front of him.

"Starters' orders," Detterling said: "don't keep 'em hanging about."

"Er . . . go," Peter said absurdly, and each contestant leapt to his own pitch.

The Khan did not bother to undress his girl; he merely opened his legs slightly (showing two ugly white scars, one on each hairy thigh and both about three inches below his crutch) and made her apply a simple manual technique. Alister was more elaborate; he fiddled rather foolishly with the skirts of the Malayan before bringing the other girl's head to his lap. Crudity paid off : for the Khan was the first to show, inside a minute, with a magnificent rainbow which arched over the table and splashed down, amid a delighted cheer from the Cadets, within a foot of Detterling's hunter. But Alister was not far behind; twenty seconds later he lifted the head of the Indo-Burmese and showed himself to Peter as he scored a palpable point, though less spectacular than the Khan's. Meanwhile he had succeeded in uncovering the Malayan; he spread her thighs quickly, plunged in while still erect, and set to work with a powerful yet unhurried action of the hips and pelvis.

At the same time the Khan, who had dismissed his first Indian, was toying gently with his Malayan's fesses, while encouraging the second Indian to amuse herself just in front of him. Rightly considering that it would be some minutes before he was called on to judge a second coup for either party, Peter took a look round the audience. Murphy, as might have been expected, was stroking himself glutinously and taking no trouble to hide the fact; Zaccharias was doing the same, but furtively, with prim, genteel little movements. Other Cadets, in twos and threes, were setting up primitive mutual arrangements, while yet others were simply staring at one or other of the two principal tableaux as though at the ark of God. Barry, sitting next to Murphy, was ignoring him entirely and gazing, with an attention that was part puzzled, part wistful and part resentful, straight at the Khan's swelling groin . . . on to which, having first lifted her into the air with both hands and dangled her over him while he took aim, the Khan now clapped the splayed Malayan, making her buttocks squelch like a sponge. He then proceeded to joggle her quickly up and down, looking intently, the while, at the gracefully self-administering Indian, and thirty seconds later, with a yell of triumph, extricated himself from his subordinate position just in time to give Peter clear proof of a second score.

Alister, once again, was not far behind. He had been going

very, very easily in the conventional position, and now flattened one of his Malayan's legs, rolled sideways off her and over it, and presented Peter with an ungenerous but indubitable emission. Eight minutes to go and all square: could either – or both – of them manage another goal?

Once again, Peter glanced round at the audience. Most of the twosomes and threesomes were still going full swing, but the facile Murphy had finished his business and shut up shop, and was lugubriously eyeing Zaccharias, who just then gave a mean little moan of fulfilment and sat quite still. Barry was looking as intently as ever at the Khan, though now with a thoughtful and academic air, his former hurtness and bewilderment having given place to an objective appreciation of efficacy and style.

But the Khan was now failing. His weapon had drooped and died; the first Indian girl, whose expert touch had done so much for him at the outset, was powerless to rouse it; and the auto-erotic exhibition of the second Indian had now lost all interest for him. For a moment his eyes hardened while he took a snap decision . . . as a result of which he turned on to his stomach and called on all three of his hand-maidens to gouge at his bottom with their finger-nails.

Alister, who was also fading, hit on an equally sophisticated means of resuscitation: he commanded the pair at his disposal to make love to one another while he took himself in hand. The girls obeyed with such evident enthusiasm that they set up an almost visible aura of lust all about them, thus giving a powerful stimulus to Alister, who lubricated his renewed rigidity from a small decanter of olive oil thoughtfully provided by Ley Wong and then, sweating fiercely, half forced and half insinuated himself through the back entrance of the Indo-Burmese. The latter raised her head and mewed horribly, a protest which might seriously have disrupted Alister's concentration – had not the Malayan swiftly forced her friend's face down again, back to the feast which she was proffering, and so closed her mouth for good.

Since the Khan was still on his belly, no one could tell how he was faring. His eyes were closed and his face was calm; but every now and then he would beat the couch sharply with his right palm, indicating to his girls that they should operate yet faster and fiercer on his bottom, which was already flecked with blood. At last he gave a kind of stentorian yap, turned on his side to show incipient renascence, pulled his Malayan down beside him, and sited his piece between her large, firm breasts, which she squeezed together until they engulfed it. The Khan now sought to complete the process of repriming it by a series of slow, heaving thrusts. His face was no longer calm; it was split by a savage grin, while his eyes seemed to be staring desperately into the distance, as though at a quarry which he could just see flickering before him through the trees.

"You must give them the time, old chap," said Detterling to Peter.

"Three minutes to go, gentlemen," said Peter, reading from Detterling's watch.

Alister was now working with a steady and elegant circular movement of his crutch, giving huge and slobbering grunts that might have signalled the oncome either of success or of exhaustion. The Khan was grinding like a millstone, jaw locked and teeth clenched, while drops of sweat bubbled on his bald scalp. His two Indians stood close to his face, fingering themselves and each other, and the Khan now brought his eyes back from the far quarry in the forest to dwell on their activities. As he did so, a light of triumph appeared on his face and he started to grind faster and shorter. Alister, meanwhile, kept the same steady rhythm, but with each revolution his action was growing just perceptibly weaker.

"Sixty seconds, gentlemen," Peter said.

And now, all other amusements being either concluded or suspended, the entire Platoon was watching the two champions as they bid for the winning throw. The look of triumph on the Khan's face was growing fiercer every moment, while Alister was visibly sagging in trunk and thigh.

"Eleven to four on Gilzai Khan," said Detterling.

And indeed the match seemed all but finished in the Khan's favour – when suddenly the goddess, laughter-loving Aphrodite, flew down from Olympus to Alister's aid. For just as he was about to sink back defeated, his Malayan girl, who had been twitching and jerking for some time under the clever tongue of the Indo-Burmese, let out a high, thin wail of ecstasy. Since her face was directly below the loins of the Indo-Burmese and Alister's dangling sack, the breath of her long cry warmed his prostate at the same moment as her gross abandonment refurbished his desire. His whole body pricked and quivered; he gave four short but savage stabs at intervals of three seconds; and then withdrew to show a tiny but palpable pearl at the end of his blood-red wand.

There was a gasp of applause from the Cadets and a quick, wry pout from the Khan, who knew that this must mean a third notch for his rival. But there was still a good chance that he would score an equaliser. For at this very moment he was easing out from under his Malayan's breasts and kneeling up to show himself rampant and ready. A last fond stroke with his own palm, and a mighty quivering ensued. A mighty, an heroic, a magnificent quivering : but no moisture. Gilzai Khan had already been drained dry.

Peter looked at Detterling.

"Does that count?" he said, handing back Detterling's watch.

"No, huzoor, it does not," said Gilzai Khan, cradling his throbbing but infertile tuber. "No rain, no harvest." He rose from his couch and limped, gallant and priapic, to where Alister lay panting and sobbing into the Malayan's navel.

"You have beat me fair and square, Mortleman huzoor," said the Khan. "With this weapon" – he tweaked himself – "you are the better man. And now we shall be brothers, shall we not?"

Alister thrust out a trembling hand and the Khan took it in both of his own. Then he removed his right hand only, turned and beckoned to Barry, and hugged him, when he came, with his right arm.

"You must see your friend safe home, little Officer Cadet," he said; "and then you will come to me, that we may talk of the day's events."

Barry nodded gravely, and bent over Alister. The Khan

dragged himself back to his couch, sat down very heavily, and started to dress. Detterling rose from his chair.

"An interesting old luncheon," he said to Peter. "I should like to see Canteloupe's face when he gets the bill . . . particularly with those girls added on. Good afternoon to you, Mr Morrison."

Peter shoved Detterling aside, trampled through upturned chairs and sprawled Cadets to the door, and galloped down the corridor to the public restaurant, which was empty at this hour of the day except for Ley Wong, who was counting his till.

"Ley Wong," Peter said : "find me one piece girlie. NOW."

The next morning the Cadets of No. 2 Pl. were both excited and morose; excited by their memories of the previous afternoon, and morose because the common round appeared, by contrast, to be somewhat drab. For them, they felt, there could now be no new thing under the sun. In order to restore them to a sense of duty, the Khan devoted an entire period, which was scheduled as 'Current Affairs', to a conscientious account of the sources and symptoms of venereal disease.

"Gonorrhoea," said the Khan, "or the clap. This disagreeable sickness declares itself between three days and three weeks after intercourse with an infected person. It is important that the men whom you will command should be clearly instructed as to the signs which herald its arrival, so that they may report sick immediately and before infecting their comrades."

"But how could they do that, Gil' Khan?"

"A diseased male," said the Khan patiently, "can infect the anus of another male, who can in turn infect the penis of a third."

"Oh, *Gil' Khan*. . . ."

I wonder if I've got it, thought Peter Morrison. But surely not; she was such a sweet little thing that she must have been clean. Three days to three weeks, the Khan says. I can't be sure for three weeks. But I *am* sure. 'Something rather special,' Ley Wong said – and he wouldn't want to risk his good name by serving up damaged goods. Something rather special, a Eurasian, a blackie-white, but more white than blackie, 'Oooh,' she said, 'how big and hard he is, put 'im between my breasts, no, first show me how you do it to yourself, naughty boy, and I will show you how I do it to myself . . . so, with the handle of the hair-brush, it passes the time when you are lonely, but we are not lonely now, there, between my breasts, and I will kiss 'im, so, he is so strong, he is throbbing, he is throbbing – a fountain, a fountain, welling up between my breasts. . . . All gone, naughty boy, all gone. But you are a strong naughty boy, and you have time (yes?), and money (yes?), so you will stay longer and I will teach you many things. But first we wash 'im . . . and then we dry 'im . . . and then we powder 'im – so – and then we leave 'im for a little, and kiss, and tickle on the neck and the ears, and talk of other matters. . . .'

"Morrison huzoor, do you hear me?"

"I hear you, Gil' Khan."

"Your customary look of intelligent attention is absent from your face."

"I apologise, Gil' Khan. Just for a moment I was thinking of . . . other matters."

"Well, huzoor, you will not think of other matters if you get the pox, so hear what Gilzai Khan now says of it. Syphilis, my brothers, or the Great Pox. Unlike gonorrhoea, syphilis is a killer for sure. It makes itself evident, any time between ten and a hundred days after intercourse with an infected person, in the form of a lesion or chancre or ulcer at the point of infection. This lesion or chancre or ulcer is a wet sore which takes on all the hues of the rainbow, and gradually spreads itself, unless treated, eating away the fair flesh, whether it be your white flesh, or my brown, or Ley Wong's yellow, or the nigger's black. The most memorable description of such a sore and its growth is to be found in a piece of traditional English verse:

" 'I took it to the doctor,' "

Gilzai Khan incongruously quoted,

" 'Who said, "Where did you knock her?"
I said, "Down where the green grass blows."
He said, "Quicker than a twinkle
That pimple on your winkle
    Will be bigger than a red, red rose." ' "

A red rose, thought Peter. 'My name is Margaret Rose,' the girl had said, as they lay there lazily scratching each other's buttocks, 'Margaret Rose Engineer, I am named after our princess. What is your name?' 'Peter.' 'Peter what? You need not fear to tell me.' 'Peter Morrison.' 'Where do you live, Peter Morrison?' 'I live in England, Margaret Rose, on a farm in Norfolk, not far from the sea. It is winter there now, and the fields are black and hard. But soon the spring will come and then the summer, and my fields – for they will be mine when my father dies – my fields will be rich with the new corn.'

'Tell me more about your home, Peter Morrison.' 'There are clumps of birch and pine, which whisper in the breezes which blow from the sea. There is a church too, and near the church a little field . . . where we play at cricket from the first day of May until the first day of October.'

'And all this will be yours?' 'Yes. I had an elder brother, Margaret Rose, but he was killed some time ago, fighting for the King. Like the brothers of many of my friends. We are the lucky ones, I suppose. We were too young to fight, and so we inherit the land for which they fell.'

'Do not be sad, Peter. Kiss me. And now there. And now there – see how the nipple rises. There too, lest the other nipple be jealous. And there. And there. And with the point of the tongue . . . just . . . *there* . . . And now I will kiss you. There, and there . . . and there. And see, he is big and strong again. Now, what shall we do to make 'im pleasure? Tickle him, so, and stroke him, so, and scratch 'im, very lightly, so. . . .' 'God oh God, how marvellous. Oh God Oh Christ Oh God.' 'And then . . . we mount 'im, very carefully, so. And then we ride 'im . . . ride 'im . . . ride 'im. . . . Oh sweet God, I am coming, Peter Morrison, you must come too when I tell you, not just yet, he is making me come, he is so big and strong, swelling inside me, making me come, now, Peter, now, Peter, *now*, Peter, NOW . . . spurt, spurt, spurt, *spurt your hot lovely spunk.*' '*Sweet Jesus Christ,* MAKE IT NEVER STOP.'

". . . So do not forget, my Cadets. Tell your men to wear sheaths, and wash themselves immediately after, and use the disinfectant cream that is for issue. And tell them that if they do not, the spirochaete will smash their noses and leave twin black holes between their rotting cheeks. . . ."

'. . . So we wash 'im and dry 'im and powder 'im and give 'im one last kiss. There. And now you must go, Peter.' 'Why?' 'Please do not ask.' 'Very well. But I can come again soon?' 'Of course. But give warning. Through Ley Wong is best.' 'I understand. This is for you, Margaret Rose.' 'Good. That is a generous present, most generous. And do not forget the old lady who will show you out. She is shrivelled and ugly now; but once she was so beautiful, just like me. Come again soon, Peter Morrison, and tell me more of your home in England. . . .'

"Morrison huzoor, let me repeat my question. What precautions will you tell your men to take?"

"Wash 'im and dry 'im and powder 'im – I mean, wear a sheath, wash afterwards, and use the disinfectant cream that is for issue."

"Good, huzoor. Perhaps you have been listening after all."

The old woman who had shown him out. When he had given her ten rupees, she had made a salaam. Something in the gesture had been familiar; it had been precisely the same in style and timing as the gesture which Margaret Rose had made when he handed her her 'present'. His immediate thought had been that the older woman must have taught the younger. 'Once she was so beautiful, just like me.' She still was rather like her – though very much darker in the face. The same eyes, the same mouth, the same hands (which had accepted the ten-rupee note). Her mother. Margaret Rose's mother, serving her daughter as a whore's maid. What kind of woman did that make of her? For that matter, what kind of woman did it make of Margaret Rose? 'We mount 'im, very carefully, so . . . and then we ride 'im . . . ride 'im . . . ride 'im.

. . .' That was the kind of woman it made of her, and for that he would go again, though the maid were twenty times her mother and his own to boot.

The next 'Current Affairs' period, one week later, was not about venereal disease and it was not taken by Gilzai Khan. It was about the situation which the British faced in India and it was taken by Captain Detterling.

"Riots," Captain Detterling said : "in Bombay, in Madras, in Calcutta, there have been ugly riots. The Commandant thought it would be more . . . tactful . . . if I were to discuss these with you instead of Gilzai Khan, who is rather annoyed as a result. He says that his assessment would have been quite as accurate as mine, and come to that, gentlemen, he is right. The Commandant requires, however, that on this issue British Cadets should be instructed by a British Officer.

"These riots, gentlemen. They have arisen because the Indians are still uncertain what we intend. Now that the war is over they want us to declare ourselves. As indeed, you might say, we have – because the Prime Minister has made it known that he wishes to quit India. But this is too vague, the Indians reply : no date has been given, no concrete arrangements have been made. The Indians are asking when and how, and as yet there has been no answer.

"But then how could there be, gentlemen? To hand over the rule of a vast continent – of an Empire, no less – is a serious matter. One cannot just get up and go, leaving one's empty chair to the first bully boy who can sit down in it. Suitable replacements must be found, money must be discussed, continued restraint and protection must be ensured for those who should be protected and restrained. Good men must be trained and their weapons tested; bad men must be disarmed and their guns spiked. In short, there must be a complex and laborious programme – such as no one has yet had the time or the presumption to draw up.

"And how long will it now take to draw up? Gentlemen, you may well ask. India is an Augean stable which we must cleanse before leaving it; how does one even begin to schedule such a terrible task? Unlike Hercules, we are not of divine descent...."

"So what did Detterling bahadur say?" asked Gilzai Khan, when he saw No. 2 Pl. later. "About the riots?"

"He said that they have been caused by our failure to declare our detailed plans," Peter Morrison told him.

"That is right."

"And he said that even to formulate such plans is almost impossible."

"Again, that is right. And you will be under such pressure to leave that you will go before the plans are properly formulated. In any case, what plans does one formulate to keep greedy and superstitious men from each other's throats? How will you satisfy both Moslem and Hindu?"

"Some sort of compromise, Gil' Khan?"

"Neither side will be satisfied unless it is given everything. I hear this afternoon that there are new riots – Moslem riots – in Karachi. The Moslems are demanding the complete expulsion of the Hindu community. What does one do with people who make demands such as these? They are my people, but I say they are mad. Listen to me, my children." Gilzai Khan lifted the empty sword-frog from his flank and slapped it back again. "Such people must be ruled with a long, sharp sword, and the King Emperor alone is strong enough to wield it."

"I was looking forward to coming to India," said Barry Strange at dinner in Wellesley Mess, "but now I'm jolly glad we'll be leaving it when we're commissioned. All these riots and things. It makes a man uncomfortable."

"According to what Colonel Glastonbury said at Khalyan," Peter reminded him, "most of us are now intended for British Battalions in the Far East. That could easily mean British Battalions here in India."

"There's a lot of the Far East which isn't India," said Barry.

"And a lot which is."

"You sound as if you want to stay here."

"I never want to stay where I'm not wanted," Peter said. "But we may be *needed*. To see that the hand-over goes smoothly."

"Not much chance of it doing that, from what the Khan was saying."

"And from what Detterling was saying," Alister Mortleman put in, "it'll be years before we hand over anyhow."

"And meanwhile, more and more nasty temper and more and more riots," said Barry. "Myself, I don't at all look forward to putting down riots."

"It 'ud be a sight easier," Alister said, "if we were allowed to shoot 'em dead. But for every dead wog, a hundred politicians howl their heads off."

"That's as it should be," said Peter. "The rights of the Indian population must be respected."

"Even when they're rioting against us?"

"They don't know what they're doing, most of them. They're the dupes of trained agitators, who whip 'em into mob hysteria."

"Rabble," said Alister.

"People," said Barry. "One can't just mow them down."

"You two just wait till you're on the wrong end of a riot," Alister told them, "and find out how you feel then."

"I hope I shall never find out," Barry said. "I might be ashamed of myself when I did."

"Just so, Barrikins. You might be ashamed of yourself, but you'd still be feeling what I'm saying – that you wanted to shoot them all dead. But I don't think you need worry." Alister leaned across the table and addressed his two friends in a confidential whisper. "I picked up a rumour today. It seems that after we're commissioned here, they'll probably send us all home. *Not* to units in the Far East, but home."

"Why on earth should they do that?"

"The Labour Government are keen to bring everyone home as soon as possible. They want the Army demobilised because

they think it'll make them popular and anyway they don't care
for Armies."

"But there's too much still to be done. We have military
responsibilities all over the place."

"They're getting shot of those as fast as they can – even if it
means just dropping them down the lats. Bring the boys home,
that's the cry. And apparently that includes us."

"Where did you hear this?"

"It's pretty clear from the English papers."

"About *us*, I mean."

"C.S.M. Cruxtable. He's trying to find out what's happened to poor Muscateer's Part One Pay Book, and he had me
in to ask if I could help. I told him what little I knew about it,
and then we got chatting for a bit. He's a chatty sort of bloke."

"I don't know that one need pay much attention to Cruxtable," Peter said. "There's been nothing official – not as far
as we're concerned."

"Always listen to a Sergeant-Major," Alister said. "One
word from a Sergeant-Major is worth three official announce-
ments."

"My brothers used to say that too," mused Barry, "or something of the kind. The Sergeant-Major's jokes, they used to
say, are the Field Marshal's nightmares."


"So that's what they're saying," said Barry to Gilzai Khan
later that evening: "that we'll all be sent back to England as
soon as we're commissioned."

"I do not know how that will be," said the Khan. "I am not
in the Commandant's confidence here. Nor in anyone else's."

"Oh, surely. Everyone likes you. *We* do."

"You are not on the staff, huzoor."

"Captain Detterling does, I know."

"The bahadur Detterling likes me well enough, I think. But
I am not in his confidence. I am an Indian, to whom he does
not tell secrets."

"This isn't a secret. It's a rumour going around everywhere."

"But the truth, or the falsehood, behind the rumour – that is still secret."

"I suppose so. . . . Does it make you sad, Gil' Khan? When they don't tell you things, I mean."

"It makes me uneasy. One does not know . . . quite what is in store."

"None of us can know that."

"One can be told what is *intended*. It is a very uncomfortable thing, little Cadet, when all one's colleagues know what is intended and oneself does not. People break off what they are saying, and give knowing looks at one, and take each other into corners so that one shall not hear them."

"Is that what they're doing to you?"

"Lately. They always did, of course, but lately I have noticed it more."

"Why?"

"You ask too many questions, huzoor. The whole evening you have been asking questions."

"I'm sorry, Gil' Khan. There. . . . Does that make up for it?"

"It does, and more. But you must go now. It is late and you are tired."

Gilzai Khan started to lift the mosquito net.

"No, I'm not. Please let me stay a little longer. Please . . . my Khan."

"How can I refuse? Oh, my little Englishman, you make my heart to yearn."

"And you make mine, Gil' Khan, and you make mine."

". . . Oh, God, Peter, you will make me die, Peter, now, Peter, *now*, Peter, NOW."

"Now, now, now, now . . . NOW."

Some while later, Margaret Rose said:

"Next time I will teach you to do it like the dogs do it. When shall you come?"

"Not for a little, I'm afraid. We're going to Jungle Camp."

"You are going away?" (Sharply.)

"Not far. Not for long."

"How long?"

"Ten days. Starting the day after tomorrow."

"Then you can come tomorrow evening."

"No, Margaret Rose. Tomorrow evening we must pack and make ready. We leave soon after midnight."

"But you will come as soon as you get back?"

"You know I shall."

"I will be lonely for you. I shall use the hair-brush and think of you. You too must do it to yourself and think of me. Let us agree on a time, and then we shall both know that the other is doing it too."

"There is not much privacy in camp."

"You will find a place. Let us say . . . ten o'clock at night."

"Every night?"

"No. Too often will spoil it. Two nights from now, and every third night after that."

"All right."

"Yes. For now – for ten days – it is all right. But what shall I do when you go for ever?"

To this question there could be no answer.

"Some time you will go," said Margaret Rose, "and then all the British will go. Then they will murder us, me and my – old lady."

"Murder you?"

"Yes. They hate us because we are neither one thing nor the other. Blackie-whites. Half-castes."

"No one could murder anyone as lovely as you."

"You do not know them. 'Half-caste whore,' they call me. 'Kill her,' they will say, 'kill her because she is unclean' – not because I am a whore, you understand, but because I am a half-caste. 'Kill her,' they will scream, '—and take her money.' "

"Oh, Margaret . . . Margaret Rose. But the British are still here now. We shall be here for some time yet. And so shall I."

"You. You do not care about me. You pay me and you mess me and that is all."

"Don't be bitter. I'm . . . very fond of you."

"And you forget me the minute you go out of the door. Until your flesh gets hard again."

"It's hard again already. Margaret Rose: teach me to do it like the dogs do it."

"You will be generous?"

"You know I will."

"With your heart as well as your rupees?"

"I will think of you when I go out of the door, if that's what you mean. And I've promised to remember you when I'm away at camp."

"Then I will give you something good to remember. Before we do it like the dogs, we must court each other like the dogs. Get on to your hands and knees, Peter. So. Now. I am wagging my tail, see, and I give a sniff-sniff there, and a lick-lick there, and then I squat like this. . . . And now you, Peter, wag your tail – good, good – and a sniff and a lick and a nip, and a sniff and a lick and a nip. . . . Nice doggie, nice doggie, lift your back leg so, and oh my goodness me. . . ."


Jungle Camp was rough. On the first day the Cadets did a forced march through the jungle (which was really only heavy bush, but quite disagreeable enough) with no rations for twelve hours and only as much water as they could carry in their water-bottles. After this, Peter was too tired to think of Margaret Rose, though their first engagement had been fixed for ten that night. On the second day, No. 2 Pl. was 'cut off' and had to man a defensive position for twenty-four hours; this time they were allowed rations but no fires to cook them. On the third day, Gilzai Khan taught them about jungle ambushes, with particular emphasis on garotting scouts: 'Over his head with the noose, my Cadets, and then squeeze till his eyes burst like plums.' On the fourth day, they practised wading along jungle streams (about twenty miles of them), after which Peter was again too tired to keep his second mental tryst with Margaret Rose. And on the fifth day Captain Detterling arrived at the camp with a face as long as a tunnel.

At first no one could understand why he looked so despondent, for the news which he brought was good. Substantially, it consisted of official confirmation of the rumour that all the Cadets, when commissioned, were to be posted back to the U.K., or at any rate to Europe, and not to units in the Far East. What was more, Detterling told them, the date on which they would pass out from the O.T.S. had been provisionally brought forward by one month, which meant that they now had barely eight weeks' training left. There were, however, some awkward complications about the regiments to which they would be assigned, particularly in the case of the so-called 'Indian Army Cadets'. The British Infantry, it appeared, was shortly to be much reduced in strength, and vacancies in all infantry regiments, especially the smarter ones, would be correspondingly fewer; yet on the other hand there were more Cadets than ever to be accommodated, as no Cadet (it now went without saying) would be going to an Indian Regiment. This meant that none of them could depend on being accepted by the regiment of his previous choice, and that many of them (perhaps 100 of the 300 which made up their intake) would be seconded to other arms altogether, such as the Artillery or the Signals, despite their manifest lack of qualification. But with all this, every effort would be made to suit individual preferences; and if they would all be so good as to write careful answers to the questions on the forms which Captain Detterling would now distribute, they might rest assured that action in their interests would be initiated as soon as he and the forms were back in Bangalore.

The prospect of getting their pips a month early and the certainty of returning to Europe more than consoled the Cadets for the possibility of having to serve in banausic regiments. While the more keen-sighted of them might suspect some instability in arrangements which had been so radically and so suddenly revised, they were all too busy filling in Detterling's forms to bother much about that.

" 'First Choice of Regiment'," Alister said: "The Rifle Brigade. I see we have to list four more. I suppose one may as well put down Barry's shower second."

"The Wessex Fusiliers are not a shower," Barry said.

"Will they still take you?" Peter asked Barry.

"I hope so. Captain Detterling said that family connections would still count for a good deal."

"Well, I've got none there, but I shall try for them too," Peter said, "since the Indian Army's out. What chance do you think I've got?"

"You're a J.U.O. You should get your choice if anyone does."

"We'll see about that. 'Choice of Station in Europe other than U.K.' I think Italy might be rather nice."

"The Macaronis all steal things," said Alister. "What about Germany? I hear you can have all the women you want for a packet of Gold Flake."

"Or Austria," said Barry: "I've always wanted to go to Vienna."

"Excuse my interrupting your plans for the Grand Tour," said Detterling from behind them, "but I want a private word with Morrison."

This took just two minutes, and incidentally explained why Detterling was looking so unhappy. For it appeared that when he left for Bangalore the next morning, he was to take with him not only the completed forms but also 14477929 Officer Cadet (J.U.O.) Morrison, P., who was required for interview with the Commandant in order to defend himself against a complaint laid against him by Miss Margaret Rose Engineer.

They travelled back to Bangalore in a fifteen-hundredweight truck. Detterling was in the cab with the driver; Peter was in the open and very dusty rear, along with Detterling's expensive camping equipment, which took up most of the room, and Sergeant-Major Cruxtable, who took up all the rest.

"And what, Sergeant-Major," said Peter with false cheeriness from his place inside Detterling's camp bath, "is taking *you* back to Bangalore?"

"Lord Muscateer's Part One Pay Book," Cruxtable said. "It's still not been found, so I've got to make an extra special search of everywhere. Office, bashas, messes, hospital – the lot."

"Why the fuss?"

"He's not officially dead until his Part One Pay Book has been handed over to Records for cancellation. So he's still on the roll for rations and pay. It's downright embarrassing. Next thing you know, they'll want to dig him up again, because the poor bleeder's not entitled to his coffin. Being as how he's not dead, you understand."

"He first missed it up at Khalyan. It's probably still there."

"Only we can't tell 'em that, Mr Morrison, because when you all got here the Company Commander signed for you as having arrived complete with Scale Nine Equipment and all requisite documents. We didn't check, you see. So we can't go back on that now, or the Company Commander will be down shit alley."

"What'll happen if you never find it?"

"Lord Muscateer's pay will be docked by so much a week until he's paid for one grave, Officer Cadet for the use of, which he's occupying under false pretences."

"You can't mean it."

"Stranger things have happened, laddie. Still, I dare say he can afford it. He'll have quite a nice credit balance building up with the Paymaster by now. . . . And what's this spot of bother you've gone and got into?"

At first Peter would not answer this; but when Cruxtable displayed total indifference as to whether he was told or not, Peter changed his mind and told him.

". . . Only I don't know what she's complaining about. I never made her do anything she didn't want to and I paid up on the nail."

"It's some trick to get more, Mr Morrison. Does she think you're rich?"

"I don't know why she should. Yes, I do. I told her once that my family has land in Norfolk."

"That'll be it, then. She's smelt money."

"Then why didn't she ask for it? She didn't need to go to the Commandant; the threat would have been quite enough.

Anyhow, I can't think what she can possibly have told him."

"Doesn't matter," said Cruxtable with sombre relish; "as things are nowadays, these bloody wogs only have to open their mouths and dribble, and everyone in the world's on their side against us. No one wants to know the truth of it. They're just for the wogs and against us – and so are half our own people, come to that."

"But she's a half-caste. Which means that proper Indians won't support her."

"They'll support her all right," said Sergeant-Major Cruxtable, "if they think it'll do down *you*."


"The sum of the thing is this," the Commandant said. "That girl swears that you promised to marry her, and that on the strength of that promise she let you have your wicked way with her. And now, she says, she's pregnant."

"So she may well be, sir. By anyone in Bangalore."

"My dear fellow, we all know that." The Commandant arranged his stubby hands as though he were holding reins and then spurred the chair-leg beneath him. "But the point is, she's threatenin' trouble and she'll get support. You know how vulnerable we are just now. Any excuse will do to get at us, and this one's good for riots all over Southern India."

Oh, Margaret Rose, how could you? I lusted, yes, but so did you (or so you made me believe), and I was always tender.

"What does she want, sir?"

"She wants you to marry her. Which really means that she wants a passage to England. I don't think she cares for the smell of things out here, and I can't say I blame her."

A passage to England. For her and (no doubt) her old mother.

"I never promised anything of the kind."

"Of course not."

"And of course I can't marry her."

"My dear Morrison, you don't have to tell me that. Now, if you were an N.C.O., it might be different. N.C.O.s often marry whores, and I believe that they can make very good wives. But a gentleman can't marry a chee-chee."

"And so where, sir, do we go from there?"

"That's just it." The Commandant shook up the reins and petulantly spurred the chair-leg. "If only you chaps would do as we ask. We do *ask* you to keep away from girls like that, because this is just the sort of thing that always comes of it. As you now see for yourself."

"If it's money she wants, sir, I think my father—"

"—No. I gathered from Detterling that you could run to plenty of conkers, so I put it to her straight. No good. She wants marriage. As I say, she wants to get out of India – because the way the wicket's goin' to start shapin' here, Morrison, she reckons it needs much more than money to keep her bails on. So if she doesn't get her way, she's goin' to make trouble; and to stop that trouble I shall have to punish you, and the only punishment severe enough to have the desired effect will be your dismissal from this O.T.S. And even then we shan't have heard the last of it."

"Punish me for what, sir?"

"In *their* eyes, for abusin' this girl's confidence; and in our eyes, for stickin' yer finger in the wrong honey-pot. *You were told when you got here not to go ruttin' with native sluts.* Not that we'd bother about that, if the wind was right, but as it is we just can't help it. It's not really a punishment, it's . . . it's an act of policy."

"But whichever it is, it's been settled on?"

"Yes. I'm sorry, Morrison."

"And if I *should* agree to marry her?"

"You'd go even quicker." A vicious back-kick at the chair-leg. "Officers don't marry Eurasian trash. We had to put up with it from a few ranker officers during the war, but all that's over now."

"So there's no hope at all, sir?"

"None . . . unless you yourself can persuade her to haul down her colours. I've done my best, God knows, and I've got nowhere at all. But I can give you five days, Morrison – until your intake returns from Jungle Camp. If you fix her before

then, and show me that you've fixed her, then everything will
be toodle-pip. If not, then it's juldi jao, my dear Morrison,
for you."


Peter's first movement was to go to see Ley Wong.

"This girlie, Ley Wong : she do me one piece harm."

Ley Wong was very sorry, but there was no accounting for
human vagary.

"Colonel Glastonbury, he be angry when he learn."

Ley Wong regretted to hear it; but the Colonel was a man
of the world and would doubtless perceive, on due consideration, that such misfortunes were bound to occur from time to
time and owed nothing to the malice of Ley Wong. Had not
the English a saying, that those who touched pitch must risk
defilement?

"You can do nothing then?"

But of course Ley Wong could do something. He could
arrange another girl for the Sahib during the remainder of his
stay in Bangalore. In all the circumstances, he would allow the
Sahib a very generous discount indeed.

"Listen, Ley Wong. I no want new girlie. I want that *this*
girlie closee one piece mouth."

The Sahib should recollect that the spoken word was beyond
recall. As Ley Wong understood the matter, the damage was
already done.

*"Not if you get her to unsay what she has said."*

Ley Wong deposed that since Margaret Rose had already
refused money the only thing which would now change her
mind was fear. Although he would normally have been able to
operate very effectively on this basis, in the present instance the
girl had solicited the protection of the authorities and was
therefore not to be tampered with by prudent men.

Then Peter called Ley Wong a fucking yellow bastard and
was politely bowed out of the Restaurant.


It was only after this futile exhibition of ill temper that Peter
began to realise the true nature of the disaster which now faced

him. Hitherto he had assumed, despite Detterling's doleful face and the Commandant's very lucid exposition of the guiding factors, that there must be some fairly easy way of settling the affair. In all his career to date, whether at school or in the Army, Peter had behaved with intelligent propriety; which is to say that he had informed himself which rules were seriously enforced by the authorities (as opposed to those rules which were kept on the books merely for the look of the thing) and had obeyed them to the letter. On arriving in India, therefore, he had paid keen attention to Colonel Glastonbury and Captain Detterling, and from their tone and attitudes he had concluded (among much else) that the rules which enjoined sexual abstinence need not be closely observed, provided only that one paid one's way like a gentleman. The official exhortation to the contrary he had taken to be simply a form of satisfying residual public hypocrisies; and indeed the Commandant, in one of his softer utterances during the recent interview, had in effect upheld this view. 'Not that we'd worry about that,' the Commandant had said, 'if the wind was right....'

But now that he came to look at it all more carefully, Peter saw just how significant this last clause was. 'If the wind was right. ...' The trouble about the wind was that it was something elemental, something which could not be controlled or 'fixed'. The wind blew where it listed; and while it was not, as a rule, strong enough to disrupt upper-class amusements, every now and again it gave a maleficent blast from the wrong quarter and ruined the picnic. This was what had happened now. He had taken his trousers off to frolic on the grass, and the wind had caught them up and carried them off to the tree-tops. Nor was this wind a mere sportive breeze, sent by one of the minor and more corrupt rural deities who might have been bought off by a congenial offering; the wind, in this case, was an ice-cold gale, and it blew from political Necessity. Whether the British authorities liked it or not, they were now compelled to punish him.

As the victim of Necessity, then, he would receive a great deal of sympathy, had indeed already received some from the

Commandant; but the fact remained that he was trouserless and would cut a very sorry figure when he went home to his friends and parents. He was threatened both with disgrace and with ridicule. The voices of sympathy would soon be replaced by the reproaches of his father and the snickers of light-minded contemporaries. ('Have you heard about po-faced Peter Morrison? Chucked out of Bangalore for humping a black tart.') But there was even worse to it than that; for while he could endure reproach and could certainly face down malice, he could not bear to go home unworthy of his land. He had come forth, as all men who held land should do, to show his love and loyalty to his sovereign, whose vassals, in a sense, his father and himself still conceived themselves to be. If he returned having been refused the King's Commission he would have dishonoured the land for which, as he saw it, he was now doing his knight-service.

And if he had dishonoured his land, he could not return to it. He could not thrive on acres to which he had been false and his title to which would now be a mockery. As he set out to visit Margaret Rose, his mood was not one of anger or indignation or even of anxiety, it was simply one of sorrow. It was his intention to go down on his knees and plead with her to spare his fields from the shame which threatened them and to spare himself from being exiled for ever.


But when he reached the handsome suburban house in which Margaret Rose had her apartments, he found Gilzai Khan on the doorstep. The Khan smiled savagely and played a tattoo on his left buttock with his empty sword-frog.

"Do not go in, huzoor."

"Gil' Khan. . . . When did you get back from Jungle Camp?"

The Khan shrugged and smiled again, dismissing the question as trivial. For a few moments Peter played with the theory that he too was one of Margaret Rose's clients, and that his desire for her had become so fierce that he had arranged the day off from camp in order to come to her. But if so, he would hardly be spending his time on the doorstep, and in any case it was clear from his demeanour that he regarded himself in some sort as a sentry.

"Excuse me, Gil' Khan, but I want to go in and see someone."

"The person you want, huzoor, will soon be coming out."

And sure enough, the door now opened and four large men emerged through it. Two of them were holding Margaret Rose, and two of them her old maid (or mother). A van sidled up the drive from nowhere, and inside ten seconds the four men and the two women had disappeared into the back of it. Margaret Rose neither spoke to Peter, as she was taken past, nor looked at him; he was not sure she had even known he was there.

Gilzai Khan, who had stepped down to the rear of the van behind the rest of them, thrust his bald head into it.

"It was as I told you?" he called.

"It was as you told us," said a voice from inside.

Then the back doors slammed and the van drove unobtrusively off.

Gilzai Khan remounted the steps, took the stupefied Peter by the arm, and walked him away down the drive.

"And now, my dear Peter," said the Khan, using the Christian name for the first time, "we will go to see the Commandant. Later you will eat with me, and then we shall return to the camp together tomorrow morning."

"I think I'm supposed to stay in Bangalore."

"No need, not now."

"I don't understand, Gil' Khan."

"By and by," said the Khan, "it will all be made very plain."

"You're lucky, Mr Morrison," the Commandant said some hours later. "The cloak and dagger boys have got a quarrel with that slut of yours, so *she* won't be shouting the odds any longer."

"Do you mean, sir . . . they're going to charge her with something?"

"Not charge her," said Gilzai Khan; "do a deal with her. Her offence is not really serious as such offences go. It will be enough if she will undertake to leave Mysore State and not to reside within twenty-five miles of any military cantonment or establishment."

The Commandant took up the reins and spurred his chair-leg.

"She's been warned off the course," he said. "Provided she stays off, no one will trouble her. But just let her stick the tip of her nose back into the ring . . . leave alone start pestering me with complaints about my Cadets . . . and she'll go down till Domesday."

"But what is her offence, sir? Trying to blackmail me?"

"No. So far as that went she had a pretty good board, as I told you. She was sure of native support, for one thing. But now she's done something else which will make the Indians drop her flat."

"What, sir?"

"I don't understand the ins and outs, but according to the chappies who flushed her out today she's been running a cloak and dagger racket of her own."

"Surely the Indians will approve of that?"

"No. She doesn't seem to be connected with any of the Indian movements – so that means she's been doing it just for the cash. Her game was papers and passports – that sort of thing – which might have been very useful to them. But she was just pulling in the mangoes on her tod. In short, she's been unpatriotic, as they'll see it, and her a half-caste anyhow, so they'll leave her to rot."

"But if she's been selling passports and so on, sir, she'll surely go to prison as well?"

"It seems the evidence isn't very ample. Our people in that line would sooner do a deal than throw the lawbooks at her. Captain Khan knows more than I do, so ask him."

Gilzai Khan, standing just behind Peter, chuckled lightly.

"And meanwhile," the Commandant said by way of peroration, "all this gets you off the hook. So thank your stars, young Morrison, and don't go gobbling the first juicy fly that floats along the water, because next time you may get reeled in and gaffed in the guts for good."

"You are no doubt thinking," said Gilzai Khan to Peter (in a curry kitchen, out of bounds to all ranks, to which he had taken Peter for dinner), "that the unmasking of Miss Engineer has been most opportune. I have reason for wishing you to know rather more about it."

"I'm not sure I want to."

"It will be good for you, huzoor. For some people – like our beloved Commandant – it is good that they should know only what suits them. They do not appreciate life's ironies and would only be perturbed by them. However, in you I think we have a genuine student of human folly, and as one such student to another I shall be happy to tell you certain things which I know and the Commandant does not. Try this chutney: it contains an interesting spice based on the seed of the poppy."

"Would that be sensible?"

"For you, yes, because you are a stable man and firm of purpose. In the same way, this knowledge I shall now impart is safe with you but would not be with all men. Now, huzoor, as I say: there are some things the Commandant does know and some he does not. What he does know is that a certain document was found in Miss Engineer's apartment, and that this has created a strong suspicion that she was trafficking in military and other identification papers. Since the evidence is scanty, however, the authorities are prepared to waive prosecution on condition she goes away and, as you would say, keeps her nose clean. 'You stick to being a whore,' they will tell her, 'and we will all love you. But no more documents, if you please, and keep your pretty fingers off the soldiers. And now, Miss Engineer, you may show us how grateful you are to us before you depart.' That is how it will be with her. Have some more of the pilau, Peter, and another stuffed paratha with this sauce."

"Thank you, Gil' Khan."

"All this, the Commandant knows. He also knows, though

he did not see fit to tell you, that the document that was found was Lord Muscateer's Part One Pay Book—"

"—Good lord. I never thought that Muscateer—"

"—Which," continued the Khan, "since Part One Pay Books carry no photographs, could serve someone for a short time as a very useful means of identification. A small thing really, and not worth much, but if Miss Engineer could steal pay books, she could also steal Officers' Identity Cards and whichever; and hence it has been deduced that she was running a market in such things. Deduced but not really proven; and herself not arraigned but simply removed."

"Sergeant-Major Cruxtable has been going mad looking for that Pay Book. He says Muscateer won't be officially dead till it's found."

"Well, now it is found, and the Muscateer bahadur can sleep in official peace."

"But look here, Gil' Khan. Muscateer went into hospital only a day or two after we got here. He *couldn't* have been with Margaret Rose."

"He *could* have been, huzoor. In that first day or two."

"She was one of Ley Wong's girls. Muscateer didn't meet Ley Wong until two hours before he was taken ill."

"That," said the Khan, "is one of the things the Commandant does not know. Another thing he does not know – and neither do those perspicacious gentlemen from the Special Branch – is that I myself, as you would say, planted Lord Muscateer's Pay Book."

Gilzai Khan paused for this to sink in.

"When the bahadur was ill," he went on, "I was with him one morning, and he said to me, 'Gilzai Khan, I am much troubled, I have lost my Part One Pay Book, and they keep asking for it.' 'Very well,' I said, 'I will look for it in your basha.' I looked for it and I found it – in the middle of the bahadur's Holy Bible, a present from the Begum his mother. But before I could give it to him he was dead, and in my sorrow I thought of other things than his Pay Book.

"But then, my dear Peter . . . when I heard from Captain Detterling at the Camp about your trouble . . . I remembered.

So I came back to Bangalore on the ration truck early this morning, and I took the Pay Book, and I presented myself as a client to Miss Engineer, with whom I had much jolly pleasure. But when she leaves the room to put the money which I give her in a safe place, I open a drawer and pop in the Pay Book – and later I go to the authorities to tell them that I have suspicions of Miss Engineer. They come to search – and in ten minutes it is all finished, as you saw. Tell me, my friend: was this not well done?"

Gilzai Khan looked like a boastful ten year old.

"You did it for me?" said Peter slowly.

"For you, and for your friend Mortleman, who is now my friend, and for your friend, the little Strange, who . . . who is also my friend. They would be sad if you were to leave them now. And I, Morrison huzoor, if you were to leave me."

"I was going . . . to beg her to stop what she was doing to me. She might have listened, perhaps."

"No. She is hard, that one. She is frigid, did you know?"

"But I always found . . . strong signs of response."

"So did I. Faked, huzoor. A little olive oil, clever use of the muscles and the voice while pretending to orgasm. 'Oh, he is spurting inside me,'" Gilzai Khan mimicked in a high voice, "'he spurts so beautiful that I shall die of it.' Well done and worth the money, huzoor: nevertheless, faked."

"You're sure?"

"Of course. If she came like that – really came – with all of her clients, she'd be dead before the sun went down."

"I thought . . . that it was only for me."

"You were meant to think that. Did she teach you to make love like the dogs do it?"

"Ye-e-es."

"Well," said Gilzai Khan, "you should have lifted your leg and pissed down her lying throat."


Peter had missed the better part of two days at Jungle Camp by the time he arrived back there with Gilzai Khan, and as far as that went he was not at all sorry. While he was away, he now heard, there had been more forced marches and almost continual deprivation. Both Barry and Alister had strange, lean looks on their faces, as if they had just joined a religious sect and were obsessed with their own new-found righteousness. It was plain that they regarded Peter, however irrationally, as a deserter; and the account which he gave of his absence (a prosaic story about personal documents which had gone astray in Delhi and needed immediate renewal and signature) did nothing to diminish their contempt. Gilzai Khan's defection had also been marked, and he too was coldly received.

But by the end of the eighth day, during which No. 2 Pl. stormed a derelict temple and Wanker Murphy had his thigh broken by falling masonry, good humour had been restored all round. Murphy's misfortune made everyone feel even more manly than before; and the inconvenience of having to carry him back to camp on a stretcher was largely borne by Peter and the Khan, whose popularity revived in consequence. On the ninth day they swam across a reservoir in battle order, cut their way through ten miles of trackless bush, and climbed from inside a ravine to attack a position from the rear; and on the tenth and last day they erected an *ad hoc* jungle fortress big enough to hold a Company and then burnt it down by way of celebration. In their own minds (thought Peter sadly) they were now lords of the jungle.

But when they arrived back in Bangalore late on the day after, loud and swaggering as Mohocks, the pride of No. 2 Pl. was instantly brought to the dust. Their leader, they learned, was to be taken : Gilzai Khan was dismissed the O.T.S.

"But *why*, sir ?"

"He's broken the rules," Captain Detterling said : "an Indian can't get away with that."

"What rules ?" Peter asked.

"Regulation Safety Precautions for Use of Live Ammunition from Automatic Weapons during Training on Assault Courses.

He neglected to fire on a fixed line, and sprayed bullets under your noses."

"That was *weeks* ago."

"Another thing," Captain Detterling said: "his political attitudes – i.e. pro-British – are not considered suitable."

*"What?"*

"I mean it. The Labour Government wants to hand this country over to the Indians, and the Indians can't wait to get hold of it. So the correct attitude for a King's Indian Officer just now is friendly obedience to the British, qualified by determination to be independent as soon as it's feasible; *not* feudal loyalty, openly proclaimed, to the Crown. It's been decided that his appointment here was a mistake."

"Decided by whom?"

"In one word, Delhi."

"Even so, sir, we might have been told more tactfully. Why was it all so sudden? We get back from Jungle Camp, and hardly has Gil' Khan got out of his truck when he's hustled away to the Commandant. And five minutes later the news is all round the bashas. That's no way to treat a good man – even if his politics are out of the fashion."

"My dear fellow, I entirely agree. But there is something else."

They've found out what he did for me, Peter thought, and trembled at the backs of his knees.

"This man Murphy, who was broken up at camp. He was brought into the hospital here delirious. The Matron reported that he was . . . babbling about an orgy at Ley Wong's."

"Oh?"

"Yes. But of course nobody believed *that* story."

"Of course not."

"The trouble was, Murphy was also carrying on about Gilzai Khan and one of the Cadets. He wasn't very clear, but it seems he wanted to own up to spotting 'em through a window one afternoon and tossing himself off while he watched. He thought he was dying, you see."

"And that story they do believe?"

"Yes. The Commandant's very old-fashioned about what he

calls 'the vices of Sodom'. Hence his lack of ceremony with the Khan."

"Did Murphy name the Cadet?"

"No. And now that he's come to his senses he denies the whole thing."

Peter gave a snort of relief.

"Which means," said Detterling, "that the Cadet's in the clear, whoever *he* may be. But Murphy was plain enough about the Khan, whatever else, so there's an end of him."

"He'll have to leave the Army?"

"No – or not for the time being. It's clear that Murphy's not going to tell the tale a second time, and anyhow they don't want a scandal of that kind. So the official reason they'll give for relieving the Khan of his job here will be that business on the Assault Course – which will look much better in the book. But if it were only that . . . that and his politics . . . they'd have let him stay till you all passed out, which would have looked better still."

"When does he go?"

"Day after tomorrow."

"We must give him a dinner – say good-bye."

"The Commandant won't like it."

"It will . . . 'look much better'."

"Yes," said Detterling. "Yes, I think we can get the Commandant to see it like that. I'll promise him that I'll be there to make sure there are no vices of Sodom."

So once again they all assembled at Ley Wong's. Although the feast provided was not quite as elaborate as that with which they had celebrated the obsequies of Muscateer, it was quite splendid enough. Ley Wong had proposed that he should serve the classical Chinese fare which friends offered to one who was going into long exile, and the suggestion had been judged apt. Exile, it appeared, warranted only twenty-three courses, as compared to the thirty-five which they had consumed in honour of the dead; but as Captain Detterling observed, on that occasion the bill had gone to Lord Canteloupe (who had paid without demur and by return of post), whereas this time they must foot it themselves.

And quite apart from the food and drink, there was another substantial item of expense. After dinner had been eaten but while the wine was still plentiful, Barry Strange left the room and returned with Gilzai Khan's black Sam Browne belt. This he buckled on to the Khan, after which he invited him to stand. Peter Morrison now came forward, bearing a sheathed Light Infantry sword, which he fastened into Gilzai Khan's empty sword-frog, kneeling in the manner of a 'squire.

"To show gratitude," he said, "and to pay honour. Go well, Gilzai Khan."

"Go well," chorused the Cadets, raising their glasses to drink : "go well, Gilzai Khan."

Gilzai Khan grinned like a fiend. He stepped up on to his chair and thence on to the table. Then he drew his new sword, kissed the hilt and brought it to the carry, raised the hilt to his lips to kiss it once again, and dipped the point in salute.

"Stay well," he said, his voice cracking very slightly : "stay well, my children . . . my brothers . . . my Cadets."

# PART THREE

# THE YOUNG KNIGHTS

DOWN THE STEPS from the rostrum on the saluting base came the Right Honourable Edwin Turbot, M.P., late Minister for Public Order in the wartime coalition Government, now the Conservative third of a three-man all-party Parliamentary fact-finding mission to British India. Having quit the steps for *terra firma*, the ex-Minister thrust his rump out behind him, as if inviting the Commandant in his immediate rear to commit a carnal act, clasped his hands over the shaft of his buttocks to make sure that nothing of the kind in fact occurred, and set off at a brisk shuffle to review the ranks of Officer Cadets.

Passing Out Parades at Bangalore were normally presided over by General Officers or distinguished members of the Indian Administration. On this occasion, however, since the local prestige of the Raj was insecure to say the least of it and since riots were threatening for one reason or another in every corner of Mysore State, it had been felt that discretion was more requisite than ceremony, and that such discretion might be combined with propriety by inviting one of the three M.P.s from the fact-finding mission (which was associated in the Indian mind with arrangements for Independence) to inspect the parade and take the salute. The Labour M.P., who had been approached first both as a member of the ruling party and as the dowdiest and therefore most suitable of the trio, had declined to take part in any military function; the Liberal M.P. had shown altogether too much interest in the whole affair; and so the job had fallen at last to Edwin Turbot, who was an old hand at this sort of game but who, it was feared, might lend rather too grand (or even imperial) an air to the proceedings.

Although the ex-Minister had been dissuaded from dressing in a frock coat and had eventually been coaxed into an appropriate suit of dark grey flannel, now that he was out in front of the parade he was beyond any man's control and intended to give himself full value. Later on he would be making a speech; just now he was face to face with the Cadets at close quarters and he was determined they should know it. None of this sneaking down the line with a neutral simper aimed over everybody's head – not for the Right Honourable Edwin Turbot.

"You there," he barked at the third Cadet he came to; "who won the Battle of Plassey?"

"Clive, sir," said the Cadet, who luckily belonged to one of the Grammar School platoons and so had a working acquaintance with history.

I hope, thought Peter Morrison, who as J.U.O. was standing out in front of No. 2 Pl. C Coy, that he's not going to ask my lot that kind of question. Nor did he; Edwin Turbot recognised proper gentlemen when he saw them and was too much of one himself to take advantage of their predictable lack of common knowledge. In any case, he had more important questions for *this* particular class of young officer.

"These rows with the natives," he said to Peter : "have they taught you how to cope with them?"

"We have been trained in Duties in Aid of the Civil Power," Peter said, and followed Turbot along the front rank of No. 2 Pl.

"Ump," said the ex-Minister, and stopped in front of Barry. "You're Barry Strange," he said.

"Sir."

"How's your father?"

"Well, thank you, sir, when last I heard."

"And your brothers?"

"Dead, sir."

"Ump," said Turbot lightly. "Lucky thing your mother's still got you. . . . Duties in Aid of the Civil Power," he resumed to Peter as they passed on, "and what do you" – to Zaccharias – "understand by *those*?"

"Keeping order, sir."

"Yes. I know a thing or two about that. Easy in England –

so far, that is – because the lower classes have always been a pretty decent lot. But the point is" – this over his shoulder to the Commandant – "what do you teach these boys here?"

"To keep their heads," said the Commandant, giving a sharp tug on the reins, "when things get rough."

"And have *you*," said Turbot to Zaccharias, "been taught to keep your head?"

"Yes, sir, of course, sir," said Zaccharias with a giggle.

"Ump," said Edwin Turbot, and shuffled on to the next platoon.

But of course, reflected Peter, as he saluted and went back to his station, keeping one's head was something which one could only learn by experience, and none of them had had so much as five seconds of that. What the Commandant presumably meant was that they had all been instructed in the set procedure which, if they followed it exactly, would guarantee that no one could blame them for anything later on. The great thing (as Gilzai Khan's dull but decent successor had repeated to them every five minutes in all three of their 'Action in Aid' periods) was that an Officer must never order his men to fire on a mob unless requested to do so by a Magistrate or equivalent representative of the Civil Power; and that even after such a request had been received, an Officer should still not give a fire order until the request had been put into writing and the Magistrate induced to sign it. For it appeared that panicky officials (of whatever colour) were apt to urge the use of bullets and then deny, at all subsequent Enquiries, that they had done so, thus leaving the military commander to sink in the quagmires of shit into which the least drop of spilt blood was always transformed by the politicians.

'And as we all know,' Gil' Khan's successor had said, 'Labour politicians are particularly adept at doing this and particularly keen on it. If you want to lose your commission, the fastest way I know is to scratch an Indian. He may be an escaped murderer, and leading a mob which has already sacked every town from Karachi to Cape Cormorin, but you just touch him – without a Magistrate's signature – and every socialist in Westminster will be squealing for your head.'

All right, thought Peter now, as he watched Edwin Turbot mount the rostrum and take out the notes for his address; so far it's simple; get a signature before you shoot, and even the politicians can't touch you; but what about the Furies, the avengers of crime against brotherhood do *they* respect the contract?

"For all of you," said Edwin Turbot in a mellow, effortless voice which carried easily over the parade ground, "this is a very great day: certainly the greatest in your young lives so far, and possibly the greatest which you will ever know. For you are receiving the King's Commission. You are being entrusted with the care and command of His Majesty's soldiers – and more than this: there is a sense in which you are being dubbed as knights. These days, of course, titular knighthoods go only to old men, most of whom have served their sovereign at the desk rather than on the battle field – many of whom, indeed, have done nothing more than present large sums of money to approved causes. But there was a time when knighthoods went to the young – to the young, the pure and the brave, who took a vow to fear God, honour their liege lords and where possible to exercise their skill and chivalry in aid of the weak, the poor and the oppressed.

"As it happens," Turbot went on, his tone shifting from the exhortative to the confidential, "there are plenty of such people around you here." He smiled in embarrassment and apology, like the headmaster of a preparatory school about to explain the facts of life of those leaving that term. "Despite many years of British rule, this is still a corrupt and superstitious country, in which peasants are strangled by moneylenders, priests obstruct necessary social reform in the name of unspeakable gods, and smooth-tongued native politicians urge the innocent to revolt in order that they may the more savagely exploit them after we, their British protectors, have gone."

The Commandant stirred uneasily, hoping that no Indian reporters were present. Edwin Turbot smiled even more apologetically than before (the headmaster now explaining to his leavers that certain older boys would try to touch their 'parts' and that this must on no account be permitted) and started to mix a well-practised huskiness into his otherwise bland speech-making voice.

"The result is that there is and will be riot and bloodshed, for which you will be blamed and which, at the same time, you will be relied upon to prevent. In such circumstances, there is one overwhelming temptation to which you must never succumb. I refer, of course, to that weakness which is sometimes called 'pity' or 'compassion' : being sorry for the poor misguided rioters, among whom there will be many young men of your own age and even little children, you may feel an impulse of mercy, you may, in a fatal moment of softness, wish to give in, to hold your hand, to put by the rod of justice which is yours to wield. If you do, you are lost. You will be failing those poor wretches of rioters, the very people to whom you owe your knightly aid – which should be given in the form of a short, sharp, memorable lesson that will teach them, in their own interest, to desist."

Dear God, thought Peter, rocking back and forth on his toes to prevent himself from feeling dizzy : how much longer will he keep us? Has no one told him that 99 per cent of those who stand here are starting tomorrow morning for Bombay and the boat back home? That only three of us out of 300 will ever come near a riot? And if someone has told him, thought Peter, light-headed in the blazing sun, has he nevertheless decided to give this lecture just for those three? Just for those three – aye, there's the rub. . . .

'You'll be glad to know,' Captain Detterling had said to Peter a few days earlier, 'that the three of you will be staying together.'

'In the Wessex Fusiliers, sir ?'

'That's right. Strange always had them down as first choice. As for you and Mortleman, the Rifle Brigade won't touch Mortleman, because his father's a bad lot, and the Indian Army won't touch you because you're white. So since both of you named the Wessex Fusiliers on those forms you had, there it is.'

'But the Wessex Fusiliers must know we both really wanted something else. Didn't they resent that? I mean, some regiments have to take what they can get, but the Wessex Fusiliers are rather grand.'

'In their middle-class way, yes,' said Detterling. 'Quite grand enough to pick and choose rather than be picked and chosen. In fact, I think they'd have turned you and Mortleman down if it hadn't been for one thing.'

'Oh?'

'Barry Strange wrote to the Colonel of the Regiment and said you were his friends.'

'Rather bold for a Cadet?'

'They know him there, you see . . .

> You come here where your brothers came,
> To the old school years ago . . .

. . . That kind of thing. One quite sees why they're a good regiment – *in* their middle-class way.'

'Well, sir, thank you for telling me.'

'That's not quite all. You're staying out here – all three of you.'

'But . . . the whole lot of us are going home.'

'Except the three of you. There's a Battalion of the Wessex Fusiliers at Berhampore. The First.'

'There are British Battalions all over India,' said Peter, refusing to believe, 'but they said that none of us was going to them. They *said* we were all going home.'

'And now I'm *saying* that Strange and Mortleman and you are staying out here. Just before the First Wessex moved to Berhampore, something went wrong with the water in the Officers' Mess and seven of 'em died of cholera. So they're very short and they've asked Delhi to let them have you.'

'That's all very well, sir. But I was *told* I was going home, I was looking forward to going h—'

'—Oh, for God's sake stop whining,' Detterling had said. 'What would they think of you – and of Strange's letter to the Colonel – if they could hear you now?'

'I'm sorry, sir.'

'I'm afraid you're going to be even sorrier. The Wessex Fusiliers,' Detterling went on thoughtfully, '*are* a good regiment, they're dead loyal to their own people, and they'd sooner burn in Hades than show their backs. But . . .'

'But what?'

'You know what Wellington said of them? "The steadiest Officers in England – and the dullest in Europe." Something like that.'

But at least, Peter thought now, they couldn't be as dull as the Right Honourable Edwin Turbot, who was at last (thank God) winding up.

"You may think," said Turbot, "that it has been rather odd of me to say so much about your duties in Aid of the Civil Power, when most of you, as I understand it, are going home to England very shortly. But let me put it to you like this. Even back in England the times are . . . peculiar. Certain classes of people have expected a great deal of a new popular Government, and have been, inevitably, disappointed. They are going to go on being disappointed until they learn that even popular Governments cannot perform miracles. Meanwhile, suppose, just suppose, that discontent were to give rise to widespread strikes – a National Strike perhaps – with the serious civil disorder that might well be concomitant? I think you take my point, gentlemen. Not the least duty of a knight at arms is to defend his own hearth against the lawless . . . whether they come from without or within. What I have said today, about dealing with riots in this country, can be applied, *mutatis mutandis*, to events which might occur considerably nearer home."

You cunning old bugger, Peter thought, keeping the sting in the tail. Well, if I've got to shoot civilians, I'd sooner shoot brown ones than white, and that's all about that. So perhaps it's as well that I'm staying in India after all. Not that it could ever come to shooting in England . . . *or could it*?

But this train of speculation was now interrupted by commands in preparation for the March Past. The Cadets would march past, in Column of Platoons . . . by the *right*, wham, tampity bam, and slam into Old Towler. Away they marched at a sharp light infantry pace to the end of the parade ground, where they wheeled and wheeled again to march back past

Edwin Turbot, who raised his hat in response to the 'Eyes Right' and let fall a tiny tear (which nobody saw) as he thought how soon these clean bright limbs would be shrunk to skin and gristle, and that of these 300 lovely paladins not one would be alive in ninety years. But the young knights themselves were discommoded by no such reflections; for in a few minutes they would put on for the first time the emblems of authority, and a man who dons a new uniform has ever thought himself immortal. The time had come at last to gird themselves in new splendour, to sit in glory and drink deep.

Most of them, of course, drank much too deep, and on the morning after it was rather a sorry crowd of new Officers that boarded the train at Bangalore Station, bound for the boat at Bombay. Peter, Alister and Barry, who were not leaving for Berhampore until the next day, were there to see them off.

"It's too bad," Second Lieutenant Zaccharias complained to them on the platform : "they're making us travel just like when we came here. Like cattle in so many trucks."

"When you're moving 300 people all together," Peter explained rather heavily, "you can't afford to pamper them."

"You should have proper respect for their rank."

"Where everyone has the same rank, nobody has any rank," said Alister contentiously : "moving 300 subalterns is the same as moving 300 sepoys. If you all had Wagon Lits, the train would stretch from here to Poona."

"No one said anything about Wagon Lits," grizzled Zaccharias : "all I want is the respect which is due to me as an Officer."

"You're not an Officer yet," said Barry, "not a real one. You won't be that until you're doing an Officer's job in a proper unit."

"That's right," said Alister; "for the time being you're just cargo."

"Well, at least," said Zaccharias spitefully, "the cargo's going home." He shoved a beggar out of the way with the flat of his foot and moved off to join the queue of disgruntled

Second Lieutenants who were slowly filing into the nearest coach. "Go and see poor old Murphy in hospital before you go," he called back to Peter, "and tell him not to beat his meat to pieces before they let him out."

Peter, Barry and Alister stood and watched as the row of new-dubbed knights, sweaty and twitching with crapula, crept past them and into the train.

"Good-bye, Julian . . . good-bye, George . . ."

The metal crests above the vizors glittered in the sun, the Sphinx, the Bugle Horn, the Cross of Malta; Britannia and the Castle and the Lamb. "Good-bye, Jimmy . . . good luck, Monty . . . happy days, Jeremy . . . see you, Paul . . ."

"What are you three doing, hanging about? Get in the queue, will you."

This from an unknown R.S.M. accompanying an unknown Captain who was commanding the train to Bombay.

"We're seeing our friends off, Sergeant-Major."

"I am an R.S.M. You don't call *me* plain Sergeant-Major."

"I am an Officer. You call *me* 'sir'."

"Then stop cluttering up this platform, *sir*."

"We shall stay here as long as we please, *Regimental Sergeant-Major*."

"I am speaking, sir, for the Officer i/c Train."

"For Christ's *sake*," said the Officer i/c Train and shambled on up the platform.

The R.S.M. pranced about at his heels.

"Must keep a tidy platform, sir."

"For Christ's *sake*, R.S.M. Clapham. Too early in the morning."

The Harp of Ulster, the Rose of Lancaster, the Horse of Kent. "Good-bye, Nicholas . . . good-bye, Sandy . . . keep it clean, Oscar . . ." The Crown of Cornwall and the Plume of Wales.

"Good-bye. Good-bye. Good-bye."

And then the train was gone and the platform was empty, except for several hundred Indians, who were sleeping in neat rows, and for Sergeant-Major Cruxtable, who was still waving down the line.

"Lonely, now they're all gone," said Cruxtable, as he turned towards the three who were left.

"Yes,' said Peter. All four looked at each other with drooping mouths.

"Zaccharias was right," said Barry, breaking the long silence : "we must go and see Murphy before we leave."

"I'm going that way too, gentlemen," said Cruxtable; "I've got some documents for him to sign."

They picked their way out of the station.

"What will happen to Murphy?" asked Alister. "Has he been commissioned like the rest of us?"

"He has been, sir," said Cruxtable, "and then he hasn't."

"Well, which?"

"He's been in hospital ever since Jungle Camp," the Sergeant-Major explained patiently, "so he's missed too much training to be commissioned with the rest of you gentlemen. By rights, he ought to be back-squadded to another company when he comes out and finish his training with them."

"But there's only Indians left here."

"Precisely, sir. He can't go in with them but equally he can't pass out with you, and then again he can't stay in hospital as a Cadet because official as from yesterday there are no white Cadets on strength in this station. It'd be unfair to bust him down to Private, and he wouldn't do as a Sergeant, so he's been posted across – on paper – to the Education Corps, on the ground he's passed his School Certificate in French and Scripture, and it just so happens the Education Corps has a vacancy for one Officer in their establishment at Delhi. Now, Captain Murphy's done enough basic officer training for *that* mob, so—"

"—*Captain* Murphy?"

"Yes, sir," said Cruxtable with grim amusement. "The vacancy carries an acting Captaincy. Odd how things turn out."

But Acting Captain Murphy, whose thigh was still in plaster, was not a happy man. "I sometimes think I'm going to be lying here for ever," he whined, while Cruxtable fussed about arranging the documents.

"Zaccharias says you're not to beat your meat," said Alister.

"That's no way to talk to your superior."

"As Regimental Officers," said Barry, "we are not accountable to Captains in the Education Corps. If you and I were washed up on a desert island, *I* should be in command of us both."

"But *I* should be drawing a Captain's screw."

"Not yet you're not, sir, anyway," said Cruxtable, giving Murphy a pen and a pile of papers. "You can call yourself 'Captain' but you don't start drawing the money till you get to Delhi."

"What's the use?" moaned Murphy. "I'll be here at least another month. You three are going away tomorrow. There's no one left at the O.T.S. but blacks. There'll be no one to come and see me except C.S.M. Cruxtable—"

"—And not even him in a week or so," said Cruxtable gently, "but I'll make sure the local padre remembers you're here."

"Oh, fuck the padre. Everyone's leaving. And for the last month the staff in here has been changing every day. Very soon now no one will even know who I am. Don't you see?" Murphy concentrated his features as if making some abnormal mental effort. "A man only has an identity," he said slowly, "if he's among people who recognise him . . . who can vouch for who and what he is. When everyone who knows me has left Bangalore, I might be anyone at all."

"You sign them papers," said Cruxtable soothingly, "and you'll get written order from Delhi in good time. They'll say exactly who and what you are."

"*If* they ever get to me. I can't receive written orders unless someone knows that I'm the person they're meant for . . . or unless I can prove it. Now," said Murphy in shrill accusation, "have you got an Officer's Identity Card for me?"

" 'Fraid not, sir. You're a special case. Your Officer's Identity Card will come from Delhi with your orders."

"There you are, you see. Until I get it I'm nobody, and as long as I'm nobody I can't possibly get it."

From the looks on their faces, Alister and Barry were thinking that Murphy was making a silly fuss. Peter was not so sure, and neither, he fancied, was Cruxtable, for all his reassuring words.

Although Murphy was not the brightest of men, he had clearly examined his situation with some care, while lying in his distressful bed, and somehow he had hit upon an important truth : that it was no good a man's knowing who he was unless other people knew it too. Leave aside the metaphysical questions which it raised, this truth had always been particularly applicable to official or military matters; better soldiers than Murphy had slipped through a crack in the floor, so to speak, and been left forgotten to rot beneath the boards. Cruxtable, Peter now thought, had probably sensed this uneasy factor in Murphy's predicament and sensed, moreover, that in the present fluid state of the Raj in India such a factor was more than usually liable to operate. But what could Cruxtable do about it? He was a Sergeant-Major whose job it was to fill in forms and collect signatures. No one would thank him to interfere further. So it was up to him, Peter, as a commissioned Officer, to make sure that Murphy's fears were allayed and his affairs put on a sound footing.

"I'll see Detterling about it," he said to Murphy.

"Captain Detterling's off, sir. In three days' time, to Delhi."

"Then he can put in a word there. He can make sure that everyone concerned knows exactly how Mr – er, Captain Murphy is placed down here."

Murphy brightened a little. Cruxtable shook his head gloomily, thereby admitting that his smooth bedside manner of minutes before had been fraudulent, and collected up the signed documents. They all said Good-bye to Murphy and trooped down the empty ward. Looking back to wave from the door, Peter observed that Captain Murphy was already beating his meat under the bed-clothes.

Outside the hospital they met Captain Detterling, who, he told them, had been there to sign a certificate which exonerated the hospital staff from any blame for losing Lord Muscateer's Part One Pay Book.

"Why worry, now it's been found?" said Peter.

"They always like to find out just who it was that lost things in the first place," Cruxtable told him.

"Murphy's afraid they're going to lose *him*," said Peter to Detterling. "I've promised him you'd see things straight in Delhi."

"Oh, yes," said Detterling easily. "But of course it's a long way . . . these days . . . between here and Delhi."

Cruxtable sniffed audibly, as if to observe that fate would take its course despite all human intervention.

"Well, at least *you* lot have got your orders signed and sealed," he said. "Look in at the office this afternoon to say good-bye, and I'll give you your railway warrants for to-morrow."

He saluted Detterling and waddled off.

"Where will he go from here?" asked Alister.

"Regimental stores somewhere," said Detterling, "or a desk in an Orderly Room. I see him next to a huge stove, full of red hot coke, drinking endless mugs of thick, sweet tea."

"Not in India surely?"

"Metaphorically," said Detterling, "men like Cruxtable take their stoves and their mugs of tea with them wherever they go, much as wandering players carry their props. The stove is the symbol and the centre of Cruxtable's entire way of life – or any other old soldier's. And talking of old soldiers, I have news of a friend of ours. Gilzai Khan."

Barry shuffled his feet about. Alister looked up with interest and affection. Peter smiled rather daintily. A squad of Sikh Cadets marched past them and gave them an 'Eyes Right'. Although the movement was punctiliously executed, it was somehow an accusation rather than a courtesy, reminding them all that their time was running out and that in a few days, even a few hours, they would no longer have the right to loiter on this ground. So they began walking slowly towards the Commandant's Headquarters, where, after all, they might still be acknowledged to have some business; but as they walked unfamiliar orders given in unfamiliar accents came to them from the parade ground, declaring that this was now an alien place. Crowded but empty, Peter thought; empty of all

that for us has made it both school and home for the last sixteen weeks. As far as we four are concerned the O.T.S. is now
as deserted as if grass were already growing through the floors
of our bashas and jungle weeds were creeping along the
verandahs.

"So what news, sir," he said at last, "what news of Gilzai
Khan?"

"He's resigned his commission."

"Because . . . because of what happened here?"

"On the face of it, one must suppose so. But there's something very odd about it all."

"I'm sure," said Barry, "that whatever Gilzai Khan has done
is as plain and honest as the day."

"Hear, hear," Alister said.

"Well, you're both wrong," said Detterling, his voice crackling with irritation. "When he left here he went to his Regimental Depot up in the North and was given a job training
recruits. Not exactly what one would have expected after
everything that went on here" – he glanced with a mixture of
malice and apology at the blushing Barry – "but then the
Indian Army, just like the British, is notorious for repeating its
mistakes. Anyhow, after a month or so all was going quite well
– when suddenly he formed up, out of the blue, and said he
wanted to resign immediately. And it turned out that because
of his age and the terms of his engagement and one thing and
another they'd have to let him do just that. They couldn't even
make him stay till he'd finished training his current intake of
recruits."

"How do you know all this, sir?" Peter asked.

"Giles Glastonbury has been taking an interest . . . for this
reason and that."

"What reason?" said Barry.

Detterling shrugged this to one side, implying with a quick
twist of his mouth that men of the world must answer some
questions for themselves.

"According to the letter I had from Giles this morning," he
went on, "they begged Gilzai Khan to stay on till they could
find a replacement, but he just wouldn't listen. He wanted to

go, and he was entitled to go, and he was going – there and then. Now what strikes any of you as being peculiar about all this?"

"Gil' Khan was a loyal man," said Peter, "who loved the Army and his Regiment. You'd think he'd agree to waive his rights and help them out for a few weeks more."

"Exactly. And come to that, why resign at all? He has no other life, and if the Indian Army was prepared to keep him on after the row here—"

"—Was it prepared to keep him on?"

"Giles says yes. Strictly speaking, a decision still had to be taken at the time the Khan resigned, but it was pretty certain that he was going to be forgiven – or at any rate pardoned – and so he had already been told. Officers like Gilzai Khan don't grow on bushes."

"So he couldn't have been resigning in order to get out before he was kicked out?"

"It seems not."

"Perhaps," said Barry, "he didn't like the idea of being 'pardoned'?"

"Then why wait as long as he did? He'd known the form for weeks and was apparently quite happy. Then he's into the Colonel's office like a jack-in-the-box one morning, and waving them all good-bye three days later. Only he didn't even wave them good-bye. As soon as his papers were stamped he vanished without a word. And this from his Regimental H.Q., remember. There were men there he'd known for over twenty years, and he didn't even bother to say good-bye."

"But this is dreadful," said Barry. "He always set such store by proper good-byes. Even if it was just for a few hours—" He broke off in some confusion. "I mean, something must have been terribly wrong," he said. "But whatever could it have been?"

" 'What song the Sirens sang,' " Detterling said, " 'or what name Achilles assumed when he hid himself among women, though puzzling questions, are not beyond all conjecture.' I'll be seeing Giles in a few days, and I'll let you know if there's anything new. Good-bye for now, chums," he said, abruptly but pleasantly. "I'll hope to see you some time in Berhampore. It's not that far from Delhi."

"Good-bye, sir . . ."

"You shouldn't call me 'sir' any more."

He shook hands with the three of them and then walked away down the avenue which led to the Commandant's office. Indian Cadets saluted him as he went, and he returned their salutes; but they did not look at his face, nor he at theirs.

"Now," said the Senior Subaltern, "repeat after me: 'I, Peter Morrison, do most faithfully swear, on this drum and by my blood . . .' "

"I, Peter Morrison, do most faithfully swear, on this drum and by my blood . . ."

" '. . . That this regiment shall be my house . . .' "

". . . That this regiment shall be my house . . ."

" '. . . That its sons shall be my brothers . . .' "

". . . That its sons shall be my brothers . . ."

" '. . . And that its honour shall be my honour to cherish and avenge. . . .' "

Peter was kneeling on his right knee and resting his right hand, palm upward, on the parchment of a corded drum. The Senior Subaltern, who was reading the oath from what looked like a small leather diary, knelt opposite him, also on one knee and on either side of the Senior Subaltern knelt the two Subalterns next in standing, both of them pointing bare swords at Peter's throat. To one side stood the Adjutant, in mounted dress, his sword sheathed; behind Peter were Barry and Alister, waiting their turn; and behind them again were all the Subaltern Officers of the First Battalion, the Wessex Fusiliers, who were there to bear witness.

" '. . . And this, I swear it by my blood . . .' "

The Subaltern on Peter's left shifted his point from Peter's throat and dipped it down and across to nick his palm. Peter turned his hand over and pressed his palm hard down on the parchment.

". . . And this, I swear it by my blood, on this drum do I

swear it, and by the souls of all those who have answered its call."

"I stand here for them," said the Adjutant, "and I am to tell you this. Now that your blood is on the drum, you must answer its call, as they did, to the death. From now until your dying day, if you receive word, written or spoken, that 'The drum is beaten', you are thereby summoned to return to it, wherever you may be and wherever it may be. And so now, for the first time : The drum is beaten, friend; the drum is in Berhampore."

"I have come to Berhampore," Peter said, "to answer the drum."

"He has come to Berhampore," said all the Subalterns together (except Barry and Alister), "to answer the drum. Come, friend, and stand among us."

Then Peter went to stand among his new comrades while Barry and Alister took the oath in their turn. After this the Adjutant led the Subalterns, with the newcomers at their head, through double doors and into a spacious dining room, which was almost filled by a table some forty yards long and ready laid for dinner. There was no cloth; the table was polished jet black; at the centre was a grotesque representation, nearly four feet high, of an Edwardian castle keep; and at the far end was a huge and triangular pile of drums, which made a kind of wigwam or canopy over the President's chair. Seated on this was the Lieutenant-Colonel Commanding and grouped about his wigwam were his Field Officers and Captains. Peter, Barry and Alister stood in a row at the bottom of the table and, "We have come to Berhampore," they shouted down its length, "to answer the drum."

"Then sit, friends, and eat," replied the Colonel, indicating that they and the Adjutant should occupy the four places nearest to him. At last, Peter felt, someone was showing a little common sense; but in fact they were not allowed to sit down until the invitation had been repeated to each one of them by each one of the Captains and Majors present, all of whom had to be personally assured that they had come to Berhampore to answer the drum.

Nor was the food up to much when they finally sat down to eat it. Although there was plenty of it, smoothly served by immaculate bearers, it was coarse in substance and unloved in the cooking; and as for the wine, it was beyond human charity.

"We usually drink beer," said the Adjutant to Peter, "but of course we make a special thing of it when we dine new fellows in. Sorry there's so little of the silver here – we had to pack it away for the duration."

"But you've got the centre-piece, I see," said Peter: "it's very ... remarkable."

"That, with the drums and this table, we take everywhere we go. It's a model of part of the Depot. Reminds us of home."

"What about the Colours? Haven't you brought them?"

"No. The drums serve much the same purpose and in war-time one must save space on troopships. By the way, Morrison," said the Adjutant shyly, "I think I should tell you that in this regiment the Adjutant, like the Field Officers, is addressed as 'sir' by subalterns, even off duty."

"As you say, sir."

"I know it's not the fashionable thing to do, but we have our own ways, you see."

The Adjutant, who was called Captain Thomas Oake, was an exceedingly nice man, Peter thought, and probably not a fool, but he did rather put one in mind of Wellington's remark, as quoted by Detterling, about the dullness of the Wessex Fusiliers. A quick look down the table now confirmed the Duke's apophthegm: the square, honest, weathered faces, all guzzling away as if this were the first and last meal of the month, gave little promise of wit or gaiety (though some promise of jollity, perhaps, which was another matter). Captain Oake's face differed from the rest in being slightly rhombic; no doubt it had once been square enough, but some accident of life or war had given its entire structure a right-handed slant, which endowed its owner with the look of a benevolent ghoul. As for the Colonel, who was called Brockworthy, his make and scale were massive; his capital block sat on his body block like a cornice on a very squat column. To such men as these, Peter reflected, his two friends and even himself must seem dainty to the point of decadence; and indeed the Colonel, between vast mouthfuls of meat and potato, was already directing some very suspicious looks at Alister.

"Interesting ceremony we've just been through," said Alister, pushing away a plate still two-thirds full; "but the thing is, Colonel, what do you do if someone doesn't turn up? When he's summoned by the drum, I mean."

"We obliterate his name, Mr Mortleman; he ceases to exist."

Alister took a draught of wine and winced energetically.

"But isn't that rather . . . unreal? Like those Jewish families who hold a funeral if one of their children marries a gentile."

"I am not well up in Jewish customs."

"Take it from me, Colonel, that's what they do. They behave as if the offending son or daughter were dead."

"Then there is no comparison between their behaviour and ours. We do not behave as if the offender was dead: we behave as if he had never existed."

The Colonel turned sharply from Alister to Barry Strange, whom he had known since Barry was in the nursery.

"Do you think," he said in a small, petulant voice which came oddly from such an exterior, "that we shall . . . understand Mortleman here? He seems rather big in the mouth."

"Nerves, sir," Barry said. "He always tries to impress new people. It's because of that he can't eat his dinner."

"Nerves, boy? This is not, you know, a nervous regiment."

"Not quite nerves, sir. Over-excitement."

"This is not an excitable regiment."

"Take my word for it," said Barry boldly: "Alister Mortleman is all right."

"We have taken your word for it, Strange; that's why he's here. Let's hope you weren't wrong about him, that's all. But I like the look of your other friend, Morrison; he seems so calm. A J.U.O. at Bangalore, I hear?"

"That's right, sir."

"And talking of Bangalore, Strange, there's some tale going round about an Indian you were friendly with."

"Our Platoon Commander. We all liked him."

"But he left very suddenly?"

"A mistake, sir. There was a bad mistake."

"So long as it wasn't yours, boy. I've known your family a very long time, and I should hate you to make a bad mistake."

"No one could be mistaken about Gilzai Khan."

"Ah, but you've just told me that someone was."

"Gilzai Khan himself, sir. He made the mistake of being too good for the place. He broke silly little rules and upset silly little men. And he made no secret of being pro-British. With politics as they are now, a pro-British Indian teaching British Cadets was bound to be inconvenient."

"Inconvenient to whom?"

"To Delhi, sir. It would annoy all the politicians both at home and in India, and they'd take it out on Delhi. So the Khan had to go, from Bangalore at any rate. He made the mistake of being the only honest man among a crew of jackals."

"I must say, Strange, you too seem to be getting a bit big in the mouth. In my day we never even mentioned such matters. Is that what Bangalore has done for you all?"

"Not Bangalore, sir. Just two officers – Gil' Khan and another one called Detterling. They enjoyed frank conversations."

"Detterling . . . Detterling . . . There's some story there, if only I could remember. A cavalryman, was he?"

"Yes, sir. Earl Hamilton's Light Dragoons."

"By God, yes. I've got it now."

"Got what, sir?"

"It's not a story for your ears, boy, though you'll hear it some day, I suppose." And then leaning forward, "Did you hear that, Oake?" called the Colonel to the Adjutant. "Detterling was instructing at Bangalore."

Captain Oake shook his rhombus in gentle deprecation.

"Understand this," the Colonel yapped next: "I'll thank you all to forget anything that Captain Detterling may have taught you." He turned on Alister like an inquisitor. "What have *you* got to say about Bangalore?" he asked.

While Alister was saying it, and the Colonel was not much liking it, and Barry was trying to hold the ring, Peter turned to Captain Oake.

"What's wrong with Detterling?" he inquired.

"Nothing was ever proved," said Oake, "so I'm not even going to hint at it. It might not be true, after all. The C.O. hates the cavalry and always believes the worst of them."

"Hates the cavalry . . . sir?"

"He thinks they're flashy and rich. This is a poor regiment, Morrison, as you've probably gathered already." Captain Oake searched his teeth with his tongue, as though seeking for some consolation in this state of affairs. "Which is a good thing," he said, suddenly finding it. "You see, all we have is the regiment, so we think the more of it. Hence all that business you went through just now. Mind you, you won't find any of that in the wartime battalions. But the First Battalion's still got quite a lot of regulars who know the proper form." He searched his teeth again and again found what he sought. "Most regulars go looking for cushy appointments in wartime," he said without malice, "like Detterling. But with us the regulars stay put with the regiment."

" 'The drum is beaten'?"

"Not only that. We just . . . feel more at home. This is *our place*. That's why we always bring this table along. By the way, did they teach you about riots in Bangalore? Duties in Aid of the Civil Power?"

"A few periods, sir. Are you expecting trouble?"

"We've been told to, and we're making preparations. The C.O. doesn't like it because he says it interferes with proper training. . . ."

". . . Good solid training," the Colonel was saying to Barry and Alister; "you don't seem to have had nearly enough of it at Bangalore. Well, that's what we believe in here. Good solid training six days of the week and Church Parade on the seventh."

"What for?" said Alister.

"Obvious, isn't it? Got to give 'em something to do, even on Sunday."

"Not the Church Parades, Colonel. The good solid training. What for? What *role* are you contemplating?"

Barry shuddered.

"Doing what has to be done," the Colonel said.

"Precisely. And what will that be?"

"Not your business to know. Or mine, come to that."

"Then how can we train for it?"

"We keep fit, sir, and we learn to do as we're told without asking damn silly questions. That's how we train for it," the Colonel said.

After a number of toasts, to the King, the Colonel in Chief, the Colonel Commandant, the Five Counties of Wessex, and absent friends, there followed a series of party games such as the Fusiliers always played after dinner on great occasions. Alister had been hoping for a little roulette, but nothing of that kind ever occurred among the Wessex Fusiliers; *their* games consisted in making someone lie down on the floor and seeing how many people could stand on him all together before he fainted, that kind of a thing. There was a particular favourite called Blind Man's Buffet, in which the 'Buffer', having been blindfolded, was turned loose to rove round the room swinging heavy punches wherever he would. He might punch the furniture, in which case he could hurt himself very nastily; or he might punch his fellow Fusiliers, in which case he could hurt them very nastily. Since he was in any case bound to keep punching at a steady rate no matter what he might hit, while the rest of the players were on their honour to remain absolutely still throughout (even when a knockout punch was coming straight at them), this game was held with good reason to be a test of character.

Alister, who was one of the first to have his eyes covered, earned general contempt by punching too softly and only at stomach level.

"Aim them hard at the jaw, man," the Colonel said.

Whereupon Alister, judging the direction and elevation by the voice, aimed one hard (as he thought) at the Colonel's jaw, and cracked his knuckles viciously on a stone wall-bracket. This misfortune raised hearty Fusilier laughter; for it seemed that the Colonel had some minor ventriloquial skill and was accustomed to undo tiros in this manner.

Peter, who didn't care much for this sort of game, took up his ground in what he thought would be a safe place, in the

rear of the Mess Piano. But this was just the area in which
experienced players, who knew the local course, went looking
for skulkers; and he received a terrific clout across the chops
from the 'Buffer' who succeeded Alister, an elderly lieutenant
whe resembled a peasant *en fête* by Brueghel and had been
commissioned in the field at Imphal.

In accordance with the rules of this entertainment, and after
the ten seconds allowed for his recovery, Peter as having been
'buffed' now became the 'Buffer'. While he was being blindfolded, most of the other players shifted, as was permitted, to
new ground; only Barry and one or two more elected to stay
put, this being an old stratagem based on the assumption that
no 'Buffer' would try to find a target in a place which would
probably have been vacated. Meanwhile the Adjutant finished
knotting the handkerchief behind Peter's head and gave the
traditional command 'Buffo', whereupon all present assumed
the correct upright position (with jaw slightly jutting to give
the 'Buffer' a sporting chance) in which they were bound to
remain frozen all through the coming 'Buffaloo' or 'Buff-up'.

"Buffo-Buffo," Captain Oake then said – the signal for
Peter to start buffing.

Peter, not much wishing to hit anyone and particularly not
wishing to hit Barry, buffed his way to where he knew Barry
had previously been and therefore ought not to be now. He
swung mightily into what he thought was empty air, buffed
Barry bang between the eyes and laid him as flat as a flounder
– except, that is, for Barry's head, which cracked against the
leg of the Second in Command's armchair and there remained,
fixed in a vertical position, as though split and secured by the
sharp edge at the angle of the chair-leg.

"Wango," the Adjutant said, indicating by this formula a
disaster of sufficient magnitude to unfreeze all other players.

These gathered round Barry, silently (since Wessex Fusiliers
do not greet catastrophe with chatter) and leaving a decent
space, so that Barry might breathe, should he still be able to,
and the M.O. might do his stuff. But the wretched fellow
couldn't even begin; for Peter, not understanding the command 'Wango', and forgetting in his dismay at having hit

someone that a 'Buff' automatically terminated the current 'Buffaloo', went on thrashing and caught the M.O. a horrible blow in the throat, causing him to crumple like a Guy in a bonfire. "Wango-wango," insisted the Adjutant to Peter – and himself went down for the count.

"Wango-wango-*wango*," the Colonel piped.

And now the Colonel himself would have been felled by Peter's leg-of-mutton fist, had not Alister deflected it in its path, and then whipped the handkerchief up over Peter's eyes.

"Lay off, Peterkin," Alister said.

Several Fusilier faces twitched with disapproval of the endearment, but in the main concern lay with the fallen. Captain Oake was speedily revived when someone squirted soda into his face; the doctor was eventually brought to his feet by some sharp kicks in the anus from the Colonel ("Get up, damn your eyes, and do your job"); but Barry, beneath whose neck was a pool of blood, was not to be dealt with, as even the Colonel saw, by such peremptory means. In the end, Peter and Alister got him laid out on a sofa; and the rather shaky Adjutant examined the back of his skull, while the medico retired, after his first look, to be violently sick in a corner.

"Plucky performance," said the Colonel. "All the same, those Strange boys. Stood there as steady as a rock and took what was coming."

"For Christ's sake," said Captain Oake in a casual tone (to avoid creating alarm), "fetch that doctor back here."

But the M.O. was still being sick.

"Pity we can't train our own," said the Colonel; "these outside fellows never come up to the scratch."

"It's this bleeding," said Alister: "it won't stop."

"Oh God, oh Christ, oh God," said Peter. "It's all my fault."

"Don't *you* start," said the Colonel. He went over to the sideboard and seized the whisky bottle. "First disinfect in case," he said, sluicing whisky into the red crevice which gaped beneath Barry's fair hair, "and then sew the bloody hole up. Have to shave the hair first, though. You" – to Alister – "fetch a razor. Cut-throat – you're the sort of chap that has one. *You*" – to the Senior Subaltern – "go to the M.I. Room for the kit. And *you*" – to Peter – "get ready to hold his hand if he comes to. There's nothing to it," he announced to his officers at large : "done it dozens of times."

"Perhaps, sir," the Adjutant began, "if we were to wait until the M.O.—"

"—Bloody man's pissed as a dhobi's arsehole. You leave it to me. Took a dooli-bearer's leg off once – beautiful job – and dug a bullet out of Bunjy Brewster's guts in '41. Common sense, that's all you need," said the Colonel, taking a razor from the breathless Alister, "and a bit of an eye for the thing."

He opened the razor and balanced it with care; then, with surprising gentleness, he began to coax the hair away from Barry's scalp.

"More whisky," he said, and swabbed the blood away with it. "Give me that needle and thread. . . . And now, just watch, all of you, and then you subalterns can have a go for yourselves. One stitch each should just about do the job – like . . . *that*. Bloody useful bit of training," he said, straightening up again, "so you're lucky to have the chance. And don't botch the poor little bugger up."

And then all the subalterns queued up, without a word and in strict order of seniority, to take their turn at stitching Barry's head.

Peter stuck a neat little flag into the area marked 'Ranges' on his wall-map of Berhampore. That was where Alister's Platoon was spending the day : Alister's Platoon, as he now reflected, but not commanded by Alister, who had been detailed off, as 'second-in-command and under instruction', to a Rifle Platoon which was commanded by one of the senior Lieutenants. Alister's conversation on the dining-in night had displeased the Colonel, and this rather humiliating appointment had been the result.

Barry, on the other hand, had won everybody's approval by his stout behaviour during the 'Buff-up', and so he had been given a Rifle Platoon all of his own. In fact, however, this was the first day on which he had been fit enough to command it;

for on the morning after the 'Buff-up', the M.O., pale and smelling of vomit, had examined his stitches, given a low moan of horror, and sent Barry off, heavily drugged, to remain under observation in the Military Hospital at Delhi. There Barry stayed for some days, then returned, minus the stitches and apparently none the worse, except for an ugly bump at the base of his skull (which in the Colonel's opinion only made him look more 'manly'); but the instructions he carried said he was to go to bed immediately and stay there for another week. Why? the Colonel wanted to know : it was all mere pampering. Possible delayed concussion, the M.O. told him, and threatened to report him to the Director of Medical Services unless Barry was allowed to follow the instructions to the letter. So to bed Barry had gone, and was much visited by all his new colleagues, who sat round him in groups of five or six for hour after hour, apparently concerned to prevent his being bored but neither saying nor doing anything at all to obviate boredom. 'The Colonel's sent them to make sure he doesn't play with himself,' Alister explained to Peter : 'it's the kind of thing they worry about here.' But however that might be, Barry had now at last been declared fit for duty, and this very morning he was taking the field with his new Platoon to practise the Frontal Assault on the Old Polo Ground. . . .

. . . In the centre of which Peter now pinned another flag to record Barry's location. He now had just three more flags to dispose of : one for the C.O., who was out inspecting the Training; one for the Adjutant, who was sitting in the office next door; and one for himself, as Intelligence Officer. The Adjutant and himself ('ADJ' and 'I.O.') he stuck side by side in a shaded area marked 'Admin. Block'; that much was easily done. But what to do about the Colonel? Since Peter had the whole of the rest of the morning to give to the problem, he took his time about it. Should he work out the C.O.'s probable route and move the flag every few minutes accordingly? Or should he pin the flag at a point equidistant from every place at which training was in progress? The latter method would be inexact; the former too conjectural.

The Adjutant now came in, as he quite often did. He liked

Peter, so Peter had very soon realised, and this was why Peter had been given his present job.

'It sounds very grand – Intelligence Officer,' Thomas Oake had said; 'but in fact, you know, you're just a glorified messenger boy. And when you're not being fagged for messages all you do is keep the map, which is simple routine. But you'll be at the centre of things . . . if you take my point.'

Peter took the point and had been very glad of the appointment. The work, if leisurely, had more subtleties to it than the Adjutant had suggested. What was more, the Adjutant's propinquity was pleasant, provided one observed the proper forms, and his conversation rich in unexpected insights.

"Getting on all right?" the Adjutant said now.

This was his unvaried excuse for dropping in for a chat.

"Slight problem over the C.O., sir. He's moving about this morning. I'm not sure how to place him."

"Ah," said Oake, frowning slightly. "He should have given you a breakdown of his route and the exact times at which he intends to reach every stage of it."

"Perhaps I should have asked him?"

"No. It's not for you or me to ask our Commanding Officer where he's going. It's for him to tell us. If he doesn't, we assume he has reasons for secrecy."

"He can't want to be secret this morning, sir."

"No. He just forgot."

Not a very serious omission, Peter thought; but it was clear that the Adjutant took a different view. His face was puzzled, hurt and apprehensive.

"The Colonel," he said at last, "is a marvellous fighting soldier, but he doesn't bother much about standard procedure. Suppose the General paid us a visit and asked to be taken to him? We'd have quite a job finding him, and that wouldn't look good."

Oake smiled wistfully at Peter and then went on:

"You think I'm making a silly fuss, don't you? And probably, as far as this morning goes, no harm will have been done. But this kind of casual behaviour . . . this disregard of the *rules* . . . presents serious dangers."

"I should have thought . . . sir . . . that the Colonel was very keen on keeping the rules."

"Keen that others should, certainly. For himself . . . he has his own set. I'm going to say something rather disloyal, Peter, because I think that you and I have to prepare ourselves for . . . possible difficulties."

The Adjutant closed his eyes and was silent for so long that he might have fallen asleep on his feet. But eventually he opened his right eye, then his left, and lumbered over to Peter's map.

"A Company," he said, rapping it lightly with his forefinger, "is going over the Assault Course. B is on the Range, C engaged in elementary tactical movements by platoons. The Band is practising for the Retreat Parade next month, and everyone else is busy with administration or interior economy. What does all this suggest to you?"

"An infantry battalion engaged in routine training."

"Which is to say training for a field role. The only trouble is that we have been warned – we have been commanded – to train with a view to something else as well – to keeping the King's peace. Duties in time of civil disorder, action in case of riot – that is what Delhi has told us to prepare for, and that is why we are really here. And so we are repeatedly reminded by missives from Brigade, and higher, two or three times a week. But how much training, since you have been here, Peter, has this Battalion done to prepare it to cope with civil riot?"

"Surely," said Peter slowly, "we have to submit copies of our Training Programmes. So Brigade . . . and higher . . . must be satisfied from these that we're doing as they wish. Otherwise they'd be down here like a ton of bricks."

"They would be if they knew what was really happening. They *ought* to be, Peter. But as it is, well, Berhampore is rather out of the way, and the war's just over, and they're all having a good time while the set-up still lasts – so they're taking our Programmes on trust. And of course on paper it's all sound enough. On paper, according to the Programmes, each Company is spending three days a week training for Duties in Aid of the Civil Power. Just as it should be. But the truth is that those days never dawn. At the last minute the Colonel always thinks of something else. 'A Coy's looking sluggish,' he tells me: 'route march for them tomorrow.' 'But sir,' I say, 'tomorrow's one of their days for Riot Drill.' 'Never mind that,' he says; 'they won't be fit for anything at all until they've had some exercise.' " The Adjutant lifted both arms from his sides. "And it's the same all the time." He let his arms fall again. "Not one Company has done a day's training in Riot Drill for the last six weeks."

"Why has the C.O. . . . . discountenanced it?" said Peter carefully.

"He thinks other things are more important. He thinks we're still training for the war."

"Sir?"

"Oh, he knows it's over, of course. But part of him, a big part, refuses to admit it. You see, all his life he's wanted one thing – to lead this regiment in battle. He's seen enough action, God knows, but to him that was just a preparation for his real destiny – to command the First Battalion, *his* Battalion, of the Wessex Fusiliers in the face of the enemy. And now he's got command all right – but it's just too late. And much of the time he can't believe it. He *can't believe* that God would have given him the command he's always prayed for without also giving him the battle."

"Won't riot duties do instead, sir?"

"Fighting civilians, Peter? You might just as well offer St. George a stray dog instead of a dragon."

"Yet stray dogs must be dealt with, I suppose?"

"Indeed they must. But they have to be captured, not killed. The techniques are different."

"The net and not the lance?"

"You might say so. But meanwhile the Colonel is sharpening his lance . . ."

". . . And disdains to learn to cast the net . . ."

". . . Which takes a light hand and lots of practice."

A long silence.

"What are you going to do, sir?" Peter said at length.

"I'm going to give lectures to the Platoon Commanders.

Every evening, starting next Monday. I shall tell the C.O. they're on Regimental History, but in fact they'll be about Riot Duties and the rest. I shall suggest ways in which chaps might practise their Platoons, at such odd times as may be available. They'll take the hint, I think."

"No good having a quiet word with the Company Commanders as well?"

"No. Most of them think like the Colonel. Action involving civilians is beneath their dignity as soldiers. And they'd think I was going beyond myself to interfere."

"I see, sir. But suppose the C.O. turns up at these lectures?"

"Then for as long as he stays they'll be about Regimental History. No harm done, as far as that goes. Though the whole thing's going to seem a bit odd, I'm afraid. . . ."

"As you say, sir, the chaps will take the hint. They'll see what's going on all right. But there's something else." Peter pondered for a few seconds. "Have you thought . . . how the Colonel will react . . . when and if there *are* riots? Will he be able to face facts? And take charge of the situation?"

"He'll hang his head in shame, that he and his regiment should have to do with any action so grubby and contemptible. Meanwhile, the Platoon Commanders will do what is necessary . . . I hope . . . and in the intervals of overseeing them, I shall offer the Colonel what comfort I may, by pretending that he is coping with it all without dishonour. I'm fond of him, you see, and I don't want his feelings to be hurt."

Thomas Oake wandered to the door, gently shaking his head.

"And for this morning, sir?" Peter called after him. "What shall I do with his flag?"

Peter held this up and waved it in front of the map. Captain Oake looked back and considered.

"Stick it in by the Assault Course," he advised. "That's where he'll be happiest, bless his heart."


"What I want to know," said Alister a few evenings later, "is what the hell we're doing here anyhow."

"Routine training prior to undertaking an active role in the field – for one thing," Peter said.

"What field?"

"In time of peace," said Barry rather earnestly, "the Army prepares itself for the next war."

"The next war will be a different affair. The Atom Bomb will see to that. Frontal attacks and field firing – that's all I've done for a fortnight. Now one Atom Bomb," said Alister sourly, "could do the work of a million frontal attacks and ten million men in five seconds."

"The Atom Bomb's not fair," said Barry. "Anyhow, no one will dare use it."

"The enemy will if we don't. Anyway, we *have* used it."

"And learnt how horrible it is. In future," said Barry, "there will have to be an agreement by both sides not to use it any more. Otherwise the whole earth will be blown up."

"Big red balls to that," Alister said. "That's just what people like you were saying when gun-powder first came in – but they all went on using it like anything . . . except for a few poor suckers who still insisted on training archers. Which is more or less what they're doing to us here. All this rubbish they're teaching us – it's as though they were training us to use the longbow after the invention of the musket."

Alister was not enjoying being second-in-command of a Platoon. The snub rankled, and the crustiness and pedantry of his Platoon Commander had completed his disillusionment with those processes of warfare which were favoured by the Wessex Fusiliers. But although Alister's bitterness was largely due to personal slight, he had, as Peter reflected, a sound point for debate. "One has to accept," Peter now said, "that there will always be a *local* need of the military methods which we are at present practising. You can't plaster every square inch with Atom Bombs."

"I don't see why not."

"They're expensive," Barry said.

"All right," Alister conceded, "let's say we're training for a local and tactical role in the next war. Why are we doing it in Berhampore, of all places?"

"We're here because we're here," said Barry, quoting his Platoon Sergeant.

"Not entirely," said Peter, who now felt it was up to him to do a little proselytising on the Adjutant's behalf. "We're here to maintain internal security in India. During a time of political transition."

"We are, are we? A fat lot of training we've done for that."

"Ah," said Peter tactfully. "The Adjutant tells me that from now on we shall be hearing more about it. He's giving lectures on Riot Duty and so on – starting Monday."

"Riot Duty," said Barry with disdain. "I don't care for the sound of that."

"No more does the Colonel. But something has to be done in preparation, so the Adjutant says."

Barry looked stubborn.

"That's for the Colonel to decide."

"No doubt," said Peter disingenuously; "but I'm sure Tom Oake would never start on anything without the Colonel's approval. Or at least his tacit approval."

But Barry shook his head sternly, repudiating the Civil Role. Barry had loved the Colonel since childhood and instinctively shared his attitudes; quelling riots was no business for a soldier, he thought; he had not won his spurs for that.

"What it is to be near the seats of the mighty," Alister was saying to Peter. "So we're really here to keep the natives in order?"

"We were warned it might come to that a long time ago. You remember what Gil' Khan used to say? We've discussed the possibility often enough between us."

"As a hypothesis," Alister said.

"As a nightmare," capped Barry.

"I never believed it could happen," Alister went on. "Or not after we were told we were going home. And then, when we came here after all, I'd somehow managed to forget about it. Picketing streets, firing on mobs – it just doesn't fit with all this." He waved a hand in the direction of the Mess, the home of the Drum. "It's not what a Regiment like this is for."

"I entirely agree," Barry said.

"All this field firing and what have you, it may be a bloody waste of time, but one *can* just about put up with it – even with the temperature at 190 in the shade. Exhausting and futile, yes, but at least it doesn't make one positively sick to think about."

"And do Civil Duties make you positively sick to think about?"

"Like Barry, I loathe the idea of them."

"You used to take a tougher view," said Peter. "Back at Bangalore."

"I told you, that was all hypothetical. The reality smells rather different."

"It hasn't come to reality yet. But if it does," said Peter, "need one be so faddy about it? After all, we shall only be doing what is needed. We shall be protecting the people of India against agitators and bullies. We shall be preventing looting and chaos. We shall be upholding the rights of religious minorities."

"We shall be doing the dirty work," said Barry; "*we* shall become the untouchables."

"That's right," said Alister: "I didn't come all this way to be a street-cleaner. That's what it'll add up to – cleaning up the mess. *Their* fucking mess."

"We helped to make it."

"Nonsense. If we hadn't been here, things would have been far worse. This country is such a bleeding shambles that no one could have done any better. All this filth and disease, all these damn silly sects and flea-bitten cows. Millions of syphilitics breeding like flies in dung. The truth is, we ought to be glad they want to rule themselves. Let 'em get on with it, I say. Let's for God's sake go away and leave them to rot in their own muck. And then at least no one will be able to blame us any more."

"We shall be blamed all right," said Peter. "Haven't you understood? There's a new way of thinking these days. We are always wrong, however hard we try, and *they* – the subject races, the natives, the masses wherever they may be – *they* are always the wronged, no matter how stupid or dirty or criminal they may be. That's what democracy means, Alister. So when we leave this country, if anything at all goes right, *they'll* be congratulated and what they've achieved without us will be paraded endlessly under our noses. But if the least little thing goes wrong—"

"—And just about everything will—"

"—It'll be *our* fault because we once presumed to govern them, and the failure will be flung in our faces. I tell you, we'll have them hanging round our necks until the end of time."

"Well, if we're going to be blamed whatever happens," said Alister, "about the best thing we can do is let 'em massacre each other – as that's what they seem to want. The more riots the better. So many less mouths to feed."

"It won't just be Hindu against Moslem. It'll be both of them against us. But whatever it is, we can't just ignore it. We owe them better than that."

"We owe them nothing."

"Then we owe ourselves better than that. We want to be able . . . to stand right with ourselves when it's over."

"I'll settle for keeping my hands clean," said Alister; "quite literally, just that."

"Right," Barry said.

"In fact," said Peter, "we shall all three of us do just what we are told to do. That much at least is clear. So if I were you, I'd wait and see what the Adjutant has to say in his lectures. . . ."

"The whole thing begins and ends with this," the Adjutant said: "everything will be all right so long as you stay on your side of the line and they stay on theirs."

The Adjutant was addressing the Senior Subaltern and all Subaltern Officers. Since the lecture was being delivered in their spare time, some of those present looked sulky or impatient; most, however, were listening with an appearance of polite attention. They had been told to be there, so there they were; and if Captain Oake was talking about riots and not about Regimental History (the subject proclaimed in Orders), that was all the same to them. No doubt he had his reasons; or possibly the programme had been changed at the last minute without their hearing of it. In any case, it did not do to show surprise or curiosity, leave alone resentment; in the Wessex Fusiliers one took things as they came, giving thanks that they were no worse. An hour's lecture on any topic under the moon was much preferable to (say) an all-night exercise. If you only sat still and pretended to listen, it would soon be over.

"So the first thing you do," Captain Oake pursued, "is to paint a long, straight, thick white line right across the street. When you've done that, you set up notices in every language spoken locally and any others you happen to know, stating that anyone who crosses the line is in danger of being shot. You then retire some way behind it and set up a barrier. Any questions so far?"

As it happened, the Adjutant had decided not to deceive the Colonel, who would have been very offended if he had ever found out. Having received his commander's willing permission, some days before, to lecture the Subalterns on their Regimental History, Tom Oake had then approached him, on the afternoon before this first session, and diffidently enquired whether it might not be prudent to give a little instruction about Riot Duties instead – 'just to keep those Johnnies in Delhi happy'. Although the Colonel had not much cared for this proposal, he had conceded that it could do no harm, and he had apparently felt (so Oake told Peter later on) that the Adjutant's purpose of lecturing Subalterns and Subalterns only put the distasteful subject of Aid to the Civil Power in its correct and inferior place. Since Captains and Majors were not to be bothered, the whole affair became an unimportant chore, much like fire drill, which was offhandedly thrown at junior men to be gone through once a month 'just in case'. On this basis, the C.O. had given Oake his blessing, merely requiring of him that he would in fact deliver the more seemly lectures on Regimental History as soon as the course on Civil Aid was concluded.

"You set up a barrier," the Adjutant repeated. "Any questions?"

"Yes, sir," said Peter (by pre-arrangement, in order 'to wake 'em all up'): "suppose you haven't time to do all this? Suppose you're called out in a hurry and things are already in full swing?"

"Good question," said the Adjutant. "I wonder no one else thought of it. Let's have more attention, gentlemen, please."

The polite faces of the Subalterns now became serious. If the Adjutant wanted a show of more attention before he got it over with, then by all means let him have it. It was as easy to look serious as to look merely polite, and doubtless the Senior Subaltern would frame a question or two later on to complete the pretence. Come to that, it was a pity he hadn't been the first to break; bad show, letting this Peter-come-lately-Morrison get in ahead like that, making them all look fools. Officious fellow, Morrison; the Adjutant's new favourite, it seemed.

"But although the problem which Mr Morrison has raised is very pertinent," Thomas Oake went on, "we'll leave it until later. First, let's get the basic procedure straight. As things are, then, we've got a thick white line and notices saying, 'So far but no farther'; and some twenty yards behind it we have ourselves, in platoon strength, let us say, and stationed behind a barricade, if materials for one are available. There is one more important item of equipment: a loud-speaker, through which, for the benefit of the illiterate, the prohibitions on the notice-boards may be conveyed from mouth to ear. . . ."

"Platoon will move to the left in threes," shouted Alister: "le-e-e-ft . . . *hunnn.*"

"Don't bray, man," his Platoon Commander said from behind him. "You can't expect to be given a platoon of your own if you're going to bray at them like a donkey."

"I should leave all that to the Platoon Sergeant," Alister said. "It's his job."

"Don't answer back. Now march the Platoon up to the Rifle Butts and wait there till I join you. And I don't expect to find you all sitting about smoking. Think of something useful for them to do—"

"—Like what?—"

"—And see that they do it. And any more insolence out of you, Mr Mortleman, and I'll wheel you in front of the Commanding Officer."

"I am instructed," said Barry to his Platoon, which was seated round him in a half circle on the ground, "to issue a routine reminder about the use of Early Treatment Packets."

The men guffawed.

"Quiet," the Sergeant said: "listen to Mr Strange."

"Thank you, Sergeant. If you intend to go with a woman, any of you, you should call at the Early Treatment Centre and collect a small packet – this – which contains a tube of disinfectant cream and one rubber sheath. During intercourse you will wear the sheath—"

"But sir," said the Platoon wag, "wearing them things spoils it."

"And not wearing them may spoil you. If you want to rot away with sores," said Barry vigorously, "like that beggar outside the barrack gate who's got no lips left, then by all means do it without a sheath. Meanwhile, my friend, you will listen without interrupting. . . ."

"Very good, Mr Strange, sir," said the Platoon Sergeant later on; "that bit about the beggar, very good. They can see him for themselves, you see. You really had them listening after that."

"Our position on the map, Mr Morrison?"

"Map reference 076492, sir. Small casuarina copse at southwest corner of tank."

The Battalion was having a night exercise.

"I can't see the tank."

"Just over that rise, sir. . . ."

". . . And there we are, bang on. Very good, Mr Morrison," the Colonel said. "Now kindly make a round of the Company Commanders and tell them all to prepare to advance at dawn."

"Excuse me, sir," said the Adjutant, "but can't we use the wireless for that?"

"They'll all have ballsed their sets up by now. Word of mouth is more reliable. They won't be able to balls Morrison up. Got that, Morrison? Tell 'em, ready to advance at dawn."

"Exact time, sir?" said the Adjutant apologetically.

"How the hell should I know? What time is dawn, Mr Morrison?"

"0452 hours, sir."

"You seem to have all the answers. 0452 hours it is then. Now on your way. But before you go . . . have a nice swig from my flask."

"Thank you, sir."

"Thank *you*, Mr Morrison, thank *you*."

". . . Right," said Tom Oake to the assembled Subalterns; "so you've got the Magistrate's written permission to fire. Now you must give a proper fire order. Don't just tell 'em to loose off into the crowd; pick out the leader, and order them to aim at him. . . ."

And so the days went on, bringing Alister to proficiency in his word of command but not to a command of his own; bringing Barry to undisputed mastery of his Platoon; bringing Peter to the kind of Intelligence required of an Intelligence Officer; bringing Thomas Oake to the end of his lectures on Duties in Aid of the Civil Power, and to the beginning of those on Regimental History; and bringing, of all things, Wanker Murphy to Berhampore.

"There's a Major Murphy to see you, sir," said the Orderly Room Quartermaster Sergeant one morning.

"*Who?*" Peter said.

"Major Murphy, sir, of the Education Corps."

And Murphy rolled into the room, all got up in riding boots and breeches and carrying an ivory-handled hunting crop.

"Peter, my dear chap. No formalities, please."

Murphy preened and postured, then sat down on Peter's desk and started pleasuring himself with the crop-handle.

"Murphy. What the devil are you doing in that rig?"

"A Field Officer, as you may have heard, is entitled to wear mounted dress."

"If he rides a horse. I didn't know they had them in the Education Corps."

"I'm only in the Education Corps nominally. Actually I'm now a courier. That's why I'm here. To liaise with you."

"And you came here on a horse?"

"The uniform is symbolic of the office," said Murphy, very seriously. "In fact I have my own staff car and a driver to drive it."

"I see. And how did all this come about?"

"Well, my commission as Captain came through all right – it seems Detterling saw after that, like you asked him to – but when I got to Delhi they said that the appointment had been dispensed with after all because the Education Corps in India was packing up. But there *was* an appointment for a Major, to go round doing secret liaison. Carrying messages which were 'for hand of Officer only'. Top level stuff. I'm known," said Murphy with pardonable pomp, "as the Viceroy's Galloper."

"And why did *you* get the job?"

"No one else wanted it, and I was spare. Funny, that. You'd have thought they'd all have jumped at it."

"Yes. . . . Shouldn't the Viceroy's Galloper be transferred to a smarter Regiment?"

"I was told about that. It seems they're all very busy and it'll take some time for the transfer to come through. Eventually I'm going to belong to Lord Curzon's Horse. But for the time being, they said, would I mind continuing in the Education Corps?"

"Nominally."

"That's it."

"Did Detterling have anything to do with it all?"

"As a matter of fact, yes. He knew what had happened about the other thing, of course, so he suggested me for this.

He took me to see that fellow Glastonbury, the one who came to Khalyan that time. 'You're just the chap we're looking for,' Glastonbury said. Then he explained about Lord Curzon's Horse and all that, and I was promoted on the spot."

"Well, congratulations. What happened to the last chap who had the job?"

"I didn't think to ask."

"Hmm. And what brings you here, Murphy? You want the Colonel, I suppose?"

"No. I want you."

"The Adjutant, you mean? He's just next door."

"No. You."

"I'm only the Intelligence Officer."

"You," Murphy said.

"For Christ's sake, Murphy. What does the Viceroy's Galloper want with me?"

"It's what Colonel Glastonbury wants with you. It's so secret I wasn't even allowed to write it down."

"Then I'm not sure I want to hear it. There's a nasty smell here, Murphy."

"Anyway, I've got to tell you and you've got to listen. It's all about Gilzai Khan."

"Ah," said Peter, abandoning caution at the sound of the well-loved name.

"He's somewhere in this area, getting up trouble among the Mohammedans. He's telling them that they'll be massacred by the Hindus if the British leave India. He's urging them to oppose self-government and to petition for us to stay on here."

"Sounds true to form."

"I dare say. But Delhi doesn't like it."

"Why not? He's pro-British, isn't he?"

"That's just what's embarrassing them. Official British Policy, Labour Party Policy, is *anti*-British, if you follow me. The idea is to hand the whole bloody boiling over to the Indians as soon as possible, and then run for it before the balloon goes up."

"Surely . . . we're going to stay until we've made proper arrangements."

"That might have been the idea once, but the wheeze now is just to get out fast. So we don't want people asking us to stay. And the better the reasons they give, the less we want it."

"In other words, the Khan is telling the plain but inconvenient truth—"

"—Which is getting on Delhi's tits—"

"—So they want him to shut his mouth."

"They want *you* to shut his mouth," Murphy said.

"Don't be absurd."

"I'm not being. I am to remind you of that awkward affair about Margaret Rose Engineer, which could still be dug up again and used against you, and I am to tell you that Delhi expects your absolute co-operation."

"What can I possibly do about it? The Khan wouldn't listen to me about a thing like this . . . even if I knew how to find him."

"There's someone else who could find him easily enough, isn't there?" Murphy said.

Peter opened his mouth and shut it again. Murphy stroked himself voluptuously with his riding crop.

"If Barry Strange put the word round the bazaar that he wanted to see Gilzai Khan," said Murphy, "the Khan would come running with his mouth watering and his tail wagging. I wonder he hasn't come already."

"Murphy. We simply cannot be having this conversation."

"I don't see why not. We are wondering why Gil' Khan, given he's in the neighbourhood, hasn't yet been to see his little friend, and we conclude, I think, that he's having a busy time of it and just hasn't heard that Barry is here. As I was saying, however, a word in the bazaar will soon put that right. And once you've tethered the juicy little kid, along comes the tiger."

"Perhaps. But the Khan is not going to be persuaded – not even by Barry – to hold his tongue over this Moslem business. You know how he feels about it."

"My dear Peter, when the tiger comes for the bait, you don't argue with him or try to reform him. You take more radical measures."

"WHAT ARE YOU SAYING, MURPHY?"

"That it would be easier and neater if Gilzai Khan's mouth was closed for good. At least, that is the opinion in Delhi."

"Glastonbury's opinion?"

"He certainly passed it on. But I think it must have originated a bit higher."

"Does Detterling know anything about it?"

"If he does, he hasn't favoured me with his comments."

"Let's get this straight, Murphy," said Peter carefully. "Gilzai Khan is a retired officer of comparatively low rank who is trying to influence local Moslem opinion in a way which annoys Delhi—"

"—And London . . ."

"—And are you seriously telling me that just because of that they want him . . . done away with?"

"Not just because of that. They're afraid of what he may become. He's a remarkable chap, as both you and I are well aware. If he once gets started, there's no knowing where he'll end. Berhampore today, all India tomorrow."

"And so they have sent you . . . to tell me . . . to . . . to do *what* exactly?"

"They didn't go into detail. The general drift is clear enough, I think."

"But Murphy, Gil' Khan is my friend. And even if he wasn't, I'm not a trained assassin. I just would not know how to do this."

"Then you'd better start thinking, Peter. Because if you disoblige Delhi, Delhi is going to disoblige you by raking up dear little Margaret Rose Engineer and using her to get you cashiered. Drummed out, my dear."

"I did nothing wrong."

"You consorted with a Eurasian girl of under sixteen – statutory rape, even if she was a whore – made her pregnant, and deserted her. That's what they're going to throw at you, Morrison – unless they hear good news from Berhampore within four weeks from now. Four weeks, I was told to say. Quite generous, really."

Then Major Murphy of the Education Corps, Galloper to the

Viceroy of India, removed his bum from Peter's desk, raised his riding whip to the peak of his cap in salute, and waddled out of Peter's office.

"Who was that chap with you this morning?" the Adjutant asked.

"An old chum from Bangalore, sir. Friendly visit."

"He took up enough of your time, I must say."

"I had to be polite, sir. Through some preposterous series of chances he's become Viceroy's Galloper – or that's what he calls himself."

"Oh. It used to be a splendid thing, but the character of the appointment has changed, I'm told. There's no more galloping to be done, just crawling about with secret orders. The kind of orders no decent man would dare send through the post."

"I see. He was never really a friend, just a Cadet in my Platoon. But I thought it as well to be polite. Anyone from Delhi . . ."

"You were quite right about that, Peter. I only hope he had no secret orders for you, ha ha."

"Ha ha."

"The last chap who had the job died of D.T.s," said Tom Oake, reminiscing, "and I think the one before was killed in a street brawl somewhere. Let's hope your friend is more lucky."

"He isn't a friend."

"Your fellow Cadet then. You should really have brought him through, you know, and introduced him. Anyone from Delhi, as you say . . ."

"He was in a hurry."

"Not to judge from the time he spent with you."

"You wouldn't have liked him, sir."

"I could have judged for myself about that."

"Please believe me, sir," said Peter desperately; "I was doing you a service by keeping Murphy out of your office. He leaves a trail of slime like a slug."

"If you put it like that," said the Adjutant gently, "I'll say no more about it. But on the next occasion someone from out-side calls on you in your office, Peter, just let me know what's going on, will you? We're not running a coffee house, you know, we're running a Battalion Headquarters."

The next occasion came just three days later, and the caller was Gilzai Khan. He was dressed in European clothes, baggy grey trousers, a crumpled alpaca jacket and an open-necked shirt, all of which made him look like a mildly left-wing don of the late nineteen-thirties. Since both the Colonel and the Adjutant were out on the drill square, supervising a rehearsal of the forthcoming Retreat Parade, Peter had no need to introduce his guest.

"Morrison huzoor."

"Gilzai Khan."

They shook hands politely.

"I'd been told you were round here," said Peter, picking his words, "and I was going to try to get hold of you."

"Were you indeed, huzoor? And who told you I was in the vicinity?"

"I had word from Delhi. They say . . . that you have gone into politics."

"They told you what kind of politics?"

"Yes."

"Then why did you want to see me?"

"For old times' sake."

Gilzai Khan accepted this and smiled his pleasure.

"Ah. That is why I have come."

Peter nodded and smiled back. Both men waited for the other to speak.

"How did you get in?" said Peter at last.

"They think I am a Munshi who has come to be interviewed. An Intelligence Officer might wish to keep up his Urdu."

"He might. In fact, I think my Adjutant would rather approve."

"But in fact, huzoor, you will not be employing this particu-lar Munshi. I have come for the first and last time. I found out by accident that you and your two friends were here, and I have come . . . to see you only, Peter . . . and to tell you a message."

"You don't want to see Barry Strange?"

The Khan shrugged.

"Have you told him I am in Berhampore?"

"Not yet. I only heard a few days ago, and I've been thinking it over."

"Like a good Intelligence Officer. No, huzoor. I do not wish to see Barry Strange. He liked the soldier but might not care for the politician. It is the same with Master Mortleman. Salute them from me, if you will, and there let it rest. And now, my message."

"What message, Gilzai Khan?"

"I learnt you were here," said the Khan, "because we have procured a roll of your Battalion. We wished to know your exact strength, you understand?"

"I understand."

"And we have made our plans accordingly." The Khan nodded as though commending his own ingenuity. "To begin with, a petition will go to Delhi, asking for a guarantee that the British will stay at least long enough and in at least sufficient numbers to protect Moslem communities – and Hindu communities too, come to that – wherever it may be necessary. The petition will be ignored. At best there will be an evasive reply. We shall then organise strikes and riots, very much the usual kind of thing; and we also propose, at a later stage, to block the railway line. We shall lie across it, huzoor, and there will be too many of us for your Battalion to remove. We have worked it all out very carefully, you see. But what I most wish to tell you is this. If it is possible, stay away from the railway line – you, and the little Strange, and the lanky Mortleman – right away from the railway. It is a warning, Peter, from one friend to another, and, as you say, for old times' sake."

There was a long silence. Then Peter said: "How did you get into this, Gil' Khan? Why did you ever leave the Army?"

"I care for my poor country, huzoor. The only hope of avoiding unbelievable massacres is for the British to stay. Or if they must leave, to leave very gradually. *Someone* must urge this."

"When we go, surely the Indian Army will keep order?"

"An Indian Army with Indian Officers?" The Khan spat on the floor. "The kind they are now training at Bangalore? Most of them could not command a pi-dog. Besides, the Army itself will be split – into Mohammedan regiments and Hindu regiments – and their way of keeping order will be to add to the slaughter. Hindu regiments will be sent to Hindu towns where they will simply kill the Moslems. It will be easier and far less dangerous than trying to restrain their Hindu brethren. But that is still in the future and none of it need concern you. I am here to tell you to keep away from the railway here in Berhampore."

"When will the trouble here start?"

"Soon. Our local petition goes to Delhi tomorrow. If we hear nothing after two weeks, the trouble will start. Slowly, then more quickly later on. It is later on you must avoid the railway."

And now Peter had decided what to do. For three days and nights after the apparition of Murphy he had pondered and found no answer: now he began to see his way plain.

"You have helped me twice, Gilzai Khan," Peter said. "You saved me from disgrace at Bangalore, and you have warned me here. What use your warning can be to me—"

"—Obey it, huzoor, obey it—"

"—What use it can be to me, or to my friends, I am not sure. Soldiers, as you know better than anyone, must go where they are told. But the warning is kindly meant and kindly taken. Now I must repay the debt."

"There is no debt. There has simply been truth between friends."

"And now there must be more of it." Peter paused. "They mean to kill you, Gilzai Khan," he said, "and they don't at all care how they do it."

The Khan bared his teeth and rubbed his nose.

"I am not surprised," he said. "How do you know of it?"

"By the same means I knew you were here. You remember a Cadet called Murphy?"

"I remember," said the Khan. "Mean and rather fat. His thigh was broken."

"And has now mended, leaving him meaner and fatter."

And then Peter told Gilzai Khan of Major Murphy's visit and all that had been said.

"Truth," he concluded, "between friends."

"So they want you to do it, do they?" The Khan grinned like a vampire. "On pain of disgrace?"

"That could be a bluff, of course. They'd have to find the girl for a start. God alone knows where she is by now."

"There are ways of discovering."

"They'd have to explain why they'd dropped it for so long."

"They could do that too. New evidence, they could say."

"I dare say they could. . . . Meanwhile, I thought I should warn you of their intentions."

"And your own, huzoor?"

"I intend to obey the rules," Peter said, "as I was always taught."

"The rules of honour? Or the rules for survival?"

"I have been taught to regard them as the same. Tell no lies and do as you would be done by. That way one cannot go far wrong."

"Let us indeed hope not." Gilzai Khan rose and walked to the door. "Stay well, huzoor," he said. "Stay well, and stay away from the railway, and see your friends do the same."

"I shall do my best. Go well . . . Gilzai Khan."


"Who was that Indian coming away from your office?" the Adjutant said.

"I thought of employing a Munshi. But that one won't do."

"Why not? He looked a better type than most of 'em. Held himself well. Walked smartly."

"And an excellent teacher for all I know. But he is . . . too familiar."

"That's no good then," the Adjutant said.

"Sir . . . ?"

"Yes, Peter?"

"I was wondering if I might have a day or two's leave. I rather want to go to Delhi."

"Why?"

"To see friends. To check up on something."

"Afraid not, old chap. I'd like to oblige, but this morning we had a special order over the wire. No leave to be granted to any personnel for any reason whatever until further notice. It looks as if they think trouble's really on the way."

"I need only be gone for thirty-six hours."

"Sorry, Peter," said Tom Oake rather sharply; "no can do."

So that's that, Peter thought: he was on his own, and had no way of confirming that Murphy's message was genuine. But then why should he doubt it? Murphy had neither the imagination nor the motive to fake it, and Murphy's credentials – the staff car and the Corporal Driver, if not the riding boots – were impressive. True, he had offered only oral authority for the instructions which he had passed on; but then, as he had remarked at the time, prudent men did not put their signatures under instructions of this nature. They just employed the Murphies of this world. So be it.

"Sorry to have bothered you, sir," he said to the Adjutant; "it isn't really as pressing as all that."


As Peter saw it, he had four duties: one to his Battalion in Berhampore, one to his superiors in Delhi, one to Gilzai Khan, and one, not the least, to himself. The problem was to reconcile them all: to perform each one without dereliction of any other.

His duty to his Battalion was simple enough: all he had to do was to obey whatever orders he was given. Much the same, he supposed, was true of his duty to Delhi. If, as he must now assume, Murphy's message was genuine, he must understand that Delhi wanted the Khan to be silenced and had chosen himself to silence him. Nor did Delhi's decision, objectively regarded, seem altogether unreasonable (though hardly very 'British'). These were difficult days, and if the Khan was setting out to make them yet more difficult, he deserved just about everything he got. If a man deliberately sowed violence, no matter how selfless his intentions, he must expect to reap it.

In Peter's view, Gilzai Khan was probably right: the withdrawal of the British would certainly lead to hideous bloodshed and was therefore to be deprecated. However, it was not Peter's duty to hold views, it was his duty to act in accordance with those of his seniors. Plainly, Delhi meant business; very well then; if one Indian must die in order that he should cease to vex an already sorely vexed Administration, on a political level at least Peter saw no particular objection. His experience as a Head of House at school had inclined him to believe in a broadly democratic method, which, however, must necessarily be liable to certain, as it were, backstairs adjustments. In order to keep people quiet, one either had to suppress them or let them have their way; it was easier and more civilised to let them have their way; but in order to let them have it, one had quietly to remove certain nuisances, from time to time, and undertake certain very dirty jobs. The removal of Gilzai Khan was just such a job: a democratically elected government in England, and a huge majority of Indian citizens, wanted the British out of India; and if the Khan was trying, by violent means, to sabotage those who were working to this end, then the Khan was better . . . out of the way. Politically the thing was as clear as a bell; Gilzai Khan's passing bell.

But there were other levels, personal and moral, on which it was not so clear. To begin with, it was Peter himself who had been given charge to . . . put the Khan out of the way; and secondly, the Khan was a friend of whom Peter was very fond and to whom he owed nothing but gratitude. What then, in all the circumstances, was his duty to Gilzai Khan? To respect the friend, Peter thought, and therefore to warn the man. This he had done. But on the other hand he owed no duty to the Khan as rebel. He might shoot down a rebel Indian with no scruple whatever. And yet . . . could he really separate the two in his mind? For there was always love to be reckoned with. When the rebel's body crumpled, would he not see the lineaments of Gilzai Khan? If he destroyed the criminal, would he not still mourn the man? Worst of all, would not killing the

Khan be a sin against brotherhood? A sin – *the* sin – which the Furies punished above all others and from which there could be no absolution at all, no matter how invidious the Khan's own offence might be.

Peter did not wish to be pursued by the Furies, a reflection which brought him, at last, to his duty to himself. This duty, on consideration, he defined as continuing in his career with his honour, both public and private, still intact. To do this, it was apparently necessary, first, to kill the Khan (else Delhi would destroy Peter himself); secondly, to do so in such a way that he need feel no personal blame (or remorse and the Furies would consume him); and thirdly, to avoid scandal or remark in the course of performance (for Delhi, that dealt in oral messages through Major Murphy, would certainly never acknowledge its responsibility for his orders).

There was only one way of achieving all this in combination – the way he had suddenly seen just before he gave the Khan his warning. He must obey the old rules of conduct : he must (to put it very generally) tell no lies and do as he would be done by. Translated into a scheme of action, these rules could not only save his public face and his private conscience, they could also solve for him the very tough physical and psychological problems of how to effect the actual killing. As he had told Murphy, he was not a trained assassin; in this particular, as in every other, he would need a rule book to guide him. Well, he had his rule book – the old code of the old school. This he had so far rigorously applied in his dealings with the Khan (to whom he had indeed told no lies and done as he would be done by), and this he would rigorously apply from now on, in his dealings with the Khan and with everybody else. It might be necessary to interpret the text with some subtlety, to read the small print with care and to search out special cases in the Appendices; but he was sure that his plan lay there (if he only read aright), a plan which the good old rules, in their wisdom, both suggested as practicable and recommended as honourable. Of the details, as yet, he was not quite sure; from now on he must read diligently, line by line, until he had sought them out.

*PART FOUR*

# TATTOO

THE BAND of the First Battalion, the Wessex Fusiliers, marched and counter-marched for the last time, halted in the centre of the parade ground, and executed a left turn, in order to face the spectators. The Drum-Major strutted from behind to take post in the van, turned about to face the Band, and raised his silver staff. Holding it vertically to the ground, he carried it slowly away to his right, conjuring a roll of kettle drums, which mounted in prelude to the evening hymn. At last the drums hovered towards climax, and then sank away again as the wind instruments went into the first luscious notes of 'The Day Thou Gavest, Lord, has Ended'.

The Retreat Parade, for which the Band had been rehearsing in the appalling heat every day for over two months, was nearing its end. Two verses of the hymn (unsung) would be followed by the Call itself. Then the Officers and the Guests (who included the Resident and his wife, and a local Nawab) would retire to the Mess for 'sundowners', while the rest of the Battalion tidied up under the R.S.M.

Not that there would be much tidying up to be done. The parade ground must be swept and raked, and the chairs put away. Since only Officers and Guests had these, and since Guests in any number had been reluctant to come to Berhampore for the occasion, there could not be more than 150 chairs set out, and two-thirds of them were empty . . . which made a very lonely and conspicuous figure of a worried little soldier with a huge cane (the Battalion 'Stick-man', or orderly of the day) who could now be seen picking his way through the barren seats towards the two occupied rows at the front of the block.

In the middle of the front row sat the C.O., with the Resident on the right of him and the Resident's Mem-sahib on the left. On the Resident's right was the Nawab, and on the left of the Resident's Mem was Thomas Oake, Adjutant. Peter Morrison, who had been observing the worried little orderly from a standing position (as Steward) on one flank, could now perceive that he was aiming at the Adjutant's rear; and indeed, as the Band went into its second stanza of the Evening Hymn, the orderly managed to squirm between two thin and pith-helmeted ladies in the second row, touched Tom Oake on the shoulder, and saluted fiercely (dislodging one pith helmet with his backward-jutting cane) as Tom turned his head. Peter, still observing from the wing, was now treated to the following silent sequence: as soon as Tom had acknowledged the orderly, the orderly bent forward to talk most urgently into Tom's ear, while the lady whose pith helmet had been knocked off reached indignantly down for it, apparently pressing her nose into the orderly's bottom as she did so; whereupon the orderly, still talking to Tom, gave a wag of his behind, as if to dislodge a fly or some other minor nuisance, and struck the lady hard on the chin with his coccyx. The lady flopped off her chair to the ground; the Stick-man saluted and swivelled, inadvertently trampled on the lady, was walloped by her companion in the pit of his stomach, and barged rapidly away, scattering the empty chairs as he went. Meanwhile, Thomas Oake had leaned across the Resident's Mem (whose face tightened ominously), tapped Colonel Brockworthy on the knee and started to mouth at him through the music. After three seconds of this the Colonel went bright orange, swelled up like a frog, and brought the silent sequence to a close by bawling, over the penultimate bar of the hymn:

"Be damned to all that, Oake. Sit still, will you, and let the thing go on."

But now, in fact, as the Call itself was about to begin, was the proper time to rise. The audience, however, mistaking the import of the C.O.'s outburst and vaguely imagining that some contrariness of Fusilier custom required them to remain seated after all ('Sit still, will you'), sat steadily on . . . except, of course, for the Fusilier Officers, who were certain of the proper drill and now rose as one man – but then, not wishing to embarrass the Guests by pointing up their solecism, immediately sat down again. But by this time the Guests had realised their error and were rising themselves . . . then started to sit again when they saw the Officers do so . . . only to find that the Officers were now rising once more – a split second too late – to join the Guests. At this stage it occurred to both factions that neither could catch the other up unless one of them waited. So each decided to wait for the other to conform, the Officers on their feet and the Guests on their bottoms, until, ten seconds having elapsed with no movement whatever, there was a failure of nerve all round, and both parties moved simultaneously, thus merely reversing their roles yet again and remaining as far as ever from desiderated harmony.

Whether this farce would resolve itself before the end of the Call, and if so, which faction would finally impose its will on the other, were interesting sources of speculation to those not among the privileged. Peter, standing out on his wing, had an absurd desire to shout the odds to the soldiers nearest him, but at once remembered his responsibilities, and also remembered that those responsibilities, to judge from the urgent manner of the now vanished orderly, would very shortly require his presence at Battalion Headquarters. Whatever nonsense was in train among the spectators, there was nothing he could do about it, so he might just as well be first on the scene of action and find out what was going on. If this was what he thought and hoped it was, then his big chance had now come and he could not afford to lose a moment.

He slipped quietly away round the back of the seats and caught up with the little Stick-man not far from the Orderly Room. The Stick-man was being sick, the excitement and the blow in his belly having been too much for him, and at first he was less than helpful.

"Fuckin' whoarre, sir, thumpin' me in ma bloddy ballocks" – vomit, vomit – "how the hell was I to help it?"

"Bad luck," said Peter soothingly. "But what's happened?" Vomit.

"Now can you tell me what's happened?"

"Fuckin' whoarre banged ma bloddy balls, that's what happened."

*"What were you telling Captain Oake?"*

"Bloddy wogs seized the station, sir. Pulling up the lines and breaking the lavatory windows. The station maisster rung up – sounded like a bloddy wog hisself – and then the police rung up and all – and told me I'd got to get the Adjutant and the Colonel at once."

"Are the police still on the telephone?"

"Ah s'pose so. They was when Ah went for the Adjutant. Ah feel as if ma bloddy sweetbreads had fell out on the floor and that cowing old whoarre were stomping on them."

Vomit.

Peter went inside. The receiver of the telephone on the Adjutant's desk (which the Stick-man had been left to answer in case of emergency) was off the hook. He picked it up.

"Hullo?"

"Captain Oake? You've taken your time, I must say."

"Second Lieutenant Morrison here; Intelligence Officer."

"I don't want a pip-squeaking wart. I want your Adjutant or your C.O."

"The Adjutant will be here soon. Is there any way I can help meanwhile?"

"I told you, I don't want to talk to a bloody little wart."

"You can keep a civil tongue in your head all the same."

"Don't be insolent. Do you know who I am?"

"I know you're a policeman of some kind."

"I'm Superintendent Willis."

"You can still use a civil tongue, I suppose? Now; what is it you want, Superintendent? The Adjutant may be delayed a few minutes, but I can help to get things going."

Although there was heavy breathing at the other end, Superintendent Willis had apparently seen reason. He answered now with something like respect.

"Very well, Mr Morrison. If you will kindly relay the following information to your Adjutant, and thus set me free to attend to my own duties at last, I shall be most grateful.

"One. Rioters in strength of approximately one thousand

are smashing the station to pieces. An attempt is also being made to tear up the line. Special squads of rioters are wrecking the signal boxes at either end of the station.

"Two. The line at both ends of the station is being blocked by rioters who are lying across it. There are about three hundred of them at either end. No trains can get in or out."

"Are there any trains waiting to get out?"

"Not immediately. But there is a small goods train, with engine, on the station siding, which is due to leave tonight at 2300 hours.

"Three. There is every sign that this operation has been carefully pre-planned and that the rioters are being organised and led by experts."

That fits, Peter thought.

"Four," continued Superintendent Willis. "The police are hopelessly outnumbered and are having little success in checking the activities of the rioters. We are concentrating on the protection of the line itself and other vital equipment. But although both signal boxes have been cut off and surrounded by detachments of policemen, these detachments have been unable to recapture the boxes from the rioters or to prevent them continuing to do serious damage inside.

"Five. The Magistrates have given their reluctant permission for the employment of two Companies of armed riflemen to assist the police in dealing with the emergency. However, no ammunition, repeat, no ammunition, will be issued either to police or Army personnel without the Magistrates' authorisation.

"Six. The First Battalion, the Wessex Fusiliers, is requested to provide forthwith the two Companies of riflemen aforesaid, and to convey them to the north end of the bazaar which lies half a mile to the east of the station.

"Have you got all that, Mr Morrison?"

"I've got it, Superintendent Willis."

"Then kindly get things moving at the juldi."

The Superintendent rang off sharply. Peter replaced his own receiver with the care and respect that were due to the King Emperor's property, then went outside to look for the Stick-man, who was sitting on the ground groaning and coddling his groin.

"Go and find the Adjutant and the Colonel," said Peter, "and ask them to be so kind as to come here without delay."

"Ma fuckin' knackers, sir."

"Never mind your knackers. They'll be all right if you only stop thinking about them. Now get moving, Fusilier. *At the double*."

The wretched fellow clambered to his feet and trotted away like an agitated duck, his legs widely splayed, his head well forward, his clasped hands still cradling his parts. Peter returned to the Adjutant's office and began to write down the gist of the Superintendent's message in the appropriate sequence.

Muddle, he thought as he wrote: there is going to be the most God-awful muddle. For the truth was that the Adjutant's lectures on riot procedure had covered only conventional and theoretical situations in which plenty of time was allowed for the preparation and deployment of troops who were already on the ground when the trouble started. Although Peter himself had been put up to enquire what was to be done in more urgent circumstances, when troops might have to be despatched *in medias res*, and although a reply had been promised for later, Thomas Oake had never got round to giving it. He had used the question as a rod for beating an apathetic audience, but had forborne to scourge himself with it . . . for the very simple reason, Peter now surmised, that neither Tom Oake nor anyone else really knew the answer. To contain riotous civilians from carefully established positions was one thing; to go into an attack against them at a few minutes' notice was quite another. The text book had a lot to say about keeping rioters out of stations but precious little helpful advice as to their ejection when once they were in. It was hopefully assumed that anything so embarrassing would never occur.

And indeed it very seldom did occur, because as a rule strong guards were mounted, at the first sign of trouble, over all important areas. In this case, however, that had not been done, or had only been half-heartedly done, because despite official forebodings (and contrary to what the Khan himself had foretold to Peter) there had been no activity whatever to give early warning. There had been no preliminary strikes, no minor or prefatory riots, no visible disturbance at all. Doubtless, Peter thought, the Khan had changed his plans – and very wisely. He had ordered total peace and quiet – and then WHAM, into a station guarded only by two dozy policemen before anyone could so much as draw breath, the whole plan being conceived and executed with a professional military competence which was not often found among mob agitators, however expert in their trade, and was not, therefore, anticipated in the calculations of the authorities.

All of which, as Peter told himself once more, meant that there was now about to be one enormous muddle; a muddle to which the dilatory behaviour of Tom Oake and the Colonel (where on earth could they be?) would contribute most handsomely. And muddle, of course, was what he, Peter, most wanted. It would give him the framework, or rather the lack of framework, which he needed to come at his object. For in time of muddle a man who had a plan, like his own, which was carefully conceived and founded on definite rules, was in a very strong position; such a man would be the only person who really knew what he was doing, and furthermore the fact that there was muddle would give him ample excuse for bending the rules, his own or other people's, should this be necessary. In the murky conditions which were now about to obtain Peter would have every chance of discharging each one of his four somewhat disparate duties – to Battalion, to Delhi, to the Khan as friend, and to himself – without prejudicing any of the other three.

There was also a fifth and subsidiary duty, to which, having finished his summary of the Superintendent's information, he now gave brief attention. Gilzai Khan had warned him to keep himself, Barry and Alister away from the railway. Whatever changes of plan the Khan had made since his visit, it was reasonable to suppose that the warning still stood, and it was incumbent on him to apply it if this were possible. Where he went himself was his own affair, but he was bound to give Barry and Alister the benefit of the Khan's advice. He had told neither of them that the Khan was in Berhampore (it would only have puzzled Alister and upset Barry), he had therefore said nothing of the visit or the warning, and he did not propose to do so now. (His rule, 'tell no lies', did not bind him to obtrude superfluous truth.) What he did propose was to use his relatively privileged position to keep his friends out of harm's way . . . if he could. In this fashion he would both be conforming with the second of his guiding rules ('do as you would be done by') and also assisting his purpose; for that purpose would not be furthered if either Alister or Barry were to reach the barricades and get a chance view of the Khan on the other side. Quite how they would react, he was uncertain; but he did feel very strongly that their mere presence would inhibit him in his cause.

Having reached this conclusion, Peter was about to go to his own office to examine his map, when the Colonel entered stumpily, made a breathy transit of Oake's office, and disappeared through a connecting door into his own. Tom Oake, who was bringing up in the rear and looking like a cur caught thieving the Sunday joint, beckoned limply to Peter to follow on with him after the Colonel.

"Well?" snapped the Colonel as they came through the door. Peter lifted his summary.

"Telephone message from Superintendent Willis," he began, "taken by me at 1745 hours on—"

"—I never saw anything like it," the Colonel said: "bloody spectators farting about like a lot of potty sheep."

"Yes, sir," said Tom Oake.

". . . At 1745 hours," Peter continued, "on Wednesday, June the—"

"—And on top of that," said the Colonel, "I'm chivvied out of my own Mess by my own Adjutant, positively bundled out, in front of the Regiment's guests, like a drunk Lance-Corporal in the canteen, just to listen to all this rubbish about riots. Policemen's business. Why can't they cope?"

"It seems there are rather a lot of rioters," Peter said.

"Do please listen to Morrison, sir," implored Tom Oake.

"All right. But this is not soldiering as I understand it. Bloody ignorant spectators who don't know when to stand up at a Retreat parade, and everyone shitting themselves because of a few dozen Indians yelling in the bazaar."

"In the Railway Station, sir," Peter said, and was then allowed to continue without interruption.

"Two Companies?" said Tom Oake when Peter had finished. "Six Platoons. The six Platoons commanded by the six most experienced Subalterns, I think, sir, and never mind what Companies they come from."

"No," said the Colonel. "Can't mix everything up like that. Two proper Companies, as such."

"With respect, sir," said Peter. "All Companies have at least thirty per cent of men down with this new epidemic of diarrhoea. No Company, as such, can muster at proper strength. We'll have to pick right through the Battalion."

"Who asked you?" snapped the Colonel.

But Tom Oake gave Peter a grateful look, and the C.O., on reflection, acknowledged the force of the argument. Peter, who very much favoured Tom Oake's scheme of employing the six senior Subalterns (and thus cutting out Barry's Platoon at least), had slightly fudged his figures to make his point; but figures were not the Colonel's strong suit and Tom Oake was certainly not going to correct them.

"Six separate Platoons then," the Colonel said, "made up to full strength where necessary by other men from their respective Companies. Lieutenants Saunders, Burrows, Clerkhurst, Gieves, Robinson and Flitchley."

Flitchley was the Subaltern who had Alister as second-in-command.

"Flitchley may have something the matter himself, sir," said Peter. "He was complaining in the rears this morning after breakfast."

In fact Flitchley had complained of constipation, but Peter had spoken the truth as far as he went : Flitchley had indeed complained, in the rears, about his bowels, that morning.

"Very well : Massingburd Mundy."

"Good decision, sir," said Tom. "And might I suggest that you take personal command? Since all the Company Commanders will have men out, they'll all have a case for being there if we let them. Which will make a nonsense. One senior commander, and one only : you."

"*You*," said the Colonel, as Tom had hoped. "This isn't my kind of thing. Indians monkeying about in Railway Stations, it's not what I was brought up to. You run it, Oake, and we'll think again if you get buggered up."

"Right, sir. I'll go and get it all moving. Peter, you stay in Headquarters here and keep the map. Put a bed in my office so that you can answer the telephone twenty-four hours a day. I may ring through at any time."

"But, sir, can't I come with you? The Orderly Officer can stand by the phone and my Sergeant is quite competent to keep the map."

The Adjutant pondered.

"Besides, sir, you'll need someone to keep the official log. Minute by minute. You know how important that is – in case there are complaints against us later."

But Thomas Oake, although he would have liked Peter with him, wanted even more to have someone whom he could trust to deal with messages and requests back at base.

"No, old chap. I'll keep my own log. You attend to the telephone and your map, so that you can explain it all to the C.O. whenever he wants."

"I shan't want," said the C.O. miserably. "Mobs in Railway Stations. I haven't given my whole life to the Army to finish up with that."

"There you are, sir. The Colonel doesn't—"

"—You shut up," said the Colonel, "and do what you're told. And if *you're* going to do your stuff, Oake, you'd better get started. It's already dark."

"Sir," said Oake.

Having saluted carefully, he withdrew from the C.O.'s presence at a calm and becoming pace. Peter retired to his own office and prepared special riot flags to stick in his map. The Colonel went back to the Mess, whence all his guests had

departed, and sulked most horribly over a long series of barra
pegs. In such fashion did the Wessex Fusiliers prepare to quell
the insurrection at Berhampore.

"Hullo seven for one," said the R.T. Set in the Adjutant's
office : "how do you hear me ? Over."

"One for seven," said Peter : "loud and clear. Over."

"Seven for one. Captain Oake speaking." (The Wessex
Fusiliers were not very strong on radio procedure and security,
both of which the Colonel disdained utterly, 'provided the
bloody things work'.) "Situation report. I confirm that we
have now cleared the station of rioters, also the track itself
within station limits. But about thirty yards – sorry, figures
three-o yards – of the track have been pulled up. Roger so
far?"

"One for seven. Roger so far."

"Seven for one. Continuation of situation report. We have
been unable to clear either of the two – sorry, figures two –
signal boxes, but we have both of them surrounded. It is feared
that all equipment inside them has been effectively dis-
mantled." Tom Oake was fond of occasional litotes. "Nor have
we been able to clear the line outside the station of the rioters
who are lying on it. Both sections on which they are lying
are half a mile in length, and we cannot exert the control
necessary over so large an area. As soon as we take a man
off, he goes along the line and lies down again. Roger so far?
Over."

"One for seven," said Peter. "Suggest as precedent Jebblepoor, 1943."

"You mean figures one-nine-four-three. What happened at
Jebblepoor?"

"The troops were ordered to pee on the rioters, who all went
home for ritual purification. The line was cleared in ten
minutes."

"I think that's rather disgusting, Peter. In any case, the
problem is academic, as there is no point in clearing the line
till the track is repaired in the station."

"What about that goods train? You might get that out off the siding."

"Forgot to tell you. The wagons on the goods train were burnt out last night."

"What was in them?"

"Food for the famine areas round Kisengarh."

"Food for their starving Moslem brothers. Did they know that?"

"Captives report they believed the wagons to be full of whisky en route for G.H.Q. Delhi. They didn't think of checking the crates first."

So even Gilzai Khan's control was not total. Nor was his intelligence service very accurate. Not for the first time, it occurred to Peter that a man accustomed to command trained soldiers must find it a debilitating task to lead rabble. He was just thinking of some pertinent enquiries along these lines, when:

"Seven for one," resumed Tom Oake's voice rather severely. "We are allowing our R.T. procedure to deteriorate, and I can't spend the whole day chatting. Injury state: three men slightly hurt with knife wounds; at least fifty badly affected by heat exhaustion this morning, and another thirty immobilised by diarrhoea.. Please send one Sergeant, four Corporals and seventy-five Fusiliers to replace these. The approaches to the station from the bazaar are clear and well guarded."

"One for seven. Roger. Figures eight-o personnel in all. What are your intentions? Over."

"Seven for one. Superintendent Willis has asked me to hold the station and approaches in case of further attack, which he believes to be imminent."

Ah.

"You agree with him about that?"

"More or less. Those chaps lying on the rails might decide to start up."

"Not if you all pee on them first."

Tom, though he had already disapproved of the suggestion, would enjoy the joke, Peter thought. Tom had a weakness for lavatory jokes, and might wish Peter were there in person to make more of them. Peter himself disliked that kind of humour, but was prepared to serve it up to his master, and now had his reward in the suppressed chuckle which he could hear in Tom's voice.

"That's enough, Peter. Send me those eighty replacements, and rations, et cetera, for a further twenty-four hours. And tell the Colonel that everything's in hand."

"No further instructions, sir? I still can't join you myself?"

Hesitation. Then :

"No. Sorry, Peter. Over and out."

It was now not quite twenty-two hours since the ill-starred Stick-man had first raised the alarm. Through all that time Peter had been confined to his own office or the Adjutant's, in which latter, shortly after the show began, an R.T. Set had been installed to supplement the telephone and ensure for Tom Oake direct contact with his Battalion H.Q. During the course of the night and the morning which followed it reports had come in regularly, and what they amounted to was this : the rioters, unarmed save for knives and clubs, had gradually been driven out of the station at bayonet point. Not a single shot had been fired nor even a single round issued (for the Magistrates had remained resolute about that) and injuries on both sides had been few and minor. But without the use of firearms it had been impossible (as Captain Oake had just said in his latest report) either to recapture the signal boxes (natural forts) or to remove the Moslems who were reclining on the railway line – a job which would in any case require yard by yard control of a large area. Furthermore, one had to remember that although few men had been wounded, over eighty had been put on the sick list.

And so now, at 1500 hours or 3 p.m. on the day which followed the rising, although a reckonable victory had been won, the situation was extremely untidy. Captain Oake's force, inadequate from the beginning, was now badly run down; while the remainder of the Battalion, itself depleted by diarrhoea and responsible for the protection of the barracks, would be able to do no more than provide the bare replacements which had been requested for the station. There, it seemed, further attack might be expected at any moment, attack mounted either by those rioters who had withdrawn or possibly by their hitherto passive brethren just up and down the railway line; and since the Moslem leadership was evidently of high calibre, as these affairs went, and had large numbers at its disposal, the prospect for the Fusiliers in the line was uneasy, to say the least of it. Indeed Tom Oake, Peter thought now, was going to have his work cut out to hold them together; one sharp counter-attack from the rioters, or just one more degree of this heat, might turn the morale, even of the healthy, as fluid as their comrades' bowels.

But he had no time to worry about that now. It was his business, first, to find eighty replacements, second to despatch supplies for another twenty-four hours, and third to reassure Lieutenant-Colonel Brockworthy, who was still sulking, that all was in order ... more or less.

The replacements he instructed the R.S.M. to raise through the Company Sergeant-Majors: one Sergeant, four Corporals and seventy-five Fusiliers. No Officer replacements? the R.S.M. enquired. No; Captain Oake had asked for none.

To raise the supplies, he sent a note by hand of his Intelligence Sergeant: rations and water for 204 men were to be despatched to the station; also cigarettes, soft drinks, etc., which the men could buy if they would. It seemed to him that he had left something out, something that no one had mentioned but was nevertheless essential, yet try as he might he could not think what. Food, drink, purchasable comforts – these had all been arranged for. Medical supplies? The Medical Orderlies were responsible for them. Bedding? Each man took his own as part of the drill. Ammunition? It was already there in Tom's charge, should ever the Magistrates authorise him to issue it. Early Treatment Packets? Don't be silly, they won't have time for *that*. No, whatever it was, he was damned if he could place it, and since no one else had thought of it either, no blame could attach to him. Best drop it then. This was no time to fabricate supererogatory problems.

As for the third of his immediate tasks, which was to reassure the Colonel, this was disagreeable but brief.

"Sir, I've come to tell you—"

"—You're a mess, Morrison. That uniform looks as if you slept in it."

"As a matter of fact, sir, I did. You see—"

"—Yes, I know. You had to stand by the telephone or whatever it was. Understand this, Morrison: in this Regiment we accept no excuse – none at all, sir – for sloppy turn-out. Now what have you come to tell me?"

"Captain Oake says everything's under control."

"So I should hope. Six Platoons of Fusiliers against a few prancing natives. When will he be back?"

"The police want his assistance for a while longer."

"Useless lot, the police. All of them failed for Sandhurst, you know, and went for the second best – tenth best, I should say. All right, Morrison. Now for God's sake go and clean yourself up."

So Peter, leaving the O.R.Q.M.S. to keep watch on the R.T. Set, went to his quarters for a shower and a change. For a few minutes he relaxed, standing in the shower and stroking himself, thinking of Margaret Rose Engineer. ('It's spurting up inside me, more, more, more . . .') But when the fantasy had come to fulfilment ('All gone, all gone') he started to think seriously of serious things. For he now had to decide, within a few hours at most, how to get himself down to the Railway Station. Preferably with Tom Oake's permission, but if this were refused, then without it, he *must* get there before the next morning. If he did not reach the scene of action while action there still was, there would be an end of his plan for God knew how long and almost certainly for much too long. ('Four weeks, I was told to say. Quite generous, really.') Even when he got there, and for all his careful calculations, he would need a lot of luck, and even if he had it he could still very easily fail. But there was no point in dwelling on that; the thing to remember was this – that unless he reached the station while some sort of emergency was still in train, he would have no chance worth the name now or ever.

So how to get there? That evening, at latest that night? It was now four o'clock, so he must act very soon indeed. The

best thing, of course, would be to bamboozle Tom into ordering him to come – much better than turning up unbidden and
probably being turned back. But how to bamboozle Tom, who
had already denied him twice? 'You know, Morrison huzoor,'
Gilzai Khan had once said, 'in the Army there is one way,
fallible but always worth trying, of obtaining the orders you
wish to obtain, and that is to pretend that you no longer want
them.' Yes; given Tom Oake's military philosophy, which held
that it was both good and right for junior men to do what they
least wanted, the Khan's formula might well provide the
answer.

As soon as he had put on a clean uniform and had a cup of
tea in the Mess, Peter returned to the Adjutant's office to
relieve the O.R.Q.M.S.

"Any news, Q?"

"Nothing from Captain Oake, sir. The Quartermaster
reports that he has already sent off the supplies, but the R.S.M.
came in to say that there'd be a slight delay over the replacements of personnel."

"Oh, why?"

"The C.O. sent what's left of the Battalion on a route march
this morning. They've only just got back."

"*Route march?* Then who's been guarding the barracks?"

"Normal piquet, sir."

Choking back any further comments on the Colonel's
intransigence, Peter nodded briskly and stepped up to the R.T.
Set.

"Very well, Q. I'll warn Captain Oake. You go and have
your tea."

"Glad to stay with you, sir. It's all quite exciting, isn't it?"

So it might be; but for the next ten minutes or so Peter particularly wanted to be left alone with the wireless.

"I'd be most grateful, Q, if you could find the R.S.M. and
ask him to expedite those replacements."

"He's got all that in hand, sir. As soon as they've had a
meal—"

"—Please do as I ask, Q. I want you to go, yourself in person, and tell the R.S.M. that there is no time at all to be lost."

"Very well, sir."

Hurt by Peter's rejection of his company, irritated by the superfluity of the errand, humiliated at being ordered about by a mere one-pipper, the O.R.Q.M.S. saluted with extreme officiousness and stamped out of the room.

"One for seven," Peter said into the mouthpiece: "fetch Captain Oake. Over."

After a long and sweaty delay (would the O.R.Q.M.S. come bounding back as soon as he'd seen the R.S.M.?) Tom Oake's voice came up over the set.

"Seven for one. Where are my replacements?"

"One for seven. All spare personnel up here have been on a route march. They've just returned, and we're sending your replacements down as soon as possible."

"Route march? Christ, they'll be worn out."

"One for seven. Important information has been received from Delhi. Intelligence sources report that the leader of these riots is almost certainly Captain Gilzai Khan, repeat Gilzai Khan, late of the 43rd Khaipur Light Infantry and recently an instructor at the O.T.S., Bangalore."

And what was wrong with that? He had indeed had the information from Delhi, from the Viceroy's Galloper himself. Tell no lies, and do as you would be done by.

"The suggestion is," Peter continued (his own suggestion, as it happened, but it wasn't his fault if the phrase had an official and authoritative ring), "that in case of further attack you make every effort to seize Gilzai Khan's person, thus depriving the rioters of an experienced and determined leader."

"That's all very well, but he won't be parading about in the front row, now will he?"

"From what is known of his character, that's just what he may be doing."

"Anyhow, I shan't know which he is."

Careful now.

"Second Lieutenants Strange and Mortleman are both

capable of identifying him. Shall I send one of them down to you?"

An easy and natural proposal of the kind which always aroused instant opposition in military minds, just because it *was* easy and natural.

"You know him too, Peter. Better than they do, because you were his J.U.O. It might be best for you to come down here."

Good. He wants me with him. So far he's left me here because he knows I'm reliable on the set and he thinks it would be self-indulgent to take me away from it for the sake of my company. But here's his excuse, made to measure and totally respectable, to do what he really wants. Steady, boy: don't show willing.

"One for seven. Sorry, sir. I've got a lot on here."

"Seven for one. This is an Intelligence Officer's job if ever there was one. Tell Flitchley to take over on the R.T. Set, and come down with the replacements."

So that was it, for the record. 'At 1625 hours, 2/Lt. Morrison was ordered down to the station by Captain Oake.' He had been sent for; though he had pleaded the importance of other duties, had actually displayed reluctance, he had been commanded to go.

"Roger," Peter said : "over and out."

The O.R.Q.M.S. came in and saluted with a bang.

"R.S.M. reports the replacements will be ready to leave in five minutes, sir."

"Tell him to hold it for half an hour, Q. I've got to go with them myself."

"Half an hour, sir?"

"I've got to leave everything in order first."

"The men could have finished their tea properly if we'd known."

"We didn't know. Please send for Mr Flitchley to come and take over the set, while I tidy up the map for him next door."

"Sir."

"And please send instructions to have my kit loaded on to the column. Camp-bed and wash-stand included."

"SIR."

While the furious O.R.Q.M.S., like Lars Porsena, bade messengers go forth in all directions, Peter went into his own office. There was nothing to do on the map; he and his Sergeant had kept that up to the minute. But there was something else that must be done – and thank God the Sergeant was still at tea. Peter unlocked a drawer in his desk, unlocked a sturdy cash box that was inside the drawer, took out six rounds of .38 ammunition, and fitted them carefully into the drum of the revolver which he was carrying on his belt. He should not have possessed these rounds and he should certainly not be taking them with him (let alone loading them) now, as he had no permission to do so. But it was essential that he should have them by him; for the probability was that no ammunition would be officially issued unless matters came to crisis, whereas his plans required that he himself should be able to fire at need. Only as a last resort, to which he prayed that he would never come ('do as you would be done by'); but fire-power he must have in case. Not that he could do much with a .38 revolver, a ladies' weapon, as they always said. However, it would have to serve. It would look very odd if he toted a rifle about, or even a sten gun. Intelligence Officers carried revolvers, and that was that.

He snapped the drum back into the stock, fastened the safety-catch, replaced the pistol in his holster, and returned to the Adjutant's office to wait for Flitchley. In fact he could be ready to leave in ten minutes if Flitchley was prompt and his servants didn't dally with his kit; but he had stipulated half an hour to impress on everybody how little he had expected to be summoned and how difficult it was for him to leave his present charge. To all eyes, he must appear as one who had been surprised and upset by his orders, very far from the man who had anticipated and indeed contrived them.

To further the illusion of his unreadiness, Peter joined the column only seconds before it left for the bazaar, running up in a state of visible agitation and bundling himself into the cab of the leading lorry. It was only when they reached the bazaar, therefore, and the men climbed down to make a tactical approach to the station, that he discovered that both Barry and Alister were there with him – had in fact been travelling in the lorry immediately behind him.

"What the hell are you two doing? No Officers were called for except me."

"Over half my Platoon's among these replacements," said Barry. "Of course I had to come."

"They'll be distributed among the other Platoons. You won't be able to command them."

"I know that. I've come here to be with them."

"Same here," Alister said. "Flitchley can't come with our lot, so I did."

There was a ripple of pleasure among the soldiers near enough to hear this conversation.

"No one told you to come. You'd both better stay here and go back with the lorries."

"I think," said Barry, "that we'll let Captain Oake decide that."

"And now," said Alister, "let's get this lot to the station. Why couldn't we take the lorries right into the station yard?"

"Tom Oake's worried about booby traps."

"Then how does he want us to move?"

"Single file; alternate sections on opposite sides of the street."

"Right," said Alister, and started cheerfully bawling a string of appropriate orders which he had learned, painfully and therefore indelibly, as Flitchley's second-in-command. In thirty seconds flat the men were ready to move off.

"The men are ready to march, sir," said Alister in the correct Fusilier style to Peter, who was technically the senior Officer present. "May I have your permission to give the order?"

"Pray proceed, sir," said Peter, conforming to the idiom.

Alister took post at the head of the leading section and ordered the advance. Barry wanted to join the two sections of his own men, but was asked by Peter to walk with him in the rear.

"Why come looking for trouble?" Peter grumbled: "you said you loathed the very idea of this kind of thing."

"So I do. But if my men must be here, then I must. You've just been in an office these last weeks, Peter. So you haven't had a chance to discover what the whole thing's about. It's only about one thing, really : being there when you're wanted."

"No one wanted you here."

"My men might. They'll feel very awkward and lonely, being scattered round different platoons. But if I'm there to go round and say a word or two, they may not mind so much."

"Flatter yourself, don't you? A little touch of Barry in the night."

Barry flushed and then blinked.

"Do you think I learnt nothing," Peter went on, "being J.U.O. all that time?"

"That was different. Bangalore was a training establishment and we were all Cadets."

"Yes, Officer Cadets. Who are meant to learn that the first thing – the only thing in the end – is to obey orders. You've come here against orders, Barry. So don't blame me if you get more than you bargained for."

"What on earth do you mean by that?"

Remembering the events of that evening months and even years later, Peter often wondered how he would have replied to this question, in what terms, vague or precise, in what tone, wheedling or minatory. In fact, however, he never had to give an answer; because even as the possible combinations of words began to pass through his mind, there was a deafening hiss which seemed to fill all heaven, and they were suddenly walking in cataracts of rain.

The Monsoon.

Which, as every schoolboy knew, had been due in this area any time these last three days. Every schoolboy perhaps, Peter thought, but not, apparently, the Commanding Officer of the First Battalion, the Wessex Fusiliers, to judge from the date he had chosen for his Retreat Parade (no wonder so few guests came), nor indeed the Adjutant and the Quartermaster, who had neglected, between them, to issue the troops with water-

proof capes. It was of these he had been thinking, or rather
failing to think, when earlier in the afternoon he had told himself that something had been forgotten. Now he knew what.
The men only had ground-sheets, which would be pitifully
inadequate; by the time the Q.M. had sent down proper capes,
they would all be soaked through and through, and since the
short-term effect of the heavy rain would be a sharp drop in
temperature, there would be some atrocious fevers and an
increase in the already endemic diarrhoea.

Splendid, Peter thought. The more disease, the more
muddle; the more muddle, the greater his chances of success.
True, the arrival of Alister and Barry was a nasty shock, as
these two, if once they recognised Gilzai Khan or even knew
he was among the rioters, might well prove serious obstacles
to Peter's plan; but Tom Oake would probably send them back
to barracks, and even if he didn't, the Monsoon, the steaming,
streaming, eye-dulling, mind-splitting Monsoon, would be an
ally that offered far more assistance than Barry or Alister could
possibly effect in hindrance. Thinking of all this, Peter grinned
roundly at Barry through the rain and spread his hands, palms
upwards, miming the need for charity in their new predicament; and was answered, after just perceptible hesitation, by
Barry's puzzled but forgiving smile.


A few minutes later, Alister and the leading section turned into
the station yard.

This was an area of sandy earth, some seventy yards square,
the top or north side of the square being the façade of the
station and the bottom or south side being a continuation of
the street along which Alister had led the replacements in a
westerly direction from the bazaar. On its east and west sides,
the station yard was closed off by high stone walls; while all
along the south side it was open to the street, from which it
was separated only by a thin strip of concrete that was flush
with both yard and street and passed as a kind of pavement.
Lining the south of the street was a high and rickety structure
of wood, which continued unbroken from a crossing some fifty

yards east of the yard to another crossing fifty yards west of it. Into this somewhat rococo building there were doors at every thirty yards or so, these being about ten feet above ground level and approachable from the street by means of exterior staircases, which were most of them little better than step-ladders.

Normally the station yard was crowded with rickshaws, gharries and motor-taxis, all of which would mill round in front of the façade in chaotic competition for custom, except in wet weather, when they would assemble, the yard being un-negotiable, along the street. It was for this alone, in fact, that Berhampore was mildly famous: if you arrived there during the rainy season, you had to convey yourself and your baggage across seventy yards of deep orange mud (the 'Berhampore Quag') to the line of vehicles beyond the concrete strip.

This evening, however, both yard and street were deserted; naturally enough, of course; but the total emptiness of the square was nonetheless disquieting and reminded Peter, as he came into view of the yard, of something more disquieting still. Thomas Oake had said that the approaches to the station from the bazaar were secure and well guarded; yet there had been no signs of guards or patrols. Possibly these were in the houses which lined the street, and certainly they themselves had made the approach safely enough (so far). But Peter did not like it, and liked it even less when he reflected that, apart from the entrance to the station through the centre of the façade, the only way out of the square was along the street, which was particularly narrow at the two points of egress, or (presumably) up one of the staircases and into the huge wooden shanty, which might not prove a very wholesome refuge.

But it was too late to worry about that. Alister, who was leading the replacements (now in one long file) along the east wall of the yard, was already half way to the station façade. When he reached it, he would only have another thirty yards or so to go – along half of the façade itself and then under the fake portcullis and into the Gothic portal. Looking through the rain towards the station (whose pert turrets and dotty battlements reminded him of the silver model of the Depot

Keep in the Mess), and observing Alister as he turned left and started along the façade, Peter breathed a sigh of relief and began to squelch through the mud (not quite a 'Quag' yet, but already glutinous) behind Barry at the rear of the column.

Then two things happened. The late afternoon became night and the rain almost doubled in volume. One moment he could see the façade, could even distinguish turrets and embrasures, and had a clear view of Alister as he walked beneath them; the next moment he could see Barry before him and up to the third man in front of Barry and no further at all. Not to worry. But why has there been no sign of sentries under the portcullis, no sign of anyone to greet us, come to that no sign of life whatever since we arrived in this accursed mud-patch? Do be sensible. This isn't Windsor Castle. Of course there aren't any sentries strutting about in the open, they've all been posted tactically at windows, behind those embrasures . . . out of which they can now see nothing, any more than I can, oh, do get a move on in front.

"Get a shufti on," he rasped at Barry : "pass it down."

Muddle all right, I wanted it, I've got it : nothing but muddle and mud.

"Shufti, shufti," he said.

But Barry, of course, couldn't hear, not unless Peter shouted, and that would be undignified. Anyway, what was he panicking about? They must be within twenty yards of the façade by now, only fifty yards to go in, a thick wall on the right of them, open ground on the left, no one could cross it without the sentries saw them, only of course the sentries couldn't see anything now – *so look left quick.*

Nothing. A wall of water. Look front. Why were there no lights in the windows? Surely *lights* would be visible? What game was Tom playing? Playing possum, playing dead? Someone coming down the line towards him, a huge, menacing figure, striding down like a moving statue . . . Alister, thank God. Alister smiling, waving them on, nothing to fear, Alister receding into the rain now, going up and down the line, no doubt, to keep them moving and reassure them : *there when wanted*, 'that's what it's all about'. Turn left down the façade

. . . look up at the windows, false of course, that's why there wasn't any light out of them, everything easily explained if only a man kept his head.

Under the portcullis and into the porch at last. There was no rain now but even less light than outside. It seemed that some way ahead there was a large inner gate, like a cathedral door. Just in front of Peter in the porch was Barry, and in front of Barry was a queue of figures up to the gate, at which Alister, just recognisable in the torch-light which now and then flicked through the narrow opening, was checking the men through. Over to Peter's left and somewhat to his rear, in a niche in the wall beneath one end of the fake portcullis, a Fusilier was crouching on one knee. A sentry. Not strutting, of course, not out in the open, a proper sentry, crouching in a recess, keeping watch from behind cover as a sentry should.

"An inclement evening, Morrison huzoor," the sentry said.

Peter stood quite still. Barry turned and went to the crouching figure.

"Khan," Barry said.

The figures ahead of Peter shuffled on, soaked, miserable and unnoticing, towards the gate.

"Khan, what are you—?"

"—Don't you know, little Cadet? Get Mortleman here. Make some excuse."

"I'll do that," said Peter.

He walked the twenty yards up the porch to the inner gate, where Alister was admitting the last of the soldiers. On the other side of the gate, visible through the foot-wide gap, was Tom Oake and a Sergeant.

"Good evening, sir," Peter said.

"Peter . . . What's Mortleman doing here?"

"He helped me bring the replacements down. He's going back now."

"I don't understand. Why did you need him?"

"I'll explain later, Tom."

This was the first time he had ever so addressed the Adjutant, who for the moment was too surprised (as he was meant to be) to call for a more ample account. Peter seized Alister by the wrist and swung him away from the gate.

"What the hell?"

"The Khan," whispered Peter. "Come on."

"The Khan?" repeated Alister, loudly and stupidly.

"What was that?" said Tom Oake from behind the gate.

"The car, Tom. The C.O.'s in it, waiting for Mortleman."

"I still don't understand."

"He came to see we got here all right. He's taking Mortleman back."

"But why—"

"—Please don't delay us, Tom, or the road may be flooded." He dragged Alister down the porch.

"Don't forget the password," Tom Oake called after them: " 'The Drum is in Berhampore Station.' "

The inner gate now closed behind them. Peter and Alister reached the portcullis end of the porch and huddled into the recess with Barry and Gilzai Khan.

"What have you done with the real sentry?" Peter asked at once.

"Two of them, huzoor. They're unconscious out there in the yard. You must not blame them when they recover. The rain was very thick."

"Gilzai Khan," said Alister, "what are you doing here?"

"He's leading tne riots," said Barry, with a mixture of apprehension and pride. "He hasn't had time to explain properly, but it's all pro-British, in a way. He wants us to stay in India."

"For as long as is necessary," the Khan said, "to prevent the Hindus from slaughtering us Mohammedans – and us from butchering them back."

"But why the riot?" Alister said.

"To make them listen to us in Delhi. They refuse to listen, huzoor."

"Why choose Berhampore?"

"Chance, huzoor. One must start somewhere."

"Peter's known he was here for some time," Barry said.

"You didn't tell us?"

"Yes, why not?" Barry rounded on Peter in accusation, then looked at the Khan as at a man betrayed.

"I suppose he had his reasons," said the Khan lightly.

"He should have told us," Barry huffed.

"But now we know," said Alister to the Khan, "I imagine we ought to arrest you. Beating our sentries about like that. But one can't arrest one's old instructor; it would be like arresting one's housemaster. In any case, I gather your visit is amicable?"

"Yes, Mortleman huzoor. I saw you arrive in the bazaar, and—"

"—What have you done with our guards?" Peter interrupted. "In the bazaar and on the route here?"

"Nothing, huzoor. They don't worry us. They spend most of their time watching the people in the houses. But we are like lice in the woodwork. We come and we go."

"Never mind all that," said Alister: "just what is this visit here in aid of? You saw us get out in the bazaar, you say, and you've followed us here to the station—"

"—I was here before you were, huzoor—"

"—You *came* here to the station. Alone, I hope—"

"—Alone indeed, huzoor—"

"WHY?"

Gilzai Khan gave a sad little grin.

"I have come here . . . to exonerate myself," he said. "You see, some time ago I asked Peter Morrison to keep you, you and the little Strange, away from here when trouble started. Not because there is any real danger – we only wish to gain attention, you understand, not to kill anyone – but because I did not choose to be seen by you in my new role. I am not ashamed of what I am doing, but nevertheless I wished your memories of Gilzai Khan to end with Bangalore. There we were friends, and parted in love and honour. All this, I thought, would be spoiled if I now became for you . . . another wog agitator."

Alister considered this, shivering slightly in the damp.

"And yet you told Peter what you were doing? And you thought he would tell us?"

"I did not mind your knowing, indeed I realised that you must all hear of it sooner or later, but I mind your *seeing*. In the imagination, a rebel leader can be a romantic, even a heroic figure, especially if his cause is good. But when seen in the flesh, screaming and mouthing and spitting and clawing – for that is what leaders of riots must do, my brothers – such a person is without appeal to gentlemen like yourselves. You might say . . . that I did not wish to lose face before you, for in doing so I should lose face in my own eyes too. After all, it is a disgraceful thing to embarrass one's friends.

"But here you are, despite my request, and soon the rioting will be renewed, and so soon you must see me, capering about like a moon-man, throwing stones and exhorting the scum of the Moslem quarters. . . . No, my brothers, I cannot endure that it should be so. And yet it must be so, it seems. So I have come to make the only amends I can." He reached behind him and brought out a long thin object with what looked, in the darkness, like a ball of silver at one end of it. "The sword you gave me when I left you all. It is the dearest gift that I have ever had, and I have kept it bright and sharp for love of you. Now I must give it you back."

"But *why*?" Barry said. "We don't think any the worse of you."

"Don't you?" said Peter. "It was you that said, only the other day, that the very thought of riots made you sick."

"Alister said that."

"And you agreed with him."

"I said I didn't want any part in helping to put riots down. It made me sick to think of pointing a rifle at unarmed civilians. But to *be* a rebel, to fight for something you think worthwhile – there's nothing wrong in that."

"Nevertheless, huzoor, to see the rebel Gilzai Khan leading his rioters will make you truly sick. When you see me, frothing at the lips and calling with arms upraised upon Allah in whom you know I do not believe, *it will make you sick*. There is no time for more talk. Take back this sword."

Holding it parallel to the ground with his two hands, he passed the sword to Barry.

"What difference will that make?" Alister said.

"It is a kind of resignation. Just as I resigned the King Emperor's commission before I could undertake such work as this, so I am now resigning my claim to your friendship. Because I am now unworthy."

Gilzai Khan rose to his feet.

"But you are not unworthy," Barry said desperately. "I don't say it's what I would have wished for you, and I'm afraid it may lead to a lot of trouble, but that doesn't mean I don't want you for a friend any more."

"Right," said Alister. "One doesn't disown a friend just because he makes an ass of himself."

"I am not making an ass of myself, Mortleman huzoor. What I am doing must be done."

"Then why are you unworthy?"

"Because by my acts I am lowering myself in your eyes – and in mine. I cannot explain any more. You will understand when you see me leading my rabble . . . myself a part of it."

Now or never, Peter thought. It hadn't come about at all as he had envisaged, and the presence of Barry and Alister was a factor unforeseen, but nevertheless a variant of his plan could now be set in train. Some attempt, at any rate, could be – must be – made. As for Barry and Alister, if he watched them carefully, they might be less of a nuisance than he had feared. They might even, just conceivably, serve his ends, if only as witnesses. Very well, Peter thought, bracing himself : do as you would be done by and tell no lies.

"I disguised myself in the uniform of one of those sentries," Gilzai Khan was saying, "and left my poor rags over him in exchange. Please see that he is not out of pocket." He passed some coins to Alister. "The rifles of both men are safe in here" – he pointed to the back of the recess – "and I do not think that either will take much harm from his experience, beyond a nasty headache. Indeed, it may teach them to be more alert for the future."

He waved his hand at them, palm outwards, in a limp movement to and fro across his chest, and stepped out into the rain, which was now slackening a little.

"I suppose he's got to take that uniform with him," Barry said reluctantly.

Peter looked quickly into Barry's rumpled face, and was at once made glad by what he saw there. *Of course*; but how could he use it?

"Gilzai Khan," Peter said.

The Khan turned.

"Those rifles," said Peter: "did you think they were loaded when you assaulted our sentries?"

"I thought they might be, huzoor. Later I found they were not."

"No. Because no ammunition has been issued. But you didn't know that. And anyhow, the bayonets were fixed?"

"Yes, huzoor."

"So you had to surprise two men, with fixed bayonets, who for all you knew might have shot you. Quite an undertaking, even for a man of your experience?"

"There was darkness and rain, huzoor. You saw what rain. And they were nearly twenty yards apart."

"Even so. . . . How did you do it?"

"From behind. With a garotte. First one, then the other." Barry shuddered.

"With a garotte? You might have killed them."

"No, huzoor. I know how long to apply the garotte in order to make a man faint without killing him."

"And then what?" Peter said. "They've been unconscious a very long time."

"A powder, huzoor, down the throat. I have no more time for these questions."

"All this trouble just to return a sword? There were a hundred ways you could have done it. You could have slipped it into the porch in the rain. You could have sent it through the post, come to that."

"I wished, very much, to try to explain."

"Let him go, Peter," Alister said. "What are you trying to prove?"

"I've proved it. In order to satisfy his personal pride, his honour I suppose he would call it, Gilzai Khan has endangered the lives of two Fusiliers. Not only has he strangled them and filled them with drugs, he's left them lying in the mud – drowning in it for all he knows – and exposed to torrential rain. Before you leave, Gilzai Khan, you're going to take us to those sentries, and we're going to make sure they're all right."

The Khan shrugged.

"Very well. But please be quick."

So far, so good, Peter thought. Tell no lies and do as you would be done by. I'm not deceiving him or being false to him; I'm merely displaying a proper concern for the Regiment's soldiers – which the Khan of all people will understand.

The little procession set off through the 'Quag' (as now indeed it was). First the Khan, moving quickly and neatly in the Fusilier sentry's jungle green; then Peter, clumsily tramping; Alister likewise; and Barry bringing up in the rear, still holding the Khan's sheathed sword. The two sentries were in fact at the west end of the façade, propped up against it in a sitting position, and to some degree sheltered by the corner which the façade made with the side wall. One was naked, except for socks and underpants, but as the Khan had said, his own clothes (linen breeches and a long shirt) had been thrown over the man as covering. Both soldiers were sleeping quietly.

"There you are," said the Khan.

Peter bent down to examine their throats. The rain had almost stopped now, and the moon was giving a little light through the cloud . . . enough to enable Peter to see that the weals made by the garotte were not serious. They were not even raw.

"Right," said Peter. "Take off that uniform so that we can dress this poor fellow properly. And put these things back on yourself."

He picked up the breeches and the shirt and passed them to the Khan. Barry nodded fiercely in approval.

"I have no time. I've paid for the soldier's clothes—"

"—That's right," said Alister, jingling the coins in his pocket; "forty rupees and the odd anna—"

"—And now I must go. I have a council to attend and I am already late. Good-bye, gentlemen; stay well."

The Khan dropped his clothes and turned. Barry swallowed and scowled. Peter drew his pistol and blocked the Khan's way.

"Gilzai Khan. You are wilfully impersonating a soldier of His Majesty. Pick up those clothes and change."

"Don't be silly, Peter," said Alister.

"He's not being silly," Barry said, earnest and excited. "That's a Fusilier uniform, and Gilzai Khan has no business to wear it. He's going to use it to come spying or something. He can have his own clothes back now, and he hasn't got the slightest excuse."

"Don't be childish, Barrikins."

"He's no right to a Fusilier uniform," Barry said. "*My brothers died in that uniform.* He'll use it to make fun of us to the mob – it's the sort of thing he has to do, he said so himself."

"Do you grudge me a uniform, little Cadet?"

"I won't have Fusilier dress on a rebel," babbled Barry.

"You approved of me as a rebel just now."

"Not in that uniform. You can't sneak round with a filthy garotte wearing that badge in your hat."

The Khan made to pass Peter. Peter cocked his pistol. Alister laughed.

"No use trying that old trick on Gil' Khan," he said: "there's no ammunition been issued."

The statement was true; let it pass. Peter said nothing, but lowered the pistol and looked apologetically at Barry. Now let it work.

"Off you go, Gil' Khan," said Alister, "or you may really embarrass us. If anyone could see us now . . ."

"Take off that uniform first," howled Barry. "My brothers died in that uniform, and you're only an Indian, you're not even in the Army any more, not even the Indian Army, you're just a dirty wog."

For a moment Gilzai Khan faltered and seemed about to turn. Then he shrugged slightly and moved on.

"Stop," wailed Barry.

The Khan walked on. Barry ran up behind him. He drew

the Khan's sword from its sheath and thrust crazily at the Khan's hips. From where Peter stood, the steel strip seemed to stop and buckle, then somehow to straighten after all and to be sliding back into its hilt like a toy or a weapon used on stage. But the Khan slumped to the ground, and when Barry released the sword hilt it wagged on the partly buried blade.

Barry, Peter and Alister stood over the fallen body. The Khan bared his teeth and grinned up at them.

"Morrison huzoor," he said, "I wish you the long and successful career which your ingenuity deserves." He gasped slightly. "Oh Strange huzoor," he said, "oh my little Cadet, why should I not wear your brothers' uniform? We were brothers, you and I, were we not? I only wished to wear, for just a little time, the same badge as you."

"Khan. Oh khan my khan my khan."

And Barry bent to kiss the grinning face, and was too late, for the lips now grinned in death.

### REPORT of a SPECIAL ENQUIRY
held at BERHAMPORE (PUNJAB)
on June 20, 1946
By Order of His Excellency the
VICEROY OF INDIA

*Subject of Enquiry:* The Death by Stabbing of the Moslem agitator, Gilzai Khan, formerly Captain in the 43rd Khaipur Light Infantry.

*Members of the Board:* The Investigating Officers appointed by H.E. the Viceroy were Lieutenant-Colonel Glastonbury and Captain Detterling, both of the 49th Earl Hamilton's Light Dragoons but presently serving on the Military Staff of H.E. the Viceroy.

*Report:* Colonel Glastonbury and Captain Detterling, having examined the three Officers of the Wessex Fusiliers who were present at Gilzai Khan's death and also a Medical Witness, and having taken their depositions on oath, have established to their entire satisfaction the following sequence of events :

1 At approximately 1800 hours, on June 18, 1946, at Berhampore Station, Second Lieutenants P. Morrison, B. Strange and A. Mortleman were conducting a draft of Fusiliers into the station hall through the main entrance.

2 Just as they had completed their duties in this respect, they discovered and apprehended (Captain) Gilzai Khan, who was disguised as a Fusilier sentry and lurking, under cover of darkness, in an alcove by the main entrance.

3 All three Officers had known Gilzai Khan for some weeks between January and March of this year, as they had been instructed by him, during the said period, at the Officers' Training School at Bangalore. They therefore recognised him at once.

4 Knowing that Gilzai Khan no longer had any connexion with the Armed Forces of the Crown, the three Officers warned him that he was under arrest. They then searched the alcove and removed from Gilzai Khan's possession two rifles, unloaded but with bayonets fixed, which he had taken from two unconscious sentries (see below), and one sheathed sword, his own personal weapon.

5 2/Lt Mortleman then challenged Gilzai Khan to explain his presence and his dress. Gilzai Khan then admitted that he was the leader of the Moslem rioters in Berhampore (a fact which has subsequently been confirmed by the Special Branch) and had been observing the arrival of the draft of Fusiliers at the station. He further admitted that he had garotted two Fusilier sentries, the uniform of one of whom he was now wearing as disguise.

6 The three Officers then ordered Gilzai Khan to take them immediately to the sentries. These had been left lying in the thick mud some thirty yards from the station entrance. They were still unconscious and had been visibly marked by the garotte. One of them was naked.

7 2/Lt Morrison now ordered Gilzai Khan to remove the uniform which he was wearing, in order that it might be put back on to the naked and seriously exposed sentry who was its rightful owner.

8 Gilzai Khan refused. 2/Lt Morrison threatened him with his empty revolver (no ammunition had been issued to British personnel) but Gilzai Khan was not deceived by the bluff and now attempted to escape.

9 2/Lt Strange, who had been given charge of Gilzai Khan's sword, drew it from its scabbard and tried to detain Gilzai Khan by threatening a pass at his body.

10 Gilzai Khan ignored the threat and was pierced, in the ensuing confusion, between hip-bone and rib-cage at his left rear. Gilzai Khan was dead within a minute.

11 *Expert Statement by Lt. Col. Glastonbury*, British Army Sabre Champion (1938) and selected member of the British Fencing Team for the 1940 Olympic Games:

i) If any thrust delivered from the level and the direction recorded is to prove lethal, the swordsman must pierce part of a very small target area.

ii) The evidence of 2/Lt Strange and his two colleagues makes it plain beyond doubt that he was not aiming at this area, or indeed at any particular area, of Gilzai Khan's body. He was merely making a clumsy general effort to stop a fast-moving man in the dark.

iii) That the thrust went home where it did, and deeply enough to prove fatal, must therefore be deemed the purest chance.

"There we are," said Colonel Glastonbury, looking up from the text which he had been reading aloud to Peter: "no difficulties there, I think."

He took up his pen and poised it over the bottom of the last page.

"No difficulties at all," said Peter; "unless they show it to Major Murphy and ask for his opinion."

"They'll have to be very persistent to get one," said Captain Detterling. "Murphy's dead."

"One of those accidents which Viceroy's Gallopers are heir to," Glastonbury said : "a bomb in his engine."

"Had his transfer come through?" asked Peter stupidly. "To Lord Curzon's Horse?"

"No."

"Pity. He'd have liked that. You might at least have done that for him before he was killed."

"My dear fellow, you speak as though I were somehow responsible for his death."

"Who was?"

"Messengers who carry bad news," said Detterling, "are never popular. It was Major Murphy's job to carry very bad news, far and wide, to all sorts and conditions of people. One of them was a certain Maharajah – Dharaparam, as it happens – in whom H.E.'s Government had rather a pressing interest. . . ."

"Dharaparam used to come to our cricket matches at Bangalore. He wouldn't have killed a fly, let alone Murphy."

"But he had loyal servants who might have been more energetic. Mind you, we can't prove anything. Nor, where Murphy is concerned, do we want to. You see," said Giles Glastonbury, "we quite like a quick turnover in this particular appointment."

"I do see," said Peter. "No names, no pack drill?"

"That's about it. . . ."

Glastonbury signed the report at last and handed the pen to Detterling, who signed in his turn. Glastonbury then piled all the sheets together and worked carefully at them with his two middle fingers until they were absolutely flush.

"You'd better show this to your two chums," he said, rapping the neat pile. "You'll all three have to countersign it. And then you'd better spruce yourselves up and get out your best uniforms."

Peter gave him a puzzled look.

"In order that there should be general recognition," Glastonbury said, "of your timely action in apprehending the rebel leader, and of your steady performance of duty in the very difficult circumstances thereafter, you are each to receive a scroll of commendation from the Viceroy. I shall have to telephone Delhi for final confirmation first, but I've no doubt . . . none at all, Morrison . . . that it will be forthcoming. The scrolls will be publicly presented to you by myself at a parade of your Battalion – such of it, that is, as is still fit to be mustered. We do not intend to make much noise by the presentation : just enough to make it absolutely clear to everybody concerned that your honourable and resourceful behaviour was in no way compromised by the death of Gilzai Khan, any attributable blame for which is solely his own."

Peter stood quite still, looking at the sheaf of paper which Glastonbury was now holding out to him.

"Don't stand there like an imbecile," Glastonbury said. "Take this Report off to Strange and Mortleman, and tell them to get their servants busy on their kit. I'm now going to telephone Delhi to assure them that everything's *thik hai*" – he rose from his seat and stretched languorously – "and then I shall arrange with your C.O. for the presentation parade to take place this afternoon."

"God, I feel horrible," Barry said, after Alister and he had read the Report of the Enquiry.

"It wasn't your fault," said Alister. "Glastonbury's made that clear enough. It was an accident."

"That's all whitewashing. Because they're glad he's dead and the riots have fizzled out."

"Not whitewashing," Peter said. "They're just . . . putting it all in the correct official perspective, so that no one can be got at later on."

"Same thing. Whitewashing."

"Look, Barrikins," said Alister : "the one thing they've established beyond any doubt at all is that we were not responsible for the Khan's death. There *is* nothing to whitewash."

"They're glad he's dead. So they don't care whether we're responsible or not, but they want it to look good on paper. Then no one can make trouble for Delhi or the Government in the House of Commons. Those scrolls they're going to give us – they're about as genuine as a three-pound note."

"That just isn't true," Peter said. "We're being commended for what we did *before* the Khan was killed. They're saying to us that we did exactly what we should have done in very tricky conditions, and it's not our fault that Gil' Khan got killed at the end of it."

"But all the same they're jolly pleased he's dead. Don't tell me that these . . . commendations . . . haven't got something to do with their satisfaction at his death. Some of that satisfaction has got into their feelings about us."

"Even if that's true," said Alister, "we're not to blame for it. Why can't you just accept the facts? The Khan's death was an accident. You were quite right to try and stop him when he was escaping, but you didn't mean to kill him, and you couldn't have killed him even if you had meant to – had it not been for a chance of one in a thousand."

"How can you know what I did mean or didn't?"

"All right," said Alister crossly : "do you want me to go and tell Glastonbury that you meant to kill the Khan after all and ought to be charged with murder?"

Barry bit his lip till the blood came.

"It's not as simple as that," he said; "and I don't suppose I could have meant to, not really. But what makes me feel so rotten is all this pretence, all this business of scrolls and parades and speeches. Whatever you say, it's a kind of celebration. Why can't they just shut up and leave it at that?"

"Because," said Peter, "they've got to put their message over, for their sake and for ours – particularly yours. They're not celebrating the Khan's death; they're disowning it. What they're saying is this : we grant that a lot of good has come of this death, which has therefore been very convenient for us, *but*, they're saying, we insist that no one in the Army, near or far, was responsible for it. They're commending us in order to assure everyone that we were absolutely above-board all through and *didn't* kill Gilzai Khan."

"Except that we did. Or at least I did."

"Not *culpably*. That's the point they want to make."

"Then they're protesting too much," Barry said. "Why can't they just keep quiet?"

"Because they want to create an atmosphere of normality, of routine. You can't do that by keeping quiet. Normality requires that people who behaved as we did—"

"—As they like to think we did—"

"—*That people who capture rebel leaders* should be mildly commended for their services. So that's just what is being done. A small parade, nothing out of the way, but just noticeable and probably recorded in two lines at the bottom of a column in the *Telegraph*. A small parade, I say, and three scrolls of fake parchment, and a few words from the Viceroy's representative. Just what everyone would expect after a decent sort of show. Entirely suitable – and therefore entirely forgettable. That's what they want, Barry, and that's how it will turn out: the whole thing will be forgotten by most people within ten days."

"Not by me, it won't," Barry said.

". . . And furthermore," said Colonel Glastonbury to the assembled Battalion (of which about half, in the event, had been fit for parade), "I know that His Excellency would wish me to add this: that another reason why the conduct of these Officers is felt to be truly commendable is that it was based upon consideration, upon good manners. Consideration for their own soldiers, consideration for their opponent – even though they were bound to restrain him. Gentlemen of the Wessex Fusiliers, next to duty it is courtesy that we are rewarding this afternoon."

Alister, Barry and Peter stepped forward, in reverse order of seniority, to receive their handshakes and their scrolls. As Glastonbury handed his to Peter, it started to rain again, and under cover of this Captain Detterling (who was a yard behind

Glastonbury and a yard to his right) just perceptibly winked. Only for a split second, and his face, both before and after, was as heavy and blank as a tomb : but during that split second the serene surface of things was rent by Detterling's wink, and through the crack which opened the devil smiled out at Peter in joyless amusement at the joke.

Nobody else much smiled that afternoon, except Colonel Brockworthy, who was pleased that the disagreeable duties connected with the riot were now over, and that credit (albeit of a kind he himself valued little if at all) seemed somehow to have accrued to the Regiment. Most officers, being wet through and somewhat puzzled by the whole affair, simply looked cross and slunk off to change as soon as possible. Even the three who had just been distinguished seemed to think that modesty (or discretion) required them to stay out of the way; so that very soon after the parade was over only Glastonbury, Detterling, Colonel Brockworthy and Thomas Oake were left in the Mess. After a very long silence, Tom Oake looked into his whisky and said :

"Too many lies. There's something fishy in all this."

"They rather like the smell in Delhi," said Detterling lightly. "I'd remember that if I were you. Anyway, what lies?"

"About Mortleman, for example. He shouldn't have been there."

"That was all explained," said Glastonbury : "Mortleman and Strange came to be with their men."

"I wasn't told at the time that Strange was there at all. And as for Mortleman, Morrison said he was going straight back – in the C.O.'s car, of all things."

"I expect," said Detterling, "that Morrison had a lot to think about. His immediate concern, remember, was to fetch Mortleman to help guard Gilzai Khan. He had no time to lose, so he probably told you the first thing that came into his head."

"He could just as well have told me the truth and fetched *me* to Gilzai Khan. That's what he should have done."

"That," said Glastonbury, "is a tricky area, I admit, but it's covered by the Old Chums Act."

"Old Chums Act?"

"Gilzai Khan had been their commander and their friend. They wanted to sort it all out themselves if they could."

"Their duty was nonetheless plain. And there are a lot of other things which don't add up. What do you say, sir?" he said to his C.O.

Colonel Brockworthy pondered.

"I say," he said at last, "that when you have bloody things like riot duty there's no good in stirring up trouble afterwards. Riot duty isn't proper soldiering; you must expect peculiar things to happen – and then do your best to forget about 'em. They don't really count."

"A very sensible attitude," said Glastonbury. "Of course there are a few inconsistencies here. There always are on these occasions. But if," he said to Tom Oake, "you had anything of importance to raise, you should have done so before the presentation parade."

"How could I? You never even called me as witness at your Enquiry."

"Because you couldn't possibly have had anything relevant to say, my dear fellow. You were stuck behind that gate the whole time."

Tom Oake took a swig at his drink.

"Then allow me to say something that is relevant now, Colonel Glastonbury. When you telephoned Delhi before luncheon . . . to ask them to confirm that you could hand out those bits of cardboard . . . you didn't get through. The wires have been down for the last twelve hours. And yet you went ahead with the presentation."

"During the Monsoons," said Colonel Glastonbury, very patiently, "telephone wires are coming down all the time. This being so, a man of foresight always obtains provisional instructions, in case. Mine were quite clear. I was to use my judgment in the matter – a judgment in which those about the Viceroy were sufficiently confident to advise His Excellency to sign those scrolls before I left. I was given permission, in case of losing contact with Delhi, to award them or withhold them, as I saw fit."

"So much the worse for you," snarled Oake, "if your judgment turns out to have been at fault."

"Come, come, Oake," said the C.O.

"So much the worse for nobody," Detterling said. "The whole thing's over, man. Don't you know what those scrolls mean? They mean that the Viceroy, and therefore the King Emperor whom he represents, considers that those three boys behaved in a praiseworthy and honourable fashion. The *King* has said that this is so, and if the King says it, it is so. If the King ennobles a man, that man is noble, no matter what the shifts which procured him his patent. If the King has honoured three of your Officers, then they are honourable, and it ill becomes you, who carry the King's commission, to say else."

"I suppose that's true," said the C.O. wearily; "in the context," he added, and looked at Tom Oake guiltily, as though he were somehow letting down the Regiment by using such a sophisticated phrase.

"You'll excuse me, sir," said Tom to Brockworthy alone, and walked stiffly out.

"The poor fellow can't understand," said Detterling, "that this is the only way of making a hopeless situation at all tolerable."

"I don't quite follow," the C.O. said.

"We are soon to leave India," Glastonbury told him, "in circumstances of confusion and disrepute. It's a bad thing, Colonel, and it entails every kind of treachery and deceit, daily and at all levels. The formula which we have devised, and used successfully here, ensures that at least *some* semblance of order and of honour is retained."

"There has been deceit here?" said the bewildered Brockworthy.

"I'm not saying that. I'm saying that if there had been, then here as elsewhere our formula would guarantee ... an impression of seemliness."

"I see," said the C.O. at long last. "Correct me if I am wrong, but I don't think this formula of yours is altogether new."

"Far from it. We have merely adapted it to the time and the place. We use it to save face, Colonel, to keep things ticking over . . . and to protect men who can't really help what they do."

"My three Officers?"

"One of them, perhaps," said Captain Detterling, and shrugged. "Never mind which. For whichever it may or may not be, he's not to blame. He's not so much a fraud as a victim – a victim of the Necessity of the times through which we are passing."

"All that's a bit beyond me," the C.O. said. "But mum's the word, if I hear you right. I'll see you to say good-bye before you go back to Delhi. But just now I think I've got this diarrhoea coming on."

Colonel Brockworthy wandered lugubriously out. Colonel Glastonbury faced Captain Detterling.

"Promising fellow, Morrison," said Glastonbury. "I'm glad he's had a pat on the back."

"It couldn't happen to a more suitable chap. Just where it's wanted. From now on the upper class is going to need all the heroes it can get."

"Or fabricate. Not that we've quite made a hero of Morrison."

"No," conceded Detterling, "and a good job we haven't. We don't want to overdo it. But a Viceroy's commendation is the sort of thing that can tip the scales heavily in a man's favour, if it's used in the right way, and so it could help him a lot later on."

"In what?"

"Oh, I don't know. But he's the kind of man who might become prominent in something. Those other two will never get anywhere, they've not got the right stuff in them – not enough shit. But Peter Morrison – he's full of it."

"I thought Morrison was quite decent," Glastonbury said, "as people go."

"Oh, he likes to do the right thing . . . to be seen to do the right thing, and even to believe it himself, if he possibly can. But he's got a lot of shit in his tanks – else he'd never have come through all this in one piece."

"I suppose you're right," said Glastonbury. "But I'm not sure we want chaps like him becoming prominent. I mean, could you trust in him, knowing what you know? If you met him in the City, say, or in Parliament?"

"*Vanitas vanitatum,*" said Captain Detterling, "*omnia vanitas.* I don't trust in anybody, myself. But at least Peter Morrison knows what to wear and what noises to make, which is something to be thankful for, I suppose."

# COME LIKE
# SHADOWS

Ulysses: Time hath, my lord, a wallet at his back,
Wherein he puts alms for oblivion . . .

SHAKESPEARE: *Troilus and Cressida*
Act III, Scene iii

# Contents

Witches: Show his eyes, and grieve his heart;
Come like shadows, so depart!

SHAKESPEARE: *Macbeth*
Act IV, Scene i

# PART ONE

# THE LAND OF THE PHAEACIANS

Therein grow trees, high and luxuriant, pears and pome-granates and apple-trees with their coloured fruit, and sweet figs and teeming olives. Of these the fruit fails not nor fades in winter or in summer, but stays throughout the year; and ever does the west wind, as it blows, quicken to life some fruits and bring to ripeness others; pear upon pear, apple upon apple, cluster upon cluster, and fig upon fig.

Homer : *The Odyssey*; Book VII

"A thousand pounds a week," said Tom Llewyllyn. "Are you interested?"

"I could be," said Fielding Gray.

"Don't be blasé."

"I'm not. But with that sort of money there's always a great, big snag. To say nothing, in this year of the proles 1970, of great, big taxes."

"They'd do their best for you about those. They'd pay you a lot of your money in hard cash as legitimate expenses, and if you asked nicely they might bank the rest for you in Zurich."

"I thought you socialists disapproved of all that."

"Tax," said Tom, "is a matter of law, not morals. There are legal methods of doing this kind of thing, and these people understand them."

"Did they bank your money in Zurich?"

"No, because I needed it here. Here and now. Patricia's being difficult about her money . . . says she's saving it all for Baby . . . and insists that we use mine for everything."

"Silly bitch."

"Don't call my wife a silly bitch," Tom said equably.

"By making you bring your money back here, she's made you lose half of it to the Revenue."

"More than half. But that isn't your worry. They'd fix something for *you* all right . . . Zurich or Bermuda or the Virgin Islands . . . *provided,* Fielding, that you asked them nicely, like I said."

"Fielding could always talk nicely," Tessie Buttock put in.

Fielding Gray and Tom Llewyllyn were having tea in their old haunt, Buttock's Hotel, where they both still lodged when in

London. Although Tessie had been offered a huge sum, years since, for the site in Cromwell Road, she had refused out of hand. Her lease was good for another twenty years, she said, and so with luck was she, and they could bleeding well wait to put up their squitty new tower of tin and matchwood until she was in her box. So Buttock's had survived into the seventies as furtive and cosy as ever . . . and a good deal less filthy since Tessie's incontinent terrier, Albert Edward, had gone to his ancestors five years before.

"I remember how Fielding used to talk so nice to poor Albert Edward," Tessie now said, and dropped a tear into her saucer.

"Did I?" said Fielding, who neither remembered nor cared. "That's not saying I want to talk nice to all these bloody Jew-boys of Tom's."

"How do you know they're Jews?" Tom said.

"I told you. With this sort of money there's always a snag, and as a rule it's called Moishe or Isaac. Real Jewy Jews, I mean. Not like Daniel or Gregory."

"Oh, come off it, love," Tessie said. "You can't turn down a thousand a week just because it's a shonk signs the cheque."

"I don't mind 'em signing cheques," Fielding said. "It's what they want in return. Muck for the millions, delivered with an air of unction. Turds wrapped in tinsel. They won't even let you be honest about it and call a turd a turd. You've got to quiver with arty enthusiasm, pretend each fart's a divine afflatus of inspiration, so that they can ease their squalid little consciences by babbling about being creative."

"Like that, is it?" said Tessie. "I can't say I'm surprised. I remember from the Bible they always did go in for hocus-pocus. But anyway," she said, "you haven't answered Tom's question : how do you know this lot are Jews?"

"Tom is talking about films," said Fielding, "and the film world is heaving with them."

"Look," said Tom : "do you, or do you not, want to hear what I have to say about this rather spectacular offer? If you do, stop talking like Himmler and listen for a minute."

"That's right, Fielding dear," said Tessie, settling comfortably. "You just park your tongue and let Tom tell us all about it. I'm interested in film biz, shonks and all. I get a film book called *Titty Bits* every week, but there's nothing like hearing it personal."

"All right," said Fielding, and turned his one eye morosely to Tom. "Let's hear it personal. I hope it's up to *Titty Bits'* standard."

"Early in July," Tom began, "I was approached by Pandarus..."

"...How very apt..."

"... Which is a London film company," said Tom rather wearily, "and itself a subsidiary of Clytemnestra Films of New York."

"How on earth had such people ever heard of *you*?"

"If you'll just keep quiet," said Tom, flushing slightly, "you'll find out by and by. Now Pandarus, with the support of Clytemnestra, is mounting a new production of *The Odyssey*. Much of the finance, as they call it, is coming from a thing called the Oglander-Finckelstein Trust..."

"...You *must* be joking..."

"... An American fund, administered by Montana University, which hands out slabs of money for cultural and creative projects such as it has somehow been persuaded this version of *The Odyssey* is going to be."

"And is it?"

"It is going to be a valid cinematic equivalent," said Tom carefully, "with the emphasis on the action rather than the poetry. The Oglander-Finckelstein Trust would probably prefer it the other way round . . . in fact definitely wants it the other way round . . . and since the trustees have so far punted in only two million dollars of the eight million they have promised, the producer is having to tread warily. He commissioned a very serious and poetic script for Og-Finck's approval, and further to assure everyone of his artistic integrity he announced that he was going to employ a high-powered academic adviser, none less than the Regius Professor of Greek at Oxford University. This gentleman, as you may know, is called Hugh Lloyd-Jones;

but through some grotesque misinterpretation of *Who's Who* the post was in fact offered to our old chum, Somerset Lloyd-James. . . ."

And he, it appeared, had not bothered to clear up the mistake, though well aware of what must have happened. Being too busy to take up the job himself, since he had just become front man in the House of Commons for the Marquis of Canteloupe (Minister of Commerce in the new Conservative Government), Lloyd-James had politely declined the Pandarus/Clytemnestra offer, but at the same time had recommended 'a very learned and versatile Fellow of Lancaster College, Cambridge, Mr. Tom Llewyllyn'.

"He's done me so many bad turns in his time," said Tom, "that I suppose he thought I was due a good one. Old Somerset can be quite a brick . . . when he's nothing to lose by it."

However *that* might be, Foxe J. Galahead, the producer, had weighed the name of Tom Llewyllyn, had confused it with that of the famous novelist (Richard), had decided that this was just what he wanted (a novelist *and* don must surely impress the pundits of Og-Finck), and had descended on Lancaster College in the depth of the Long Vacation to clinch the matter. But Tom, at first, had not much wanted to be clinched.

'*The Odyssey*'s not my period,' Tom had said. 'I'm a modern historian, Mr. Galahead. I know nothing about the Mycenean Age.'

'Is that when it happened?'

'Roughly. The epic was written, or collated from oral traditions, around 650 B.C. It purported to be about events which happened 500 years before, in the so-called Heroic Age, which was a kind of epilogue to the Mycenean Age, which itself was a kind of epilogue to the Bronze—'

'. . . Just hold it there, baby,' said Foxe ('call me Foxy') J. Galahead. 'You seem to know enough about it to me.'

'Everyone knows that much.'

'You English, you're so modest you crucify me. But sorry, Mr. Llewyllyn . . . I guess you're Welsh.'

'English by habit and dwelling. And preference.'

'But that book you wrote about Welsh miners . . .'

'. . . What book about Welsh miners?'

'Christ's balls, Tom, if I'd written that book . . . they made a movie of it, I remember . . . *How Green Was My Valley* . . . if I'd written that marvellous, marvellous book, I'd go about like I had two pricks. But I guess this English modesty . . . I mean Welsh modesty . . . I mean . . .'

At which moment Patricia Llewyllyn had arrived in Tom's college rooms with their ten-year-old daughter, Baby, just in time to stop Foxy Galahead from remembering that *How Green Was My Valley* had in fact been published in 1939 and filmed soon afterwards, and that Tom, though now over forty, must have been in knickers at the time. Not that this would have made much difference, because Foxy had taken to Tom and been very impressed by his impromptu exegesis on the date of *The Odyssey*, particularly by his use of the word 'purported'. This was the guy to show Og-Finck, and no smegma. So as far as Foxy was concerned, Tom was Foxy's man all right; and as far as Patricia was concerned, Tom was Foxy's man all right, since the job carried an enormous screw; and as far as Tom himself was concerned . . . well, he had always wanted to go to Corfu, where the film was being shot, and here was Foxy waving a first-class air ticket to the place right under his nose.

"Did Patricia and Baby go too, dear?" Tessie now said.

No, answered Tom. Pandarus didn't like wives and children round the place and would have made him pay their fare, which Patricia, in line with her ever-mounting passion for economy, refused to let him do. She and Baby would be quite content at home in Grantchester, she had told him, and though Baby nearly blew the roof off ('Baby wants to go to Corfooo-ooo-ooo') and was then sick in malignant mauve all over her Levis, it had been settled that Tom should go alone. So there he was, back in July, newly appointed Academic, Historical and Literary Adviser to the Pandarus/Clytemnestra production of Homer's *Odyssey*, at £800 a week, with a bloody great suite in the Corfu Palace Hotel.

"Corfu," said Fielding, "Greece. Greece, Colonels. Colonels, Fascism. You didn't mind all that?"

"It had nothing to do with *The Odyssey*. Or with Pandarus Films."

"But Pandarus Films had to do with *it*. By bringing money into Greek territory, Pandarus Films gave comfort and even recognition of a kind to an oppressive régime of the right."

"A fat lot you care," Tessie said.

"I'll bet somebody cared," said Fielding; "the unions for a start. Some time ago there was a gloating bit in the *Guardian* which said that most unions connected with films and television had forbidden their members to assist in productions anywhere in Greece or its islands."

"That's quite true," Tom told him. "In order to spite the Colonels the union leaders would have been quite happy to shit on their own members . . . to say nothing of the ordinary Greeks who stood to benefit. But in this case there was an odd twist. You see, Pandarus is going to need four million more than the eight million dollars offered by Og-Finck, and Foxy could only raise the extra if he promised to shoot in Corfu."

"How was that?"

"The money was put up by two old gambling associates of Foxy's. Max de Freville . . ."

". . . I've met him . . ."

". . . And a Greek chum of Max's called Lykiadopoulos. They own extensive tourist installations in Corfu, and some sort of share in the casino."

"The last I saw of Max, it was Cyprus he was interested in."

"So it was. But that was no good when the rows there started up again, so they muscled in on the Corfu boom, right at the beginning. And boom it's been ever since. They could find four million for Foxy all right, and were happy to do so . . . on the absolute condition that he made the film on Corfu."

"To the great benefit, every possible way round, of their own tourist enterprises?"

"Right. But that was no skin off Foxy's nose, and he definitely needed the extra money, so in the end he put it to the unions flat : either the film would be shot on Corfu or it could not be shot at all."

Whereupon the union leaders had sneered and shrugged their shoulders; but not so the rank and file, who were sick of being out of work and watching their industry totter into its tomb. They wanted to make films, they said; their leaders had already botched up three big productions in a row by excessive demands and infantile quibbling; and if the twelve million dollar *Odyssey* was now to be cancelled just because a few grubby students disapproved of the Government in Athens, that was the last straw. In no time at all quite a rebellion had flared up; and the union leaders, seeing that they had badly misjudged this particular situation, were looking for a face-saver to enable them to back down with dignity. It was Foxy, or rather his shrewd director, Jules Jacobson, who had found a formula for them. This film, the union leaders were told, would be of great cultural and educational value (witness the backing from Og-Finck), and it was a film which, for essential artistic reasons, must be made on Corfu. For Corfu (the Homeric Scheria or Island of the Phaeacians) was where much of the story had actually happened. Not only were the territory and the coast line ideal, but immortal scenes could be shot in their exact historical locations, thus gaining both in spirit and verisimilitude (etcetera, etcetera). This did the trick : a pompous document was issued, from the headquarters of the unions concerned, announcing that a special exception to the embargo on Greece would be made in favour of the producers of *The Odyssey* because of their unique endeavours in the cause of creative international enlightenment (etcetera, etcetera). And so although a number of trendy bishops and otherwise unoccupied dons continued to snarl and screech about 'this betrayal of the Greek people', the director and his two units had taken wing on 1 July for Corfu, where they had been joined by the newly recruited Tom some seven days later.

"It's all balls," Fielding now said, "about historical locations. The whole thing's a legend . . . where it's not a fairy tale."

"I made out a very good geographical case," said Tom primly, "for positing that Odysseus was washed ashore on the beach at Ermones and then taken to what is now Palaeocastritsa."

"You had to do something for your eight hundred quid a week. Your director could have found that theory, for what it's worth, in any ten drachma guide book."

"Maybe," said Tom. "But it was the sort of thing which kept the unions happy. 'Topographico-historical fidelity,' we called it. And the director thinks the same tactic will pay off with Montana University and the Og-Finck Trust. 'Topographico-historical fidelity' might be good evidence of Foxy's *bona fides* . . . when he starts asking for the rest of the money."

"They'll never be taken in," said Fielding, his eye flickering in irritation. "American scholars are grindingly accurate about that sort of thing."

"Never mind all this book-talk," snapped Tessie all of a sudden. "What I want to know is, what happened to Tom when he got out there?"

"The first thing," Tom said, "was that I had dinner with the director, Jules Jacobson, who filled me in about the whole set-up."

"Jacobson. A shonk?"

"A very special one, Tessie. East End boy who finished the war with a commission and a Military Cross, and started in the film business in 1946 as cameraman for his uncle's blue movies. He'd come a long way since then, and hadn't forgotten an inch of it. . . ."

'The first rule here,' Jules Jacobson had told Tom in the restaurant of the Corfu Palace, 'is that I give the orders. I *direct*. Foxy Galahead *produces,* which means that he comes up with the cash and is entitled to common civility. But no more. If he tells you to do anything, you listen politely, and then go away and don't do it.'

Jules Jacobson was a lean, dark man with close and narrow green eyes. He wore a silk shirt, the tie of a superior though now defunct regiment of Fusiliers, no coat, and very tight trousers. He looked absolutely cool in the sticky July evening, while Tom was dripping with sweat so copiously that he would normally have felt quite embarrassed. But not with Jacobson : for Jacobson had that kind of sophisticated courtesy that refrains from noticing (and thereby increasing) discomfiture which it cannot alleviate. He also had authority of the same subtle order : for while his words (though succinct) were not especially remarkable, his manner, one of self-assured indifference, made them law, as absolutely as if they had been engraven on stone tablets.

'So just remember that,' Jacobson had said. 'Listen to Foxy, if you have to, smile if you can raise the energy, but whatever he wants, don't do it. Unless you know I want it too.'

'I suppose that could be awkward. After all, he is my employer.'

'And mine. He pays me to direct . . . among other things, to direct you. You'll find that a film company is a very hierarchical affair; there's a strict chain of command and everyone has his own clearly defined function. There's a pretence of equality . . . Christian names from top to bottom . . . but every man jack out on location has his own duties, his own status and his own privileges, and woe betide him if he tries to step outside them.'

Tom wiped his brow.

'A chain of command, you said ?'

'Right.'

'Well, surely Mr. Galahead is at the head of that chain.'

'Administratively, yes. Not as regards technical or creative processes.' Jacobson used the phrase quite seriously, Tom had noted with regret. 'The staging, the acting, the shooting, the lighting, the dialogue . . . everything to do with the film as such is up to me. I've got it in my contract. It follows that you're here to advise *me;* to find the answers to the questions which *I* shall ask. So don't let Foxy send you off on wild goose chases. He's got his own ideas about this film . . . which aren't mine.'

'So he's paying his money for you to make your film ?'

'Wrong. The money isn't his . . . he raises it. And I certainly can't make the film I'd like to. You've heard of the Oglander-Finckelstein Trust ?'

'Mr. Galahead said something about it when he came to see me in Cambridge.'

'Just call him Foxy. As I told you, we keep up an illusion of equality; it's traditional in the trade.'

'Foxy to his face?'

'Yes. Everyone does, even the prop men. Everyone except for myself and the two top stars. We can call him "Foxy baby" if we want . . . our privilege.'

'Written into your contract, I suppose?'

Jacobson grinned.

'That's the spirit,' he said, 'Now then: the Oglander-Finkelstein Trust. . . .'

And he had begun to explain the situation, which at that time was still largely unknown to Tom. The Oglander-Finckelstein Trust, it appeared, had provided two million dollars at once, with a promise of six million to be paid later, on condition of 'satisfactory progress'. Since the initial two million had been spent on 'getting the picture off the ground' and transporting the company to Corfu, the production was now being currently financed by the four million which Max de Freville and Stratis Lykiadopoulos had paid over. Now that the company was firmly installed on its location, money would not be used so fast; but, even so, present resources would be exhausted by the end of October, and it was very important that Og-Finck should come up with its next contribution by 1 November at latest.

'Which means,' said Tom, 'that you must show proof of "satisfactory progress"?'

'What they mean by "satisfactory progress",' Jules Jacobson had emended.

And here was the rub. Proof of progress must take the form of rough-cut sequences edited out of such film as could be shot during the next three months. Apart from that, it was quite possible that representatives of Og-Finck would turn up in Corfu to inspect the company in action, and if so it would be important to create an impression of industry and dedication; but far more important, indeed essential to the whole enterprise, was that the syndics of the Trust should be pleased by 'what was already in the can'. Now, what they wanted was what was promised by the existing script: a faithful version of Homer's masterpiece, which would include much of the bard's original dialogue and even of his narrative and descriptive passages, these latter to be recited over the visual scenes as a running poetic commentary.

'And all that,' Jules had said, 'is just too much. The conception is too literary. It won't work as cinema. And yet I shall have to go as far as I can to meet them, or no more lolly.'

'And what does Mr. Gala . . . what does Foxy say?'

'He goes to the other extreme from Og-Finck. He wants to cash in on the film when it's finished, which as he sees it means filling the thing with fighting and fucking, and not a speech longer than "crap".' Jules clicked his teeth savagely and then went on : 'I suppose he thinks he can con Og-Finck along till it's too late for them to back down. *Caveat emptor*. But if he wants an Errol Flynn extravaganza, he's chosen the wrong director. I'm going to make a quality movie, Tom, and I only hope Foxy baby won't squeal too loud when he finds out.'

'But surely your contract covers you there. You said just now that you're empowered to take decisions on all the artistic questions.'

'That's certainly true, and it's also true that I can do most of the shooting when Foxy isn't here. But when he is he hangs over my neck all day yelling for blood, cunt and hurricanoes, and that, believe me, is no help at all.'

Jules, in fact, had two sets of demands to meet, each irreconcilable with the other and each hyperbolic in itself. He had a producer who wanted the crudest kind of box-office and financial sponsors who wanted the purest form of art.

'But the point is,' said Jules, 'that it wouldn't *be* art. That Homeric dialogue, for example. Hulking great five-minute speeches, marvellous pieces to read or declaim, but guaranteed to kill any film stone dead. And I don't just mean that they'd empty the cinema, which is what bugs Foxy about them, I mean that artistically and dramatically they could not work on the screen. That's what I'm concerned with, Tom : the screen.'

And so what, Tom had enquired, did Jules propose to do about it all? Well, as far as Foxy was concerned, Jules proposed to keep him happy by really going to town on the more famous Homeric spectaculars (which were packed with blood and hurricanoes if a little short on cunt), and at the same time to defend the 'culture' scenes by telling Foxy that they could always omit them from the final version but would definitely need them, in the short run, to show to Og-Finck and secure the next lot of money. Thus Foxy would receive the impression that Jules was a faithful ally in the conning of Og-Finck. . . .

'. . . And that should keep him off my back for the time being. With people like Foxy Galahead the time being is all one can worry about.'

'So we've got blood and thunder to keep Foxy happy, and "culture" scenes for the Oglander-Finckelstein Trust. But what about these culture scenes, Jules? Will they satisfy Og-Finck?'

'I hope so. They'll be authentically set up for one thing . . . that's where you come in . . . and they'll carry a full load of Homer's dialogue and so on to please the egg-heads. I can always strip that down in the cutting room later on.'

'After the money's all paid and it's too late for Og-Finck to turn awkward?'

'You're learning fast. Cognac?'

'Please. I've certainly learnt more than I'd expected to in one evening. Tell me, Jules : why are you letting a stranger into the skeleton cupboard?'

'I like your face and I'm going to need your help. I've read your books . . . some of them . . . and I fancy we're going to get on.'

As indeed they had, so much so that Tom had soon become a confidential assistant rather than a mere academic adviser. Officially he was there to give Jules the benefit of his antiquarian knowledge and his literary taste; he was required to explain precisely what such and such a phrase or passage would have signified in its Homeric context. But after he had explained, he was increasingly often invited by Jules to join him in considering whether one or other of the actors had the capacity to render a valid interpretation, and if not, what should be done about it. This in turn led to long discussions of the idiosyncrasies, careers and case histories of the entire cast, and of the best tactics Jules could use to elicit good performances or soothe wounded vanities.

'That stupid bitch,' Jules would say, of, for example, the actress who played Penelope. 'She says she's not got enough big scenes in the first half.'

'The story doesn't need them. Homer doesn't provide them.'

'So Homer doesn't provide them. So she wants them written in.'

'Then write them in. Shoot them . . . and lose them.'

'Too expensive . . . in time and money both.'

'Then say so.'

'She'll say nothing's too expensive for the star.'

'She isn't the star.'

'She thinks she is. And God help us if she ever stops.'

'Tell her it's a part of quality rather than length.'

'She wouldn't understand, Tom. She's over forty, she's been a household name for twenty years, and she's made her career in a world in which the star is all-important and has the longest and juiciest part.'

'So he does—Odysseus. She can't think she's as important as he is.'

'Not quite that. But she thinks she's the only woman in the piece that counts.'

'Then she must be potty. There's Circe, Calypso, Nausicaa . . .'

'. . . She won't know about them, Tom. She'll only have read her own scenes, and all she knows is there's not enough of them.'

*'Only have read her own scenes?'*

'You don't know these people. They're barely literate, some of them—they're moronic. Morons who have the right kind of faces and a gift of mimicry, which on a good day they can pass off as acting. Compared with a lot of 'em this Penelope of ours is a queen. At least she learns her lines . . .'

'. . . And doesn't get drunk by ten in the morning, like Odysseus.'

'Let's leave him out for now. Today's problem is Penelope.

She wants more scenes, she can't have them, and she's going to piss all over everybody if she doesn't get them. Just what does a man do?'

'Start pissing on her first,' Tom said. 'Tell her it'll be time to think about new scenes when she gets her present ones right.'

'But she is getting them right . . . as right as she ever will. No good wrecking her confidence by crabbing decent work.'

'Then find her a lover to keep her quiet.'

'She likes police-women. *London* police-women.'

'So dig up some brawny dyke and tell her it's a London police-woman on holiday here in Corfu.'

'She prefers them in uniform.'

'Sweet Jesus Christ, Jules. . . .'

But eventually the problem had been settled simply by extending Penelope's speeches in her existing scenes to their maximum Homeric length. In this way the wretched woman was given so much homework that she had no time left for further complaint; and although, as Jules observed, it would mean another massive job in the cutting room, that worry could wait.

Comparable problems, of which there were many, were solved by comparable devices. The most serious and persistent difficulty was the inebriety of Odysseus, a grizzled and internationally loved survivor of wartime naval romances, who gave of his best only when he had drunk two-thirds of a bottle of whisky but gave out altogether when he had emptied the whole. The amounts of liquor involved were constant and exact, nor was there ever any variation by so much as the tenth of a gill : at one-third of a bottle the star became passable, at two-thirds (dead on the line) he became brilliant, and at three-thirds he was a goner . . . to the drop. Fortunately the very precision of these mathematics made Jules's job just possible : a specially graded decanter was procured which served the function of a clock, the whole of the day's shooting being governed, not by the passing of the hours, but by the sinking level of Odysseus's bourbon. On days when the level was sinking too fast, and that meant most days, Jules had to work desperately to keep the hero on set and finish the take before the final and fatal measure went down the red lane and Odysseus slumped into unbreachable coma; but at least, as Jules told Tom, a quick glance at the scale on the decanter would always tell him exactly where he was with Odysseus and exactly what quality of acting he could expect, which made it a lot easier than working with most of the booze-artists he'd known.

And so, since Jules and Tom between them found some sort of formula to control everything from Odysseus's dipsomania to the home-sickness of the clapper-boy (who was allowed one free telephone call a week to his mother in Islington), the film had begun, as Jules expressed it, to build. Throughout July and August, while the Second Unit busied itself with stunts for the spectaculars, Jules had divided his time between the early scenes in the absent Odysseus's palace and the amorous and knock-about escapades on Circe's island. During the former he had been able to make much therapeutic and exhausting work for the exigent Penelope; and by his speedy completion of the latter he had happily made possible the early departure for England of the actress cast as Circe, a venomous little witch who had only got the part 'by doing a blow-job on Foxy' and was upsetting the entire company by the airs she put on in celebration of this achievement.

With Circe gone and Foxy, for one reason or another seldom present, Jules had good cause to be pleased with himself. The work (even Circe's) had been excellent; the company's morale stood high; progress went on well up to schedule; expenses were not quite as savage as they might have been. But there was one ugly fly buzzing in the ointment, one anxiety which inexorably mounted : the quality of the script.

"Lawks," Tessie Buttock almost shouted. "More bloody book-talk. What I want to hear about is that Circe . . . her and those blow-jobs."

"You've heard all I know about that," said Tom, "and by this time Circe was gone."

"Didn't give you a turn before she went then?"

"No, Tessie. I'm a married man . . ."

". . . Phooey . . ."

". . . And whether you like it or not I was much too busy with this script. Whatever *Titty Bits* may imply, it's scripts and not blow-jobs that get pictures made."

And the script from which they were working in Corfu had started to present more snags with every hour that passed. It was, as it had to be, the same script as had been shown to the Oglander-Finckelstein Trust, specially prepared by a well briefed and corrupt screen-writer to keep the trustees sweet, short of action, long on poetry and talk. But despite this Jules was confident, as he had explained to Tom, that he could expand the action as he went along and strip away any excess of talk (with or without the approval of Og-Finck) when the film was finally edited. The immediate problem for both of them was something else again : not the length of the dialogue but its language. For the author had totally failed to find an English idiom which in any way answered their needs. In the heavier and bloodier scenes he had merely used, *verbatim,* the pastiche-biblical language of the translation by Butcher and Lang; while for social or domestic events he had switched straight over, ignoring the stylistic contrast, to the demotic version by Rieu, occasionally and fortuitously inserting a chunk of T. E. Lawrence.

In all fairness, the result, though heterogeneous, read rather well; but it was deadly difficult in the acting. For a start, none of the three translations came at all trippingly off the tongue, or not off the tongues which had been hired by Pandarus; and then the juxtaposition of different styles (heroic in one scene, folksy in the next) imposed far too great a strain on the talents of Odysseus and Penelope. Although both could manage not implausibly a wide range of facial expressions, neither was capable of frequent and radical shifts in verbal usage, for after all, as Jules remarked, they weren't 'bloody Gielgud and Evans'.

All this being so, what was needed was new dialogue throughout. The poet's narrative, Jules conceded, such of it as he would retain, might possibly be left, as it was cast at present, in antique English; for this would give the thing a certain 'background', and Jules had a very good man (an unfrocked priest) who could do the unseen Homer's 'voice over' in tones appropriately bardic; but when it came to the speeches of the characters themselves, Jules said, these must all be rewritten in one style, and that a modern one, which should be uniform enough to suit the limited elocutive powers of the actors, yet flexible enough to compass all the passions with which the poet had endowed his *personae*. The new version, Jules had enthused, must have Lang's dignity without his archaism, Rieu's fluidity without his commonplace, and Lawrence's subtle insight without his preciosity : it must also breathe the aristocratic spirit of the legend without being in any way offensive to egalitarian nostrils.

'Rather a strong order,' as Tom had observed. 'Whom shall you get to do it?'

'You and me between us. We've done a good bit already.'

'We've done a bit of tinkering where we could. What you're talking about now is a complete rebore.'

'We'll take it piece by piece as it comes.'

'We can't do it, Jules. It's a job for an expert.'

'Look, Tom. What we want are speeches which make sense of the story and which our crumby actors can enunciate without swallowing their false teeth. On these actors we *are* experts.'

'But not on translating Homer.'

'It doesn't have to be too exact. We just get the gist of what they've got to say and give 'em words in which to say it as naturally as possible. You've written a novel . . .'

'. . . One novel, years ago . . .'

'. . . So you can knock out natural dialogue.'

'But this isn't natural dialogue, Jules. It's governed by all sorts of conventions. These people are gods and kings and heroes and ghosts, and they talk in a special way.'

'Then find an equivalent of that special way, in clear, sharp English which the Odeon audience will understand.'

'Odeon Leicester Square, or Odeon Leyton Orient?'

'Both. Straight, simple stuff, but with an air about it. Like Robert Bolt writes.'

'Like Robert Bolt gets paid for.'

'So you want more money?'

'No,' said Tom the socialist. 'I'm already paid far too much.'

'Then earn it by writing me this dialogue.'

'I can try, I suppose.'

'That's my boy,' Jules had said. 'Start with that bit where Telemachus calls on Nestor.'

'Oh, Jesus Christ, Jules, have a heart. The old sod talks for pages. . . .'

But Tom had sat down and done his laborious best, the more laborious in that Jules, who would normally have helped him, was suddenly preoccupied with an absurd local crisis.

This had its origin in the tactless social behaviour of the company's ten starlets. These girls, who were there to play handmaidens and the like, had a habit of sitting in the Arcade outside the Corfu Bar through the long hot evenings and soliciting the attentions of any Greek youth who was not still in knickers. The authorities were long since inured to the immodest costume and predatory custom of tourists of all sexes, but the starlets' goings-on went beyond all previous limits. There were violent scenes of exploratory passion on the cricket ground just over the road from the bar; and on two occasions liaisons had been consummated on the pitch itself, to the applause of hysterical schoolboys, who packed the close field. Fearing lest such performances should become fashionable, the Corfiot police had at last asked Jules to give the young ladies a warning. He had done so and been (for once) flouted : their private lives, the girls said, were their own. Not, said Jules, if they were carried on in public. Even in easy-going Corfu, he told them, the Greeks had a strain of puritanism which was to be respected. But all to no avail. Two nights later the youngest and juiciest starlet had been apprehended by the police while wailing like a banshee in the extreme throes of orgasm, which had been induced by a waiter from a neighbouring restaurant in an open car parked on the boundary line. She had been led off with her lover to the lockup, still spasmodically jerking, amid cries of 'Filthy Fascists' from her colleagues at the tables in the Arcade, who had been narrowly restrained by a senior cameraman from active intervention.

So it was now Jules's job to get the wretched girl out from behind bars and save her from criminal prosecution under about ninety-nine different headings.

'What was the man like,' Tom had asked Jules, 'this waiter?'

'An absolute beast. Youngish, but with a face like a hog. All snout and jowl.'

'Then try saying she was raped.'

'They'll know that's not true,' said Jules. 'Girls from outside Greece actually *prefer* men like that. There's plenty of nice English and American boys about this summer, but all the women from nine to ninety are hot for black bristly Greeks.'

'Well, why?'

'Novelty. They think the Greeks want it much more and bang it in much harder.'

'Exactly,' Tom insisted. 'They're as good as getting themselves raped. Every woman's dream, I'm told . . . to be tied to the bed and shagged by a gorilla. Nasty, brutish and quick.'

'Maybe. But Elena wasn't tied and she wasn't forced. And it certainly wasn't quick. They were both bawling away for a good ten minutes. That's why the police came.'

'Bawling?'

'With pleasure, Tom. Quite unmistakably, I'm told. Whatever you say, we cannot get this thing up to look like rape. So what are we to do?'

'Push it all on to Foxy's plate.'

'He won't be here for at least a week. Max de Freville or his pal Lykiadopoulos might have been able to cope, but they're both in Athens.'

'Look,' said Tom. 'As far as I can make out there's nothing these people won't do to bring tourists in . . . except let them use hash. They're ravaging the whole coast with their obscene package hotels, they're killing half the trees on the island to widen the roads for charabancs, and they wouldn't at all mind turning the whole place into one huge air strip. Now, we're not exactly tourists but we're all the things which go with tourism . . . foreign money, advertisement, mass entertainment . . . we're the whole modern world rolled into one, and they're keen as Beelzebub to have us. So don't you tell me that a few crisp bank notes won't get that little girl out of quod before you can say *efcharisto*.'

'A few years ago, perhaps. But the new régime likes to boast about not being corrupt or coercible. They don't like arresting foreigners, but when they have to they show no fear or favour. It's all to do with what they call the new Hellenic sovereignty.'

'But in the case of a major film company . . . which they're jolly lucky to have here at all. . . .'

'In such a case,' said Jules, 'they draw the line very low on the page. Very low indeed. But where they do draw it, Tom, they draw it very firmly. You mentioned hash just now. They could easily take a soft attitude on that, at any rate for foreigners, but they just won't do it; it's below their line and there's a score of young Americans in their prisons with five-year sentences to prove it.'

'And Elena's fallen below the line too, you reckon?'

'I know damn well she has. A public fuck on the cricket ground . . .'

'. . . On the boundary . . .'

'. . . Within fifty yards of the Arcade, Tom, making a racket-like the entire London Zoo in rut, *and* after due warning about such behaviour had been very civilly given. Of course it's below any possible line, and no amount of crisp bank notes can change that.'

'Then what will? We need her out to start getting her ready for the Nausicaa sequence.'

The two of them had paused in their walk along the Peripatos and stared across the bay towards the fortress.

'What makes it worse,' Jules had said, sitting heavily down on the balustrade, 'is all that yelling about Fascists when she was arrested. She joined in, you see.'

'Resisted arrest, in fact?'

'They could say so.'

'Face,' said Tom : 'that's the key to it all. I'm sure they'd let her out if they could do it without losing face. What does the Greek lawyer say?'

'Shrugs his shoulders and pouts.'

'And the Vice-Consul?'

'Doesn't want to know about it.'

'Impasse.'

'It certainly seems so.'

And the bay darkened as the sun went down behind the western hills. But two days later Elena had reappeared, as juicy as ever and quite unrepentant, for a preliminary fitting of the costumes for the Nausicaa scenes; and Jules, whom Tom had hardly seen since their conversation on the Peripatos, had arrived in the dressing room to supervise, grinning like a monkey. 'How did you do it?' Tom said during the first break.

'A graceful compliment from Pandarus Films to the Administration. I went round to the Nomarch and two or three other big-wigs and offered 'em walking-on parts as Phaeacian nobles . . . for the palace scenes and the games. An appropriate way of memorializing all the kindness and cooperation we had received from them, I said—oh, and just one little problem : if we didn't have Elena for the Princess Nausicaa's handmaid we couldn't do the Phaeacian scenes at all. She was out within the hour.'

'Very neat.'

'It was your remark about face that made me think of it. Concern for face is a symptom of unsatisfied vanity, and that's what's the matter with all these ridiculous Greeks. Excessive vanity with nothing whatsoever to be vain about. So if only, I thought, one could find some pabulum for their hungry egos, they could afford to relax and make themselves amenable about Elena. And hey-presto, my dear, I was right.'

'It may not be much fun . . . trying to direct a bevy of screen-struck bureaucrats.'

'Only three or four of them. And when they find out how boring and exhausting it is to be on set all day doing the same thing fifty times over, they'll probably back out. Meanwhile, we've got little Elena back, and now we can really buckle down to the Nausicaa bits. I want you to drop everything else and start re-scripting the scene where they discover Odysseus on the beach.'

'You agree it should be done at Ermones?'

'If that's where you think it really happened. The Nausicaa sequence is going to be our big thing to show Og-Finck, and we want every mark for culture we can get.'

'I'm going to have torture with the script, Jules. The girl Nausicaa is one of the most touching figures in literature.'

'So why is that torture?'

'It's all so delicate. Her speeches are some of the subtlest and most beautiful in *The Odyssey* . . . and you want them re-written for your Odeon audience. Can't you conceive how hideously hard that will be? It's one thing to do Odysseus being brave or Penelope being faithful : but Nausicaa . . . she'll shrivel at a touch.'

'So it's difficult,' said Jules. 'So don't stand here talking. Go back to your expensive suite in the Corfu Palace and get to work. I'll look in on you this evening. Now I've fixed this bother about Elena I'll have more time free to help you again.'

So Tom had gone back to the Corfu Palace Hotel, and sat down at his desk, and gazed out towards Epirus over the wine-dark sea; and then he had opened his *Odyssey* at the beginning of Book VI. . . .

. . . "Look," said Tessie in Buttock's Hotel. "What I want to know is, where does Fielding come in on all this?"

"Very soon now, Tessie. You'll see."

"I mean, that's what it's all leading up to? Fielding getting a job?"

"His being offered a job, Tessie. We don't yet know if he'll take it."

"Get on with the story," Fielding said. "There you were, sitting in your plush hotel. . . ."

. . . And reading Book VI of *The Odyssey,* for about the nine-tieth time. Odysseus, newly washed ashore on the island of the Phaeacians, was huddled beneath the brushwood near a river-mouth, 'overcome with weariness and sleep'; and meanwhile the goddess Athene had gone up into the city to rouse the little princess Nausicaa and send her to find and succour the naked voyager. . . .

' . . . Ἡ δ'α'νέμου ὡς πνοιή . . . *Like a breath of air the goddess sped to the couch of the maiden, and stood above her head, and spoke to her, taking the form of the daughter of Dymas, a girl of like age with Nausicaa and dear to her heart:*

' *"Nausicaa, how comes it that thy mother bore thee so heedless? Thy bright garments are lying uncared for.; yet thy marriage is near at hand, when thou thyself shalt be clad in fair raiment and must give other such to the companions of thy train . . . Nay, come, let us go out early in the day to wash thy robes . . . for thou shalt not long remain a maid unwed. Even now thou hast wooers in the land, the noblest of all the Phaeacians."* '

So Nausicaa rose with the dawn, persuaded the king her father to lend her mules and a waggon for the day, and set out with her handmaidens and the dirty laundry, which latter she proposed to wash near the sea-shore, 'in the fair streams of the river, where were the washing tanks that never failed'.

At this stage, Tom reached for the script. The original script-writer had handled all this by cutting straight from the beach, on which the waves had just deposited the exhausted Odysseus, to the Palace yard, where Nausicaa and her handmaids were loading the laundry on to the waggon while her kindly mother brought out provisions for a picnic. This method satisfactorily dispensed with Athene's divine interference (a recurrent embarrassment), but it did not give a proper idea (Tom thought) of the family's role and importance. However, this was easily rectified. Tom scribbled a note in the margin, recommending that a regal Alcinous and several attendant noblemen (a good scene for the Nomarch and his chums) should make an imposing appearance to wave the princess off. So far, then, no real difficulties.

Tom now went back to Homer. Nausicaa and her handmaidens (including Dymas's daughter, the pick of the bunch, who was to be played by the juicy and delinquent Elena) arrived at the river, did the washing, put it out to dry on the beach, had a bathe, ate their picnic, and then 'put off their headgear and began to play at ball, and white-armed Nausicaa was leader of their song.'

No difficulty here, Tom thought. The script followed the Homeric text in giving a full account of the girls' activities, which Jules would stage as he thought fit. But what about this song they were singing as they played with their ball? Had anyone thought of that? Not that Tom knew of. And yet a song was surely essential to this enchanting scene, a song of the dreams of maidenhood, a modest epithalamium in anticipation of the wedding days they all longed for. 'SONG,' Tom wrote in the margin : 'suggest it be based on VI 11. 30 to 40 (thoughts of marriage) which do not otherwise appear in script.' And who would write it? Not his worry, for God's sake.

His worries really began (and how) with Homer's next incident.

Just before it was time to load up the waggon and start for home . . . 'the princess tossed the ball towards one of her handmaids, and threw it wide of her, and cast it into a deep eddy, and thereat they all cried out aloud' . . . and woke up Odysseus, who was still sleeping off his marine exertions under some nearby bushes. 'Thus he spoke in his heart : "O woe is me, to what land of men am I now come?" ', and got up to go and find out. 'Forth he came like a mountain lion', having only a branch of leaves to shield his nakedness, and at once the girls panicked and ran off to hide . . . all except Nausicaa, who, being a princess, stood her ground. All *that* was all right : what was very much not all right was the exchange of speeches which now followed.

Odysseus flattered the princess and asked for help; the princess fell for Odysseus's caddish weather-beaten charm and promised to take him to her royal parents. That was the essence of it; but of course the situation was far too delicate, and the nuances beneath the exchange were far too subtle, for the whole thing to be settled just like that. The speeches, in consequence, were canny, sensitive, elaborate, highly stylised and exceedingly long. As literature they worked superbly, but on the screen they just could not work, no matter how one translated them. How the devil, Tom asked himself desperately, was the thing to be done?

The existing script simply gave the speeches straight out of Homer, in Rieu's translation. Sound stuff but flat. Tom himself had been reading from the Greek, as far as he could manage, and otherwise from a standard translation of the 'biblical' school : this, he knew, was quite adequate but far too heavy and mannered for the screen. As Jules had said, a new idiom was required. But what idiom could possibly achieve what was needed? How could a modern audience ever be made to sit through Odysseus's speech of rococo flattery and accept it as plausible, accept that it would do the trick? And what on earth was one to do with the passage later on about the joys of marriage? 'For nothing is stronger or better than this, that a man and his wife dwell in their home of one accord, a great grief to their enemies and a joy to their friends; but best of all do they know it themselves.' A beautiful and moving passage in itself, but the very last thing one wanted tacked on to this already voluminous supplication. Of course these lines could be cut out . . . but oh the pity if they were. And of course they could be kept in . . . but then what about the sheer unreality which would result?

"Well, what about it?" said Fielding Gray in Buttock's Hotel. "It's part of the Homeric convention?"

"But the conventions of Homer and those of the modern cinema just cannot be reconciled. Or not by me. I sat there all the rest of the morning. I had no lunch . . ."

". . . That was silly, dear . . ."

". . . And I sat there half the afternoon, sweating and striving, willing myself to do it. And still I was no nearer even beginning to find the sort of language Jules wanted."

"I wonder you weren't ill, dear."

"Oh, I was. Sick at the heart, Tessie. So in desperation I rang down for a company car and I drove out to the beach at Ermones. Hoping for . . . inspiration . . . comfort . . . God knows what. Peace and quiet at any rate, for it's a lonely little place. They're putting a hotel there, of course, but it won't be up till next year; and for the time being there's just an arc of sand, a hundred yards or so, with rocks and then sheer cliffs at either end, a few olive trees on the bare slopes above it, and this stream, which still flows right down across the beach and into the sea. And when I got there . . . Tessie . . . Fielding . . . I could see it. The girls doing the washing in the stream, a little way up in the tanks, and then bathing and eating their picnic on the beach, and playing with their ball and singing . . . until suddenly the ball goes into the water, and everyone starts squealing and giggling . . . and out of the scrub comes the old rotter himself, covered with salt brine and goat-shit, and only the princess has the guts to stand still and listen to him. A ravishing scene, Fielding, Tessie, and so bloody right . . . right for the screen too, if only it hadn't been for those speeches. And here was I, being given the chance to make them right too, to do the one thing still needed to put this miraculous scene on film . . . and I just couldn't do it. I knew I couldn't do it. I tell you, I sat there and wept . . . the driver thought I was potty . . . till the sun started to go down, just about the time Nausicaa and her party would have been setting off home after they'd cleaned up Odysseus. So I watched them starting from the beach and up along the river, Odysseus walking with the handmaids behind the waggon; and then I made the driver take me to where I could see them all turning away across the fields, towards Palaeo-castritsa as it's called now, getting smaller and smaller as I waved to them over the new golf course; and then I cried a bit more; and then at last I drove back to Corfu and went straight to Jules Jacobson and told him that I'd failed."

'You haven't had time to try,' Jules had said.

'I can't do it, Jules. And that's final.'

'You've done all right up till now.'

'You haven't asked for much up till now. Just a bit of fiddling with the dialogue. But now that you want it . . . transformed . . .'

'You're damn right I do. *And* for the scenes we've already shot, Tom. I've been thinking about them and they won't do now. We've got to go back and shoot them again . . . the bits with dialogue, that is . . . so that there'll be the same sort of language all through.'

'I wonder,' Tom had said, 'that any films ever get made, if this is the way you all go on. We've been here since July, Jules, two solid months, and *now* you decide to begin again from scratch. You really mean you're going to scrap all you've done?'

'Only the dialogue. The action can stand.'

'That still means a hell of a lot of work . . . and money . . . just thrown into the gutter. What'll Foxy say?'

'That's my business. I shall tell him my decision . . . or a version of it . . . when he arrives tomorrow. What we've done hasn't been wasted, Tom. You could say that we've been experimenting with different styles.'

'And still haven't found the right one.'

'I was relying on you to do that.'

The voice had been neutral, not reproachful, and all the more hurting for that.

'You were asking too much. I'm sorry, Jules, but I'm not a magician. And even if I were, I haven't time. Three weeks at most, and I must be back in Cambridge.'

'You could postpone that.'

But Tom could not postpone that. Until recently he had been only a supernumerary fellow of Lancaster, more or less free to come and go as he pleased, but the previous spring he had been elected to a full college fellowship and appointed a Tutor in Modern History. Besides, he had a book to see through the University Press. By 5 October at latest he must be back for the new academic year; back, he now told himself, in the real world, having quitted these realms of fantasy for good. Not that he hadn't enjoyed his time on Nausicaa's island; but the dream was beginning to turn into a nightmare, and he was very glad to have an ungainsayable reason to be gone.

And Jules had understood. With the versatility of his kind, he immediately abandoned a plan which could no longer hold and felt up into the air for a new one.

'Right,' he said; 'so here's what I'll tell Foxy. Tom's done all

he can for us, I'll say, and he's set us well on the right lines.
The only thing is, there's a bit of a hang-up over the dialogue ...
which we must get right, if only for the sake of Og-Finck. So,
I'll say to Foxy, what we do is this : we go ahead shooting action
scenes only, and meanwhile we get a good man to rewrite the
talk from A to Z. A man who knows Greek, who has a taste for
this kind of story, a man who can handle character and conversation, a man ...'

'... Fielding Gray,' Tom had said without really thinking.

'And who might he be?'

'A novelist who is well thought of for his dialogue and has
a knowledge of Greek Literature.'

'Any scripts?'

'Not that I know of. So you'll get him cheap . . . by your
standards.'

'Shall I like him?'

'Probably ... if you like me.'

And that had been enough. The next day Jules had put it to
Foxy in Tom's presence. Tom (he learned to his own surprise)
had been one of the most clear-sighted and creative advisers
with whom it had ever been a director's good fortune to work;
but now he had fulfilled his task and must return to his college.
The only thing which Tom and Jules hadn't *quite* settled between them, Jules said, was the final cast of the dialogue, and
Tom had recommended a friend who would come out and
deal with that.

'A lovely friend of Tom's?' mused Foxy. 'And what might he
be called?'

'Fielding Gray.'

'Man who wrote *Tom Jones*?'

'Pretty much in the same class,' said Jules, without moving a
muscle. 'He's won all the best prizes, Foxy, and Tom reckons
he'll understand our problem.'

'Well, I dunno, Jules. Any friend of Tom's, but I dunno.'

'Look, Foxy. While you've been away, little Elena's been in
the Greek pokey.'

'*Elena?* However did little El ...'

'. . . And the only reason she's out again now, and sitting in her room this minute waiting to wrap her boobies round your prick, is because Tom thought up a way to spring her.'

'Gee, Tom baby, I sure am . . .'

'. . . So if Tom recommends someone to do a job, Foxy, then we trust him, baby boy, because Tom Llewyllyn knows what he's at.'

'Well, I'll have to take a little time . . .'

'. . . We've no time to take, Foxy. So just say the word . . . and then you can run off to Elena.'

'Okay, okay. So we'll have this Fielding guy. Any friend of Tom's, like I said. . . .'

'Why did you press it so hard?' said Tom when Foxy had gone panting off.

'Because I want someone . . . different from all these . . . to talk to. Someone like you. Of course, Foxy will want something in return.'

'Like what?'

'When the new dialogue's ready, we'll have to re-shoot the scenes on Circe's island. Ten to one he'll want Circe's part for Elena . . . or whoever's chewing him by then.'

'You'll agree to that?'

'No. I'll get the original Circe back here from England. She's a crabby little bitch but she can act.'

'What'll you give Foxy then?'

'I'll see when the time comes. We'll think of something.'

'We?'

'Me and this Fielding Gray. He'll help me over things like that?'

'I dare say. But watch him, Jules. He's had a few shocks in his life and he can get some funny ideas.'

'Now you tell me. But I'll chance that if he's everything else you say. You'd better be off, Tom. Since you're going, go fast. Go fast, and send me Fielding Gray.'

"So they've got a contract ready for you," said Tom to Fielding in Buttock's Hotel. "A thousand a week for two weeks on probation. If Jules likes your work, and if he likes you, they'll sign you up for three months further. Fourteen thousand pounds, my dear : go there and get it."

"How do I know they'll like my work? What they want is impossible."

"But what is not impossible," Tom said, "is to make them think that they're getting it. They're short of time, Fielding; anything that reads straight and clear will pass for genius."

"Then why didn't you serve it up?"

"Because I'd have known I was giving short measure, and I didn't want to do that either to Homer or to Jules Jacobson. Your conscience, I fancy, is less delicate. You can settle quite happily for second best."

"That's what we all do in the end." Fielding narrowed his eye at Tom. "Don't be so damned smug."

"Sorry. But one thing more, Fielding. Don't let Jules down. Don't cheat him."

"You've as good as said I've got to. You've told me that this dialogue he wants can't ever really be written . . . you've admitted that he'll have to be fobbed off."

"I'm not talking about the dialogue now. As to that, do the best you can and there an end of it. I meant in other ways, Fielding. Don't do what you did to me over that BBC business in Athens. *Don't desert.*"

"There were special circumstances."

"There always are for men like you."

"If you feel like that, I wonder you've recommended me this time."

"Off the top of my head. But come to think of it, it's time you got off your arse and went somewhere."

"I don't yet know that I shall."

"Oh, don't be a drag, dear," said Tessie. "Think of all them girls . . . waiting to wrap their boobies round your prick. I must say, Tom seems to have wasted his time . . . just talking to that dreary shonk Jacobson."

"From the sound of it," said Fielding, "that's just what I'll be expected to do."

"You'll like him, Fielding. And you'll get plenty of chances to amuse yourself . . . if you want to."

"Of course he'll want to," Tessie said. "And perhaps he'll have something worth telling at the end of it. Not all this crap about maidens dancing on beaches."

"Be quiet, you wretched old bag," said Fielding. And to Tom, "When does he expect to hear?"

"There's a ticket waiting for you at Pandarus' London office in Curzon Street. Just book a flight and wire your time of arrival."

"I see. But I'm still not sure, mind you. I'll have to discuss it with Harriet."

Harriet Ongley was Fielding's mistress, with whom he had lived on the Norfolk coast for the last eight years. He had also to some extent lived off her, and still did. For although his novels were reputable and even, as novels go, quite profitable, his income was seldom more than £3000 a year; and had it not been for the very comfortable number of dollars which the widow Ongley had inherited ten years before from her husband, Fielding would have lacked for many of his favourite refinements, to say nothing of the large and pleasant villa in which they lived at Broughton Staithe. This looked out over the end of the golf course and on to the salt-marshes, where Fielding and Harriet were now walking in the early evening after his return from London. Harriet, her round face glowing with sea-side health and her round legs (not bad for fifty) bare and brown above her sandals, was trying to make a brisk pace, since she took a puritanical view of walks; but Fielding, who did not, only lagged behind her every time she put on pressure, and after a minute at most she had to turn and wait while he sauntered over the gap.

"You'll never take off weight this way," she said.

"I don't want to. A certain solidity is becoming in a middle-aged man."

"And leads to coronary thrombosis. What did Dr. La Soeur have to say?"

It was to visit the doctor that Fielding had been in London.

"Dr. La Soeur is a man of the world. He is tolerant of middle-aged solidity."

"He can't think that you're fit."

"We didn't discuss that," Fielding said. "He talked about my face."

Harriet, who had been just about to race ahead again, slackened her step.

"There's nothing wrong?"

"No more than there has been for the last twelve years. The fittings are sound. The Cyclops' eye will continue to see."

"Oh," said Harriet, relieved. "I thought there might be an infection or something."

"No. The Army surgeons did a good job . . . by the standards of 1958. But it seems there are people who could do a much better job now . . . aesthetically, I mean. For a high price, of course."

"We can pay it."

"You can, perhaps. But I told him 'no'."

"Oh Fielding, sweet. Why?"

"I'm only just getting used to this face. I don't want to spend the next ten years getting used to another."

This was true; but it was also true that Fielding did not wish to become further beholden to Harriet Ongley than he already was. To owe her for his very face would be too much.

"Besides," Fielding went on, "a handsome artificial face . . . if it *were* handsome . . . would be even more obscene than a hideous one. And think of the embarrassment when one's friends didn't recognise one. 'I'm Fielding Gray,' I'd have to say. 'Oh no, you're not,' they'd say. 'Fielding's got a face like a marzipan pig.' I'd probably have to get my prick out to prove it, and not *all* my friends would recognise me by that."

This was the sort of remark which Harriet hated more than anything, as Fielding well knew. Now, as so often lately, he was very keen to annoy Harriet, in order to prove to himself, and to her, that he could risk her anger, that she hadn't bought him, that he was still, at bottom, independent. But Harriet knew this particular game as well as he did; she stopped to examine a marsh shrub, picked off a small spray which she tucked into the top of her skirt, and then said, in a reasonable and slightly bored tone of voice :

"If you don't intend to have it done, why mention it in the first place?"

"To show you that I no longer care about it. Any more than I care about getting fat. And let me tell you, I've got nowhere near so fat as Tom Llewyllyn."

"You've seen him?" said Harriet, without much pleasure. I'll soon get her bate going now, Fielding thought.

"Yes," he said. "He'd just got back from Corfu and was spending the night at Tessie's. Now, Tom had something *really* interesting to say."

Harriet, playing at the game with some skill, showed no desire to hear it, but Fielding told her, even making the effort to keep up with her in her brisker spurts of walking, so that she shouldn't miss a word. He was not trying to tell her good news; he was spitefully (as he thought, subtly) demonstrating that after all he was famous, that he could be rich, that he could do without Harriet Ongley. But Harriet, still playing cleverly, merely turned her face away, whenever she thought it might show how much he was hurting, and pretended to gaze at the distant dunes.

"Of course you must go," she said when he had finished.

She wasn't meant to say this. She was meant to say that he would be prostituting himself and his art, she was meant to beg him to stay there in Broughton, so that he could round on her and accuse her of bossing and possessing and managing, of stifling and maiming his whole life.

"Ongley had a cousin," she went on blandly and carefully, "whose brother-in-law was something to do with the Oglander-Finckelstein Trust. It's a very fine organisation, Fielding. You're lucky to work for it."

"I'm not working for it," he grated through his twisted mouth : "I'll be working . . . if I do work . . . for Pandarus Films.

And the whole point of what I've been telling you is that Pandarus Films are taking Og-Finck for a ride."

"I don't know. From what you say Tom said, this director . . . Jacobson . . . is going to do a serious job."

"But not quite the job that Og-Finck wants him to do."

"He's going some way to meet them. They'll come to terms, you see. That's the best anyone can hope for in this world . . . to come to terms."

"You really are very naïve, Harriet. With a man like Foxe J. Galahead producing, the whole affair will turn into a tit-show."

"But Tom said that the director has the first and last word on how the film's actually made."

"And Galahead has a great many words in between. Half the girls have been hired to lick his cock."

That would surely do the trick : both Harriet the feminist and Harriet the maternal protectress would hate and fear this crude vision of the seraglio. As indeed Harriet did; but far greater than her distaste for such a vision was her sorrow over the unkindness and ingratitude which had made Fielding conjure it. He had accepted her in the role of mother as well as mistress from the very beginning, when she had first picked him out of the dirt, both literally and figuratively, eight years ago in Greece. Now, as she knew, he was rejecting her in the mother-role, so she had tried to slough it; yet here he was scheming to push her back into it, so that he might have the better target to resent and to violate. Well, she would not be caught that way.

"It's no good telling me all this," she said. "You must decide for yourself : either you take the job or you don't. If I were you I'd take it. It'll do you good, and your work good, to get a change of air. And it'll be nice for us both if you can make a bit of money."

All of which was exactly what Fielding thought. But it was not what Harriet was meant to think. He, Fielding, might know that he needed a change of air—that for the last three years he had been growing slacker and slower both in body and mind, that he had been self-satisfied and perfunctory in his work, that he was, in every sense, running to fat, and needed brisk and prolonged movement, in almost any direction, to sweat him out. Oh yes, he himself might know this, but Harriet was not meant to know it, far less to say it; Harriet was meant to think him perfect as and where he was and to plead with him to stay there, so that he, with his supreme understanding of himself, could upbraid and defy the silly, whining cow in the cause of his own good. Or again, as to money, he, Fielding, might acknowledge that up to a point he ... well ... found her contributions convenient; but *she* was definitely not required even to hint at such a thing. I'll pay you back, he thought, for that. I'll teach you to bray about money. I'll go away and make so much that I'll never need to think of you again. And then you can just sit here by these salt-marshes and rot. But that would be the end of the match; meanwhile he must win this first round.

"Oh, I shall go to Corfu," he told her, "if only for a good laugh and some new material. But I'm afraid that you can't come."

"Oh?" she said, and turned round, slowly and casually, to indicate that it was time to make for home.

"They won't pay your fare or your hotel," he said as he turned too, "only mine."

"I dare say I could pay my own. If I wanted to come."

"Of course you could. But I wouldn't if I were you. The director's not keen on having wives ... and so on ... about the place. He thinks that they disrupt things. That they pester. That they're always wanting treats or patent medicines or love ... irrelevant things like that. The director wants a working company on Corfu, not a miniature welfare state. Or so Tom said."

"No one could stop me going."

"You'd just be ignored. Totally."

Although Fielding had already said a lot of nasty things to Harriet that evening, this was the first time he had expressed naked contempt. Hitherto his utterance, however harsh in meaning, had been softened by some pretence of wit or irony, so that it had been just possible to think of the conversation as a civilised contest between two intelligent people who were working off a mild disagreement; but this last threat was so brutal and direct a statement of antipathy that he might just as well, Harriet felt, have struck her. Her knees sagged slightly, her eyes pricked and blinked, she put both hands to her stomach.

"Would you ignore me, Fielding?" she said.

Ah, he thought; an appeal for mercy. She's had enough for now; the moment I stopped playing about and let her have it straight, she caved in, just like that. And yet he felt no relish in his victory, now it was won. As he looked at the tears springing in her big round eyes and the plump fingers entwined and twisting over her belly, he felt, first of all, disgust with himself that he could have been so violent, and then boredom with Harriet, that she should have buckled so quickly just when things were really warming up.

"Would you ignore me, Fielding?" she said for the second time.

Careful now, he thought. For it was essential, he knew, to his own inner comfort that he should rid himself of the guilt which always followed on his acts of violence; and this he could never do by self-justification, even when he had reason whereby to justify himself, but only by expressing tenderness, however counterfeit, to his victim. He looked at the crumbling gun-sites which were still left among the dunes from the war, and remembered how the blood had welled up from his mother's mouth, here in Broughton twenty-five years ago. . . .

'Mama, I'm sorry, so sorry. *Please,* mama. I didn't mean . . .'

'. . . Nasty little pansy,' she had lisped through the streaming blood; 'nasty, vicious little pig.'

"Would you ignore me, Fielding?" said Harriet yet once more.

Blackmailing sow, he thought; just like my mother. But the guilt will torture me unless I can soothe her into forgiveness. And besides, she's still paying for my wine and my whisky, for my lobster and even for my house. I'm not independent of her yet, and I may never be. Salve your guilt, Fielding Gray : salve your guilt and look to your meal-ticket. A few pleasant words are not a high price to pay for such ample insurance.

"I'm sorry, sweet," he said. "I'm rather on edge about it all.

I only meant that making a film is a very busy, expensive and complicated affair. People get very tired, Tom says . . . tired and wrought-up both at once, and they are always short of time."

"So I'd be in the way." Already slightly mollified. "I'd amuse myself, you know."

"But for the time being . . . until I've found my feet . . . and had a chance to arrange things, to spy out the land . . . best stay here, sweet. Really."

With his left hand he lifted her two hands from her belly, which he massaged gently with his right.

"Piglet pie," he said.

"Don't wheedle, Fielding. I know what it is. You don't want to share this with me."

"But I do, Harry. Only I want to find out what I'm getting into first. And after all, Tom says that this hotel the film people stay in . . . the one I'll be staying in . . . is packed out by Pandarus. So I'll have to enquire where else we could go when you came."

"You'll have a suite. Suites always have double bedrooms."

"For the first two weeks I'm on probation. I've got to work very hard and do everything to please them. If I move you into my suite, and if this man Jacobson doesn't like wives there anyway . . . You must see it, Harry."

"I'm not sure you should go at all. There's something . . . corrupt about it. Something rotten. That producer and those girls. . . ."

"He's not there very much. Harry, you said yourself I need a change."

"A change of *air*."

"That's all it'll be. You know that. Piglet."

She clasped her hands over his and pressed them to her belly very tightly.

"When shall you go?" she said at last.

"No time to be lost. Tomorrow, if I can make London in time for a 'plane."

"That's right, of course. If they need someone so badly. When can I come, Fielding?"

"I'll let you know after the first fortnight. If they take me on permanently, I'll arrange it as soon as possible after that."

"Yes. That's sensible, I suppose."

"You know it is, Harry."

And now, he thought, as he took a last look back at the gun-sites among the dunes, I suppose she'll want to be fucked three times because it's my last night.

# PART TWO

# NAUSICAA

". . . So the way I see it," said Foxy J. Galahead in the bar at Corfu Airport, "we get that little Nausicaa laid right there on the beach."

Fielding looked at Jules Jacobson, who said nothing and waited patiently for Foxy to continue. Since Fielding had only flown in ten minutes before, he was not at his best. Since Foxy was about to fly out, and was always excited at the prospect of a journey, he was at his worst.

"Out comes Odysseus, raw as a carrot," Foxy was saying, "and there's Nausicaa standing there dazed, because she's never seen a pair of balls till now, and she knows that this is it, and an electric message flashes between them, and he screws her right there on the beach . . . POW."

"While the handmaids stand round them fingering each other?" said Jules Jacobson, poker-faced.

"No," said Foxy. "We don't want any perversions in this picture. Good straight sex and plenty of it : bom, bom, bom and no filth. Got that?" he blared at Fielding.

"The handmaids," said Fielding slowly, "would be bound to know what was going on. Are they peeping out through the bushes? Or do they just hide their faces?"

"No peeping; that's filth. Voyeurism. But no shutting their eyes to it, because that makes out it's disgusting. And it's not," said Foxy, flinging his arms wide, "it's beautiful. It's this little girl's first fuck, and it's the sun and the moon and the stars . . . so what those handmaids do, they stand up above the beach, looking out over the sea, and they sing a love song about wandering mariners and how they all hope there'll be one for them too before very long."

669

"Like 'One day my Prince will come'?" Jules Jacobson said.

"Yeah, Jules, yeah. Something like that, I guess."

"And who shall we get to write it?"

"Fielding here can start with the words. That's what we pay him for, words. Like to write a song, Fielding?"

"All right with me, Foxy," said Fielding for the sake of peace.

"That's my baby. I like a guy that don't raise difficulties. And that reminds me, Jules : Elena."

"What about her, Foxy? Raising difficulties, is she?"

"She's not the old Elena. She won't play the old games like she used to. Maybe she's hung up on that Greek waiter who stuffed her?"

"Bom, bom, bom and no filth," Jules said. "I don't think Elena has hang-ups, Foxy. She's not the type. Anyway, what can I do about it?"

"Let Gretel have her part as Nausicaa's chief handmaid. Gretel . . . why that face, and those eyes, and that mouth . . . that lovely, lovely mouth . . ."

". . . She can't sing out of it, Foxy. She's tone-deaf."

"So she can't sing. So what the hell?"

"The handmaids have got to sing this great song, remember? While Odysseus pops the weasel with Nausicaa."

"Dub the song."

Foxy's flight to Athens was announced.

"Too late to change now, Foxy. Elena's been dressed and rehearsed in the part . . ."

". . . But it's a different part, now Odysseus is going to lay Nausicaa."

"Different for Nausicaa. Not for the handmaids."

"Yeah, different for them too. Now they've got this love song."

"Which Gretel can't sing."

"Which we're going to have dubbed. Just you listen to me, Jules. That Gretel . . . she's an artist."

"So she's an artist. But she's not Nausicaa's chief handmaid. That's for little Elena . . . even if she won't play the old games like she used to."

"Jules baby, you make me sore as an arsehole. All I'm ask . . ."

". . . Go on now, Foxy baby, or you'll miss your 'plane. I'll do something for Gretel, don't you worry, but it's Elena for Nausicaa's chief handmaid."

As Foxy waddled huffily off, two henchmen moved up to escort him.

"I'm sorry to subject you to that the minute you get here," Jules said, "but he wanted to meet you before he left and tell you his ideas. You heard 'em : now forget 'em."

Foxy turned at the gate and gave them a gleeful, almost childish wave of farewell, his grievance already, it seemed, forgotten.

"Who's Gretel?" Fielding said as they waved back.

"Swedish slut with an underlip like a shovel. Means she can scoop his balls in too, I suppose."

"*Not* a handmaid by the sound of it."

"No. I had her in mind for a cannibal when we get to the Laestrygonians. Which," said Jules, "will be a very long while yet. And meanwhile, Fielding Gray, our business is Nausicaa. Tom told you what's wanted?"

Fielding nodded.

"Well now," said Jules, "I'm going to tell you again, while we go over the ground. I've got a car outside."

"A porter for my luggage?"

Jules shrugged and picked up Fielding's very substantial suitcase. Carrying it without difficulty, he led the way out to the car park, where he stopped by a small Renault and slung Fielding's case up on to the roof-rack. Fielding, who was only carrying his typewriter and a small grip, was a good fifteen seconds behind Jules and collapsed into the co-driver's seat panting.

"You notice I haven't brought a driver," said Jules. "They're not only damned bad, Greek drivers, but they think they have a democratic right to muscle in on their employers' conversations. And this afternoon," he said, as he turned fast but very smoothly on to the main road, "I want your undivided attention. Because on Nausicaa and the Phaeacians depends our next lot of cash from the Oglander-Finckelstein Trust."

"Which you'll want by early November. So we've got to finish shooting the scenes well before then . . . so that you can cut together all the best takes?"

"Right. I want four days' shooting in the palace and ten on the beach at Ermones. Two weeks. So I'll need the new lines for those scenes just as soon as you can have them ready."

"And I'm to forget all Foxy's blah? No fucking and no singing."

"No fucking, certainly. But there *is* to be singing . . . just where Homer says there is, while the girls are playing with their ball. Tom said that would be right, and I agree."

"But I don't suppose either of you wrote the song?"

"No," said Jules with a pleasant smile. "What I want is a kind of refrain. I want one simple, four-line stanza from you, Fielding, two couplets of rhymed iambic pentameters. Subject: the happy marriages they all hope to make."

"And the music?"

"I'll find that."

"You'd be better off with a proper poet to compose the verse. I don't really write poetry."

"For a thousand a week you write everything. You're getting twenty-five per cent up on Tom because you're bound to turn out all the words I want. Tom was only an adviser; I couldn't *make* him write. But I'll make you write what I want, Fielding Gray, or I'll break your sodding neck."

Fielding found this speech rather exciting. It was fun to work for a man who was in earnest . . . though surely he needn't have driven quite so fast over these pot-holes. Thankfully, Fielding saw that they were now approaching a golf course, flat and green on the left of the road, lightly flecked with young trees.

"Surely . . . Ermones is left and just over the course?" Fielding said, remembering Tom's description of the environment.

"Well done. But we're going to the Palace first. We're using the monastery at Palaeocastritsa for that. With a bit of faking it'll pass quite well."

Jules hooted at an oncoming lorry which was taking up the entire road. Just in time the lorry gave way, but the driver shook his fist from the window as they passed.

"Road-works vehicle," said Jules. "Public employees here like to think they take precedence over the public." Then, noticing that Fielding had gone white, "Am I driving too fast for you?"

"These days," said Fielding with a great effort, "all menials put on the airs of officials, just like that driver. It gives them an illusion of status and a chance to get their own back for the tedium of their existence. The usherettes in English cinemas bully one around like drill sergeants."

"Very good," said Jules, "very good. You were scared to shit by that lorry but you thought of an answer."

"The least I can do for a thousand a week. And I want to be clear from the start exactly what else I do for the money. I re-write the speeches in that script but nothing else. Right?"

"Right. The sequence of action and movement will stay as it is, and neither you nor Foxy nor God Himself can change it. However," said Jules, "I myself just might. We're coming to the first of the bays by Palaeocastritsa. . . ."

And for the next three hours Fielding was taken over every inch of the ground. The Palace/monastery courtyard, probable places for shots of Nausicaa and her girls while *en route,* the point at which they would meet the river, the approaches, along the river and through the low rocky hills near the sea, to the washing tanks, the tiny estuary and the beach; Odysseus's distressful bed in the scrub, the shady nook for the girls' picnic, the sand banks on which they would spread the washing to dry, the flat space near the estuary on which they would play at ball and sing, the hiding places to which all but the Princess would scatter as the hero emerged. . . .

"Can you see it?" said Jules at last.

"Yes . . . but so could Tom."

"Never mind Tom. Make them talk for me, Fielding; please make them talk."

"I must see the actors first. See and hear."

"Quite right," said Jules, with evident approval which overlaid a slight and puzzling reluctance. "I've got them coming to dinner. Odysseus if he's not too drunk . . . and Nausicaa." Again the hint of reluctance. Why, Fielding wondered.

"I've also asked someone else," said Jules, visibly brightening. "The chief handmaid . . . the daughter of Dymas, as Homer calls her."

"Otherwise little Elena . . . who refused to play games any longer with Foxy?"

"Rather impressive that," said Jules. "The rest of 'em would have gone on doing whatever Foxy told 'em, however disgusting, and purring all over him. But not, it seems, Elena. Good, honest girl, Elena; says what she means and stands by it."

"I think," said Elena to Fielding, "that your face is not as bad as I was warned."

For of course everyone had been warned, Jules and Foxy by Tom, then the whole company by Jules, which was why no one had shown any surprise.

"Rather *plastic*," Elena went on, "but I quite like your one eye. Isn't there a character in this film somewhere who only has one eye?"

"Polyphemus," said Fielding, "otherwise known as the Cyclops. Not an attractive fellow. He eats some of Odysseus's sailors."

"My, my. I hope you're not going to eat any of us."

"I shall very soon feel like it . . . if we don't go into dinner."

Jules's dinner party was assembled in the bar of the Corfu Palace, with the unexpected addition of Penelope, who had invited herself at the last minute 'to say hallo to the new writer', and with the exception of Odysseus, for whom they would wait, Jules now said, for five more minutes. Penelope, whose real name was Margaret Lichfield, heaved a long sigh at the announcement and went to work with her lipstick.

"Trouble with these old pissers," Penelope said, "they've got no consideration."

"It's an illness," said Nausicaa, a delicious red-head, of small

yet gangling build, who had been introduced as Sasha Grimes.
"I do feel so sorry for him."

"It's easy to be understanding at your age, darling. But at
mine one's ulcers start barking if they're not fed."

"Poor Margaret," said Nausicaa, in a voice creamy with pity
for the whole suffering world. "Have one of these olives."

"And lose my appetite? My intestinal juices, Sasha dear, are
very precariously balanced."

"That's what comes of having to rush. Because you weren't
really expecting . . . were you, Margaret darling? . . . to be
asked out this evening at all."

"The young red vixen has sharp teeth," Elena murmured to
Fielding, "but the old black crow has very strong wings. After
all, they've carried her all the way from a gutter in Bermondsey
to a pinnacle in this profession."

"But she's still afraid," suggested Fielding, "that the young
red vixen will creep up behind her and chase her off it?"

"All old-timers are afraid of something like that. But in fact,"
said Elena, "Sasha Grimes will never be in the same class as old
Margaret. Margaret's a star; Sasha's just a very good actress.
She got the Oglander-Finckelstein Award at nineteen . . . that's
one reason why she's here now . . . she's had some marvellous
parts at the Old Vic and so on, but she'll never make it as a
star, or not in the sense that Margaret has. Margaret Lichfield
is to Sasha Grimes as Greer Garson to Jane Asher."

"If you get much sharper, Sasha darling," Margaret Lichfield was saying, "you're going to cut your own pretty little
throat without knowing it. If you want to know why I've made
such an effort to get to this dinner," she said, clamping her
martini into her fist and marching across to Fielding, "it's because I was anxious to meet Mr. Thingummy here. Now, what
are you going to do about my speeches, Mr. Thingummy darling? That's what I want to know. They're as chewy as a hunk
of rubber."

"We'll discuss your speeches later on, Margaret," said Jules
rather coolly.

"Yes, Margaret darling, later on," cooed Nausicaa. "Tonight, you see, we have to discuss *my* speeches." She simpered like a mischievous angel. "Or didn't Jules explain when he invited you?"

Margaret Lichfield drew strongly on her martini.

"First things first, little one," she said. "Penelope is the lead . . . as even you may know."

"For such an *experienced* person, Margaret, you do say the oddest things. What has Penelope got to do with my scenes on the beach? That's what darling Jules is worried about just now."

"*Worried*, darling, he may well be."

"Dinner, dears," said Jules, with just a hint of despair. "We won't wait any more for Angus."

Dinner was unexpectedly agreeable, at any rate for Fielding, largely because he was sitting next to Elena. Jules had honoured Margaret Lichfield, as a senior star, by placing her on his right but had punished her as a party-crasher by leaving vacant for Odysseus the seat which was on her own right. To the right again of the empty chair was Elena, to her right Fielding, and to his Sasha Grimes, who sat on Jules's left. As long as Elena had no one to her immediate left, it was Fielding's clear duty to devote himself to her, and this he was happy to do : for although Sasha/Nausicaa was by far the more beautiful of his two neighbours, she was a girl of didactic utterance and anti-septic disposition, constantly clearing the space about her with fierce little movements of her fingers, as if to protect herself from the touch and taint of imaginary intruders. Elena, on the other hand, was brown, appetising, rather sweaty young flesh, which she distributed, so to speak, by the handful. She plonked her thigh firmly against Fielding's from the moment they sat down and frequently nudged him in the chest with her bare upper arm, letting it linger beneath his chin as though to say 'have a nice juicy mouthful if you want one'.

But this would have been to insult the admirable dinner which Jules had ordered. Elena ate hers voraciously (another strong point in her favour), the Lichfield chomped away with content-ment, ulcers appeased, and even the delicate Sasha, who surveyed her food as if its presence were a gross affront to her sensitivities, took a few patronising mouthfuls. The result was an immediate improvement in everybody's temper. Jules and Margaret speculated with cheerful malevolence about the future fate in the film world of the departed Circe; Sasha/Nausicaa listened with bright, reproving eyes and smugly enjoined them to charity; while Fielding, reserving half an ear for the professional purpose of recording the genteel accents of Sasha, lent the other one and a half to the babbling Elena.

"I hope Angus Carnavon doesn't make it to dinner," she said. "I don't like the way he paws."

"Oh?"

"Or rather, it's not the pawing I mind, it's the pathetic pretence behind it. He wants you to think he's uncontrollably randy, when all he ever has is a snail between his legs. Drink, of course. But they say it was always the same even before he hit the bottle."

"Perhaps that's why he hit the bottle."

"*You* look a bit boozy to me."

"I am a bit boozy."

"Because of all that plastic on your face? It doesn't put me off, you know."

"I'm glad. But I was boozy before the plastic, as you call it."

"Why? Snail trouble, like Angus?"

"No. Not snail trouble. Mother trouble, you might say."

"You queer?"

"Some of the time. Not much of it, these days."

"Some of them say Angus Carnavon is queer, but I don't think he fancies anything. Except whisky, of course."

"But can he act?"

"You must have seen him for yourself . . . he's starred in enough pictures in his time."

"In his time. Can he *still* act?"

"Yes," said Elena with plain and generous admiration. "He's bloody fine as Odysseus. Or at any rate he twitches that craggy face of his about with marvellous results. And his voice sends me. Sometimes dry and sad, sometimes rasping and cruel, sometimes. . . . Here he comes now, not too stoned, I hope." She ran her fingernails lightly up the inside of Fielding's thigh and let her hand linger briefly. "No," she said, "no snail trouble for you. Come to my room . . . 527 . . . when the party's done. I want another word with you, and now I'll have to talk to this bladderful of hooch."

After some confusion while Carnavon, not a large man but very chunky, manoeuvred himself into dock, demanded scrambled eggs in place of Jules's menu, and then started to paw Elena, Fielding was addressed by Sasha Grimes, who was now gazing at him with schoolmarmish reproach.

"One should never allow oneself," she said, "to be distracted from one's creative responsibilities."

"Indeed not. Especially when one is being well paid."

"Ah," she diagnosed briskly. "The cynical pose of an unfulfilled artistic spirit. I can tell. I have empathy, you see."

"It isn't a pose. One tries to do sound work and hopes to get good money."

" 'Sound work'," she echoed, shaking her head. "What has that to do with the ecstasy of creation?"

"I know nothing about the ecstasy of creation."

"But you would like to. That is why you are unfulfilled. And why you welcome trivial distraction."

She nodded towards Elena, who was glumly trying to fork food into her mouth without spilling it on to Odysseus's grizzled head, which was burrowing about in her bosom.

"We all welcome a bit of that," Fielding said.

"Speak for yourself," she said thinly.

"Oh, I do."

"Then wallow like an animal, if you must; I can't stop you. But don't let yourself be taken in, my friend. Jules won't like it."

"I don't understand."

"Even if you adopt a professional rather than a creative approach to your task, you must still value your integrity?"

"I suppose so."

"Then don't swerve from it" . . . again she nodded towards Elena . . . "whatever the temptation."

At this stage Fielding began to be curious, and more than curious, about Miss Sasha Grimes, alias Nausicaa. Prim and self-protective she might be, forbidding in her tone and priggish in her sentiments; but it was precisely this governessy aspect which, combined with the loose limbs and the flowing red hair, made her so fascinating. Her sexual appeal was less immediate than Elena's but far more subtle and evocative; somehow she conjured distant memories, which awakened not so much desire as yearning, of a prudish girl cousin who had turned suddenly shameless in the back of the car on the way home from a panto-mime, or of one stern young nanny whose hands had strayed into his pyjamas even as she rebuked his naughtiness. The nanny had left soon afterwards; the cousin, though often approached, had never again been accommodating; but nothing could take away the remembered and magical moments, those moments when something had occurred of such delicious enor-mity that it briefly revealed another world in which all natural routines and processes were confounded or reversed. It was to this world, Fielding thought, that Nausicaa might give one re-admittance : if ever one went to bed with her, the mere fact of its happening at all would be miraculous, against nature; it would be like pleasuring, and being pleasured by, someone absolutely unattainable, the Queen or the Virgin Mary.

Perhaps Sasha Grimes sensed something of what he was thinking. At all events she smiled mysteriously, put one finger nervously on the back of his hand, and said :

"I hope we shall understand one another. I'm very anxious you should get my speeches right."

She then proceeded to talk, with precision and intelligence, about her own merits and limitations as an actress. Her voice was small, she said, but clear and accurate. Although she was quite at home with difficult language, long sentences were apt to leave her breathless, despite all the expensive lessons which she had taken in voice-control. She was more suited to pique than passion, better at demanding than sympathising, which might not help her in the role of Nausicaa; however, she could do the Princess, she promised him, without making her suburban or coy, and she would be excellent as the nubile maiden upon whose innocent heart concupiscence was beginning to obtrude. To get down to more detail, she preferred iambic or trochaic rhythms of speech to dactyllic or anapaestic (though she realised there must be variety) so would dear Mr. Gray, with whom she now saw she was going to agree perfectly in such matters, very kindly remember . . .

". . . BITCH," shouted Odysseus, making the whole dining-room rattle.

Elena had stuck her fork into his hand.

"I'm very sorry," Elena said, "and I'll put up with almost anything for the sake of peace, but I'm not going to have my dugs bitten off . . . even if you do use Steradent."

Carnavon shook his wounded hand, shambled to his feet and started his farewells.

"Cow," he said quite mildly to Margaret; "Yid," he growled at Jules; "Tight-twat," more fiercely to Sasha; "You writer fairies," with a snarl at Fielding; and to Elena once more, "BITCH."

He leant forward, took a single spoonful of his scrambled egg, then reversed sharply into the Maître d'Hôtel, who spun him round cleverly and trotted him out.

"Rotten dinner," said Carnavon to the Maître d'Hôtel as they went. "No taste at all in that slut's teats."

"Ungrateful hound," said Elena to the rest of the party. "He nearly drew blood."

"At least," said Fielding, "I've got a good idea of his vocal range. He seems at his best with monosyllables . . . pity we can't confine him to those."

"He ought to be confined to grunting," Elena said. "Ignorant pig."

"We must all try to help him," said Sasha. "It's a sickness. you see."

"You're too good to be true," said Elena.

"And just you wait," put in Margaret Lichfield, "till you have to smell the stale whisky on his breath right through five hours' shooting."

"We don't know what he may have suffered."

"Or care."

"I only know he's nearly killed me with whisky fumes this last month."

"Poor darling Margaret. I've often wondered what made you look so tired on set."

"And now you're going to find out, Sasha dear, during those wonderful scenes of yours on that beach."

"I shall rise above it, Margaret dear. I shall disengage myself from crude physical sensations and float like a spirit, directing my body from above."

"Shall you, darling? He won't want to act opposite a waxwork, you know, even one as life-like as you."

"No," said Elena. "He likes tits made of flesh and blood."

"He'd never dare forget himself so far with me."

"Perhaps he wouldn't want to. What was it he called you just now? Tight-twat?"

"Shut up, the lot of you," said Jules, firmly but amiably, "and go to bed. Not you, Fielding, I want a word with you."

"And so do I, don't forget," whispered Elena as she rose to leave. "Room 527."

"I must say," said Fielding as the women all trooped out, "they're very obedient."

"They're worn out after a long day, and they've got to be up again by six. We start early, you know."

"They seemed lively enough."

"Keeping up an act. The show must go on . . . even off-stage."

"There's a lot to be said for the precept. Old Margaret Lichfield keeps marching on like a guardsman. You wouldn't think it's twenty years since she starred in *Zenobia*."

"Guardsman is right. She tramples. She had no business at dinner tonight. She knew very well I wanted to discuss the Nausicaa scenes, but as it was I had the devil's own job keeping her quiet so that the rest of you could get on with it. How did you manage?"

"Quite well, thank you. I had a vivid if brief impression of Odysseus's capacities, and an interesting talk with little Nausicaa."

"What did you make of her?"

"Intelligent when she talks about her acting. Otherwise a pretentious and self-righteous little ninny."

"Sasha models herself on Vanessa Redgrave. She picks up all the progressive clichés, and says it would be frivolous and anti-social just to be an actress. She has to be . . . what's that phrase she told me? . . . compassionately and ideologically orientated."

"But anyone can see she's only *acting* all that."

"She's too stupid to see it herself. Just wait till you hear her on politics."

"She told me that the only thing which mattered was creative ecstasy."

"You mustn't expect her to be consistent. She'll parrot any jargon which takes her fancy. An atrocious little ninny, as you say . . . but potentially an admirable Nausicaa."

"And rather beguiling in a way."

"What way?"

"All this *noli me tangere* of hers. Just suppose," said Fielding, "that she did let one touch her, it would be like touching a goddess. It would be to enjoy what was utterly unexpected and utterly forbidden."

"So already you're beginning to covet it?"

"I didn't say so."

"But I saw you thinking so . . . at dinner. Which is why I asked you to stay behind just now, though I'm more than ready for bed. Hands off my Nausicaa, Fielding. I don't want her disturbed or in any sense diverted. I just want her to concentrate on her acting until those vitally important scenes of hers are safely in the tin."

"I was only theorising, Jules. In a poetic sort of way."

"Which means your mind is on the subject. So get your mind off the subject, Fielding, and on to Elena instead . . . even if she is less poetic. That's why I asked *her* tonight. To provide you with any . . . needful amusement."

"You detailed her off, Jules?"

"More or less. She's as tough as tungsten . . . nothing would disturb *her* . . . and she owes me a good turn for getting her out of clink."

"Tell me . . . did you detail anyone off for Tom?"

"No. He didn't seem to need anyone," said Jules with strong retrospective approval. "But he warned me you would."

"Well, I could certainly do with a change of women. How kind of you and Tom to think of it. You'll be glad to know that Elena is at this very moment awaiting me in her room. 527."

Jules nodded rather heavily.

"I saw you getting on well together," he said.

"So did little Sasha. And do you know, Jules, little Sasha gave me a warning against Elena. Veiled, but an unmistakable warning. Now, what would you say was at the bottom of that?"

"Sasha's not jealous, if that's what you're hoping. She probably disapproves of Elena . . . thinks she's cheap or coarse."

"It's more complicated than that, Jules. Sasha implied that Elena was in some way a threat, that she was going to take me in . . . those were Sasha's words . . . and that *you wouldn't like it.* And yet now I find that it was you who arranged it all. So just what could Sasha have meant?"

Jules's face sagged in weary irritation.

"She's trying to be clever and make mysteries," he said. "Take my word for it, Fielding, there's nothing devious or dangerous about Elena. An honest girl who speaks her mind."

"But a whore."

"A whore?"

"You said so yourself. She's entertaining me, you said, in return for favours received from you."

"All right, a whore. But an honest one. She'll give full value."

"I'm delighted to hear it. But whores . . . even honest ones . . . always ask for *more* favours, particularly if they've been paid in advance."

"You wouldn't grudge her a small present? Not on a thousand a week."

"Oh no. But I'd still like to know what Sasha meant."

"I told you. She was just trying to seem profound. Part of her act. But if you're worried about any of this, just go straight to your room and forget it. All I require is that you stay clear of Sasha. If you want a girl, Elena's laid on for you; if you don't, that's fine by me."

"Oh, I want Elena all right. She saw to that at dinner. But whatever you say, Jules, there's more to this than meets the eye."

"Then go and find out what it is," said Jules, yawning hugely. "And don't wake me up to tell me."

"Sod you then, you rotten sod," said Elena in Room 527.

"Why am I a rotten sod?" asked Fielding.

"You come in here, and you help yourself to the sweet trolley . . . "

" . . . At your invitation . . ."

" . . . And then you refuse to write any lines for a girl."

For Sasha Grimes had been right and Jules Jacobson wrong. Elena did have a game of her own to play : she wanted Fielding, as script-writer, to write in some speeches for her. As Sasha had warned, Jules certainly wouldn't like it.

"I haven't refused," said Fielding carefully. "I've simply tried to explain that my job is not to write in new speeches but to re-write the old ones."

"You could cut one of the old ones in two and give me half of it."

"Look," said Fielding with a slight sigh. "I write . . . or rather rewrite . . . under the instructions of the director, Jules Jacobson. This afternoon Jules took me through your scenes very carefully, telling me exactly who would do and say what, and showing me exactly where and when they would do and say it. You and the other handmaidens have a lot to do but nothing at all to say. Homer gives you no lines, the present script gives you no lines, Jules doesn't want you to have any lines. If I wrote any for you, Jules would simply cut them out."

Elena gave a twitch of her naked breasts and considered this. Then she put a hand across and started to scratch Fielding, very delicately, at the base of his stomach.

"I see what you mean," she said in a commonsense voice; "but you could always try to persuade him."

"He'd say I was interfering with his direction."

Elena went on scratching. Fielding put one hand over and caressed both her nipples, one with his thumb and the other with his little finger.

"Save that for your typewriter," Elena said. But she didn't try to stop him and she didn't leave off scratching.

"You'd have had a better chance of getting a speaking part," said Fielding, "if you'd gone on being nice to Foxy Galahead."

"I couldn't stand Foxy. He was so damned sentimental. And then he wanted me to shave my bush off and pretend I was only nine."

"What would you have done about these?"

Fielding gave her breasts a wobble.

"He was going to buy me a special kind of high-neck nightie, nursery style. I was going to lie there in this nightie, and Foxy was going to come in and pretend he was Daddy come to say goodnight to his little girl. Then there was to be some routine about how I had a pain in my tummy. I ask you."

"It doesn't sound very exacting."

"I suppose not. And Gretel said he made it rather fun. But me, I like being myself, lover. I like sex every way it comes, straight as a ram-rod or bent as a spring in the mattress, but I want it to be *me* it gets done to, not some fantasy kiddy-wink of Foxy's."

"So you wouldn't play, and now you've lost yourself an ally."

"Lost myself a big fat slob."

Elena stopped scratching Fielding's stomach. She put her hand between his thighs and started pricking lightly with the points of her nails at the bottom of his buttocks. Fielding raised his knees to give her a larger area to work on.

"I suppose," Fielding said, "it's no good your trying to get at Jules yourself?"

"You think I haven't tried?"

The pricking sensation on Fielding's buttocks was really exquisite. Elena now removed Fielding's hand from her breasts, rested her head on his chest, and started sliding it slowly down.

"Elena . . . what shall I do to you?"

No answer. Prick, prick, prick on the buttocks and a warm circling tongue. Whereas Fielding's first dish from the sweet trolley had only been a conventional recipe, this second offering was an individual confection of genius. Prick, prick, prick . . . and a finger straying to find the valve in the cleft, probing softly for entrance.

"Christ, Elena . . . What do you want me to do to you?"

Tongue withdrawn. Exposed flesh dank and chilly.

"Promise to write me some lines, lover. That's what."

"Oh, Elena. I've told you . . ."

". . . Just you promise."

"But Elena. . . ."

Finger withdrawing its charity. Buttocks untouched, unloved.

"Listen, Elena. . . ." Jules would never consent to a speech for her, certainly not at his, Fielding's, suggestion. He'd be accused of meddling, of disregarding his very clear brief, of wasting time and money. He couldn't afford that sort of trouble while still only on probation. But what was it Jules had said about a song to be written? Yes: a refrain for the girls to sing while they played at ball. "Elena. I suppose I *could* write you some lines and just try them on Jules."

Prick, prick.

"I can't promise he'll like them, but I'd do my best."

Finger poised on valve.

"How many lines, lover?"

Two couplets, Jules had said. Two rhymed couplets.

"A few. Four, perhaps."

"All in one speech? Or separate?"

"All of them . . . I think . . . would be together."

"That's a good lover."

The warm tongue soothed away the chill. Prick, prick on the buttocks. Finger easing snugly into place. *Jubilate*.

"I wish," Fielding said, "that I could feel like this for ever."

But of course he couldn't, and the next morning he felt awful.

To begin with, he had promised to write some lines for Elena. By this she understood a speech; whereas he himself knew that all he would ever write for her was what he had been told to write by Jules . . . four lines of a refrain to be sung in chorus with the other handmaids. That she herself had not behaved well, having forced the promise out of him under duress, did not excuse him; and even if it did, she was going to be absolutely furious when she found out how he had misled her.

None of which boded well for his future relations either with Elena or, more important, with Jules. He could just imagine Jules's face if an enraged Elena formed up to him, on set or elsewhere, and demanded the speech that Fielding had promised her. The confrontations, the explanations, the protestations . . . oh, Christ. Yet the fact remained that it had been Jules who had got Fielding into this mess by 'laying Elena on' for him in the first place; and the question now presented itself, why had Jules done it? Surely, if Sasha was able to foresee Elena's embarrassing and demanding behaviour, Jules himself, wise in the ways of starlets, could have done so too . . . especially as Fielding had prompted him by remarking on Sasha's misgivings. But Jules had simply pooh-poohed all that and told Fielding to go ahead or not as he chose. Again, why? Jules's ostensible motive was to protect the delicate Sasha/Nausicaa from Fielding's attentions by channelling them off on to Elena; but could Jules really think that Sasha was so vulnerable and he, Fielding, so uncontrollable, that it was necessary to provide sexual distraction for him on his very first night in Corfu? Whatever warning Tom had given Jules, he could hardly have made Fielding out to be such a monster of incontinence as that.

Altogether, there were some uncomfortable questions here

to which Fielding badly needed the answers. But since the only
answers must come from Jules, and since Jules was in some
distant corner of the island watching the stunt men of the
Second Unit, Fielding would have to wait till the evening.
Meanwhile, he told himself firmly, there was one thing he *could*
be sure of . . . the necessity to work, and to work well, if he was
to secure confirmation of his contract at the end of the first two
weeks. He rose from the balcony on which he had been break-
fasting and went inside to his desk.

> "So take, while there is time, the gifts that the gods
> have granted :
> Taste ten thousand kisses, you will yet have tasted
> too few. . . ."

Fielding had decided to start by writing the words of the song
which Jules wanted. Four lines, Jules had said, two couplets of
rhymed iambic pentameters, in praise and hope of marriage.
But it was clear to Fielding that iambic pentameters would not
do as the basis of a chant which the girls must sing while they
played with their ball. It would be a big ball, which they would
throw, in the afternoon heat, with long languorous movements;
and these would be far better accompanied by a relaxed and
lulling rhythm than by the crisp rattle of iambs, which would
be more suitable to P.T. instructors slapping a basket ball about
in a gym. So Fielding had devised or remembered a spondaeo-
dactyllic line which would go most exquisitely, he thought, with
the slow curve of the ball through the shimmering sandy heat
and the indolent lapping nearby of the calm blue sea. As for
what the verses would say, they would celebrate desire rather
than marriage (for desire was what these girls were really on
about), and the appropriate sentiments were to be found in an
Elegy of Propertius which he had once been made to memorise
at school. So now he would translate the remembered lines into
his chosen measure, and make rhymes, he thought, at alternate
rather than proximate line-endings, in order to keep the ear
longer expectant and therefore more attentive through the
deliberately dragging words.

"So take, while there is time, the gifts that the gods
                                    have granted;
Taste ten thousand kisses, you will yet have tasted
                                    too few. . . ."

Now, what followed? If you don't do this, Propertius went on, your beauty will decay, like fallen rose-petals, before you and others have been able to enjoy it. Exactly. So:

"For as the leaves fall from the rose which but now
                                    hath flaunted. . . ."

'Flaunted' to rhyme with 'granted'? All right, if the other rhyme were made strong. 'Flaunted' used intransitively? Yes, it would pass in a song. 'Leaves' . . . or petals? Leaves for the metre, petals, he supposed, for botanical accuracy. Botanical accuracy not necessary in context, rose-leaves being sound poetic currency. All right; now clinch it:

"So take, while there is time, the gifts that the gods
                                    have granted;
Taste ten thousand kisses, you will yet have tasted
                                    too few;
For as the leaves fall from the rose which but now
                                    hath flaunted,
As the leaves fade and fall, the same it must be
                                    with you."

Very pretty, Fielding thought, if I do say it myself.

"Not what I asked for," Jules Jacobson said that evening.

He frowned over the sheet of paper which Fielding had shown him, then read the lines a second time, silently mouthing the words.

"No," he said at last; "not at all what I asked for. But I think it might do rather well. The slow rhythm . . . I can see it and hear it in a slow rhythm."

"So can I," Fielding said.

"You weren't asked to. You were asked for iambs. Now you've done it this way I'll have to hunt around for some other music."

"You already had some music?"

"Handel's setting for 'Where e'r you walk'. Out of copyright, you see. But now you've dispensed with iambic pentameters I'll have to look for something else. Please, Fielding, do not disobey my instructions again." He mouthed the first couplet once more. "But I agree," he said, "it could work. How are you getting on with the actual speeches?"

"Quite well, I think. I'll have a good deal to show you tomorrow."

"Not now?"

"It needs checking very carefully, Jules. Tomorrow, if you don't mind."

"All right. So long as you're not disregarding instructions."

"No," said Fielding, "I'm not. But I very well might have been." He told Jules about Elena's request. "Did you realise," he asked, "that something of the sort might happen?"

"Oh yes," said Jules.

"Then why did you tell me there was nothing to worry about with Elena? Why did you say Sasha was talking nonsense when you knew all the time that she was probably right?"

"I didn't want to put you off."

"Why were you so keen to put me on?"

"I told you. I wanted to be sure you wouldn't pester Sasha. Tom had warned me . . ."

". . . That I liked a bit of flesh. And so I do. But I don't jump in where I'm not wanted, Jules. I learned that lesson long ago."

"I didn't want to take any risk over Sasha."

"Risk? Did you think I was going to rape her or something . . . and kiss good-bye to a thousand a week? A simple request to keep away from her would have been quite enough. I can take a hint, Jules, and even if I couldn't I've no doubt whatever that little Sasha can take care of herself. So why all this fuss? Why did you go to such pains to bundle me into bed with Elena . . . knowing that she might make trouble of her own . . . on my very first night in Corfu?"

Jules considered Fielding carefully. He looked into his one eye and then into the puckered slit where the other should have been. After this he nodded heavily, just as he had nodded on the previous evening when Fielding had told him that he was expected by Elena in her bedroom.

"I wanted to see what you'd do," said Jules at last. "I wanted to see whether you'd really jump into bed with the first girl who touched you up . . . just like a randy little boy."

"Now you know. And much good may it do you."

"Oh, it does," said Jules. "You see, I've got a theory about you, Fielding. After Tom left, I made a few enquiries. I was determined to have you here anyhow, since he'd recommended you . . ."

". . . You must think very highly of his advice . . ."

". . . Oh, I do, and also of his warnings. So I decided, as I say, to make a few enquiries, and I started, on the off chance he'd be able to help me, with Max de Freville."

"The man who knows too much," said Fielding bitterly, remembering his last meeting with Max. "Tom said he was here."

"With a stake in this film, and so most anxious to help me. And what he didn't know, that woman of his did. Mrs. Angela Tuck."

"*Christ*. Is she still with him?"

"Oh yes indeed. You'll appreciate, then, that I've been very fully informed. All that squalid business of yours at school at the end of the war; your Army career; how you got your face smashed in Cyprus; how you started up as a novelist . . . and not least, what happened when you went back to Cyprus on that job for the BBC in 1962 and got taken for a ride . . . in every sense . . . by that cute little Greek. I've got a dossier on you, Fielding Gray, on everything from your sexual pranks over the last twenty-five years down to the fillings in your teeth. And on the strength of all this I formed a theory. Do you want to know what it is?"

"I don't need you to tell me, Jules. All my friends have the same one . . . that early frustrations and traumas have warped my nature, left me in a permanent state of retarded adolescence, and rendered me incapable of any kind of love higher than promiscuous and juvenile sexuality. I've heard it all before."

"Cut away the jargon, and what it comes down to is, you're just a shit. That's my theory, Fielding. Never mind early frustrations and the rest; we all had them to contend with. You're simply on old-fashioned shit who'll ride rough-shod over anything or anybody to get what he wants . . . and who dissolves into floods of self-pity on the rare occasions when he doesn't get it."

"Perhaps those occasions have always been the important ones," said Fielding, shivering slightly. "The few things I didn't get . . . Cambridge, for instance . . . those have been the things which I really . . . Oh, to hell with it," he said. "What's all this got to do with Elena? We were talking about her, remember?"

"I remember very clearly. Elena was a test. I wanted to see whether my theory was right. After all, you've spent eight years living quietly and perhaps even faithfully with a certain Mrs. Ongley, Max says, and that might have changed you for the better. Or so I thought."

"So you laid on Elena, who showed you I was still a retarded adolescent."

"That you're still a howling shit. Still riding rough-shod, still entirely careless of people as people. Elena could have been an animated dummy for all you cared. Which means you're still a danger, whatever you say to the contrary, to girls like Sasha . . . who may be a ninny but doesn't deserve to be treated as a piece of prey. A director of a large company of highly strung actors likes to know these things."

"And now you know. So you're going to send me home tomorrow, I suppose?"

"Of course not," said Jules lightly. "I need to know your personal form . . . which is contemptible . . . in order to control you within my company; but I've hired you, Fielding, as a professional. Which brings us to the second part of the test. Elena asked you, as I thought she might, to write in some lines for her. Now, here we have to do with a professional problem . . . one brought on to yourself by personal indulgence, but still a professional problem in its essence. How did you cope with that?"

"I told her I couldn't oblige her," said Fielding, "because you wouldn't allow it. So then she stopped what she was doing, which was delicious .. and I said I'd try."

"Just what did you mean by that?"

"This song." Fielding tapped the sheet of paper which Jules was still holding. "I promised I'd try to write her up to four lines, and there they are."

"Shit," said Jules equably. "You knew she meant a speech of her own."

"She used the word 'lines'. And so did I, very scrupulously."

"Shit," said Jules again. "But at least you're not shitting on me. From a professional point of view you get full marks. What are you going to do when she finds out?"

"Nothing. Nothing, that is, that might bugger up you or the script. Didn't Max tell you, Jules? Whatever else may be said of me, my professional record is immaculate."

"Except," said Jules, "when you ran out of that assignment in 'sixty-two to go off with the Greek boy."

"That was exceptional."

"Let's hope so. But you quite see I had to make some tests."

"You lied to me in making them."

"I also showed you the easy way out of them. You can always go to your own room, I reminded you, and straight to your own bed."

"All right. But now get this plain, Jules : my loyalty is to that script . . . or to the money I shall get for rewriting it as you want it rewritten. Nothing will get in my way there, least of all a little tart like Elena. So let's have no more lies and no more tests. Agreed?"

"No more lies. But one more test . . . the proper test, Fielding : can you write my speeches?" Jules fluttered the song-paper. "This is well enough in its way . . . if not quite what I asked for. But can you write me speeches that will work?"

"I told you," Fielding said : "I'll have some to show you tomorrow night."

So far, thought Fielding, so good. He's made his tests, found out that I'm just the sort of bounder he thought I was . . . and he don't care one little bit, provided that I shag only the girls he wants me to shag, and that I get on with the work. He is now convinced that professionally I am *serieux,* and he has deduced from the song I knocked up that I probably know what I'm doing.

But what, thought Fielding, am I in truth doing? He placed a flagon of whisky on his desk with a glass and a bottle of mineral water. Then he sat down and looked through the night, over the narrow sea and on to the black mountains of Epirus. I have, he thought, one aim : to do this work in such a way that I shall be taken on for the full fourteen weeks and shall then pull in £14,000. As Tom said, that shouldn't be too hard : they're in a hurry, they'll be desperate to believe that I can find their answers, and anything that reads clearly and with a bit of a ring to it will make them happy. But all the same, he thought, there's a bit more to it than that.

For the one thing which Fielding could not abide was the idea that he might make a fool, so to speak, out of Homer. Homer had always been his favourite poet, ever since the Senior Usher had read aloud the first lines of *The Odyssey,* one morning long ago, when Fielding was just fifteen and newly promoted into the Under Sixth. . . .

*Ἄνδρα μοι ἔννεπε, Μοῦσα, πολύτροπον* . . . .

*Tell me, Muse, of the man of many wiles, who wandered many ways after he had sacked the sacred citadel of Troy. Many were the men whose cities he saw and whose mind he learned, and many the woes he suffered in his heart upon the sea. . . .*

The lines had thrilled him then, and they still did. Whenever he had read them, slouched on a bunk in a frowsty Nissen hut in Ranby Camp, or walking up and down outside the little white house which had been his Squadron Headquarters in Santa Kytherea, or sitting in one of Tessie's rooms that smelled of Albert Edward . . . wherever and whenever he had read them, they had promised breezes singing and waves running, they had promised mountains and haunted woods and secret rivers, little bright ports at morning and fires on the beach at evening, strange faces looking down from high windows, lotus, wine and love. And always the poet had kept his promise; for here in *The Odyssey* was the old gods' plenty, that brought to Fielding, whether at fifteen or at forty, blood's quickness and heart's delight.

And so now, as Fielding considered the task before him, he recognised a duty as well as a mere means to money. He must keep faith with Homer and show his gratitude even while supplying his greed. Not only must he please Jules and produce speeches of the kind Jules wanted, he must also ensure that these speeches were worthy of the poet from whom they were derived and that when spoken they would not injure the poet's honour. Cuts, omissions and much editing by Jules there would have to be—this he fully understood—but it was incumbent on him to work in words of such strength and purity that, however much they might be chopped about, they would still convey the spirit of Homer.

Now, Foxy would not give a damn about this spirit; and he could, as Fielding had already learned, bring strong pressures to bear, should he wish to pervert the tone of the film in his commercial interest. As for Jules, he could and would resist Foxy's pressures, for he had the terms of his contract to uphold him and a most evident integrity; but he had his own ideas of how Homer should be interpreted on film, ideas which, though not Foxy's, were not necessarily Fielding's. Faced, therefore, with the prospect of powerful coercion by Foxy or by Jules or by both, Fielding now formulated to himself some preparatory propositions.

In the first place, he reflected, he must avoid any kind of row, any slightest appearance of disaffection, for the two weeks of his probation; only when he had secured a contract for the full period could he exert himself in Homer's interest with real confidence. Secondly, surely it would be better, even when his position were secured, to eschew violent confrontation. If he were to differ from his employers as to the substance or method of what was to be done, let him hide his disagreement and proceed to his own end by stealth, allowing Jules and/or Foxy to think that the end which he sought was theirs. If they wanted something, then let them think they were getting it; in this way he would be left in peace to contrive for them what he himself wanted them to have. As to his ability to cozen them in this way, Fielding was in no doubt whatever : Foxy was an unlettered booby; Jules, while shrewd and in some ways sensitive, had not had the benefit of a classical education. Fielding alone knew the ground properly, and he was therefore free to play his own game on it. *Caveat emptor.*

His immediate task now was to rewrite the speeches for the scenes on the beach. Rather tricky, Fielding thought, for his first exercise. The speeches in question, as Tom had observed, were particularly beautiful and subtle, and to cast them plainly enough to satisfy Jules yet delicately enough not to betray Homer was going to be a difficult matter. Although he had already done some work on them, he had not done as much as he had implied to Jules, and now he had only until the following evening to produce a solid sample. He scowled at the mountains of Epirus, and then transcribed the first speech, both in Greek and in literal English :

*Alas for me. To a land of what mortals am I come? Are they savage and wild and unjust? Or do they love strangers and have the fear of the gods in their hearts? . . .*

But this, of course, was not really a speech, though printed as such in the text; it was Odysseus's first thoughts on being woken. In any case, none of it either need be or should be spoken aloud; it must be implied by the hero's actions (peering through the bushes at the beach and the squawking maidens) and by the expressions which passed over his face. First doubt, then determination, as he made ready to do the only thing he could . . . go out, naked as he was, and confront Nausicaa.

So Fielding crossed out the speech and scribbled a note ('Face, gestures, etc.') in the margin. He then read the existing directions for Odysseus's appearance out of the brush and the hysterical flight of all the girls save the Princess herself. What he was now left with was the Princess standing there, courageous but astonished, gaping at the masculine limbs 'all befouled with the brine' and plainly requiring immediate explanation, which Odysseus, on any reckoning, must surely supply. There could be no further evasion, no substitution of gestures or expressions: in all the circumstances Odysseus had got to say a mouthful and a good one at that, and Fielding now had to write it for him.

So Fielding transcribed, again both in Greek and in literal English, the first few lines of Odysseus's 'gentle and cunning speech':

> *I beseech thee, O queen . . . a goddess are you, or are you mortal? If you are a goddess, one of those who hold wide heaven, to Artemis, daughter of great Zeus, do I liken you most nearly in fairness and in height and in form. . . .*

Here was the text: how to make what Jules wanted of *this*? Now he was finally up against it. Have at it then: neck or nothing. He took a deep drink, then a deep breath, and began to write. . . .

". . . So have kindness, lady," said Angus Carnavon, "for I come to you out of the sea after much toil and danger, and of those who live here I know not even one. Show me where is your city, and give me clothes to put about my body; and then may god be kind to you also, and give you all that your heart desires, a husband and a home, when you would have them, and fellowship to bind you, which is the best gift of all."

"Cut," called Jules. "Take fifteen minutes."

Angus/Odysseus tottered away over the beach, sat down under an awning, and applied himself to a gigantic drink which was waiting. Sasha/Nausicaa, seeming taller than usual in a white ankle-length dress, swished up to Jules and Fielding, who were sitting together beside one of the cameras.

"Well?" she said.

"Well enough," said Jules. "You stood there like a picture,

my dear. If you can get your speech off as well as Angus did
his . . ."

". . . It's not the speech that worries me. Will Angus still be
conscious when I get to the end of it?"

"He's a sixth of his bottle still left, I'm told. He'll be good
for the next take, which is all we want of him today. You go and
rest, honey. Ready for take 137," he called to those round him,
"in ten minutes' time."

Jules rose and beckoned to Fielding. They walked away from
the cameras and the groups of hunched technicians towards the
sea.

"It seems to be working," said Jules with cautious congratu-
lation. "The rhythm's right and the style's right. When you
showed me the first draft ten days ago, I had my doubts. But
now . . . I think we shall be all right."

"Then I'd better get back to my desk, Jules. I've got the rest
of the book to work on."

"You'd better just wait and hear Sasha say her first piece.
If that's all right too, then you can get going with the rest as
fast as possible."

"She was all right in rehearsal."

"Not the same thing as a proper take. Don't ask me why,
Fielding, but you can only be certain it's all right when the
cameras are rolling for real . . . as Foxy would put it. Well, the
cameras are now doing just that; and if Sasha's bit goes as well
as Angus's, I'll take your stuff as proven, and I'll extend your
contract to the full period as soon as I get in tonight."

"Without asking Foxy?"

"He's left that decision with me. So back to the barricades,
my dear, and just you pray that little Sasha makes a go
of it."

They turned to walk back to their chairs.

"What the devil's this?" Jules said.

'This' was a procession of three people winding down from
the rocks above the beach. First, a dapper figure in tropical
whites and a wide panama; then a fat little fellow (apparently
made up, like the Michelin man, of pneumatic rings) who was

wearing a dark suit and a grey homburg; and finally an enormous, scarlet-faced woman, with heaving torso and legs like flabby Doric columns.

"Max de Freville in the lead," Fielding said.

"And Lykiadopoulos. Come to watch. It's a nuisance but they've paid for the privilege."

"Who's the woman?" Fielding asked.

"Max's woman. Angela Tuck."

"CHRIST. She's got grotesque."

"Come and meet 'em. We'll have to settle them down before we start the take."

As Jules and Fielding went forward to greet the procession, Fielding saw that Max had hardly changed since their last meeting eight years before. The furrows between his nose and the two ends of his mouth, always very noticeable, had deepened and widened a little; but that was all. Angela, on the other hand, he would not have recognised, if Jules had not warned him who she was. Eight years ago, although she had undoubtedly been coarse to look at, her legs had still been brown and firm and her face not without a bawdy and suggestive charm. Now she was just a mass of meat : her face was smothered under three huge sweaty rolls . . . two cheeks and the chin . . . which toppled inwards to overlap the corners of her lips and almost to envelop her nostrils; and the trunk-like legs, in thick white stockings, wobbled at every step.

"You there, you one-eyed satyr," she called, with all her old bitchy authority, "long time no see. Come and thrill me with tales of your sex-life."

In the end, after the more decorous grettings were done, the colonial Max and the Edwardian (Greek version) Lykiadopoulos were seated one each side of Jules, while Fielding and Angela were parked together a little way behind. When they were all comfortable, Jules gave a signal, on which Angus/Odysseus was trundled by three assistants into his position and Sasha/Nausicaa strode fiercely forward into hers.

"Interesting build," said Angela; "well honed hussy. Unusual."

"Strict silence during the take, please," said Jules over his shoulder.

"This is very important," Fielding whispered to Angela; "if this goes right I'll get a full-length contract . . . another twelve weeks."

"Here's luck, then," she growled back, and clamped one hand over the inside of his thigh in what he hoped was intended only as moral support. She gave a squeeze that made him wince, then relaxed her grip but did not remove her hold; and he was just wondering whether or not this ogress risen from his past was indeed contemplating a trip with him down Memory Lane, when all thoughts of Angela were temporarily driven from his head by the clack of the clapper that heralded Take 137.

What was to be filmed now was Nausicaa's answer to Odysseus's plea for help. Close-up of Nausicaa, the script ordained, her lips trembling. Close-up of Odysseus, who sank on to one knee and bowed his head. Then pull back slowly to see and hear the Princess as she answered. Now; now she must speak the words which could mean £12,000 to Fielding.

She opened her mouth, seemed to gag slightly, and closed it. Oh Christ, the silly bitch was going to fluff. Fielding trembled all along his body with chagrin and anxiety . . . and was then reminded of Angela, whose hand moved up his thigh in a light caress and settled snugly into his groin, not to excite, it seemed, but to soothe, or rather, to soothe by partly exciting, as an unscrupulous mother might calm a fractious child by mildly pleasuring its innocent body. Nice, thought Fielding, nice, easing his thighs apart to accept the comfort and placing his hand on Angela's to show his gratitude. As he did so, he became aware that Sasha Grimes was now moving splendidly through her speech, was indeed already more than half way through it.

". . . Since it is to this land you have come, you shall lack for nothing. I will show you our city and tell you the name of our people : we are called the Phaeacians, and I myself am the daughter of Alcinous, who is first in power among them."

She stretched out her hand to Odysseus to raise him, and he took it in both of his, turned it over and lowered his lips into the palm, while the Princess went taut with pleasure. First she gave a slight shudder at the male proximity, then she went rigid at the moment of Odysseus's kiss on her palm, her lips just parted and her belly slightly arched towards him, then she closed her eyes, willed her body to subside, and opened her eyes again in time to smile back brilliantly as Odysseus raised his head to smile up at her in his thankfulness. Oh you wonderful, clever little cat, Fielding thought, and without either surprise or warning he felt himself throb with violent release, three, four, five times, under Angela's hand.

"Cut," called Jules. "Bloody marvellous."

Sasha stalked off. Odysseus remained down on one knee, being unable to rise without assistance. Angela very slowly withdrew her hand from Fielding, while he eased his copy of the script over his lap to disguise any damage. Max and Lykiadopoulos nodded pleasantly to each other behind Jules's back. Three henchmen appeared to carry Odysseus back to the awning. Lykiadopoulos winked with almost regal dignity at the clapper-boy, who crossly pouted back. Jules rose and turned to Fielding and Angela.

"That's it, Fielding," he said. "Go and do the rest of the book just like that."

"Bully for you, sweetie," Angela said.

Odysseus fell forward out of his armchair and lay prone under the awning.

"Cart him off home," called Jules : "we're through with him for today. Take 138 in twenty minutes. Nausicaa rounding up the handmaids and organising them to feed and bath Odysseus. What are you waiting for, Fielding? I don't need you here any more. Go and write speeches."

"I'll walk up with you," Angela said.

It seemed that for all Jules's preoccupations Max and Lykiadopoulos wanted a few words with him; at any rate they took one arm each and walked him away from his chair, leaning in towards him, each talking alternatively into one of his ears. So Angela and Fielding were left by themselves to make their progress off the beach, Angela waddling breathily, Fielding stepping carefully in pace with her and clasping his script before him.

"You want that actress girl, don't you?" Angela said.

"Not particularly. What happened was because of the nervous strain. "

"Not very flattering, are you? But I know it wasn't me. It was me at first, warming the works up, but it wasn't me at the end, and it wasn't the nervous strain, it was little Miss Prim Airs going stiff and sticking out her fanny. That's when it really started. One moment you just had a rise, the next you were half an inch longer and beginning to twitch."

"Need you be so analytic, Angela?"

"Yes. It's the only way I get my fun these days. Watching and working out the form. This has been a rare treat for me, I can tell you."

"I'm glad. But you're wrong about Sasha. She's locked, so to speak, into armour. It'd be like lusting after Joan of Arc."

"People did that, I dare say. And if ever the armour came off . . ."

"There'd probably be something very, very wrong underneath it. Not worth the trouble and the risks, Angela. I've got something quite good enough to be going on with . . . over there." He pointed to Elena, who was being carefully arranged under the olive tree from behind which she was to emerge at Nausicaa's summons. "Succulent, as you see, and inventive."

"Muck," said Angela. "A pretty little bit of muck. Now Miss Prim Airs . . . Sasha . . . she's altogether out of the ordinary."

"Perhaps. But even if she's worth the labour of unbolting all that armour, the director has issued an embargo. He won't have her touched, in case she gets put off her acting."

"He needn't worry about that. She's full up to the eyes with ambition and tough as they breed 'em. Anyway, now you've got your contract you don't need to bother so much about the director."

They began to climb a rocky path up from the beach towards a small plateau which had been cleared and levelled for privileged cars. Angela breathed still more heavily. You poor old bag, Fielding thought : when I think of you in that summer of 1945, striding over the turf like an Amazon and flaying the arse off your golf ball . . . twenty-five years ago, so you're still well short of fifty. What on earth's done this to you? Cheap Greek brandy? But Max can afford the best . . . which of course is also the strongest.

"Do you mind," said Angela, "if we rest for a moment?"

She propped her bottom on a convenient rock. Fielding stood facing her, still shielding his crutch with his script.

"You remember when we last met," she said eventually, "and had that rather jolly afternoon together?"

"Very clearly. On Hydra."

"That's right. 1962 it must have been, just before Max and I went to Cyprus. Well, as you see, I've changed a bit since then. No more jolly afternoons in the hay for me."

"You're still . . . an impressive woman," said Fielding dutifully.

"As impressive . . . and as bedworthy . . . as a female gorilla. Max, you understand, has never wanted me in that way . . . not even at the beginning. As for other men," she said equably, "I suppose I could pay. I've done that before. But in fact there are very good reasons why I should leave it alone from now on . . . just leave it alone."

She looked at Fielding as if expecting him to ask what the reasons were. But he scented danger and even horror in this topic, and merely nodded.

"So," she continued, "any pleasure I get these days comes, as I said just now, from watching and weighing the form. Procuring too. I've always had the soul of a bawd." She laughed merrily, raised her bottom from the rock, and started slowly on up the path. "If you like," she said, "I'll help you get that girl . . . Sasha. You would like, wouldn't you? It'd be worth it, if only for the experience. Not every man gets to do it with Joan of Arc."

Fielding helped her over a large rock which was embedded in the path.

"What's in it for you?" he asked. "A peep-hole in the bed-room door?"

"Very uncomfortable, and not at all easy to arrange in the Corfu Palace Hotel. Now, back at Max's and my place there's a room with a fake mirror in the wall. . . ."

"Fair enough. It might be rather exciting . . . knowing that you were watching behind a fake mirror. But first things first, Angela. First you have to help me to her bed. Now, little Sasha shows no sign at all of wanting anybody. She's a serious girl, dedicated to social causes. Why should she want to put out the honey pot for a cynical old wreck like me?"

"Just because you are a cynical old wreck." Angela led the way across the little car park to a maroon Rolls-Royce. "A serious girl with a sense of duty might respond to an appeal. 'I'm so unhappy,' you might say: 'I'm so ugly and horrid, and you're so beautiful and pure.' So then she thinks of you as deprived; she thinks she owes you something to repair the inequity."

"She'll hardly think she owes me her maidenhood."

"Why not . . . if it *is* her maidenhood? It would show her sacrifice was really sincere. But if she still holds out, you go a stage further. You pretend to be guilty and wretched because you're prostituting your literary art to the movie moguls and thereby raking in more money every day than twenty Indian peasants in a year. Really pile on the agony. Little girls like Sasha won't do anything for fun; but if you spread enough sheer misery around, down come their knickers at the last, because misery's their substitute for romance."

She opened the rear door of the Rolls.

"End of lesson one," she said. "Pile on the agony and see what happens. If it works, I'll invite you both to Max's place so that I can collect my fee in kind. If not, we must think again."

Very suddenly the high colour drained from her face.

"Angela . . . are you all right?"

"Go now."

She scrabbled her way into the car and sprawled along the back seat.

"Angela . . ."

". . . Go away, damn you. No. Turn on the air cooler first. Yellow knob on the dashboard. . . . Thanks."

"I'll stay till Max comes."

"Just you bugger off," she croaked, "and write your pretty speeches."

When Fielding arrived back at the Corfu Palace, he ordered a bottle of champagne to be sent up to his room, though it was not his custom, these days, to drink in the afternoon. I've got the contract, he thought, as he toasted himself in the wall-mirror: whatever disagreements there may be now, over Homer or anything else, I've got myself another twelve thousand quid.

He had also got himself some immediate personal problems. The first was Elena. Since there was a lot of work with Nausicaa and the handmaids still to be done, and since not all of the amended script for these scenes had yet been passed round, Elena still did not know that she hadn't been given the lines which he had promised her. But every day she was becoming more suspicious, every night more perfunctory in her services. Very soon she was going to ask him straight out where and when her lines were coming, and she was not going to be amused when told, 'You've had 'em, duckie . . . I thought you knew . . . that pretty little song you all sang with the ball.'

So Elena would be angry and would be off with Fielding; and even after two weeks of her, he would feel the lack. Which led to an interesting but perturbing question: should he follow Angela's advice and make a set for Sasha instead? This would certainly be intriguing; but leave aside any trouble it might bring with Jules if he found out, Fielding was very uneasy about the possible reactions of Sasha herself. Let him assume that Angela was right, let him assume that a pretence of unhappiness would indeed bring him into Sasha's bed, he must still pause at the question of what he might find when he got there. For as he had told Angela, a man who dared to unbolt armour as impregnable as Sasha's appeared to be might discover something very disconcerting underneath.

To have or not to have? On the whole, and despite his misgivings, he inclined to have, if he could, especially if Elena withdrew her present offices. But whichever way it all worked out, one thing was quite certain : he did not want Harriet Ongley cluttering up the ground. Since he had been in Corfu she had written twice and then, the day before, sent a cable, wanting to know urgently what plans he was making for her to join him. If he ignored her, she would just turn up unbidden; it had happened before. The only way to keep her off was to write . . . to wire . . . that there was delay over the decision on his contract and that he could make no firm plans as yet. He could play it that way for another two weeks, perhaps; then he would have to think of a new lie. What a bore women were, whether wanted or unwanted . . . more boring, on the whole, when wanted, because more powerful to command their own witless way. There were times when he could wish that that bomb in Cyprus had made him a eunuch.

But since it hadn't, he must proceed as a whole man. He rehearsed to himself what he would say to Elena when she accused him of double-crossing her; he drafted a cable to Harriet attributing the delay over settling his contract, and hence his own inability to make arrangements, to the absence of Foxy Galahead; and he wrote a polite little note to Sasha Grimes, praising her performance that afternoon and asking her to dine with him and discuss her remaining scenes on the evening after the next.

Nausicaa watched her maidens as they stowed the last bundle of dry washing on to the waggon, and then strode to the front of it, beckoning to Odysseus, now clean and properly dressed, to follow her. He offered her an arm to help her up into the driving seat, but she shook her head, came close under his shoulder, and began to talk very earnestly.

"Listen, stranger from the sea. Now you are fed and clothed I will bring you to my people, and this is how it must come about. As long as we are passing through the woods and the fields, walk with my handmaids behind the waggon; but when we draw near the city, you will see a harbour set on either side of it, and all along the road you will see the curved ships of the Phaeacians, drawn up in their posts, and many men busied about them in the last of the evening light. It is their mocking speech that I fear, should they see you following my waggon. So do you look about you for a grove of poplar trees that is near to the road. . . ."

Ideal, thought Fielding, as Nausicaa went on, at some length, to tell Odysseus exactly where he must hide, and for how long, and what he must do when it was dark : ideal; they couldn't have come on a better day's schedule.

For there had been an unexpected visitation of enormous importance, and hence Fielding's presence on the beach when he should have been sitting in the Corfu Palace writing speeches for the rest of the film. He was there on set to answer such questions on dialogue or related matters as might be put to him by Dr. Emile Schottgatt or any of his three colleagues on The Creative Authentication Committee of the Oglander-Finckelstein Trust. The Committee had flown in unobserved on the previous afternoon (that on which Max de Freville and his friends had come to the beach) and had emerged from nowhere this morning, all of them wearing calf-length linen shorts and fawn ankle-socks, avid, it seemed, to commence creative authenticating.

'Christ,' Jules had said to their courier, a plump but rather wan P.R.O. from Clytemnestra Films. 'Why didn't you warn us you were bringing this lot?'

'They like snap visits. I was given just ten minutes' notice by Foxy Galahead to bring 'em over from New York.'

'You could have wired.'

'I did. To the hotel for rooms.'

'You could have wired me.'

'Foxy said not. He said you'd cope much better if it came as a surprise.'

'Why should he think that?'

'Because you'd just carry on naturally and not get all ballsed up with making special arrangements.'

'A lot of help Foxy is.'

'He's coming over himself tomorrow. Meanwhile, he says have the script-writer do any explaining they want. He thinks the script-writer's a sharp cookie.'

So it was at this stage that Julies had sent for Fielding, to tell him to accompany them out to the beach for the day's shooting.

'This is Burke Lawrence,' Jules had said, introducing the P.R.O.

'We met some years ago.'

'Christ,' said Burke Lawrence; 'so we bloody did.'

'No time to talk over old days now,' Jules had said. 'We've got problems.' And he had rapidly briefed Fielding on the proposed course of the day's shooting, before sending him to join the Inquisition in their minibus and ride out with them to Ermones.

And now Sasha was going great guns in a scene which, Fielding thought, Dr. Schottgatt and his chums must surely approve. For it was faithful to Homer, rather static, definitely poetic and somewhat verbose. A 'culture' scene beyond any possible doubt. What precisely their reactions were, however, Schottgatt & Co. were not letting on just yet. They sat in a little row of canvas chairs, their hands clasped in their laps, their thin, white, hairless legs planted in four prim parallel pairs, their faces spongy and totally impassive. What a crew, thought Fielding : God alone knew what sort of questions he was to expect from a tribunal like that.

"And when you have reached our house," Nausicaa was saying, "and have passed through the court and entered the great hall, walk on swiftly till you come to my mother, who sits by the hearth in the firelight spinning the purple yarn. . . ."

Interesting hint here, thought Fielding, that the Phaeacians had still to some extent preserved matriarchal customs. It was getting in with the Queen that mattered, or so Nausicaa seemed to be saying. But for all the learned gentlemen from Montana University appeared to care, Nausicaa could be reciting her three-times table or repeating an old wives' cure for warts. No poker-table had even known such absolute poker faces. They looked as if they had been sealed silent by the hand of God; and indeed the only words they had spoken to Fielding so far that whole day were 'good morning', which Schottgatt, as their leader, had pinged at him as he entered their minibus. Nothing more had been said on the way to the beach; and when Fielding attempted to interest them in a brief description of the topography, as they were crossing the golf course towards the sea, they had not even troubled to turn their heads in his direction. Americans, think what you might of them, were generally so courteous and pleased when you tried to tell them something; but this lot might just as well have been zombies . . . zombies under the total control of Dr. Schottgatt, at whose nod they had alighted from the minibus, behind whom they had walked in Indian file on to the beach, and at whose nod, once more, they had seated themselves in identical postures which they had then held without moving for the entire morning. How was one to communicate with such a party? Perhaps Burke Lawrence would know? But communication with Lawrence himself was going to offer yet another awkward problem, Fielding thought, in view of the curious circumstances in which they had last met.

"Cast your hands about my mother's knees," Sasha was concluding, "for if you find her favour, then, though you come from the end of the earth, you can hope to see your friends once more and return to your own sweet country."

"Cut," called Jules.

Schottgatt beckoned to Fielding. Now at last the silence was going to be broken, perhaps, now at last the questions and the criticisms would begin.

"Four glasses of water, sir, if you will be so good," Dr. Emile Schottgatt said.

After fetching water for the committee-men, each of whom took his glass in his right hand and rested it carefully on his right knee, and after being thanked by Schottgatt on behalf of all four of them, Fielding felt that however embarrassing it might be, he must now have a word with Burke Lawrence. This seemed to be his only hope of achieving some understanding of the bizarre ensemble which the P.R.O. had brought with him from New York. Having spotted Lawrence slip away with a tin of beer into the labyrinth of rock at the south end of the beach, Fielding now followed him and ran him to ground where he sat hunched into a tiny cave in a low wall of incipient cliff.

"Last time we met," Fielding said, grasping the nettle, "you were beastly drunk and in bad trouble."

"I remember well enough," said Lawrence, and sucked at his beer.

"What happened to you all? You and that Holbrook woman and her ex-husband?"

"We all kept as quiet as little mice, and after a time it was safe to come out of our holes. After all, the big row was in Venice and we were in England."

"But I should have thought the Italian police could have interested Scotland Yard in your activities?"

"We were very peripheral, you know . . . even Jude Holbrook, and he was the most involved of us. Besides," said Lawrence, who seemed amiably or at last equably disposed, "when it came to the point there wasn't any evidence. The wop police thought they had bushels of it, but it crumbled under their noses. Hearsay, conjecture, a lot of Venetian tattle . . . that's all they had. They barely managed to fix three years on Salvadori himself."

"But the writing was on the wall?"

"Oh yes. I cleared out to Canada. Somebody said that the Canadians wanted young film directors . . . which was what I was meant to be. It didn't quite work out as I hoped, but I'm not complaining."

"And the other two?"

"Penelope Holbrook still lives in London on alimony which Jude sends her . . . or did when I last saw her five years ago. The money comes in from Hong Kong. God knows what Jude does there. . . . Why are you asking all these questions?"

"I like tidying things up. And I wanted to know where I stood with you . . . after our last encounter."

"I'm P.R.O. of an outfit which employs you as script-writer. That's where you stand with me."

"Good. But I'm damned if I know where I stand with those four wise men you've brought here. What do you know about them?"

"The Creative Authentication Committee of the Oglander-Finckelstein Trust," said Burk Lawrence, "consists of four senior members of Montana University who are nominated by the Professor of English Literature. At present the four nominees are Dr. Emile Schottgatt, an expert on early Aegean dialects; Dr. Gayland Webb, an archaeologist who made his name investigating Viking settlements in Greenland; Dr. Gabriel Rutter, an anthropologist who specialises in the Australian aborigine; and Dr. Pym K. Zimmerei, a sociologist, who is currently writing a treatise on Post-Menopausal Masturbation in the Affluent Female."

"Christ." Fielding turned away from Lawrence and peered back through the rocks to the beach, where the four magi were still seated in line, clasping their glasses of water. "How do you tell 'em apart?"

"You don't have to. Schottgatt answers for all of them."

"And what do *they* know about being creative?"

"Search me. I dare say they know a bit about being authentic."

"But listen, Lawrence. It appears that the future of this film depends on the report which those four curios turn in when they get home. Now, we were reckoning on quite a tough job when it came to getting the rest of the money, but no one expected to have to deal with four old spiders out of the Sibyl's Cave. Will you, as P.R.O., kindly explain to me just how I'm meant to approach them?"

"You're not. You wait till they approach you."

"That's what Foxy wants?"

"Sure is. So just sit tight, Major Gray, and obey your orders."

"I don't use the rank these days."

"But I shall. I like ranks," said Burke Lawrence. "I get sick of all these damn silly meaningless Christian names. 'I'm Si, meet Syd.' Do me a favour, and let me call you by your proper title."

"I don't see why not."

"Thank you. And now, Major Gray : would you care for a little tip?"

"I always appreciate tips."

"Then steer clear of that red-head, Sasha Grimes. I saw you looking at her just now . . . with that certain look. Forget all that and forget it fast. Sasha Grimes is Calamity Jane . . . in that department at least."

"How can you be sure?"

"P.R.O.s," said Lawrence, "are paid to be sure about these things."

"I've already been warned off by Jules," said Fielding. "He doesn't want her disturbed."

"I bet he doesn't . . . and especially not just now. Sasha Grimes, you see, could be a great help in keeping Og-Finck happy."

"She's certainly acting well enough."

"It's not just her acting. Miss Grimes, Major Gray, has a privileged relationship with the Og-Finck Trust. A year or two back she won the Oglander-Finckelstein Award for Drama . . ."

". . . So I've heard . . ."

". . . And the twelve-month Fellowship at Montana University that goes with it. Youngest person ever to get it, and the first from Britain."

"They must have thought very highly of her."

"They did, Major Gray. And during the year she held the award, she got herself in even better with them. Not only as an actress but as a . . . lovely, sensitive person . . . full of compassion and conscience . . . all that crap. By the end of that year, Sasha Grimes was the apple of Og-Finck's eye, which is why she got this part . . . a condition of their deal with Foxy. And so those old men in knickers will listen breathless to anything she has to say . . . on or off the set."

"I see. Handle with care."

"Not to be handled at all, Major Gray. As Jules Jacobson

says, do not disturb. For every possible reason. Leave aside that she's the darling of Og-Finck, just remember that I'm warning you on a purely sexual level as well : it's you too that will be *disturbed*, Major Gray, if you start anything with Sasha Grimes."

"Would she let me start anything?"

Burke Lawrence cocked his head, focused his eyes, and then swivelled them from left to right and back again several times, as though consulting an invisible dossier in the air before him.

"She might," Lawrence said at last. "For your sake I hope she doesn't. Not but what you could get into a big enough mess just by *trying*."

"I'm meant to be having dinner alone with her tomorrow night. That is, I've sent a note to ask her."

"Then you'd better pray she writes back to say 'no, thank you'," Burke Lawrence said, and tossed his empty beer tin into the never-resting sea.

But as it happened, Sasha Grimes had already written back to say 'yes, please', and Fielding found her note as soon as he returned to the Corfu Palace. That engagement, however, was for the next evening; meanwhile he had to get through this one, which was to be devoted to the entertainment of the Creative Authenticators. Jules was to be host (in Foxy's absence) and he had bidden Fielding to come along and assist him; Sasha, as the favourite of Og-Finck and an ex-member of Montana, would also be in attendance. The scheme was that the three of them should conduct the Committee plus Burke Lawrence on a tour of 'traditional' Corfiot evening amusements, these to consist of eating a dinner of crawfish somewhere on the coast, watching peasant dancing at a rural Taverna called the Persephone, and admiring the Castle of St. Angelo by moonlight.

Since three of the four committee-men did not eat shell-fish, and since the keeper of the Persephone had forgotten to hire any dancers, and since the Greek driver missed the track which would have brought them to the Gorge of St. Angelo, the outing was not a success. Jules had hoped that his guests would give

some idea of whether or not they had liked what they had seen
on set that day; but the four wise men had eyes and ears for no
one but Sasha, and even with her they refused to discuss any
subject connected with the film or its making, though she tried
hard to elicit their reactions. She gave up this attempt when it
was at last clearly hopeless, and switched her conversation to
'compassionate' statements about the miseries of Greek workers,
statements which the Committee (though as ignorant of the matter as Sasha was) complacently endorsed by ponderous iteration.

"It's all very well," said Fielding to Burke Lawrence in the
putrescent loo of the Taverna Persephone, "but when *are* they
going to talk about what they're here for?"

"Remember your orders, Major Gray: just sit quiet until
challenged."

Which was sound enough precept; but by now Fielding was
starting to jitter. If even the much respected Sasha could not
make the Committee talk about the film, there must be something wrong somewhere. Such total silence on the one topic
which really concerned everyone present, though an optimist
might have attributed it to discretion, seemed to Fielding to be
discourteous to the point of malignance. It could not bode well.
After he had said good-night to the four doctors, he came away
feeling rather as though he had dined with a posse of under-
takers on the eve of a mass funeral. The Committee smelt of the
graveyard; and if they buried the Odysseus project, there was
an end of Fielding's contract; for although Jules had now
extended this for the next three months, Fielding's engagement,
like everyone else's, was contingent on the funding of the production. All in all he was in a bleak mood as he went up to bed
and he was not at all cheered, as he opened the door of his drawing room, to see Elena sitting at his desk.

"Sorry, sweetheart," he said. "My evening's already gone
on too long. That Committee . . ."

". . . It won't take you long to hear what I've got to say."

"Drink?" said Fielding, scenting trouble.

"No. Just a straight answer. Where the hell are my lines?"
She thumped both fists down among the papers on his desk.

"I've been through your copy of the script, I've been through every scrap of paper on this fucking desk, and nowhere can I see my lines."

Ah, well. It had to come sooner or later.

"You've got a short memory," he said: "don't you recall that song?"

"Song?"

" 'So take, while there is time, the gifts that . . .' "

". . . Like a heap of crap I recall it. What about it?"

"Your lines, sweetheart. And you were jolly lucky to get them. Jules was very doubtful at first."

"But we *all* sang that bloody song. Including bloody Nausicaa."

"Exactly. It might have been *only* Nausicaa. I interested Jules in sharing it out a bit. Why, you had one whole line to yourself."

"Half a line the second time through. You promised me *lines* . . . four lines, you said . . . to myself."

"I said I'd try, and I did try, and that's what came of it. It was always a strong order, most unlikely to get past Jules, and so I said at the time. But I did my best, I positively got a song for you to sing, so now let's have a little gratitude."

"Why didn't you tell me that my lines were that song?"

"I thought you'd realise."

"But we were always going to have a song, even before you came. Jules had been discussing it with Tom Llewyllyn. It's not true what you're saying, lover." Reproachful now rather than angry, he noticed, even though giving him the lie direct. "You never tried to write my lines. You've just been doing me a load of dirt."

"All right," Fielding said. "But you didn't play it very clean yourself. Getting a fellow's balls bubbling and then threatening to stop. What sort of a game is that?"

"Horrid," she admitted, and gave him a sad little grin. "But then I'm just a slut, and I haven't any real talent, so it's the only sort of game I can play if I want to get on in this business. Almost all of them . . . even those who have got talent . . .

started out like that. You ask Margaret Lichfield. It's the only way, lover, at any rate for scrubbers like me."

"But you must know by now that promises extracted in bed are apt to be dishonoured. They always have been, Elena. There's a rule which says they don't count, and it was the gods themselves who made it."

"And of course all the shits in this trade take full advantage of it. But I'll tell you what it was with you, lover. You had just a slight thing about you of being a gentleman. Oh, I knew that most of it had worn off years ago, but it was still possible to see that once upon a time you'd been brought up to open doors for ladies and to be kind to underdogs and to tell the truth. It was in your cut, in your style, in a way it isn't in Jules's or Foxy's or Angus's . . . or even in Max de Freville's . . . though you might find it in that little Greek pal of his, come to think of it now. Anyway, lover, when I saw you, I said to myself, 'Elena, my dear,' I said, 'this here is the remains of an old-fashioned English gent, and he might, he just might, keep his promise to a girl.' Well, it turns out you just didn't. One more in a long line of disappointments, but a bigger one than most, lover, because it was wrapped up in a gentleman's word."

She smiled at Fielding quite kindly, and then left.

The next three days had been set aside by Jules as an interval. The scenes on the beach had now been finished bang on schedule; and since Odysseus, Nausicaa and her maidens would all be working in the scenes next to come (Odysseus's appeal for passage home in the hall of Alcinous, and the Games given for his entertainment), it had seemed to Jules, when he was drawing up the programme, that they would be glad about now of a rest. Furthermore, a three-day respite would give Jules himself the chance to make his final preparations on the new sets to which they would now be shifting, and also—or so he had hoped—the time to rough-edit some clips of the beach scenes for despatch to the Oglander-Finckelstein Trust.

But now these sensible and leisurely plans must be changed. The O/F Trust, instead of biding quietly on its own side of the

Atlantic, had sent scouts and outriders to demand and disrupt, and their leader had made it plain that they would brook neither idleness nor delay. If there was no shooting for them to watch, they would watch rehearsals, and if there was none of these either they would see what film had already been made—every single foot of it, and now. There was no time to prepare special sequences, Jules decided; he would have to make do with the rushes, *mal soignés* as these might be. With some difficulty the Authenticators were induced to take the morning off and were promised, to make up, a bumper afternoon screening of every inch of celluloid that could be found for them. The occasion would be graced by the presence of Foxe J. Galahead, who was flying in at noon.

"Jesus wept, baby," said Foxy to Jules as they drove from the airport. "They can't be as bad as that."

"Worse, Foxy. Why did you let 'em come?"

"Couldn't stop 'em. It was always on the cards that Og-Finck would send someone."

"But why these four scarecrows?"

"How do I know why? Can't Burke Lawrence handle them? Or Fielding Gray?"

"Foxy. Three of them are vegetarian, two are also teetotal, and one is a sociologist. How does anyone handle a crowd like that? They just sit there in a row waiting to be shown things. This afternoon they have to be shown what there is of this film, and you've got to be there helping out."

"Helping out?"

"Laughing and crying and falling about in the right places."

"But I was going to spend the afternoon with Gretel. I cabled ahead to ask her to lunch. Can't this show wait till to-morrow?"

"No, Foxy. They are sitting like vultures on a fence, and they got very impatient when I said that no carcasses would be served this morning. If they don't get something by two-thirty, they'll be on the wing back to Montana. And you know what that means."

"Okay, Jules. How did they like what they've seen so far?"

"They just don't say. They watched the seven last takes out at Ermones yesterday, and not one word did they say to anyone."

"More like mummies than vultures?"

"Like both," sighed Jules.

"All right. So I'll give them lunch," Foxy said, "and strictly no Gretel. Tell Fielding to be there and Burke Lawrence. Where's the screening?"

"In the hotel. The large room they use for their Winter Casino."

"And that gives me an idea. Ring Max de Freville and Lyki, and get them to come. Not that Angela, she'd give J. Christ himself the creeps, just Max and Lyki. And tell 'em I'd like a word with 'em before we join the rest for lunch."

What Jules had to show the Committee was as follows: some high-class stunting, by the men of the Second Unit, which would later be cut into the battles, brawls and storms; a lot of sound work by Penelope and the suitors in Odysseus's palace on Ithaca (a cleverly decked-out Corfiot castle); the sequence on Circe's island, shot on the lush hillsides near Corfu's Benitses; and the scenes in which Nausicaa and her handmaids set out from Alcinous's palace and discovered Odysseus on the beach. It was these latter, the only ones to have been made so far from Fielding's revised script, by which Jules set much the most store and by which alone he would have chosen, had matters been left to him, to have the quality of his achievement assessed.

But matters had not been left to him. The assessors were now on the spot and breathing heavily down his neck; they were insisting on seeing *all* the film available; and it was tolerably clear to everyone, even if it had not been stated in so many words, that on the strength of that afternoon's exhibition the Committee was going to hand down a straight and irreversible verdict as to whether or not the Trust would release the further six million dollars which were needed to complete the production. No doubt about it, thought Fielding as the umpteenth reel unwound in the Winter Casino; the chips were finally down.

At Foxy's luncheon party the committee-men had spoken hardly a word. Max and Fielding had tried to engage the archaeologist in a discussion of the site at Pylos; Burke Lawrence had rallied Zimmerei the sociologist with some choice tales from his early days in advertising; Foxy and Lykiadopoulos had done their best with Rutter and Schottgatt, Lykiadopoulos being particularly fluent about the erosion and inevitable destruction (as he predicted) of Venice : but none of this had drawn more than curt nods and cold smiles from the committee-men... who were now, some three hours later, watching Nausicaa's reception of the naked Odysseus, a passage which they had requested should be put on for them a second time. They alone were paying any attention to it; the rest of the audience had long since been reduced, by weariness and anxiety combined, to a state of stunned hysteria. Even Foxy, who for hours had reacted with vigorous and appropriate noises to every shadow which passed over the screen, had now exhausted his repertoire and was sitting absolutely still with his head hanging almost between his knees.

On the screen Odysseus turned over Nausicaa's hand and kissed the palm; the Princess arched her back, closed her eyes, and opened them to smile down at the battered hero; then the blue and yellow of the beach suddenly flicked to a gleaming blank; and somebody switched the light on.

"That's the lot," Jules said, "except for the scenes you gentlemen saw being shot yesterday."

"Can we not see those on film ?"

"They're still being developed."

"Still being developed?"

"They have to go to Athens; it takes thirty-six hours before we can get them back."

"Very well," said Dr. Emile Schottgatt with hatchet face; "and now we should like to ask a few questions of the scriptwriter, Mr. Gray."

"At your service, gentlemen," said Fielding, trying to summon up some strength.

"Mr. Gray . . . would you describe your speeches as natural language?"

"No, sir. As formal language. Simple to speak and easy to understand, but definitely formal."

"And are we to infer, Mr. Gray, that in the late Bronze Age everyone habitually spoke in this formal and stylised manner?"

"Of course not. It is a poetic convention to suit the legend and the kind of people about whom it was written."

"What kind of people was that, Mr. Gray?"

"Gods and goddesses. Kings and queens and heroes."

"No ordinary people? What about Odysseus's sailors?"

"The only ones who matter in the story were his chosen officers and companions. Nobles and heroes like himself."

"I see. So the story excludes all but the pagan gods and the human upper classes?"

"Effectively, yes."

"Then will not the average audience feel itself to be excluded? Will it not understand that the common people, the equivalent of itself, was confined in those days entirely to menial tasks and was unfit even to be mentioned in literature or legend?"

"If the audience understands that," said Fielding, irritated and reckless, "it will be quite correct."

"And so we are to compound the insult which that particular social system inflicted on the people at large by repeating it in this film? And by parading it under the noses of all those who watch the film, thus making them feel, albeit at a historical distance, degraded and inferior?"

"A bit far-fetched, surely?"

"No," said Dr. Zimmerei, speaking for the first and only time. "To portray a hierarchical system in a work which extols the actions of the hierarchical leaders is to condone the methods of hierarchy."

"I thought you gentlemen were here as judges of our artistic authenticity."

"There are more important things in this modern age," said Dr. Schottgatt, "than considerations of pure art. Social questions must be paramount."

"But this whole story is happening in another world."

"Whose values differ totally from the democratic and egalitarian values of our own."

"That is inevitable."

"It is also unacceptable. You see, Mr. Gray, the world of Odysseus has so far been represented in this film as being better and nobler than ours is. Despite its indifference to the plight of the common people, indeed just because of this indifference, Odysseus's world is made out to be beautiful, joyous and heroic. We find that the appeal of your *Odyssey* depends very largely on sheer snobbery and brutal contempt for the labouring classes, who are treated as merely invisible."

"Look," said Foxy, "I don't get it. We went over all *that* stuff when the Trust agreed to back us. The Trustees said that *The Odyssey* was high-class cultural entertainment, just the sort of thing they were meant to subscribe to, and the best of luck to everyone. So why are you fellows making such a fuss?"

"Because we want the tinsel stripped off it," said Schottgatt. "We want Odysseus and his gang seen for the nasty thugs they were, and to this end we want their victims to be shown, and shown as suffering . . . not just neglected altogether."

"You haven't answered Mr. Galahead's question," Jules said. "When this production was first mooted, the instructions of the Trust were that we should stick as close as possible to Homer's text. The original script was prepared and approved on that basis. There was no suggestion whatever that we should superimpose the kind of . . . social realism . . . which you apparently advocate."

"There have been changes since then, Mr. Jacobson. Changes in our University and therefore changes in the administration of the Trust."

"No one warned us of a change of policy about our film."

"That's one reason why we're here now."

"Then would I be right in saying," Jules asked carefully, "that you do not object to our portraying a hierarchical society, *provided* that we give a square deal to those at the bottom of it? What you resent is the Homeric technique of leaving the ploughboy and the scullion right out of it."

"We want it made clear," said Schottgatt, "that the superficial splendour and romance of the world in which Odysseus moved depended to a great extent on the misery and exploitation of the working class as it then existed."

"Should be possible," said Max de Freville languidly. "Dot a few scraggy peasants round the fields, put a few louts to turn the spits at the banquets. . . ."

"The treatment," said Schottgatt, "must be a compassionate study of a forcibly brutalised slave caste."

"If that's what you want," said Jules, "I could use locals. You don't want them to speak?"

"Not necessarily. So long as they are visibly there and are seen to be ill-used. In those scenes in Odysseus's Palace, for example."

"I've explained to you," said Jules, "that I've got to shoot those scenes and several others again, with Mr. Gray's new dialogue. A change in the domestic flavour can be introduced then."

Schottgatt pursed his lips and nodded coldly, conceding this possibility.

"Look here," said Foxy to Schottgatt. "Are you saying that you're going to play ball? That providing we do all this about these peasants and so on, you'll recommend we get our money from the Trust?"

"As to that," said Schottgatt, "my colleagues and I must now retire to decide. You have made your attitudes plain enough, I think. Can I trouble you, Mr. Galahead, to come to my room in an hour's time?"

"Dear me," said little Lykiadopoulos after the Committee had retired, "so now American professors are doctoring the Classics to suit their political ideas?"

"It's an old left-wing trick," said Fielding. "Like the Russians rewriting history."

"Not unheard of on the right wing," said Max de Freville.

"Right wing, schmight wing," Foxy said. "What bugs me is, how do we pay for these damn peasants? The budget's stretched to busting already."

"You'd better just pray, Foxy babe," said Jules, "that we've still got a budget. I don't think Dr. Emile Schottgatt cares about our ethical tone."

"We said he could have his mother-fucking peasants, so what the hell more does he want?"

"Compassion," said Lykiadopoulos, "and he didn't hear much in your voices. Let us hope that when you present yourself in an hour's time you are going to hear more of it in his."

"You must understand," said Schottgatt to Foxy, "that matters are no longer as simple as they were."

Foxy and Schottgatt were alone in Schottgatt's room.

"There have been . . . structural changes in our University," Schottgatt went on, "which have affected our operation of the Oglander-Finckelstein Trust. The provision of money by the Trust must now be ratified, not only by me and my colleagues, but by a select committee of students. Even if we assume that you will abide by our conditions, and that you will do so in the spirit intended, the student committee may reject the whole project as being irrelevant."

"Just who tells who what to do in Montana?" Foxy said.

"As things are at this time," replied Schottgatt, "the students must be allowed to feel that they tell us. However, I think I can guarantee that they will vote you the rest of your money."

"Well thank sweet Jesus for that."

"No," said Schottgatt, "thank me. For the point is that the students will be told by myself and my committee that for political reasons we are compelling you to tear Homer to shreds. They will enjoy the idea of that . . . those of them who have heard of Homer . . . and so they will allow us to continue funding you. Out of spite to an established classic."

"Do I detect a hint, Dr. Schottgatt baby, that you're on our side?"

"Mr. Galahead, the Trust has already invested a large sum

of money in a film which is being directed, we have reason to think, with considerable expertise. It would be folly to withdraw at this stage. While student idealism would of course reject such a calculation, my colleagues and I are more sensible of mundane necessities. So we are prepared to compromise along the lines already discussed."

"Yeah, squads of peasants. But what about this stuff you'll tell the students . . . about tearing Homer to shreds? What we've discussed doesn't add up to that."

"No."

"And so when the kids see the film, and realise that you've been stringing them along? What then?"

"By the time this film is publicly shown, Mr. Galahead, we shall have an entirely new student committee. The great thing to remember about students is that even the most troublesome of them are impermanent."

"I see. But you *do* still want peasants?"

"Insurance, Mr. Galahead."

"In case the kids get nosy while we're still shooting?"

"Correct. What's more, the students will wish to know that they have effective means of exerting control right through to the end of production. In order to induce them to vote the way we wish, I shall have to say that your funds are being paid by instalments, each instalment being conditional on your continued obedience. I suggest instalments of three hundred thousand dollars a week."

"But it was to have been paid all at once."

"Three hundred thousand a week," said Schottgatt very firmly, "over the next twenty weeks. Always provided, as I shall have to tell the student committee, that our representative here continues to send in favourable reports."

"Your representative here?" said Foxy. "Will one of you gentlemen be staying on?"

"No," said Schottgatt. "We propose to appoint someone whom we think will report responsibly to ourselves and the student body. Someone," he went on blandly, "who is in sympathy with progressive political ideals and understands the ideological connotations of a collective enterprise of this kind."

"Look," said Foxy in a moment of rebellion, "you needn't think you're buying the whole show. De Freville and Lykiadopoulos have a one-third investment in this film."

"Then perhaps they would care to invest a further six million dollars . . . in the event of the Trust's withdrawing?"

For once Foxy said nothing.

"Very well," Schottgatt summed up, "the Trust will pay you three hundred thousand dollars a week, for twenty weeks, starting on Monday, 2 November. These payments to be conditional on the good reports, with respect to the future tone of the production, from our representative here in Corfu . . . who, we have decided after deep consultation, shall be that talented and concerned young lady, Miss Sasha Grimes."

"Dr. Schottgatt, baby," said Foxy after a long pause, "you have to be joking."

"Far from it. Look at it this way, Mr. Galahead. If you are to have your money, as you and I both wish, the students must be convinced that they hold an effective watching brief or that someone they can trust is holding it for them."

"Yeah, I get that. But why Sasha Grimes?"

"She was quite a personality in Montana, Mr. Galahead. Most of the students have heard of her, and some of the older ones met her while she was still with us. She is now a well-known actress . . . but not yet so rich and famous as to arouse their disapproval or mistrust. She is modest in her demeanour and manner of living, she eschews lavish social occasions, she is a professed egalitarian with revolutionary sympathies."

Foxy shuddered and Schottgatt grinned.

"That is just why she is so useful to us, Mr. Galahead. Because if *she* says that the progress and management of this production are satisfactorily in line with current left-wing orthodoxies, then the student committee will believe her and let the thing go on. But they must be sure that they have the power to interfere if they should want to. So we set up the young and idealist Miss Grimes as the symbol of that power, and we tell them that her appointment as their representative here will be its guarantee. There is no better way, Mr. Galahead, of securing their necessary consent."

Foxy pondered this.

"Okay," Foxy said. "I agree."

"You have no choice."

"But listen, Dr. Schottgatt baby. What if Sasha starts to go overboard about all these peasants and things? Peasants we gotta have, I know this, but too much of them could wreck the whole film . . . and you know *that*."

"You and Mr. Jacobson are very experienced men. Let us hope," said Dr. Emile Schottgatt, "that between you you can contain Miss Grimes's enthusiasms."

"Let's hope so, Dr. Schottgatt baby. Let's hope so indeed."

"So what it comes to," said Jules to Fielding later on, "is that they've appointed Sasha as a kind of commissar. There was nothing, Foxy says, that he could do to stop it."

"Where's Foxy now?"

"Prostrate with relief and with Gretel."

"Oh. . . . Can you manage Sasha, do you think?"

"I don't know. I've never thought of her in these terms."

"Nor have I. But now that I'm starting to, I think they stink."

"Foxy says we're stuck with the arrangement. I'd as soon have a crate of dynamite under my bed. . . ."

What would Jules have thought, Fielding wondered, if he'd known that Fielding was taking the dynamite out to dine that very evening?

But Jules would have had little time to worry about Fielding's social arrangements even if he had known of them. As soon as he left Fielding he was summoned by Schottgatt, and what Schottgatt had to say sent him post-haste to Foxy, though Foxy, he knew, would still be prostrate with Gretel.

"Aw, piss," said Foxy, after Gretel had been bundled out by Jules, "I hardly got my socks off. What is it now, for Christ's sake?"

"I've just been with Schottgatt."

Foxy got off the bed and put on a dressing gown which was embroidered with sumptuous silk erotica.

"So what's with Schottgatt? He already said his mouthful for today."

"And now he's said another. The Committee's leaving tomorrow, he said . . ."

". . . Thank God for that . . ."

". . . And he just wanted me to know that from now on a copy of our accounts out here is to be sent direct each week to the accountant of the Oglander-Finckelstein Trust. Did you agree to that, Foxy?"

"Yes. No choice, baby. Anyway, they've always been entitled to ask how their money was being spent. They have done once or twice already."

"I know. But they always used to be content with a rough breakdown. Now it looks as if they mean to go through it all with a toothcomb."

"So what? We're not cheating them."

"No," said Jules, "but we are doing things of which they may not approve very much. Your expenses, for example, all those air passages and helicopter rides, have a privileged look about them."

"I have to travel. They know that."

"And they know you could do it cheaper. Or take this arrangement with Margaret Lichfield. Instead of paying her money down for the part, we're going to 'employ her' at £5000 a year for the next ten years, thus saving her as much as twenty thousand in tax. I don't say it's illegal, but I don't think schemes like that will give the new régime at Montana much pleasure."

"Too late to change that now."

"You realise that those students only have to get hold of one little thing they don't like, and they can cut off supplies just like that?"

"Yeah."

"Then what have you done about alternative backing?"

"Jules baby, you are bugging me. Because you know as well

as I know that just now there is no backing to be had in the whole wide world—except maybe for James quim-cranking Bond. It did occur to me that our friend Max de Freville might think of upping his stake if things got really rough for us, which was why I asked him and Lyki to drop by before lunch. But no joy there. The best they could do would be half a million."

"Then what happens if O/F cuts us off?"

"They won't, if we do like Schottgatt tells us. He may look like Oliver Cromwell's arsehole, but it seems he wants this film finished and he's got it all added up. Which is why he wants the accounts from now on . . . to stop any trouble he sniffs out before it can start really stinking."

"Like the Lichfield tax racket?"

"That's a back number, baby, and it's too well hidden. Come to that, our accountant is probably more than a match for Og-Finck's any day of the week. But from now on, Jules, we play it straight, just in case. Until the last of those cheques for three hundred grand is into the bank and cleared, we keep those accounts so clean that Schottgatt could eat his nut cutlets off them. No help with tax dodges, no special currency rates, not for nobody . . . nothing whatever that could bring the lightest blush of indignation to the purest student cheek. Get it?"

"No helicopters for Foxy?"

"All right. No helicopters for Foxy," Foxy said.

"We've still got to keep Sasha Grimes sweet."

"Then keep her sweet, if you have to dish out pictures of Chairman mother-fucking Mao to the whole damn company. Now for Christ's sake go and find Gretel and get her back here before my balls drop off."

Fielding had arranged to take Sasha Grimes to the restaurant out at the Achilleion, where the Summer Casino was. (In the Casino's system of chronology, summer didn't end till mid-November.) It would make a nice change, he felt, and then the Achilleion was far enough from the town to lessen the likelihood of their being discovered by Jules, but not far enough for Fielding to be accused of deliberate concealment if they were—

quite the contrary, in fact, as it was a resort of some fashion.

Fielding's ostensible reason for asking Sasha to dine, and the one which he would offer to Jules if caught and castigated, was that he wished to discuss her remaining lines. These were very few but very important; for Nausicaa, though appearing prominently in several more scenes, would remain brooding and silent until at last she caught the hero alone to deliver a bitter and poignant farewell.

"The point is," said Fielding, dutifully pursuing this official topic, "that Odysseus isn't actually leaving for some while yet, and they both know it. So what she's really saying is, 'I may as well say good-bye now, because I know you're too important to be having any more time for me. But do just remember, it was me that helped you in the first place'."

"In short," said Sasha, "he's treating her with typical masculine brutality."

"No, dear. He realises, first that it will make scandal if he pays too much attention to her, and second that she's in love with him, which must be stopped for her own good. So although he has to answer her dismissively, the dismissal is as kind as he can make it. 'I'll always remember you,' he says, '*after* I get back safe to my own country.' Or in other words, 'There's nothing in it for either of us here and now' . . . a point which has to be made for everybody's sake. So he makes it, and then goes straight off to join her father before there can be any tears or trouble."

"Yes," she said, "that makes sense. I'll remember it all when we get to the scene. Thank you, Fielding."

This subject now being exhausted, Fielding bethought himself of his second and undeclared reason for dining Sasha, which was to give a try-out to Angela Tuck's formula for arousing her pity and hence her concupiscence. 'Really pile on the agony,' Angela had said, 'misery's their substitute for romance.' Well, yes: but how did one begin? Declarations of agony weren't much in Fielding's line. He could be Stoical, Cynical, Cyrenaic or even Socratic without much trouble, but personal concern or guilt about the woes of the world (woes which in his view it did much to invite by its own sheer folly and greed) he did not find easy to simulate.

"I'm glad," he said rather awkwardly, "that you'll be staying on in this . . . er . . . new capacity. We could do with a voice like yours round here."

"Oh," she said, "do you mean that? I could do with some support."

"In what way?"

"Well, for the next two weeks I'm still under contract and finishing my acting schedule, so I can keep an eye on things without being conspicuous. But after that I shan't be in the company any more, I shall just be employed by the Trust to report. I shall feel . . . alien from you all."

"No need to feel that," Fielding said. "Why don't you just attach yourself to me, as a kind of assistant script-writer? You'll have suggestions to make about how to bring in all these servants and workmen . . ."

". . . Yes, for a compassionate *Odyssey* . . ."

". . . If you like to call it that," he said, suppressing a shudder. "What more natural than that you should convey your suggestions through the script-writer, who can keep a running record of them?"

"You'd be prepared to help me?"

She fluttered her fingers in the air between them, half as if beckoning him towards her, half as if repelling and exorcising his probably evil intentions.

"It'd make me feel better," he said, trying grimly. "It isn't always comfortable, you know . . . earning all this money and wondering what one's doing for it."

"I shouldn't have thought you were the type to feel sensitive about that."

"One can't but notice a certain contrast," he ground out, "between our own lives and that of most Greeks."

"There are many people much worse off than the Greeks," she instructed him. "You should see them in Egypt or India."

For the life of him he couldn't bring himself to mouth any more hypocrisies just yet. Instead he nodded solemnly.

"It's shameful," he said, "it's disgusting . . . that people are coming to this place tonight to gamble with money they don't need. Every penny in their pockets ought to be seized and given to Oxfam."

Will she ever learn, he wondered, that if you stop people starving, they just breed more people to starve? And then aloud : "Unfortunatly there's not much we can do about that. But I suppose we can try to get some things right . . . this film, for instance. I'd like to think I was being of some use to you."

"Should you, Fielding? Well then, let me tell you what I'm planning."

What she was planning was quite hideous. Not content with dragging menials and mechanicals into every scene (*and* sometimes giving them speeches about their deprivations), she wanted to plant a social conscience in Odysseus himself. He would begin by repenting his killing of the Cyclops (an innocent shepherd), he would later be racked with guilt at having exploited Circe and Calypso (instead of helping them to 'fulfilled womanhood and sexual equality'), and when he finally returned to Ithaca he would give away all his lands and money to found a commune in place of his kingdom. The only parts of the film Sasha did not propose to change were those in which she appeared herself : there would be no beachcombers or fishermen around to catch the eye when Miss Grimes was on the screen.

"I see," Fielding said at last. "But I'm not sure that we can manage a programme quite as radical as that."

"Why not ?"

"The changes you propose would cost a lot of money. I don't know that the Trust would authorise an increased investment."

"It's a question," she said, "of making proper use of the money which *is* coming. We can move the company out of that expensive hotel for a start."

"No, dear," he said quickly. "There is a pre-paid contract with the hotel for bookings up to March. If we moved out, we'd lose the money altogether." He had no idea whether this was true, but it sounded plausible. "Once a concern is actually go-ing, it is difficult to change the pattern of expenditure."

"I thought you were going to be on my side."

"I am. But there are certain realities to be faced. What other economies did you have in mind?"

"I thought . . . that everyone might agree to a cut in their salary."

Yes, he thought: you'll have finished drawing yours.

"You might have a little trouble with the unions," he said, trying not to sound ironical.

Although she pouted at this, she took the point. She is not, thought Fielding, a complete imbecile; just young and ignorant and, like all left-wingers, rather spiteful; in the end she thinks more of bringing ruin to Dives than relief to Lazarus.

"It'll be exciting, working on the script together," he said. "What do you say we go back and make a start tonight?"

"I don't know about tonight."

"It's been so lonely, working on that script in the evenings," Fielding said. "But with someone to help, and something worth-while to aim at. . . ."

"All right," she said, "let's start tonight."

God, Fielding thought, you really are delicious. That long, luscious red hair, those little breasts, those rather clumsily circ-ling arms; that dedicated, priggish face . . . oh, to see it sweat and grin with lust.

"Evening, Major Gray," said Burke Lawrence from behind him. "Going into the gaming rooms?"

"No."

"I am. My last night, you know. I'm taking the Four Stooges away tomorrow morning."

Sasha frowned. Fielding signalled for his bill.

"Come and have a flutter," said Lawrence, "you and Miss Grimes. That old regiment of yours . . . Lord Hamilton's Dragoons—"

"—Earl Hamilton's Light Dragoons," Fielding emended automatically, "or Hamilton's Horse—"

"—They were great ones for gambling, I heard. Come to the tables and show us."

"Thank you, no. Miss Grimes and I have work."

Burke Lawrence belched audibly and tottered on his way. The bill came. Fielding paid it at once but they had to wait for change.

"What was that 'Major Gray' bit?" Sasha said.

"A long time ago I was in the Army. Everyone was then."

"Not everyone was a Major in Earl Hamilton's Light Dragoons. Rather repulsive, all that."

"Oh, come off it, dear. We had to have soldiers, and someone had to tell them what to do."

Too late, he saw from her face that he had made a grave mistake. His guilt, if it was to convince Sasha, would have to embrace his Army career.

"I mean," he said, "that was how it seemed then. Over the last ten years we've all come to see it differently." God, he thought, why should I be apologising to this stupid slut for one of the few things in my life I'm proud of?

"Then why do you still call yourself 'Major'?"

"I don't. Burke Lawrence does. It's a kind of joke."

"Yes. A joke on the side of Majors. Against all the poor people they order about and kill. I heard it in his voice."

"You're reading too much into it, Sasha. He was drunk. . . . And here's my change. Let's go home and get to work on that script."

"You corrected him when he got the name of your regiment wrong."

"So would you have done if you'd been in the bloody thing twelve years."

"I'd have made myself forget it. . . . I don't think I want to work on the script this evening."

God damn Burke Lawrence.

"All right. But I'll see you home."

"Stay and play roulette with Burke Lawrence."

"I hate roulette and I don't much care for Burke Lawrence. He used to push drugs in the old days."

"Better than being a Major and getting people killed."

How mindless could she get? But he would have to cry *'peccavi'* over the Army or lose Sasha for good.

"Look, Sasha," he said, hating himself for his treachery, not to her, but to his past. "I was forced into joining the Army when I was still very young" . . . that, in a sense was true . . . "and I've had nightmares about it ever since I left it." And so was that true : the hum of cicadas in the afternoon, the bodies being moved from the truck into the ambulance, the sudden shout of warning from the Corporal-Major, and the black grenade curving through the air . . . *despite the agreed truce.* Oh, the swine, the scum; bloody Cypriot scum. Now as often when he thought of it he started to tremble in despair and rage, and only stopped when Sasha placed one hesitant finger on his wrist.

"Peace," she said, "peace."

"Thank you. . . . You'll come and start work on that script?"

"Not tonight. I think you'll still be Major Gray for the rest of tonight. But tomorrow, Fielding, if you're feeling well again. . . ."

The next day Burke Lawrence and the Creative Authentication Committee flew away early in the morning and were followed by Foxy early in the afternoon. Foxy was going to stop in London to consult with Pandarus and in New York to consult with Clytemnestra, and then go on to Montana to make sycophantic noises at the Oglander-Finckelstein Trust.

"Which means," Foxy said to Jules and Fielding at the airport, "that I shall wave my new social conscience at them as big as blown up tits in a nudie show. To make good and sure they get the weekly payments ready. Meanwhile, you two stop that Grimes dame from gumming up the ball-cocks round here."

"Rather a stiff order," Jules said.

"I know, Jules babe, I know. But do your best, huh? Otherwise we'll all be in the crap. Right up to our teeth."

After which Foxy's flight was called, and he went to join his henchmen at the gate. As he went, Fielding noticed, he was perceptibly less jaunty than usual and he didn't turn to wave. When he reached his henchmen, he gave them a polite and apologetic nod and motioned them to go ahead of him. Foxy, it seemed, wished to be alone.

"He'll have to get rid of that retinue from now on," Jules said : "Og-Finck will never stand for a private bodyguard."

"Is that what they are?"

"Not really. Just two actors who flopped, so he employs them for old times' sake. Og-Finck still won't stand for it."

They went out to Jules's car and started to drive towards the little inland valley where Jules was going to stage the games of the Phaeacians. Fielding ought really to have returned to the Corfu Palace to get on with his speeches, but since they were all rather winded after yesterday's events it had been agreed that he take the afternoon off to bear Jules company.

"I've got a request," Fielding said.

"Not a good time for requests, Fielding."

"This one must be made now or never."

"Well?"

"Now that you've taken me on for the next three months, can you send my money to a bank in Switzerland?"

"What have we done so far?"

"My first two weeks' salary is going to my bank in England."

"But you don't fancy paying tax on the rest?" grinned Jules. "There's schools and hospitals rotting into the ground for lack of cash, but Fielding Gray wants all of his for Fielding Gray."

"I need money for my old age, Jules. £12,000, even now, is a useful sum of capital. Cut off the taxes, and it's merely money to piss up the wall."

"That's the intention, boy. They don't want you to collect any capital, because capital makes you independent, and independence is the new dirty word."

"Will you help or not, Jules?"

"No. I sympathise, my dear. I quite understand that you don't want your money used to provide seaside outings for imbeciles or universities for verminous rabble. But you see, little Sasha Grimes thinks otherwise. So if she found out we were helping you dodge your social duties, she might say something very damaging to her friends at Og-Finck."

"She need never know."

"They might find out for themselves. We've got to send in the accounts."

"Saying how much you pay out and to whom. Not where you put it for them."

"Look, Fielding," said Jules. "If I went to the accountant who's here with us, and asked him to do this for you, he could certainly do it. I don't know the details . . . I expect the money would be transferred through a Clytemnestra account in Switzerland . . . but somehow or other he could do it. So normally I'd get him to oblige. But not now. Now we keep our noses clean, Foxy says, and polish up our social ethics. As of now we're taking not the teeniest, weeniest risk. So that's how it is, my dear, and there's an end of that."

They turned off the main road and drove down a track, through trees on either side, until they came to a large meadow. On three sides of this rose a gentle slope scattered with olive trees, while on the fourth, from which Fielding and Jules had approached, was a long wall of poplar mingled with cypress. Although the meadow was square, the slopes which ascended from it formed a rough semi-circle, so that the whole made a natural theatre. Here they would film the games which the Phaeacians held for Odysseus, and here Jules now busied himself with checking areas and angles.

"You know," said Fielding later on, as they sat to rest in the shade of the olives, "I could make it worth your while."

"Make what worth my while?"

"The risk, such as it is, of paying my money in Switzerland."

"Don't go on about it, Fielding. You've had my answer."

"There's something you don't know, Jules." And Fielding, having admitted to his dinner with Sasha the previous evening, proceeded to describe Sasha's ideas for a 'compassionate' *Odyssey*. "But it's possible," he concluded, "since she can't change the script without my help, that I can keep all this within limits. It is also possible, if Sasha likes me as much as I'm beginning to think, that I can influence her reports to Og-Finck."

Jules chewed his lower lip vigorously.

"If you're trying to bed her," he said, "remember what I told you at the start. I don't want her upset."

"Neither do I. I want her purring with pleasure."

"I don't want her mind taken off her acting."

"Jules. She only has two weeks' acting left and only one more really important scene. After that she'll just be here as an informer . . . and an interferer. We need to get her into a pleasant and acquiescent state of mind as soon as possible— even if it should mean taking her mind off her acting."

"And what makes you think that *your* treatment will get her into a pleasant and acquiescent state of mind?"

"She's beginning to believe that I'm a convert to her way of thinking—equality and all that. Women like making converts. And she's also beginning to pity me."

"Beware of pity."

"Indeed . . . if you are the one that pities. It dulls the faculties and stirs up false affections, even false passions. But if this happened to Sasha, it would keep her out of mischief. Sasha engrossed in an object of pity would have less time to meddle with your film."

"Until she snapped out of it, as sooner or later she would. When she saw she'd been conned, she'd tear you apart."

"I'm not deceiving her as much as you think."

"Oh yes, you are. Pretending to be converted to her socialist fads while dreaming of numbered accounts in Zürich."

"About that, I agree; but I'm not conning her altogether. She pities me, Jules, because she's convinced that I was cruelly victimised while I was in the Army. And so I was . . . though not in the way she thinks. When I remember what happened to me in Cyprus, I sometimes get a kind of fit . . . I start shaking with sheer hatred of the Cypriots who destroyed my face. That was how it was with me last night . . . and she pitied me because she thought I was trembling with horror and guilt for all the wicked things I'd been made to do when in uniform."

"So she was conned."

"The fit was genuine."

"But she was conned, because she thought it meant something it didn't mean, and you didn't put her straight. She'll sort it out in time . . . and then God help you."

"But meanwhile . . . if I can keep her from ruining this production?"

"In that cause," said Jules casually, "I don't mind if you kill her."

"That would be overdoing it and might not please Og-Finck. I'll stick to conning her, if it's all the same to you."

"Then make a good job of it."

"And in return . . . you'll tell the accountant to send my salary to Switzerland?"

"It's totally against Foxy's new policy."

"But a very small price to pay for what you'd be getting."

"If we get it." Jules scowled in reluctant agreement. "I'll see how things go this next fortnight," he said. "And then if I'm convinced you've really got your thumb on her, I'll tip off the accountant to fix you up any way you want for the last ten weeks of your contract. Fair enough?"

"Fair enough."

"So be it," said Jules rising. "Now then: where's the best place for the King and Queen to watch these games from? The King and the Queen and of course our dear little Princess. . . ."

It was the dear little Princess who entirely occupied Fielding's thoughts as he bathed, dressed and ate the dinner which he had ordered in his room. For he was to meet Sasha later that evening for their first session together on the script. This was to be a general discussion, in which Sasha would outline her proposed reforms over wide areas and they would then take a preliminary look at possible methods of applying them. This evening, then, no very definite decision would be taken; but Sasha was bound to press for these before long and, it was essential, Fielding considered, that he should get his thumb on her, as Jules had put it, without any further delay. So many things depended on this : the quality of the film and indeed its continued production; his own money and his plans to have it banked in Switzerland; his future prestige and influence with Jules . . . and, it now occurred to him, with Foxy. For if he could bring this off, if he could contain the menace which Sasha now represented, then Foxy would surely, as they said in this world, *owe* him; and it was interesting to speculate on ways in which he might be persuaded to discharge the debt.

But that was for the future. Here and now the problem was how to get his thumb on Sasha. Since she had an eye and an ear for a good scene, he could possibly get her to agree that it would be a shame to spoil too many of Homer's by crowding them out with proletarian extras; she had already made it clear that her own scenes were not to be altered at the dictates of social realism, and she might be induced to extend this indulgence. Again, feigned sympathy with her aims, and feigned co-operation in them, might help him to limit and reduce them. After all, he could tell her, too much misery on the screen would bludgeon the spectator insensible. She could make her political point much more effectively by showing one mutilated stump than by parading a regiment of beggars, because she would have given one clear-cut image which was easily retained in the memory. This was the sort of thing which Sasha instinctively understood. 'Yes, you're so right,' he imagined her saying, 'and it would save us money. . . .'

All of which was very well, but Fielding had a strong idea that the kind of hold he needed to gain on Sasha must be, in the end, personal. Aesthetic argument, pretended but qualified agreement, calculated deceit . . . all these might achieve something; but final victory could only be won by making her like him (which she was already disposed to do) and then depend on him. If he was to soften up Sasha to the degree she would have to be softened, he must first make her trust him and hold to him for purely personal reasons. She must do as he said because it was he that said it.

And now came the big question : with a view to bringing this about, would her seduction be a help or a hindrance? If he made a good thing of it, it would clearly be a great help. As he had already told himself and others, however, seducing Sasha would be one hell of a job and might lead to horrors and complications beyond imagining. (What had Burke Lawrence called her? A sexual Calamity Jane, something like that.) On balance then, Fielding concluded, he would be wise to keep out of Sasha's bed even if she gave him the most cordial invitation to climb into it. But at the very same time as he formulated this prohibition he knew he would never obey it. For the truth was that Sasha, as a carnal prospect, was so elusive, alluring, perilous and unpredictable, so hedged about with sanctions and tabus, that to Fielding, with his taste for the arcane, she had now become irresistible.

". . . Two good examples of what I mean," Sasha was saying to Fielding: "Nestor and Menelaus. They are both presented as kindly if boring old men. But in fact both were authoritarian princes who trod on everyone near them. As for Menelaus, let's not forget that he had allowed tens of thousands of lives to be lost in a long and brutal war simply so that he could get his unfaithful wife back. All those people butchered just so that one man could keep his property. Because that's how he saw her. . . ."

At least, thought Fielding, she's read it all. I do wish to God that she hadn't. As Sasha went grinding on, he wondered if he could pour himself a whisky. They were, after all, in his sitting room. But Sasha did not approve of stimulants and would consider any suggestion of a pause for refreshment to be disrespectful of her exegesis. But ah, he had it . . .

". . . Sound point, dear," he said, "but if you don't mind I must mix my draught." A quick look at the clock on his desk. "I have to be very punctual about that."

He went to his bedroom, poured himself half a large tumbler of whisky, dripped half an inch of mineral water on top, and rejoined Sasha in the sitting room.

"Draught?" she said. "What for?"

Fielding pointed vaguely at his face. Let her make what she

could of that. But in the event she didn't, apparently, bother to make anything.

"And another point," she droned: "those people down in Hades. Why are they all lords and ladies? Why aren't there any ordinary soldiers and their wives to say what *they* thought of it all?"

"You've got to allow for the convention, Sasha. In the same way as Shakespeare never gave a serious or important part to ordinary men, so Homer, being much earlier, gave them no parts at all."

"What about that soldier of Shakespeare's on the eve of Agincourt? He was serious."

"But very brief. Exceptional in any case."

"Exceptional but there. It's up to us to make a few exceptions in Homer . . . since he didn't do it himself. Now, for this scene in Hades I'm going to suggest. . . ."

Followed a quarter of an hour of suggestions, of which Fielding dutifully scribbled notes. This can't go on, he thought. She must be stopped, or at least brought within reasonable limits. A personal approach is the only way, and of all personal approaches the sexual is the strongest. If it goes wrong, it'll just have to go wrong; if she explodes, then at least my little world here will end with a bang and not a whimper. But there's no point, he thought, in rushing things, in being crude or violent; there is still, for all these intolerable suggestions, a day or two of grace before anything need be done about them. So first try the gradual way; softly softly catchee little red monkey.

"I think," he said, when she next took a split second's pause for breath, "that that's about all I can assimilate in one evening. I'll analyse these ideas of yours and break them down, and tomorrow I'll tell you how we might incorporate them in the script."

This seemed to satisfy her, and she began to make gathering up and going movements.

"Don't go," he said. "I've got something different to discuss with you. Let me send . . . for a glass of lemonade or something?"

"Thank you. Water will do."

"Mineral water?"

"Out of the tap. What all the Greeks drink."

Fielding fetched it from the bathroom.

"I've been thinking," he said, "about when you say good-bye to Odysseus."

"We've already talked about that. I'm sad because I know I'm no more use to him . . . however kind he may be about it."

"I think you're something else as well as sad. I think you're a bit provocative . . . a bit 'come hither' . . . forgive me, Sasha . . . sexy."

"Oh?" Cold eyes, intelligent interest.

"You want him to pay you attention, although you know it's almost hopeless. Your only chance is to tempt him . . . not right into bed, because a Princess doesn't do that, but into feeling a bit randy for you, so that you'll at least have the satisfaction of seeing that look in his eyes. And since you're attracted by him, as you've already shown on the beach, it's easy for you to try to rouse him. You just show him that you've got an itch for him, which is the surest way of giving a man an itch for you. As it happens, Odysseus is far too wary and wily to respond, but that's no reason why you shouldn't try."

"How should I play it, do you think?"

"That must be for Jules to say, if he accepts this line of thought." He came and stood close to where she sat. "But as I see it you've got to be hinting at offering yourself . . . rather like you did on the beach, though then it was almost unconscious and anyhow he didn't see. This time it'll be deliberate, a consciously worked version of what you did without meaning to on the beach." He paused for a moment and brought his mouth close to her ear. "You could do it marvellously, Sasha. Show me how you think it might go."

While Fielding drew back a yard or two to give her room, Sasha sat very quiet, her eyes as cold and dull as iron. Then suddenly a light smile flicked over her face, her eyes dipped and rose again, shining now, and she rippled upright in front of him. She circled one of his wrists with a single finger and brought one thigh almost up to his crutch, making it tremble till it seemed ever closer, till its warmth seemed to flow into his groin.

" 'Farewell,' " she said, " 'stranger from the sea. Perhaps you will remember me hereafter, when you have your wish and come safe home. Then, perhaps, you will remember me, for it was I who first heard you and gave you back your life.' "

"My God," Fielding said, as the warmth came in waves from her trembling thigh. "this is superb. You really understand it."

He put his arms out to bring her to him, but almost before he had moved she was half way to the door.

"As an actress," she said, "I had an intuitive understanding of what you meant." Her eyes were cold again, holding neither desire nor disgust nor reproach, totally neutral. Fielding thought she would leave immediately, but in fact she lingered, looked at him very calmly, and said,

"Tell me, Fielding. How did Burke Lawrence know you'd been a Major and all that?"

"I met him once a long time back. We didn't talk much about it, but he could always have enquired later."

"I keep remembering that when he called you 'Major' last night, you didn't mind."

"Why should I, if it amused him?"

"I keep remembering it. What you said about how it gave you nightmares to think of what you did in the Army . . ."

". . . So it does . . ."

". . . And how ill it suddenly made you. *And yet,* when he first called you 'Major', you didn't at all mind."

"I scarcely heard."

"Perhaps not."

"I was concentrating on you."

"Perhaps."

"Forget it, Sasha. It's all been over too long to bother with."

"I hope so. Good-night, Fielding. And thank you for your ideas about Nausicaa."

Harriet wrote in answer to Fielding's telegram :

Dearest Fielding,

    All this is very muddling. If they promised you a decision about your contract after two weeks, then a decision there should be. We can't go on like this. I want to know whether I'm to join you or whether you're coming back home. It's very lonely here without you. Do please, dearest, *make* them give you an answer and cable me as soon as you can. I'm very unhappy and upset.

Then you'll just have to go on being unhappy and upset, thought Fielding. I've got a very big bank running and I don't want you out here nagging in my ear-hole. But how to keep you away. . . . ?

    As you will see (Harriet went on) I enclose a letter from Gregory Stern. I'm afraid I opened it by mistake when it came...

. . . Not half you didn't, you prying bitch . . .

. . . and once having done so I thought I might as well read it. It seems to me a very good suggestion of Gregory's, and just the sort of work you ought to be doing. So if those film people refuse to commit themselves and go on playing about with you like this, why not show them that you know your value if they don't and just come on home and start this book for Gregory?

Why not? I'll show you twelve thousand reasons why not.

    Although he says nothing about dates, I don't suppose his offer will be open indefinitely. It would be nice to have something settled with him, even if it did mean giving up part of that film money you're earning.

That's it. You don't care how much money I lose so long as I'm sitting safe under your beady eyes. And yet when all this started you said you wanted me to make money. Bloody bird-brained woman.

    But perhaps things have altered since you last cabled. Perhaps Pandarus has now confirmed the contract. In that case, of course, you'll have to continue, and we must hope that Gregory can wait another three months before you make a start for him. At least I'll be able to join you in Corfu, which will be all the comfort I really need.

All my love, pumpkin,

Harry.

Jesus, Joseph and Judas. Another lie needed for her within twenty-four hours. Should it be a small and temporising lie, which would be easy to devise but would only keep her off for a few days? Or should he risk a real whopper, which might raise the siege for weeks but might equally well bring her down on him, in desperation and disbelief, with her biggest battering ram. Seeking temporary distraction from this problem, he applied himself to the enclosed letter from his publisher, Gregory Stern.

It appeared that Gregory was planning a new series of biographical and critical studies of Modern English Novelists. 'Modern' meant going back, in Gregory's view, as far as Joseph Conrad, who was to be the subject of the inaugural volume. Would Fielding like to undertake this? Gregory's rates (unspecified, needless to say) would take account of time and effort needed for research, and expenses within reason (whose reason?) would also be paid. As Harriet had observed, no dates were mentioned, but Fielding had the impression that Gregory was keen to up-anchor and be off.

It was, no doubt about it, a very promising notion. Notwithstanding his sour reflections just now about Gregory's shifty attitude to payment, Fielding knew of old that Gregory would be as generous as possible within his means, which these days were rapidly increasing. But even so any offer of Gregory's would be peanuts as compared with the princely provision of Pandarus; and the task, particularly the research, would be quite gruelling. But yet again it was good work, the kind that ought to be done, the kind that ought to be done by *him*. For while he had never pretended to be committed or inspired as a writer, he did claim to be a conscientious professional who gave good value; and here was a worthwhile professional job to be done if ever there was one. What was more, there would be no intrigue or backbiting in this assignment, no psychopaths or paranoiacs such as filled the Corfu Palace to the brim, no dirty little schemes about Swiss banks . . . just scholarly peace and quiet, and Harriet bringing in the tea-trays.

And there, of course, was the rub. He could not go back to peace and quiet and Harriet's tea-trays . . . not yet. Corfu, at the moment, smelt of money, sex, excitement, power and popular fame. Although not all of these would be for him, the scent of them, floating in the air about him, was very sweet in his nostrils. Uneasy and ungrateful as he might feel at shilly-shallying over Gregory Stern's most seemly proposal, he could not bring himself to quit the halls of Sybaris until he had penetrated its innermost chambers and gathered up his share of the goodies which were going there.

And after all, he now told himself, there was this to salve his conscience : amid all his other activities, he was using his skill and taste to promote the honour of Homer. All this deceiving and flattering and seducing . . . its chief end was to protect the poet against the abuses of commercial hucksters on the one hand and political fanatics on the other. True, there might be both profit and pleasure in it for Fielding himself; but the poet would surely have been too large-hearted to grudge a man that.

To Gregory he now wrote briefly, expressing his pleasure at being chosen and stating his willingness to devote himself unswervingly to Conrad as soon as his contract with Pandarus was done, if Gregory would wait that long. He could, he added untruthfully, find the leisure to do a little general research while he was still with Pandarus.

To Harriet he wired that his contract was now fixed (he could hardly disguise this any longer in view of what he had told Gregory) but that she must wait in England until she received the letter which he was posting that very day. The composition of this was a ghastly job; for Fielding had decided on the second method of dealing with Harriet . . . an enormous fib which would keep her away from Corfu for at least a month . . . and adroit through he was in this line, to find and frame a falsehood of the superior quality needed here was almost beyond him. However, he eventually ran up quite a plausible tale to the effect that for a month or more he was to go on tour through Greece and the Aegean in order to spot out possible new locations, as it now appeared that Corfu was in many respects inadequate. He would communicate, he said, from various points *en route*, but he could give no definite schedule of his movements, since these must depend on local information which he could only gather as he went.

He then scribbled four notes of the 'much in haste, just off again' category, on four different kinds of paper and with four different pens. These he dated over the next month at rough intervals of a week; he sealed them, stamped them, addressed them to Harriet, and sent them with covering letters to four trusted and worldly expatriot acquaintances, two of whom lived in the Peloponnese, one on Skyros and one on Mitylene. Each correspondent was adjured, for love of Fielding, to post the enclosed envelope in or near his own district on or near such and such a date. Finally, Fielding made a record, to refresh his memory later, of his supposed peregrination.

Harriet, he reckoned, was just vague enough to believe that a script-writer could be employed as he had told her. If she didn't, if she came to Corfu to check, that particular balloon would go up with a nasty bang; but this was just one more risk he had to take. Meanwhile, were there any loopholes which he could close but hadn't? There was certainly one. After he had posted his packets at the concierge's desk, he had a friendly talk with the concierge, at the end of which it was agreed that any lady who might telephone for him *from England* should be told that the Kyrios Gray had left the hotel and was not expected back for the next four or five weeks. For this service there would be a weekly charge, payable in advance and in cash, of three thousand drachmae, but the concierge proudly guaranteed a faultless professional performance.

The next thing Fielding did was to ring up Angela Tuck, who asked him to a tête-à-tête luncheon at 'Max's place'. This was a restored Venetian palazzo which overlooked a bay some miles north of the town; it had a lawn which sloped down to a private beach, and on either side of this lawn were a number of little arbours, most of which sheltered rather good Hellenistic statues of life-size nymphs or demi-gods. One of them, however, was furnished with benches and a table, and it was here that Angela had arranged for them to have lunch.

"Max is in Athens with Lyki," Angela said, "drumming up more Government support for their bloody tourist hotels."

She pointed across the bay, on the far side of which three hideous erections, looking like Martian forts in a cheap science fiction film, occupied two-thirds of the visible coast line.

"What's the use of having a lovely place like this," said Angela, "if you've got to sit and stare at that?" She was looking better than when Fielding had last seen her, just as massive and flabby but not so high-coloured. Yet now her hatred of the hotels was bringing her rapidly out in a kind of orange sweat, as though her face were smeared with marmalade. "They're going to murder this island," she said. "Look at the way they're destroying the trees. Don't they know what happened on other islands? Once they all looked as green and beautiful as this, but their trees were destroyed and they turned into lumps of rock."

"That was a very long time ago," Fielding said, "and modern Greeks don't know any history. Not that they'd change their ways if they did. Greeks destroy trees—it's almost a natural law. The only reason there are any left here is that the Venetians and the British kept planting them."

"The good old raj, eh? There was a lot to be said for it. But Max and Lyki between them are going to turn Corfu into a desert. Hotels, roads, camping sites . . . there isn't a square inch of the place which they're not going to change into something hideous."

"Tell 'em to stop."

"They just laugh. 'My dear lady,' Lykiadopoulos says, 'you might as well try to stop the flow of time itself. Someone will make money here : why not us?' And Max is just as bad. He's a kind and civilised man is Max, he's been all over Europe *and* looked at what he's seen, so he knows exactly what horrible damage he's doing here; and yet nothing, short of the Last Trump, is going to make him stop. It's not just for money either. He resents nature, Fielding. He resents something which can get on perfectly well, indeed much better, without *him*. So he's out to teach nature a lesson . . . chop it and change it and pull it about until it's quite sure who's master."

She took a huge gulp of vodka and tonic and then wiped the marmalade off her face.

"That's why those hotels are so ugly," she said, "to spite nature."

She clawed the air in the direction of the Martian forts, immediately started to exude more marmalade, dabbed at it rather despairingly, and then sat still.

"I'm not supposed to excite myself," she said, "so to hell with it. Now, duckie : Max has been asking after Harriet Ongley. I must confess I'd forgotten her."

"Why is Max interested?"

"She's a friend from way back. You must have known that."

"She used to talk of him when we first met, but she hasn't mentioned him in years. Even when I told her that Max was out here, she said nothing."

"There's not a lot in it. Just that her late lamented husband sometimes played in the chemmy games which Max used to run in the fifties."

"Tell him Harriet's staying in England." He outlined his plan for keeping her there. "Will Max mind?"

"Not in the least. He just likes to know what's going on. We'll back you up, if Harriet would get in touch with us. Speaking for myself, I'm delighted, because I suppose this means you're going ahead with little Sasha Grimes?"

Two waiters appeared with cold *hors d'œuvres* and wine. Angela, when served, took only a small piece of egg and a mushroom. Fielding, hungry after a long morning, helped himself liberally; he noticed that Angela gave his plate a look of repulsion and then hurriedly turned her face away.

"So what's cooking with little Sasha?" said Angela when the waiters had gone. She kept her face turned from Fielding as he ate, and was visibly compelling herself to eat her own food, forking it to her mouth crumb by crumb. Where does she get all that flesh, he wondered.

"Little Sasha," he said, "has become a very important person." He gave a full account of this, and also of his own sessions alone with Sasha. "I think," he said, "that the sooner I have her the better. It's urgent, Angie. What shall I do?"

Angela pushed her plate away and carried her wine glass up to her bosom, where she held it in both hands.

"You're sure," she said, "that all that business with her thigh was only faked."

"Yes. She was acting Nausicaa. She turned it on and off like a light."

"So that means that the time she really liked you best was when you told her about the Army?"

"I suppose so. I trembled a lot and she put her hand out to calm me. She meant to be kind and she was."

"Well there's your line. You keep it up about the Army, she pities and soothes you . . . and finally you end up in bed."

"It's a tricky area, Angela."

"I don't see why. Just tell her what happened . . . how you were blown up in Cyprus and had your face ripped off . . ."

". . . But that's just what I can't tell her. She thinks I was trembling with *guilt* that evening, for having been a nasty fascist soldier. If I tell her about that grenade, she'll know the real reason . . . that I'd like to kill every Greek in Cyprus and was trembling with rage because I can't. If she knew that, I'd be finished. She's suspicious about the Army anyhow; she keeps going on about how I was a Major in a smart regiment. Best keep away from all that."

"Then we must find something that you really are guilty about."

"That's it. I've got to cry '*mea culpa*' and mean it. That's the only sort of misery to satisfy her."

The two waiters returned with two mullet. Angela accepted hers, took a tiny mouthful, and gagged on it. Fielding was about to commiserate on her lack of appetite but then wisely decided to keep quiet. He watched her swallow a whole glass of wine in one pull and shakily refill from the bottle.

"You've got plenty of things you can work up guilt about," she said when she was recovered. "That time you hit your mother down at Broughton . . . or better still, the way you let down that wretched little boy at your school. Christopher."

He had almost forgotten how much Angela knew of his past. He had seen her so seldom over the years, and thought so little about her, that it was hard to realise quite how deep their relations went. Yet of course she knew all about his mother and all about Christopher too. She had been there in Broughton when it all came to a head, in 1945, and had indeed used it for her own ends at the time. And for her own pleasure later on. 'Show me, Fielding,' she had said that afternoon on Hydra eight years ago, 'show me what you did with Christopher.' Oh yes; she knew it all.

"You could even make her read that novel you wrote about it," Angela now said.

"I haven't got a copy."

"I have. Somewhere up in the house."

"She might not approve. Turning it into a book . . . into money."

"Then pretend you're guilty about that too."

"I am."

"So you'll really be able to wallow in it, won't you? Lust, betrayal, incestuous love-hate, and violent death. Topped off with dollops of tears, because you used it all to make money. She'll think she's hearing a play by Webster."

Funny, thought Fielding. The Angela he used to know would never have referred to Webster, or worried about the trees on Corfu, come to that. She seemed to have picked up a certain literate wisdom during her wanderings with Max . . . while still unmistakably remaining her old coarse and cynical self.

"And when you've finally got up her," this self now remarked, "don't forget the fee for my advice. You remember what that is?"

"Very clearly. I'll bring her out here as soon as I can, so make sure your fake mirror's working properly. If Sasha saw you standing there on the other side she might be rather cross."

"But you've got to get her first," Angela said. "So one last hint. Blame it all on your wicked public school. She'll like that. Tell her you were maimed and perverted by pedagogues and pigs."

"In fact they were extremely nice and understanding men."

"That's not what she wants to hear, duckie. You just get your part straight : I'm guilty, I'm guilty, I'm guilty . . . but so are those public school pigs."

The waiters brought fruit, sweet wine from Samos, and coffee. After a little while Fielding said he must go.

"No," said Angela, slipping her hand between his thighs, "don't go yet. Sit here and let me hold you. For old times' sake."

"Come with me," said Sasha Grimes late that night, and led Fielding towards his bedroom.

"Lie down," she said. "No, don't undress. Just lie down and be still."

While Sasha moved about the bedroom making preparations, Fielding went on muttering and blubbering about pigs of parents and schoolmasters, and what they had all done not only to long dead Christopher but to Fielding too. By now he was no longer sure which parts of this were sincere and which were simulated; but to judge from the results so far, enough of it was genuine to lend conviction to the whole. He was just getting ready to do the bit about his mother again (perhaps two-thirds sincere, this) when something in Sasha's activities stopped him dead. He lay absolutely quiet now, watching her during every second, and with each that passed he became more puzzled. At length, after she had looked carefully round to make sure that everything was ready, she began to walk, still fully clothed (as he was) towards the bed; she turned aside to Fielding's dressing table, from which she took a clean hand- kerchief and a bottle of Eau de Cologne; then she continued towards the bed, until she was standing right over Fielding. She unscrewed the top of the bottle which she was carrying, poured some Eau de Cologne on to the handkerchief, and began to bathe Fielding's forehead and cheeks. As she did so she whispered.

"Sasha," he said at last, looking up at her rather wildly, "Sasha, are you sure?"

"Just lie still," she said, "and later do exactly as I say."

She put down the bottle and the handkerchief on the bedside table, then lifted her dress up over her thighs and tucked it into the patent leather belt round her waist.

"Filthy bitch, Sasha," she said, "you filthy, filthy bitch."

She started to lower the tights which she was wearing under the dress.

"You like it when he looks at you, Sasha, don't you?" she said. "Poor Fielding, he's suffered so much. So you think that's an excuse to let him look. *You filthy bitch.*"

She went on carefully lowering her tights. Fielding seeing her narrowed eyes and remembering the way she had whispered to him, was strongly minded to get up and send her away before it was too late. But already it was too late . . . her eyes and her parted lips told him that. He had deliberately tried to start this and now he must see it through. Only one thing for it : lie there still, as she said.

"Poor Fielding," she murmured, "so many tears. Will you take this dirty whore to make up? Will you let her comfort you for what you suffered on the cross?"

She raised both hands as high as she could, and as he saw what was next to happen he stiffened violently along the bed.

## PART THREE

# A MAN OF MANY WILES

"Thank God," said Jules to Fielding, "that we're finally finished with the Phaeacians. That bloody Nomarch and his friends. . . ."

"Were they so awful?"

"Yes, Fielding, they were. Larking about like a lot of schoolboys. If I hadn't owed them for getting Elena out of clink, I'd have sent them home after the first morning."

"How do they come out in the rushes?"

"Not too badly, as it happens. We hardly see them during the games, and in Alcinous's palace they look quite sombre and dignified. It was between shots that they were so trying. They'd start feeling up the girls and wouldn't come back on set. So then I'd have to shout, and they got all puffed up and offended, and the girls got right out of hand, and on one occasion Elena lost her knickers and came back on with her bush showing under her tunic . . ."

". . . There, there," Fielding said. "It's all over now. On to the next thing. Are you happy with the dialogue for Odysseus and Calypso?"

"Yes, thanks."

"And the scenes in Hades? I had rather a tussle with Sasha about those. She wanted more lower-class ghosts, but I managed to keep her down to one."

"Which we can always cut out later. . . . Anyhow, you've done a fine job. Thank you, Fielding."

"We aim to please. What shall I work on now?"

"The scenes after Odysseus's return to Ithaca. And then start rewriting Circe. I'm not sure when I can get that little madam back here, but I want to be ready for her. And now, my dear, my turn to do something for you."

"Oh yes?" said Fielding, pretending that he had forgotten.

"The stipulated two weeks have gone by since we discussed that bargain about Sasha. She seems to be behaving very reasonably, and I'm prepared to give the credit to you . . . though sometimes I wonder how long it can last."

"I'm well into gear. But it has been an effort, Jules."

"I believe you. And now you shall have your reward. If you go and see the accountant, you'll find him cooperative."

"About Switzerland?"

"Anywhere you name. But if I were you," said Jules with a funny glint in his eyes, "I'd ask the accountant's advice."

In order to avoid predators, the Pandarus accountant in Corfu lived in a small hotel some way from the Corfu Palace and operated from a tiny office which had been rented for him at the back of the American Express. Since it was a warm and clear November day, Fielding decided to walk there along the sea.

There was no doubt about it, he thought; things were going very well indeed. To everyone's relief, the Og-Finck money was coming in as promised, three hundred grand weekly and bang on time. Jules was still on schedule with the filming, despite his troubles with the ill-disciplined Nomarch, and was evidently pleased with the script. Sasha had acted out her final scenes beautifully and in other respects, though occasionally intransigent, was being by and large biddable. She had been coaxed out of imposing much change on the script, while the two reports which she had so far sent to Og-Finck and the student committee were known to be quietly favourable.

But of course, Fielding thought, as he breasted a slope and came into sight of the gardens, Sasha would continue volatile. There were few easy moments with her around, and if ever a man had earned his employers' gratitude, it was he. There were times when he woke in the night sweating with anxiety, thankful to God that Sasha was not there beside him (for she hated sharing beds after it was over) but all the more fearful of whatever feverish and guilt-ridden fantasy she might even now be devising against their next encounter. Which of them would crack first, he wondered; how long could it go on? Yet one way or the other it must go on; he must maintain his authority. And certainly (he now comforted himself) that was still unquestioned; for Sasha, unwilling as she had been to accept Angela's invitation to Max's place, had nevertheless done so purely because Fielding said it would please him, and they were to go there for 'dinner and the night' the day after next.

For the time at least, then, that front was holding up. Fielding turned left and skirted the cricket ground, on which a fat little schoolmaster was superintending an autumnal game. In England, Fielding thought, the stumps were put away weeks ago . . . much too early. He had always felt that cricket was at its best late in the year, a dying game in the dying year. Not that he thought the game was dying, or at least he prayed not, but Harriet had once said . . . Ah, he thought, bringing himself sharply back from reverie to current reality : Harriet. Well, here too was cause for satisfaction. Harriet had apparently accepted what he had written about his fictitious tour away from Corfu, and had sent back to wish him a good trip.

'I hope this finds you somewhere,' she had written. '. . . Have you been in touch with Gregory? If you convince him you're really keen on the Conrad proposal, I expect he'll wait till you're ready.'

So there was no need to worry about Harriet . . . though he must remember that the weeks were going on. As for Gregory and Conrad, there was nothing to be done until he heard from Gregory, and meanwhile he had prepared himself to abide, without regret or recrimination, by whatever decision should be made. If Gregory would wait, good; if not, there was an end of it. After all, there were more urgent matters than Conrad . . . such as enjoying, and using, what little was left of his youth. Just now that meant concentrating on Corfu and Sasha (who, however hazardous, was certainly a high-class enjoyment) and, not least, on making money. There would be time enough later for research and biographies, when he had had his fill and made his packet and could settle in comfort to the work. All things being equal, he would like to write about Conrad, but there would doubtless be other subjects and other offers quite as good.

Soothed by this philosophy, and satisfied that his concerns in general were going as right as any rational man could expect, he entered the American Express and made for the accountant's office.

"Hi, man," said the accountant, who was perhaps thirty years old and dressed in an expensive Red Indian outfit with his hair styled to match. "What's with you?"

Fielding explained what was with him.

"Yeah, that checks. Mr. Jacobson warned me," said the accountant, adopting a more official but hardly more respectful manner. "So what are your instructions, sir?" he leered.

"Mr. Jacobson suggested I should ask your advice."

"The two best places for your money are Malta and Switzerland. Don't touch the Carribean; the blacks may start grabbing." The accountant spoke concisely and confidently but also with an air of scepticism, as if he was telling a lucky player how best to make use of a wad of Monopoly money. "Some say Portugal is safe, but you'd never get it out again. Ditto South Africa. There's always Japan, but in my book that's just too far away."

"In mine too. Malta or Switzerland then: which is the better?"

"The Swiss are beginning to get a conscience about all the loot which crooks and politicians stash away there. One day they may fling their accounts wide open . . . say in two hundred years."

"Not a very pressing conscience?"

"Insulated by layers of cream cake. In Malta, on the other hand, you might get interest on your money, which would be much harder to arrange in Switzerland."

"Interest is always nice."

"Then I'd suggest a deposit account in Malta. The only

thing is . . . Malta I don't quite trust. It looks good, it should be good, it will be good, as long as the Church there goes on calling the old tunes. But that may not be for as long as some people think."

"Why not?"

"The Holy Catholic Church," said the accountant, adjusting the Red Indian riband round his forehead, "is getting ready to jump on the liberal juggernaut. Just look at the recent record : no more Noble Guard or papal creations of nobility; duller gear for the Cardinals; Masses in the vernacular instead of Latin. The next step could be giving money away . . . not the Church's money, natch, but somebody else's, for there's nothing your liberal likes better than giving away somebody else's money."

"I hardly see that the Church could give away mine."

"If your money was in Malta; and if Rome told the Church in Malta to stop being anti-socialist; and if the socialists got in as a result : then it might not look so good for your money. And the Church could say, look, everybody, we've stopped supporting privilege : on the most Catholic island of Malta we've just allowed the People to sequester all the wicked tax-evaders' pelf."

"Switzerland then. It's what I always had in mind. I'm sorry to have taken up so much of your time."

"No trouble, man. Just a professional service, for which I shall charge you £50 against your salary. Now then. We get you to open an account with the same bank as Clytemnestra uses in Zürich, and then we work a straight little transfer job."

"How will it appear in the accounts?"

"It'll appear okay. Leave that to me. What concerns you is that £1000 a week . . . less my fifty . . . will go smoothly into your lovely new account in your lovely new Swiss bank."

He passed Fielding some papers to fill in and busied himself with others.

"And I trust I see another satisfied client," he said when they were both finished.

"Indeed you do," said Fielding, and then remembered something in one of the documents he had just signed. "Am I to understand that your fee of £50 is *weekly*?"

"That's right, man." The accountant collected up all the papers. "Perhaps Mr. Jacobson didn't make it quite clear. In specialised cases like this, you are, of course, bound to take advice; and this case is so specialised, if you follow me, that the fee comes rather high."

"I follow you," said Fielding crossly.

"What the hell, man. It's all dream money. Or rather, it would be, if there weren't people like me to help you hang on to it after you've woken up. It's quite a trick, bringing money out of dreams and into the real world, and the man who does it for you deserves his five per cent."

"A very fair point. I'm sorry if I sounded annoyed."

"That's okay, man. They all get annoyed but not all of them apologise like you. So here's a tip for free. Your money will be safe in Switzerland, and you can spend it anywhere on the continent; but dream gold is apt to turn to dross if you carry it across the English Channel."

"The tax man smells it?"

"Yeah. The odd hundred quid's worth now and then . . . that's all right. But don't take it over in sacks."

"Thank you. I'll remember."

"You do that, man. Most of them don't. They forget, you see, where the money first came from, and then they get careless. To keep dream money, Mr. Gray, you've got to stay very wide awake."

When Fielding returned from the accountant's office to his room in the Corfu Palace, he found a letter from Gregory Stern:

My dear,

I want you and no one else to do the book on Conrad, as I think both your style and your sympathies will suit the subject. You match Conrad in pessimism, and you understand, if you do not share, his belief that some sort of hope is to be found in the discipline and decency of those few men who have succeeded in clearing and for a while defending small patches in the universal jungle.

I am sorry that we must wait three months before you can make a proper start, but I accept this. We will go into details about the terms when you get back.

Detterling asks me to tell you that he is probably coming to Corfu at Christmas, to stay with his old friend Max de Freville. He hopes to see something of you, and to tell you more of our plans and aspirations for the 'Modern English Novelist' series.

Meanwhile, my dear, take care that you are not eaten alive by the Movie Moguls.

Love as ever (and from Isobel)
Gregory

Excellent, thought Fielding. His day was going very well. A sound arrangement just made with Mammon and now a gratifying letter from (so to speak) God. What was more, it would be nice to see Detterling at Christmas and very convenient; for as Gregory's partner and Fielding's old friend Detterling was always a useful ally in getting Fielding good terms for his books, and this would be a timely chance to raise the topic re Conrad . . . even if he did have to endure a lecture on his publishers' 'plans and aspirations' first.

But the important thing, Fielding thought, was that he was now engaged and trusted to undertake a reputable and serious literary task as soon as his allotted days in Corfu were done. Work on Conrad would wipe out the professional indignity of having played the whore in Cockaigne, while the profits of his whoredom would still remain intact. He would be having it both ways: he would be winning esteem as a man of letters and yet still eating caviar when he fancied it. . . .

Or would he? By the time he left Corfu there would be £10,000 (less the accountant's five hundred) safely banked for him in Zürich. But this was money which he had intended as a capital reserve; it was not to be frittered away on caviar, it was not to be spent at all until it was really needed. But then again, if this money was not to be used, he must go back to live in Harriet's house on the Norfolk coast; and one of the pleasures of Cockaigne which he did not at all wish to forgo was independence of Harriet.

The simple truth was, as he had always known, that he needed more, much more, than £10,000 . . . less the accountant's five hundred. Not only did he need enough to live in ease and independence while he was working on Conrad, he also needed a really large sum of capital behind him (even if preserved, ten thou. was merely marbles) in order to alleviate old age and to subsidise future failures. He was, after all, already well over forty; tastes were changing all the time; so that even if his talent did not desert him, his public might.

Dream money. He must drum up more dream money while he was yet in dreamland, and this gave him just ten weeks.

Very well, Fielding asked himself : who mints the dream money?

Foxy Galahead does.

And why should he give any more of it to you, Fielding Gray?

Because he *owes* me for my good offices with Sasha Grimes.

But surely Pandarus has paid that debt already, by helping you to dodge your taxes?

Not so, not so; the Swiss arrangement, however 'specialised', will cost Pandarus nothing, and my services with Sasha are worth a lot more than that.

Perhaps; but will Foxy acknowledge the obligation? And if he does, will he discharge it?

As to that, we shall see. . . .

"Tell me," said Fielding to Max de Freville during dinner at Max's place, "how does Foxy Galahead stand with Pandarus and Clytemnestra? On what terms do they employ him?"

"He is a director of both firms," said Max, "and as such is highly salaried. He also produces films for them and takes a cut of the profits."

"He's just a leech," Sasha said, "sucking money."

"But first," said Lykiadopoulos, "he must find a host to suck it from. He must find means to finance productions beyond the relatively very small sums which Pandarus or Clytemnestra can put up for themselves. These days this is hard to do, but Mr. Galahead is good at doing it . . . thus finding money not only for himself to suck but for you and Mr. Gray and many others."

"A clown like that," said Angela; "I wonder anyone trusts him with a penny."

"He has a name for being a lucky clown," Lykiadopoulos said. "So men with money to invest, who like most powerful men are often superstitious, think maybe he will be lucky for them too."

"And that being a clown," added Max, "he will later be easy to cheat of more than he owes them."

"Is that why you invested in this film?" Sasha enquired.

"No," said Max. "You see, I happen to know he isn't a clown. It just suits him to appear as one."

"Has anyone ever seen him," asked Fielding, "without his motley?"

"Yes," said Max : "wearing a mask and a long black apron at the Board of Clytemnestra. They listen to him there all right, and they don't laugh while he's talking."

This information pleased Fielding. He was beginning to make plans for doing his deal with Foxy, plans which would run a lot smoother if Foxy's writ was respected inside Clytemnestra. But despite what Max had just said he found it hard to conceive of Foxy in the role of authoritarian.

"I must say, I can't quite see it," he now said.

"Let's hope you'll never have to," said Max.

"I can see it," said Sasha. "It was just the same with Hitler. He looked like a clown to Chaplin and everyone outside, but in Germany itself he was an ogre. Underneath it all, Foxe J. Galahead is just another bloody Nazi."

"You are surely too young to remember the Nazis," said Lykiadopoulos with avuncular reproof of such crudeness.

"The German ones, yes," said Sasha, annoyed by Lykiadopoulos's tone, "but there are some good examples here in Greece just now."

There was a brief and embarrassed silence, after which Max began to talk of the guests he was expecting for Christmas. "Detterling you know," he said to Fielding. "He may be bringing his cousin, Canteloupe . . ."

". . . Don't just pretend I haven't said it," shouted Sasha challenging the whole table. "I've said it and I meant every word."

"My dear," said Lykiadopoulos, "do not upset yourself. We cannot all see these things alike. Greece is a poor country, and if it is to have the wealth it needs to be truly free, it must first have discipline."

While Lykiadopoulos talked on calmly, despite Sasha's angry interruptions, about the essentially practical nature of the régime, Fielding reflected that if Sasha was still in such a taking at bed-time Angela would have but poor entertainment watching from behind the fake mirror. He was here to pay Angela her 'fee', and he wanted to pay the poor old bag generously; but Sasha in her angry mood would later make for a dismal spectacle at best and possibly for none at all.

"No compassion," Sasha snapped now, "no dignity, no justice. Nothing but talk of tourism and trade. What are your lights, your guiding lights? I know the people have them if their leaders haven't."

"Yes," said Lykiadopoulos, losing patience at last, "our people have a guiding light, and as with any other people it is greed. The régime here caters for that, and so it is accepted by the people. All this talk some of them put out about yearning to return to democracy is simply to save face. You have heard, Miss Grimes, how important is *face* in our country? Φιλοτίμη , as we call it?"

Sasha sniffed a graceless confession of ignorance.

"Then I shall explain to you one good example. So long as the colonels make us richer, we shall bear with them and crawl; but at the same time we shall strike Byronic attitudes about liberty and justice, in order to disguise from the world the fact that we are crawling. That, Miss Grimes, is saving face."

Sasha sniffed again, rose from the table, and marched from the room.

"I'm going to pack," she said as she went.

Fielding rose to follow her and Angela to follow Fielding.

"It'll have to be now or never," Fielding whispered back to Angela. "You'd better go and take post."

A minute or two later, Angela was installed in a small booth behind the fake mirror. Although the air was very close in there, for some time at least she did not notice this, so absorbed she was by the scene in Sasha's bedroom.

When Angela had arrived in the booth, Sasha was already busy packing a small grey Revelation suitcase, while Fielding stood nearby and appeared to be arguing with her. Angela could not hear what Fielding said, but it was clear that he was trying to be calm and persuasive; his manner was not in the least aggressive, his countenance had a quiet sorrow which its deformities rendered more sorrowful. At first Sasha hardly troubled to answer him; but when her packing was almost finished, she turned to him and seemed to pay him closer attention.

Fielding now went into a long monologue. Though his manner was still calm, every now and again he made strange and intense gestures, one of which made Angela shiver in her closet : it was as though Fielding had mimed his own evisceration; he splayed his fingers over his heart, then over his belly, then in the region of his groin. As soon as he did this, Sasha's whole demeanour changed; she was no longer merely listening to him, she was suddenly possessed. Her eyes narrowed, her body tightened; and after a few more words from Fielding, she gave a brief, eager nod, and started to move very quickly and precisely about the room, stopping here or there to trace lines and circles on the floor with her finger, rather as if she were arranging a stage or set for a preliminary rehearsal and must mark out the boards with chalk to assist the actors in remembering their movements and their stations.

Meanwhile Fielding, fully clothed as he was, had gone to lie on the bed. After he had been there about a minute, Sasha transferred her efforts to the walls; on these too she traced imaginary figures, but figures very different from the ones on the floor. Whereas those had been pure geometrical forms, the designs which she indicated against the walls, while not entirely random, were variable and fluid. They were in fact, as Angela at length realised, the outlines of human bodies—though in one case Sasha reverted to her geometrical style with what appeared to be two long rectangles arranged to form an upright T.

A real nutter, Angela thought; a judgment which was confirmed when Sasha suddenly knelt down in front of the invisible T, hitting her forehead sharply on the floor and raising her rump high in the air as she did so. Perhaps she likes it like that, from behind, thought Angela; but already Sasha was on her feet and rummaging through her suitcase, from which she produced a bottle of Eau de Cologne and a small towel. She then walked briskly to the bed.

Angela's motive in watching Fielding and Sasha was not to obtain overt sexual excitement, which these days she thought to be impossible, but to associate herself with a sexual occasion (thus gratifying a life-long habit which persisted despite the disappearance of desire) and also to feed an almost intellectual curiosity. She expected, that is, to be amused, interested, informed, perhaps to be made mildly and theoretically envious of pleasures no longer available to her. What she had not expected was to be in any way stirred; and she was therefore surprised and discommoded by the sheer yearning . . . not lust, not immediate desire, but for all that a bodily yearning . . . which came over her as she witnessed the events that now followed. It was not that she was sexually excited but that she overwhelmingly wished to be; her body ached in vain to melt with the old abandon, to twitch with the remembered spasms.

What happened, hardly three yards from where she stood, was this. Sasha came to Fielding, moistened her towel from her bottle, and bathed his forehead. Then she put by the bottle and the towel, lifted her skirt, muttered fiercely, tucked the skirt into her belt, and began to lower her tights, still muttering fiercely and pushing her crutch forward as though presenting it for Fielding's closer inspection. When her tights reached her ankles, she stepped out of them and straddled slightly, said something directly to Fielding, then stretched both arms up above her head. For a few seconds she stood beautifully poised, as though about to sweep down into a ballerina's curtsy at the finish of a dance; but when her hands descended they did not spread wide for a curtsy, they came rending through the upper part of her dress, bringing it down in tatters to her waist and exposing two pointed and naked breasts, both of which were flecked with blood where her nails had passed over them.

Christ, thought Angela, and noticed old scars on Sasha's breasts and chest : if she does this very often, she won't have any tits left. Or any dresses either. What in God's name will she do next?

What Sasha did next was to leave the bed and go from place to place on the floor. At each place where she had traced a circle, she stopped, clawed her fingers through her hair and down her bare torso, and then appeared to address one of the invisible figures she had outlined on the wall. To judge from her face she was whining and howling, but very low, for Angela could still hear no sound at all. At last she went and stood before the space in which she had drawn the big T; she looked at the blank wall with horror, rent her hair once again, then ran back to the bed, where she stooped over Fielding, weeping and shuddering, and enfolded his inert body with her arms and shoulders. She stayed there a long time, during which Angela began to understand.

She understood still more when Sasha began, very slowly and with no help from Fielding, to remove Fielding's clothes, a difficult task which she performed with surprising neatness and dignity. So that's it, Angela thought : she wants to think that he's. . . . No, she couldn't. But oh yes, she could. That big T, sketched by her finger on the wall, that was the clue : a T, the Roman means of execution, which hadn't been a †, as most people supposed, but a large wooden T; it was like that in some of the old pictures. And when the body came down from the T, who tended it? His mother? Or the other Mary, Mary Magdalene? Both; at least, both were there in the old pictures. The Magdalene, thought Angela, had tried to tempt Him and failed; but she still loved Him and followed Him and was there at His execution; and when the body came down, she surely helped anoint it . . . which is just what that crazy girl is doing now. For Sasha had placed the towel over Fielding's crutch and was steadily rubbing the rest of him with Eau de Cologne from the bottle. Fielding lay absolutely still, eyes closed. Dead. But I am the body and the life; there's something stirring under that towel. God, thought Angela, why is this so troubling? Why do I tremble so and sweat?

Sasha now bowed herself reverently away from the anointed body of Fielding, then turned to face the wall. Once more she addressed the figures that only she saw there; but this time she implored rather than howled. Once more she turned to go back to the bed; but this time she did not run back to it, she walked. Walked slowly, paused once to say something to someone, smiled, and slowly walked on. And on the third day. . . . Open the tomb, take off the towel, and Fielding is risen indeed. No more lamentation, thought Angela; rejoice, Sasha, rejoice; rejoice now, as you kneel up over him in that torn and rucked up dress; wipe away the tears from your face and the blood from your bosom, yes, and use the tears and the blood . . . yes, like that . . . to anoint his quickening body, until it stands wet and gleaming, streaked with salt and gore. And now sink on to him, Sasha, and as you impale yourself give a great cry of triumph, and then plunge on down, Sasha, down, down and down.

"Good," said Jules to Fielding, "very good."

He stacked the sheets of script which he had been reading and put them away in a folder.

"You carry on like that," he said, "and there'll be no problems. I take it that Sasha is still under control?"

"Yes. She still tries to drag the proles in where they're not wanted but she's far less insistent. Nevertheless, it's a strain, Jules."

"You're being well rewarded . . . Foxy arrives back tomorrow. Will you come to the airport with me to meet him?"

"What time?"

"Twelve-thirty."

"Sorry, Jules. I've got an appointment."

"Change it. Foxy likes people to meet him."

"This appointment," said Fielding, "is quite unalterable."

Fielding waited under the cypress trees to keep his tryst.

So Foxy arrives today, Fielding thought: he's arriving at this very minute. I'll get hold of him this evening. No; this afternoon . . . as soon as he's finished his reunion with Gretel. He'll be at his most tractable then, poor booby. I've got everything I've wanted so far from these people, so why not this?

If only *this* came off as he hoped, there would be peace and quiet and comfort while he worked on Conrad, and no more truck with Harriet. But did he want to ditch her completely? She had been very loyal and kind. No; he wouldn't desert her altogether; he would just stay away from her when he wanted to . . . which would be for about ten months in every twelve. How would she take it? But that problem was for later, when his time was up in Corfu. Just now what he must remember was that in a fortnight or so Harriet would assume that his 'tour' was over and start pressing again to come and join him. That was the trouble with women: they were so relentless, they never let a man off. Take Sasha . . . no, he would not think about Sasha now. Now he was waiting for another woman . . . and here she was, coming towards him up the path.

Fielding stepped out of the shade of the cypress trees and went to meet her. Up the path she came: Angela Tuck, riding in her coffin. The Church of England chaplain fussed along behind it, and behind him walked Lykiadopoulos and Max de Freville.

The cortège halted by a newly dug grave, and Max came up to Fielding.

"This is a private funeral," he said.

"That's why I didn't come to the service."

"You've come here."

"She was a very old friend."

"You killed her."

"No. It was all her idea."

"You should never have agreed."

"Please, gentlemen," said Lykiadopoulos. "This is not a scene out of 'Amlet."

So Fielding stood his ground and the priest raised his book. "Man that is born of woman. . . ."

Poor old cow. What on earth had happened to her? Heart attack, the doctors had said. The absurd thing was that Fielding hadn't even heard about it until late the following day. For after Sasha and he had finished on that evening up at Max's villa, Sasha had still insisted on their leaving. Max, with characteristic efficiency, had procured a taxi for them within five minutes, and Fielding had not wished to make further embarrassment by asking for Angela before they left. So he had just said to Max, 'Say good-bye to Angie for me', and Max had nodded and said, 'She's probably gone to bed . . . she goes very early these days,' and that had been that.

Then, the next afternoon, he had heard the news on the telephone. From Lykiadopoulos.

'The doctor says it was a heart attack, Mr. Gray. We found her unconscious, Max and I, and we carried her to her bed, and the doctor came and told us she was dead. The authorities are quite satisfied . . . after all, she's been ill for some time— but then again, they don't know exactly where we found her, and they might think it—rather curious . . . if they did. Do *you* know where we found her, Mr. Gray?'

'I've a very shrewd idea.'

'Yes; Max thought you might have. But none of us wants any scandal, so if the authorities should happen to call on you, you of course know nothing at all. You left the dinner table with Miss Grimes, you both packed your cases, and you went.'

"Suffer us not, at our last hour. . . ."

Angela's last hour had been passed behind that mirror. Heart attack. Over-excitement, Fielding supposed. Round about the time that Sasha had started to scream in her orgasm it must all have proved too much for poor Angie, and down she fell stone dead. A good way to go. But was it that way? Or had there been a long agony of gradual suffocation and hideous cramps? He would never know. She had been found unconscious and had later been pronounced to be dead. That was all . . . and that was enough. It was not Fielding's business to pry into what went on through the looking glass. He had kept his bargain on this side of it, and however much Max might blame him, his conscience was quite clear.

"We therefore commit her body to the ground. . . ."

Good-bye, Angie; Angie, good-bye. No trumpets for *you* on the other side, I fear, but doubtless some of your dead lovers will turn out to meet you. There must be a regiment of them there by now. My own father among them . . . though God knows what sort of welcome he'll give you. Because you did for him, Angela, you did for him all right, twenty-five years ago, that summer back in Broughton Staithe. My God, how sexy you were then; no wonder he dropped dead with fucking you, and serve the bastard right. And now it seems that you've gone in much the same way. Funny, that. Oh, Angela, I wish I'd fucked you more often myself. Only that once in Hydra . . . Christ, your honey thighs in those stockings, your wet crotch on my belly, I could almost come just thinking of it. My God, how you'd laugh if you knew : me standing over your coffin with a cock as stiff as you are.

Somewhat invigorated by the funeral, Fielding had a large and late luncheon and then rang up Foxy Galahead's suite to ask if he could drop by for a 'little talk'. Foxy said Gretel couldn't bear to leave him just yet, but he'd be glad to see Fielding in an hour.

And he looked it.

"Jules says you've got Miss Sasha eating out of your hand," he greeted Fielding. "That's my boy."

"If only it can last. But we'll come to that later."

Foxy, alerted by something in Fielding's voice which Fielding had hoped wasn't there, gave him a quick, sharp glance.

"Later?" Foxy said. And then, smiling broadly, "So where did you want to begin?"

*In medias res,* Fielding thought.

"Has it ever occurred to you," Fielding asked, "to have a good dialogue writer permanently attached to Pandarus and Clytemnestra? I mean . . . if you did employ such a man, on a retainer basis, you could call him in whenever you wanted a script to be patched up . . . as you wanted this *Odyssey* of ours patched up . . . for a much lower fee than you have to pay a writer on a temporary contract. And you'd be saving yourselves a great deal of trouble as well as money."

"Would we now?" Foxy said amiably. "And suppose this man wasn't right for a particular job when he was needed? Suppose he could re-dialogue some things quite okay, but we just happened to want some extra cracks for Jack Lemmon, let's say, and this writer couldn't write cracks?"

"Of course you'd have to choose someone pretty versatile."

"Like Fielding Gray, I suppose," said the grinning Foxy.

"Well, why not?"

"Yes. Why not? Other companies have done something like it. What sort of terms would you propose?"

He's making it too easy for me, Fielding thought.

"I should have reckoned," said Fielding, "that a lump sum... paid into a Swiss bank . . . of $50,000 would be a fair retainer for the next ten years. I would then guarantee to be on call for up to six months in any one year, and would only ask a relatively small fee, say $1000 a week, for working while wanted."

The best of both worlds, he thought. All this and lots of time for Conrad too.

"Six months at $1000 a week," said Foxy, "is about $25,000. In ten years you'd have made $250,000. $300,000 with the retainer. Isn't that rather a lot for a part-time dialogue-writer?"

"It would only be as much as that if you called me in for

the maximum period, which I take to be unlikely. But just suppose you did. You'd be getting a total of five years' solid work for $60,000 a year. That's a much lower fee than you're paying me at this minute."

"We need you at this minute. We might never need you again."

"Then all you'd have lost would be your initial investment of $50,000 . . . my retainer. Peanuts."

"Then why do you want them?"

"Not peanuts to me, Foxy. Peanuts to Pandarus and Clytemnestra."

"They're not all that rich, you know. Why do you think I spend so much time finding backers for them?"

"Because they need backers to mount a multi-million dollar picture. But not to pay out a mere fifty thousand to me. They'd do it without thinking twice . . . if you suggested it."

As to that, Fielding wasn't really sure. Was Foxy's pull truly as strong as Max had implied the other night? Never mind : the compliment would help his cause.

"Yes," said Foxy, "I think they'd go along with me. Like you say, they wouldn't think twice . . . which means, baby, that I have to think twice for them. Otherwise I shall screw them up—and find myself walking the plank. You savvy?"

"I savvy, Foxy. So you think twice . . . and then what do you say to my proposition?"

"I say you've made a good try, but no go. It's the fifty thousand that sticks in my arse. Money for work when wanted, yes . . . if it's work we think you can do. But an investment of fifty thousand in your future . . . no." Foxy paused. "You're not all that good, Fielding Gray," he said, smiling affectionately as he spoke. "This *Odyssey* thing suits you, but you're not all that good, and you'll probably get worse, and for all I know you may fall under a bus. There's always others glad of a job. We don't have to retain you . . . not even for peanuts."

Now for it, Fielding thought.

"So that's your decision after thinking twice?"

"That's it, baby."

"Then I'd appreciate it if you'd think three times."

"Why should I do that, baby?"

Foxy smiled more affectionately than ever.

"Sasha Grimes, Foxy. We don't want to upset her. Our money comes from Og-Finck every week for just as long as she says so. Right?"

"Right, baby."

"Well, it's me," said Fielding, "that's keeping her sweet."

"So Jules tells me, baby boy."

"And believe me, Foxy, it's hard work. Now, if I got all depressed and didn't feel up to that work any more . . . and stopped keeping her sweet . . . or even did something that turned her sour. . . ."

Foxy shrugged and went right on smiling.

"Okay, Fielding babes. So you squeeze the lemon, and you turn her sour. Then the money stops . . . and your job with it."

"And your film with it."

"So you've cut off your nose to spite your face." Foxy looked at Fielding's ruined face. "Sorry, baby," he said.

"That's all right. You see, Foxy, I've got other work to go to. Not as well paid as this but far more satisfying. So satisfying, in fact,"—now for the big bluff—"that I'd just as soon go and do it straight away . . . *unless,* Foxy, there's something extra to keep me here . . . like that fifty thousand retainer we were talking of."

Foxy smiled on and said nothing.

"For the rest," Fielding continued, "I shouldn't be heartbroken if this film folded tomorrow. But it would be different with you, I think. You'd have a lot of explaining to do . . . to Pandarus in London and Clytemnestra in New York. You'd have screwed them up good and proper, Foxy . . . and you'd find yourself walking the plank."

"What a cute little cookie you are," Foxy said. "You mean, you'd see all these people we've got here in Corfu done out of a job . . . a job they're relying on for months to come . . . unless I pay you $50,000 to keep on humping Sasha Grimes?"

"Let's not get crude, Foxy. Let's say what I've been saying . . . that if you can't see your way to retaining me under my very reasonable terms, I might just lose heart and start neglecting Sasha. Or I might get so nervous that I'd have a row with her. And then, of course, the consequences for most of us could be very unfortunate."

"All right, baby," said Foxy, "let's say that. And let's add that I appreciate your warning."

"Enough to act on it?"

"Sure, baby, sure. You say that you may get to feeling insecure and then do the wrong thing by Sasha. So I aim to keep you secure, right? What you want is I should take care of your future . . . so now I do just that. Then no more insecurity and no more trouble. Right?"

"Right. Thanks, Foxy."

Fielding gave a grin of genuine gratitude.

"But you'll understand," said Foxy, "that I have to talk to some people first. I have to get agreement."

"But you'll get it?"

"Yeah, I'll get it. They'll listen to me, Fielding baby. Give me three days?"

"A week if you need it, Foxy."

Be generous in victory.

"That's mighty fine of you, Fielding," Foxy said, and slapped Fielding on both shoulders. "I really do appreciate that."

It had all been too easy from the start. Much too easy, Fielding now thought. Was Foxy up to anything? But then . . . what could he be up to? Nothing hostile, Fielding was sure. Because if Foxy tried to pull the rug from under him, he'd bring Sasha down at the same time, and Foxy simply could not risk trouble with her. He might try to stall and cheat over Fielding's $50,000 for a bit; but he could never go into a positive attack without attacking Sasha too.

Fielding's telephone rang. He sighed, picked up the receiver, listened to Sasha, and then told her he'd be along to her room in ten minutes. She had had a new idea for the script . . . and a new idea for later on that night. The long day wasn't by any means over yet. Dear God, Fielding thought : if Foxy knew all that I go through, he couldn't grudge me $50,000.

About the time that Sasha was talking to Fielding on the telephone, Foxy Galahead was talking to Max, Jules and Lykiadopoulos out at Max's villa.

"So we're all agreed," Foxy said. "All of us here have put a lot of effort or a lot of money into this film, and we don't propose to let it be wrecked by Mr. Fielding Gray."

"He could be bluffing," Jules said.

"We can't risk that," said Max.

"Surely," said Lykiadopoulos, "even if Miss Grimes did report unfavourably to the Trust, they wouldn't want to throw away all the money they've already invested. That's what they'd be doing if they stopped remitting now."

"The Trust wouldn't want to bitch us up," said Foxy, "but the Student Committee would. With them it's politics, not money. No, gentlemen : we have to keep Sasha Grimes happy, and that means looking after Fielding Gray."

"You mean, pay him what he asks?" Jules said. "This retainer, as he calls it."

"It's one way, certainly."

"A bad way," said Max. "We couldn't trust him even when he'd been paid."

"Never trust a blackmailer," said Lykiadopoulos, "believe me. Besides, it is bad morals to pay blackmail. And very annoying."

"And very expensive," Foxy said. "Though mind you, Pandarus or Clytemnestra could find the money."

"No money," said Max, thinking of Angela dead in the cemetery, "no money for Fielding Gray."

"Then what else do you suggest?"

Max thought of Angela. He had never been in love with her, but she had been his companion for over ten years. He had never made love to her, but they had often slept together just for fellowship. Now she was there no longer. Ill though she might have been, she would have stayed with him a while yet . . . if it hadn't been for Fielding Gray.

"Suppose," said Max slowly, "suppose we were to get him arrested. Imprisoned for the next few weeks."

Three faces looked at him blankly.

"Listen," said Max, "and I will make it all very plain."

"So you think it won't work?" Sasha said mournfully.

"No, love," said Fielding, "not in this film."

Fielding was having quite a job to persuade Sasha that her new idea for the script (though fundamentally brilliant, Sasha darling) would not do in the context of *The Odyssey*. Sasha wanted Penelope, on being reunited with Odysseus, to burst into a passionate speech about women's rights and how she did not propose to be his chattel just because he had at last condescended to come home. With considerable patience, Fielding had urged first that this would be out of character, and secondly that it would ruin the overall balance of the film. Why should it? Sasha asked. Because, Fielding told her, a sensational and socially aware Penelope would distract both popular and critical attention from the quiet perfection of Nausicaa. This, thank God, seemed to have done the trick, though Sasha was still sputtering on a bit for the look of the thing.

"All right. If you're sure," she said, and finally sputtered out.

So that was task one safely performed. Now for task two.

"And what was your *other* idea?" Fielding asked.

"Aaah," she said.

"But surely," Jules was saying at Max's place, "to get rid of Gray will do more harm than good. Sasha will resent it and then turn on us."

"Only," said Max, "if she thinks we have got rid of him deliberately. But if he were arrested for something entirely outside our scope . . . and if we appeared to sympathise with him and to be making every effort to get him released . . . then she would be both grateful and tractable."

"Good thinking," Foxy said.

"But for what," said Lykiadopoulos, "is Mr. Gray to be arrested?"

*"In 1962," Max said, "Fielding Gray conducted an investigation in Greece and Cyprus for BBC Television. He came to me for some hints . . . I was living on Hydra at the time . . . so I helped him and followed his progress. He was gathering information about the Grivas campaign in Cyprus, and he managed to put his hand on some stuff which was potentially very damaging, not only to Grivas himself, but also to Greek national prestige, and, incidentally, to the American secret service."

"What had *they* got to do with Cyprus?" Foxy asked.

"These days they have something to do with almost everything. . . . Now, as it turned out, Gray failed to establish proper proof . . . those concerned saw to that . . . so he was unable to broadcast what he knew on the BBC. But he did know it, and he still does, and all interested parties must have remained aware of this ever since."

"They'll be keeping on eye on him?"

"No," said Max. "They dealt with him very nastily last time he stuck his nose in, and they'll reckon to have cured him of his curiosity for good. As indeed they did. Fielding Gray will never trouble them again if he can help it."

"Then what's in this for us?"

"Suppose," said Max, "that they thought he *was* sniffing about again."

"But he isn't."

"But suppose they thought he was. Suppose they thought that after eight years he'd decided to have another look for the proof he never found . . . or, rather more likely after what happened last time, to sell a big tip about it all to someone else. There'd be quite a market for a tip-off like that. A possible chance to injure Greek . . . and American . . . prestige. . . ."

"Better still," said Foxy, entering into the spirit of the thing:

*See *The Judas Boy* passim. S.R.

"suppose they thought he'd *already sold* the tip, and they wanted to find out where."

"Good thinking," said Max.

"Corrupt thinking," said Jules. "Not decent."

"He's threatening to wreck our film," said Lykiadopoulos. "He started it all. Do you wish to offer the other cheek?"

"I don't want to smash him to pieces."

"Nor do we," said Lykiadopoulos. "We just want him safely out of the way for a time. Now, Max, my friend. These people you call 'they.' Who are they?"

"People . . . who are concerned for Greek 'face', Lyki. For American 'face' too."

"Not exactly policemen?"

"They have an understanding with the police."

"I am a Christian man, Max," Lykiadopoulos said. "Last time 'they' dealt with Mr. Gray, they were very brutal, you have told us."

"Not physically. They thought of a better way."

"Good. I deprecate physical violence. And so now we interest . . . 'them' . . . in Mr. Gray once more. They are not watching him, you say, but they can be made to think that they should. You know 'their' address?"

"One of their addresses. You'd be very surprised by it."

"I don't wish even to know of it. But what exactly, my friend, are you going to write and tell them?"

"What Foxy suggested just now. That Fielding Gray has just sold . . . or has agreed to sell . . . the injurious story which he found out eight years ago . . ."

". . . Found out but never *proved*, you say . . ."

". . . But can substantiate just far enough to put their enemies on a very strong scent."

"That's it," Foxy said. "Then they'll be wild to find out just how much he's said and to whom. They'll want very badly to have a nice long talk with Fielding Gray."

"And how," said Lykiadopoulos, "do you propose to make

them believe you . . . these gentlemen at the so surprising address?"

"Very fair question," Max said. "I see it all going something like this. . . ."

"Oh Sasha," said Sasha, "you foul bitch. You filthy, disgusting . . . oh, Christ, it's so marvellous . . . dirty, loathsome bitch."

". . . So you see," said Max, " 'they' may not believe what we tell them, but they won't ignore it, because it is not impossible and they'll be able to check up on it with so very little trouble. They've nothing to lose by checking, except a few minutes of their time, and a very great deal to gain. Just a quick look . . . and then they can take it or leave it alone."

"They'll take it," chuckled Foxy. "When do we fix it for? Mr. Fielding Gray is graciously allowing me a week to drum up the money."

"So we fix it for this day week," said Max. "That will give me very good time to make sure that 'they' are ready. Any problems, gentlemen?"

"Yes," said Jules, glad of a chance to diminish Foxy's satisfaction, "who's going to write the rest of the script?"

But Foxy was ready for this.

"Get as much as you can out of him this next week," Foxy said, "and then you finish it."

"Oh hell, Foxy. It won't be the same."

"Look, Jules baby. He's not writing a new script, he's rewriting an old one. You must know by now pretty much how he goes about making the changes. You must be familiar with his cute little tricks . . . his . . . what d'ya call it? . . . ."

"Idiom?" suggested Lykiadopoulos.

"Yeah, yeah. His idiom. You've handled a lot of his stuff, baby, and now you start writing it yourself, see, and bingo."

"Yes. Bingo and little Sasha jumps on my back."

"Little Sasha, Jules baby, is going to be our friend. She thinks we're trying to get her lovely Fielding out of the clinkeroo, and so she loves us, little Sasha does, and helps us all she can to produce a script worthy of her martyred darling who is languishing in the hands of the wicked fascists."

"I think it's a damned shame," said Jules. "He's worked very hard on that script."

"If only," said Lykiadopoulos, "he had confined himself to that, we wouldn't be having this disagreeable conversation. Poor Mr. Gray. He's a classical scholar himself, he should have known better than to indulge his own *hybris*."

"*Hybris*?" said Foxy.

"Insolence," said Max.

"Head-in-air," said Lykiadopoulos, "for which the traditional punishment assigned by the gods is to slip on an unobserved banana skin."

"And tomorrow," chortled Foxy, "we start getting that banana skin ready."

*PART FOUR*

# THE JOURNEY TO ACHERON

Exactly a week after Fielding had first solicited a 'retainer' contract, Foxy Galahead sent for him to come up to his suite.

"I'm sorry it's taken all this time," Foxy said from behind his desk, "but now I've got good news for you."

"Ah."

"Clytemnestra and Pandarus have agreed to retain you," said Foxy, "and instructions have gone from New York to Zürich that $50,000 be paid into your account there. It will be credited to you by tomorrow at the latest."

"Thank you, Foxy. I'm sure you won't regret it."

"I'm sure I shan't, baby. A contract will be prepared in due course on the basis of our discussion last week, and meanwhile will you please sign this receipt?"

"Receipt?"

"For $50,000, baby. Such sums must be accounted for."

"But I don't actually . . . know . . . it's there. Not yet. I'm sorry to be difficult, Foxy. Could I telephone the bank, do you think?"

"Why not go there yourself?" Foxy said. "It'll only take a day or so, and they'll want to see you and talk to you, now all this money's coming in."

Well, and why not? His work was well in hand, despite recent pressures from Jules, and he could do with a rest from Sasha.

"Yes, you go see the bank in Zürich," Foxy said. "Take a long loving look at your statement and introduce yourself to the manager. Have yourself a holiday."

"Thanks, Foxy. I will."

Fielding waved at Foxy across the desk and started to go.

"Oh, and take this receipt form, will you, baby, and post it off as soon as you're happy. Then they can get cracking on the contract."

Fielding went back to Foxy's desk.

"Which shall I send it to?" he asked. "Clytemnestra or Pandarus?"

"Neither."

Foxy passed Fielding an envelope which bore an address typed in capitals: LAMPAS, WILLIAM-TELLRING, 31, ZURICH.

"Lampas?" Fielding said. "Lampas?"

"Clytemnestra subsidiary for handling things in Zürich. They arranged this money of yours, so the receipt goes back through them. You can drop it in yourself if you're passing."

Foxy now handed Fielding the receipt form. It too was typed, and it read:

Received of Lampas, Zürich, the sum of Fifty Thousand Dollars ($50,000) in respect of contractual obligations orally agreed.

Underneath this was an empty space for the date and Fielding's signature, and underneath this again was his name typed in capitals: FIELDING GRAY.

"Fair enough," Fielding said.

He put the receipt form in the envelope and the envelope in his breast pocket.

"Don't forget about it. These accountants like things cut and dried. . . . And just have a word with Jules before you leave. Tell him your trip's got my blessing. One must never," said Foxy, "neglect professional etiquette."

"When shall you be back?" said Sasha crossly.

"I can get a plane on from Athens this evening . . . spend the night in Zürich . . . do my business tomorrow morning . . . and be back here tomorrow night or the morning after."

"What business," said Sasha, "have you got in Zürich?"

Steady now. Sasha did not approve of dealings done through Swiss banks.

"A publisher there is bringing out one of my novels."

This seemed to satisfy her. Lucikly she was not in the mood for conducting cross-examinations.

"Oh Fielding, I'm going to miss you. Can we . . . before you go. . . . ?"

Always part friends.

"Yes," he said. "That would be nice."


In the reconstructed Stoa of Attalus in the Athenian Agora there is a statue of a boy playing a flute. This statue is about a third of the way down the Stoa from the northern end, and next to it there is a door. About the time that Sasha was lowering her tights to take her pleasure with Fielding, a tall man in his early middle age knocked on the door in the Stoa and was admitted into a small and windowless room which was furnished with several metal filing cabinets and a lot of battered statuary.

"Well, Restarick?" said the man who had admitted him, a man with a nose like a hockey-stick and a thin, down-turned mouth.

"Our man's leaving Corfu. Probably leaving Greece."

"For good?"

"I can't say," said Restarick. "But the police have agreed to pick him up at the airport here in Athens. They'll hand him over to us and our Greek colleagues. And if we find anything on him. . . ."

"It's my bet there'll be nothing. Why should he start again after all this time? I simply don't trust your information. An anonymous letter. . . ."

"Anonymous letters have a way of being true. Ask any tax collector."

"Well, we'll see."

"Yes, we shall see," said Restarick. "Because if we do find anything on him, the police will let us keep him for investigation."

"That could be tricky, Restarick. This man's quite a well known writer."

"Only in England."

"Even the English can still make a fuss."

"But it's us Americans the Greeks want to please. The régime needs money, Aloysius. And in any case, if Gray is up to anything, the Greeks will be as interested as we are."

"I still say there could be a nasty fuss if this man is detained for very long."

"Well, yes," said Restarick. "You could be right. So I have a little plan. The American School of Greek Studies."

"What about it?" said the man with the hockey-stick nose.

"You are employed by it." Restarick waved a hand at the stumps of statuary littered round the floor. "You can arrange for Gray to be offered its hospitality."

"Like hell I can."

"Not in Athens, of course. In one of those remote hostelries of yours . . . which are empty at this time of the year. Mr. Gray, let us say, is taken ill somewhere out in the country, he is given temporary shelter in your hostelry, and you then 'discover' who he is . . . an English novelist, with strong antiquarian interests, who is scripting a film about Odysseus. So what more natural than that the American School of Greek Studies should offer so sympathetic a guest all the care and comfort he needs until he is fully recovered? The world hears this and the world is happy."

"His friends hear this and come to call."

"And find that he is indeed ill. Very ill."

"And at once they ask why he hasn't been moved to a hospital."

"Don't nag. Details later. Trust me for that."

"I hope I shan't need to. Because I still think," said the man with the hockey-stick nose (about the time that Sasha was pulling her tights on again), "that we shan't find anything on Fielding Gray."

Jules saw Fielding off at the airport.

"I'm sorry you're going," Jules said.

"Not for long."

"Suppose I need to refer to the script? I mean, those bits I haven't seen yet."

"You've had all I've done so far except for a few pages. They're in the left-hand drawer of my desk."

"I still wish you weren't going."

"Hell, Jules, I've earned a break. It'll be two days at most." Jules shrugged miserably.

"Well, good luck," he said.

They shook hands and Fielding went to the barrier.

Oh Christ, Jules thought, he's deserved everything he's going to get. Foxy and Max are quite right : he's a dangerous threat to the film . . . my film . . . and he's got to be dealt with. And yet . . . he did seem to love the film and he's worked like a slave at it. Worked at it, loved it . . . and threatened to destroy it. So you go to hell, Fielding Gray; but I hope you don't get fried there, and I'm going to miss you very much.

Could this really be true? thought Fielding in the plane to Athens. Was he really richer by $50,000? (To say nothing of a potentially lucrative contract for work over the next ten years . . . a contract under which they would surely employ him occasionally, in order to get value for the retainer.) Could it really be as easy as this?

But what could possibly be wrong? Foxy himself had sent him off to see that all was well, had given him a receipt to sign and post when he was satisfied. Nothing could be wrong . . . now. All this last week he had watched for signs that Foxy or Jules might be meditating some treacherous riposte, but everything about them had been entirely normal. True, Jules had seemed anxious to make him get on with the script rather quicker than usual, but Jules was subject to such fits of restlessness from time to time, and his demands had not been too difficult to meet. The only odd thing had been that Jules had never once indicated that he knew what Fielding was up to, though Foxy must surely have discussed it with him. But probably Jules disapproved . . . how could he not disapprove? . . . and preferred simply to keep silent on the topic. Anyway, why should Fielding worry? He could put up with a good deal of disapproval in exchange for $50,000.

Fielding's plane from Corfu landed at the domestic airport outside Athens shortly after half past three. He took a taxi straight to the international airport, from which his plane for Zürich would leave at five. He presented his ticket at the flight-desk, and received it back together with his boarding card and an exit card, which latter he at once filled in. He then moved towards the Departure Lounge, where he proposed to examine the bookstall and have some tea while waiting for his flight to be called.

Before he could enter the Departure Lounge, he must go through Passports and Customs at the barrier. The Passport man took his passport, his boarding card and his exit card, looked at them, stamped all three, put the exit card on a pile to one side, and flicked the passport and the boarding card back to Fielding. The Customs man just nodded. Fielding went down the stairs into the Departure Lounge and started to thumb through a paperback copy of *My Secret Life* which was prominently displayed on the bookstall.

Restarick and his friend with the nose like a hockey-stick watched Fielding as he went down the stairs.

"That over-night bag he's carrying . . . that's his only luggage," said the man with the hockey-stick nose.

"So I've noticed," said Restarick.

"So it hardly looks as if he means to leave Greece for good."

"But he *is* leaving, Aloysius. Or rather, he isn't. Just you watch. It will be very nice and quiet. No one will even notice what is happening. So when we produce him down in Vassae, we can tell any story we wish."

"Suppose we find nothing on him?"

"Then he will still be in good time for his plane. Now just watch. . . ."

At the bookstall, Fielding was approached by a very ordinary airport policeman, who saluted rather sloppily and explained in passable English that Fielding had forgotten to record his passport number on his exit card. Would he kindly now come and repair the omission? Fielding was pretty sure that he had filled in the card correctly, but if they said he hadn't. . . . After all, he knew himself to be a little light-headed. He hurriedly purchased *My Secret Life* for 200 drachmae, picked up his over-night bag, and started towards the stairs in order to remount them to the barrier. But the policeman shook his head, pointed politely to a door near the duty-free counter, and walked off, leaving Fielding, who was mildly puzzled but well accustomed to the quirks of Greek bureaucracy, to make his own way.

"There you are, Aloysius," said Restarick. "No fuss. He just walks placidly through that door of his own accord, and nobody blinks an eyelid."

Fielding walked through the door.

In Corfu, Max de Freville rang up the international airport at Athens. Several times he was put through to the wrong desk, but at last he was connected with Swissair and learned what he wanted to know.

"So what's happened?" Foxy said.

"He didn't take the plane to Zürich. Swissair say he checked in for the flight, but then someone returned his boarding card to the desk, about ten minutes before the flight was called, and said that Mr. Gray would not be going."

"So they've got him in Athens."

"It seems like it."

"Good," said Foxy. "What now?"

"We simply sit here and know nothing. As far as we're concerned, Fielding Gray set out from here to Zürich early this afternoon and is expected back tomorrow night or the morning after. When he fails to turn up we shrug our shoulders and wonder why he's been delayed. After another twenty-four hours, we start to get worried. You make enquiries on behalf of your company, and eventually you get on to the Greek police: your British employee, Mr. Fielding Gray, is missing . . . has there been an accident?"

"And has there?"

"The police promise to enquire. Some time later they ring you back and give you the official hand-out. They very much regret that Mr. Gray is being held for investigation. *My* script-writer, you scream : *what* investigation? The police are sorry, *kyrios,* but the matter is . . . confidential. You start yelling about consuls and lawyers. Please, *kyrios,* this will not improve matters : the police will inform you as soon as there is anything more you should know. Then you tell everyone here what is going on, and you comfort the outraged Sasha, and assure her that everything possible is being done to get her Fielding back from those fascist beasts."

"The trouble is," said Foxy, "that something *will* have to be done. Just for the look of it. If I do too little, Sasha will get savage; and if I do too much, they might actually let him out."

"We shall have to strike a very delicate balance," said Max. "Exactly how we manage it must depend on the official version of what's going on."

"They'll claim he's being held for investigation . . . so you said."

"That's what I'm expecting. But there are other formulae, and a wide range of official attitudes to go with them. When they've spoken their lines, Foxy, we can start scripting yours. . . ."

When Fielding had been gone for two days, Jules Jacobson went to his room to collect the sheets of script which Fielding had said were in his desk. Jules took them from the drawer and read them, and then poured himself a whisky from Fielding's bottle. He drank it down in one, looked sadly round the room, and then went downstairs, where he instructed the management to pack up all Fielding's belongings and put them in store until further notice.

Fielding was being driven out of Athens. Restarick was at the wheel, while Fielding was sitting in the back with a stocky man who had a dark skin and close-cut hair. This was the first time Fielding had seen this particular man, and he did not like the look of him. Greek, Fielding thought; or perhaps Greek-Cypriot. Aloud he said :

"Where are we going?"

"We are going to a place called Vassae," said Restarick.

"Where the temple is?"

"Not far from it."

"Why?"

"So that you can have a nice rest," said the man beside Fielding, "after which you will be able to explain yourself more satisfactorily than you have done so far."

"There is nothing to explain."

"There is an unsigned receipt for $50,000 to explain," said Restarick from the front.

"I've told you. I've been telling you for two days. That is for money which is being paid to me by the film company Clytemnestra."

"The receipt says it is being paid by Lampas of Zürich."

"A Swiss subsidiary of Clytemnestra."

"Which Clytemnestra has never heard of," said Restarick. "We have rung Clytemnestra in New York, and they know of no subsidiary called Lampas. And they know of no payment to you other than £1000 a week for your present engagement."

Fielding shifted sweatily from ham to ham.

"Then there's been a mistake. Did you try Mr. Foxe J. Galahead in Corfu?"

"We did. He knows of no payment either."

Fielding went cold.

"All he knows is that you asked his leave to go to Zürich for a day or so. Private business, he understood. He expected you back this morning at latest and was beginning to get worried. We were able to reassure him."

"What did you tell him?"

"That you were in good care. We asked him too about Lampas of Zürich. It meant nothing to him."

Fielding went colder.

"But he suggested," Restarick continued, "that perhaps this private business you mentioned to him was to do with a company called Lampas. Although he had not heard of it, it might nevertheless exist. The only trouble is, Mr. Gray, that the company does not exist. Nor does the address on that envelope. A little work with Swiss directories has made that very plain."

"For Christ's sake," Fielding said, "what the hell can it matter to you?"

"We have memories," said the man beside him. "We remember your escapade in 1962."

"The devil you do. And what's it got to do with all this?"

"Lampas," said Restarick. "A Greek word in origin."

"Meaning a beacon," said the man beside Fielding.

"Thank you, Savidis." Restarick started to accelerate along the highway to the Isthmus. "A beacon. Just the sort of silly symbolical name such organisations always adopt."

"Organisation?" said Fielding stupidly.

"Yes. Not a company, that appears in respectable directories, but an organisation of another kind. You should know."

And he did know. Lampas. The word had struck a faint, uneasy chord when he first saw it on the envelope, but Foxy's plausible words had reassured him at once. Now he remembered: Harriet, years ago, babbling away about some new movement which they ought to subscribe to, an anti-fascist, anti-neo-colonialist movement, Lampada, she thought it was called, she had the details in a letter from a friend upstairs; and himself, Fielding, snarling that he was sick of all this left-wing rubbish, that he wouldn't give a penny; then a minor row and Lampada forgotten by mutual consent. Until now. Lampada : accusative singular of Lampas, feminine, a beacon.

"Just the sort of organisation," Restarick said, "that would be interested in what you discovered in 1962."

"Balls."

"It wasn't balls. You know that."

"I could never prove it. You know *that*."

"But you could put anyone who was interested on the right

track, and you can bet your life where it would lead 'em. To new knowledge of American interference . . . past and then present, Mr. Gray . . . in Greece and the eastern Mediterranean. Just the job for Lampas."

"At a price of $50,000?"

"Lampas has come a long way these last few years. Russian money. Guilty liberal money. This sort of thing is very much in fashion among the trendy rich."

"But $50,000 . . . just for a lead?"

"A great deal, certainly. We'll come to that in a moment. But first, Mr. Gray, do please recognise the logical case against you. We receive an anonymous tip-off that Mr. Fielding Gray, who is in Greek waters for an ostensibly innocent purpose, is in fact up to his old tricks and may be carrying evidence to that effect. The next thing we know, you are trying to leave Greece . . . carrying an unsigned receipt for a large sum of money which we deduce that you are going off to collect."

"From a non-existent company," said Fielding wearily, "at a non-existent address."

"From an existing organisation, whose representative you are obviously going to meet. Somewhere, anywhere in Zürich or Switzerland. Only you know the rendezvous."

"Only you . . . so far," Savidis said.

"The receipt, already prepared, is clearly your warrant of *bona fides*," Restarick went on. "The fictitious address on the envelope is probably some coded instruction for the person you are to meet. So off you go to meet him, to deliver your information and collect your fee . . ."

". . . But never even got there," said Fielding crossly. "So where does that leave us?"

"Sitting in this car," said Restarick, "wondering what you would have said if you *had* got there. And how much you have already said here in Greece. Because the receipt, already prepared, proves that you had already agreed a price with somebody . . . in Corfu, we presume. You wouldn't have told him everything, as he wasn't paying you out himself, but in order to get him to agree such a very large price, you must have dished out a very tasty appetiser. What was it, Mr. Gray? And to whom did you serve it?"

Fielding shrugged hopelessly.

"We shall ask again," said Savidis.

"Indeed we shall. You see, plainly the man in question is highly regarded by Lampas. He must be, so to speak, their resident expert here in Greece. The resident expert, responsible to chiefs who are based in Switzerland or elsewhere. He assesses the quality of information on offer, he sends those like yourself, who offer it, to Switzerland to deliver it, and he authorises—or at least suggests—the payment of very important sums. So he himself must be very important to Lampas . . . and to us, Mr. Gray."

"He is a fiction of your own making."

"Who is he, Mr. Gray? And how much did you tell him before he sent you off? In Vassae we shall have plenty of time to find out."

"It seems," said Foxy Galahead, "that he never went to Zürich but had some kind of nervous breakdown instead."

Foxy was talking to Jules and Sasha in his suite. Sasha was drinking fresh lemon juice and Jules was gloomily drinking gin. Every now and then Sasha looked with disapproval at Jules's gin, though in fact it had cost rather less than her own lemon juice.

"Someone rang up," Foxy said, "and told me he was Aloysius Sheath of the American School of Greek Studies. He was down at one of the School's hostelries, he said, at a place called Vassae, he said . . . does either of you know where that is? . . ."

". . . Ancient site," muttered Jules, "in the western Peloponnese."

". . . And he'd found someone wandering round a temple or something who afterwards turned out to be Fielding Gray. Fielding was in a terrible state, according to this Mr. Sheath, and hardly knew who he was. He talked a lot of rubbish about lump payments and banks and holding companies . . . can either of you make sense of *that*? . . ."

". . . He never spoke of money to me," said Sasha.

"Jules baby?"

Jules just shook his head and wished that Sasha weren't there, so that Foxy could stop putting on an act and tell him what had really happened.

". . . But eventually," Foxy was saying, "Fielding talked about Corfu and what he'd been doing here, so Mr. Sheath got my name out of him and was able to call me up. He says that finally Fielding went on a terrible crying jag, sobbing his heart out about Greek hexameters and compressed prose equivalents and oh, Homer, Homer, and was he worthy . . ."

". . . Oh, poor Fielding," Sasha said.

". . . So this Aloysius Sheath gave him a lot of sleeping tablets and sent for the doctor. The doctor said keep him quiet and don't move him and send for a specialist. So Mr. Sheath and his friends are taking care of Fielding in this hostelry, and they've sent for the psychiatrist who attends the American School in Athens. Very sensible, I'd say."

"I'd like to go there and see him," Sasha said.

"I'd wait here, baby, until they know exactly what's to be done. Mr. Sheath will call me again as soon as he's learned what the psychiatrist has to say."

"You'll tell me at once, Foxy?"

"Of course, Sasha baby."

"Then I think, if you'll excuse me, I'll go and lie down."

Foxy saw Sasha solicitously to the door.

"Now what is all this?" said Jules when Foxy came back.

"Just like I told you. A man rang up calling himself Aloysius Sheath and gave me that spiel about Vassae and nervous breakdowns."

"It can't have been like that."

"I don't know how it was, Jules baby, but that is obviously how . . . they . . . wish us to think that it was. This is what Max calls the official hand-out. You see, *they* don't know that we want them to keep him, so they think they've got to find a respectable excuse."

"They certainly have . . . if the American School backs it."

"The American School backs it, baby. I called them to check. Yes, they have a man called Aloysius Sheath, yes, he's down at their hostelry at Vassae, and yes, he's been on to them with some tale about a stray Britisher he's taken in."

"But if they're doing it this way," said Jules, "they'll have trouble on their hands before long. Sasha Grimes, for one, is going to be knocking on their door at Vassae."

"No trouble," Foxy said. "There are lots of good reasons why a psycho patient might not be allowed to see company."

"But sooner or later . . ."

". . . Sooner or later, Jules, they'll realise that he's no use to them, and then they'll let him go anyway. I don't think he'll show his face back here . . ."

". . . But he might tell Sasha or someone what had happened. That he'd been framed."

"And Sasha or someone might think, 'What the hell, he's had a nervous breakdown.' "

"Too many 'mights', Foxy."

"Very true baby. So now we use every second we've got, and we get to finish this mother-fucking film on the double."

Aloysius Sheath, with the nose like a hockey-stick, took Fielding for a walk round the temple of Apollo the Saviour at Vassae. Savidis, with the close-cut hair, came along too, walking always just behind them.

"The odd thing about this temple," said Aloysius Sheath, "is that it was erected in the loneliest part of the country. Pausanias says it was paid for by the people of Phigalia in gratitude to Apollo for their deliverance from the plague. But Phigalia was a long way from here . . ."

". . . And now," said Savidis, "there's nothing left of it. The only thing round here is this temple."

The grey columns sprouted from the grey rock. To the south a shallow mountain valley, broken by spurs, receded towards a backdrop of angular and intermittent peaks. To the north the same valley became a huge, swirling rift, which debouched on to a plain many hundreds of feet below. Grey sky and grey scrub and grey rock. Not a man, not an animal in sight anywhere. Not a house either . . . except the House of Apollo the Saviour.

"Four thousand feet up, we are," Savidis said.

"And yet outside Athens there is not a better preserved temple in Greece. Of course," said Aloysius Sheath, "we've helped a lot with that. They're very grateful. Now then. . . . You'll notice that it has six columns front and back, and fifteen on either side instead of the usual twelve. There are thirty-seven of them still standing here, but twenty-three panels of frieze have been carted away by . . . guess whom . . . the British. . . ."

Later on they walked back along the narrow, stony track that led up the valley to the hostelry. This was built between two spurs, sheltered from winds both north and south, and hidden from the road which ran past the temple.

"Very snug," said Aloysius. "We'll do very well here for a time. Very snug and very discreet."

"My friends in Corfu will find me."

But which of them were still his friends?

"My dear fellow," said Aloysius, who spoke a very anglicised American, "they already know where you are. I was the one who telephoned to tell them. They were very anxious about you, but I was able to reassure them. No one will come up here until we give the word."

"What did you tell them?"

"That you were ill with overwork and needed rest."

"They believed it?"

"Why shouldn't they? Responsible members of the American School of Greek Studies do not go round disseminating lies about distinguished English novelists."

"Except that *you* do."

"But you are ill with overwork. You took on too much when you took on this business with Lampas. And now you must be cured of your illness."

"Yes," said Savidis, "by having the truth sweated out of you."

And now, at last, Fielding more or less understood the nature of the trap which had caught him. These people thought he was the real thing and no one would ever undeceive them. They would keep him here till he told what they thought he had to tell, and Foxy would be only too happy to let them keep him. No one at all would agitate or protest, because on the face of it there was nothing whatever to protest about : he was the sick guest of the American School of Classical Studies.

"What do your superiors at the American School think?" he asked Aloysius.

"That I am down here studying such carving as remains in the temple, and have given graceful assistance to a distressed English traveller."

"Oh God," said Fielding, "what am I to do?"

"Tell us what we want to know. If you do it nicely, *we* might even pay you a bit."

"I've nothing to tell that you don't know already. Can't you believe that?"

"No," said Savidis.

"You see, my dear chap," said Aloysius, "your record is against you. You have gone in for this kind of thing before; you know your way around in these circles. So when we find a piece of paper on you that says 'Lampas', we take it at face-value . . . especially as no one at all supports your own explanation."

"You can't get blood out of a stone."

"You're not a stone," Savidis said.

"Come along, both of you," said Aloysius, "it's time for tea."

The next evening Aloysius Sheath telephoned Foxy Gala-head again. Foxy listened carefully, then sent for Sasha and Jules.

"Good news about Fielding," he told them. "On the whole, that is. Apparently the psychiatrist says that all he needs is rest and quiet. Vassae's a splendid place for that, so his good friends there will look after him."

"Sounds all right," muttered Jules.

"The only thing is," said Foxy, who was reporting absolutely truthfully, "they say no visitors for the next week. It's definitely overwork that has caused the trouble, and if one of us went to see him, he'd start asking about the film and the script, and get all upset again."

"He must want to know about it all," Sasha said.

"I told them to tell him we could manage. Tell him 'Jules is making out', I said."

"I am too," said Jules, looking more cheerful. "I've studied the way he went to work, and Sasha," he put in tactfully, "is giving me some useful tips. I shall be able to finish off that script."

"Surely," said Sasha, "he'll be back to do that himself."

"One can't be sure," said Foxy.

"Well," said Sasha, "I shall go to see him as soon as the week is up. Is that all right with you, Foxy?"

"You forget, baby," said Foxy, "it's no longer me that employs you. You go where and when you please."

"'Jules is making out'," said Aloysius to Fielding. "That was the message."

"So you see," said Restarick, "they're quite happy without you. No one is ever indispensable."

Restarick was standing in front of a log fire in the hostelry, holding a glass of ouzo. Savidis was cooking the dinner in the next room, whither Aloysius, who fancied his culinary gifts, now went to assist. The hostelry, as Aloysius had said, was very snug and despite its remote situation was well supplied from Andritsaena, the nearest town. In other circumstances, thought Fielding, one could have been very happy here : even as it was, he was getting quite attached to the cosy domestic routine. He got up from his chair and helped himself to another drink.

"That's right," said Restarick, "I'm glad you're feeling at home."

"One makes the best of things."

"Of course. We hope you will do just that. We don't want to be nasty," Restarick said. "All we want is for you to tell us who you were in touch with and how much you had to reveal in advance to get an offer of $50,000. As soon as you've told us the truth about that . . . the truth, of course, Mr. Gray . . . we shall let you go and give you $1500 for your time and trouble. I cannot say fairer than that."

"No," Fielding agreed. "But I've been in touch with nobody and revealed nothing. I cannot say truer than that."

"We think you can. And if you don't, we shall have to turn nasty after all. Now, let me see. Physical violence? Torture? No, of course not. Much too crude, and makes a bad impression with the public if it comes out later. But there are other ways. You see, your friends know that you've had a bad nervous breakdown; so they wouldn't be at all surprised at some further failure, mental or perhaps moral. For example, we could arrange it all something like this. . . ."

As Restarick started to tell him how they could arrange it, Fielding forgot about his drink and rapidly lost the excellent appetite which he had been building up for his dinner.

A week later, Sasha Grimes took an aeroplane to Athens, where she hired a car and set out for Vassae. She was looking forward very much to seeing Fielding, whom she expected to find almost recovered. At Foxy's sensible suggestion, she had telephoned ahead to say that she was coming, and Aloysius Sheath had sounded very pleased.

'We'll get a room ready,' he had said, having first given her some helpful directions about the route.

Sasha reached Vassae towards evening, as Aloysius Sheath had told her she would, and parked her car in the small park near the temple of Apollo the Saviour. Then, following Aloysius's instructions, she walked along the path up the valley, skirted the first of the two spurs, and approached the hostelry, which looked like an elaborate German hunting lodge. When she knocked on the front door, a polite servant appeared, very trim with his white jacket and close-cut hair, and took her suit-case from her.

"Mr. Sheath is in the sitting room," the servant said, and opened the door for her before carrying off her case.

"My dear Miss Grimes, an honour," said Aloysius Sheath. "I was privileged to see you as Katharina last year in London."

"My favourite part," said Sasha. "I am a shrew, you see."

"You don't look it. Have a drink."

"I'd rather see Fielding," Sasha said.

"Of course. Just a moment, Miss Grimes."

Aloysius went out and almost immediately afterwards Fielding came in. How nice of that nice man to leave us alone, Sasha thought. She went to Fielding and kissed him warmly on the lips. He looked well and very happy to see her.

"Fielding. . . ."

"Elena. . . ."

"Fielding?"

"Oh, Elena, I am glad you've come. We can leave tomorrow morning and go back to Corfu together. You've got a car, Elena?"

"*Fielding.*"

"Well, have you?"

"Yes."

"Good. It'll be all right now you're here. They've given you the room next to mine, so we can do it tonight. I've been looking forward to that. Do it tonight and leave for Corfu tomorrow? What do you say, Elena?"

Sasha was about to say a good deal, in her best shrewish style at that, but then she thought about Fielding's breakdown and smiled bravely instead.

"Good," said Fielding, "I thought you'd like the idea of that."

He looked at her happily, then nodded his head. His eyes glazed over, he peered about him and sat down in an armchair, slobbered and then fell asleep.

Sasha went to the door and opened it.

"Somebody, please," she called.

The white-coated servant came across the hall and into the sitting room, took one look at Fielding, lifted the recumbent body from the chair (he must be very strong, Sasha thought), and carried it out. Aloysius Sheath appeared in the doorway.

"Thank you, Savidis," he called over his shoulder. "You know what to do, of course?"

"He . . . sort of fainted," Sasha said.

"Coma," said Aloysius. "I hoped he was over that. I thought he was so much better . . . so did the nurse."

"Nurse?"

"The fellow in the white coat. Very experienced. Doctor Harocopos the psychiatrist sent him down from Athens to help. I was going to send him back tomorrow, but now . . ."

". . . Mr. Sheath. He . . . Fielding . . . thought I was someone else."

Aloysius shook his head.

"What can we do?" said Sasha.

"Harocopos said there might be relapses."

"You'll send for Doctor Harocopos?"

"If the nurse thinks it's necessary. Miss Grimes, I am sorry. We thought he was ready to see people. I don't quite know how to say this" . . . Aloysius wrinkled his hockey-stick nose all down the shaft and round up the hook . . . "but let's put it this way. The nurse understands this illness. The School in Athens will send any help we need. Meanwhile, it seems that . . . you can't do much good."

"You mean, I've already done harm?"

"Perhaps. It's our fault for letting you come. But there it is."

Sasha, full of compassion, uneasiness, and resentment (which she knew to be irrational) at being called 'Elena'; rather disgusted by the slobbering object that had been carried away by the nurse; rather impressed by the nurse himself and by Aloysius Sheath's good will; confident in the resources of the American School in Athens; agonised at the thought of sleeping under the same roof as Fielding yet not being able to go near him : Sasha, confused yet reassured, desiring Fielding yet loathing him, wanted only one thing : out.

"There is an hotel the other side of Andritsaena," she said, "which I passed on the way up. I'll spend the night there."

"You'll come back tomorrow?" said Aloysius kindly.

"No."

He nodded in sad approval.

"You don't think he should go to a . . . to a hospital, Mr. Sheath?"

"Not in Greece," said Aloysius with gentle emphasis, "not in Greece. I'm sorry you can't take a better report back to Corfu, Miss Grimes, but let's hope he'll improve before long."

When Fielding woke up, Restarick and Savidis were standing over his bed.

"What happened?" he said.

"You had a visitor," said Restarick. "Can you remember? Miss Sasha Grimes."

"Yes, Sasha. Where is Sasha?" said Fielding sitting up urgently.

"She didn't much care for your behaviour, and she's gone. You mistook her for someone else, you see. And then passed out."

"Oh Christ. What have I done?"

"You've done nothing," said Savidis. "We did it."

"We gave you a preparation," said Restarick, "which made you suggestible. In your tea. Then we told you that you were going to see an old friend. You were talking to Aloysius the other day about a starlet called Elena . . . and very amusing you were, Aloysius says . . . so we decided to tell you it would be her. Elena was coming to see you after tea, we said. Elena . . . Elena . . . Elena."

"And I fell for this?"

"You couldn't help it. You saw, as you were bound to, this Elena. We understand these things," Restarick said. "These days they play an important part in our profession."

Fielding gave a little moan and lay back.

"That's right," said Restarick, "you stay there and have a

good rest. But remember. If you don't tell us what we want to know, we shall very soon have to start the treatment of which I told you the other day. After what's happened this evening, I think you can understand that it will be effective. The stuff we used just now is harmless in small doses; but there are other things which are less so."

When Restarick and Savidis left him, Fielding lay and thought about 'the treatment'. Restarick had explained very carefully about this. They did not wish to use it, Restarick had said, because it would make for permanent mental damage; but since the world was now amply prepared for Fielding to exhibit signs of mental oddity when he emerged, they could probably get away with using it, and were ready to take the risk if they had to. They would start by trying a truth drug. Not much harm in that, but little good either, from Restarick's point of view, because someone who had been given a truth drug was just as likely to start spouting childhood secrets or to confess a fondness for shoplifting as to reveal what was actually required of him. Truth drugs were random in their operation : Restarick desired relevance and precision. So when, as was probable, the results of administering the truth drug proved unsatisfactory, they would try something else . . . a moral strategy rather than a pharmaceutical one, though it too involved some use of drugs. It could be described, perhaps, as a kind of spiritual blackmail, and as Fielding thought about it now he hugged himself in terror beneath the sheets.

How long before they would start? Clearly they were indeed reluctant to do so, or they would have begun long since. How long had he been at Vassae? Well over a week. Time was going on. . . . Harriet, he thought suddenly : yes, *Harriet*. She would think that by now he was back in Corfu from his 'tour' ('a month or so', he had said). When he failed to communicate with her by letter or by cable, she would do one of two things : either she would come straight out to Corfu to confront him . . . God knew, she had done that often enough in the past . . . or she would telephone the Corfu Palace first to find out what was going on. And when she did find out, as in either case she was bound to, when she heard that he was 'ill at Vassae', she would come there to gather him up. Harriet would not be put off if he thought she was someone else or called her once or twice by the wrong name. She would know he was in trouble, she would love him as she always had, she would stay with him, stand by him, and take him home. Oh Harriet, Harriet in Norfolk, hear my call *de profundis* and come to take me home.

Harriet behaved just as Fielding thought she would . . . up to a point. About a week after she received the last of the four hasty jottings which he purported to have written while on tour, she began to expect further word, to tell her that he was or soon would be back in Corfu. Further word of some kind at any rate. Since none came, she decided to telephone the Corfu Palace, and began by asking for Mr. Fielding Gray.

The concierge, with whom she was connected, knew exactly where Fielding was: he was convalescing from some illness at Vassae, and his belongings were being held for him in a storeroom until there should be further instructions. But this was not what the concierge told Harriet. For he remembered that the *kyrios* Gray had been paying him regularly to be prepared to tell a simple lie to inquisitive ladies who might chance to telephone from England. True, the weekly payments had now lapsed, but the *kyrios* had been very generous, there was no reason to suppose that his wishes had changed, and here was a chance to perform an effortless act of kindness for which the *kyrios* would doubtless reward him should he return to the hotel.

The concierge therefore consulted the note he had made when the matter was originally discussed, and politely informed Harriet that Fielding was to be gone from the hotel for some four or five weeks and had not, as yet, sent back a forwarding address.

"But surely," Harriet wailed, "he's *already* been gone for four or five weeks."

The tone of Harriet's voice aroused the concierge's compassion . . . for Fielding and not for Harriet. So he simply repeated what he had told her and put down the receiver, congratulating himself on having done a good turn to a fellow male.

Oh dear, oh dear, thought Harriet in Broughton Staithe. He must have changed his plans. Why hasn't he told me? He said nothing in those beastly letters except how busy he was on his tour, and busy he doubtless was, but when he knew his plans were changing, why didn't he say? If he could tell the hotel in Corfu, he could have told me, three words by wire would have been enough, *why didn't he tell me* instead of leaving me to find out from some foolish concierge . . . who couldn't even give an address. How thoughtless, Harriet told herself, how careless, how very, very unkind. He doesn't care, he can't, whether I come or not, it's been like this a long time now, I should have woken up to it before, he doesn't want me to come, that's what it is, he doesn't want me there at all.

Always before, when she had thought this, she had simply packed and gone right after him. But this time she had no idea whatever where to go; and something about this particular piece of cruelty, so easily avoidable, so shabbily prolonged, had stricken all present will to act and poisoned all hope. Leave him be, wherever he is, she thought : there's nothing I can do now. Sooner or later, I suppose, he will come back to England . . . but after this, do I really want to see him any more?

In Corfu things carried on quite smoothly. Foxy went away and came back; Lykiadopoulos went to Milan on business and stayed there; Max de Freville went nowhere. Circe came out again from England to re-make her scenes with Odysseus, remade them, and departed; and Sasha Grimes, who was rather subdued these days, cooperated with Jules over the script, doing everything as she thought Fielding would have wanted it done. She felt guilty about the way she had left him in Vassae and spoke of him often, wanting reassurance.

"There's nothing you can do for him," said Jules day after day, "except hope that he gets better. You know that."

Sasha, remembering the glazed eyes and the slobbering lips,

was compelled to agree. After all, Aloysius Sheath and the nurse were there to take care of Fielding; they did not need her at Vassae, and to be honest with herself she was very glad they didn't.

"Now," Jules was saying to her, "here is a list of the scenes I want to get finished before Christmas. They cover Odysseus's stay with the swineherd and the earlier episode with the Cyclops. I've pencilled in the camera directions on my script, but I want you to look 'em over for me before I go firm on them. Okay?"

It was an honour to be asked for such specialised advice, and well Sasha knew it. She spared a quick, sad thought for Fielding and settled to her work.

"As I thought," said Restarick to Fielding, "truth drugs have proved no good on you. You've told me nothing."

"I've nothing to tell, that's why."

"You had plenty to say, mind you. Stories about hitting your mother and God knows what. But nothing I wanted to hear."

"I can't tell you what I don't know."

Restarick sighed.

"I'm going away for a little while," he said. "Savidis and Aloysius will take care of you as usual. When I come back, we start the treatment proper."

Fielding shrank.

"Yes," said Restarick, seeing this. "Think about it while you have time. Small doses at first, you'll resist them of course, but you'll be given more and more, and eventually you'll be hooked. You know what happens to people who get hooked on heroin. They deteriorate. They gibber, and go grey, and stop washing. They do no work, even if they're offered it; they live, while they do live, only for their vice. Sad . . . but just what people might expect . . . or so they'll say when we turn you loose . . . of someone who's had a nervous breakdown. That was only the beginning, they'll say; that was when he started to crack up. Poor Fielding Gray."

"Please," said Fielding, "please don't do that to me."

"I must. I must frighten you into telling me what I *must* know, and in order to frighten you I must mean what I threaten. I do mean it, Mr. Gray. You choose; either you come clean or you turn dirty. Into a dirty, shambling junky . . . human refuse."

"Look," said Fielding, "I am a reasonable man and I am not brave. In the face of a threat like this, if I had anything that I could tell you, I should certainly yield. Can't you believe that?"

"Oh, I do. I believe that you will yield. The only question is when. For $50,000, which may still be waiting in Zürich, you obviously think it's worth resisting us till the very last moment. In the forlorn hope, I suppose, that something will turn up. Or perhaps you still think that we're bluffing?"

Fielding bowed his head.

"Well, nothing will turn up," Restarick said, "and as soon as I get back here you'll find out that we aren't bluffing. I'll be with you again just before Christmas, Mr. Gray; whether or not we shall make merry at that season must depend on you."

*PART FIVE*

# THE WILL OF ZEUS

A few days before Christmas, Max de Freville's guests arrived at his villa. They were the Marquis Canteloupe, Minister of Commerce in the new Conservative Government, Somerset Lloyd-James, M.P. (Canteloupe's understrapper in the House of Commons), and Captain Detterling, M.P. and publisher, a distant cousin of Canteloupe.

"We'll have a nice quiet time this evening," Max told them as they sat drinking in one of the little arbours off his lawn. "Party night tomorrow."

"Good sort of party?" asked Canteloupe.

"Pandarus's Christmas piss-up."

"Pandarus?"

"The film company out here. Making *The Odyssey*."

"Good," said Detterling, "I'll be able to get hold of Fielding Gray."

"I don't think so," said Max, and told them about Fielding's nervous breakdown at Vassae.

"What's his trouble this time?" Canteloupe asked.

"Overwork," said Max.

"He's used to hard work," said Lloyd-James.

"This time he took on too much."

"You mean," said Detterling, "that he couldn't cope with writing for films?"

"More or less that."

"Well, I hope there's no permanent damage," said Detterling. "He's doing a book on Conrad for me and Gregory Stern. That's what I wanted to talk to him about. I'd better go and see him at Vassae."

"I wouldn't," said Max, "not until he's better."

He told them of the report which Sasha had brought back with her.

"Then I'll leave it till after Christmas," Detterling said. "He sounds a real mess. Has he been drinking?"

"He's always been drinking," said Lloyd-James, "but I thought I'd heard that this woman of his . . . Harriet something . . ."

". . . Ongley . . ." put in Detterling.

". . . I thought I'd heard that she kept him straight about his drinking."

"Harriet Ongley hasn't been here to keep him straight," said Max de Freville.

"You never know with boozers," Lord Canteloupe said, "but talking as an old soak myself, I find it very odd that he should have gone all the way to this Vassae place just to get himself sozzled. I mean to say, he could have done that here."

"No one said it *was* drink," Max reminded them. "The doctors say nervous breakdown."

"Whatever that may mean. Look at that fellow, Peter Morrison. They said he had a nervous breakdown, but all it was," said Canteloupe, "was a fit of pique because he didn't get a job when we came to power in June."

"He never expected one," said Detterling; "he couldn't have. He was out of the House for a good twelve years . . . right up till that by-election in sixty-eight."

"He expected something," insisted Canteloupe, "so when we gave him nothing he got into a tantrum, and they called it a nervous breakdown."

"He doesn't want anyone to know this," said Detterling, "but his elder son's got meningitis. That's what upset Peter."

"Oh," said Canteloupe bleakly. "Will the boy die?"

"Worse. He'll be potty for life. He'd just got a scholarship to Oxford."

"Oh," said Canteloupe again. "Let's go back to Fielding Gray."

"There's nothing to go back to," said Max. "He's had a mental breakdown, and some fellow from the American School of

Greek Studies found him in a bad way at Vassae. They're looking after him in a hostelry there. We'll be told when he's fit for visitors."

"I still don't understand," said Canteloupe, "why the devil he went to Vassae."

"Apparently he'd just wandered off there."

"He was always wandering off somewhere," said Somerset Lloyd-James.

"And so far," said Detterling, "he's always wandered back. But I do want to see him before I go home."

"Leave it a few days," said Max. "There'll be plenty of time to think about it after Christmas."

When Restarick arrived back at Vassae, he handed a small and stoutly wrapped parcel to Savidis.

"We'll be needing the things in there," said Restarick, "starting tomorrow. Unless he's changed his mind."

"He hasn't."

"No choice then. Where is he?"

"In his room. Playing chess with Aloysius."

Restarick went to Fielding's room and knocked on the door. Aloysius Sheath's voice told him to enter.

Fielding was lying on the bed, apparently asleep. Aloysius Sheath sat over a chess board on which the pieces were set ready for a game. Opposite Aloysius was an empty chair, at which he now pointed.

"He couldn't start," Aloysius said. "He lay down instead."

"Frightened, is he?"

"Sort of . . . numb. While you were away, he kept saying, 'I'd tell him everything . . . if only there were anything. Whatever he does, there's nothing new to say.' You don't suppose," suggested Aloysius, very low, "that he's telling the truth about that?"

"We can't give up now. Mr. Gray," said Restarick, shaking Fielding, "Mr. Gray."

Fielding stirred but did not open his eyes.

"I hear you," he mumbled. "So you're back?"

"Back to keep my word. We'll start tomorrow."

About the same time as Restarick was talking to Fielding, Max de Freville and his friends arrived at the Corfu Palace Hotel for the Pandarus Christmas piss-up.

Since Sasha Grimes had insisted that this should not be elaborate or expensive, Foxy had concentrated on basic essentials. He had provided an ample but plain buffet, two bottles per head of cheap Thracian red wine for the entire company, and a demotic band. The cheap Thracian wine was far stronger than anyone had anticipated, and by the time Max and his party got there it had wrought pretty fair havoc. Angus Carnavon had long since been carried off unconscious, and Margaret Lichfield was dancing frantically with Gretel.

"That lousy Lichfield wants my Gretel," Foxy greeted Max. "Come to the bar."

On the way to the bar, they passed Sasha, who was dancing in a refined but egalitarian way with the clapper-boy, and Elena, who was sitting by the wall munching a huge plate of cold fish.

"Come and meet the guests," said Foxy to Elena. "This here is Dook Canteloupe, and Mr. Devonshire Lloyd-Thing, and Colonel Dett. Dook, Devonshire, Colonel . . . this is li'l Elena, luscious li'l Elena, lovely, luscious, prick-lifting li'l Elena, lovely, luscious, lecherous . . ."

". . . For Christ's sake," said Elena, "give them food and drink."

Food they declined, having prudently dined before coming, but they accepted huge beakers of red wine. When Canteloupe heard it was Thracian, he proposed a Thracian sconce.

"Sconce?" said Foxy.

"All down in one," said Canteloupe, and poured his whole beaker into himself without even swallowing.

Foxy tried to do the same, but he gagged painfully half way through and spouted a jet of wine into the air which came down again on to Elena.

"You mother-fucking pig," said Elena, and put down her

fish with a clonk. "You ruined my dress."

"Elena baby . . . you come with me, and we'll take off that dress and dry it and—"

"—Balls," Elena said.

"Absent friends," said Canteloupe, raising another beaker. "Here's to that one-eyed bugger, Fielding Gray."

Canteloupe poured down his beaker and Elena gave him a quick look.

"You know Fielding Gray?"

"We all do," said Detterling.

"Never mind Fielding," said Foxy, "he's gone off his nut. Nice uncle Foxy-woxy buy li'l Elena a new dress . . . if li'l Elena come and take off the old one."

"I don't go for trips down memory lane," said Elena. "You get Gretel to take off her dress."

But Gretel was leaping through the exit arm in arm with Margaret Lichfield.

Meanwhile, Jules came over to talk with Max, and Somerset Lloyd-James went off to dance with a starlet. Detterling said he was going to have a little go in the Casino (which had now moved in from the Achilleion to the Corfu Palace) and Lord Canteloupe tackled his third beaker, listening vaguely to the conversation between Jules Jacobson and Max. Max had heard from his Greek pal Lykiadopoulos, and it seemed that Lykiadopoulos had got on to something in Italy which might suit Pandarus Films rather well after they were finished in Corfu.

"Can't talk properly in all this racket," Jules said. "Come up to my room for a bit."

"Back before long," said Max to Canteloupe. "Make yourself at home. They're a friendly bunch."

Max and Jules moved off together, and Canteloupe thought it would be nice to make himself at home with that jolly little girl who'd had all the wine spewed over her. Just at the moment, however, she still seemed to be having a pretty fierce conversation with the producer-chappie or whatever he was who'd done all the spewing. Leave them to it, Canteloupe thought: have another mug of this red infuriator first, and *then* we'll see. He moved off to the filling-point.

"Li'l Elena come with nuncle Foxy-woxy," Foxy was saying.

"What's in it for li'l Elena?" said Elena.

"I just said. A lovely new dress."

"Like a lovely new dress which costs five hundred quid," Elena said, "or a mink coat while we're about it."

"That's asking high, baby."

"Not for chewing your old cod, it's not."

"You listen to me, Elena baby. You're bugging me. I don't like greedy girls. You know what happens when people get greedy with Foxy? They come unstuck, baby, when they get too greedy with Foxy J. Galahead."

"Knackers."

"You don't believe me, baby? Then you think what happened to Fielding Gray. He got too greedy with Foxy, too greedy and too smart Master Fielding got . . . so now he's having a breakdown on the top of some fucking mountain."

"You mean . . . that was your work?"

Foxy sucked his wine.

"Sort of, baby. So you watch out, and you come and play pee-wee pies with uncle Foxy, or . . ."

". . . How did you do it, Foxy?" Elena said.

Foxy winked obscenely and belched, then sat down hard on the floor. Elena went over to Canteloupe, confiscated his beaker, and swept him on to the dance floor.

"Zow-eee," said Canteloupe, and put his right hand in the cleft of Elena's bottom.

"Dook Canteloupe . . . you're a friend of Fielding Gray's?"

"I know him a bit."

"This business at Vassae. There's something wrong."

"Thought it was odd when Max told me."

"I don't know the whys and the hows," Elena said, "but there's something in the oven that stinks. Fielding behaved like a swine to me, but I'm not letting him be done down like this. It just isn't decent."

Canteloupe stopped dancing, unhanded Elena's fesses, and looked at her carefully.

"What's not decent?" he asked.

"What they're doing to Fielding."

"How do you know?"

"Because of something I've just heard. Don't ask me any more, because I've got to live here till this lousy film's done. Just you go to Vassae and have a look for yourself."

"We thought of going after Christmas."

"Better go now," Elena said. "Now."

She hurried back to Foxy, who was now slumped against the bar.

"Come on," she said. "Let's go and play pee-wee pies."

"Great, baby." Foxy blundered up against her, spilling more wine on her dress. "Did I say anything just now?"

"Nothing much," Elena said.

"But you went away from me, baby."

"Just saying good-night to a friend. Come on, uncle Foxy-woxy, you come on with li'l Elena. . . ."

A good girl, that, thought Canteloupe. Nice botty. A warm, honest girl. She thinks Fielding Gray's a bastard, but some bigger bastard's shat on him a bit too hard, even for a bastard like Fielding Gray. 'Just you go to Vassae and have a look for yourself . . . now.'

Canteloupe rumbled off to the room which served as the Winter Casino, waved aside the doorman who asked for his ticket, and shipped Detterling off from the Chemmy table.

"But it's my bank next," said Detterling as Canteloupe led him out.

"Go to the telephone," said Canteloupe, "and see if the airport can fix us a private plane. To the airfield nearest Vassae . . . whatever it is."

"Kalamata, I'd say. Can't I run my bank first?"

"No," said Canteloupe, and sent Detterling reeling towards the concierge's desk.

Canteloupe then returned to the Pandarus piss-up and looked for Somerset Lloyd-James, who was prancing gawkily about with a fat girl whose navel was showing.

As the pair passed Canteloupe, he put both hands on Somerset's shoulders.

"Say good-night to Maisie," he said to Somerset.

"I'm called Beryl," the girl said.

"He knows what I mean."

"I'm damned if I do," said Somerset, his pimples glowing with resentment.

"We're going on a trip," said Canteloupe as he ushered Somerset off. "Fielding Gray's in trouble. I've been warned."

"Rubbish. You heard what Max said last night."

"And I heard what I've just heard now."

"Can't it wait till tomorrow? I was hoping to have one of these starlets. I've never had a starlet before."

"They're really only chorus girls."

"Then they'd be that much cheaper, wouldn't they? I can't imagine," Somerset said, "why you want to spoil the evening like this."

"Look," said Canteloupe. "Once upon a time we helped to sod up Fielding Gray, you and I. We had good reason, and I'm not ashamed of it, but we did sod him about something rotten, and now we've a chance to make it up. If my information is correct, that is."

"And if not?"

"We lose nothing except the price of a plane to Kalamata."

"*You* can pay for that," said Somerset lisping with annoyance, "ath you're tho keen. I'm thaving up for a thtarlet."

"Chorus girl," said Canteloupe. "Half of them have got clap. If you start bunking up with that lot, it's six to four on you'll be pissing fish-hooks within a week."

"That's not saying I want to spend good money on lunatic trips to Kalamata. Anyway, we couldn't possibly get there at this time of night."

"Yes, we can," said Detterling, who had just joined them. "We leave in thirty minutes flat. The pilot says there's room for four passengers, so Max can come too."

"Good," said Somerset, "that'll cut the cost."

"No," said Canteloupe, "no Max."

"Why on earth not?"

"Instinct. If my informant was right, there's something nasty going on. Why didn't Max tell us?"

"Perhaps he didn't know."

"Perhaps he didn't. But then again," said Canteloupe, "being Max, perhaps he did. So we go without him."

"But we can't just push off and say nothing."

"That's exactly what we must do," said Canteloupe. "Luckily Max has gone upstairs to talk business with that shonk called Jules something. When he comes down and doesn't see us, he'll think we've all got off with dirty girls from Pandarus, and he'll leave us to find our own way home. We'll be later than he thinks."

In the taxi on the way to the airport, Canteloupe told the others what Elena had said to him.

"But what in the world *can* be wrong?" said Detterling sceptically. "Why should anyone be . . . doing Fielding down . . . as this woman says?"

"Perhaps he's been up to his old tricks," said Somerset, "and underrated the opposition."

Now they were under way, Somerset was enjoying the expedition. Since he himself had no axe to grind (for once), he could simply go along and see the fun. He had always been amused by Fielding's antics and was glad of a chance to find out what was at the bottom of this one.

"Depend upon it," Somerset said, "he's been putting his hot little hand where he shouldn't, and somebody's got out a chopper."

"I only hope he can still use his typewriter," Detterling said. "Gregory and I are setting a lot of store on this book about Conrad."

But far better, Detterling reflected, that Fielding should be the victim of human malice (as now seemed to be the case) than that he should be suffering from a mental breakdown. With malice to combat one could at least see how one stood; with mental disorder there was no knowing where the thing began or ended.

"I rather hope," Detterling now said, "that your little girl was right, Canteloupe. Otherwise we're going to look frightfully silly, charging off like this."

"Better look silly now," said Canteloupe, "than soppy later."

The reason why Canteloupe had got everyone moving so quickly was that he was fiercely offended by the idea that anything untoward could happen to an Englishman (a gentleman at that, more or less) in a foreign country. He believed Elena because he had seen that she was amiable and honest; and believing her, he must assume that Fielding Gray was somehow being got at. Why or by whom was not clear, but one thing certainly was: it was all happening in some mucky little foreign state, and that it should be allowed to happen there showed a lack of respect for the English and for England. These days there was much too much of this kind of thing. Englishmen were being constantly abused and maltreated all over the globe, and no one lifted a finger, let alone despatched a gunboat. It just wouldn't do, thought Canteloupe, and here, thank God, was one instance at least in which the right man (himself) was on the spot when wanted.

"Remember, you two," Canteloupe said, "whatever's going on, we're English and we're on the side of Fielding Gray. We'll take no bloody nonsense from anyone . . . least of all from the natives."

Fielding turned sweatily in his bed. We start tomorrow, Restarick had said; tomorrow, which was now today. Three or four doses, Restarick had said, and you'll need it, you'll have to have it. And when we refuse it you'll talk. After that, of course, we'll set you free, but by then it'll be too late for you, you'll be hooked. So why, oh why, won't you tell us before we begin?

*I've nothing to tell.*

Oh dear, oh dear, oh dear, Restarick had said: then we start tomorrow.

Canteloupe and his chums reached Kalamata airport at four-thirty a.m. After a lot of telephoning Detterling procured them a taxi. "Vassae," said Canteloupe to the driver.

The driver shook his head.

"Near Andritsaena," said Detterling.

The driver spread his hands. Detterling took a touring map from his pocket and showed the driver the route. The driver laughed scornfully. Canteloupe took a large wad of money from his pocket and passed it under the driver's nose. The driver shrugged petulantly.

"He thinks it's too far," said Somerset. "Let me try."

Somerset took off his glasses and tapped the driver on the shoulder. As the driver turned, Somerset looked him in the eyes and grinned. The driver made a quick gesture with the fingers of one hand, turned back to the wheel, clicked off the inside light, and started up the car.

"What was all that about?" said Canteloupe.

"My irises are rather peculiar," said Somerset, replacing his glasses. "Simple people very often think that I have the Eye."

"Savidis knows how to give the injection," said Restarick. "It will be much easier for all of us if you don't struggle."

On the table lay a syringe, which Savidis now picked up.

"Take off your coat," said Savidis to Fielding, "and roll up your sleeve."

Aloysius Sheath came in.

"There are three men in dinner jackets," he said, "coming up the path. They can only be English."

Restarick went with Aloysius to the window. There in the bright morning were three black figures, walking in Indian file : an old man, tall and stooping but with a certain spring in his tread, was leading; a man of vaguely military style came second; and a shambling weed in spectacles brought up in the rear.

"Roll up your sleeve," said Savidis to Fielding.

"Put that thing down," said Restarick to Savidis, "and come with me to the front door." And to Aloysius : "You stay here with Mr. Gray."

When Savidis opened the front door, the old man in the dinner jacket nodded very politely.

"My name is Canteloupe," he said. "These gentlemen are Captain Detterling and Mr. Lloyd-James. We have come to see Major Fielding Gray."

Neither Savidis nor Restarick answered.

"This building does belong to the American School of Greek Studies?" Canteloupe said.

Savidis pointed to a plaque by the door which confirmed this.

"Well, we've had a devil of a job finding you, and now, if you please, we wish to speak with Major Gray."

"He is not well," said Restarick from behind Savidis.

"He will be none the worse for seeing three old friends."

"You don't understand . . ."

". . . That is why I am here. Kindly let me in." Savidis barred the door.

"I am a Minister of Her Britannic Majesty," said Canteloupe, "and these two gentlemen are members of the British Parliament. We demand to see Major Fielding Gray."

"Your writ does not run here," said Restarick.

"And we want none of your British arrogance," Savidis said.

Somerset took off his glasses, looked Savidis straight in the eye, and grinned. Savidis flinched and drew back.

"Peasants never change," said Canteloupe as he walked under the lintel. "You can educate them and dress them up and tell them they're free and equal . . . and the very first owl that screeches they're back on their knees, crossing themselves and snivelling. But you," he said to Restarick, "are not a peasant. You have not even that excuse for your obstinacy. What am I to say to you?"

"You can ask my pardon," said Restarick, "for trespassing on American property. And I shall grant it, on condition that you leave."

There was a scuffling noise from behind a door across the hall, and Fielding shot out, followed by a red-faced Aloysius.

"Oh Canteloupe," said Fielding breathily, "is it really you?"

"It is," said Canteloupe. "What the hell's going on?"

"They're keeping me here," sobbed Fielding. "They're giving me drugs and—"

"—Details later. You're not potty or anything?"

"I shall be if I don't get away."

"Then you can come with us. I ask your pardon," said Canteloupe to Restarick, "for trespassing on American property, and whether you grant it or not we shall now leave."

"Not with Gray."

"Yes, with Gray."

"He's ill, I tell you. Those drugs he's babbling about, he has to have them for his illness."

"Never mind all that." Canteloupe turned to Fielding. "Do you, or do you not, wish to come with us?"

"Yes," said Fielding, "for God's sake, yes."

"Then that is settled," Canteloupe said.

Restarick made a slight movement of menace in Fielding's direction.

"Don't be a cunt," Canteloupe said. "You cannot detain him by force without our bearing witness against you. You cannot detain us by force, because whoever you may be you dare not lay hands on a peer of the British Parliament and a Minister of the British Crown. I don't know what you were up to," said Canteloupe, "and I don't much care; but now I'm here, and that's an end of it. Major Gray is an Englishman and he's leaving with his English friends."

"He won't get far without his passport. You'll never find that without my help."

"If he travels with me," said the Marquis Canteloupe, "he won't need to worry about his passport." And to Fielding, "Come along, my dear fellow, I fancy we're no longer welcome here."

"Ridiculous foreigners," said Canteloupe as they all walked down the path. "All they need is to be *told*. The trouble is, no one's told them for so long that most people have forgotten how."

"It's considered wicked to tell them," Detterling said slyly. "It degrades them, you see."

"Degrades them? A superstitious Greek peasant and a couple of bent Yankees? Who the hell cares," said Canteloupe, "about degrading a shower of shit like that?"

"They were . . . very frightening," said Fielding.

"That's because there was no one there to put them in their place. Of course people can be frightening," Canteloupe said, "if you let them get out of hand. It's happening everywhere: students, coons, labourers, all getting out of hand because no one dares to *tell* them and put them in their place."

"They don't want to listen," said Somerset.

"They've never wanted to listen, but they always have if they were handled right. You just have to bounce them into it, that's what. Frighten them," said Canteloupe, "before they can frighten you."

"Superior fire-power," said Aloysius to Restarick. "You couldn't say no to an English Minister. Unfair opposition."

"If we'd had more time we might have managed. If we'd been warned. . . . Ah, well," said Restarick, "that's that. This round we lose." He picked the syringe off the table on which Savidis had left it half an hour before. "I wonder," he said, "if Gray would ever have realised that there was only a mild tranquilliser in this syringe. That was what really interested me, you know. Lampas we can deal with when and as they show their hand. What fascinated me was not so much what Gray might have had to tell us as the process of breaking him down . . . of reducing him to a gibbering wreck by entirely illusory means. Illusory threats," he mused, "are so much cheaper and less harmful and less incriminating than substantial ones. And just as effective. But there's one thing wrong with them."

"As we've just seen," Aloysius said.

"Yes. It only needs some coarse brute like Canteloupe to appear," said Restarick, "and the whole delicate structure crumbles at the sound of his voice."

"Well," said Canteloupe in the taxi back to Kalamata, "what now? Back to Corfu?"

"No," said Fielding, "or not for me." And he gave a broad account of all that had happened, as far as his own knowledge would serve, playing down his own treachery and playing up everyone else's.

"So it looks as if Max had a hand in it," said Somerset.

"If you remember," said Canteloupe with satisfaction, "I said something of the kind last night. In all the circumstances, we can hardly go back to his villa."

"We can't walk around in dinner jackets for the rest of our lives," said Detterling.

"Well now," said Canteloupe. "You know Max best, so you can go back to Corfu and collect our kit."

"And mine, please," said Fielding. "It's still in the Corfu Palace, I suppose."

"And then you can rejoin us," said Canteloupe, "and we can all go somewhere *nice* for Christmas before going on home. How about Monte? It can be very agreeable in December."

"I wath looking forward to a free holiday," Somerset whined.

"So were we all. But whichever way you look at it," Canteloupe said, "I think we should be wise to leave Greece without undue delay. We'll call in at the Embassy in Athens, to arrange about a passport for Gray and make sure there are no other little difficulties . . . and then we'll take an aeroplane for Nice. And I for one," he said, peering out of the window at the grey scrub and the grey rock, "shall not be sorry to be gone."

From his office behind the American Express in Corfu, the Pandarus accountant in the Red Indian get-up put through another routine weekly payment to Zürich for credit of Fielding Gray. That Fielding was absent, and had been for some time, he was well aware; but no one had told him to suspend Fielding's salary. Although this was probably an oversight, he wasn't going to enquire into the matter, because he was glad of his own five per cent every week, and what was more, he had rather liked Fielding.

'Let him have his dream money,' the accountant thought, 'and much good may it do him, wherever he may be.'

Some weeks after he left Vassae, Fielding had a letter from Jules Jacobson.

'. . . And so now we are nearly finished with the shooting, almost a month ahead of the original schedule. This means that all the more time and money will be available for cutting and tidying, and when that's been done I think I can promise a very passable picture.

'I missed you after your departure, in every way. However, I flatter myself that I got by rather well with completing the script, and Sasha was very clever at going over my stuff and adapting the style to match what you had already written for us. She was upset when she heard that your chums were removing you to England, because until then she'd always hoped you would come back to her in Corfu; but Max de Freville assured her it was all for the best, as your friends had your welfare much at heart. So Sasha settled back to work and was if anything more helpful than ever; I think she saw herself as performing a loyal duty, *in piam memoriam* to you, so to speak. But her piety did not extend to fidelity : she has consoled herself by an affair with the clapper-boy, and there is even talk of their being married some time soon.

'But to get back to our film . . . and when I say "our" I mean it. I have not forgotten the excellent work you put in before other ambitions intervened, and I have arranged that you shall have a full-screen credit. We are not ungrateful, you see. As for money—well, you probably know by now that Foxy, amid all his other preoccupations, forgot to cancel your salary payments. You were paid out for the full period of your contract. Foxy was furious when he found out, but eventually he agreed with me that all things considered justice of a kind had been done.

'So all's well that ends well, except that it might have ended so much better. You see, Fielding, after what you tried to do to Pandarus we can never employ you again. This is a great pity, as Lykiadopoulos has just returned, after a long absence in Italy, with news of a really splendid project of Cine-Milano's . . . in which, at Lyki's suggestion, they have invited Pandarus and Clytemnestra to cooperate. They are to film *The Golden Ass*; I am to direct. Preliminary work starts in six months' time (when I shall be finally finished with Odysseus) and next July or August I must begin preparing a script with the assistance of a suitable script-writer. We have all been telling each other that it would have been just the thing for you. Only now, of course, it is not for you. . . .'

Just the thing for me, Fielding thought, as he looked across the salt marshes to the sea. Six months to get well on with Conrad, and then a nice fat fee for scripting *The Golden Ass*. Only now, of course, it is not for me.

And yet . . . all things considered, as Jules had said . . . he had got much of what he wanted. He had got £10,000 in a Swiss bank, and he had, it appeared, got rid of Harriet. For the time at least. When he had reached London, after Christmas with Canteloupe at Monte, he had telephoned Broughton Staithe to announce that he would arrive there the evening after next. (He would have to live somewhere while deciding on his next move, and even to old friends of Tessie's Buttock's Hotel did not, these days, come cheap.) A rather small-voiced Harriet had said yes, everything would be ready for him; and so it had been . . . a fire in the grate, the water hot for his bath, and a nice stew cooking in the oven. But there had been no Harriet. The car was still in the garage and there was no message on the pad in the hall, so at first he had thought she must have gone out just for a few minutes (perhaps they were short of whisky and she had walked up the road to the off-licence): but the minutes had become hours and the hours days, and still there was no sign or word of Harriet. She's rumbled me at last, he thought when a week had passed by; she's rumbled me and she's left me and now there will be peace and quiet.

£10,000 (or rather £9500) tax free; no Harriet; peace and

quiet. But how was he to get the money to England? Dream gold, the Pandaras accountant had said, would turn to dross if carried over the English Channel. Should he go abroad then? After all, he could suit himself. But where to? There was no point in going anywhere unless there were people to wish it and resent it, unless there were people to weep at his departure and others to welcome his arrival. If no one cared where he went, there was no pleasure in going. Anyway, he wanted to be in England for a while; England, as Canteloupe was always saying, was the only decent country left. But England without Harriet? For at least Harriet had been something to fuck (however tedious the process) and somebody to swear at. At least Harriet had cared what he did. And Harriet had money. . . .

Well, perhaps she would be back and perhaps she wouldn't. Meanwhile, he had enough money of his own in England for the time being: after all, his first four weeks' salary from Pandarus had been sent to his English bank, and Gregory Stern was to pay a very fair advance for his book on Conrad. Conrad; work; there was his consolation. Work never let a man down . . . as long as he could still do it. Work suffereth long, and is kind; work vaunteth not itself, is not puffed up. Doth not behave itself unseemly. . . . He would sit down at Broughton and work. In loneliness? Yes, but also in tranquillity. In happiness? No, but in seemly acceptance of his lot. And there could have been many worse lots. The hours would pass quickly, he knew, the weeks would be gone almost before he noticed them, and always at his left hand the pile of written sheets would grow steadily thicker, witness and measure of his work.

So now he would walk on the salt marshes for a little and look at the crumbling gun-sites, and remember, as he always did, that first summer after the war. Then along the beach and across the golf course (oh Angela, Angela, striding over the turf); and then back to the empty house, to sit at his desk and make some notes on *Nostromo,* lifting his head from time to time to look at the never-resting sea.

# THE HISTORY OF VINTAGE

The famous American publisher Alfred A. Knopf (1892–1984) founded Vintage Books in the United States in 1954 as a paperback home for the authors published by his company. Vintage was launched in the United Kingdom in 1990 and works independently from the American imprint although both are part of the international publishing group, Random House.

Vintage in the United Kingdom was initially created to publish paperback editions of books acquired by the prestigious hardback imprints in the Random House Group such as Jonathan Cape, Chatto & Windus, Hutchinson and later William Heinemann, Secker & Warburg and The Harvill Press. There are many Booker and Nobel Prize-winning authors on the Vintage list and the imprint publishes a huge variety of fiction and non-fiction. Over the years Vintage has expanded and the list now includes great authors of the past – who are published under the Vintage Classics imprint – as well as many of the most influential authors of the present.

For a full list of the books Vintage publishes, please visit our website
www.vintage-books.co.uk

For book details and other information about the classic authors we publish, please visit the Vintage Classics website
www.vintage-classics.info

www.vintage-classics.info